PARAMOUNT PICTURES PRESENTS A MACE NEUFELD/JERRY SHERLOCK PRODUCTION

A JOHN McTIERNAN FILM

SEAN CONNERY   ALEC BALDWIN

THE HUNT FOR RED OCTOBER

SCOTT GLENN JAMES EARL JONES SAM NEILL

MUSIC BY BASIL POLEDOURIS PRODUCTION DESIGNER TERENCE MARSH

DIRECTOR OF PHOTOGRAPHY JAN DE BONT

EXECUTIVE PRODUCERS LARRY DE WAAY AND JERRY SHERLOCK

SCREENPLAY BY LARRY FERGUSON AND DONALD STEWART

BASED ON THE NOVEL BY TOM CLANCY

PRODUCED BY MACE NEUFELD

DIRECTED BY JOHN McTIERNAN

READ THE BERKLEY BESTSELLER A PARAMOUNT PICTURE

Berkley Books by Tom Clancy

THE HUNT FOR RED OCTOBER
RED STORM RISING
PATRIOT GAMES
THE CARDINAL OF THE KREMLIN

TOM CLANCY

THE HUNT FOR RED OCTOBER

BERKLEY BOOKS, NEW YORK

This Berkley book contains the complete
text of the original hardcover edition.
It has been completely reset in a typeface
designed for easy reading and was printed
from new film.

THE HUNT FOR RED OCTOBER

A Berkley Book / published by arrangement with
Naval Institute Press

PRINTING HISTORY
Naval Institute Press edition published 1984
Berkley edition / October 1985

A BERKLEY BOOK ® TM 757,375
Berkley Books are published by The Berkley Publishing Group,
200 Madison Avenue, New York, New York 10016.
The name "BERKLEY" and the "B" logo
are trademarks belonging to Berkley Publishing Corporation.

PRINTED IN THE UNITED STATES OF AMERICA

70 69 68 67 66 65 64 63 62 61

Acknowledgments

For technical information and advice I am especially indebted to Michael Shelton, former naval aviator; Larry Bond, whose naval wargame, "Harpoon," was adopted for the training of NROTC cadets; Drs. Gerry Sterner and Craig Jeschke; and Lieutenant Commander Gregory Young, USN.

For Ralph Chatham,
a sub driver who spoke the truth,
and for all the men who wear dolphins

THE FIRST DAY

FRIDAY, 3 DECEMBER

The Red October

Captain First Rank Marko Ramius of the Soviet Navy was dressed for the Arctic conditions normal to the Northern Fleet submarine base at Polyarnyy. Five layers of wool and oilskin enclosed him. A dirty harbor tug pushed his submarine's bow around to the north, facing down the channel. The dock that had held his *Red October* for two interminable months was now a water-filled concrete box, one of the many specially built to shelter strategic missile submarines from the harsh elements. On its edge a collection of sailors and dockyard workers watched his ship sail in stolid Russian fashion, without a wave or a cheer.

"Engines ahead slow, Kamarov," he ordered. The tug slid out of the way, and Ramius glanced aft to see the water stirring from the force of the twin bronze propellers. The tug's commander waved. Ramius returned the gesture. The tug had done a simple job, but done it quickly and well. The *Red October,* a *Typhoon*-class sub, moved under her own power towards the main ship channel of the Kola Fjord.

"There's *Purga*, Captain." Gregoriy Kamarov pointed to the icebreaker that would escort them to sea. Ramius nodded. The two hours required to transit the channel would tax not his seamanship but his endurance. There was a cold north wind blowing, the only sort of north wind in this part of the world. Late autumn had been surprisingly mild, and scarcely any snow had fallen in an area that measures it in meters; then a week before a major winter storm had savaged the Murmansk coast, breaking pieces off the Arctic icepack. The icebreaker was no formality. The *Purga* would butt aside any ice that might have drifted overnight into the channel. It would not do at all for the Soviet Navy's newest missile submarine to be damaged by an errant chunk of frozen water.

The water in the fjord was choppy, driven by the brisk wind. It began to lap over the *October*'s spherical bow, rolling back down the flat missile deck which lay before the towering black sail. The water was coated with the bilge oil of numberless ships, filth that would not evaporate in the low temperatures and that left a black ring on the rocky walls of the fjord as though from the bath of a slovenly giant. An altogether apt simile, Ramius thought. The Soviet giant cared little for the dirt it left on the face of the earth, he grumbled to himself. He had learned his seamanship as a boy on inshore fishing boats, and knew what it was to be in harmony with nature.

"Increase speed to one-third," he said. Kamarov repeated his captain's order over the bridge telephone. The water stirred more as the *October* moved astern of the *Purga*. Captain Lieutenant Kamarov was the ship's navigator, his last duty station having been harbor pilot for the large combatant vessels based on both sides of the wide inlet. The two officers kept a weather eye on the armed icebreaker three hundred meters ahead. The *Purga*'s after deck had a handful of crewmen stomping about in the cold, one wearing the white apron of a ship's cook. They wanted to witness the *Red October*'s first operational cruise, and besides, sailors will do almost anything to break the monotony of their duties.

Ordinarily it would have irritated Ramius to have his ship escorted out—the channel here was wide and deep—but not today. The ice was something to worry about. And so, for Ramius, was a great deal else.

"So, my Captain, again we go to sea to serve and protect the *Rodina!*" Captain Second Rank Ivan Yurievich Putin poked his head through the hatch—without permission, as usual—and clambered up the ladder with the awkwardness of a landsman. The tiny control station was already crowded enough with the captain, the navigator, and a mute lookout. Putin was the ship's *zampolit* (political officer). Everything he did was to serve the *Rodina* (Motherland), a word that had mystical connotations to a Russian and, along with V. I. Lenin, was the Communist party's substitute for a godhead.

"Indeed, Ivan," Ramius replied with more good cheer than he felt. "Two weeks at sea. It is good to leave the dock. A seaman belongs at sea, not tied alongside, overrun with bureaucrats and workmen with dirty boots. And we will be warm."

"You find this cold?" Putin asked incredulously.

For the hundredth time Ramius told himself that Putin was the perfect political officer. His voice was always too loud, his humor too affected. He never allowed a person to forget what he was. The perfect political officer, Putin was an easy man to fear.

"I have been in submarines too long, my friend. I grow accustomed to moderate temperatures and a stable deck under my feet." Putin did not notice the veiled insult. He'd been assigned to submarines after his first tour on destroyers had been cut short by chronic seasickness—and perhaps because he did not resent the close confinement aboard submarines, something that many men cannot tolerate.

"Ah, Marko Aleksandrovich, in Gorkiy on a day like this, flowers bloom!"

"And what sort of flowers might those be, Comrade Political Officer?" Ramius surveyed the fjord through his binoculars. At noon the sun was barely over the southeast horizon, casting orange light and purple shadows along the rocky walls.

"Why, snow flowers, of course," Putin said, laughing loudly. "On a day like this the faces of the children and the women glow pink, your breath trails behind you like a cloud, and the vodka tastes especially fine. Ah, to be in Gorkiy on a day like this!"

The bastard ought to work for Intourist, Ramius told himself, except that Gorkiy is a city closed to foreigners. He had been there twice. It had struck him as a typical Soviet city, full of ramshackle buildings, dirty streets, and ill-clad citizens. As it was in most Russian cities, winter was Gorkiy's best season. The snow hid all the dirt. Ramius, half Lithuanian, had childhood memories of a better place, a coastal village whose Hanseatic origin had left rows of presentable buildings.

It was unusual for anyone other than a Great Russian to be aboard—much less command—a Soviet naval vessel. Marko's father, Aleksandr Ramius, had been a hero of the Party, a dedicated, believing Communist who had served Stalin faithfully and well. When the Soviets first occupied Lithuania in 1940, the elder Ramius was instrumental in rounding up political dissidents, shop owners, priests, and anyone else who might have been troublesome to the new regime. All were shipped off to fates that now even Moscow could only guess at. When the Germans invaded a year later, Aleksandr fought heroically as a political commissar, and was later to distinguish himself in the Battle of Leningrad. In 1944 he returned to his native land with the spearhead of the Eleventh Guards Army to wreak bloody vengeance on those who had collaborated with the Germans or been suspected of such. Marko's father had been a true Soviet hero—and Marko was deeply ashamed to be his son. His mother's health had been broken during the endless siege of Leningrad. She died giving birth to him, and he was raised by his paternal grandmother in Lithuania while his father strutted through the Party Central Committee in Vilnius, awaiting his promotion to Moscow. He got that, too, and was a candidate member of the Politburo when his life was cut short by a heart attack.

Marko's shame was not total. His father's prominence had made his current goal a possibility, and Marko planned to wreak his own vengeance on the Soviet Union, enough, perhaps, to satisfy the thousands of his countrymen who had died before he was even born.

"Where we are going, Ivan Yurievich, it will be colder still."

Putin clapped his captain's shoulder. Was his affection feigned or real? Marko wondered. Probably real. Ramius was an honest man, and he recognized that this short, loud oaf did have some human feelings.

"Why is it, Comrade Captain, that you always seem glad to leave the *Rodina* and go to sea?"

Ramius smiled behind his binoculars. "A seaman has one country, Ivan Yurievich, but two wives. You never understand that. Now I go to my other wife, the cold, heartless one that owns my soul." Ramius paused. The smile vanished. "My only wife, now."

Putin was quiet for once, Marko noted. The political officer had been there, had cried real tears as the coffin of polished pine rolled into the cremation chamber. For Putin the death of Natalia Bogdanova Ramius had been a cause of grief, but beyond that the act of an uncaring God whose existence he regularly denied. For Ramius it had been a crime committed not by God but the State. An unnecessary, monstrous crime, one that demanded punishment.

"Ice." The lookout pointed.

"Loose-pack ice, starboard side of the channel, or perhaps something calved off the east-side glacier. We'll pass well clear," Kamarov said.

"Captain!" The bridge speaker had a metallic voice. "Message from fleet headquarters."

"Read it."

"'Exercise area clear. No enemy vessels in vicinity. Proceed as per orders. Signed, Korov, Fleet Commander.'"

"Acknowledged," Ramius said. The speaker clicked off. "So, no *Amerikantsi* about?"

"You doubt the fleet commander?" Putin inquired.

"I hope he is correct," Ramius replied, more sincerely than his political officer would appreciate. "But you remember our briefings."

Putin shifted on his feet. Perhaps he was feeling the cold.

"Those American 688-class submarines, Ivan, the *Los Angeles*es. Remember what one of their officers told our spy? That they could sneak up on a whale and bugger it before it knew they were there? I wonder how the KGB got that bit of information. A beautiful Soviet agent, trained in the ways of the decadent West, too skinny, the way the imperialists like their women, blond hair . . ." The captain grunted amusement. "Probably the American officer was a boastful boy, trying to find a way to do something similar to our agent, no? And feeling his liquor, like most sailors. Still. The American *Los*

Angeles class, and the new British *Trafalgar*s, those we must guard against. They are a threat to us."

"The Americans are good technicians, Comrade Captain," Putin said, "but they are not giants. Their technology is not so awesome. *Nasha lutcha,*" he concluded. Ours is better.

Ramius nodded thoughtfully, thinking to himself that *zampoliti* really ought to know something about the ships they supervised, as mandated by Party doctrine.

"Ivan, didn't the farmers around Gorkiy tell you it is the wolf you do not see that you must fear? But don't be overly concerned. With this ship we will teach them a lesson, I think."

"As I told the Main Political Administration," Putin clapped Ramius' shoulder again, *"Red October* is in the best of hands!"

Ramius and Kamarov both smiled at that. You son of a bitch! the captain thought, saying in front of my men that *you* must pass on my fitness to command! A man who could not command a rubber raft on a calm day! A pity you will not live to eat those words, Comrade Political Officer, and spend the rest of your life in the gulag for that misjudgment. It would almost be worth leaving you alive.

A few minutes later the chop began to pick up, making the submarine roll. The movement was accentuated by their height above the deck, and Putin made excuses to go below. Still a weak-legged sailor. Ramius shared the observation silently with Kamarov, who smiled agreement. Their unspoken contempt for the *zampolit* was a most un-Soviet thought.

The next hour passed quickly. The water grew rougher as they approached the open sea, and their icebreaker escort began to wallow on the swells. Ramius watched her with interest. He had never been on an icebreaker, his entire career having been in submarines. They were more comfortable, but also more dangerous. He was accustomed to the danger, though, and the years of experience would stand him in good stead now.

"Sea buoy in sight, Captain." Kamarov pointed. The red lighted buoy was riding actively on the waves.

"Control room, what is the sounding?" Ramius asked over the bridge telephone.

"One hundred meters below the keel, Comrade Captain."

"Increase speed to two-thirds, come left ten degrees." Ramius looked at Kamarov. "Signal our course change to *Purga,* and hope he doesn't turn the wrong way."

Kamarov reached for the small blinker light stowed under the bridge coaming. The *Red October* began to accelerate slowly, her 30,000-ton bulk resisting the power of her engines. Presently the bow wave grew to a three-meter standing arc of water; man-made combers rolled down the missile deck, splitting against the front of the sail. The *Purga* altered course to starboard, allowing the submarine to pass well clear.

Ramius looked aft at the bluffs of the Kola Fjord. They had been carved to this shape millennia before by the remorseless pressure of towering glaciers. How many times in his twenty years of service with the Red Banner Northern Fleet had he looked at the wide, flat U-shape? This would be the last. One way or another, he'd never go back. Which way would it turn out? Ramius admitted to himself that he didn't much care. Perhaps the stories his grandmother had taught him were true, about God and the reward for a good life. He hoped so—it would be good if Natalia were not truly dead. In any case, there was no turning back. He had left a letter in the last mailbag taken off before sailing. There was no going back after that.

"Kamarov, signal to *Purga:* 'Diving at—,'" he checked his watch, "'—1320 hours. Exercise OCTOBER FROST begins as scheduled. You are released to other assigned duties. We will return as scheduled.'"

Kamarov worked the trigger on the blinker light to transmit the message. The *Purga* responded at once, and Ramius read the flashing signal unaided: "IF THE WHALES DON'T EAT YOU. GOOD LUCK TO *RED OCTOBER!*"

Ramius lifted the phone again, pushing the button for the sub's radio room. He had the same message transmitted to fleet headquarters, Severomorsk. Next he addressed the control room.

"Depth under the keel?"

"One hundred forty meters, Comrade Captain."

"Prepare to dive." He turned to the lookout and ordered him below. The boy moved towards the hatch. He was probably glad to return to the warmth below, but took the time for one last look at the cloudy sky and receding cliffs. Going to sea on a submarine was always exciting, and always a little sad.

"Clear the bridge. Take the conn when you get below, Gregoriy." Kamarov nodded and dropped down the hatch, leaving the captain alone.

Ramius made one last careful scan of the horizon. The sun

was barely visible aft, the sky leaden, the sea black except for the splash of whitecaps. He wondered if he were saying good-bye to the world. If so, he would have preferred a more cheerful view of it.

Before sliding down he inspected the hatch seat, pulling it shut with a chain and making sure the automatic mechanism functioned properly. Next he dropped eight meters down the inside of the sail to the pressure hull, then two more into the control room. A *michman* (warrant officer) shut the second hatch and with a powerful spin turned the locking wheel as far as it would go.

"Gregoriy?" Ramius asked.

"Straight board shut," the navigator said crisply, pointing to the diving board. All hull-opening indicator lights showed green, safe. "All systems aligned and checked for dive. The compensation is entered. We are rigged for dive."

The captain made his own visual inspection of mechanical, electrical, and hydraulic indicators. He nodded, and the *michman* of the watch unlocked the vent controls.

"Dive," Ramius ordered, moving to the periscope to relieve Vasily Borodin, his *starpom* (executive officer). Kamarov pulled the diving alarm, and the hull reverberated with the racket of a loud buzzer.

"Flood the main ballast tanks. Rig out the diving planes. Ten degrees down-angle on the planes," Kamarov ordered, his eyes alert to see that every crewman did his job exactly. Ramius listened carefully but did not look. Kamarov was the best young seaman he had ever commanded, and had long since earned his captain's trust.

The *Red October*'s hull was filled with the noise of rushing air as vents at the top of the ballast tanks were opened and water entering from the tank floods at the bottom chased the buoying air out. It was a lengthy process, for the submarine had many such tanks, each carefully subdivided by numerous cellular baffles. Ramius adjusted the periscope lens to look down and saw the black water change briefly to foam.

The *Red October* was the largest and finest command Ramius had ever had, but the sub had one major flaw. She had plenty of engine power and a new drive system that he hoped would befuddle American and Soviet submarines alike, but she was so big that she changed depth like a crippled whale. Slow going up, even slower going down.

"Scope under." Ramius stepped away from the instrument after what seemed a long wait. "Down periscope."

"Passing forty meters," Kamarov said.

"Level off at one hundred meters." Ramius watched his crewmen now. The first dive could make experienced men shudder, and half his crew were farmboys straight from training camp. The hull popped and creaked under the pressure of the surrounding water, something that took getting used to. A few of the younger men went pale but stood rigidly upright.

Kamarov began the procedure for leveling off at the proper depth. Ramius watched with a pride he might have felt for his own son as the lieutenant gave the necessary orders with precision. He was the first officer Ramius had recruited. The control room crew snapped to his command. Five minutes later the submarine slowed her descent at ninety meters and settled the next ten to a perfect stop at one hundred.

"Well done, Comrade Lieutenant. You have the conn. Slow to one-third speed. Have the sonarmen listen on all passive systems." Ramius turned to leave the control room, motioning Putin to follow him.

And so it began.

Ramius and Putin went aft to the submarine's wardroom. The captain held the door open for the political officer, then closed and locked it behind himself. The *Red October*'s wardroom was a spacious affair for a submarine, located immediately forward of the galley, aft of the officer accommodations. Its walls were soundproofed, and the door had a lock because her designers had known that not everything the officers had to say was necessarily for the ears of the enlisted men. It was large enough for all of the *October*'s officers to eat as a group—though at least three of them would always be on duty. The safe containing the ship's orders was here, not in the captain's stateroom where a man might use his solitude to try opening it by himself. It had two dials. Ramius had one combination, Putin the other. Which was hardly necessary, since Putin undoubtedly knew their mission orders already. So did Ramius, but not all the particulars.

Putin poured tea as the captain checked his watch against

the chronometer mounted on the bulkhead. Fifteen minutes until he could open the safe. Putin's courtesy made him uneasy.

"Two more weeks of confinement," the *zampolit* said, stirring his tea.

"The Americans do this for two *months,* Ivan. Of course, their submarines are far more comfortable." Despite her huge bulk, the *October*'s crew accommodations would have shamed a gulag jailer. The crew consisted of fifteen officers, housed in fairly decent cabins aft, and a hundred enlisted men whose bunks were stuffed into corners and racks throughout the bow, forward of the missile room. The *October*'s size was deceptive. The interior of her double hull was crammed with missiles, torpedoes, a nuclear reactor and its support equipment, a huge backup diesel power plant, and bank of nickle-cadmium batteries outside the pressure hull, which was ten times the size of its American counterparts. Running and maintaining the ship was a huge job for so small a crew, even though extensive use of automation made her the most modern of Soviet naval vessels. Perhaps the men didn't need proper bunks. They would only have four or six hours a day to make use of them. This would work to Ramius' advantage. Half of his crew were draftees on their first operational cruise, and even the more experienced men knew little enough. The strength of his enlisted crew, unlike that of Western crews, resided much more in his eleven *michmanyy* (warrant officers) than in his *glavnyy starshini* (senior petty officers). All of them were men who would do—were specifically trained to do—exactly what their officers told them. And Ramius had picked the officers.

"You want to cruise for two months?" Putin asked.

"I have done it on diesel submarines. A submarine belongs at sea, Ivan. Our mission is to strike fear into the hearts of the imperialists. We do not accomplish this tied up in our barn at Polyarnyy most of the time, but we cannot stay at sea any longer because any period over two weeks and the crew loses efficiency. In two weeks this collection of children will be a mob of numbed robots." Ramius was counting on that.

"And we could solve this by having capitalist luxuries?" Putin sneered.

"A true Marxist is objective, Comrade Political Officer," Ramius chided, savoring this last argument with Putin. "Objectively, that which aids us in carrying out our mission is good, that which hinders us is bad. Adversity is supposed to hone one's spirit and skill, not dull them. Just being aboard a submarine is hardship enough, is it not?"

"Not for you, Marko." Putin grinned over his tea.

"I am a seaman. Our crewmen are not, most never will be. They are a mob of farmers' sons and boys who yearn to be factory workers. We must adjust to the times, Ivan. These youngsters are not the same as we were."

"That is true enough," Putin agreed. "You are never satisfied, Comrade Captain. I suppose it is men like you who force progress upon us all."

Both men knew exactly why Soviet missile submarines spent so little of their time—barely fifteen percent of it—at sea, and it had nothing to do with creature comforts. The *Red October* carried twenty-six SS-N-20 Seahawk missiles, each with eight 500-kiloton multiple independently targetable reentry vehicles—MIRVs—enough to destroy two hundred cities. Land-based bombers could only fly a few hours at a time, then had to return to their bases. Land-based missiles arrayed along the main East-West Soviet rail network were always where paramilitary troops of the KGB could get at them lest some missile regiment commander suddenly came to realize the power at his fingertips. But missile submarines were by definition beyond any control from land. Their entire mission was to disappear.

Given that fact, Marko was surprised that his government had them at all. The crew of such vessels had to be trusted. And so they sailed less often than their Western counterparts, and when they did it was with a political officer aboard to stand next to the commanding officer, a second captain always ready to pass approval on every action.

"Do you think you could do it, Marko, cruise for two months with these farmboys?"

"I prefer half-trained boys, as you know. They have less to unlearn. Then I can train them to be seamen the right way, my way. My personality cult?"

Putin laughed as he lit a cigarette. "That observation has been made in the past, Marko. But you are our best teacher and your reliability is well known." This was very true. Ramius had sent hundreds of officers and seamen on to other submarines whose commanders were glad to have them. It was an-

other paradox that a man could engender trust within a society
that scarcely recognized the concept. Of course, Ramius was
a loyal Party member, the son of a Party hero who had been
carried to his grave by three Politburo members. Putin waggled
his finger. "You should be commanding one of our higher naval
schools, Comrade Captain. Your talents would better serve the
state there."

"It is a seaman I am, Ivan Yurievich. Only a seaman, not
a schoolmaster—despite what they say about me. A wise man
knows his limitations." And a bold one seizes opportunities.
Every officer aboard had served with Ramius before, except
for three junior lieutenants, who would obey their orders as
readily as any wet-nosed *matros* (seaman), and the doctor, who
was useless.

The chronometer chimed four bells.

Ramius stood and dialed in his three-element combination.
Putin did the same, and the captain flipped the lever to open
the safe's circular door. Inside was a manila envelope plus four
books of cipher keys and missile-targeting coordinates. Ramius
removed the envelope, then closed the door, spinning both dials
before sitting down again."

"So, Ivan, what do you suppose our orders tell us to do?"
Ramius asked theatrically.

"Our duty, Comrade Captain." Putin smiled.

"Indeed." Ramius broke the wax seal on the envelope and
extracted the four-page operation order. He read it quickly. It
was not complicated.

"So, we are to proceed to grid square 54-90 and rendezvous
with our attack submarine *V. K. Konovalov*—that's Captain
Tupolev's new command. You know Viktor Tupolev? No? Viktor
will guard us from imperialist intruders, and we will conduct
a four-day acquisition and tracking drill, with him hunting us—
if he can." Ramius chuckled. "The boys in the attack submarine
directorate still have not figured how to track our new drive
system. Well, neither will the Americans. We are to confine
our operations to grid square 54-90 and the immediately surrounding squares. That ought to make Viktor's task a bit easier."

"But you will not let him find us?"

"Certainly not," Ramius snorted. "Let? Viktor was once my
pupil. You give nothing to an enemy, Ivan, even in a drill. The
imperialists certainly won't! In trying to find us, he also prac-

tices finding their missile submarines. He will have a fair chance of locating us, I think. The exercise is confined to nine squares, forty thousand square kilometers. We shall see what he has learned since he served with us—oh, that's right, you weren't with me then. That's when I had the *Suslov*."

"Do I see disappointment?"

"No, not really. The four-day drill with *Konovalov* will be interesting diversion." Bastard, he said to himself, you knew beforehand exactly what our orders were—and you do know Viktor Tupolev, liar. It was time.

Putin finished his cigarette and his tea before standing. "So, again I am permitted to watch the master captain at work—befuddling a poor boy." He turned towards the door. "I think—"

Ramius kicked Putin's feet out from under him just as he was stepping away from the table. Putin fell backwards while Ramius sprang to his feet and grasped the political officer's head in his strong fisherman's hands. The captain drove his neck downward to the sharp, metal-edged corner of the wardroom table. It struck the point. In the same instant Ramius pushed down on the man's chest. An unnecessary gesture— with the sickening crackle of bones Ivan Putin's neck broke, his spine severed at the level of the second cervical vertebra, a perfect hangman's fracture.

The political officer had no time to react. The nerves to his body below the neck were instantly cut off from the organs and muscles they controlled. Putin tried to shout, to say something, but his mouth flapped open and shut without a sound except for the exhalation of his last lungful of air. He tried to gulp air down like a landed fish, and this did not work. Then his eyes went up to Ramius, wide in shock—there was no pain, and no emotion but surprise. The captain laid him gently on the tile deck.

Ramius saw the face flash with recognition, then darken. He reached down to take Putin's pulse. It was nearly two minutes before the heart stopped completely. When Ramius was sure that his political officer was dead, he took the teapot from the table and poured two cups' worth on the deck, careful to drip some on the man's shoes. Next he lifted the body to the wardroom table and threw open the door.

"Dr. Petrov to the wardroom at once!"

The ship's medical office was only a few steps aft. Petrov was there in seconds, along with Vasily Borodin, who had hurried aft from the control room.

"He slipped on the deck where I spilled my tea," Ramius gasped, performing closed heart massage on Putin's chest. "I tried to keep him from falling, but he hit his head on the table."

Petrov shoved the captain aside, moved the body around, and leapt on the table to kneel astride it. He tore the shirt open, then checked Putin's eyes. Both pupils were wide and fixed. The doctor felt around the man's head, his hands working downward to the neck. They stopped there, probing. The doctor shook his head slowly.

"Comrade Putin is dead. His neck is broken." The doctor's hands came loose, and he closed the *zampolit*'s eyes.

"No!" Ramius shouted. "He was alive only a minute ago!" The commanding officer was sobbing. "It's my fault. I tried to catch him, but I failed. My fault!" He collapsed into a chair and buried his face in his hands. "My fault," he cried, shaking his head in rage, struggling visibly to regain his composure. An altogether excellent performance.

Petrov placed his hand on the captain's shoulder. "It was an accident, Comrade Captain. These things happen, even to experienced men. It was not your fault. Truly, Comrade."

Ramius swore under his breath, regaining control of himself. "There is nothing you can do?"

Petrov shook his head. "Even in the finest clinic in the Soviet Union nothing could be done. Once the spinal cord is severed, there is no hope. Death is virtually instantaneous—but also it is quite painless," the doctor added consolingly.

Ramius drew himself up as he took a long breath, his face set. "Comrade Putin was a good shipmate, a loyal Party member, and a fine officer." Out the corner of his eye he noticed Borodin's mouth twitch. "Comrades, we will continue our mission! Dr. Petrov, you will carry our comrade's body to the freezer. This is—gruesome, I know, but he deserves and will get an honorable military funeral, with his shipmates in attendance, as it should be, when we return to port."

"Will this be reported to fleet headquarters?" Petrov asked.

"We cannot. Our orders are to maintain strict radio silence."
Ramius handed the doctor a set of operations orders from his

pocket. Not those taken from the safe. "Page three, Comrade Doctor."

Petrov's eyes went wide reading the operational directive.

"I would prefer to report this, but our orders are explicit: Once we dive, no transmissions of any kind, for any reason."

Petrov handed the papers back. "Too bad, our comrade would have looked forward to this. But orders are orders."

"And we shall carry them out."

"Putin would have it no other way," Petrov agreed.

"Borodin, observe: I take the comrade political officer's missile control key from his neck, as per regulations," Ramius said, pocketing the key and chain.

"I note this, and will so enter it in the log," the executive officer said gravely.

Petrov brought in his medical corpsman. Together they took the body aft to the medical office, where it was zippered into a body bag. The corpsman and a pair of sailors then took it forward, through the control room, into the missile compartment. The entrance to the freezer was on the lower missile deck, and the men carried the body through the door. While two cooks removed food to make room for it, the body was set reverently down in the corner. Aft, the doctor and the executive officer made the necessary inventory of personal effects, one copy for the ship's medical file, another for the ship's log, and a third for a box that was sealed and locked up in the medical office.

Forward, Ramius took the conn in a subdued control room. He ordered the submarine to a course of two-nine-zero degrees, west-northwest. Grid square 54-90 was to the east.

THE SECOND DAY

SATURDAY, 4 DECEMBER

The Red October

It was the custom in the Soviet Navy for the commanding officer to announce his ship's operational orders and to exhort the crew to carry them out in true Soviet fashion. The orders were then posted for all to see—and be inspired by—outside the ship's Lenin Room. In large surface ships this was a classroom where political awareness classes were held. In *Red October* it was a closet-sized library near the wardroom where Party books and other ideological material were kept for the men to read. Ramius disclosed their orders the day after sailing to give his men the chance to settle into the ship's routine. At the same time he gave a pep talk. Ramius always gave a good one. He'd had a lot of practice. At 0800 hours, when the forenoon watch was set, he entered the control room and took some file cards from an inside jacket pocket.

"Comrades!" he began, talking into the microphone, "this is the captain speaking. You all know that our beloved friend and comrade, Captain Ivan Yurievich Putin, died yesterday in a tragic accident. Our orders do not permit us to inform fleet headquarters of this. Comrades, we will dedicate our efforts and our work to the memory of our comrade, Ivan Yurievich Putin—a fine shipmate, an honorable Party member, and a courageous officer.

"Comrades! Officer and men of *Red October!* We have orders from the Red Banner Northern Fleet High Command, and they are orders worthy of this ship and this crew!

"Comrades! Our orders are to make the ultimate test of our new silent propulsion system. We are to head *west,* past the North Cape of America's imperialist puppet state, Norway, then to turn southwest towards the Atlantic Ocean. We will pass all of the imperialist sonar nets, and we will *not* be detected! This will be a true test of our submarine and his capabilities. Our own ships will engage in a major exercise to locate us and at the same time to befuddle the arrogant imperialist navies. Our mission, first of all, is to evade detection by anyone. We will teach the Americans a lesson about Soviet technology that they will not soon forget! Our orders are to continue southwest, skirting the American coast to challenge and defeat their newest and best hunter submarines. We will proceed all the way to our socialist brothers in Cuba, and we will be the *first ship* to make use of a new and supersecret nuclear submarine base that we have been building for two years right under their imperialist noses on the south coast of Cuba. A fleet replenishment vessel is already en route to rendezvous with us there.

"Comrades! If we succeed in reaching Cuba undetected by the imperialists—and we will!—the officers and men of *Red October* will have a week—*a week*—of shore leave to visit our fraternal socialist comrades on the beautiful island of Cuba. I have been there, comrades, and you will find it to be exactly what you have read, a paradise of warm breezes, palm trees, and comradely good fellowship." By which Ramius meant women. "After this we will return to the Motherland by the same route. By this time, of course, the imperialists will know who and what we are, from their slinking spies and cowardly reconnaissance aircraft. It is intended that they should know this, because we will again evade detection on the trip home. This will let the imperialists know that they may not trifle with the men of the Soviet Navy, that we can approach their coast at the time of our choosing, and that they must respect the Soviet Union!

"Comrades! We will make the first cruise of *Red October* a memorable one!"

Ramius looked up from his prepared speech. The men on watch in the control room were exchanging grins. It was not often that a Soviet sailor was allowed to visit another country, and a visit by a nuclear submarine to a foreign country, even an ally, was nearly unprecedented. Moreover, for Russians the island of Cuba was as exotic as Tahiti, a promised land of white sand beaches and dusky girls. Ramius knew differently. He had read articles in *Red Star* and other state journals about the joys of duty in Cuba. He had also been there.

Ramius changed cards in his hands. He had given them the good news.

"Comrades! Officers and men of *Red October!*" Now for the bad news that everyone was waiting for. "This mission will not be an easy one. It demands our best efforts. We must maintain absolute radio silence, and our operating routines must be *perfect!* Rewards only come to those who truly earn them. Every officer and every man aboard, from your commanding officer to the newest *matros*, must do his socialist duty and do it well! If we work together as comrades, as the New Soviet Men we are, we shall succeed. You young comrades new to the sea: Listen to your officers, to your *michmanyy*, and to your *starshini*. Learn your duties well, and carry them out exactly. There are no small jobs on this ship, no small responsibilities. Every comrade depends for his life upon every other. Do your duty, follow your orders, and when we have completed this voyage, you will be true Soviet sailors! That is all." Ramius released his thumb from the mike switch and set it back in the cradle. Not a bad speech, he decided—a large carrot and a small stick.

In the galley aft a petty officer was standing still, holding a warm loaf of bread and looking curiously at the bulkhead-mounted speaker. That wasn't what their orders were supposed to be, was it? Had there been a change in plans? The *michman* pointed him back to his duties, grinning and chuckling at the prospect of a week in Cuba. He had heard a lot of stories about Cuba and Cuban women and was looking forward to seeing if they were true.

In the control room Ramius mused. "I wonder if any American submarines are about?"

"Indeed, Comrade Captain," nodded Captain Second Rank Borodin, who had the watch. "Shall we engage the caterpillar?"

"Proceed, Comrade."

"Engines all stop," Borodin ordered.

"All stop." The quartermaster, a *starshina* (petty officer), dialed the annunciator to the STOP position. An instant later the order was confirmed by the inner dial, and a few seconds after that the dull rumble of the engines died away.

Borodin picked up the phone and punched the button for engineering. "Comrade Chief Engineer, prepare to engage the caterpillar."

It wasn't the official name for the new drive system. It had no name as such, just a project number. The nickname *caterpillar* had been given it by a young engineer who had been involved in the sub's development. Neither Ramius nor Borodin knew why, but as often happens with such names, it had stuck.

"Ready, Comrade Borodin," the chief engineer reported back in a moment.

"Open doors fore and aft," Borodin ordered next.

The *michman* of the watch reached up the control board and threw four switches. The status light over each changed from red to green. "Doors show open, Comrade."

"Engage caterpillar. Build speed slowly to thirteen knots."

"Build slowly to one-three knots, Comrade," the engineer acknowledged.

The hull, which had gone momentarily silent, now had a new sound. The engine noises were lower and very different from what they had been. The reactor plant noises, mainly from pumps that circulated the cooling water, were almost imperceptible. The caterpillar did not use a great deal of power for what it did. At the *michman*'s station the speed gauge, which had dropped to five knots, began to creep upward again. Forward of the missile room, in a space shoehorned into the crew's accommodations, the handful of sleeping men stirred briefly in their bunks as they noted an intermittent rumble aft and the hum of electric motors a few feet away, separated from them by the pressure hull. They were tired enough even on their first day at sea to ignore the noise, fighting back to their precious allotment of sleep.

"Caterpillar functioning normally, Comrade Captain," Borodin reported.

"Excellent. Steer two-six-zero, helm," Ramius ordered.

"Two-six-zero, Comrade." The helmsman turned his wheel to the left.

The USS Bremerton

Thirty miles to the northeast, the USS *Bremerton* was on a heading of two-two-five, just emerging from under the icepack. A 688-class attack submarine, she had been on an ELINT— electronic intelligence gathering—mission in the Kara Sea when she was ordered west to the Kola Peninsula. The Russian missile boat wasn't supposed to have sailed for another week, and the *Bremerton*'s skipper was annoyed at this latest intelligence screw-up. He would have been in place to track the *Red October* if she had sailed as scheduled. Even so, the American sonarmen had picked up on the Soviet sub a few minutes earlier, despite the fact that they were traveling at fourteen knots.

"Conn, sonar."

Commander Wilson lifted the phone. "Conn, aye."

"Contact lost, sir. His screws stopped a few minutes ago and have not restarted. There's some other activity to the east, but the missile sub has gone dead."

"Very well. He's probably settling down to a slow drift. We'll be creeping up on him. Stay awake, Chief." Commander Wilson thought this over as he took two steps to the chart table. The two officers of the fire control tracking party who had just been establishing the track for the contact looked up to learn their commander's opinion.

"If it was me, I'd go down near the bottom and circle slowly right about here." Wilson traced a rough circle on the chart that enclosed the *Red October*'s position. "So let's creep up on him. We'll reduce speed to five knots and see if we can move in and reacquire him from his reactor plant noise." Wilson turned to the officer of the deck. "Reduce speed to five knots."

"Aye, Skipper."

Severomorsk, USSR

In the Central Post Office building in Severomorsk a mail sorter watched sourly as a truck driver dumped a large canvas sack on his work table and went back out the door. He was late— well, not really late, the clerk corrected himself, since the idiot had not been on time once in five years. It was a Saturday, and he resented being at work. Only a few years before, the forty-hour week had been started in the Soviet Union. Unfortunately this change had never affected such vital public services as mail delivery. So, here he was, still working a six-day week—and without extra pay! A disgrace, he thought, and had said often enough in his apartment, playing cards with his workmates over vodka and cucumbers.

He untied the drawstring and turned the sack over. Several smaller bags tumbled out. There was no sense in hurrying. It was only the beginning of the month, and they still had weeks to move their quota of letters and parcels from one side of the building to the other. In the Soviet Union every worker is a government worker, and they have a saying: As long as the bosses pretend to pay us, we will pretend to work.

Opening a small mailbag, he pulled out an official-looking envelope addressed to the Main Political Administration of the Navy in Moscow. The clerk paused, fingering the envelope. It probably came from one of the submarines based at Polyarnyy, on the other side of the fjord. What did the letter say? the sorter wondered, playing the mental game that amused mailmen all over the world. Was it an announcement that all was ready for the final attack on the imperialist West? A list of Party members who were late paying their dues, or a requisition for more toilet paper? There was no telling. Submariners! They were all prima donnas—even the farmboy conscripts still picking shit from between their toes paraded around like members of the Party elite.

The clerk was sixty-two. In the Great Patriotic War he had been a tankrider serving in a guards tank corps attached to Konev's First Ukrainian Front. That, he told himself, was a man's job, riding into action on the back of the great battle tanks, leaping off to hunt for the German infantrymen as they cowered in their holes. When something needed doing against those slugs, it was *done!* Now what had become of Soviet fighting men? Living aboard luxury liners with plenty of good food and warm beds. The only warm bed he had ever known was over the exhaust vent of his tank's diesel—and he'd had to fight for that! It was crazy what the world had become. Now sailors acted like czarist princes and wrote tons of letters back and forth and called it work. These pampered boys didn't know what hardship was. And their privileges! Every word they committed to paper was priority mail. Whimpering letters to their sweethearts, most of it, and here he was sorting through it all on a Saturday to see that it got to their womenfolk—even though they couldn't possibly have a reply for two weeks. It just wasn't like the old days.

The sorter tossed the envelope with a negligent flick of the wrist towards the surface mailbag for Moscow on the far side of his work table. It missed, dropping to the concrete floor. The letter would be placed aboard the train a day late. The sorter didn't care. There was a hockey game that night, the biggest game of the young season, Central Army against Wings. He had a liter of vodka bet on Wings.

Morrow, England

"Halsey's greatest popular success was his greatest error. In establishing himself as a popular hero with legendary aggressiveness, the admiral would blind later generations to his impressive intellectual abilities and a shrewd gambler's instinct to—" Jack Ryan frowned at his computer. It sounded too much like a doctoral dissertation, and he had already done one of those. He thought of dumping the whole passage from the memory disk but decided against it. He had to follow this line of reasoning for his introduction. Bad as it was, it did serve as a guide for what he wanted to say. Why was it that introductions always seemed to be the hardest part of a history book? For three years now he had been working on *Fighting Sailor,* an authorized biography of Fleet Admiral William Halsey. Nearly all of it was contained on a half-dozen floppy disks lying next to his Apple computer.

"Daddy?" Ryan's daughter was staring up at him.

"And how's my little Sally today?"

"Fine."

Ryan picked her up and set her on his lap, careful to slide his chair away from the keyboard. Sally was all checked out on games and educational programs, and occasionally thought that this meant she was able to handle Wordstar also. Once that had resulted in the loss of twenty thousand words of electronically recorded manuscript. And a spanking.

She leaned her head against her father's shoulder.

"You don't look fine. What's bothering my little girl?"

"Well, Daddy, y'see, it's almost Chris'mas, an . . . I'm not sure that Santa knows where we are. We're not where we were last year."

"Oh, I see. And you're afraid he doesn't come here?"

"Uh huh."

"Why didn't you ask me before? Of course he comes here. Promise."

"Promise?"

"Promise."

"Okay." She kissed her father and ran out of the room, back to watching cartoons on the telly, as they called it in England. Ryan was glad she had interrupted him. He didn't want to forget to pick up a few things when he flew over to Washington. Where was—oh, yeah. He pulled a disk from his desk drawer and inserted it in the spare disk drive. After clearing the screen, he scrolled up the Christmas list, things he still had to get. With a simple command a copy of the list was made on the adjacent printer. Ryan tore the page off and tucked it in his wallet. Work didn't appeal to him this Saturday morning. He decided to play with his kids. After all, he'd be stuck in Washington for much of the coming week.

The V. K. Konovalov

The Soviet submarine *V. K. Konovalov* crept above the hard sand bottom of the Barents Sea at three knots. She was at the southwest corner of grid square 54-90 and for the past ten hours had been drifting back and forth on a north-south line, waiting for the *Red October* to arrive for the beginning of Exercise OCTOBER FROST. Captain Second Rank Viktor Alexievich Tupolev paced slowly around the periscope pedestal in the control room of his small, fast attack sub. He was waiting for his old mentor to show up, hoping to play a few tricks on him. He had served with the Schoolmaster for two years. They had been good years, and while he found his former commander to be something of a cynic, especially about the Party, he would unhesitatingly testify to Ramius' skill and craftiness.

And his own. Tupolev, now in his third year of command, had been one of the Schoolmaster's star pupils. His current vessel was a brand-new *Alfa*, the fastest submarine ever made. A month earlier, while Ramius had been fitting out the *Red*

October after her initial shakedown, Tupolev and three of his officers had flown down to see the model sub that had been the test-bed for the prototype drive system. Thirty-two meters long and diesel-electric powered, it was based in the Caspian Sea, far from the eyes of imperialist spies, and kept in a covered dock, hidden from their photographic satellites. Ramius had had a hand in the development of the caterpillar, and Tupolev recognized the mark of the master. It would be a bastard to detect. Not quite impossible, though. After a week of following the model around the north end of the Caspian Sea in an electrically powered launch, trailing the best passive sonar array his country had yet made, he thought he had found a flaw. Not a big one, just big enough to exploit.

Of course there was no guarantee of success. He was not only in competition with a machine, but also with the captain commanding her. Tupolev knew this area intimately. The water was almost perfectly isothermal; there was no thermal layer for a submarine to hide under. They were far enough from the freshwater rivers on the north coast of Russia not to have to worry about pools and walls of variable salinity interfering with their sonar searches. The *Konovalov* had been built with the best sonar systems the Soviet Union had yet produced, copied closely from the French DUUV-23 and a bit improved, the factory technicians said.

Tupolev planned to mimic the American tactic of drifting slowly, with just enough speed to maintain steerage, perfectly quiet and waiting for the *Red October* to cross his path. He would then trail his quarry closely and log each change in course and speed, so that when they compared logs in a few weeks the Schoolmaster would see that his erstwhile student had played his own winning game. It was about time someone did.

"Anything new on sonar?" Tupolev was getting tense. Patience came hard to him.

"Nothing new, Comrade Captain." The *starpom* tapped the X on the chart that marked the position of the *Rokossovskiy,* a *Delta*-class missile sub they had ben tracking for several hours in the same exercise area. "Our friend is still cruising in a slow circle. Do you think that *Rokossovskiy* might be trying to confuse us? Would Captain Ramius have arranged for him to be here, to complicate our task?"

The thought had occurred to Tupolev. "Perhaps, but prob-

ably not. This exercise was arranged by Korov himself. Our
mission orders were sealed, and Marko's orders should have
been also. But then, Admiral Korov is an old friend of our
Marko." Tupolev paused for a moment and shook his head.
"No. Korov is an honorable man. I think Ramius is proceeding
this way as slowly as he can. To make us nervous, to make us
question ourselves. He will know we are to hunt him and will
adjust his plans accordingly. He might try to enter the square
from an unexpected direction—or to make us think that he is.
You have never served under Ramius, Comrade Lieutenant.
He is a fox, that one, an old gray-whiskered fox. I think we
will continue to patrol as we are for another four hours. If we
have not yet acquired him then, we will cross over to the
southeast corner of the square and work our way in to the
center. Yes."

    Tupolev had never expected that this would be easy. No
attack submarine commander had ever embarrassed Ramius.
He was determined to be the first, and the difficulty of the task
would only confirm his own prowess. In one or two more years,
Tupolev planned to be the new master.

THE THIRD DAY

SUNDAY, 5 DECEMBER

The Red October

The *Red October* had no time of her own. For her the sun neither rose nor set, and the days of the week had little significance. Unlike surface ships, which changed their clocks to conform with the local time wherever they were, submarines generally adhered to a single time reference. For American subs this was Zulu, or Greenwich mean time. For the *Red October* it was Moscow standard time, which by normal reckoning was actually one hour ahead of standard time to save on utility expenses.

Ramius entered the control room in mid-morning. Their course was now two-five-zero, speed thirteen knots, and the submarine was running thirty meters above the bottom at the west edge of the Barents Sea. In a few more hours the bottom would drop away to an abyssal plain, allowing them to go much deeper. Ramius examined the chart first, then the numerous banks of instruments covering both side bulkheads in the compartment. Last he made some notations in the order book.

"Lieutenant Ivanov!" he said sharply to the junior officer of the watch.

"Yes, Comrade Captain!" Ivanov was the greenest officer aboard, fresh from Lenin's Komsomol School in Leningrad, pale, skinny, and eager.

"I will be calling a meeting of the senior officers in the wardroom. You will now be the officer of the watch. This is your first cruise, Ivanov. How do you like it?"

"It is better than I had hoped, Comrade Captain," Ivanov replied with greater confidence than he could possibly have felt.

"That is good, Comrade Lieutenant. It is my practice to give junior officers as much responsibility as they can handle. While we senior officers are having our weekly political discussion, *you* are in command of this vessel! The safety of this ship and all his crew is *your* responsibility! You have been taught all you need to know, and my instructions are in the order book. If we detect another submarine or surface ship you will inform me at once and instantly initiate evasion drill. Any questions?"

"No, Comrade Captain." Ivanov was standing at rigid attention.

"Good." Ramius smiled. "Pavel Ilych, you will forever remember this as one of the great moments of your life. I know, I can still remember my first watch. Do not forget your orders or your responsibilities!"

Pride sparkled in the boy's eyes. It was too bad what would happen to him, Ramius thought, still the teacher. On first inspection, Ivanov looked to have the makings of a good officer.

Ramius walked briskly aft to the ship's medical office.

"Good morning, Doctor."

"Good morning to you, Comrade Captain. It is time for our political meeting?" Petrov had been reading the manual for the sub's new X-ray machine.

"Yes, it is, Comrade Doctor, but I do not wish you to attend. There is something else I want you to do. While the senior officers are at the meeting, I have the three youngsters standing watch in control and the engineering spaces."

"Oh?" Petrov's eyes went wide. It was his first time on a submarine in several years.

Ramius smiled. "Be at ease, Comrade. I can get from the wardroom to control in twenty seconds, as you know, and Comrade Melekhin can get to his precious reactor just as fast. Sooner or later our young officers must learn to function on their own. I prefer that they learn sooner. I want you to keep an eye on them. I know that they all have the knowledge to do their duties. I want to know if they have the temperament. If Borodin or I watch over them, they will not act normally. And in any case, this is a medical judgment, no?"

"Ah, you wish me to observe how they react to their responsibilities."

"Without the pressure of being observed by a senior line officer," Ramius confirmed. "One must give young officers room to grow—but not too much. If you observe something that you question, you will inform me at once. There should be no problems. We are in open sea, there is no traffic about, and the reactor is running at a fraction of its total power. The first test for young officers ought to be an easy one. Find some excuse for traveling back and forth, and keep an eye on the children. Ask questions about what they are doing."

Petrov laughed at that. "Ah, and also you would have me learn a few things, Comrade Captain? They told me about you at Severomorsk. Fine, it will be as you say. But this will be the first political meeting I have missed in years."

"From what your file says, you could teach Party doctrine to the Politburo, Yevgeni Konstantinovich." Which said little about his medical ability, Ramius thought.

The captain moved forward to the wardroom to join his brother officers, who were waiting for him. A steward had left several pots of tea along with black bread and butter to snack on. Ramius looked at the corner of the table. The bloodstains had long since been wiped away, but he could remember exactly what it looked like. This, he reflected, was one difference between himself and the man he had murdered. Ramius had a conscience. Before taking his seat, he turned to lock the door behind him. His officers were all sitting at attention, since the compartment was not large enough for them to stand once the bench seats were folded down.

Sunday was the normal day for the political awareness session at sea. Ordinarily Putin would have officiated, reading some *Pravda* editorials, followed by selected quotations from the works of Lenin and a discussion of the lessons to be learned from the readings. It is very much like a church service.

With the demise of the *zampolit* this duty devolved upon the commanding officer, but Ramius doubted that regulations anticipated the sort of discussion on today's agenda. Each officer in this room was a member of his conspiracy. Ramius outlined their plans—there had been some minor changes which he had not mentioned to anyone. Then he told them about the letter.

"So, there is no going back," Borodin observed.

"We have all agreed upon our course of action. Now we are committed to it." Their reactions to his words were just what he expected them to be—sober. As well they might be. All were single; no one left behind a wife or children. All were Party members in good standing, their dues paid up to the end of the year, their Party cards right where they were supposed to be, "next to their hearts." And each one shared with his comrades a deep-seated dissatisfaction with, in some cases a hatred of, the Soviet government.

The planning had begun soon after the death of his Natalia. The rage he had almost unknowingly suppressed throughout his life had burst forth with a violence and passion that he had struggled to contain. A lifetime of self-control had enabled him to conceal it, and a lifetime of naval training had enabled him to choose a purpose worthy of it.

Ramius had not yet begun school when he first heard tales from other children about what his father Aleksandr had done in Lithuania in 1940 and after that country's dubious liberation from the Germans in 1944. These were the repeated whisperings of their parents. One little girl told Marko a story that he recounted to Aleksandr, and to the boy's uncomprehending horror her father vanished. For his unwitting mistake Marko was branded an informer. Stung by the name he was given for committing a crime—which the State taught was not a crime at all—whose enormity never stopped pulling at his conscience, he never informed again.

In the formative years of his life, while the elder Ramius ruled the Lithuanian Party Central Committee in Vilnius, the motherless boy was raised by his paternal grandmother, common practice in a country savaged by four years of brutal war. Her only son left home at an early age to join Lenin's Red Guards, and while he was away she kept to the old ways, going to mass every day until 1940 and never forgetting the religious education that had been passed on to her. Ramius remembered her as a silver-haired old woman who told wonderful bedtime stories. Religious stories. It would have been far too dangerous for her to bring Marko to the religious ceremonies that had never been entirely stamped out, but she did manage to have him baptized a Roman Catholic soon after his father had deposited him with her. She never told Marko about this. The risk would have been too great. Roman Catholicism had been brutally suppressed in the Baltic states. It was a religion, and as he grew older Marko learned that Marxism-Leninism was a jealous god, tolerating no competing loyalties.

Grandmother Hilda told him nighttime stories from the Bible, each with a lesson of right and wrong, virtue and reward. As a child he found them merely entertaining, but he never told his father about them because even then he knew that Aleksandr would object. After the elder Ramius again resumed control of his son's life, this religious education faded into Marko's memory, neither fully remembered nor fully forgotten.

As a boy, Ramius sensed more than thought that Soviet Communism ignored a basic human need. In his teens, his misgivings began to take a coherent shape. The Good of the People was a laudable enough goal, but in denying a man's soul, an enduring part of his being, Marxism stripped away the foundation of human dignity and individual value. It also cast aside the objective measure of justice and ethics which, he decided, was the principal legacy of religion to civilized life. From earliest adulthood on, Marko had his own idea about right and wrong, an idea he did not share with the State. It gave him a means of gauging his actions and those of others. It was something he was careful to conceal. It served as an anchor for his soul and, like an anchor, it was hidden far below the visible surface.

Even as the boy was grappling with his first doubts about his country, no one could have suspected it. Like all Soviet children, Ramius joined the Little Octobrists, then the Young Pioneers. He paraded at the requisite battle shrines in polished boots and blood-red scarf, and gravely stood watch over the remains of some unknown soldier while clasping to his chest a deactivated PPSh submachinegun, his back ramrod straight before the eternal flame. The solemnity of such duty was no accident. As a boy Marko was certain that the brave men whose graves he guarded so intensely had met their fates with the same sort of selfless heroism that he saw portrayed in endless war movies at the local cinema. They had fought the hated Germans to protect the women and children and old people behind the lines. And like a nobleman's son of an earlier Russia, he took special pride in being the son of a Party chieftain. The Party, he heard a hundred times before he was five, was the Soul of the People; the unity of Party, People, and Nation was the holy trinity of the Soviet Union, albeit with one segment more important than the others. His father fit easily into the cinematic image of a Party apparatchik. Stern but fair, to Marko he was a frequently absent, gruffly kind man who brought his son what presents he could and saw to it that he had all the advantages the son of a Party secretary was entitled to.

Although outwardly he was the model Soviet child, inwardly he wondered why what he learned from his father and in school conflicted with the other lessons of his youth. Why did some parents refuse to let their children play with him? Why when he passed them did his classmates whisper *"stukach,"* the cruel and bitter epithet of informer? His father and the Party taught that informing was an act of patriotism, but for having done it once he was shunned. He resented the taunts of his boyhood peers, but he never once complained to his father, knowing that this would be an evil thing to do.

Something was very wrong—but what? He decided that he had to find the answers for himself. By choice Marko became individual in his thinking, and so unknowingly committed the gravest sin in the Communist pantheon. Outwardly the model of a Party member's son, he played the game carefully and according to all the rules. He did his duty for all Party organizations, and was always the first to volunteer for the menial tasks allotted to children aspiring to Party membership, which he knew was the only path to success or even comfort in the Soviet Union. He became good at sports. Not team sports— he worked at track and field events in which he could compete as an individual and measure the performance of others. Over the years he learned to do the same in all of his endeavors, to watch and judge the actions of his fellow citizens and officers with cool detachment, behind a blank face that concealed his conclusions.

In the summer of his eighth year the course of his life was forever changed. When no one would play with "the little *stukach*," he would wander down to the fishing docks of the small village where his grandmother had made her home. A ragtag collection of old wooden boats sailed each morning, always behind a screen of patrol boats manned by MGB—as the KGB was then known—border guards, to reap a modest harvest from the Gulf of Finland. Their catch supplemented the local diet with needed protein and provided a minuscule income for the fishermen. One boat captain was old Sasha. An officer in the czar's navy, he had revolted with the crew of the cruiser *Avrora,* helping to spark the chain of events that changed the face of the world. Marko did not learn until many years later that the crewmen of the *Avrora* had broken with Lenin— and been savagely put down by Red Guards. Sasha had spent twenty years in labor camps for his part in that collective in-discretion and only been released at the beginning of the Great Patriotic War. The *Rodina* had found herself in need of experienced seamen to pilot ships into the ports of Murmansk and Archangel, to which the Allies were bringing weapons, food, and the sundries that allow a modern army to function. Sasha had learned his lesson in the gulag: he did his duty efficiently and well, asking for nothing in return. After the war he'd been given a kind of freedom for his services, the right to perform back-breaking work under perpetual suspicion.

By the time Marko met him, Sasha was over sixty, a nearly bald man with ropy old muscles, a seaman's eye, and a talent for stories that left the youngster wide-eyed. He'd been a midshipman under the famous Admiral Marakov at Port Arthur in 1906. Probably the finest seaman in Russian history, Marakov's reputation as a patriot and an innovative fighting sailor was sufficiently unblemished that a Communist government would eventually see fit to name a missile cruiser in his memory. At first wary of the boy's reputation, Sasha saw something in him that others missed. The boy without friends and the sailor without a family became comrades. Sasha spent hours telling and retelling the tale of how he had been on the admiral's flagship, the *Petropavlovsk*, and participated in the one Russian victory over the hated Japanese—only to have his battleship sunk and his admiral killed by a mine while returning to port. After this Sasha had led his seamen as naval infantry, winning three decorations for courage under fire. This experience—he waggled his finger seriously at the boy—taught him of the mindless corruption of the czarist regime and convinced him to join one of the first naval soviets when such action meant certain death at the hands of the czar's secret police, the *okhrana*. He told his own version of the October Revolution from the thrilling perspective of an eyewitness. But Sasha was very careful to leave the later parts out.

He allowed Marko to sail with him and taught him the fundamentals of seamanship that decided a boy not yet nine that his destiny lay on the sea. There was a freedom at sea he could never have on land. There was a romance about it that touched the man growing within the boy. There were also dangers, but in a summer-long series of simple, effective lessons, Sasha taught the boy that preparation, knowledge, and discipline can deal with any form of danger; that danger confronted properly is not something a man must fear. In later years Marko would reflect often on the value this summer had held for him, and wonder just how far Sasha's career might have led if other events had not cut it short.

Marko told his father about Sasha towards the end of that long Baltic summer and even took him to meet the old seadog. The elder Ramius was sufficiently impressed with him and what he had done for his son that he arranged for Sasha to have command of a newer, larger boat and moved him up on the list for a new apartment. Marko almost believed that the Party could do a good deed—that he himself had done his first manly good deed. But old Sasha died the following winter, and the good deed came to nothing. Many years later Marko realized that he hadn't known his friend's last name. Even after years of faithful service to the *Rodina*, Sasha had been an unperson.

At thirteen Marko traveled to Leningrad to attend the Nakhimov School. There he decided that he, too, would become a professional naval officer. Marko would follow the quest for adventure that had for centuries called young men to the sea. The Nakhimov School was a special three-year prep

school for youngsters aspiring to a career at sea. The Soviet
Navy at that time was little more than a coastal defense force,
but Marko wanted very much to be a part of it. His father
urged him to a life of Party work, promising rapid promotion,
a life of comfort and privilege. But Marko wanted to earn
whatever he received on his own merits, not to be remembered
as an appendage of the "liberator" of Lithuania. And a life at
sea offered romance and excitement that even made serving
the State something he could tolerate. The navy had little tradition to build on. Marko sensed that in it there was room to
grow, and saw that many aspiring naval cadets were like himself, if not mavericks then as close to mavericks as was possible
in a society so closely controlled as his own. The teenager
thrived with his first experience of fellowship.

Nearing graduation, his class was exposed to the various
components of the Russian fleet. Ramius at once fell in love
with submarines. The boats at that time were small, dirty, and
smelled from the open bilges that the crews used as a convenient
latrine. At the same time submarines were the only offensive
arm that the navy had, and from the first Marko wanted to be
on the cutting edge. He'd had enough lectures on naval history
to know that submarines had twice nearly strangled England's
maritime empire and had successfully emasculated the economy of Japan. This had greatly pleased him; he was glad the
Americans had crushed the Japanese navy that had so nearly
killed his mentor.

He graduated from the Nakhimov School first in his class,
winner of the gold-plated sextant for his mastery of theoretical
navigation. As leader of his class, Marko was allowed the
school of his choice. He selected the Higher Naval School for
Underwater Navigation, named for Lenin's Komsomol,
VVMUPP, still the principal submarine school of the Soviet
Union.

His five years at VVMUPP were the most demanding of
his life, the more so since he was determined not to succeed
but to excel. He was first in his class in every subject, in every
year. His essay on the political significance of Soviet naval
power was forwarded to Sergey Georgiyevich Gorshkov, then
commander in chief of the Baltic Fleet and clearly the coming
man in the Soviet Navy. Gorshkov had seen the essay published

in *Morskoi Sbornik (Naval Collections)*, the leading Soviet naval journal. It was a model of progressive Party thought, quoting Lenin six different times.

By this time Marko's father was a candidate member of the Presidium, as the Politburo was then called, and very proud of his son. The elder Ramius was no one's fool. He finally recognized that the Red Fleet was a growing flower and that his son would someday have a position of importance in it. His influence moved his son's career rapidly along.

By thirty, Marko had his first command and a new wife. Natalia Bogdanova was the daughter of another Presidium member whose diplomatic duties had taken him and his family all over the world. Natalia had never been a healthy girl. They had no children, their three attempts each ending in miscarriage, the last of which had nearly killed her. She was a pretty, delicate woman, sophisticated by Russian standards, who polished her husband's passable English with American and British books— politically approved ones to be sure, mainly the thoughts of Western leftists, but also a smattering of genuine literature, including Hemingway, Twain, and Upton Sinclair. Along with his naval career, Natalia had been the center of his life. Their marriage, punctuated by prolonged absences and joyous returns, made their love even more precious than it might have been.

When construction began on the first class of Soviet nuclear-powered submarines, Marko found himself in the yards learning how the steel sharks were designed and built. He was soon known as a very hard man to please as a junior quality control inspector. His own life, he was aware, would ride on the workmanship of these often drunk welders and fitters. He became an expert in nuclear engineering, spent two years as a *starpom*, and then received his first nuclear command. She was a *November*-class attack submarine, the first crude attempt by the Soviets to make a battleworthy long-range attack boat to threaten Western navies and lines of communication. Not a month later a sister ship suffered a major reactor casualty off the Norwegian coast, and Marko was first to arrive on the scene. As ordered, he successfully rescued the crew, then sank the disabled sub lest Western navies learn her secrets. Both tasks he performed expertly and well, a noteworthy tour de force for a young commander. Good performance was something he had always felt it was important to reward in his subordinates, and the fleet commander at that time felt the same way. Marko soon moved on to a new *Charlie I*–class sub.

It was men like Ramius who went out to challenge the Americans and the British. Marko took few illusions with him. The Americans, he knew, had long experience in naval warfare—their own greatest fighter, Jones, had once served the Russian navy for the Czaritza Catherine. Their submariners were legendary for their craftiness, and Ramius found himself pitted against the last of the war-trained Americans, men who had endured the sweaty fear of underwater combat and utterly defeated a modern navy. The deadly serious game of hide-and-seek he played with them was not an easy one, the less so because they had submarines years ahead of Soviet design. But it was not a time without a few victories.

Ramius gradually learned to play the game by American rules, training his officers and men with care. His crews were rarely as prepared as he wished—still the Soviet Navy's greatest problem—but where other commanders cursed their men for their failings, Marko corrected the failings of his men. His first *Charlie*-class submarine was called the Vilnius Academy. This was partially a slur against his half-Lithuanian blood—though since he had been born in Leningrad of a Great Russian, his internal passport designated him as that—but mainly recognition that officers came to him half-trained and left him ready for advancement and eventual command. The same was true of his conscripted crewmen. Ramius did not permit the hazing and low-level terrorism normal throughout the Soviet military. He saw his task as the building of seamen, and he produced a greater percentage of reenlistments than any other submarine commander. A full ninth of the *michmanyy* in the Northern Fleet submarine force were Ramius-trained professionals. His brother submarine commanders were delighted to take aboard his *starshini*, and more than one advanced to officer's school.

After eighteen months of hard work and diligent training, Marko and his Vilnius Academy were ready to play their game of fox and hounds. He happened upon the USS *Triton* in the Norwegian Sea and hounded her mercilessly for twelve hours. Later he would note with no small satisfaction that the *Triton* was soon thereafter retired, because, it was said, the oversized vessel had proven unable to deal with the newer Soviet designs. The diesel-powered submarines of the British and the Norwegians that he occasionally happened across while snorkling he dogged ruthlessly, often subjecting them to vicious sonar lashing. Once he even acquired an American missile submarine, managing to maintain contact with her for nearly two hours before she vanished like a ghost into the black waters.

The rapid growth of the Soviet Navy and the need for qualified officers during his early career prevented Ramius from attending the Frunze Academy. This was normally a *sine qua non* of career advancement in all of the Soviet armed services. Frunze, in Moscow near the old Novodevichiy Monastery, was named for a hero of the Revolution. It was the premiere school for those who aspired to high command, and though Ramius had not attended it as a student, his prowess as an operational commander won him an appointment as an instructor. It was something earned solely on merit, for which his highly placed father was not responsible. That was important to Ramius.

The head of the naval section at Frunze liked to introduce Marko as "our test pilot of submarines." His classes became a prime attraction not only for the naval officers in the academy but also for the many others who came to hear his lectures on naval history and maritime strategy. On weekends spent at his father's official dacha in the village of Zhukova-1, he wrote manuals for submarine operations and the training of crews, and specifications for the ideal attack submarine. Some of his ideas had been controversial enough to upset his erstwhile sponsor, Gorshkov, by this time commander in chief of the entire Soviet Navy—but the old admiral was not entirely displeased.

Ramius proposed that officers in the submarine service should work in a single class of ship—better yet, the same ship—for years, the better to learn their profession and the capabilities of their vessels. Skilled captains, he suggested, should not be forced to leave their commands for desk-bound promotions. Here he lauded the Red Army's practice of leaving a field commander in his post so long as the man wanted it, and deliberately contrasted his view on this matter with the practice of imperialist navies. He stressed the need for extended training in the fleet, for longer-service enlisted men, and for better living conditions on submarines. For some of his ideas he found a sympathetic ear in the high command. For others he did not, and thus Ramius found himself destined never to have his own admiral's flag. By this time he did not care. He loved his submarines too much ever to leave them for a squadron or even a fleet command.

After finishing at Frunze, he did indeed become a test pilot of submarines. Marko Ramius, now a captain first rank, would take out the first ship of every submarine class to "write the book" on its strengths and weaknesses, to develop operational routines and training guidelines. The first of the *Alfa*s was his, the first of the *Delta*s and *Typhoon*s. Aside from one extraordinary mishap on an *Alfa*, his career had been one uninterrupted story of achievement.

Along the way he became the mentor of many young officers. He often wondered what Sasha would have thought as he taught the demanding art of submarine operations to scores of eager young men. Many of them had already become commanding officers themselves; more had failed. Ramius was a commander who took good care of those who pleased him—and took good care of those who did not. Another reason why he had never made admiral was his unwillingness to promote officers whose fathers were as powerful as his own but whose abilities were unsatisfactory. He never played favorites where duty was concerned, and the sons of a half-dozen high Party officials received unsatisfactory fitness reports despite their active performance in weekly Party discussions. Most had become *zampoliti*. It was this sort of integrity that earned him trust in fleet command. When a really tough job was at hand, Ramius' name was usually the first to be considered for it.

Also along the way he had gathered to himself a number of young officers whom he and Natalia virtually adopted. They were surrogates for the family Marko and his wife never had. Ramius found himself shepherding men much like himself, with long-suppressed doubts about their country's leadership. He was an easy man to talk to, once a man had proven himself. To those with political doubts, those with just grievances, he gave the same advice: "Join the Party." Nearly all were already Komsomol members, of course, and Marko urged them to take the next step. This was the price of a career at sea, and guided by their own craving for adventure most officers paid that price. Ramius himself had been allowed to join the Party at eighteen,

the earliest possible age, because of his father's influence. His
occasional talks at weekly Party meetings were perfect reci-
tations of the Party line. It wasn't hard, he'd tell his officers
patiently. All you had to do was repeat what the Party said—
just change the words around slightly. This was much easier
than navigation—one had only to look at the political officer
to see that! Ramius became known as a captain whose officers
were both proficient and models of political conformity. He
was one of the best Party recruiters in the navy.

Then his wife died. Ramius was in port at the time, not
unusual for a missile sub commander. He had his own dacha
in the woods west of Polyarnyy, his own Zhiguli automobile,
the official car and driver those which his command station
enjoyed, and numerous other creature comforts that came with
his rank and his parentage. He was a member of the Party elite,
so when Natalie had complained of abdominal pain, going to
the Fourth Department clinic which served only the privileged
had been a natural mistake—there was a saying in the Soviet
Union: Floors parquet, docs okay. He'd last seen his wife alive
lying on a gurney, smiling as she was wheeled towards the
operating room.

The surgeon on call had arrived at the hospital late, and
drunk, and allowed himself too much time breathing pure oxygen to sober up before starting the simple procedure of removing an inflamed appendix. The swollen organ burst just as
he was retracting tissue to get at it. A case of peritonitis immediately followed, complicated by the perforated bowel the
surgeon caused by his clumsy haste to repair the damage.

Natalia was placed on antibiotic therapy, but there was a
shortage of medicine. The foreign—usually French—pharmaceuticals used in Fourth Department clinics had run out.
Soviet antibiotics, "plan" medications, were substituted. It was
a common practice in Soviet industry for workers to earn bo-
nuses by manufacturing goods over the usual quota, goods that
bypassed what quality control existed in Soviet industry. This
particular batch of medication had never been inspected or
tested. *And the vials had probably been filled with distilled
water instead of antibiotics,* Marko learned the next day. Natalia
had lapsed into deep shock and coma, dying before the series
of errors could be corrected.

The funeral was appropriately solemn, Ramius remembered

bitterly. Brother officers from his own command and over a hundred other navy men whom he had befriended over the years were there, along with members of Natalia's family and representatives of the Local Party Central Committee. Marko had been at sea when his father died, and because he had known the extent of Aleksandr's crimes, the loss had had little effect. His wife's death, however, was nothing less than a personal catastrophe. Soon after they had married Natalia had joked that every sailor needs someone to return to, that every woman needs someone to wait for. It had been as simple as that—and infinitely more complex, the marriage of two intelligent people who had over fifteen years learned each other's foibles and strengths and grown ever closer.

Marko Ramius watched the coffin roll into the cremation chamber to the somber strain of a classical requiem, wishing that he could pray for Natalia's soul, hoping that Grandmother Hilda had been right, that there was something beyond the steel door and mass of flame. Only then did the full weight of the event strike him: *the State had robbed him of more than his wife, it had robbed him of a means to assuage his grief with prayer, it had robbed him of the hope—if only an illusion—of ever seeing her again.* Natalia, gentle and kind, had been his only happiness since that Baltic summer long ago. Now that happiness was gone forever. As the weeks and months wore on he was tormented by her memory; a certain hairstyle, a certain walk, a certain laugh encountered on the streets or in the shops of Murmansk was all it took to thrust Natalia back to the forefront of his consciousness, and when he was thinking of his loss, he was not a professional naval officer.

The life of Natalia Bogdanova Ramius had been lost at the hands of a surgeon who had been drinking while on call—a court-martial offense in the Soviet Navy—but Marko could not have the doctor punished. The surgeon was himself the son of a Party chieftain, his status secured by his own sponsors. Her life might have been saved by proper medication, but there had not been enough foreign drugs, and Soviet pharmaceuticals were untrustworthy. The doctor could not be made to pay, the pharmaceutical workers could not be made to pay—the thought echoed back and forth across his mind, feeding his fury until he decided that the State would be made to pay.

The idea had taken weeks to form and was the product of

a career of training and contingency planning. When the construction of the *Red October* was restarted after a two-year hiatus, Ramius knew that he would command her. He had helped with the designing of her revolutionary drive system and had inspected the model, which had been running on the Caspian Sea for some years in absolute secrecy. He asked for relief from his command so that he could concentrate on the construction and outfitting of the *October* and select and train his officers beforehand, the earlier to get the missile sub into full operation. The request was granted by the commander of the Red Banner Northern Fleet, a sentimental man who had also wept at Natalia's funeral.

Ramius had already known who his officers would be. All graduates of the Vilnius Academy, many the "sons" of Marko and Natalia, they were men who owed their place and their rank to Ramius; men who cursed the inability of their country to build submarines worthy of their skills; men who had joined the Party as told and then become even more dissatisfied with the Motherland as they learned that the price of advancement was to prostitute one's mind and soul, to become a highly paid parrot in a blue jacket whose every Party recitation was a grating exercise in self-control. For the most part they were men for whom this degrading step had not borne fruit. In the Soviet Navy there were three routes to advancement. A man could become a *zampolit* and be a pariah among his peers. Or he could be a navigation officer and advance to his own command. Or he could be shunted into a specialty in which he would gain rank and pay—but never command. Thus a chief engineer on a Soviet naval vessel could outrank his commanding officer and still be his subordinate.

Ramius looked around the table at his officers. Most had not been allowed to pursue their own career goals despite their proficiency and despite their party membership. The minor infractions of youth—in one case an act committed at age eight—prevented two from ever being trusted again. With the missile officer, it was because he was a Jew; though his parents had always been committed, believing Communists, neither they nor their son was ever trusted. Another officer's elder brother had demonstrated against the invasion of Czechoslovakia in 1968 and disgraced his whole family. Melekhin, the chief engineer and Ramius' equal in rank, had never been allowed the route to command simply because his superiors wanted him to be an engineer. Borodin, who was ready for his own command, had once accused a *zampolit* of homosexuality; the man he had informed on was the son of the chief *zampolit* of the Northern Fleet. There are many paths to treason.

"And what if they locate us?" Kamarov speculated.

"I doubt that even the Americans can find us when the caterpillar is operating. I am certain that our own submarines cannot. Comrades, I helped design this ship," Ramius said.

"What will become of us?" the missile officer muttered.

"First we must accomplish the task at hand. An officer who looks too far ahead stumbles over his own boots."

"They will be looking for us," Borodin said.

"Of course," Ramius smiled, "but they will not know where to look until it is too late. Our mission, comrades, is to avoid detection. And so we shall."

THE FOURTH DAY

MONDAY, 6 DECEMBER

CIA Headquarters

Ryan walked down the corridor on the top floor of the Langley, Virginia, headquarters of the Central Intelligence Agency. He had already passed through three separate security checks, none of which had required him to open his locked briefcase, now draped under the folds of his buff-colored toggle coat, a gift from an officer in the Royal Navy.

What he had on was mostly his wife's fault, an expensive suit bought on Savile Row. It was English cut, neither conservative nor on the leading edge of contemporary fashion. He had a number of suits like this arranged neatly in his closet by colors, which he wore with white shirts and striped ties. His only jewelry was a wedding band and a university ring, plus an expensive but accurate digital watch on a more expensive gold band. Ryan was not a man who placed a great deal of value in appearances. Indeed, his job was to see through these in the search for hard truth.

He was physically unremarkable, an inch over six feet, and his average build suffered a little at the waist from a lack of exercise enforced by the miserable English weather. His blue eyes had a deceptively vacant look; he was often lost in thought, his face on autopilot as his mind puzzled through data or research material for his current book. The only people Ryan needed to impress were those who knew him; he cared little for the rest. He had no ambition to celebrity. His life, he judged, was already as complicated as it needed to be—quite a bit more complicated than most would guess. It included a wife he loved and two children he doted on, a job that tested his intellect, and sufficient financial independence to choose his own path. The path Jack Ryan had chosen was in the CIA. The agency's official motto was, The truth shall make you free. The trick, he told himself at least once a day, was finding that truth, and while he doubted that he would ever reach this sublime state of grace, he took quiet pride in his ability to pick at it, one small fragment at a time.

The office of the deputy director for intelligence occupied a whole corner of the top floor, overlooking the tree-covered Potomac Valley. Ryan had one more security check to pass.

"Good morning, Dr. Ryan."

"Hi, Nancy." Ryan smiled at her. Nancy Cummings had held her secretarial job for twenty years, had served eight DDIs, and if the truth were known she probably had as good a feel for the intelligence business as the political appointees in the adjacent office. It was the same as with any large business—the bosses came and went, but the good executive secretaries lasted forever.

"How's the family, Doctor? Looking forward to Christmas?"

"You bet—except my Sally's a little worried. She's not sure Santa knows that we've moved, and she's afraid he won't make it to England for her. He will," Ryan confided.

"It's so nice when they're that little." She pressed a hidden button. "You can go right in, Dr. Ryan."

"Thanks, Nancy." Ryan twisted the electronically protected knob and walked into the DDI's office.

Vice Admiral James Greer was reclining in his high-backed judge's chair reading through a folder. His oversized mahogany desk was covered with neat piles of folders whose edges were bordered with red tape and whose covers bore various code words.

"Hiya, Jack!" he called across the room. "Coffee?"

"Yes, thank you, sir."

James Greer was sixty-six, a naval officer past retirement age who kept working through brute competence, much as Hyman Rickover had, though Greer was a far easier man to work for. He was a "mustang," a man who had entered the naval service as an enlisted man, earned his way into the Naval Academy, and spent forty years working his way to a three-star flag, first commanding submarines, then as a full-time intelligence specialist. Greer was a demanding boss, but one who took care of those who pleased him. Ryan was one of these.

Somewhat to Nancy's chagrin, Greer liked to make his own coffee with a West Bend drip machine on the credenza behind his desk, where he could just turn around to reach it. Ryan poured himself a cup—actually a navy-style handleless mug. It was traditional navy coffee, brewed strong, with a pinch of salt.

"You hungry, Jack?" Greer pulled a pastry box from a desk drawer. "I got some sticky buns here."

"Why, thanks, sir. I didn't eat much on the plane." Ryan took one, along with a paper napkin.

"Still don't like to fly?" Greer was amused.

Ryan sat down in the chair opposite his boss. "I suppose I ought to be getting used to it. I like the Concorde better than the wide-bodies. You only have to be terrified half as long."

"How's the family?"

"Fine, thank you, sir. Sally's in first grade—loves it. And little Jack is toddling around the house. These buns are pretty good."

"New bakery just opened up a few blocks from my place. I pass it on the way in every morning." The admiral sat upright in his chair. "So, what brings you over today?"

"Photographs of the new Soviet missile boat, *Red October*," Ryan said casually between sips.

"Oh, and what do our British cousins want in return?" Greer asked suspiciously.

"They want a peek at Barry Somers' new enhancement gadgets. Not the machines themselves—at first—just the finished product. I think it's a fair bargain, sir." Ryan knew the CIA didn't have any shots of the new sub. The operations directorate did not have a man at the building yard at

Severodvinsk or a reliable man at the Polyarnyy submarine base. Worse, the rows of "boat barns" built to shelter the missile submarines, modeled on World War II German submarine pens, made satellite photography impossible. "We have ten frames, low obliques, five each bow and stern, and one from each perspective is undeveloped so that Somers can work on them fresh. We are not committed, sir, but I told Sir Basil that you'd think it over."

The admiral grunted. Sir Basil Charleston, chief of the British Secret Intelligence Service, was a master of the quid pro quo, occasionally offering to share sources with his wealthier cousins and a month later asking for something in return. The intelligence game was often like a primitive marketplace. "To use the new system, Jack, we need the camera used to take the shots."

"I know." Ryan pulled the camera from his coat pocket. "It's a modified Kodak disk camera. Sir Basil says it's the coming thing in spy cameras, nice and flat. This one, he says, was hidden in a tobacco pouch."

"How did you know that—that we need the camera?"

"You mean how Somers uses lasers to—"

"Ryan!" Greer snapped. "How much do you know?"

"Relax, sir. Remember back in February, I was over to discuss those new SS-20 sites on the Chinese border? Somers was here, and you asked me to drive him out to the airport. On the way out he started babbling about this great new idea he was heading west to work on. He talked about it all the way to Dulles. From what little I understood, I gather that he shoots laser beams through the camera lenses to make a mathematical model of the lens. From that, I suppose, he can take the exposed negative, break down the image into the—original incoming light beams, I guess, then use a computer to run *that* through a computer-generated theoretical lens to make a perfect picture. I probably have it wrong." Ryan could tell from Greer's face that he didn't.

"Somers talks too goddamned much."

"I told him that, sir. But once the guy gets started, how the hell do you shut him up?"

"And what do the Brits know?" Greer asked.

"Your guess is as good as mine, sir. Sir Basil asked me about it, and I told him that he was asking the wrong guy—I mean, my degrees are in economics and history, not physics. I told him we needed the camera—but he already knew that. Took it right out of his desk and tossed it to me. I did not reveal a thing about this, sir."

"I wonder how many other people he spilled to. Geniuses! They operate in their own crazy little worlds. Somers is like a little kid sometimes. And you know the First Rule of Security: The likelihood of a secret's being blown is proportional to the *square* of the number of people who're in on it." It was Greer's favorite dictum.

His phone buzzed. "Greer . . . Right." He hung up. "Charlie Davenport's on the way up, per your suggestion, Jack. Supposed to be here half an hour ago. Must be the snow." The admiral jerked a hand towards the window. There were two inches on the ground, with another inch expected by nightfall. "One flake hits this town and everything goes to hell."

Ryan laughed. That was something Greer, a down-easter from Maine, never could seem to understand.

"So, Jack, you say this is worth the price?"

"Sir, we've wanted these pictures for some time, what with all the contradictory data we've been getting on the sub. It's your decision and the judge's but, yes, I think they're worth the price. These shots are very interesting."

"We ought to have our own men in that damned yard," Greer grumped. Ryan didn't know how Operations had screwed that one up. He had little interest in field operations. Ryan was an analyst. How the data came to his desk was not his concern, and he was careful to avoid finding out. "I don't suppose Basil told you anything about their man?"

Ryan smiled, shaking his head. "No, sir, and I did not ask." Greer nodded his approval.

"Morning, James!"

Ryan turned to see Rear Admiral Charles Davenport, director of naval intelligence, with a captain trailing in his wake.

"Hi, Charlie. You know Jack Ryan, don't you?"

"Hello, Ryan."

"We've met," Ryan said.

"This is Captain Casimir."

Ryan shook hands with both men. He'd met Davenport a few years before while delivering a paper at the Naval War College in Newport, Rhode Island. Davenport had given him a hard time in the question-and-answer session. He was supposed to be a bastard to work for, a former aviator who had lost flight status after a barrier crash and, some said, still bore a grudge. Against whom? Nobody really knew.

"Weather in England must be as bad as here, Ryan." Davenport dropped his bridge coat on top of Ryan's. "I see you stole a Royal Navy overcoat."

Ryan was fond of his toggle coat. "A gift, sir, and quite warm."

"Christ, you even talk like a Brit. James, we gotta bring this boy home."

"Be nice to him, Charlie. He's got a present for you. Grab yourself some coffee."

Casimir scurried over to fill a mug for his boss, then sat down at his right hand. Ryan let them wait a moment before opening his briefcase. He took out four folders, keeping one and handing the others around.

"They say you've been doing some fairly good work, Ryan," Davenport said. Jack knew him to be a mercurial man, affable one moment, brittle the next. Probably to keep his subordinates off balance. "And—Jesus Christ!" Davenport had opened his folder.

"Gentlemen, I give you *Red October,* courtesy of the British Secret Intelligence Service," Ryan said formally.

The folders had the photographs arranged in pairs, four each of four-by-four prints. In the back were ten-by-ten blowups of each. The photos had been taken from a low-oblique angle, probably from the rim of the graving dock that had held the boat during her post-shakedown refit. The shots were paired, fore and aft, fore and aft.

"Gentlemen, as you can see, the lighting wasn't all that great. Nothing fancy here. It was a pocket camera loaded with 400-speed color film. The first pair was processed normally to establish high levels. The second was pushed for greater brightness using normal procedures. The third pair was digitally enhanced for color resolution, and the fourth was digitally enhanced for line resolution. I have undeveloped frames of each view for Barry Somers to play with."

"Oh?" Davenport looked up briefly. "That's right neighborly of the Brits. What's the price?" Greer told him. "Pay up. It's worth it."

"That's what Jack says."

"Figures," Davenport chuckled. "You know he really is working for them."

Ryan bristled at that. He liked the English, liked working with their intelligence community, but he knew what country he came from. Jack took a deep breath. Davenport liked to goad people, and if he reacted Davenport would win.

"I gather that Sir John Ryan is still well connected on the other side of the ocean?" Davenport said, extending the prod.

Ryan's knighthood was an honorary one. It was his reward for having broken up a terrorist incident that had erupted around him in St. James's Park, London. He'd been a tourist at the time, the innocent American abroad, long before he'd been asked to join the CIA. The fact that he had unknowingly prevented the assassination of two very prominent figures had gotten him more publicity than he'd ever wanted, but it had also brought him in contact with a lot of people in England, most of them worth the time. Those connections had made him valuable enough that the CIA asked him to be part of a joint American-British liaison group. That was how he had established a good working relationship with Sir Basil Charleston.

"We have lots of friends over there, sir, and some of them were kind enough to give you these," Ryan said coolly.

Davenport softened. "Okay, Jack, then you do me a favor. You see whoever gave us these gets something nice in his stocking. They're worth plenty. So, exactly what do we have here?"

To the unschooled observer, the photographs showed the standard nuclear missile submarine. The steel hull was blunt at one end, tapered at the other. The workmen standing on the floor of the dock provided scale—she was huge. There were twin bronze propellers at the stern, on either side of a flat appendage which the Russians called a beaver tail, or so the intelligence reports said. With the twin screws the stern was unremarkable except in one detail.

"What are these doors for?" Casimir asked.

"Hmm. She's a big bastard." Davenport evidently hadn't heard. "Forty feet longer than we expected, by the look of her."

"Forty-four, roughly." Ryan didn't much like Davenport, but the man did know his stuff. "Somers can calibrate that for us. And more beam, two meters more than the other *Typhoon*s.

She's an obvious development of the *Typhoon* class, but—"

"You're right, Captain," Davenport interrupted. "What are those doors?"

"That's why I came over." Ryan had wondered how long this would take. He'd caught onto them in the first five seconds. "I don't know, and neither do the Brits."

The *Red October* had two doors at the bow and stern, each about two meters in diameter, though they were not quite circular. They had been closed when the photos were shot and only showed up well on the number four pair.

"Torpedo tubes? No—four of them are inboard." Greer reached into his drawer and came out with a magnifying glass. In an age of computer-enhanced imagery it struck Ryan as charmingly anachronistic.

"You're the sub driver, James," Davenport observed.

"Twenty years ago, Charlie." He'd made the switch from line officer to professional spook in the early sixties. Captain Casimir, Ryan noted, wore the wings of a naval aviator and had the good sense to remain quiet. He wasn't a "nuc."

"Well, they can't be torpedo tubes. They have the normal four of them at the bow, inboard of these openings . . . must be six or seven feet across. How about launch tubes for the new cruise missile they're developing?"

"That's what the Royal Navy thinks. I had a chance to talk it over with their intelligence chaps. But I don't buy it. Why put an anti-surface-ship weapon on a strategic platform? We don't, and we deploy our boomers a lot further forward than they do. The doors are symmetrical through the boat's axis. You can't launch a missile out of the stern, sir. The openings barely clear the screws."

"Toward sonar array," Davenport said.

"Granted they could do that, if they trail one screw. But why two of them?" Ryan asked.

Davenport gave him a nasty look. "They love redundancies."

"Two doors forward, two aft, I can buy cruise missile tubes. I can buy a towed array. But both sets of doors exactly the same size?" Ryan shook his head. "Too much of a coincidence. I think it's something new. That's what interrupted her construction for so long. They figured something new for her and spent the last two years rebuilding the *Typhoon* configuration to accommodate it. Note also that they added six more missiles for good measure."

"Opinion," Davenport observed.

"That's what I'm paid for."

"Okay, Jack, what do you think it is?" Greer asked.

"Beats me, sir. I'm no engineer."

Admiral Greer looked his guests over for a few seconds. He smiled and leaned back in his chair. "Gentlemen, we have what? Ninety years of naval experience in this room, plus this young amateur." He gestured at Ryan. "Okay, Jack, you've set us up for something. Why did you bring this over personally?"

"I want to show these to somebody."

"Who?" Greer's head cocked suspiciously to one side.

"Skip Tyler. Any of you fellows know him?"

"I do," Casimir nodded. "He was a year behind me at Annapolis. Didn't he get hurt or something?"

"Yeah," Ryan said. "Lost his leg in an auto accident four years ago. He was up for command of the *Los Angeles* and a drunk driver clipped him. Now he teaches engineering at the Academy and does a lot of consulting work with Sea Systems Command—technical analysis, looking at their ship designs. He has a doctorate in engineering from MIT, and he knows how to think unconventionally."

"How about his security clearance?" Greer asked.

"Top secret or better, sir, because of his Crystal City work."

"Objections, Charlie?"

Davenport frowned. Tyler was not part of the intelligence community. "Is this the guy who did the evaluation of the new *Kirov?*"

Yes, sir, now that I think about it," Casimir said. "Him and Saunders over at Sea Systems."

"That was a nice piece of work. It's okay with me."

"When do you want to see him?" Greer asked Ryan.

"Today, if it's all right with you, sir. I have to run over to Annapolis anyway, to get something from the house, and—well, do some quick Christmas shopping."

"Oh? A few dolls?" Davenport asked.

Ryan turned to look the admiral in the eye. "Yes, sir, as a matter of fact. My little girl wants a Skiing Barbie doll and some Jordache doll outfits. Didn't you ever play Santa, Admiral?"

Davenport saw that Ryan wasn't going to back off anymore. He wasn't a subordinate to be browbeaten. Ryan could always walk away. He tried a new tack. "Did they tell you over there that *October* sailed last Friday?"

"Oh?" They hadn't. Ryan was caught off guard. "I thought she wasn't scheduled to sail until this Friday."

"So did we. Her skipper is Marko Ramius. You heard about him?"

"Only secondhand stuff. The Brits say he's pretty good."

"Better than that," Greer noted. "He's about the best sub driver they have, a real charger. We had a considerable file on him when I was at DIA. Who's bird-doggin' him for you, Charlie?"

"*Bremerton* was assigned to it. She was out of position doing some ELINT work when Ramius sailed, but she was ordered over. Her skipper's Bud Wilson. Remember his dad?"

Greer laughed out loud. "Red Wilson? Now there was one spirited submarine driver! His boy any good?"

"So they say. Ramius is about the best the Soviets have, but Wilson's got a 688 boat. By the end of the week, we'll be able to start a new book on *Red October.*" Davenport stood. "We gotta head back, James." Casimir hurried to get the coats. "I can keep these?"

"I suppose, Charlie. Just don't go hanging them on the wall, even to throw darts at. And I guess you want to get moving, too, Jack?"

"Yes, sir."

Greer lifted his phone. "Nancy, Dr. Ryan will need a car and a driver in fifteen minutes. Right." He set the receiver down and waited for Davenport to leave. "No sense getting you killed out there in the snow. Besides, you'd probably drive on the wrong side of the road after a year in England. Skiing Barbie, Jack?"

"You had all boys, didn't you, sir? Girls are different." Ryan grinned. "You've never met my little Sally."

"Daddy's girl?"

"Yep. God help whoever marries her. Can I leave these photographs with Tyler?"

"I hope you're right about him, son. Yes, he can hold onto them—if and only if he has a good place to keep them."

"Understood, sir."

"When you get back—probably be late, the way the roads are. You're staying at the Marriott?"

"Yes, sir."

Greer thought that over. "I'll probably be working late. Stop by here before you bed down. I may want to go over a few things with you."

"Will do, sir. Thanks for the car." Ryan stood.

"Go buy your dolls, son."

Greer watched him leave. He liked Ryan. The boy was not afraid to speak his mind. Part of that came from having money and being married to more money. It was a sort of independence that had advantages. Ryan could not be bought, bribed, or bullied. He could always go back to writing history books full time. Ryan had made money on his own in four years as a stockbroker, betting his own money on high-risk issues and scoring big before leaving it all behind—because, he said, he hadn't wanted to press his luck. Greer didn't believe that. He thought Jack had been bored—bored with making money. He shook his head. The talent that had enabled him to pick winning stocks Ryan now applied to the CIA. He was rapidly becoming one of Greer's star analysts, and his British connections made him doubly valuable. Ryan had the ability to sort through a pile of data and come out with the three or four facts that meant something. This was too rare a thing at the CIA. The agency still spent too much of its money collecting data, Greer thought, and not enough collating it. Analysts had none of the supposed glamour—a Hollywood-generated illusion—of a secret agent in a foreign land. But Jack knew how to analyze reports from such men and data from technical sources. He knew how to make a decision and was not afraid to say what he thought, whether his bosses liked it or not. This sometimes grated the old admiral, but on the whole he liked having subordinates whom he could respect. The CIA had too many people whose only skill was kissing ass.

The U.S. Naval Academy

The loss of his left leg above the knee had not taken away Oliver Wendell Tyler's roguish good looks or his zest for life. His wife could testify to this. Since leaving the active service four years before, they had added three children to the two they already had and were working on a sixth. Ryan found him sitting at a desk in an empty classroom in Rickover Hall, the U.S. Naval Academy's science and engineering building. He was grading papers.

"How's it goin', Skip?" Ryan leaned against the door frame. His CIA driver was in the hall.

"Hey, Jack! I thought you were in England." Tyler jumped to his foot—his own phrase—and hobbled over to grab Ryan's hand. His prosthetic leg ended in a square, rubber-coated band instead of a pseudo-foot. It flexed at the knee, but not by much. Tyler had been a second-squad All American offensive tackle sixteen years before, and the rest of his body was as hard as the aluminum and fiberglass in his left leg. His handshake could make a gorilla wince. "So, what are you doing here?"

"I had to fly over to get some work done and do a little shopping. How's Jean and your . . . five?"

"Five and two-thirds."

"Again? Jean ought to have you fixed."

"That's what she said, but I've had enough things disconnected." Tyler laughed. "I guess I'm making up for all those monastic years as a nuc. Come on over and grab a chair."

Ryan sat on the corner of the desk and opened his briefcase. He handed Tyler a folder.

"Got some pictures I want you to look at."

"Okay." Tyler flipped it open. "Whose—a Russian! Big bastard. That's the basic *Typhoon* configuration. Lots of modifications, though. Twenty-six missiles instead of twenty. Looks longer. Hull's flattened out some, too. More beam?"

"Two or three meters' worth."

"I heard you were working with the CIA. Can't talk about that, right?"

"Something like that. And you never saw these pictures, Skip. Understood?"

"Right." Tyler's eyes twinkled. "What do you want me not to look at them for?"

Ryan pulled the blowups from the back of the folder. "These doors, bow and stern."

"Uh-huh." Tyler set them down side by side. "Pretty big. They're two meters or so, paired fore and aft. They look symmetrical through the long axis. Not cruise missile tubes, eh?"

"On a boomer? You put something like that on a strategic missile sub?"

"The Russkies are a funny bunch, Jack, and they design things their own way. This is the same bunch that built the *Kirov* class with a nuclear reactor *and* an oil-fired steam plant. Hmm ... twin screws. The aft doors can't be for a sonar array. They'd foul the screws."

"How 'bout if they trail one screw?"

"They do that with surface ships to conserve fuel, and sometimes with their attack boats. Operating a twin-screw missile boat on one wheel would probably be tricky on this baby. The *Typhoon*'s supposed to have handling problems, and boats that handle funny tend to be sensitive to power settings. You end up jinking around so much that you have trouble holding course. You notice how the doors converge at the stern?"

"No, I didn't."

Tyler looked up. "Damn! I should have realized it right off the bat. It's a propulsion system. You shouldn't have caught me marking papers, Jack. It turns your brain to Jell-O."

"Propulsion system?"

"We looked at this—oh, must have been twenty some years ago—when I was going to school here. We didn't do anything with it, though. It's too inefficient."

"Okay, tell me about it."

"They called it a tunnel drive. You know how out West they have lots of hydroelectric power plants? Mostly dams. The water spills onto wheels that turn generators. Now there's a few new ones that kind of turn that around. They tap into underground rivers, and the water turns impellers, and they turn the generators instead of a modified mill wheel. An impeller is like a propeller, except the water drives it instead of the other way around. There's some minor technical differences, too, but nothing major. Okay so far?

"With this design, you turn that around. You suck water in the bow and your impellers eject it out the stern, and that moves the ship." Tyler paused, frowning. "As I recall you have to have more than one per tunnel. They looked at this back in the early sixties and got to the model stage before dropping it. One of the things they discovered is that one impeller doesn't work as well as several. Some sort of back pressure thing. It was a

new principle, something unexpected that cropped up. They
ended up using four, I think, and it was supposed to look
something like the compressor sets in a jet engine."

"Why did we drop it?" Ryan was taking rapid notes.

"Mostly efficiency. You can only get so much water down
the pipes no matter how powerful your motors are. And the
drive system took up a lot of room. They partially beat that
with a new kind of electric induction motor, I think, but even
then you'd end up with a lot of extraneous machinery inside
the hull. Subs don't have that much room to spare, even this
monster. The top speed limit was supposed to be about ten
knots, and that just wasn't good enough, even though it did
virtually eliminate cavitation sounds."

"Cavitation?"

"When you have a propeller turning in the water at high
speed, you develop an area of low pressure behind the trailing
edge of the blade. This can cause water to vaporize. That creates
a bunch of little bubbles. They can't last long under the water
pressure, and when they collapse the water rushes forward to
pound against the blades. That does three things. First, it makes
noise, and us sub drivers hate noise. Second, it can cause
vibration, something else we don't like. The old passenger
liners, for example, used to flutter several inches at the stern,
all from cavitation and slippage. It takes a hell of a lot of force
to vibrate a 50,000-ton ship; that kind of force breaks things.
Third, it tears up the screws. The big wheels only used to last
a few years. That's why back in the old days the blades were
bolted onto the hub instead of being cast in one piece. The
vibration is mainly a surface ship problem, and the screw deg-
radation was eventually conquered by improved metallurgical
technology.

"Now, this tunnel drive system avoids the cavitation problem. You still have cavitation, but the noise from it is mainly
lost in the tunnels. That makes good sense. The problem is
that you can't generate much speed without making the tunnels
too wide to be practical. While one team was working on this,
another was working on improved screw designs. Your typical
sub screw today is pretty large, so it can turn more slowly for
a given speed. The slower the turning speed, the less cavitation
you get. The problem is also mitigated by depth. A few hundred
feet down, the higher water pressure retards bubble formation."

"Then why don't the Soviets copy our screw designs?"

"Several reasons, probably. You design a screw for a specific hull and engine combination, so copying ours wouldn't automatically work for them. A lot of this work is still empirical, too. There's a lot of trial and error in this. It's a lot harder, say, than designing an airfoil, because the blade cross-section changes radically from one point to another. I suppose another reason is that their metallurgical technology isn't as good as ours—same reason that their jet and rocket engines are less efficient. These new designs place great value on high-strength alloys. It's a narrow specialty, and I only know the generalities."

"Okay, you say that this is a silent propulsion system, and it has a top speed limit of ten knots?" Ryan wanted to be clear on this.

"Ballpark figure. I'd have to do some computer modeling to tighten that up. We probably still have the data laying around at the Taylor Laboratory." Tyler referred to the Sea Systems Command design facility on the north side of the Severn River. "Probably still classified, and I'd have to take it with a big grain of salt."

"How come?"

"All this work was done twenty years ago. They only got up to fifteen-foot models—pretty small for this sort of thing. Remember that they had already stumbled across one new principle, that back-pressure thing. There might have been more out there. I expect they tried some computer models, but even if they did, mathematical modeling techniques back then were dirt-simple. To duplicate this today I'd have to have the old data and programs from Taylor, check it all over, then draft a new program based on this configuration." He tapped the photographs. "Once that was done, I'd need access to a big league mainframe computer to run it."

"But you could do it?"

"Sure. I'd need exact dimensions on this baby, but I've done this before for the bunch over at Crystal City. The hard part's getting the computer time. I need a big machine."

"I can probably arrange access to ours."

Tyler laughed. "Probably not good enough, Jack. This is specialized stuff. I'm talking about a Cray-2, one of the biggies. To do this you have to mathematically simulate the behavior of millions of little parcels of water, the water flow over—and through, in this case—the whole hull. Same sort of thing NASA has to do with the Space Shuttle. The actual work is easy enough—it's the *scale* that's tough. They're simple calculations, but you have to make millions of them per second. That means a big Cray, and there's only a few of them around. NASA has one in Houston, I think. The navy has a few in Norfolk for ASW work—you can forget about those. The air force has one in the Pentagon, I think, and all the rest are in California."

"But you could do it?"

"Sure."

"Okay, get to work on it, Skip, and I'll see if we can get you the computer time. How long?"

"Depending on how good the stuff at Taylor is, maybe a week. Maybe less."

"How much do you want for it?"

"Aw, come on, Jack!" Tyler waved him off.

"Skip, it's Monday. You get us this data by Friday and there's twenty thousand dollars in it. You're worth it, and we want this data. Agreed?"

"Sold." They shook hands. "Can I keep the pictures?"

"I can leave them if you have a secure place to keep them. Nobody gets to see them, Skip. Nobody."

"There's a nice safe in the superintendent's office."

"Fine, but he doesn't see them." The superintendent was a former submariner.

"He won't like it," Tyler said. "But okay."

"Have him call Admiral Greer if he objects. This number." Ryan handed him a card. "You can reach me here if you need me. If I'm not in, ask for the admiral."

"Just how important is this?"

"Important enough. You're the first guy who's come up with a sensible explanation for these hatches. That's why I came here. If you can model this for us, it'll be damned useful. Skip, one more time: This is highly sensitive. If you let anybody see these, it's my ass."

"Aye aye, Jack. Well, you've laid a deadline on me, I better get down to it. See you." After shaking hands, Tyler took out a lined pad and started listing the things he had to do. Ryan left the building with his driver. He remembered a Toys-R-Us right up Route 2 from Annapolis, and he wanted to get that doll for Sally.

CIA Headquarters

Ryan was back at the CIA by eight that evening. It was a quick trip past the security guards to Greer's office.

"Well, did you get your Surfing Barbie?" Greer looked up.

"Skiing Barbie," Ryan corrected. "Yes, sir. Come on, didn't you ever play Santa?"

"They grew up too fast, Jack. Even my grandchildren are all past that stage." He turned to get some coffee. Ryan wondered if he ever slept. "We have something more on *Red October*. The Russians seem to have a major ASW exercise running in the northeast Barents Sea. Half a dozen ASW search aircraft, a bunch of frigates, and an *Alfa*-class attack boat, all running around in circles."

"Probably an acquisition exercise. Skip Tyler says those doors are for a new drive system."

"Indeed." Greer sat back. "Tell me about it."

Ryan took out his notes and summarized his education in submarine technology. "Skip says he can generate a computer simulation of its effectiveness," he concluded.

Greer's eyebrows went up. "How soon?"

"End of week, maybe. I told him if he had it done by Friday we'd pay him for it. Twenty thousand sound reasonable?"

"Will it mean anything?"

"If he gets the background data he needs, it ought to, sir. Skip's a very sharp cookie. I mean, they don't give doctorates away at MIT, and he was in the top five of his Academy class."

"Worth twenty thousand dollars of our money?" Greer was notoriously tight with a buck.

Ryan knew how to answer this. "Sir, if we followed normal procedure on this, we'd contract one of the Beltway Bandits—," Ryan referred to the consulting firms that dotted the beltway around Washington, D.C., "—they'd charge us five or ten times as much, and we'd be lucky to have the data by Easter. This way we might just have it while the boat's still at sea. If worse comes to worst, sir, I'll foot the bill. I figured you'd want this data fast, and it's right up his alley."

"You're right." It wasn't the first time Ryan had short-circuited normal procedure. The other times had worked out fairly well. Greer was a man who looked for results. "Okay, the Soviets have a new missile boat with a silent drive system. What does it all mean?"

"Nothing good. We depend on our ability to track their boomers with our attack boats. Hell, that's why they agreed a few years back to our proposal about keeping them five hundred miles from each other's coasts, and why they keep their missile subs in port most of the time. This could change the game a bit. By the way, *October*'s hull, I haven't seen what it's made of."

"Steel. She's too big for a titanium hull, at least for what it would cost. You know what they have to spend on their *Alfa*s."

"Too much for what they got. You spend that much money for a superstrong hull, then put a noisy power plant in it. Dumb."

"Maybe. I wouldn't mind having that speed, though. Anyway, if this silent drive system really works, they might be able to creep up onto the continental shelf."

"Depressed-trajectory shot," Ryan said. This was one of the nastier nuclear war scenarios in which a sea-based missile was fired within a few hundred miles of its target. Washington is a bare hundred air miles from the Atlantic Ocean. Though a missile on a low, fast flight path loses much of its accuracy, a few of them can be launched to explode over Washington in less than a few minutes' time, too little for a president to react. If the Soviets were able to kill the president that quickly, the resulting disruption of the chain of command would give them ample time to take out the land-based missiles—there would be no one with authority to fire. This scenario is a grand-strategic version of a simple mugging, Ryan thought. A mugger doesn't attack his victim's arms—he goes for the head. "You think *October* was built with that in mind?"

"I'm sure the thought occurred to them," Greer observed. "It would have occurred to us. Well, we have *Bremerton* up there to keep an eye on her, and if this data turns out to be useful we'll see if we can come up with an answer. How are you feeling?"

"I've been on the go since five-thirty London time. Long day, sir."

"I expect so. Okay, we'll go over the Afghanistan business tomorrow morning. Get some sleep, son."

"Aye, aye, sir." Ryan got his coat. "Good night."

It was a fifteen-minute drive to the Marriott. Ryan made the mistake of turning the TV on to the beginning of Monday Night Football. Cincinnati was playing San Francisco, the two best quarterbacks in the league pitted against one another. Football was something he missed living in England, and he managed to stay awake nearly three hours before fading out with the television on.

SOSUS Control

Except for the fact that everyone was in uniform, a visitor might easily have mistaken the room for a NASA control center. There were six wide rows of consoles, each with its own TV screen and typewriter keyboard supplemented by lighted plastic buttons, dials, headphone jacks, and analog and digital controls. Senior Chief Oceanographic Technician Deke Franklin was seated at console fifteen.

The room was SOSUS (sonar surveillance system) Atlantic Control. It was in a fairly nondescript building, uninspired government layer cake, with windowless concrete walls, a large air-conditioning system on a flat roof, and an acronym-coded blue sign on a well-tended but now yellowed lawn. There were armed marines inconspicuously on guard inside the three entrances. In the basement were a pair of Cray-2 supercomputers tended by twenty acolytes, and behind the building was a trio of satellite ground stations, all up- and down-links. The men at the consoles and the computers were linked electronically by satellite and landline to the SOSUS system.

Throughout the oceans of the world, and especially astride the passages that Soviet submarines had to cross to reach the open sea, the United States and other NATO countries had deployed gangs of highly sensitive sonar receptors. The hundreds of SOSUS sensors received and forwarded an unimaginably vast amount of information, and to help the system operators classify and analyze it a whole new family of computers had to be designed, the supercomputers. SOSUS served its purpose admirably well. Very little could cross a barrier without being detected. Even the ultraquiet American and British attack submarines were generally picked up. The sensors, lying on the bottom of the sea, were periodically updated; many now had their own signal processors to presort the data they forwarded, lightening the load on the central computers and enabling more rapid and accurate classification of targets.

Chief Franklin's console received data from a string of sensors planted off the coast of Iceland. He was responsible for an area forty nautical miles across, and his sector overlapped the ones east and west so that, theoretically, three operators were constantly monitoring any segment of the barrier. If he got a contact, he would first notify his brother operators, then type a contact report into his computer terminal, which would in turn be displayed on the master control board in the control room at the back of the floor. The senior duty officer had the frequently exercised authority to prosecute a contact with a wide range of assets, from surface ships to antisubmarine aircraft. Two world wars had taught American and British officers the necessity of keeping their sea lines of communication—SLOCs—open.

Although this quiet, tomblike facility had never been shown to the public, and though it had none of the drama associated with military life, the men on duty here were among the most important in the service of their country. In a war, without them, whole nations might starve.

Franklin was leaning back in his swivel chair, puffing contemplatively on an old briar pipe. Around him the room was dead quiet. Even had it not been, his five-hundred-dollar headphones would have effectively sealed him off from the outside world. A twenty-six year chief, Franklin had served his entire career on destroyers and frigates. To him, submarines and submariners were the enemy, regardless of what flag they might fly or what uniform they might wear.

An eyebrow went up, and his nearly bald head cocked to one side. The pulls on the pipe grew irregular. His right hand reached forward to the control panel and switched off the signal processors so that he could get the sound without computerized interference. But it was no good. There was too much background noise. He switched the filters back on. Next he tried some changes in his azimuth controls. The SOSUS sensors were designed to give bearing checks through the selective use of individual receptors, which he could manipulate electronically, first getting one bearing, then using a neighboring gang to triangulate for a fix. The contact was very faint, but not too far from the line, he judged. Franklin queried his computer terminal. The USS *Dallas* was up there. *Gotcha!* he said with a thin smile. Another noise came through, a low-frequency rumble that only lasted a few seconds before fading out. Not all that quiet, though. Why hadn't he heard it before switching the reception azimuth? He set his pipe down and began making adjustments on his control board.

"Chief?" A voice came over his headphones. It was the senior duty officer.

"Yes, Commander?"

"Can you come back to control? I have something I want you to hear."

"On the way, sir." Franklin rose quietly. Commander Quentin was a former destroyer skipper on a limited duty after a winning battle with cancer. Almost a winning battle, Franklin corrected himself. Chemotherapy had killed the cancer—at the cost of nearly all his hair, and turning his skin into a sort of transparent parchment. Too bad, he thought, Quentin was a pretty good man.

The control room was elevated a few feet from the rest of the floor so that its occupants could see over the whole crew of duty operators and the main tactical display on the far wall. It was separated from the floor by glass, which allowed them to speak to one another without disturbing the operators. Franklin found Quentin at his command station, where he could tap into any console on the floor.

"Howdy, Commander." Franklin noted that the officer was gaining some weight back. It was about time. "What do you have for me, sir?"

"On the Barents Sea net." Quentin handed him a pair of phones. Franklin listened for several minutes, but he didn't sit down. Like many people he had a gut suspicion that cancer was contagious.

"Damned if they ain't pretty busy up there. I read a pair of *Alfa*s, a *Charlie*, a *Tango*, and a few surface ships. What gives, sir?"

"There's a *Delta* there, too, but she just surfaced and killed her engines."

"Surfaced, Skipper?"

"Yep. They were lashing her pretty hard with active sonar, then a 'can queried her on a gertrude."

"Uh-huh. Acquisition game, and the sub lost."

"Maybe. Quentin rubbed his eyes. The man looked tired. He was pushing himself too hard, and his stamina wasn't half what it should have been. "But the *Alfa*s are still pinging, and now they're headed west, as you heard."

"Oh." Franklin pondered that for a moment. "They're looking for another boat, then. The *Typhoon* that was supposed to have sailed the other day, maybe?"

"That's what I thought—except she headed west, and the exercise area is northeast of the fjord. We lost her the other day on SOSUS. *Bremerton*'s up sniffing around for her now."

"Cagey skipper," Franklin decided. "Cut his plant all the way back and just drifting."

"Yeah," Quentin agreed. "I want you to move down to the North Cape barrier supervisory board and see if you can find her, Chief. She'll still have her reactor working, and she'll be making some noise. The operators we have on that sector are a little young. I'll take one and switch him to your board for a while."

"Right, Skipper," Franklin nodded. That part of the team was still green, used to working on ships. SOSUS required more finesse. Quentin didn't have to say that he expected Franklin to check in on the whole North Cape team's boards and maybe drop a few small lessons as he listened in on their channels.

"Did you pick up on *Dallas?*"

"Yes, sir. Real faint, but I think I got her crossing my sector, headed northwest for Toll Booth. If we get an Orion down there, we might just get her locked in. Can we rattle their cage a little?"

Quentin chuckled. He didn't much care for submarines either. "No, NIFTY DOLPHIN is over. Chief. We'll just log it and let the skipper know when he comes back home. Nice work, though. You know her reputation. We're not supposed to hear her at all."

"That'll be the day!" Franklin snorted.

"Let me know what you find, Deke."

"Aye aye, Skipper. You take care of yourself, hear?"

THE FIFTH DAY

TUESDAY, 7 DECEMBER

Moscow

It was not the grandest office in the Kremlin, but it suited his needs. Admiral Yuri Ilych Padorin showed up for work at his customary seven o'clock after the drive from his six-room apartment in the Kutuzovskiy Prospekt. The large office windows overlooked the Kremlin walls; except for those he would have had a view of the Mosow River, now frozen solid. Padorin did not miss the view, though he had won his spurs commanding river gunboats forty years before, running supplies across the Volga into Stalingrad. Padorin was now the chief political officer of the Soviet Navy. His job was men, not ships.

On the way in he nodded curtly to his secretary, a man of forty. The yeoman leaped to his feet and followed his admiral into the inner office to help him off with his greatcoat. Padorin's navy-blue jacket was ablaze with ribbons and the gold star medal of the most coveted award in the Soviet Military, Hero of the Soviet Union. He had won that in combat as a freckled boy of twenty, shuttling back and forth on the Volga. Those were good days, he told himself, dodging bombs from the

German Stukas and the more random artillery fire with which the Fascists had tried to interdict his squadron . . . Like most men he was unable to remember the stark terror of combat.

It was a Tuesday morning, and Padorin had a pile of mail waiting on his desk. His yeoman got him a pot of tea and a cup—the usual Russian glass cup set in a metal holder, sterling silver in this case. Padorin had worked long and hard for the perqs that came with this office. He settled in his chair and read first through the intelligence dispatches, information copies of data sent each morning and evening to the operational commands of the Soviet Navy. A political officer had to keep current, to know what the imperialists were up to so that he could brief his men on the threat.

Next came the official mail from within the People's Commissariat of the Navy and the Ministry of Defense. He had access to all of the correspondence from the former, while that from the latter had been carefully vetted since the Soviet armed services share as little information as possible. There wasn't too much mail from either place today. The usual Monday afternoon meeting had covered most of what had to be done that week, and nearly everything Padorin was concerned with was now in the hands of his staff for disposition. He poured a second cup of tea and opened a new pack of unfiltered cigarettes, a habit he'd been unable to break despite a mild heart attack three years earlier. He checked his desk calendar—good, no appointments until ten.

Near the bottom of the pile was an official-looking envelope from the Northern Fleet. The code number at the upper left corner showed that it came from the *Red October*. Hadn't he just read something about that?

Padorin rechecked his ops dispatches. So, Ramius hadn't turned up in his exercise area? He shrugged. Missile submarines were supposed to be elusive, and it would not have surprised the old admiral at all if Ramius were twisting a few tails. The son of Aleksandr Ramius was a prima donna who had the troubling habit of seeming to build his own personality cult: he kept some of the men he trained and discarded others. Padorin reflected that those rejected for line service had made excellent *zampoliti*, and appeared to have more line knowledge than was the norm. Even so, Ramius was a captain who needed watching. Sometimes Padorin suspected that he was too much a sailor and not enough a Communist. On the other hand, his father had been a model Party member and a hero of the Great Patriotic War. Certainly he had been well thought of, Lithuanian or not. And the son? Years of letter-perfect performance, as many years of stalwart Party membership. He was known for his spirited participation at meetings and occasionally brilliant essays. The people in the naval branch of the GRU, the Soviet military intelligence agency, reported that the imperialists regarded him as a dangerous and skilled enemy. Good, Padorin thought, the bastards ought to fear our men. He turned his attention back to the envelope.

Red October, now there was a fitting name for a Soviet warship! Named not only for the revolution that had forever changed the history of the world but also for the Red October Tractor Plant. Many was the dawn when Padorin had looked west to Stalingrad to see if the factory still stood, a symbol of the Soviet fighting men struggling against the Hitlerite bandits. The envelope was marked Confidential, and his yeoman had not opened it as he had the other routine mail. The admiral took his letter opener from the desk drawer. It was a sentimental object, having been his service knife years before. When his first gunboat had been sunk under him, one hot August night in 1942, he had swum to shore and been pounced on by a German infantryman who hadn't expected resistance from a half-drowned sailor. Padorin had surprised him, sinking the knife in his chest and breaking off half the blade as he stole his enemy's life. Later a machinist had trimmed the blade down. It was no longer a proper knife, but Padorin wasn't about to throw this sort of souvenir away.

"Comrade Admiral," the letter began—but the type had been scratched out and replaced with a hand-written "Uncle Yuri." Ramius had jokingly called him that years back when Padorin was chief political officer of the Northern Fleet. "Thank you for your confidence, and for the opportunity you have given me with command of this magnificent ship!" Ramius ought to be grateful, Padorin thought. Performance or not, you don't give this sort of command to—

What? Padorin stopped reading and started over. He forgot the cigarette smoldering in his ashtray as he reached the bottom

of the first page. A joke. Ramius was known for his jokes—
but he'd pay for this one. This was going too fucking far! He
turned the page.

"This is no joke, Uncle Yuri—Marko."

Padorin stopped and looked out the window. The Kremlin
wall at this point was a beehive of niches for the ashes of the
Party faithful. He couldn't have read the letter correctly. He
started to read it again. His hands began to shake.

He had a direct line to Admiral Gorshkov, with no yeomen
or secretaries to bar the way.

"Comrade Admiral, this is Padorin."

"Good morning, Yuri," Gorshkov said pleasantly.

"I must see you immediately. I have a situation here."

"What sort of situation?" Gorshkov asked warily.

"We must discuss it in person. I am coming over now."
There was no way he'd discuss this over the phone; he knew
it was tapped.

The USS Dallas

Sonarman Second Class Ronald Jones, his division officer noted,
was in his usual trance. The young college dropout was hunched
over his instrument table, body limp, eyes closed, face locked
into the same neutral expression he wore when listening to one
of the many Bach tapes on his expensive personal cassette player.
Jones was the sort who categorized his tapes by their flaws, a
ragged piano tempo, a botched flute, a wavering French horn.
He listened to sea sounds with the same discriminating intensity. In all the navies of the world, submariners were regarded
as a curious breed, and submariners themselves looked upon
sonar operators as odd. Their eccentricities, however, were
among the most tolerated in the military service. The executive
officer liked to tell a story about a sonar chief he'd served with
for two years, a man who had patrolled the same areas in missile submarines for virtually his whole career. He became so
familiar with the humpback whales that summered in the area
that he took to calling them by name. On retiring, he went to
work for the Woods Hole Oceanographic Institute, where his
talent was regarded not so much with amusement as awe.

Three years earlier, Jones had been asked to leave the
California Institute of Technology in the middle of his junior

year. He had pulled one of the ingenious pranks for which Cal Tech students were justly famous, only it hadn't worked. Now he was serving his time in the navy to finance his return. It was his announced intention to get a doctorate in cybernetics and signal processing. In return for an early out, after receiving his degree he would go to work for the Naval Research Laboratory. Lieutenant Thompson believed it. On joining the *Dallas* six months earlier, he had read the files of all his men. Jones' IQ was 158, the highest on the boat by a fair margin. He had a placid face and sad brown eyes that women found irresistible. On the beach Jones had enough action to wear down a squad of marines. It didn't make much sense to the lieutenant. He'd been the football hero at Annapolis. Jones was a skinny kid who listened to Bach. It didn't figure.

The USS *Dallas*, a 688-class attack submarine, was forty miles from the coast of Iceland, approaching her patrol station, code-named Toll Booth. She was two days late getting there. A week earlier, she had participated in the NATO war game NIFTY DOLPHIN, which had been postponed several days because the worst North Atlantic weather in twenty years had delayed other ships detailed to it. In that exercise the *Dallas*, teamed with HMS *Swiftsure*, had used the foul weather to penetrate and ravage the simulated enemy formation. It was yet another four-oh performance for the *Dallas* and her skipper, Commander Bart Mancuso, one of the youngest submarine commanders in the U.S. Navy. The mission had been followed by a courtesy call at the *Swiftsure*'s Royal Navy base in Scotland, and the American sailors were still shaking off hangovers from the celebration . . . Now they had a different mission, a new development in the Atlantic submarine game. For three weeks, the *Dallas* was to report on traffic in and out of Red Route One.

Over the past fourteen months, newer Soviet submarines had been using a strange, effective tactic for shedding their American and British shadowers. Southwest of Iceland the Russian boats would race down the Reykjanes Ridge, a finger of underwater highlands pointing to the deep Atlantic basin. Spaced at intervals from five miles to half a mile, these mountains with their knife-edged ridges of brittle igneous rock rivaled the Alps in size. Their peaks were about a thousand feet beneath the stormy surface of the North Atlantic. Before the late sixties

submarines could barely approach the peaks, much less probe
their myriad valleys. Throughout the seventies Soviet naval
survey vessels had been seen patrolling the ridge—in all seasons, in all weather, quartering and requartering the area in
thousands of cruises. Then, fourteen months before the *Dallas'*
present patrol, the USS *Los Angeles* had been tracking a Soviet
Victor II–class attack submarine. The *Victor* had skirted the
Icelandic coast and gone deep as she approached the ridge. The
Los Angeles had followed. The *Victor* proceeded at eight knots
until she passed between the first pair of seamounts, informally
known as Thor's Twins. All at once she went to full speed and
moved southwest. The skipper of the *Los Angeles* made a
determined effort to track the *Victor* and came away from it
badly shaken. Although the 688-class submarines were faster
than the older *Victors*, the Russian submarine had simply not
slowed down—for fifteen hours, it was later determined.

At first it had not been all that dangerous. Submarines had
highly accurate inertial navigation systems able to fix their
positions to within a few hundred yards from one second to
another. But the *Victor* was skirting cliffs as though her skipper
could see them, like a fighter dodging down a canyon to avoid
surface-to-air missile fire. The *Los Angeles* could not keep track
of the cliffs. At any speed over twenty knots both her passive
and active sonar, including the echofathometer, became almost
useless. The *Los Angeles* thus found herself navigating completely blind. It was, the skipper later reported, like driving a
car with the windows painted over, steering with a map and a
stopwatch. This was theoretically possible, but the captain
quickly realized that the inertial navigation system had a built-
in error factor of several hundred yards; this was aggravated
by gravitational disturbances, which affected the "local vertical," which in turn affected the inertial fix. Worst of all, his
charts were made for surface ships. Objects below a few hundred
feet had been known to be misplaced by miles—something
that mattered to no one until recently. The interval between
mountains had quickly become less than his cumulative navigational error—sooner or later his submarine would drive into
a mountainside at over thirty knots. The captain backed off.
The *Victor* got away.

Initially it was theorized that the Soviets had somehow staked
out one particular route, that their submarines were able to

follow it at high speed. Russian skippers were known to pull some crazy stunts, and perhaps they were trusting to a combination of inertial systems, magnetic and gyro compasses attuned to a specific track. This theory had never developed much of a following, and in a few weeks it was known for certain that the Soviet submarines speeding through the ridge were following a multiplicity of tracks. The only thing American and British subs could do was stop periodically to get a sonar fix of their positions, then race to catch up. But the Soviet subs never slowed, and the 688s and *Trafalgars* kept falling behind.

The *Dallas* was on Toll Booth station to monitor passing Russian subs, to watch the entrance to the passage the U.S. Navy was now calling Red Route One, and to listen for any external evidence of a new gadget that might enable the Soviets to run the ridge so boldly. Until the Americans could copy it, there were three unsavory alternatives: they could continue losing contact with the Russians; they could station valuable attack subs at the known exits from the route; or they could set up a whole new SOSUS line.

Jones' trance lasted ten minutes—longer than usual. He ordinarily had a contact figured out in far less time. The sailor leaned back and lit a cigarette.

"Got something, Mr. Thompson."

"What is it?" Thompson leaned against the bulkhead.

"I don't know." Jones picked up a spare set of phones and handed them to his officer. "Listen up, sir."

Thompson himself was a masters candidate in electrical engineering, an expert in sonar system design. His eyes screwed shut as he concentrated on the sound. It was a very faint low-frequency rumble—or swish. He couldn't decide. He listened for several minutes before setting the headphones down, then shook his head.

"I got it a half hour ago on the lateral array," Jones said. He referred to a subsystem of the BQQ-5 multifunction submarine sonar. Its main component was an eighteen-foot-diameter dome located in the bow. The dome was used for both active and passive operations. A new part of the system was a gang of passive sensors which extended two hundred feet down both sides of the hull. This was a mechanical analog to the sensory organs on the body of a shark. "Lost it, got it back, lost it, got it back," Jones went on. "It's not screw sounds, not whales or fish. More like water going through a pipe, except for that funny rumble that comes and goes. Anyway, the bearing is about two-five-zero. That puts it between us and Iceland, so it can't be too far away."

"Let's see what it looks like. Maybe that'll tell us something."

Jones took a double-plugged wire from a hook. One plug went into a socket on his sonar panel, the other into the jack on a nearby oscilloscope. The two men spent several minutes working with the sonar controls to isolate the signal. They ended up with an irregular sine wave which they were only able to hold a few seconds at a time.

"Irregular," Thompson said.

"Yeah, it's funny. It sounds regular, but it doesn't look regular. Know what I mean, Mr. Thompson?"

"No, you've got better ears."

"That's cause I listen to better music, sir. That rock stuff'll kill your ears."

Thompson knew he was right, but an Annapolis graduate doesn't need to hear that from an enlisted man. His vintage Janis Joplin tapes were his own business. "Next step."

"Yessir." Jones took the plug from the oscilloscope and moved it into a panel to the left of the sonar board, next to a computer terminal.

During her last overhaul, the *Dallas* had received a very special toy to go along with her BQQ-5 sonar system. Called the BC-10, it was the most powerful computer yet installed aboard a submarine. Though only about the size of a business desk, it cost over five million dollars and ran at eighty million operations per second. It used newly developed sixty-four-bit chips and made use of the latest processing architecture. Its bubble memory could easily accommodate the computing needs of a whole squadron of submarines. In five years every attack sub in the fleet would have one. Its purpose, much like that of the far larger SOSUS system, was to process and analyze sonar signals; the BC-10 stripped away ambient noise and other naturally produced sea sounds to classify and identify man-made noise. It could identify ships by name from their individual acoustical signatures, much as one could identify the finger or voice prints of a human.

As important as the computer was its programming software. Four years before, a PhD candidate in geophysics who was working at Cal Tech's geophysical laboratory had completed a program of six hundred thousand steps designed to predict earthquakes. The problem the program addressed was one of signal versus noise. It overcame the difficulty seismologists had discriminating between random noise that is constantly monitored on seismographs and genuinely unusual signals that foretell a seismic event.

The first Defense Department use of the program was in the Air Force Technical Applications Command (AFTAC), which found it entirely satisfactory for its mission of monitoring nuclear events throughout the world in accordance with arms control treaties. The Navy Research Laboratory also redrafted it for its own purposes. Though inadequate for seismic predictions, it worked very well indeed in analyzing sonar signals. The program was known in the navy as the signal algorithmic processing system (SAPS).

"SAPS SIGNAL INPUT," Jones typed into the video display terminal (VDT).

"READY," the BC-10 responded at once.

"RUN."

"WORKING."

For all the fantastic speed of the BC-10, the six hundred thousand steps of the program, punctuated by numerous GOTO loops, took time to run as the machine eliminated natural sounds with its random profile criteria and then locked into the anomalous signal. It took twenty seconds, an eternity in computer time. The answer came up on the VDT. Jones pressed a key to generate a copy on the adjacent matrix printer.

"Hmph." Jones tore off the page. "'ANOMALOUS SIGNAL EVALUATED AS MAGMA DISPLACEMENT.' That's SAPS' way of saying take two aspirin and call me at end of the watch."

Thompson chuckled. For all the ballyhoo that had accompanied the new system, it was not all that popular in the fleet. "Remember what the papers said when we were in England? Something about seismic activity around Iceland, like when that island poked up back in the sixties."

Jones lit another cigarette. He knew the student who had originally drafted this abortion they called SAPS. One problem

was that it had a nasty habit of analyzing the wrong signal—
and you couldn't tell it was wrong from the results. Besides,
since it had been originally designed to look for seismic events,
Jones suspected it of a tendency to interpret anomalies as seismic events. He didn't like the built-in bias, which he felt the
research laboratory had not entirely removed. It was one thing
to use computers as a tool, quite another to let them do your
thinking for you. Besides, they were always discovering new
sea sounds that nobody had ever heard before, much less classified.

"Sir, the frequency is all wrong for one thing—nowhere
near low enough. How 'bout I try an' track in on this signal
with the R-15?" Jones referred to the towed array of passive
sensors the *Dallas* was trailing behind her at low speed.

Commander Mancuso came in just then, the usual mug of
coffee in his hand. If there was one frightening thing about the
captain, Thompson thought, it was his talent for showing up
when something was going on. Did he have the whole boat
wired?

"Just wandering by," he said casually. "What's happening
this fine day?" The captain leaned against the bulkhead. He
was a small man, only five eight, who had fought a battle
against his waistline all his life and was now losing because
of the good food and lack of exercise on a submarine. His dark
eyes were surrounded by laugh lines that were always deeper
when he was playing a trick on another ship.

Was it day, Thompson wondered? The six-hour one-in-three
rotating watch cycle made for a convenient work schedule, but
after a few changes you had to press the button on your watch
to figure out what day it was, else you couldn't make the proper
entry in the log.

"Skipper, Jones picked up a funny signal on the lateral. The
computer says it's magma displacement."

"And Jonesy doesn't agree with that." Mancuso didn't have
to make it a question.

"No, sir, Captain, I don't. I don't know what it is, but for
sure it ain't that."

"You against the machine again?"

"Skipper, SAPS works pretty well most of the time, but
sometimes it's a real *kludge*." Jones' epithet was the most

perjorative curse of electronics people. "For one thing the frequency is all wrong."

"Okay, what do you think?"

"I don't know, Captain. It isn't screw sounds, and it isn't any naturally produced sound that I've heard. Beyond that . . ." Jones was struck by the informality of the discussion with his commanding officer, even after three years on nuclear subs. The crew of the *Dallas* was like one big family, albeit one of the old frontier families, since everybody worked pretty damned hard. The captain was the father. The executive officer, everyone would readily agree, was the mother. The officers were the older kids, and the enlisted men were the younger kids. The important thing was, if you had something to say, the captain would listen to you. To Jones, this counted for a lot.

Mancuso nodded thoughtfully. "Well, keep at it. No sense letting all this expensive gear go to waste."

Jones grinned. Once he had told the captain in precise detail how he could convert this equipment into the world's finest stereo rig. Mancuso had pointed out that it would not be a major feat, since the sonar gear in this room alone cost over twenty million dollars.

"Christ!" The junior technician bolted upright in his chair. "Somebody just stomped on the gas."

Jones was the sonar watch supervisor. The other two watch-standers noted the new signal, and Jones switched his phones to the towed array jack while the two officers kept out of the way. He took a scratch pad and noted the time before working on his individual controls. The BQR-15 was the most sensitive sonar rig on the boat, but its sensitivity was not needed for this contact.

"Damn," Jones muttered quietly.

"Charlie," said the junior technician.

Jones shook his head. *"Victor. Victor* class for sure. Doing turns for thirty knots—big burst of cavitation noise, he's digging big holes in the water, and he doesn't care who knows it. Bearing zero-five-zero. Skipper, we got good water around us, and the signal is real faint. He's not close." It was the closest thing to a range estimate Jones could come up with. Not close meant anything over ten miles. He went back to working his controls. "I think we know this guy. This is the one with a bent blade on his screw, sounds like he's got a chain wrapped around it."

"Put it on speaker," Mancuso told Thompson. He didn't want to disturb the operators. The lieutenant was already keying the signal into the BC-10.

The bulkhead-mounted speaker would have commanded a four-figure price in any stereo shop for its clarity and dynamic perfection; like everything else on the 688-class sub, it was the very best that money could buy. As Jones worked on the sound controls they heard the whining chirp of propeller cavitation, the thin screech associated with a bent propeller blade, and the deeper rumble of a *Victor*'s reactor plant at full power. The next thing Mancuso heard was the printer.

"*Victor I*–class, number six," Thompson announced.

"Right," Jones nodded. "*Vic*-six, bearing still zero-five-zero." He plugged the mouthpiece into his headphones. "Conn, sonar, we have a contact. A *Victor* class, bearing zero-five-zero, estimated target speed thirty knots."

Mancuso leaned out into the passageway to address Lieutenant Pat Mannion, officer of the deck. "Pat, man the fire-control tracking party."

"Aye, Cap'n."

"Wait a minute!" Jones' hand went up. "Got another one!" He twiddled some knobs. "This one's a *Charlie* class. Damned if he ain't digging holes, too. More easterly, bearing zero-seven-three, doing turns for about twenty-eight knots. We know this guy, too. Yeah, *Charlie II*, number eleven." Jones slipped a phone off one ear and looked at Mancuso. "Skipper, the Russkies have sub races scheduled for today?"

"Not that they told me about. Of course, we don't get the sports page out here," Mancuso chuckled, swirling the coffee around in his cup and hiding his real thoughts. What the hell was going on? "I suppose I'll go forward and take a look at this. Good work, guys."

He went a few steps forward into the attack center. The normal steaming watch was set. Mannion had the conn, with a junior officer of the deck and seven enlisted men. A first-class firecontrolman was entering data from the target motion analyzer into the Mark 117 fire control computer. Another officer was entering control to take charge of the tracking exercise. There was nothing unusual about this. The whole watch went about its work alertly but with the relaxed demeanor that came with years of training and experience. While the other armed services routinely had their components run exercises against allies or themselves in emulation of Eastern Bloc tactics, the navy had its attack submarines play their games against the real thing—and constantly. Submariners typically operated on what was effectively an at-war footing.

"So we have company," Mannion observed.

"Not that close," Lieutenant Charles Goodman noted. "These bearings haven't changed a whisker."

"Conn, sonar." It was Jones' voice. Mancuso took it.

"Conn, aye. What is it, Jonesy?"

"We got another one, sir. *Alfa 3,* bearing zero-five-five. Running flat out. Sounds like an earthquake, but faint, sir."

"*Alfa 3?* Our old friend, the *Politovskiy.* Haven't run across her in a while. Anything else you can tell me?"

"A guess, sir. The sound on this one warbled, then settled down, like she was making a turn. I think she's heading this way—that's a little shaky. And we have some more noise to the northeast. Too confused to make any sense of just now. We're working on it."

"Okay, nice work, Jonesy. Keep at it."

"Sure thing, Captain."

Mancuso smiled as he set the phone down, looking over at Mannion. "You know, Pat, sometimes I wonder if Jonesy isn't part witch."

Mannion looked at the paper tracks that Goodman was drawing to back up the computerized targeting process. "He's pretty good. Problem is, he thinks we work for him."

"Right now we are working for him." Jones was their eyes and ears, and Mancuso was damned glad to have him.

"Chuck?" Mancuso asked Lieutenant Goodman.

"Bearing still constant on all three contacts, sir." Which probably meant they were heading for the *Dallas.* It also meant that they could not develop the range data necessary for a fire control solution. Not that anyone wanted to shoot, but this was the point of the exercise.

"Pat, let's get some sea room. Move us about ten miles east," Mancuso ordered casually. There were two reasons for this. First, it would establish a base line from which to compute probable target range. Second, the deeper water would make for better acoustical conditions, opening up to them the distant sonar convergence zone. The captain studied the chart as his navigator gave the necessary orders, evaluating the tactical situation.

Bartolomeo Mancuso was the son of a barber who closed his shop in Cicero, Illinois, every fall to hunt deer on Michigan's Upper Peninsula. Bart had accompanied his father on these hunts, shot his first deer at the age of twelve and every year thereafter until entering the Naval Academy. He had never bothered after that. Since becoming an officer on nuclear submarines he had learned a much more diverting game. Now he hunted people.

Two hours later an alarm bell went off on the ELF radio in the sub's communications room. Like all nuclear submarines, the *Dallas* was trailing a lengthy wire antenna attuned to the extremely low-frequency transmitter in the central United States. The channel had a frustratingly narrow data band width. Unlike a TV channel, which transmitted thousands of bits of data per frame, thirty frames per second, the ELF radio passed on data slowly, about one character every thirty seconds. The duty radioman waited patiently while the information was recorded on tape. When the message was finished, he ran the tape at high speed and transcribed the message, handing it to the communications officer who was waiting with his code book.

The signal was actually not a code but a "one-time-pad" cipher. A book, published every six months and distributed to every nuclear submarine, was filled with randomly generated transpositions for each letter of the signal. Each scrambled three-letter group in this book corresponded to a preselected word or phrase in another book. Deciphering the message by hand took under three minutes, and when that was completed it was carried to the captain in the attack center.

NHG	JPR	YTR
FROM COMSUBLANT	TO LANTSUBS AT SEA	STANDBY
OPY TBD	QEQ	GER
POSSIBLE MAJOR	REDEPLOYMENT ORDER	LARGE-SCALE
MAL	ASF	NME
UNEXPECTED	REDFLEET OPERATION	IN PROGRESS
TYQ	ORV	
NATURE UNKNOWN	NEXT ELF MESSAGE	
HWZ		
COMMUNICATE SSIX		

COMSUBLANT—commander of the Submarine Force in the Atlantic—was Mancuso's big boss, Vice Admiral Vincent Gallery. The old man was evidently contemplating a reshuffling of his entire force, no minor affair. The next wake-up signal, AAA—encrypted, of course—would alert them to go to periscope-antenna depth to get more detailed instructions from SSIX, the submarine satellite information exchange, a geosynchronous communications satellite used exclusively by submarines.

The tactical situation was becoming clearer, though its strategic implications were beyond his ability to judge. The ten-mile move eastward had given them adequate range information for their initial three contacts and another *Alfa* which had turned up a few minutes later. The first of the contacts, *Vic 6*, was now within torpedo range. A Mark 48 was locked in on her, and there was no way that her skipper could know the *Dallas* was here. *Vic 6* was a deer in his sights—but it wasn't hunting season.

Though not much faster than the *Victor*s and *Charlie*s, and ten knots slower than the smaller *Alfa*s, the *Dallas* and her sisters could move almost silently at nearly twenty knots. This was a triumph of engineering and design, the product of decades of work. But moving without being detected was useful only if the hunter could at the same time detect his quarry. Sonars lost effectiveness as their carrier platform increased speed. The *Dallas'* BQQ-5 retained twenty percent effectiveness at twenty knots, nothing to cheer about. Submarines running at high speed from one point to another were blind and unable to harm anyone. As a result, the operating pattern of an attack submarine was much like that of a combat infantryman. With a rifleman it was called dash-and-cover; with a sub, sprint-and-drift. After detecting a target, a sub would race to a more advantageous position, stop to reacquire her prey, then dash again until a firing position had been achieved. The sub's quarry would be moving too, and if the submarine could gain position in front of it, she had then only to lie in wait like a great hunting cat to strike.

The submariner's trade required more than skill. It required instinct, and an artist's touch; monomaniacal confidence, and the aggressiveness of a professional boxer. Mancuso had all of these things. He had spent fifteen years learning his craft, watching a generation of commanders as a junior officer, listening carefully at the frequent round-table discussions which made submarining a very human profession, its lessons passed on by verbal tradition. Time on shore had been spent training in a variety of computerized simulators, attending seminars, comparing notes and ideas with his peers. Aboard surface ships and ASW aircraft he learned how the "enemy"—the surface sailors—played his own hunting game.

Submariners lived by a simple motto: There are two kinds of ships, submarines . . . and targets. What would *Dallas* be hunting? Mancuso wondered. Russian subs? Well, if that was the game and the Russians kept racing around like this, it ought to be easy enough. He and the *Swiftsure* had just bested a team of NATO ASW experts, men whose countries depended on their ability to keep the sea-lanes open. His boat and his crew were performing as well as any man could ask. In Jones he had one of the ten best sonar operators in the fleet. Mancuso was ready, whatever the game might be. As on the opening day of hunting season, outside considerations were dwindling away. He was becoming a weapon.

CIA Headquarters

It was 4:45 in the morning, and Ryan was dozing fitfully in the back of a CIA Chevy taking him from the Marriott to Langley. He'd been over for what? twenty hours? About that, enough time to see his boss, see Skip, get the presents for Sally, and check the house. The house looked to be in good shape. He had rented it to an instructor at the Naval Academy. He could have gotten five times the rent from someone else, but he didn't want any wild parties in his home. The officer was a Bible-thumper from Kansas, and made an acceptable custodian.

Five and a half hours of sleep in the past—thirty? Something like that; he was too tired to look at his watch. It wasn't fair. Sleeplessness murders judgment. But it made little sense telling himself that, and telling the admiral would make less.

He was in Greer's office five minutes later.

"Sorry to have to wake you up, Jack."

"Oh, that's all right, sir," Ryan returned the lie. "What's up?"

"Come on over and grab some coffee. It's going to be a long day."

Ryan dropped his topcoat on the sofa and walked over to pour a mug of navy brew. He decided against Coffee Mate or sugar. Better to endure it naked and get the caffeine full force.

"Any place I can shave around here, sir?"

"Head's behind the door, over in the corner." Greer handed him a yellow sheet torn from a telex machine. "Look at this."

TOP SECRET
102200Z*****38976

NSA SIGINT BULLETIN

REDNAV OPS

MESSAGE FOLLOWS

AT 083145Z NSA MONITOR STATIONS [DELETED] [DELETED] AND [DELETED] RECORDED AN ELF BROADCAST FROM REDFLEET ELF FACILITY SEMIPOLIPINSK XX MESSAGE DURATION 10 MINUTES XX 6 ELEMENTS XX

ELF SIGNAL IS EVALUATED AS "PREP" BROADCAST TO REDFLEET SUBMARINES AT SEA XX

AT 090000Z AN "ALL SHIPS" BROADCAST WAS MADE BY REDFLEET HEADQUARTERS CENTRAL COMMO STATION TULA AND SATELLITES THREE AND FIVE XX BANDS USED: HF VHF UHF XX MESSAGE DURATION 39 SECONDS WITH 2 REPEATS IDENTICAL CONTENT MADE AT 091000Z AND 092000Z XX 475 5-ELEMENT CIPHER GROUPS XX

SIGNAL COVERAGE AS FOLLOWS: NORTHERN FLEET AREA BALTIC FLEET AREA AND MED SQUADRON AREA XX NOTE FAR EAST FLEET NOT REPEAT NOT AFFECTED BY THIS BROADCAST XX

NUMEROUS ACKNOWLEDGMENT SIGNALS EMANATED FROM ADDRESSES IN AREAS CITED ABOVE XX ORIGIN AND TRAFFIC ANALYSIS TO

FOLLOW XX NOT COMPLETED AT THIS TIME XX
BEGINNING AT 100000Z NSA MONITOR STATIONS
[DELETED] [DELETED] AND [DELETED] RE-
CORDED INCREASED HF AND VHF TRAFFIC AT
REDFLEET BASES POLYARNYY SEVEROMORSK
PECHENGA TALLINN KRONSTADT AND EAST-
ERN MED AREA XX ADDITIONAL HF AND VHF
TRAFFIC FROM REDFLEET ASSETS AT SEA XX
AMPLIFICATION TO FOLLOW XX

EVALUATION: A MAJOR UNPLANNED REDFLEET
OPERATION HAS BEEN ORDERED WITH FLEET
ASSETS REPORTING AVAILABILITY AND STATUS
XX

END BULLETIN

NSA SENDS

102215Z

BREAKBREAK

Ryan looked at his watch. "Fast work by the boys at NSA,
and fast work by our duty watch officers, getting everybody
up." He drained his mug and went over for a refill. "What's
the word on signal traffic analysis?"

"Here." Greer handed him a second telex sheet.

Ryan scanned it. "That's a lot of ships. Must be nearly
everything they have at sea. Not much on the ones in port,
though."

"Landline," Greer observed. "The ones in port can phone
fleet ops, Moscow. By the way, that *is* every ship they have
at sea in the Western Hemisphere. Every damned one. Any
ideas?"

"Let's see, we have that increased activity in the Barents
Sea. Looks like a medium-sized ASW exercise. Maybe they're
expanding it. Doesn't explain the increased activity in the Baltic
and Med, though. Do they have a war game laid on?"

"Nope. They just finished CRIMSON STORM a month
ago."

Ryan nodded. "Yeah, they usually take a couple of months
to evaluate that much data—and who'd want to play games
up there at this time of the year? The weather's supposed to

be a bitch. Have they ever run a major game in December?"

"Not a big one, but most of these acknowledgments are from submarines, son, and subs don't care a whole lot about the weather."

"Well, given some other preconditions, you might call this ominous. No idea what the signal said, eh?"

"No. They're using computer-based ciphers, same as us. If the spooks at the NSA can read them, they're not telling me about it." In theory the National Security Agency came under the titular control of the director of Central Intelligence. In fact it was a law unto itself. "That's what traffic analysis is all about, Jack. You try to guess intentions by who's talking to whom."

"Yes, sir, but when everybody's talking to everybody—"

"Yeah."

"Anything else on alert? Their army? Voyska PVO?" Ryan referred to the Soviet air defense network.

"Nope, just the fleet. Subs, ships, and naval aviation."

Ryan stretched. "That makes it sound like an exercise, sir. We'll want a little more data on what they're doing, though. Have you talked to Admiral Davenport?"

"That's the next step. Haven't had time. I've only been in long enough to shave myself and turn the coffee on." Greer sat down and set his phone receiver in the desk speaker before punching in the numbers.

"Vice Admiral Davenport." The voice was curt.

"Morning, Charlie, James here. Did you get that NSA -976?"

"Sure did, but that's not what got me up. Our SOSUS net went berserk a few hours ago."

"Oh?" Greer looked at the phone, then at Ryan.

"Yeah, nearly every sub they have at sea just put the pedal to the metal, and all at about the same time."

"Doing what exactly, Charlie?" Greer prompted.

"We're still figuring that out. It looks like a lot of boats are heading into the North Atlantic. Their units in the Norwegian Sea are racing southwest. Three from the western Med are heading that way, too, but we haven't got a clear picture yet. We need a few more hours."

"What do they have operating off our coast, sir?" Ryan asked.

"They woke you up, Ryan? Good. Two old *November*s.

One's a raven conversion doing an ELINT job off the cape. The other one's sitting off King's Bay making a damned nuisance of itself."

Ryan smiled to himself. An American or allied ship was a *she;* the Russians used the male pronoun for a ship; and the intelligence community usually referred to a Soviet ship as *it*.

"There's a *Yankee* boat," Davenport went on, "a thousand miles south of Iceland, and the initial report is that it's heading north. Probably wrong. Reciprocal bearing, transcription error, something like that. We're checking. Must be a goof, because it was heading south earlier."

Ryan looked up. "What about their other missile boats?"

"Their *Delta*s and *Typhoon*s are in the Barents Sea and the Sea of Okhotsk, as usual. No news on them. Oh, we have attack boats up there, of course, but Gallery doesn't want them to break radio silence, and he's right. So all we have at the moment is the report on the stray *Yankee*."

"What are we doing, Charlie?" Greer asked.

"Gallery has a general alert out to his boats. They're standing by in case we need to redeploy. NORAD has gone to a slightly increased alert status, they tell me." Davenport referred to the North American Aerospace Defense Command. "CINCLANT and CINCPAC fleet staffs are up and running around in circles, like you'd expect. Some extra P-3s are working out of Iceland. Nothing much else at the moment. First we have to figure out what they're up to."

"Okay, keep me posted."

"Roger, if we hear anything, I'll let you know, and I trust—"

"We will." Greer killed the phone. He shook a finger at Ryan. "Don't you go to sleep on me, Jack."

"On top of this stuff?" Ryan waved his mug.

"You're not concerned, I see."

"Sir, there's nothing to be concerned about yet. It's what, one in the afternoon over there now? Probably some admiral, maybe old Sergey himself, decided to toss a drill at his boys. He wasn't supposed to be all that pleased with how CRIMSON STORM worked out, and maybe he decided to rattle a few cages—ours included, of course. Hell, their army and air force aren't involved, and it's for damned sure that if they were planning anything nasty the other services would know about it. We'll have to keep an eye on this, but so far I don't see anything to—" Ryan almost said lose sleep over "—sweat about."

"How old were you at Pearl Harbor?"

"My father was nineteen, sir. He didn't marry until after the war, and I wasn't the first little Ryan." Jack smiled. Greer knew all this. "As I recall you weren't all that old yourself."

"I was a seaman second on the old *Texas.*" Greer had never made it into that war. Soon after it started he'd been accepted by the Naval Academy. By the time he had graduated from there and finished training at submarine school, the war was almost over. He reached the Japanese coast on his first cruise the day after the war ended. "But you know what I mean."

"Indeed I do, sir, and that's why we have the CIA, DIA, NSA, and NRO, among others. If the Russkies can fool all of us, maybe we ought to read up on our Marx."

"All those subs heading into the Atlantic . . ."

"I feel better with word that the *Yankee* is heading north. They've had enough time to make that a hard piece of data. Davenport probably doesn't want to believe it without confirmation. If Ivan was looking to play hardball, that *Yankee*'d be heading south. The missiles on those old boats can't reach very far. Sooo—we stay up and watch. Fortunately, sir, you make a decent cup of coffee."

"How does breakfast grab you?"

"Might as well. If we can finish up on the Afghanistan stuff, maybe I can fly back tomorr—tonight."

"You still might. Maybe this way you'll learn to sleep on the plane."

Breakfast was sent up twenty minutes later. Both men were accustomed to big ones, and the food was surprisingly good. Ordinarily CIA cafeteria food was government-undistinguished, and Ryan wondered if the night crew, with fewer people to serve, might take the time to do their job right. Or maybe they had sent out for it. The two men sat around until Davenport phoned at quarter to seven.

"It's definite. All the boomers are heading towards port. We have good tracks on two *Yankee*s, three *Delta*s, and a *Typhoon*. *Memphis* reported when her *Delta* took off for home at twenty knots after being on station for five days, and then Gallery queried *Queenfish*. Same story—looks like they're all headed for the barn. Also we just got some photos from a Big Bird pass over the fjord—for once it wasn't covered with clouds—

and we have a bunch of surface ships with bright infrared signatures, like they're getting steam up."

"How about *Red October?*" Ryan asked.

"Nothing. Maybe our information was bad, and she didn't sail. Wouldn't be the first time."

"You don't suppose they've lost her?" Ryan wondered aloud.

Davenport had already thought of that. "That would explain the activity up north, but what about the Baltic and Med business?"

"Two years ago we had that scare with *Tullibee,*" Ryan pointed out. "And the CNO was so pissed he threw an all-hands rescue drill on both oceans."

"Maybe," Davenport conceded. The blood in Norfolk was supposed to have been ankle deep after that fiasco. The USS *Tullibee,* a small one-of-a-kind attack sub, had long carried a reputation for bad luck. In this case it had spilled over onto a lot of others.

"Anyway, it looks a whole lot less scary than it did two hours back. They wouldn't be recalling their boomers if they were planning anything against us, would they?" Ryan said.

"I see that Ryan still has your crystal ball, James."

"That's what I pay him for, Charlie."

"Still, it is odd," Ryan commented. "Why recall all of the missile boats? Have they ever done this before? What about the ones in the Pacific?"

"Haven't heard about those yet," Davenport replied. "I've asked CINCPAC for data, but they haven't gotten back to me yet. On the other question, no, they've never recalled all their boomers at once, but they do occasionally reshuffle all their positions at once. That's probably what this is. I said they're heading towards port, not into it. We won't know that for a couple of days."

"What if they're afraid they've lost one?" Ryan ventured.

"No such luck," Davenport scoffed. "They haven't lost a boomer since that *Golf* we lifted off Hawaii, back when you were in high school, Ryan. Ramius is too good a skipper to let that happen."

So was Captain Smith of the *Titanic,* Ryan thought.

"Thanks for the info, Charlie." Greer hung up. "Looks like you were right, Jack. Nothing to worry about yet. Let's get that data on Afghanistan in here—and just for the hell of it, we'll look at Charlie's pictures of their Northern Fleet when we're finished."

Ten minutes later a messenger arrived with a cart from central files. Greer was the sort who liked to see the raw data himself. This suited Ryan. He'd known of a few analysts who had based their reports on selective data and been cut off at the knees for it by this man. The information on the cart was from a variety of sources, but to Ryan the most significant were tactical radio intercepts from listening posts on the Pakistani border, and, he gathered, from inside Afghanistan itself. The nature and tempo of Soviet operations did not indicate a backing off, as seemed to be suggested by a pair of recent articles in *Red Star* and some intelligence sources inside the Soviet Union. They spent three hours reviewing the data.

"I think Sir Basil is placing too much stock in political intelligence and too little in what our listening posts are getting in the field. It would not be unprecedented for the Soviets not to let their field commanders know what's going on in Moscow, of course, but on the whole I do not see a clear picture," Ryan concluded.

The admiral looked at him. "I pay you for answers, Jack."

"Sir, the truth is that Moscow moved in there by mistake. We know that from both military and political intelligence reports. The tenor of the data is pretty clear. From where I sit, I don't see that *they* know what they want to do. In a case like this the bureaucratic mind finds it most easy to do nothing. So, their field commanders are told to continue the mission, while the senior party bosses fumble around looking for a solution and covering their asses for getting into the mess in the first place."

"Okay, so we know that we don't know."

"Yes, sir. I don't like it either, but saying anything else would be a lie."

The admiral snorted. There was a lot of that at Langley, intelligence types giving answers when they didn't even know the questions. Ryan was still new enough to the game that when he didn't know, he said so. Greer wondered if that would change in time. He hoped not.

After lunch a package arrived by messenger from the National Reconnaissance Office. It contained the photographs taken earlier in the day on two successive passes by a KH-11 satellite.

They'd be the last such photos for a while because of the restrictions imposed by orbital mechanics and the generally miserable weather on the Kola Peninsula. The first set of visible light shots taken an hour after the FLASH signal had gone out from Moscow showed the fleet at anchor or tied to the docks. On infrared a number of them were glowing brightly from internal heat, indicating that their boilers or gas-turbine engine plants were operating. The second set of photos had been taken on the next orbital pass at a very low angle.

Ryan scrutinized the blowups. "Wow! *Kirov, Moskva, Kiev,* three *Kara*s, five *Kresta*s, four *Krivak*s, eight *Udaloy*s, and five *Sovremenny*s."

"Search and rescue exercise, eh?" Greer gave Ryan a hard look. "Look at the bottom here. Every fast oiler they have is following them out. That's most of the striking force of the Northern Fleet right there, and if they need oilers, they figure to be out for a while."

"Davenport could have been more specific. But we still have their boomers heading back in. No amphibious ships in this photo, just combatants. Only the new ones, too, the ones with range and speed."

"And the best weapons."

"Yeah," Ryan nodded. "And all scrambled in a few hours. Sir, if they had this planned in advance, we'd have known about it. This must have been laid on today. Interesting."

"You've picked up the English habit of understatement, Jack." Greer stood up to stretch. "I want you to stay over an extra day."

"Okay, sir." He looked at his watch. "Mind if I phone the wife? I don't want her to drive out to the airport for a plane I'm not on."

"Sure, and after you've finished that, I want you to go down and see someone at DIA who used to work for me. See how much operational data they're getting on this sortie. If this is a drill, we'll know soon enough, and you can still take your Surfing Barbie home tomorrow."

It was a Skiing Barbie, but Ryan didn't say so.

THE SIXTH DAY

WEDNESDAY, 8 DECEMBER

CIA Headquarters

Ryan had been to the office of the director of central intelligence several times before to deliver briefings and occasional personal messages from Sir Basil Charleston to his highness, the DCI. It was larger than Greer's, with a better view of the Potomac Valley, and appeared to have been decorated by a professional in a style compatible with the DCI's origins. Arthur Moore was a former judge of the Texas State Supreme Court, and the room reflected his southwestern heritage. He and Admiral Greer were sitting on a sofa near the picture window. Greer waved Ryan over and passed him a folder.

The folder was made of red plastic and had a snap closure. Its edges were bordered with white tape and the cover had a simple white paper label bearing the legends EYES ONLY Δ and WILLOW. Neither notation was unusual. A computer in the basement of the Langley headquarters selected random names at the touch of a key; this prevented a foreign agent from inferring anything from the name of the operation. Ryan opened the folder and looked first at the index sheet. Evidently there were only three copies of the WILLOW document, each initialed by its owner. This one was initialed by the DCI himself. A CIA document with only three copies was unusual enough that Ryan, whose highest clearance was NEBULA, had never encountered one. From the grave looks of Moore and Greer, he guessed that these were two of the Δ-cleared officers; the other, he assumed, was the deputy director of operations (DDO), another Texan named Robert Ritter.

Ryan turned the index sheet. The report was a xeroxed copy of something that had been typed on a manual machine, and it had too many strikeovers to have been done by a real secretary. If Nancy Cummings and the other elite executive secretaries had not been allowed to see this . . . Ryan looked up.

"It's all right, Jack," Greer said. "You've just been cleared for WILLOW."

Ryan sat back, and despite his excitement began to read the document slowly and carefully.

The agent's code name was actually CARDINAL. The highest ranking agent-in-place the CIA had ever had, he was the stuff that legends are made of. CARDINAL had been recruited more than twenty years earlier by Oleg Penkovskiy. Another legend—a dead one—Penkovskiy had at the time been a colonel in the GRU, the Soviet military intelligence agency, a larger and more active counterpart to America's Defense Intelligence Agency (DIA). His position had given him access to daily information on all facets of the Soviet military, from the Red Army's command structure to the operational status of intercontinental missiles. The information he smuggled out through his British contact, Greville Wynne, was supremely valuable, and Western countries had come to depend on it—too much. Penkovskiy was discovered during the Cuban Missile Crisis in 1962. It was his data, ordered and delivered under great pressure and haste, that told President Kennedy that Soviet strategic systems were not ready for war. This information enabled the president to back Khrushchev into a corner from which there was no easy exit. The famous blink ascribed to Kennedy's steady nerves was, as in many such events throughout history, facilitated by his ability to see the other man's cards. This advantage was given him by a courageous agent whom he would never meet. Penkovskiy's response to the FLASH request from Washington was too rash. Already under suspicion, this finished him. He paid for his treason with his life. It was CARDINAL who first learned that he was being watched more closely than was the norm for a society where everyone is watched. He warned Penkovskiy—too late. When it became clear that the colonel could not be extracted from the Soviet Union, he himself urged CARDINAL to betray him. It was the final ironic joke of a brave man that his own death would advance the career of an agent whom he had recruited.

CARDINAL's job was necessarily as secret as his name. A senior adviser and confidant of a Politburo member, CARDINAL often acted as his representative within the Soviet military establishment. He thus had access to political and military intelligence of the highest order. This made his information extraordinarily valuable—and, paradoxically, highly suspect. Those few experienced CIA case officers who knew of him found it impossible to believe that he had not been "turned" somewhere along the line by one of the thousands of KGB counterintelligence officers whose sole duty it is to watch everyone and everything. For this reason CARDINAL-coded material was generally cross-checked against the reports of other spies and sources. But he had outlived many small-fry agents.

The name CARDINAL was known in Washington only to the top three CIA executives. On the first day of each month a new code name was chosen for his data, a name made known only to the highest echelon of CIA officers and analysts. This month it was WILLOW. Before being passed on, grudgingly, to outsiders, CARDINAL data was laundered as carefully as Mafia income to disguise its source. There were also a number of security measures that protected the agent and were unique to him. For fear of cryptographic exposure of his identity, CARDINAL material was hand delivered, never transmitted by radio or landline. CARDINAL himself was a very careful man—Penkovskiy's fate had taught him that. His information was conveyed through a series of intermediaries to the chief of the CIA's Moscow station. He had outlived twelve station chiefs; one of these, a retired field officer, had a brother who was a Jesuit. Every morning the priest, an instructor in philosophy and theology at Fordham University in New York, said mass for the safety and the soul of a man whose name he would never know. It was as good an explanation as any for CARDINAL's continued survival.

Four separate times he had been offered extraction from the Soviet Union. Each time he had refused. To some this was proof that he'd been turned, but to others it was proof that like most successful agents CARDINAL was a man driven by something he alone knew—and therefore, like most successful agents, he was probably a little crazy.

The document Ryan was reading had been in transit for twenty hours. It had taken five for the film to reach the American embassy in Moscow, where it was delivered at once to the station chief. An experienced field officer and former reporter for the *New York Times*, he worked under the cover of press attaché. He developed the film himself in his private darkroom. Thirty minutes after its arrival, he inspected the five exposed frames through a magnifying glass and sent a FLASH-priority dispatch to Washington saying that a CARDINAL signal was en route. Next he transcribed the message from the film to flash paper on his own portable typewriter, translating from the Russian as he went. This security measure erased both the agent's handwriting and, by the paraphrasing automatic to translation, any personal peculiarities of his language. The film was then burned to ashes, the report folded into a metal container much like a cigarette case. This held a small pyrotechnic charge that would go off if the case were improperly opened or suddenly shaken; two CARDINAL signals had been lost when their cases were accidentally dropped. Next the station chief took the case to the embassy's courier-in-residence, who had already been booked on a three-hour Aeroflot flight to London. At Heathrow Airport the courier sprinted to make connections with a Pan Am 747 to New York's Kennedy International, where he connected with the Eastern shuttle to Washington's National Airport. By eight that morning the diplomatic bag was in the State Department. There a CIA officer removed the case, drove it immediately to Langley, and handed it to the DCI. It was opened by an instructor from the CIA's technical services branch. The DCI made three copies on his personal Xerox machine and burned the flash paper in his ashtray. These security measures had struck a few of the men who had succeeded to the office of the DCI as laughable. The laughs had never outlasted the first CARDINAL report.

When Ryan finished the report he referred back to the second page and read it through again, shaking his head slowly. The

WILLOW document was the strongest reinforcement yet of his desire not to know how intelligence information reached him. He closed the folder and handed it back to Admiral Greer.

"Christ, sir."

"Jack, I know I don't have to say this—but what you have just read, nobody, not the president, not Sir Basil, not God if He asks, *nobody* learns of it without the authorization of the director. Is that understood?" Greer had not lost his command voice.

"Yes, sir." Ryan bobbed his head like a schoolboy.

Judge Moore pulled a cigar from his jacket pocket and lit it, looking past the flame into Ryan's eyes. The judge, everyone said, had been a hell of a field officer in his day. He'd worked with Hans Tofte during the Korean War and had been instrumental in bringing off one of the CIA's legendary missions, the disappearance of a Norwegian ship that had been carrying a cargo of medical personnel and supplies for the Chinese. The loss had delayed a Chinese offensive for several months, saving thousands of American and allied lives. But it had been a bloody operation. All of the Chinese personnel and all of the Norwegian crewmen had vanished. It was a bargain in the simple mathematics of war, but the morality of the mission was another matter. For this reason, or perhaps another, Moore had soon thereafter left government service to become a trial lawyer in his native Texas. His career had been spectacularly successful, and he'd advanced from wealthy courtroom lawyer to distinguished appellate judge. He had been recalled to the CIA three years earlier because of his unique combination of absolute personal integrity and experience in black operations. Judge Moore hid a Harvard law degree and a highly ordered mind behind the facade of a West Texas cowboy, something he had never been but simulated with ease.

"So, Dr. Ryan, what do you think of this?" Moore said as the deputy director of operations came in. "Hi, Bob, come on over here. We just showed Ryan here the WILLOW file."

"Oh?" Ritter slid a chair over, neatly trapping Ryan in the corner. "And what does the admiral's fair-haired boy think of that?"

"Gentlemen, I assume that you all regard this information as genuine," Ryan said cautiously, getting nods. "Sir, if this information was hand delivered by the Archangel Michael, I'd have trouble believing it—but since you gentlemen say it's reliable . . ." They wanted his opinion. The problem was, his conclusion was too incredible. Well, he decided, *I've gotten this far by giving my honest opinions . . .*

Ryan took a deep breath and gave them his evaluation.

"Very well, Dr. Ryan," Judge Moore nodded sagaciously. "First I want to hear what else it might be, then I want you to defend your analysis."

"Sir, the most obvious alternative doesn't bear much thinking about. Besides, they've been able to do it since Friday and they haven't done it," Ryan said, keeping his voice low and reasonable. Ryan had trained himself to be objective. He ran through the four alternatives he had considered, careful to examine each in detail. This was no time to allow personal views to intrude on his thinking. He spoke for ten minutes.

"I suppose there's one more possibility, Judge," he concluded. "This could be disinformation aimed at blowing this source. I cannot evaluate that possibility."

"The thought has occurred to us. All right, now that you've gone this far, you might as well give your operational recommendation."

"Sir, the admiral can tell you what the navy'll say."

"I sorta figured that one out, boy," Moore laughed. "What do you think?"

"Judge, setting up the decision tree on this will not be easy— there are too many variables, too many possible contingencies. But I'd say yes. If it's possible, if we can work out the details, we ought to try. The biggest question is the availability of our own assets. Do we have the pieces in place?"

Greer answered. "Our assets are slim. One carrier, *Kennedy*. I checked. *Saratoga*'s in Norfolk with an engineering casualty. On the other hand, HMS *Invincible* was just over here for the NATO exercise, sailed from Norfolk Monday night. Admiral White, I believe, commanding a small battle group."

"Lord White, sir?" Ryan asked. "The earl of Weston?"

"You know him?" Moore asked.

"Yes, sir. Our wives are friendly. I hunted with him last September, a grouse shoot in Scotland. He makes noises like a good operator, and I hear he has a good reputation."

"You're thinking we might want to borrow their ships, James?" Moore asked. "If so, we'll have to tell them about this. But we have to tell our side first. There's a meeting of the National Security Council at one this afternoon. Ryan, you will prepare the briefing papers and deliver the briefing yourself."

Ryan blinked. "That's not much time, sir."

"James here says you work well under pressure. Prove it." He looked at Greer. "Get a copy of his briefing papers and be ready to fly to London. That's the president's decision. If we want their boats, we'll have to tell them why. That means briefing the prime minister, and that's your job. Bob, I want you to confirm this report. Do what you have to do, but do not get WILLOW involved."

"Right," Ritter replied.

Moore looked at his watch. "We'll meet back here at 3:30, depending on how the meeting goes. Ryan, you have ninety minutes. Get cracking."

What am I being measured for? Ryan wondered. There was talk in the CIA that Judge Moore would be leaving soon for a comfortable ambassadorship, perhaps to the Court of St. James's, a fitting reward for a man who had worked long and hard to reestablish a close relationship with the British. If the judge left, Admiral Greer would probably move into his office. He had the virtues of age—he wouldn't be around that long—and of friends on Capitol Hill. Ritter had neither. He had complained too long and too openly about congressmen who leaked information on his operations and his field agents, getting men killed in the process of demonstrating their importance on the local cocktail circuit. He also had an ongoing feud with the chairman of the Select Intelligence Committee.

With that sort of reshuffling at the top and this sudden access to new and fantastic information . . . *What does it mean for me?* Ryan asked himself. They couldn't want him to be the next DDI. He knew he didn't have anything like the experience required for that job—though maybe in another five or six years . . .

Reykjanes Ridge

Ramius inspected his status board. The *Red October* was heading southwest on track eight, the westernmost surveyed route on what Northern Fleet submariners called Gorshkov's Railroad. His speed was thirteen knots. It never occurred to him that this was an unlucky number, an Anglo-Saxon superstition. They would hold this course and speed for another twenty hours. Immediately behind him, Kamarov was seated at the submarine's gravitometer board, a large rolled chart behind him. The young lieutenant was chain-smoking, and looked tense as he ticked off their position on the chart. Ramius did not disturb him. Kamarov knew this job, and Borodin would relieve him in another two hours.

Installed in the *Red October*'s keel was a highly sensitive device called a gradiometer, essentially two large lead weights separated by a space of one hundred yards. A laser-computer system measured the space between the weights down to a fraction of an angstrom. Distortions of that distance or lateral movement of the weights indicated variations in the local gravitational field. The navigator compared these highly precise local values to the values on his chart. With careful use of gravitometers in the ship's inertial navigation system, he could plot the vessel's location to within a hundred meters, half the length of the ship.

The mass-sensing system was being added to all the submarines that could accommodate it. Younger attack boat commanders, Ramius knew, had used it to run the Railroad at high speed. Good for the commander's ego, Ramius judged, but a little hard on the navigator. He felt no need for recklessness. Perhaps the letter had been a mistake . . . No, it prevented second thoughts. And the sensor suites on attack submarines simply were not good enough to detect the *Red October* so long as he maintained his silent routine. Ramius was certain of this; he had used them all. He would get where he wanted to go, do what he wanted to do, and nobody, not his own countrymen, not even the Americans, would be able to do a thing about it. That's why earlier he had listened to the passage of an *Alfa* thirty miles to his east and smiled.

The White House

Judge Moore's CIA car was a Cadillac limousine that came with a driver and a security man who kept an Uzi submachinegun under the dashboard. The driver turned right off Pennsylvania Avenue onto Executive Drive. More a parking lot than a street, this served the needs of senior officials and reporters who worked at the White House and the Executive

Office Building. "Old State," that shining example of Institutional Grotesque that towered over the executive mansion. The driver pulled smoothly into a vacant VIP slot and jumped out to open the doors after the security man had swept the area with his eyes. The judge got out first and went ahead, and as Ryan caught up he found himself walking on the man's left, half a step behind. It took a moment to remember that this instinctive action was exactly what the marine corps had taught him at Quantico was the proper way for a junior officer to accompany his betters. It forced Ryan to consider just how junior he was.

"Ever been in here before, Jack?"

"No, sir, I haven't."

Moore was amused. "That's right, you come from around here. Now, if you came from farther away, you'd have made the trip a few times." A marine guard held the door open for them. Inside a Secret Service agent signed them in. Moore nodded and walked on.

"Is this to be in the Cabinet Room, sir?"

"Uh-uh. Situation Room, downstairs. It's more comfortable and better equipped for this sort of thing. The slides you need are already down there, all set up. Nervous?"

"Yes, sir, I sure am."

Moore chuckled. "Settle down, boy. The president has wanted to meet you for some time now. He liked that report on terrorism you did a few years back, and I've shown him some more of your work, the one on Russian missile submarine operations, and the one you just did on management practices in their arms industries. All in all, I think you'll find he's a pretty regular guy. Just be ready when he asks questions. He'll hear every word you say, and he has a way of hitting you with good ones when he wants." Moore turned to descend a staircase. Ryan followed him down three flights, then they came to a door which led to a corridor. The judge turned left and walked to yet another door, this one guarded by another Secret Service agent.

"Afternoon, Judge. The president will be down shortly."

"Thank you. This is Dr. Ryan. I'll vouch for him."

"Right." The agent waved them in.

It was not nearly as spectacular as Ryan had expected. The Situation Room was probably no larger than the Oval Office upstairs. There was expensive-looking wood paneling over what were probably concrete walls. This part of the White House dated back to the complete rebuilding job done under Truman. Ryan's lectern was to his left as he went in. It stood in front and slightly to the right of a roughly diamond-shaped table, and behind it was the projection screen. A note on the lectern said the slide projector in the middle of the table was already loaded and focused, and gave the order of the slides, which had been delivered from the National Reconnaissance Office.

Most of the people were already here, all of the Joint Chiefs of Staff and the secretary of defense. The secretary of state, he remembered, was still shuttling back and forth between Athens and Ankara trying to settle the latest Cyprus situation. This perennial thorn in NATO's southern flank had flared up a few weeks earlier when a Greek student had run over a Turkish child with his car and been killed by a gang minutes later. By the end of the day fifty people had been injured, and the putatively allied countries were once more at each other's throats. Now two American aircraft carriers were cruising the Aegean as the secretary of state labored to calm both sides. It was bad enough that two young people had died, Ryan thought, but not something to get a country's army mobilized for.

Also at the table were General Thomas Hilton, chairman of the Joint Chiefs of Staff, and Jeffrey Pelt, the president's national security adviser, a pompous man Ryan had met years before at Georgetown University's Center for Strategic and International Studies. Pelt was going through some papers and dispatches. The chiefs were chatting amicably among themselves when the commandant of the marine corps looked up and spotted Ryan. He got up and walked over.

"You Jack Ryan?" General David Maxwell asked.

"Yes, sir." Maxwell was a short, tough fireplug of a man whose stubbly haircut seemed to spark with aggressive energy. He looked Ryan over before shaking hands.

"Pleased to meet you, son. I liked what you did over in London. Good for the corps." He referred to the terrorist incident in which Ryan had very nearly been killed. "That was good, quick action you took, Lieutenant."

"Thank you, sir. I was lucky."

"Good officer's supposed to be lucky. I hear you got some interesting news for us."

"Yes sir. I think you will find it worth your time."

"Nervous?" The general saw the answer and smiled thinly. "Relax, son. Everybody in this damned cellar puts his pants on the same way as you." He backhanded Ryan to the stomach and went back to his seat. The general whispered something to Admiral Daniel Foster, chief of naval operations. The CNO looked Ryan over for a moment before going back to what he was doing.

The president arrived a minute later. Everyone in the room stood as he walked to his chair, on Ryan's right. He said a few quick things to Dr. Pelt, then looked pointedly at the DCI.

"Gentlemen, if we can bring this meeting to order, I think Judge Moore has some news for us."

"Thank you, Mr. President. Gentlemen, we've had an interesting development today with respect to the Soviet naval operation that started yesterday. I have asked Dr. Ryan here to deliver the briefing."

The president turned to Ryan. The younger man could feel himself being appraised. "You may proceed."

Ryan took a sip of ice water from a glass hidden in the lectern. He had a wireless control for the slide projector and a choice of pointers. A separate high-intensity light illuminated his notes. The pages were full of errors and scribbled corrections. There had not been time to edit the copy.

"Thank you, Mr. President. Gentlemen, my name is Jack Ryan, and the subject of this briefing is recent Soviet naval activity in the North Atlantic. Before I get to that it will be necessary for me to lay a little groundwork. I trust you will bear with me for a few minutes, and please feel free to interrupt with questions at any time." Ryan clicked on the slide projector. The overhead lights near the screen dimmed automatically.

"These photographs come to us courtesy of the British," Ryan said. He now had everyone's attention. "The ship you see here is the Soviet fleet ballistic missile submarine *Red October*, photographed by a British agent in her dock at their submarine base at Polyarnyy, near Murmansk in northern Russia. As you can see, she is a very large vessel, about 650 feet long, a beam of roughly 85 feet, and an estimated submerged displacement of 32,000 tons. These figures are roughly comparable to those of a World War I battleship."

Ryan lifted a pointer. "In addition to being considerably larger than our own *Ohio*-class Trident submarines, *Red October* has a number of technical differences. She carries twenty-six missiles instead of our twenty-four. The earlier *Typhoon*-class vessels, from which she was developed, only have twenty.

October carries the new SS-N-20 sea-launched ballistic missile, the Seahawk. It's a solid-fuel missile with a range of about six thousand nautical miles, and it carries eight multiple independently targetable reentry vehicles, MIRVs, each with an estimated yield of five hundred kilotons. It's the same RV carried by their SS-18s, but there are less of them per launcher.

"As you can see, the missile tubes are located forward of the sail instead of aft, as in our subs. The forward diving planes fold into slots in the hull here; ours go on the sail. She has twin screws; ours have one propeller. And finally, her hull is oblate. Instead of being cylindrical like ours, it is flattened out markedly top and bottom."

Ryan clicked to the next slide. It showed two views superimposed, bow over stern. "These frames were delivered to us undeveloped. They were processed by the National Reconnaissance Office. Please note the doors here at the bow and here at the stern. The British were a little puzzled by these, and that's why I was permitted to bring the shots over earlier this week. We weren't able to figure out this function at the CIA either, and it was decided to seek the opinion of an outside consultant."

"Who decided?" the secretary of defense demanded angrily. "Hell, I haven't even seen them yet!"

"We only got them Monday, Bert," Judge Moore replied soothingly. "These two on the screen are only four hours old. Ryan suggested an outside expert, and James Greer approved it. I concurred."

"His name is Oliver W. Tyler. Dr. Tyler is a former naval officer who is now associate professor of engineering at the Naval Academy and a paid consultant to Sea Systems Command. He's an expert in the analysis of Soviet naval technology. Skip— Dr. Tyler—concluded that these doors are the intake and exhaust vents for a new silent propulsion system. He is currently developing a computer model of the system, and we hope to have this information by the end of the week. The system itself is rather interesting." Ryan explained Tyler's analysis briefly.

"Okay, Dr. Ryan." The president leaned forward. "You've just told us that the Soviets have built a missile submarine that's supposed to be hard for our men to locate. I don't suppose that's news. Go on."

"*Red October*'s captain is a man named Marko Ramius. That is a Lithuanian name, although we believe his internal passport designates his nationality as Great Russian. He is the son of a high Party official, and as good a submarine commander as they have. He's taken out the lead ship of every Soviet submarine class for the past ten years.

"*Red October* sailed last Friday. We do not know exactly what her orders were, but ordinarily their missile subs—that is, those with the newer long-range missiles—confine their activities to the Barents Sea and adjacent areas in which they can be protected from our attack boats by land-based ASW aircraft, their own surface ships, and attack submarines. About noon local time on Sunday, we noted increased search activity in the Barents Sea. At the time we took this to be a local ASW exercise, and by late Monday it looked to be a test of *October*'s new drive system.

"As you all know, early yesterday saw a vast increase in Soviet naval activity. Nearly all of the blue-water ships assigned to their Northern Fleet are now at sea, accompanied by all of their fast fleet-replenishment vessels. Additional fleet auxiliaries sailed from the Baltic Fleet bases and the western Mediterranean. Even more disquieting is the fact that nearly every nuclear submarine assigned to the Northern Fleet—their largest—appears to be heading into the North Atlantic. This includes three from the Med, since submarines there come from the Northern Fleet, not the Black Sea Fleet. Now we think we know why all this happened." Ryan clicked to the next slide. This one showed the North Atlantic, from Florida to the Pole, with Soviet ships marked in red.

"The day *Red October* sailed, Captain Ramius evidently posted a letter to Admiral Yuri Ilych Padorin. Padorin is chief of the Main Political Administration of their navy. We do not know what that letter said, but here we can see its results. This began to happen not four hours after that letter was opened. Fifty-eight nuclear-powered submarines and twenty-eight major surface combatants all headed our way. This is a remarkable reaction in four hours. This morning we learned what their orders are.

"Gentlemen, these ships have been ordered to locate *Red October*, and if necessary, to sink her." Ryan paused for effect. "As you can see, the Soviet surface force is here, about halfway between the European mainland and Iceland. Their submarines, these in particular, are all heading southwest towards the U.S. coast. Please note, there is no unusual activity on the Pacific side of either country—except we have information that Soviet fleet ballistic missile submarines in *both* oceans are being recalled to port.

"Therefore, while we do not know exactly what Captain Ramius said, we can draw some conclusions from these patterns of activity. It would appear that they think he's heading in our direction. Given his estimated speed as something between ten and thirty knots, he could be anywhere from here, below Iceland, to here, just off our coast. You will note that in either case he has successfully avoided detection by all four of these SOSUS barriers—"

"Wait a minute. You say they have issued orders to their ships to sink one of their submarines?"

"Yes, Mr. President."

The president looked at the DCI. "This is reliable information, Judge?"

"Yes, Mr. President, we believe it to be solid."

"Okay, Dr. Ryan, we're all waiting. What's this Ramius fellow up to?"

"Mr. President, our evaluation of this intelligence data is that *Red October* is attempting to defect to the United States."

The room went very quiet for a moment. Ryan could hear the whirring of the fan in the slide projector as the National Security Council pondered that. He held his hands on the lectern to keep them from shaking under the stare of the ten men in front of him.

"That's a very interesting conclusion, Doctor." The president smiled. "Defend it."

"Mr. President, no other conclusion fits the data. The really crucial thing, of course, is the recall of their other missile boats. They've never done that before. Add to that the fact that they have issued orders to sink their newest and most powerful missile sub, and that they are chasing in this direction, and one is left with the conclusion that they think she has left the reservation and is heading this way."

"Very well. What else could it be?"

"Sir, he could have told them that he's going to fire his missiles. At us, at them, the Chinese, or just about anyone else."

"And you don't think so?"

"No, Mr. President. The SS-N-20 has a range of six thousand miles. That means he could have hit any target in the

Northern Hemisphere from the moment he left the dock. He's had six days to do that, but he has not fired. Moreover, if he had threatened to launch his birds, he would have to consider the possibility that the Soviets would enlist our assistance to locate and sink him. After all, if our surveillance systems detect the launch of nuclear-armed missiles in any direction, things could get very tense, very quickly."

"You know he could fire his birds in both directions and start World War III," the secretary of defense observed.

"Yes, Mr. Secretary. In that case we'd be dealing with a total madman—more than one, in fact. On our missile boats there are five officers, who must all agree and act in unison to fire their missiles. The Soviets have the same number. For political reasons their nuclear warhead security procedures are even more elaborate than ours. Five or more people, all of whom wish to end the world?" Ryan shook his head. "That seems most unlikely, sir, and again, the Soviets would be well advised to inform us and enlist our aid."

"Do you really think they would inform us?" Dr. Pelt asked. His tone indicated what he thought.

"Sir, that's more a psychological question than a technical one, and I deal principally with technical intelligence. Some of the men in this room have met their Soviet counterparts and are better equipped to answer that than I am. My answer to your question, however, is yes. That would be the only rational thing for them to do, and while I do not regard the Soviets as entirely rational by our standards, they are rational by their own. They are not given to this sort of high-stakes gambling."

"Who is?" the president observed. "What else might it be?"

"Several things, sir. It could simply be a major naval exercise aimed at testing their ability to close our sea lines of communication and our ability to respond, both on short notice. We reject this possibility for several reasons. It's too soon after their autumn naval exercise, CRIMSON STORM, and they are only using nuclear submarines; no diesel-powered boats seem to be involved. Clearly speed is at a premium in their operation. And as a practical matter, they do not run major exercises at this time of year."

"And why is that?" the president asked.

Admiral Foster answered for Ryan. "Mr. President, the weather up there at this time of the year is extremely bad. Even we don't schedule exercises under these conditions."

"I seem to recall we just ran a NATO exercise, Admiral," Pelt noted.

"Yes, sir, south of Bermuda, where the weather's a lot nicer. Except for an antisub exercise off the British Isles, all of NIFTY DOLPHIN was held on our side of the lake."

"Okay, let's get back to what else their fleet might be up to," the president ordered.

"Well, sir, it might not be an exercise at all. It could be the real thing. This could be the beginning of a conventional war against NATO, its first step being interdiction of the sea lines of communication. If so, they've achieved complete strategic surprise and are now throwing it away by operating so overtly that we cannot fail to notice or react forcefully. Moreover, there is no corresponding activity whatever in their other armed services. Their army and air force—except for maritime surveillance aircraft—and their Pacific Fleet are engaged in routine training operations.

"Finally, this could be an attempt to provoke or divert us, drawing our attention to this while they are preparing to spring a surprise somewhere else. If so, they're going about it in a strange way. If you try to provoke somebody, you don't do it in his front yard. The Atlantic, Mr. President, is still our ocean. As you can see from this chart, we have bases here in Iceland, the Azores, all up and down our coast. We have allies on both sides of the ocean, and we can establish air superiority over the entire Atlantic if we so choose. Their navy is numerically large, larger than ours in some critical areas, but they cannot project force as well as we can—not yet, anyway—and certainly not right off our coast." Ryan took a sip of water.

"So, gentlemen, we have a Soviet missile submarine at sea when all the others, in both oceans, are being recalled. We have their fleet at sea with orders to sink that sub, and evidently they are chasing it in our direction. As I said, this is the only conclusion that fits the data."

"How many men on the sub, Doctor?" the president asked.

"We believe 110 or so, sir."

"So, 110 men all decide to defect to the United States at one time. Not an altogether bad idea," the president observed wryly, "but hardly a likely one."

Ryan was ready for that. "There is precedent for this, sir. On November 8, 1975, the *Storozhevoy,* a Soviet *Krivak*-class missile frigate, attempted to run from Riga, Latvia, to the Swedish island of Gotland. The political officer aboard, Valery Sablin, led a mutiny of the enlisted personnel. They locked their officers in their cabins and raced away from the dock. They came close to making it. Air and fleet units attacked them and forced them to halt within fifty miles of Swedish territorial waters. Two more hours and they would have made it. Sablin and twenty-six others were court-martialed and shot. More recently we have had reports of mutinous episodes on several Soviet vessels—especially submarines. In 1980 an *Echo*-class Soviet attack submarine surfaced off Japan. The captain claimed to have had a fire aboard, but photographs taken by naval reconnaissance aircraft—ours and Japanese—did not show smoke or fire-damaged debris being jettisoned from the submarine. However, the crewmen on deck did show sufficient evidence of trauma to support the conclusion that a riot had taken place aboard. We have had similar, sketchier reports for some years now. While I admit this is an extreme example, our conclusion is decidedly not without precedent."

Admiral Foster reached inside his jacket and came out with a plastic-tipped cigar. His eyes sparkled behind the match. "You know, I could almost believe this."

"Then I wish you'd tell us all why, Admiral," the president said, "because I still don't."

"Mr. President, most mutinies are led by officers, not enlisted men. The reason for this is simply that the enlisted men do not know how to navigate the ship. Moreover, officers have the advantages and educational background to know that successful rebellion is a possibility. Both of these factors would be even more true in the Soviet Navy. What if just the officers are doing this?"

"And the rest of the crew is going along with them?" Pelt asked. "Knowing what would happen to them and their families?"

Foster puffed a few times on his cigar. "Ever been to sea, Dr. Pelt? No? Let's imagine for the moment that you're taking a world cruise, on the *Queen Elizabeth 2,* say. One fine day you're in the middle of the Pacific Ocean—but how do you know exactly where you are? You don't know. You know what the officers tell you. Oh, sure, if you know a little astronomy, you might be able to estimate your latitude to within a few hundred miles. With a good watch and some knowledge of spherical trigonometry you might even guess your longitude to within a few hundred. Okay? That's on a ship that you can see from.

"These guys are on a submarine. You can't see a whole lot. Now, what if the officers—not even all the officers—are doing this? How will the crew know what's going on?" Foster shook his head. "They won't. They can't. Even our guys might not, and our men are trained a lot better than theirs. Their seamen are nearly all conscripts, remember. On a nuclear submarine you are absolutely cut off from the outside world. No radios except for ELF and VLF—and that's all encrypted; messages have to come through the communications officer. So, he has to be in on it. Same thing with the boat's navigator. They use inertial navigation systems, same as us. We have one of theirs, from that *Golf* we lifted off Hawaii. In their machine the data is also encrypted. The quartermaster reads the numbers off the machine, and the navigator gets their position from a book. In the Red Army, on *land,* maps are classified documents. Same thing in their navy. The enlisted men don't get to see charts and are not encouraged to know where they are. This would be especially true on missile submarines, right?

"On top of all that, these guys are working sailors, nucs. When you're at sea, you have a job to do, and you do it. On their ships, that means from fourteen to eighteen hours a day. These kids are all draftees with very simple training. They're taught to perform one or two tasks—and to follow their orders exactly. The Soviets train people to do their jobs by rote, with as little thinking as possible. That's why on major repair jobs you see officers holding tools. Their men will have neither the time nor the inclination to question their officers about what's going on. You do your job, and depend on everybody else to do his. That's what discipline at sea is all about." Foster tapped his cigar ash into an ashtray. "Yes, sir, you get the officers together, maybe not even all of them, and this would work. Getting ten or twelve dissidents together is a whole lot easier than assembling a hundred."

"Eas*ier,* but hardly easy, Dan," General Hilton objected. "For Christ's sake, they have at least one political officer aboard, plus moles from their intelligence outfits. You really think a Party hack would go along with this?"

"Why not? You heard Ryan—that frigate's mutiny was led by the political officer."

"Yeah, and since then they have shaken up that whole directorate," Hilton responded.

"We have defecting KGB types all the time, all good Party members," Foster said. Clearly he liked the idea of a defecting Russian sub.

The president took all this in, then turned to Ryan. "Dr. Ryan, you have managed to persuade me that your scenario is a theoretical possibility. Now, what does the CIA think we ought to do about it?"

"Mr. President, I'm an intelligence analyst, not—"

"I know very well what you are, Dr. Ryan. I've read enough of your work. I can see you have an opinion. I want to hear it."

Ryan didn't even look at Judge Moore. "We grab her, sir."

"Just like that?"

"No, Mr. President, probably not. However, Ramius could surface off the Virginia Capes in a day or two and request political asylum. We ought to be prepared for that contingency, sir, and my opinion is that we should welcome him with open arms." Ryan saw nods from all the chiefs. Finally somebody was on his side.

"You've stuck your neck out on this one," the president observed kindly.

"Sir, you asked me for an opinion. It will probably not be that easy. These *Alfa*s and *Victor*s appear to be racing for our coast, almost certainly with the intention of establishing an interdiction force—effectively a blockade of our Atlantic coast."

"*Blockade,*" the president said, "an ugly word."

"Judge," General Hilton said, "I suppose it's occurred to you that this is a piece of disinformation aimed at blowing whatever highly placed source generated this report?"

Judge Moore affected a sleepy smile. "It has, Gener'l. If this is a sham, it's a damned elaborate one. Dr. Ryan was directed to prepare this briefing on the assumption that this data is genuine. If it is not, the responsibility is mine." God bless you, Judge, Ryan said to himself, wondering just how gold-plated the WILLOW source was. The judge went on, "In any case, gentlemen, we will have to respond to this Soviet activity whether our analysis is accurate or not."

"Are you getting confirmation on this, Judge?" the president asked.

"Yes, sir, we are working on that."

"Good." The president was sitting straight, and Ryan noted his voice become crisper. "The judge is correct. We have to react to this, whatever they're really up to. Gentlemen, the Soviet Navy is heading for our coast. What are we doing about it?"

Admiral Foster answered first. "Mr. President, our fleet is pulling to sea at this moment. Everything that'll steam is out already, or will be by tomorrow night. We've recalled our carriers from the South Atlantic, and we are redeploying our nuclear submarines to deal with this threat. We began this morning to saturate the air over their surface force with P-3C Orion patrol aircraft, assisted by British Nimrods operating out of Scotland. General?" Foster turned to Hilton.

"At this moment we have E-3A Sentry AWACS-type aircraft circling them along with Dan's Orions, both accompanied by F-15 Eagle fighters out of Iceland. By this time Friday we'll have a squadron of B-52s operating from Loring Air Base in Maine. These will be armed with Harpoon air-to-surface missiles, and they'll be orbiting the Soviets in relays. Nothing aggressive, you understand," Hilton smiled. "Just to let them know we're interested. If they continue to come this way, we will redeploy some tactical air assets to the East Coast, and, subject to your approval, we can activate some national guard and reserve squadrons quietly."

"Just how will you do that quietly?" Pelt asked.

"Dr. Pelt, we have a number of guard outfits scheduled to run through our Red Flag facility at Nellis in Nevada starting this Sunday, a routine training rotation. They go to Maine instead of Nevada. The bases are pretty big, and they belong to SAC." Hilton referred to the Strategic Air Command. "They have good security."

"How many carriers do we have handy?" the president asked.

"Only one at the moment, sir, *Kennedy. Saratoga* stripped a main turbine last week, and it'll take a month to replace. *Nimitz* and *America* are both in the South Atlantic right now, *America* coming back from the Indian Ocean, *Nimitz* heading out to the Pacific. Bad luck. Can we recall a carrier from the eastern Med?"

"No." The president shook his head. "This Cyprus thing is

still too sensitive. Do we really need to? If anything . . . un-toward happens, can we handle their surface force with what we have at hand?"

"Yes, sir!" General Hilton said at once. "Dr. Ryan said it: the Atlantic is our ocean. The air force alone will have over five hundred aircraft designated for this operation, and another three or four hundred from the navy. If any sort of shooting match develops, that Soviet fleet will have an exciting and short life."

"We will try to avoid that, of course," the president said quietly. "The first press reports surfaced this morning. We had a call from Bud Wilkins of the *Times* right before lunch. If the American people find out too soon what the scope of this is . . . Jeff?"

"Mr. President, let's assume for the moment that Dr. Ryan's analysis is correct. I don't see what we can do about it," Pelt said.

"What?" Ryan blurted. "I, ah, beg your pardon, sir."

"We can't exactly steal a Russian missile sub."

"Why not!" Foster demanded. "Hell, we have enough of their tanks and aircraft." The other chiefs agreed.

"An aircraft with a crew of one or two is one thing, Admiral. A nuclear-powered submarine with twenty-six rockets and a crew of over a hundred is something else. Naturally, we can give asylum to the defecting officers."

"So, you're saying that if the thing does come sailing into Norfolk," Hilton joined in, "we give it back! Christ, man, it carries two hundred warheads! They just might use those god-damned things against us someday, you know. Are you *sure* you want to give them back?"

"That's a billion-dollar asset, General," Pelt said diffidently.

Ryan saw the president smile. He was said to like lively discussions. "Judge, what are the legal ramifications?"

"That's admiralty law, Mr. President." Moore looked uneasy for once. "I've never had an admiralty practice, takes me all the way back to law school. Admiralty is *jus gentium*—the same legal codes theoretically apply to all countries. American and British admiralty courts routinely cite each other's rulings. But as for the rights that attach to a mutinous crew—I have no idea."

"Judge, we are not dealing with mutiny or piracy," Foster noted. "The correct term is *barratry*, I believe. Mutiny is when the crew rebels against lawful authority. Gross misconduct of the officers is called barratry. Anyway, I hardly think we need to attach legal folderol to a situation involving nuclear weapons."

"We might, Admiral," the president mused. "As Jeff said, this is a highly valuable asset, legally their property, and they will know we have her. I think we are agreed that not all the crew is likely to be in on this. If so, those not party to the mutiny—barratry, whatever—will want to return home after it's all over. And we'll have to let them go, won't we?"

"Have to?" General Maxwell was doodling on a pad. "Have to?"

"General," the president said firmly, "we will not, repeat *not*, be party to the imprisonment or murder of men whose only desire is to return to home and family. Is that understood?" He looked around the table. "If they know we have her, they'll want her back. And they will know we have her from the crewmen who want to return home. In any case, big as this thing is, how could we hide her?"

"We might be able to," Foster said neutrally, "but as you say, the crew is a complication. I presume we'll have the chance to look her over?"

"You mean conduct a quarantine inspection, check her for seaworthiness, maybe make sure they're not smuggling drugs into the country?" The president grinned. "I think we might arrange that. But we are getting ahead of ourselves. There's a lot of ground to cover before we get to that point. What about our allies?"

"The English just had one of their carriers over here. Could you use her, Dan?" General Hilton asked.

"If they let us borrow her, yes. We just finished that ASW exercise south of Bermuda, and the Brits acquitted themselves well. We could use *Invincible,* the four escorts, and the three attack boats. The force is being recalled at high speed because of this."

"Do they know of this development, Judge?" the president asked.

"Not unless they've developed it themselves. This information is only a few hours old." Moore did not reveal that Sir Basil had his own ear in the Kremlin. Ryan didn't know much about it himself, had only heard some disconnected rumblings.

"With your permission, I have asked Admiral Greer to be ready to fly to England to brief the prime minister."

"Why not just send—"

Judge Moore was shaking his head. "Mr. President, this information—let's say it's only delivered by hand." Eyebrows went up all around the table.

"When is he leaving?"

"This evening, if you wish. There are a couple of VIP flights leaving Andrews tonight. Congressional flights." It was the usual end-of-session junket season. Christmas in Europe, on fact-finding missions.

"General, do we have anything quicker?" the president asked Hilton.

"We can scratch up a VC-141. Lockheed JetStar, almost as fast as a -135, and we can have it up in half an hour."

"Do it."

"Yes, sir, I'll call them in right now." Hilton rose and walked to a phone in the corner.

"Judge, tell Greer to pack his bags. I'll have a cover letter waiting for him on the plane to give to the prime minister. Admiral, you want the *Invincible?*"

"Yes, sir."

"I'll get her for you. Next, what do we tell our people at sea?"

"If *October* just sails in, it won't be necessary, but if we have to communicate with her—"

"Excuse me, Judge," Ryan said, "that is rather likely—that we'll have to. They'll probably have these attack boats on the coast before she gets here. If so, we'll have to warn her off if only to save the defecting officers. They are out to locate and sink her."

"We haven't detected her. What makes you think they can?" Foster asked, miffed at the suggestion.

"They did build her, Admiral. So they might know things about her that will enable them to locate her more easily than us."

"Makes sense," the president said. "That means somebody goes out to brief the fleet commanders. We can't broadcast this, can we, Judge?"

"Mr. President, this source is too valuable to compromise in any way. That's all I can say here, sir."

"Very well, somebody flies out. Next thing is, we'll have to talk to the Soviets about this. For the moment they can say that they're operating in home waters. When will they pass Iceland?"

"Tomorrow night, unless they change course," Foster answered.

"Okay, we give it a day, for them to call this off and for us to confirm this report. Judge, I want something to back up this fairy tale in twenty-four hours. If they haven't turned back by midnight tomorrow, I'll call Ambassador Arbatov into my office Friday morning." He turned to the chiefs. "Gentlemen, I want to see contingency plans for dealing with this situation by tomorrow afternoon. We will meet here tomorrow at two. One more thing: *no leaks!* This information does not go beyond this room without my personal approval. If this story breaks to the press, I'll have heads on my desk. Yes, General?"

"Mr. President, in order to develop those plans," Hilton said after sitting back down, "we have to work through our field commanders and some of our own operations people. Certainly we'll need Admiral Blackburn." Blackburn was CINCLANT, commander in chief of the Atlantic.

"Let me think that one over. I'll be back to you in an hour. How many people at the CIA know about this?"

"Four, sir. Ritter, Greer, Ryan, and myself, sir. That's all."

"Keep it that way." The president had been bedeviled by security leaks for months.

"Yes, Mr. President."

"Meeting is adjourned."

The president stood. Moore walked around the table to keep him from leaving at once. Dr. Pelt stayed also as the rest filed out of the room. Ryan stood outside the door.

"That was all right." General Maxwell grabbed his hand. He waited until everyone else was a few yards down the hall before going on. "I think you're crazy, son, but you sure put a burr under Dan Foster's saddle. No, even better: I think he got a hard-on." The little general chuckled. "And if we get the sub, maybe we can change the president's mind and arrange for the crew to disappear. The judge did that once, you know." It was a thought that chilled Ryan as he watched Maxwell swagger down the hall.

"Jack, you want to come back in here a minute?" Moore's voice called.

"You're an historian, right?" the president asked, reviewing his notes. Ryan hadn't even noticed him holding a pen.

"Yes, Mr. President. That's what my graduate degree's in." Ryan shook his hand.

"You have a fine sense of the dramatic, Jack. You would have made a decent trial lawyer." The president had made his reputation as a hard-driving state's attorney. He had survived an unsuccessful Mafia assassination attempt early in his career which hadn't hurt his political ambitions one bit. "Damned nice briefing."

"Thank you, Mr. President." Ryan beamed.

"The judge tells me you know the commander of that British task force."

It was like a sandbag hitting his head. "Yes, sir. Admiral White. I've hunted with him, and our wives are good friends. They're close to the Royal Family."

"Good. Somebody has to fly out to brief our fleet commander, then go on to talk to the Brits, if we get their carrier, as I expect we will. The judge says we ought to let Admiral Davenport go out with you. So, you fly out to *Kennedy* tonight, then on to *Invincible*."

"Mr. President, I—"

"Come now, Dr. Ryan," Pelt smiled thinly. "You are uniquely suited to this. You already have access to the intelligence, you know the British commander, and you're a naval intelligence specialist. You fit. Tell me, how eager do you think the navy is about getting this *Red October?*"

"Of course they're interested in it, sir. To get a chance to look at it, better yet to run it, take it apart, and run it some more. It would be the intelligence coup of all time."

"That's true. But maybe they're a little too eager."

"I don't understand what you mean, sir," Ryan said, though he understood it just fine. Pelt was the president's favorite. He was not the Pentagon's favorite.

"They might take a chance that we might not want them to take."

"Dr. Pelt, if you're saying that a uniformed officer would—"

"He's not saying that. At least not exactly. What he's saying is that it might be useful for me to have somebody out there who can give me an independent, civilian point of view."

"Sir, you don't know me."

"I've read a lot of your reports." The chief executive was smiling. It was said he could turn dazzling charm on and off like a spotlight. Ryan was being blinded, knew it, and couldn't do a thing about it. "I like your work. You have a good feel for things, for facts. Good judgment. Now, one reason I got to where I am is good judgment, too, and I think you can handle what I have in mind. The question is, will you do it, or won't you?"

"Do what, exactly, sir?"

"After you get out there, you stay put for a few days, and report directly to me. Not through channels, directly to me. You'll get the cooperation you need. I'll see to that."

Ryan didn't say anything. He'd just become a spy, a field officer, by presidential fiat. Worse, he'd be spying on his own side.

"You don't like the idea of reporting on your own people, right? You won't be, not really. Like I said, I want an independent, civilian opinion. We'd prefer to send an experienced case officer out, but we want to minimize the number of people involved in this. Sending Ritter or Greer out would be far too obvious, whereas you, on the other hand, are a relative—"

"Nobody?" Jack asked.

"As far as they're concerned, yes," Judge Moore replied. "The Soviets have a file on you. I've seen parts of it. They think you're an upper-class drone, Jack."

I am a drone, Ryan thought, unmoved by the implicit challenge. In this company I sure as hell am.

"Agreed, Mr. President. Please forgive me for hesitating. I've never been a field officer before."

"I understand." The president was magnanimous in victory. "One more thing. If I understand how submarines operate, Ramius could just have taken off, not saying anything. Why tip them off? Why the letter? The way I read this, it's counterproductive."

It was Ryan's turn to smile. "Ever meet a sub driver, sir? No? How about an astronaut?"

"Sure, I've met a bunch of the Shuttle pilots."

"They're the same breed of cat, Mr. President. As to why he left the letter, there's two parts to that. First, he's probably mad about something, exactly what we'll find out when we see him. Second, he figures he can pull this off regardless of what they try to stop him with—and he wants them to know that. Mr. President, the men who drive subs for a living are aggressive, confident, and very, very smart. They like nothing better than making somebody else, a surface ship operator for example, look like an idiot."

"You just scored another point, Jack. The astronauts I've met, on most things they're downright humble, but they think they're gods when it comes to flying. I'll keep that in mind. Jeff, let's get back to work. Jack, keep me posted."

Ryan shook his hand again. After the president and his senior adviser left, he turned to Judge Moore. "Judge, what the hell did you tell him about me?"

"Only the truth, Jack." Actually, the judge had wanted this operation to be run by one of the CIA's senior case officers. Ryan had not been part of this scheme, but presidents have been known to spoil many carefully laid plans. The judge took this philosophically. "This is a big move up in the world for you, if you do your job right. Hell, you might even like it."

Ryan was sure he wouldn't, and he was right.

CIA Headquarters

He didn't speak the whole way back to Langley. The director's car pulled into the basement parking garage, where they got out and entered a private elevator that took them directly to Moore's office. The elevator door was disguised as a wall panel, which was convenient but melodramatic, Ryan thought. The DCI went right to his desk and lifted a phone.

"Bob, I need you in here right now." He glanced at Ryan, standing in the middle of the room. "Looking forward to this, Jack?"

"Sure, Judge," Ryan said without enthusiasm.

"I can see how you feel about this spying business, but the whole thing could develop into an extremely sensitive situation. You ought to be damned flattered you're being trusted with it."

Ryan caught the between-the-line message just as Ritter breezed in.

"What's up, Judge?"

"We're laying an operation on. Ryan is flying out to the

Kennedy with Charlie Davenport to brief the fleet commanders on this *October* business. The president bought it."

"Guess so. Greer left for Andrews just before you pulled in. Ryan gets to fly out, eh?"

"Yes. Jack, the rules is this: you can brief the fleet commander and Davenport, that's all. Same for the Brits, just the boss-sailor. If Bob can confirm WILLOW, the data can be spread out, but only as much as is absolutely necessary. Clear?"

"Yes, sir. I suppose somebody has told the president that it's hard to accomplish anything if nobody knows what the hell is going on. Especially the guys who're doing the work."

"I know what you're saying, Jack. We have to change the president's mind on that. We will, but until we do, remember— he is the boss. Bob, we'll need to rustle something up so he'll fit in."

"Naval officer's uniform? Let's make him a commander, three stripes, usual ribbons." Ritter looked Ryan over. "Say a forty-two long. We can have him outfitted in an hour, I expect. This operation have a name?"

"That's next." Moore lifted his phone again and tapped in five numbers. "I need two words . . . Uh-huh, thank you." He wrote a few things down. "Okay, gentlemen, you're calling this Operation MANDOLIN. You, Ryan, are Magi. Ought to be easy to remember, given the time of year. We'll work up a series of code words based on those while you're being fitted. Bob, take him down there yourself. I'll call Davenport and have him arrange the flight."

Ryan followed Ritter to the elevator. It was going too fast, everyone was being too clever, he thought. This Operation MANDOLIN was racing forward before they knew what the hell they were going to do, much less how. And the choice of his code name struck Ryan as singularly inappropriate. He wasn't anyone's wise man. The name should have been something more like "Halloween."

THE SEVENTH DAY

THURSDAY, 9 DECEMBER

The North Atlantic

When Samuel Johnson compared sailing in a ship to "being in jail, with the chance of being drowned," at least he had the consolation of travelling to his ship in a safe carriage, Ryan thought. Now he was going to sea, and before he got to his ship Ryan stood the chance of being smashed to red pulp in a plane crash. Jack sat hunched in a bucket seat on the port side of a Grumman Greyhound, known to the fleet without affection as a COD (for carrier onboard delivery), a flying delivery truck. The seats, facing aft, were too close together, and his knees jutted up against his chin. The cabin was far more amenable to cargo than to people. There were three tons of engine and electronics parts stowed in crates aft—there, no doubt, so that the impact of a plane crash on the valuable equipment would be softened by the four bodies in the passenger section. The cabin was not heated. There were no windows. A thin aluminum skin separated him from a two-hundred-knot wind that shrieked in time with the twin turbine engines. Worst of all, they were flying through a storm at five thousand feet, and the

COD was jerking up and down in hundred-foot gulps like a berserk roller coaster. The only good thing was the lack of lighting, Ryan thought—at least nobody can see how green my face is. Right behind him were two pilots, talking away loudly so they could be heard over the engine noise. The bastards were enjoying themselves!

The noise lessened somewhat, or so it seemed. It was hard to tell. He'd been issued foam-rubber ear protectors along with a yellow, inflatable life preserver and a lecture on what to do in the event of a crash. The lecture had been perfunctory enough that it took no great intellect to estimate their chances of survival if they did crash on a night like this. Ryan hated flying. He had once been a marine second lieutenant, and his active career had ended after only three months when his platoon's helicopter had crashed on Crete during a NATO exercise. He had injured his back, nearly been crippled for life, and ever since regarded flying as something to be avoided. The COD, he thought, was bouncing more down than up. It probably meant they were close to the *Kennedy*. The alternative did not bear thinking about. They were only ninety minutes out of Oceana Naval Air Station at Virginia Beach. It felt like a month, and Ryan swore to himself that he'd never be afraid on a civilian airliner again.

The nose dropped about twenty degrees, and the aircraft seemed to be flying right at something. They were landing, the most dangerous part of carrier flight operations. He remembered a study conducted during the Vietnam War in which carrier pilots had been fitted with portable electrocardiographs to monitor stress, and it had surprised a lot of people that the most stressful time for carrier pilots wasn't while they were being shot at—it was while they were landing, particularly at night.

Christ, you're full of happy thoughts! Ryan told himself. He closed his eyes. One way or another, it would be over in a few seconds.

The deck was slick with rain and heaving up and down, a black hole surrounded by perimeter lights. The carrier landing was a controlled crash. Massive landing gear struts and shock absorbers were needed to lessen the bone-crushing impact. The aircraft surged forward only to be jerked to a halt by the arresting wire. They were down. They were safe. Probably. After a moment's pause, the COD began moving forward again. Ryan heard some odd noises as the plane taxied and realized that they came from the wings folding up. The one danger he had not considered was flying on an aircraft whose wings were supposed to collapse. It was, he decided, just as well. The plane finally stopped moving, and the rear hatch opened.

Ryan flipped off his seatbelts and stood rapidly, banging his head on the low ceiling. He didn't wait for Davenport. With his canvas bag clutched to his chest he darted out of the rear of the aircraft. He looked around, and was pointed to the *Kennedy*'s island structure by a yellow-shirted deck crewman. The rain was falling heavily, and he felt rather than saw that the carrier was indeed moving on the fifteen-foot seas. He ran towards an open, lighted hatch fifty feet away. He had to wait for Davenport to catch up. The admiral didn't run. He walked with a precise thirty-inch step, dignified as a flag officer should be, and Ryan decided that he was probably annoyed that his semisecret arrival prohibited the usual ceremony of bosun's pipes and side boys. There was a marine standing inside the hatch, a corporal, resplendent in striped blue trousers, khaki shirt and tie, and snow-white pistol belt. He saluted, welcoming both aboard.

"Corporal, I want to see Admiral Painter."

"The admiral's in flag quarters, sir. Do you require escort?"

"No, son. I used to command this ship. Come along, Jack." Ryan got to carry both bags.

"Gawd, sir, you actually used to do this for a living?" Ryan asked.

"Night carrier landings? Sure, I've done a couple of hundred. What's the big deal?" Davenport seemed surprised at Ryan's awe. Jack was sure it was an act.

The inside of the *Kennedy* was much like the interior of the USS *Guam*, the helicopter assault ship Ryan had been assigned to during his brief military career. It was the usual navy maze of steel bulkheads and pipes, everything painted the same shade of cave-gray. The pipes had some colored bands and stenciled acronyms which probably meant something to the men who ran the ship. To Ryan they might as well have been neolithic cave paintings. Davenport led him through a corridor, around a corner, down a "ladder" made entirely of steel and so steep he almost lost his balance, down another passageway, and around another corner. By this time Ryan was thoroughly lost. They came to a door with a marine stationed in front. The sergeant saluted perfectly, and opened the door for them.

Ryan followed Davenport in—and was amazed. Flag quarters on the USS *Kennedy* might have been transported as a block from a Beacon Hill mansion. To his right was a wall-sized mural large enough to dominate a big living room. A half-dozen oils, one of them a portrait of the ship's namesake, President John Fitzgerald Kennedy, dotted the other walls, themselves covered with expensive-looking paneling. The deck was covered in thick crimson wool, and the furniture was pure civilian, French provincial, oak and brocade. One could almost imagine they were not aboard a ship at all, except that the ceiling—"overhead"—had the usual collection of pipes, all painted gray. It was a decidedly odd contrast to the rest of the room.

"Hi ya, Charlie!" Rear Admiral Joshua Painter emerged from the next room, drying his hands with a towel. "How was it coming in?"

"Little rocky," Davenport allowed, shaking hands. "This is Jack Ryan."

Ryan had never met Painter but knew him by reputation. A Phantom pilot during the Vietnam War, he had written a book, *Paddystrikes,* on the conduct of the air campaigns. It had been a truthful book, not the sort of thing that wins friends. He was a small, feisty man who could not have weighed more than a hundred thirty pounds. He was also a gifted tactician and a man of puritanical integrity.

"One of yours, Charlie?"

"No, Admiral, I work for James Greer. I am not a naval officer. Please accept my apologies. I don't like pretending to be what I'm not. The uniform was the CIA's idea." This drew a frown.

"Oh? Well, I suppose that means you're going to tell me what Ivan's up to. Good, I hope to hell somebody knows. First time on a carrier? How did you like the flight in?"

"It might be a good way to interrogate prisoners of war," Ryan said as offhandedly as he could. The two flag officers had a good laugh at his expense, and Painter called for some food to be sent in.

The double doors to the passageway opened serveral minutes

later and a pair of stewards—"mess management specialists"—
came in, one bearing a tray of food, the other two pots of
coffee. The three men were served in a style appropriate to
their rank. The food, served on silver-trimmed plates, was
simple but appetizing to Ryan, who hadn't eaten in twelve
hours. He dished cole slaw and potato salad onto his plate and
selected a pair of corned-beef-on-ryes.

"Thank you. That's all for now," Painter said. The stewards
came to attention before leaving. "Okay, let's get down to
business."

Ryan gulped down half a sandwich. "Admiral, this information is only twenty hours old." He took the briefing folders
from his bag and handed them around. His delivery took twenty
minutes, during which he managed to consume the two sandwiches and a goodly portion of his cole slaw and spill coffee
on his hand-written notes. The two flag officers were a perfect
audience, not interrupting once, only darting a few disbelieving
looks at him.

"God Almighty," Painter said when Ryan finished. Davenport just stared poker-faced as he contemplated the possibility
of examining a Soviet missile sub from the inside. Jack decided
he'd be a formidable opponent over cards. Painter went on,
"Do you really believe this?"

"Yes, sir, I do." Ryan poured himself another cup of coffee.
He would have preferred a beer to go with his corned beef. It
hadn't been bad at all, and good kosher corned beef was something he'd been unable to find in London.

Painter leaned back and looked at Davenport. "Charlie, you
tell Greer to teach this lad a few lessons—like how a bureaucrat
ain't supposed to stick his neck this far out on the block. Don't
you think this is a little far-fetched?"

"Josh, Ryan here's the guy who did the report last June on
Soviet missile-sub patrol patterns."

"Oh? That was a nice piece of work. It confirmed something
I've been saying for two or three years." Painter rose and
walked to the corner to look out at the stormy sea. "So, what
are we supposed to do about all this?"

"The exact details of the operation have not been determined. What I expect is that you will be directed to locate *Red
October* and attempt to establish communications with her skipper. After that? We'll have to figure a way to get her to a safe

place. You see, the president doesn't think we'll be able to hold onto her once we get her—if we get her."

"What?" Painter spun around and spoke a tenth of a second before Davenport did. Ryan explained for several minutes.

"Dear God above! You give me one impossible task, then you tell me that if we succeed in it, we gotta give the goddamned thing back to them!"

"Admiral, my recommendation—the president asked me for one—was that we keep the submarine. For what it's worth, the Joint Chiefs are on your side, too, along with the CIA. As it is, though, if the crewmen want to go back home, we have to send them back, and then the Soviets will know we have the boat for sure. As a practical matter, I can see the other side's point. The vessel is worth a pile of money, and it is their property. And how would we hide a 30,000-ton submarine?"

"You hide a submarine by sinking it," Painter said angrily. "They're designed to do that, you know. 'Their property!' We're not talking about a damned passenger liner. That's something designed to kill people—our people!"

"Admiral, I am on your side," Ryan said quietly. "Sir, you said we've given you an impossible task, Why?"

"Ryan, finding a boomer that does not want to be found is not the easiest thing in the world. We practice against our own. We damned near always fail, and you say this one's already passed all the northeast SOSUS lines. The Atlantic's a rather large ocean, and a missile sub's noise footprint is very small."

"Yes, sir." Ryan noted to himself that he might have been overly optimistic about their chances for success.

"What sort of shape are you in, Josh?" Davenport asked.

"Pretty good, really. The exercise we just ran, NIFTY DOLPHIN, worked out all right. Our part of it," Painter corrected himself. "*Dallas* raised some hell on the other side. My ASW crews are functioning very well. What sort of help are we getting?"

"When I left the Pentagon, the CNO was checking the availability of P-3s out on the Pacific, so you'll probably be seeing more of those. Everything that'll move is putting to sea. You're the only carrier, so you've got overall tactical command, right? Come on, Josh, you're our best ASW operator."

Painter poured some coffee for himself. "Okay, we have one carrier deck. *America* and *Nimitz* are still a good week away. Ryan, you said you're flying out to *Invincible*. We get her, too, right?"

"The president was working on that. Want her?"

"Sure. Admiral White has a good nose for ASW, and his boys really lucked out during DOLPHIN. They killed two of our attack boats, and Vince Gallery was some kind of pissed about that. Luck's a big part of this game. That would give us two decks instead of one. I wonder if we can get some more S-3s?" Painter referred to the Lockheed Vikings, carrier-borne antisubmarine aircraft.

"Why?" Davenport asked.

"I can transfer my F-18s to shore, and that'll give us room for twenty more Vikings. I don't like losing the striking power, but what we're going to need is more ASW muscle. That means more S-3s. Jack, you know that if you're wrong, that Russkie surface force is going to be a handful to deal with. You know how many surface-to-surface missiles they're packing?"

"No, sir." Ryan was certain it was too many.

"We're one carrier, and that makes us their primary target. If they start shooting at us, it'll get awful lonesome—then it'll get awful exciting." The phone rang. "Painter here . . . Yes. Thank you. Well, *Invincible* just turned around. Good, they're giving her to us along with two tin cans. The rest of the escorts and the three attack subs are still heading home." He frowned. "I can't really fault them for that. That means we have to give them some escorts, but it's a good trade. I want that flight deck."

"Can we chopper Jack out to her?" Ryan wondered if Davenport knew what the president had ordered him to do. The admiral seemed interested in getting him off the *Kennedy*.

Painter shook his head. "Too far for a chopper. Maybe they can send a Harrier back for him."

"The Harrier's a fighter, sir," Ryan commented.

"They have an experimental two-seat version set up for ASW patrolling. It's supposed to work reasonably well outside their helo perimeter. That's how they bagged one of our attack boats, caught her napping." Painter finished off the last of his coffee.

"Okay, gentlemen, let's get ourselves down to ASW control and try and figure a way to run this circus act. CINCLANT will want to hear what I have in mind. I suppose I'd better decide for myself. We'll also call *Invincible* and have them send a bird back to ferry you out, Ryan."

Ryan followed the two admirals out of the room. He spent two hours watching Painter move ships around the ocean like a chess master with his pieces.

The USS Dallas

Bart Mancuso had been on duty in the attack center for more than twenty hours. Only a few hours of sleep separated this stretch from the previous one. He had been eating sandwiches and drinking coffee, and two cups of soup had been thrown in by his cooks for variety's sake. He examined his latest cup of freeze-dried without affection.

"Cap'n?" He turned. It was Roger Thompson, his sonar officer.

"Yes, what is it?" Mancuso pulled himself away from the tactical display that had occupied his attention for several days. Thompson was standing at the rear of the compartment. Jones was standing beside him holding a clipboard and what looked like a tape machine.

"Sir, Jonesy has something I think you ought to look at." .

Mancuso didn't want to be bothered—extended time on duty always taxed his patience. But Jones looked eager and excited. "Okay, come on over to the chart table."

The *Dallas'* chart table was a new gadget wired into the BC-10 and projected onto a TV-type glass screen four feet square. The display moved as the *Dallas* moved. This made paper charts obsolete, though they were kept anyway. Charts can't break.

"Thanks, Skipper," Jones said, more humbly than usual. "I know you're kinda busy, but I think I got something here. That anomalous contact we had the other day's been bothering me. I had to leave it after the ruckus the other Russkie subs kicked up, but I was able to come back to it three times to make sure it was still there. The fourth time it was gone, faded out. I want to show you what I worked up. Can you punch up our course track for back then on this baby, sir?"

The chart table was interfaced through the BC-10 into the ship's inertial navigation system, SINS. Mancuso punched the command in himself. It was getting so that they couldn't flush the head without a computer command . . . The *Dallas'* course track showed up as a convoluted red line, with tick marks displayed at fifteen-minute intervals.

"Great!" Jones commented. "I've never seen it do that before. That's all right. Okay." Jones pulled a handful of pencils from his back pocket. "Now, I got the contact first at 0915 or so, and the bearing was about two-six-nine." He set a pencil down, eraser at *Dallas'* position, point directed west towards the target. "Then at 0930 it was bearing a two-six-zero. At 0948, it was two-five-zero. There's some error built into these, Cap'n. It was a tough signal to lock in on, but the errors should average out. Right about then we got all this other activity, and I had to go after them, but I came back to it about 1000, and the bearing was two-four-two." Jones set down another pencil on the due-east line traced when the *Dallas* had moved away from the Icelandic coast. "At 1015 it was two-three-four, and at 1030 it was two-two-seven. These last two are shaky, sir. The signal was real faint, and I didn't have a very good lock on it." Jones looked up. He appeared nervous.

"So far, so good. Relax, Jonesy. Light up if you want."

"Thanks, Cap'n." Jones fished out a cigarette and lit it with a butane lighter. He had never approached the captain quite this way. He knew Mancuso to be a tolerant, easygoing commander—if you had something to say. He was not a man who liked his time wasted, and it was sure as hell he wouldn't want it wasted now. "Okay, sir, we gotta figure he couldn't be too far away from us, right? I mean, he had to be between us and Iceland. So let's say he was about halfway between. That gives him a course about like this." Jones set down some more pencils.

"Hold it, Jonesy. Where does the course come from?"

"Oh, yeah." Jones flipped open his clipboard. "Yesterday morning, night, whatever it was, after I got off watch, it started bothering me, so I used the move we made offshore as a baseline to do a little course track for him. I know how, Skipper. I read the manual. It's easy, just like we used to do at Cal Tech to chart star motion. I took an astronomy course in my freshman year."

Mancuso stifled a groan. It was the first time he had ever heard this called easy, but on looking at Jones' figures and diagrams, it appeared that he had done it right. "Go on."

Jones pulled a Hewlitt Packard scientific calculator from his pocket and what looked like a National Geographic map liberally coated with pencil marks and scribblings. "You want to check my figures, sir?"

"We will, but I'll trust you for now. What's the map?"

"Skipper, I know it's against the rules an' all, but I keep this as a personal record of the tracks the bad guys use. It doesn't leave the boat, sir, honest. I may be a little off, but all this translates to a course of about two-two-zero and a speed of ten knots. And *that* aims him right at the entrance of Route One. Okay?"

"Go on." Mancuso had already figured that one. Jonesy was on to something.

"Well, I couldn't sleep after that, so I skipped back to sonar and pulled the tape on the contact. I had to run it through the computer a few times to filter out all the crap—sea sounds, the other subs, you know—then I rerecorded it at ten times normal speed." He set his cassette recorder on the chart table. "Listen to this, Skipper."

The tape was scratchy, but every few seconds there was a *thrum*. Two minutes of listening seemed to indicate a regular interval of about five seconds. By this time Lieutenant Mannion was looking over Thompson's shoulder, listening, and nodding speculatively.

"Skipper, that's gotta be a man-made sound. It's just too regular for anything else. At normal speed it didn't make much sense, but once I speeded it up, I had the sucker."

"Okay, Jonesy, finish it," Mancuso said.

"Captain, what you just heard was the acoustical signature of a Russian submarine. He was heading for Route One, taking the inshore track off the Icelandic coast. You can bet money on that, Skipper."

"Roger?"

"He sold me, Captain," Thompson replied.

Mancuso took another look at the course track, trying to figure an alternative. There wasn't any. "Me, too. Roger, Jonesy makes sonarman first class today. I want to see the paper work done by the turn of the next watch, along with a nice letter of commendation for my signature. Ron," he poked the sonarman in the shoulder, "that's all right. Damned well done!"

"Thanks, Skipper." Jones' smile stretched from ear to ear.

"Pat, please call Lieutenant Butler to the attack center."

Mannion went to the phones to call the boat's chief engineer.

"Any idea what it is, Jonesy?" Mancuso turned back.

The sonarman shook his head. "It isn't screw sounds. I've never heard anything like it." He ran the tape back and played it again.

Two minutes later, Lieutenant Earl Butler came into the attack center. "You rang, Skipper?"

"Listen to this, Earl." Mancuso rewound the tape and played it a third time.

Butler was a graduate of the University of Texas and every school the navy had for submarines and their engine systems. "What's that supposed to be?"

"Jonesy says it's a Russian sub. I think he's right."

"Tell me about the tape," Butler said to Jones.

"Sir, it's speeded up ten times, and I washed it through the BC-10 five times. At normal speed it doesn't sound like much of anything." With uncharacteristic modesty, Jones did not point out that it had sounded like something to him.

"Some sort of harmonic? I mean, if it was a propeller, it'd have to be a hundred feet across, and we'd be hearing one blade at a time. The regular interval suggests some sort of harmonic." Butler's face screwed up. "But a harmonic what?"

"Whatever it was, it was headed right here." Mancuso tapped Thor's Twins with his pencil.

"That makes him a Russian, all right," Butler agreed. "Then they're using something new. Again."

"Mr. Butler's right," Jones said. "It does sound like a harmonic rumble. The other funny thing is, well, there was this background noise, kinda like water going through a pipe. I don't know, it didn't pick up on this. I guess the computer filtered it off. It was real faint to start with—anyway, that's outside my field."

"That's all right. You've done enough for one day. How do you feel?" Mancuso asked.

"A little tired, Skipper. I've been working on this for a while."

"If we get close to this guy again, you think you can track him down?" Mancuso knew the answer.

"You bet, Cap'n! Now that we know what to listen for, you bet I'll bag the sucker!"

Mancuso looked at the chart table. "Okay, if he was heading

for the Twins, and then ran the route at, say twenty-eight or thirty knots, and then settled down to his base course and speed of about ten or so . . . that puts him about here now. Long ways off. Now, if we run at top speed . . . forty-eight hours will put us here, and that'll put us in front of him. Pat?"

"That's about right, sir," Lieutenant Mannion concurred. "You're figuring he ran the route at full speed, then settled down—makes sense. He wouldn't need the quiet drive in that damned maze. It gives him a free shot for four or five hundred miles, so why not uncrank his engines? That's what I'd do."

"That's what we'll try and do, then. We'll radio in for permission to leave Toll Booth station and track this character down. Jonesy, running at max speed means you sonarmen will be out of work for a while. Set up the contact tape on the simulator and make sure the operators all know what this guy sounds like, but get some rest. All of you. I want you at a hundred percent when we try to reacquire this guy. Have yourself a shower. Make that a Hollywood shower—you've earned it—and rack out. When we do go after this character, it'll be a long, tough hunt."

"No sweat, Captain. We'll get him for you. Bet on it. You want to keep my tape, sir?"

"Yeah." Mancuso ejected the tape and looked up in surprise. "You sacrificed a Bach for this?"

"Not a good one, sir. I have a Christopher Hogwood of this piece that's much better."

Mancuso pocketed the tape. "Dismissed, Jonesy. Nice work."

"A pleasure, Cap'n." Jones left the attack center counting the extra money for jumping a rate.

"Roger, make sure your people are well rested over the next two days. When we do go after this guy, it's going to be a bastard."

"Aye, Captain."

"Pat, get us up to periscope depth. We're going to call this one into Norfolk right now. Earl, I want you thinking about what's making that noise."

"Right, Captain."

While Mancuso drafted his message, Lieutenant Mannion brought the *Dallas* to periscope-antenna depth with an upward angle on the diving planes. It took five minutes to get from five hundred feet to just below the stormy surface. The submarine was subject to wave action, and while it was very gentle by surface ship standards, the crew noted her rocking. Mannion raised the periscope and ESM (electronic support measures) antenna, the latter used for the broad-band receiver designed to detect possible radar emissions. There was nothing in view— he could see about five miles—and the ESM instruments showed nothing except for aircraft sets, which were too far away to matter. Next Mannion raised two more masts. One was a reed-like UHF (ultrahigh frequency) receiving antenna. The other was new, a laser transmitter. This rotated and locked onto the carrier wave signal of the Atlantic SSIX, the communications satellite used exclusively by submarines. With the laser, they could send high-density transmissions without giving away the sub's position.

"All ready, sir," the duty radioman reported.

"Transmit."

The radioman pressed a button. The signal, sent in a fraction of a second, was received by photovoltaic cells, read over to a UHF transmitter, and shot back down by a parabolic dish antenna towards Atlantic Fleet Communications headquarters. At Norfolk another radioman noted the reception and pressed a button that transmitted the same signal up to the satellite and back to the *Dallas*. It was a simple way to identify garbles.

The *Dallas* operator compared the received signal with the one he'd just sent. "Good copy, sir."

Mancuso ordered Mannion to lower everything but the ESM and UHF antennae.

Atlantic Fleet Communications

In Norfolk the first line of the dispatch revealed the page and line of the one-time-pad cipher sequence, which was recorded on computer tape in the maximum security section of the communications complex. An officer typed the proper numbers into his computer terminal, and an instant later the machine generated a clear text. The officer checked it again for garbles. Satisfied there were none, he took the printout to the other side of the room where a yeoman was seated at a telex. The officer handed him the dispatch.

The yeoman keyed up the proper addressee and transmitted the message by dedicated landline to COMSUBLANT Operations, half a mile away. The landline was fiber optic, located in a steel conduit under a paved street. It was checked three times a week for security purposes. Not even the secrets of nuclear weapons performance were as closely guarded as day-to-day tactical communications.

COMSUBLANT *Operations*

A bell went off in the operations room as the message came up on the "hot" printer. It bore a Z prefix, which indicated FLASH-priority status.

Z090414ZDEC

T O P   S E C R E T   T H E O

FM: USS DALLAS

TO: COMSUBLANT

INFO: CINCLANTFLT

//NOOOOO//

REDFLEET SUBOPS
1. REPORT ANOMALOUS SONAR CONTACT ABOUT 0900Z 7DEC AND LOST AFTER INCREASE IN REDFLEET SUB ACTIVITY. CONTACT SUBSE-QUENTLY EVALUATED AS REDFLEET SSN/SSBN TRANSITING ICELAND INSHORE TRACK TO-WARDS ROUTE ONE. COURSE SOUTHWEST SPEED TEN DEPTH UNKNOWN.
2. CONTACT EVIDENCED UNUSUAL REPEAT UN-USUAL ACOUSTICAL CHARACTERISTICS. SIG-NATURE UNLIKE ANY KNOWN REDFLEET SUBMARINE.
3. REQUEST PERMISSION TO LEAVE TOLL BOOTH TO PURSUE AND INVESTIGATE. BELIEVE A NEW DRIVE SYSTEM WITH UNUSUAL SOUND CHAR-ACTERISTICS BEING USED THIS SUB. BELIEVE GOOD PROBABILITY CAN LOCATE AND IDEN-TIFY.

A lieutenant junior grade took the dispatch to the office of Vice Admiral Vincent Gallery. COMSUBLANT had been on duty since the Soviet subs had started moving. He was in an evil mood.

"A FLASH priority from *Dallas*, sir."

"Uh-huh." Gallery took the yellow form and read it twice. "What do you suppose this means?"

"No telling, sir. Looks like he heard something, took his time figuring it out, and wants another crack at it. He seems to think he's onto something unusual."

"Okay, what do I tell him? Come on, mister. You might be an admiral yourself someday and have to make decisions." An unlikely prospect, Gallery thought.

"Sir, *Dallas* is in an ideal position to shadow their surface force when it gets to Iceland. We need her where she is."

"Good textbook answer." Gallery smiled up at the youngster, preparing to cut him off at the knees. "On the other hand, *Dallas* is commanded by a fairly competent man who wouldn't be bothering us unless he really thought he had something. He doesn't go into specifics, probably because it's too complicated for a tactical FLASH dispatch, and also because he thinks that we know his judgment is good enough to take his word on something. 'New drive system with unusual sound characteristics.' That may be a crock, but he's the man on the scene, and he wants an answer. We tell him yes."

"Aye aye, sir," the lieutenant said, wondering if the skinny old bastard made decisions by flipping a coin when his back was turned.

The Dallas

Z090432ZDEC

T O P   S E C R E T

FM: COMSUBLANT

TO: USS DALLAS

A. USS DALLAS Z090414ZDEC

B. COMSUBLANT INST 2000.5

OPAREA ASSIGNMENT //N04220//

1. REQUEST REF A GRANTED.
2. AREAS BRAVO ECHO GOLF REF B ASSIGNED FOR UNRESTRICTED OPS 090500Z TO 140001Z. REPORT AS NECESSARY. VADM GALLERY SENDS.

"Hot damn!" Mancuso chuckled. That was one nice thing about Gallery. When you asked him a question, by God, you got an answer, yes or no, before you could rig your antenna in. Of course, he reflected, if it turned out that Jonesy was wrong and this was a wild-goose chase, he'd have some explaining to do. Gallery had handed more than one sub skipper his head in a bag and set him on the beach.

Which was where he was headed regardless, Mancuso knew. Since his first year at Annapolis all he had ever wanted was command of his own attack boat. He had that now, and he knew that the rest of his career would be downhill. In the rest of the navy your first command was just that, a first command. You could move up the ladder and command a fleet at sea eventually, if you were lucky and had the right stuff. Not submariners, though. Whether he did well with the *Dallas* or poorly, he'd lose her soon enough. He had this one and only chance. And afterwards, what? The best he could hope for was command of a missile boat. He'd served on those before and was sure that commanding one, even a new *Ohio*, was about as exciting as watching paint dry. The boomer's job was to stay hidden. Mancuso wanted to be the hunter, that was the exciting end of the business. And after commanding a missile boat? He could get a "major surface command," perhaps a nice oiler—it would be like switching mounts from Secretariat to Elsie the Cow. Or he could get a squadron command and sit in an office onboard a tender, pushing paper. At best in that position he'd go to sea once a month, his main purpose being to bother sub skippers who didn't want him there. Or he could get a desk job in the Pentagon—what fun! Mancuso understood why some of the astronauts had cracked up after coming back from the moon. He, too, had worked many years for this command, and in another year his boat would be gone. He'd have to give the *Dallas* to someone else. But he did have her now.

"Pat, let's lower all masts and take her down to twelve hundred feet."

"Aye aye, sir. Lower the masts," Mannion ordered. A petty officer pulled on the hydraulic control levers.

"ESM and UHF masts lowered, sir," the duty electrician reported.

"Very well. Diving officer, make your depth twelve hundred feet."

"Twelve hundred feet, aye," the diving officer responded. "Fifteen degrees down-angle on the planes."

"Fifteen degrees down, aye."

"Let's move her, Pat."

"Aye, Skipper. All ahead full."

"All ahead full, aye." The helmsman reached up to turn the annunciator.

Mancuso watched his crew at work. They did their jobs with mechanistic precision. But they were not machines. They were men. His.

In the reactor spaces aft, Lieutenant Butler had his enginemen acknowledge the command and gave the necessary orders. The reactor coolant pumps went to fast speed. An increased amount of hot, pressurized water entered the exchanger, where its heat was transferred to the steam on the outside loop. When the coolant returned to the reactor it was cooler than it had been and therefore denser. Being denser, it trapped more neutrons in the reactor pile, increasing the ferocity of the fission reaction and giving off yet more power. Farther aft, saturated steam in the "outside" or nonradioactive loop of the heat exchange system emerged through clusters of control valves to strike the blades of the high-pressure turbine. The *Dallas'* huge bronze screw began to turn more quickly, driving her forward and down.

The engineers went about their duties calmly. The noise in the engine spaces rose noticeably as the systems began to put out more power, and the technicians kept track of this by continuously monitoring the banks of instruments under their hands. The routine was quiet and exact. There was no extraneous conversation, no distraction. Compared to a submarine's reactor spaces, a hospital operating room was a den of libertines.

Forward, Mannion watched the depth gauge go below six hundred feet. The diving officer would wait until they got to nine hundred feet before starting to level off, the object being to zero the dive out exactly at the ordered depth. Commander Mancuso wanted the *Dallas* below the thermocline. This was the border between different temperatures. Water settled in isothermal layers of uniform stratification. The relatively flat boundary where warmer surface water met colder depth water was a semipermeable barrier which tended to reflect sound waves. Those waves that did manage to penetrate the thermocline were mostly trapped below it. Thus, though the *Dallas* was now running below the thermocline at over thirty knots and making as much noise as she was capable of, she would still be difficult to detect with surface sonar. She would also be largely blind, but then, there was not much down there to run into.

Mancuso lifted the microphone for the PA system. "This is the captain speaking. We have just started a speed run that will last forty-eight hours. We are heading towards a point where we hope to locate a Russian sub that went past us two days ago. This Russkie is evidently using a new and rather quiet propulsion system that nobody's run across before. We're going to try and get ahead of him and track on him as he passes us again. This time we know what to listen for, and we'll get a nice clear picture of him. Okay, I want everyone on this boat to be well rested. When we get there, it'll be a long, tough hunt. I want everybody at a hundred percent. This one will probably be interesting." He switched off the microphone. "What's the movie tonight?"

The diving officer watched the depth gauge stop moving before answering. As chief of the boat, he was also manager of the *Dallas*' cable TV system, three video-cassette recorders in the mess room which led to televisions in the wardroom, and various other crew accommodations. "Skipper, you got a choice. *Return of the Jedi* or two football tapes: Oklahoma-Nebraska and Miami-Dallas. Both those games were played while we were on the exercise, sir. It'll be like watching them live." He laughed. "Commercials and all. The cooks are already making the popcorn."

"Good. I want everybody nice and loose." Why couldn't they ever get Navy tapes, Mancuso wondered. Of course, Army had creamed them this year . . .

"Morning, Skipper." Wally Chambers, the executive officer, came into the attack center. "What gives?"

"Come on back to the wardroom, Wally. I want you to listen

to something." Mancuso took the cassette from his shirt pocket and led Chambers aft.

The V. K. Konovalov

Two hundred miles northeast of the *Dallas,* in the Norwegian Sea, the *Konovalov* was racing southwest at forty-one knots. Captain Tupolev sat alone in the wardroom rereading the dispatch he'd received two days before. His emotions alternated between rage and grief. The Schoolmaster had done *that!* He was dumbfounded.

But what was there to do? Tupolev's orders were explicit, the more so since, as his *zampolit* had pointed out, he was a former pupil of the traitor Ramius. He, too, could find himself in a very bad position. If the slug succeeded.

So, Marko had pulled a trick on everyone, not just the *Konovalov.* Tupolev had been slinking about the Barents Sea like a fool while Marko had been heading the other way. Laughing at everyone, Tupolev was sure. Such treachery, such a hellish threat against the *Rodina.* It was inconceivable—and all too conceivable. All the advantages Marko had. A four-room apartment, a dacha, his own Zhiguli. Tupolev did not yet have his own automobile. He had earned his way to a command, and now it was all threatened by—this! He'd be lucky to keep what he had.

I have to kill a friend, he thought. Friend? Yes, he admitted to himself, Marko had been a good friend and a fine teacher. Where had he gone wrong?

Natalia Bogdanova.

Yes, that had to be it. A big stink, the way that had happened. How many times had he had dinner with them, how many times had Natalia laughed about her fine, strong, big sons? He shook his head. A fine woman killed by a damned incompetent fool of a surgeon. Nothing could be done about it, he was the son of a Central Committee member. It was an outrage the way things like that still happened, even after three generations of building socialism. But nothing was sufficient to justify this madness.

Tupolev bent over the chart he'd brought back. He'd be on his station in five days, in less time if the engine plant held together and Marko wasn't in too much of a hurry—and he wouldn't be. Marko was a fox, not a bull. The other *Alfas* would get there ahead of his, Tupolev knew, but it didn't matter. He had to do this himself. He'd get ahead of Marko and wait. Marko would try to slink past, and the *Konovalov* would be there. And the *Red October* would die.

The North Atlantic

The British Sea Harrier FRS.4 appeared a minute early. It hovered briefly off the *Kennedy*'s port beam as the pilot sized up his landing target, the wind, and sea conditions. Maintaining a steady thirty-knot forward speed to compensate for the carrier's forward speed, he side-slipped his fighter neatly to the right, then dropped it gently amidships, slightly forward of the *Kennedy*'s island structure, exactly in the center of the flight deck. Instantly a gang of deck crewmen raced for the aircraft, three carrying heavy metal chocks, another a metal ladder which he set up by the cockpit, whose canopy was already coming open. A team of four snaked a fueling hose towards the aircraft, eager to demonstrate the speed with which the U.S. Navy services aircraft. The pilot was dressed in an orange coverall and yellow life jacket. He set his helmet on the back of the front seat and came down the ladder. He watched briefly to be sure his fighter was in capable hands before sprinting to the island. He met Ryan at the hatch.

"You Ryan? I'm Tony Parker. Where's the loo?" Jack gave him the proper directions and the pilot darted off, leaving Ryan standing there in a flight suit, holding his bag and feeling stupid. A white plastic flight helmet dangled from his other hand as he watched the crewmen fueling the Harrier. He wondered if they knew what they were doing.

Parker was back in three minutes. "Commander," he said, "there's one thing they've never put in a fighter, and that's a bloody toilet. They fill you up with coffee and tea and send you off, and you've no place to go."

"I know the feeling. Anything else you have to do?"

"No, sir. Your admiral chatted with me on the radio when I was flying in. Looks like your chaps have finished fueling my bird. Shall we be off?"

"What do I do with this?" Ryan held up his bag, expecting to have to hold it in his lap. His briefing papers were inside the flight suit, tucked against his chest.

"We put it in the boot, of course. Come along, sir."

Parker walked out to the fighter jauntily. The dawn was a feeble one. There was a solid overcast at one or two thousand feet. It wasn't raining, but looked as though it might. The sea, still rolling at about eight feet, was a gray, crinkled surface dotted with whitecaps. Ryan could feel the *Kennedy* moving, surprised that something so huge could be made to move at all. When they got to the Harrier, Parker took the duffle in one hand and reached for a recessed handle on the underside of the fighter. Twisting and pulling the lever, he revealed a cramped space about the size of a small refrigerator. Parker stuffed the bag into it, slamming the door shut behind it, making sure the locking lever was fully engaged. A deck crewman in a yellow shirt conferred with the pilot. Aft a helicopter was revving its engines, and a Tomcat fighter was taxiing towards a midships catapult. On top of this a thirty-knot wind was blowing. The carrier was a noisy place.

Parker waved Ryan up the ladder. Jack, who liked ladders about as much as he liked flying, nearly fell into his seat. He struggled to get situated properly, while a deck crewman strapped him into the four-point restraint system. The man put the helmet on Ryan's head and pointed to the jack for its intercom system. Maybe American crews really did know something about Harriers. Next to the plug was a switch. Ryan flipped it.

"Can you hear me, Parker?"

"Yes, Commander. All settled in?"

"I suppose."

"Right." Parker's head swiveled to check the engine intakes. "Starting the engine."

The canopies stayed up. Three crewmen stood close by with large carbon dioxide extinguishers, presumably in case the engine exploded. A dozen others were standing by the island, watching the strange aircraft as the Pegasus engine screamed to life. Then the canopy came down.

"Ready, Commander?"

"If you are."

The Harrier was not a large fighter, but it was certainly the loudest. Ryan could feel the engine noise ripple through his body as Parker adjusted his thrust-vector controls. The aircraft wobbled, dipped at the nose, then rose shakily into the air.

Ryan saw a man by the island point and gesture to them. The
Harrier slid to port, moving away from the island as it gained
in height.

"That wasn't too bad," Parker said. He adjusted the thrust
controls, and the Harrier began true forward flight. There was
little feeling of acceleration, but Ryan saw that the *Kennedy*
was rapidly falling behind. A few seconds later they were
beyond the inner ring of escorts.

"Let's get on top of this muck," Parker said. He pulled back
on the stick and headed for the clouds. In seconds they were
in them, and Ryan's field of view was reduced from five miles
to five feet in an instant.

Jack looked around his cockpit, which had flight controls
and instruments. Their airspeed showed one hundred fifty knots
and rising, altitude four hundred feet. This Harrier had evidently been a trainer, but the instrument panel had been altered
to include the read-out instruments for a sensor pod that could
be attached to the belly. A poor man's way of doing things,
but from what Admiral Painter said it had evidently worked
well enough. He figured the TV-type screen was the FLIR
readout, which monitored a forward-looking infrared heat sensor. The airspeed gauge now said three hundred knots, and the
climb indicator showed a twenty-degree angle of attack. It felt
like more than that.

"Should be hitting the top of this soon," Parker said. "Now!"

The altimeter showed twenty-six thousand feet when Ryan
was blasted by pure sunlight. One thing about flying that he
never got used to was that no matter how awful the weather
was on the ground, if you flew high enough you could always
find the sun. The light was intense, but the sky's color was
noticeably deeper than the soft blue seen from the ground. The
ride became airliner smooth as they escaped the lower turbu-
lence. Ryan fumbled with his visor to shield his eyes.

"That better, sir?"

"Fine, Lieutenant. It's better than I expected."

"What do you mean, sir?" Parker inquired.

"I guess it beats flying on a commercial bird. You can see
more. That helps."

"Sorry we don't have any extra fuel, or I'd show you some
aerobatics. The Harrier will do almost anything you ask of
her."

"That's all right."

"And your admiral," Parker went on conversationally, "said that you don't fancy flying."

Ryan's hands grabbed the armrests as the Harrier went through three complete revolutions before snapping back to level flight. He surprised himself by laughing. "Ah, the British sense of humor."

"Orders from your admiral, sir," Parker semi-apologized. "We wouldn't want you to think the Harrier's another bloody bus."

Which admiral, Ryan wondered, Painter or Davenport? Probably both. The top of the clouds was like a rolling field of cotton. He'd never appreciated that before, looking through a foot-square window on an airliner. In the back seat he almost felt as if he were sitting outside.

"May I ask a question, sir?"

"Sure."

"What's the flap?"

"What do you mean?"

"I mean, sir, that they turned my ship around. Then I get orders to ferry a VIP from *Kennedy* to *Invincible*."

"Oh, okay. Can't say, Parker. I'm delivering some messages to your boss. I'm just the mailman," Ryan lied. Roll that one three times.

"Excuse me, Commander, but you see, my wife is expecting a child, our first, soon after Christmas. I hope to be there, sir."

"Where do you live?"

"Chatham, that's—"

"I know. I live in England myself at the moment. Our place is in Marlow, upriver from London. My second kid got started over there."

"Born there?"

"Started there. My wife says it's those strange hotel beds, do it to her every time. If I were a betting man, I'd give you good odds, Parker. First babies are always late anyway."

"You say you live in Marlow?"

"That's right, we built a house there earlier this year."

"Jack Ryan—John Ryan? The same chap who—"

"Correct. You don't have to tell anybody that, Lieutenant."

"Understood, sir. I didn't know you were a naval officer."

"That's why you don't have to tell anyone."

"Yes, sir. Sorry for the stunt earlier."

"That's all right. Admirals must have their little laughs. I understand you guys just ran an exercise with our guys."

"Indeed we did, Commander. I sank one of your submarines, the *Tullibee*. My systems operator and I, that is. We caught her near the surface at night with our FLIR and dropped noise-makers all round her. You see, we didn't let anyone know about our new equipment. All's fair, as you know. I understand her commander was bloody furious. I'd hoped to meet him in Norfolk, but he didn't arrive until the day we sailed."

"You guys have a good time in Norfolk?"

"Yes, Commander. We were able to get in a day's shooting on your Chesapeake Bay, the Eastern Shore, I believe you call it."

"Oh yeah? I used to hunt there. How was it?"

"Not bad. I got my three geese in half an hour. Bag limit was three—stupid."

"You called in and blasted three geese in a half hour this late in the season?"

"That is how I earn my modest living, Commander, shooting," Parker commented.

"I was up for a grouse shoot with your admiral last September. They made me use a double. If you show up with my kind of gun—I use a Remington automatic—they look at you like you're some kind of terrorist. I got stuck with a pair of Purdeys that didn't fit. Got fifteen birds. Seemed an awful lazy way to hunt, though, with one guy loading my gun for me, and another platoon of ghillies driving the game. We just about annihilated the bird population, too."

"We have more game per acre than you do."

"That's what the admiral said. How far to *Invincible*?"

"Forty minutes."

Ryan looked at the fuel gauges. They were half empty already. In a car he'd be thinking about a fill-up. All that fuel gone in half an hour. Well, Parker didn't seem excited.

The landing on HMS *Invincible* was different from the COD's arrival on the *Kennedy*. The ride became rocky as Parker descended through the clouds, and it occurred to Ryan that they were on the leading edge of the same storm he'd endured the night before. The canopy was coated with rain, and he heard the impact of thousands of raindrops on the airframe—or was it hail? Watching the instruments, he saw that Parker leveled out at a thousand feet, while they were still in clouds, then descended more slowly, breaking into the clear at a hundred feet. The *Invincible* was scarcely a half the *Kennedy*'s size. He watched her bobbing actively on the fifteen-foot seas. Parker used the same technique as before. He hovered briefly on the carrier's port side, then slid to the right, dropping the fighter twenty feet onto a painted circle. The landing was hard, but Ryan was able to see it coming. The canopy came up at once.

"You can get out here," Parker said. "I have to taxi to the elevator."

A ladder was already in place. He unbuckled and got out. A crewman had already retrieved his bag. Ryan followed him to the island and was met by an ensign—a sublieutenant, the British call the rank.

"Welcome aboard, sir." The youngster couldn't be more than twenty, Ryan thought. "Let me help you out of the flight suit."

The sublieutenant stood by as Ryan unzipped and took off his helmet, Mae West, and coverall. He retrieved his cap from the bag. In the process he bounced off the bulkhead a few times. The *Invincible* seemed to be corkscrewing in a following sea. A bow wind and a following sea? In the North Atlantic in winter, nothing was too crazy. The officer took his bag, and Ryan held onto the briefing material.

"Lead on, *left*enant," Ryan gestured. The youngster shot up a series of three ladders, leaving Jack panting behind, thinking about the jogging he wasn't getting in. The combination of the ship's motion and an inner ear badly scrambled from the day's flying made him dizzy, and he found himself bumping into things. How did professional pilots do it?

"Here's the flag bridge, sir." The sublieutenant held the door open.

"Hello, Jack!" boomed the voice of Vice Admiral John White, eighth earl of Weston. He was a tall, well-built man of fifty with a florid complexion set off by a white scarf at his neck. Jack had first met him earlier in the year, and since then his wife Cathy and the countess, Antonia, had become close friends, members of the same circle of amateur musicians. Cathy Ryan played classical piano. Toni White, an attractive woman of forty-four, owned a Guarnieri del Jesu violin. Her husband was a man whose peerage was treated as the convenient afterthought. His career in the Royal Navy had been built entirely on merit. Jack walked over to take his hand.

"Good day, Admiral."

"How was your flight?"

"Different. I've never been in a fighter before, much less one with ambitions to mate with a hummingbird," Ryan smiled. The bridge was overheated, and it felt good.

"Jolly good. Let's go aft to my sea cabin." White dismissed the sublieutenant, who handed Jack his bag before withdrawing. The admiral led him aft through a short passageway and left into a small compartment.

It was surprisingly austere, considering that the English liked their comforts and that White was a peer. There were two curtained portholes, a desk, and a couple of chairs. The only human touch was a color photograph of his wife. The entire port wall was covered with a chart of the North Atlantic.

"You look tired, Jack." White waved him to the upholstered chair.

"I am tired. I've been on the go since—hell, since 6:00 A.M. yesterday. I don't know about time changes, I think my watch is still on European time."

"I have a message for you." White pulled a slip of paper from his pocket and handed it over.

"Greer to Ryan. WILLOW confirmed," Ryan read. "Basil sends regards. Ends." Somebody had confirmed WILLOW. Who? Maybe Sir Basil, maybe Ritter. Ryan would not quote odds on that one.

Jack tucked it in his pocket. "This is good news, sir."

"Why the uniform?"

"Not my idea, Admiral. You know who I work for, right? They figured I'd be less conspicuous this way."

"At least it fits." The admiral lifted a phone and ordered refreshments sent to them. "How's the family, Jack?"

"Fine, thank you, sir. The day before I came over Cathy and Toni were playing over at Nigel Ford's place. I missed it. You know, if they get much better, we ought to have a record cut. There aren't too many violin players better than your wife."

A steward arrived with a plateful of sandwiches. Jack had never figured out the British taste for cucumbers on bread.

"So, what's the flap?"

"Admiral, the significance of the message you just gave me is that I can tell this to you and three other officers. This is very hot stuff, sir. You'll want to make your choices accordingly."

"Hot enough to turn my little fleet around." White thought it over before lifting the phone and ordering three of his officers to the cabin. He hung up. "Captain Carstairs, Captain Hunter, and Commander Barclay—they are, respectively, *Invincible*'s commanding officer, my fleet operations officer, and my fleet intelligence officer."

"No chief of staff?"

"Flew home, death in the family. Something for your coffee?" White extracted what looked like a brandy bottle from a desk drawer.

"Thank you, Admiral." He was grateful for the brandy. The coffee needed the help. He watched the admiral pour a generous amount, perhaps with the ulterior motive of making him speak more freely. White had been a British sailor longer than he'd been Ryan's friend.

The three officers arrived together, two carrying folding metal chairs.

"Admiral," Ryan began, "you might want to leave that bottle out. After you hear this story, we might all need a drink." He passed out his two remaining briefing folders and talked from memory. His delivery took fifteen minutes.

"Gentlemen," he concluded, "I must insist that this information be kept strictly confidential. For the moment no one outside this room may learn it."

"That is too bad," Carstairs said. "This makes for a bloody good sea story."

"And our mission?" White was holding the photographs. He poured Ryan another shot of brandy, gave the bottle a brief look, then stowed it back in the desk.

"Thank you, Admiral. For the moment our mission is to locate *Red October*. After that we're not sure. I imagine just locating her will be hard enough."

"An astute observation, Commander Ryan," Hunter said.

"The good news is that Admiral Painter has requested that CINCLANT assign you control of several U.S. Navy vessels, probably three 1052-class frigates, and a pair of FFG *Perry*s. They all carry a chopper or two."

"Well, Geoffrey?" White asked.

"It's a start," Hunter agreed.

"They'll be arriving in a day or two. Admiral Painter asked me to express his confidence in your group and its personnel."

"A whole fucking Russian missile submarine..." Barclay said almost to himself. Ryan laughed.

"Like the idea, Commander?" At least he had one convert.

"What if the sub is heading for the U.K.? Does it then become a British operation?" Barclay asked pointedly.

"I suppose it would, but from the way I read the map, if Ramius was heading for England, he'd already be there. I saw a copy of the president's letter to the prime minister. In return for your assistance, the Royal Navy gets the same access to the data we develop as our guys get. We're on the same side, gentlemen. The question is, can we do it?"

"Hunter?" the admiral asked.

"If this intelligence is correct...I'd say we have a good chance, perhaps as good as fifty percent. On one hand, we have a missile submarine attempting to evade detection. On the other, we have a great deal of ASW arrayed to locate her, and she will be heading towards one of only a few discrete locations. Norfolk, of course, Newport, Groton, King's Bay, Port Everglades, Charleston. A civilian port such as New York is less likely, I think. The problem is, what with Ivan sending all his *Alfa*s racing to your coast, they will get there ahead of *October*. They may have a specific port target in mind. We'll know that in another day. So, I'd say they have an equal chance. They'll be able to operate far enough off your coast that your government will have no viable legal reason to object to whatever they do. If anything, I'd say the Soviets have the advantage. They have both a clearer idea of the submarine's capabilities and a simpler overall mission. That more than balances their less capable sensors."

"Why isn't Ramius coming on faster?" Ryan asked. "That's the one thing I can't figure. Once he clears the SOSUS lines off Iceland, he's clear into the deep basin—so why not crack his throttles wide open and race for our coast?"

"At least two reasons," Barclay answered. "How much operational intelligence data do you see?"

"I handle individual assignments. That means I hop around a lot from one thing to another. I know a good deal about their boomers, for example, but not as much about their attack boats." Ryan didn't have to explain he was CIA.

"Well, you know how compartmentalized the Sovs are. Ramius probably doesn't know where their attack submarines are, not all of them. So, if he were to race about, he'd run the off chance of blundering into a stray *Victor* and being sunk without ever knowing what was happening. Second, what if the Soviets did enlist American assistance, saying perhaps that a missile sub had been taken over by a mutinous crew of Maoist counterrevolutionaries—and then your navy detects a missile submarine racing down the North Atlantic towards the American coast. What would your president do?"

"Yeah," Ryan nodded. "We'd blow it the hell out of the water."

"There you have it. Ramius is in the trade of stealth, and he'll likely stick to what he knows," Barclay concluded. "Fortunately or unfortunately, he's jolly good at it."

"How soon will we have performance data on this quiet drive system?" Carstairs wanted to know.

"Next couple of days, we hope."

"Where does Admiral Painter want us?" White asked.

"The plan he submitted to Norfolk puts you on the right flank. He wants *Kennedy* inshore to handle the threat from their surface force. He wants your force farther out. You see, Painter thinks there's the chance that Ramius will come straight south from the G-I-U.K. gap into the Atlantic basin and just sit for a while. The odds favor his not being detected there, and if the Soviets send the fleet after him, he's got the time and supplies to sit out there longer than they can maintain a force off our coast—both for technical and political reasons. Additionally, he wants your striking power out here to threaten their flank. It has to be approved by the commander in chief of the Atlantic Fleet, and a lot of details remain to be worked out. For example, Painter requested some E-3 Sentries to support you out here."

"A month in the middle of the North Atlantic in winter?" Carstairs winced. He had been the *Invincible*'s executive officer during the war around the Falklands and had ridden in the violent South Atlantic for endless weeks.

"Be happy for the E-3s." The admiral smiled. "Hunter, I want to see plans for using all these ships the Yanks are giving us, and how we can cover a maximum area. Barclay, I want to see your evaluation of what our friend Ramius will do. Assume he's still the clever bastard we've come to know and love."

"Aye aye, sir." Barclay stood with the others.

"Jack, how long will you be with us?"

"I don't know, Admiral. Until they recall me to the *Kennedy,* I guess. From where I sit, this operation was laid on too fast. Nobody really knows what the hell we're supposed to do."

"Well, why don't you let us see to this for a while? You look exhausted. Get some sleep."

"True enough, Admiral." Ryan was beginning to feel the brandy.

"There's a cot in the locker over there. I'll have someone set it up for you, and you can sleep in here for the time being. If anything comes in for you, we'll get you up."

"That's kind of you, sir." Admiral White was a good guy, Jack thought, and his wife was something very special. In ten minutes, Ryan was on the cot and asleep.

The Red October

Every two days the *starpom* collected the radiation badges. This was part of a semiformal inspection. After seeing to it that every crewman's shoes were spit-shined, every bunk was properly made, and every footlocker was arranged according to the book, the executive officer would take the two-day-old badges and hand the sailors new ones, usually along with some terse advice to square themselves away as New Soviet Men ought. Borodin had this procedure down to a science. Today, as always, the trip from one compartment to another took two hours. When he was finished, the bag on his left hip was full of old badges, and the one on his right depleted of new ones. He took the badges to the ship's medical officer.

"Comrade Petrov, I have a gift for you." Borodin set the leather bag on the physician's desk.

"Good." The doctor smiled up at the executive officer. "With all the healthy young men I have little to do but read my journals."

Borodin left Petrov to his task. First the doctor set the badges out in order. Each bore a three-digit number. The first digit identified the badge series, so that if any radiation were detected there would be a time reference. The second digit showed where the sailor worked, the third where he slept. This system was easier to work with than the old one, which had used individual numbers for each man.

The developing process was cookbook-simple. Petrov could do it without a thought. First he switched off the white overhead light and replaced it with a red one. Then he locked his office door. Next he took the development rack from its holder on the bulkhead, broke open the plastic holders, and transferred the film strips to spring clips on the rack.

Petrov took the rack into the adjacent laboratory and hung it on the handle of the single filing cabinet. He filled three large square basins with chemicals. Though a qualified physician, he had forgotten most of his inorganic chemistry and didn't remember exactly what the developing chemicals were. Basin number one was filled from bottle number one. Basin two was filled from bottle two, and basin three, he remembered, was filled with water. Petrov was in no hurry. The midday meal was not for two more hours, and his duties were truly boring. The last two days he had been reading his medical texts on tropical diseases. The doctor was looking forward to visiting Cuba as much as anyone aboard. With luck a crewman would come down with some obscure malady, and he'd have something interesting to work on for once.

Petrov set the lab timer for seventy-five seconds and submerged the film strips in the first basin as he pressed the start button. He watched the timer under the red light, wondering if the Cubans still made rum. He had been there, too, years before, and acquired a taste for the exotic liquor. Like any good Soviet citizen, he loved his vodka but had the occasional hankering for something different.

The timer went off and he lifted the rack, shaking it carefully over the tank. No sense getting the chemical—silver nitrate? something like that—on his uniform. The rack went into the second tank, and he set the timer again. Pity the orders had been so damned secret—he could have brought his tropical uniform. He'd sweat like a pig in the Cuban heat. Of course, none of those savages ever bothered to wash. Maybe they had learned something in the past fifteen years? He'd see.

The timer *ding*ed again, and Petrov lifted the rack a second time, shaking it and setting it in the water-filled basin. Another boring job completed. Why couldn't a sailor fall down a ladder and break something? He wanted to use his East German X-ray machine on a live patient. He didn't trust the Germans, Marxists or not, but they did make good medical equipment, including his X-ray, autoclave, and most of his pharmaceuticals. Time. Petrov lifted the rack and held it up against the X-ray reading plate, which he switched on.

"Nichevo!" Petrov breathed. He had to think. His badge was fogged. Its number was 3-4-8: third badge series, frame fifty-four (the medical office, galley section), aft (officers') accommodations.

Though only two centimeters across, the badges were made with variable sensitivity. Ten vertically segmented columns were used to quantify the exposure level. Petrov saw that his was fogged all the way to segment four. The engine room crewmen's were fogged to segment five, and the torpedomen, who spent all their time forward, showed contamination only in segment one.

"Son of a bitch." He knew the sensitivity levels by heart. He took the manual down to check them anyway. Fortunately, the segments were logarithmic. His exposure was twelve rads. Fifteen to twenty-five for the engineers. Twelve to twenty-five rads in two days, not enough to be dangerous. Not really life threatening, but . . . Petrov went back into his office, careful to leave the films in the labs. He picked up the phone.

"Captain Ramius? Petrov here. Could you come aft to my office, please?"

"On the way, Comrade Doctor."

Ramius took his time. He knew what the call was about. The day before they sailed, while Petrov had been ashore procuring drugs for his cupboard, Borodin had contaminated the badges with the X-ray machine.

"Yes, Petrov?" Ramius closed the door behind him.

"Comrade Captain, we have a radiation leak."

"Nonsense. Our instruments would have detected it at once."

Petrov got the films from the lab and handed them to the captain. "Look here."

Ramius held them up to the light, scanning the film strips

top to bottom. He frowned. "Who knows of this?"

"You and I, Comrade Captain."

"You will tell no one—no one." Ramius paused. "Any chance that the films were—that they have something wrong, that you made an error in the developing process?"

Petrov shook his head emphatically. "No, Comrade Captain. Only you, Comrade Borodin, and I have access to these. As you know, I tested random samples from each batch three days before we sailed." Petrov wouldn't admit that, like everyone, he had taken the samples from the top of the box they were stored in. They weren't really random.

"The maximum exposure I see here is . . . ten to twenty?" Ramius understated it. "Whose numbers?"

"Bulganin and Surzpoi. The torpedomen forward are all under three rads."

"Very well. What we have here, Comrade Doctor, is a possible minor—minor, Petrov—leak in the reactor spaces. At worst a gas leak of some sort. This has happened before, and no one has ever died from it. The leak will be found and fixed. We will keep this little secret. There is no reason to get the men excited over nothing."

Petrov nodded agreement, knowing that men had died in 1970 in an accident on the submarine *Voroshilov,* more in the icebreaker *Lenin.* Both accidents were a long time ago, though, and he was sure Ramius could handle things. Wasn't he?

The Pentagon

The E ring was the outermost and largest of the Pentagon's rings, and since its outside windows offered something other than a view of sunless courtyards, this was where the most senior defense officials had their offices. One of these was the office of the director of operations for the Joint Chiefs of Staff, the J-3. He wasn't there. He was down in a subbasement room known colloquially as the Tank because its metal walls were dotted with electronic noisemakers to foil other electronic devices.

He had been there for twenty-four hours, though one would not have known this from his appearance. His green trousers were still creased, his khaki shirt still showed the folds made by the laundry, its collar starched plywood-stiff, and his tie was held neatly in place by a gold marine corps tiepin. Lieutenant General Edwin Harris was neither a diplomat nor a service academy graduate, but he was playing peacemaker. An odd position for a marine.

"God damn it!" It was the voice of Admiral Blackburn, CINCLANT. Also present was his own operations officer, Rear Admiral Pete Stanford. "Is this any way to run an operation?"

The Joint Chiefs were all there, and none of them thought so.

"Look, Blackie, I told you where the orders come from." General Hilton, chairman of the Joint Chiefs of Staff, sounded tired.

"I understand that, General, but this is largely a submarine operation, right? I gotta get Vince Gallery in on this, and you should have Sam Dodge working up at this end. Dan and I are both fighter jocks, Pete's an ASW expert. We need a sub driver in on this."

"Gentlemen," Harris said calmly, "for the moment the plan we have to take to the president need only deal with the Soviet threat. Let's hold this story about the defecting boomer in abeyance for the moment, shall we?"

"I agree," Stanford nodded. "We have enough to worry about right here."

The attention of the eight flag officers turned to the map table. Fifty-eight Soviet submarines and twenty-eight surface warships, plus a gaggle of oilers and replenishment ships, were unmistakably heading for the American coast. To face this, the U.S. Navy had one available carrier. The *Invincible* did not rate as such. The threat was considerable. Among them the Soviet vessels carried over three hundred surface-to-surface cruise missiles. Though principally designed as antiship weapons, the third of them believed to carry nuclear warheads were sufficient to devastate the cities of the East Coast. From a position off New Jersey, these missiles could range from Norfolk to Boston.

"Josh Painter proposes that we keep *Kennedy* inshore," Admiral Blackburn said. "He wants to run the ASW operation from his carrier, transferring his light attack squadrons to shore and replacing them with S-3s. He wants *Invincible* out on their seaward flank."

"I don't like it," General Harris said. Neither did Pete Stanford, and they had agreed earlier that the J-3 would launch the counterplan. "Gentlemen, if we're only going to have one deck to use, we damned well ought to have a carrier and not an oversized ASW platform."

"We're listening, Eddie," Hilton said.

"Let's move *Kennedy* out here." He moved the counter to a position west of the Azores. "Josh keeps his attack squadrons. We move *Invincible* inshore to handle the ASW work. It's what the Brits designed her for, right? They're supposed to be good at it. *Kennedy* is an offensive weapon, her mission is to threaten them. Okay, if we deploy like this, she is the threat. From over here she can range against their surface force from outside their surface-to-surface missile perimeter—"

' "Better yet," Stanford interjected, pointing to some vessels on the map, "threaten this service force here. If they lose these oilers, they ain't going home. To meet that threat they'll have to redeploy themselves. For starters, they'll have to move *Kiev* offshore to give themselves some kind of air defense against *Kennedy.* We can use the spare S-3s from shore bases. They can still patrol the same areas." He traced a line about five hundred miles off the coast.

"Leaves *Invincible* kind of naked, though," the CNO, Admiral Foster, noted.

"Josh was asking about some E-3 coverage for the Brits." Blackburn looked at the air force chief of staff, General Claire Barnes.

"You want help, you get help," Barnes said. "We'll have a Sentry operating over *Invincible* at dawn tomorrow, and if you move her inshore we can maintain that round the clock. I'll throw in a wing of F-16s if you want."

"What do you want in return, Max?" Foster asked. Nobody called him Claire.

"The way I see this, you have *Saratoga*'s air wing sitting around doing nothing. Okay, by Saturday I'll have five hundred tactical fighters deployed from Dover to Loring. My boys don't know much about antiship stuff. They'll have to learn in a hurry. I want you to send your kids to work with mine, and I also want your Tomcats. I like the fighter-missile combination. Let one squadron work out of Iceland, the other out of New England to track the Bears Ivan's starting to send our way. I'll sweeten that. If you want, we'll send some tankers to Lajes to help keep *Kennedy*'s birds flying."

"Blackie?" Foster asked.

"Deal," Blackburn nodded. "The only thing that bothers me is that *Invincible* doesn't have all that much ASW capacity."

"So we get more," Stanford said. "Admiral, what say we take *Tarawa* out of Little Creek, team her with *New Jersey*'s group, with a dozen ASW choppers aboard and seven or eight Harriers?"

"I like it," Harris said quickly. "Then we have two baby carriers with a noteworthy striking force right in front of their groups, *Kennedy* playing stalking tiger to their east, and a few hundred tactical fighters to the west. They have to come into a three-way box. This actually gives us more ASW patrolling capacity than we'd have otherwise."

"Can *Kennedy* handle her mission alone out there?" Hilton asked.

"Depend on it," Blackburn replied. "We can kill any one, maybe any two of these four groups in an hour. The ones nearest shore will be your job, Max."

"How long did you two characters rehearse this?" General Maxwell, commandant of the marine corps, asked the operations officer. Everyone chuckled.

The Red October

Chief Engineer Melekhin cleared the reactor compartment before beginning the check for the leak. Ramius and Petrov were there also, plus the engineering duty officers and one of the young lieutenants, Svyadov. Three of the officers carried Geiger counters.

The reactor room was quite large. It had to be to accommodate the massive, barrel-shaped steel vessel. The object was warm to the touch despite being inactive. Automatic radiation detectors were in every corner of the room, each surrounded by a red circle. More were hanging on the fore and aft bulkheads. Of all the compartments on the submarine, this was the cleanest. The deck and bulkheads were spotless white-painted steel. The reason was obvious: the smallest leak of reactor coolant had to be instantly visible even if all the detectors failed.

Svyadov climbed an aluminum ladder affixed to the side of the reactor vessel to run the detachable probe from his counter over every welded pipe joint. The speaker-annunciator on the hand-held box was turned to maximum so that everyone in the compartment could hear it, and Svyadov had an earpiece plugged in for even greater sensitivity. A youngster of twenty-one, he was nervous. Only a fool would feel entirely safe looking for a radiation leak. There is a joke in the Soviet Navy: How do you tell a sailor from the Northern Fleet? He glows in the dark. It had been a good laugh on the beach, but not now. He knew that he was conducting the search because he was the youngest, least experienced, and most expendable officer. It was an effort to keep his knees from wobbling as he strained to reach all over and around the reactor piping.

The counter was not entirely silent, and Svyadov's stomach cringed at each click generated by the passage of a random particle through the tube of ionized gas. Every few seconds his eyes flickered to the dial that measured intensity. It was well inside the safe range, hardly registering at all. The reactor vessel was a quadruple-layer design, each layer several centimeters of tough stainless steel. The three inner spaces were filled with a barium-water mixture, then a barrier of lead, then polyethylene, all designed to prevent the escape of neutrons and gamma particles. The combination of steel, barium, lead, and plastic successfully contained the dangerous elements of the reaction, allowing only a few degrees of heat to escape, and the dial showed, much to his relief, that the radiation level was less than that on the beach at Sochi. The highest reading was made next to a light bulb. This made the lieutenant smile.

"All readings in normal range, comrades," Svyadov reported.

"Start over," Melekhin ordered, "from the beginning."

Twenty minutes later Svyadov, now sweating from the warm air that gathered at the top of the compartment, made an identical report. He came down awkwardly, his arms and legs tired.

"Have a cigarette," Ramius suggested. "You did well, Svyadov."

"Thank you, Comrade Captain. It's warm up there from the lights and the coolant pipes." The lieutenant handed the counter to Melekhin. The lower dial showed a cumulative count, well within the safe range.

"Probably some contaminated badges," the chief engineer commented sourly. "It would not be the first time. Some joker in the factory or at the yard supply office—something for our friends in the GRU to check into. 'Wreckers!' A joke like this ought to earn somebody a bullet."

"Perhaps," Ramius chuckled. "Remember the incident on *Lenin?*" He referred to the nuclear-powered icebreaker that had spent two years tied to the dock, unusable because of a reactor mishap. "A ship's cook had some badly crusted pans, and a madman of an engineer suggested that he use live steam to get them cleaned. So the idiot walked down to the steam generator and opened an inspection valve, with his pots under it!"

Melekhin rolled his eyes. "I remember it! I was a staff engineering officer then. The captain had asked for a Kazakh cook—"

"He liked horsemeat with his kasha," Ramius said.

"—and the fool didn't know the first thing about a ship. Killed himself and three other men, contaminated the whole fucking compartment for twenty months. The captain only got out of the gulag last year."

"I bet the cook got his pans cleaned, though," Ramius observed.

"Indeed, Marko Aleksandrovich—they may even be safe to use in another fifty years." Melekhin laughed raucously.

That was a hell of a thing to say in front of a young officer, Petrov thought. There was nothing, nothing at all funny about a reactor leak. But Melekhin was known for his heavy sense of humor, and the doctor imagined that twenty years of working on reactors allowed him and the captain to view the potential dangers phlegmatically. Then, there was the implicit lesson in the story: never let someone who does not belong into the reactor spaces.

"Very well," Melekhin said, "now we check the pipes in the generator room. Come, Svyadov, we still need your young legs."

The next compartment aft contained the heat exchanger/ steam generator, turboalternators, and auxiliary equipment. The main turbines were in the next compartment, now inactive while the electrically driven caterpillar was operating. In any case, the steam that turned them was supposed to be clean. The only radioactivity was in the inside loop. The reactor coolant, which carried short-lived but dangerous radioactivity, never flashed to steam. This was in the outside loop and boiled from uncontaminated water. The two water supplies met but never mixed inside the heat exchanger, the most likely site for a coolant leak because of its more numerous fittings and valves.

The more complex piping required a full fifty minutes to check. These pipes were not as well insulated as those forward. Svyadov nearly burned himself twice, and his face was bathed in perspiration by the time he finished his first sweep.

"Readings all safe again, comrades."

"Good," Melekhin said. "Come down and rest a moment before you check it again."

Svyadov almost thanked his chief for that, but this would not have done at all. As a young, dedicated officer and member of the Komsomol, no exertion was too great. He came down carefully, and Melekhin handed him another cigarette. The chief engineer was a gray-haired perfectionist who took decent care of his men.

"Why, thank you, Comrade," Svyadov said.

Petrov got a folding chair. "Sit, Comrade Lieutenant, rest your legs."

The lieutenant sat down at once, stretching his legs to work out the knots. The officers at VVMUPP had told him how lucky he was to draw this assignment. Ramius and Melekhin were the two best teachers in the fleet, men whose crews appreciated their kindness along with their competence.

"They really should insulate those pipes," Ramius said. Melekhin shook his head.

"Then they'd be too hard to inspect." He handed the counter to his captain.

"Entirely safe," the captain read off the cumulative dial. "You get more exposure tending a garden."

"Indeed," Melekhin said. "Coal miners get more exposure than we do, from the release of radon gas in the mines. Bad badges, that's what it has to be. Why not take out a whole batch and check it?"

"I could, Comrade," Petrov answered. "But then, due to the extended nature of our cruise, we'd have to run for several days without any. Contrary to regulations. I'm afraid."

"You are correct. In any case the badges are only a backup to our instruments." Ramius gestured to the red-circled detectors all over the compartment.

"Do you really want to recheck the piping?" Melekhin asked.

"I think we should," Ramius said.

Svyadov swore to himself, looking down at the deck.

"There is no extravagance in the pursuit of safety," Petrov quoted doctrine. "Sorry, Lieutenant." The doctor was not a bit sorry. He had been genuinely worried, and was now feeling a lot better.

An hour later the second check had been completed. Petrov took Svyadov forward for salt tablets and tea to rehydrate himself. The senior officers left, and Melekhin ordered the reactor plant restarted.

The enlisted men filed back to their duty stations, looking at one another. Their officers had just checked the "hot" compartments with radiation instruments. The medical corpsman had looked pale a while earlier and refused to say anything. More than one engine attendant fingered his radiation badge and checked his wristwatch to see how long it would be before he went off duty.

THE EIGHTH DAY

FRIDAY, 10 DECEMBER

HMS Invincible

Ryan awoke in the dark. The curtains were drawn on the cabin's two small portholes. He shook his head a few times to clear it and began to assess what was going on around him. The *Invincible* was moving on the seas, but not as much as before. He got up to look out of a porthole and saw the last red glow of sunset aft under scudding clouds. He checked his watch and did some clumsy mental arithmetic, concluding that it was six in the evening, local time. That translated to about six hours of sleep. He felt pretty good, considering. A minor headache from the brandy—so much for the theory that good stuff doesn't give you a hangover—and his muscles were stiff. He did a few sit-ups to work out the knots.

There was a small bathroom—head, he corrected himself—adjoining the cabin. Ryan splashed some water on his face and washed his mouth out, not wanting to look in the mirror. He decided he had to. Counterfeit or not, he was wearing his country's uniform and he had to look presentable. It took a minute to get his hair in place and the uniform arranged properly. The CIA had done a nice job of tailoring, given such short notice. Finished, he went out the door towards the flag bridge.

"Feeling better, Jack?" Admiral White pointed him to a tray full of cups. It was only tea, but it was a start.

"Thank you, Admiral. Those few hours really helped. I guess I'm in time for dinner."

"Breakfast," White corrected him with a laugh.

"What—uh, pardon me, Admiral?" Ryan shook his head again. He was still a little groggy.

"That's a sun*rise,* Commander. Change in orders, we're heading west again. *Kennedy*'s moving east at high speed, and we're to take station inshore."

"Who said, sir?"

"CINCLANT. I gather Joshua was not at all pleased. You are to remain with us for the moment, and under the circumstances it seemed the reasonable thing to let you sleep. You did appear to need it."

Must have been eighteen hours, Ryan thought. No wonder he felt stiff.

"You do look much better," Admiral White noted from his leather swivel chair. He got up, took Ryan's arm, and guided him aft. "Now for breakfast. I've been waiting for you. Captain Hunter will brief you on your revised orders. Weather's clearing up for a few days, they tell me. Escort assignments are being reshuffled. We're to operate in conjunction with your *New Jersey* group. Our antisubmarine operations begin in earnest in another twelve hours. It's a good thing you got that extra sleep, lad. You'll bloody need it."

Ryan ran his hand over his face. "Can I shave, sir?"

"We still permit beards. Let it wait until after breakfast."

Flag quarters on HMS *Invincible* were not quite to the standard of those on the *Kennedy*—but close. White had a private dining area. A steward in a white livery served them expertly, setting a third place for Hunter, who appeared within a few minutes. When they started talking, the steward was excused.

"We rendezvous with a pair of young *Knox*-class frigates in two hours. We already have them on radar. Two more 1052s, plus an oiler and two *Perry*s will join us in another thirty-six hours. They were on their way home from the Med. With our own escorts, a total of nine warships. A noteworthy collection, I think. We'll be working five hundred miles offshore, with the *New Jersey–Tarawa* force two hundred miles to our west."

"*Tarawa?* What do we need a regiment of marines for?" Ryan asked.

Hunter explained briefly. "Not a bad idea, that. The funny thing is, with *Kennedy* racing for the Azores, that rather leaves us guarding the American coast." Hunter grinned. "This may be the first time the Royal Navy has ever done that—certainly since it belonged to us."

"What are we up against?"

"The first of the *Alfa*s will be on your coast tonight, four of them ahead of all the others. The Soviet surface force passed Iceland last night. It's divided into three groups. One is built around their carrier *Kiev*, two cruisers and four destroyers; the second, probably the force flag, is built around *Kirov*, with three additional cruisers and six destroyers; and the third is centered on *Moskva*, three more cruisers and seven destroyers. I gather that the Soviets will want to use the *Kiev* and *Moskva* groups inshore, with *Kirov* guarding them out to sea—but *Kennedy*'s relocation will make them rethink that. Regardless, the total force carries a considerable number of surface-to-surface missiles, and potentially, we are very exposed. To help out with that, your air force has an E-3 Sentry detailed to arrive here in an hour to exercise with our Harriers, and when we get farther west, we'll have additional land-based air support. On the whole our position is hardly an enviable one, but Ivan's is rather less so. So far as the question of finding *Red October* is concerned?" Hunter shrugged. "How we conduct our search will depend on how Ivan deploys. At the moment we're conducting some tracking drills. The lead *Alfa* is eighty miles northwest of us, steaming at forty-plus knots, and we have a helicopter in pursuit—which is roughly what it amounts to," the fleet operations officer concluded. "Will you join us below?"

"Admiral?" Ryan wanted to see *Invincible*'s combat information center.

"Certainly."

Thirty minutes later Ryan was in a darkened, quiet room whose walls were a solid bank of electronic instruments and glass plotting panels. The Atlantic Ocean was full of Russian submarines.

The White House

The Soviet ambassador entered the Oval Office a minute early, at 10:59 A.M. He was a short, overweight man with a broad Slavic face and eyes that would have done a professional gambler proud. They revealed nothing. He was a career diplomat, having served in a number of posts throughout the Western world, and a thirty-year member of the Communist party's Foreign Department.

"Good morning, Mr. President, Dr. Pelt," Alexei Arbatov nodded politely to both men. The president, he noted at once, was seated behind his desk. Every other time he'd been here the president had come around the desk to shake hands, then sat down beside him.

"Help yourself to some coffee, Mr. Ambassador," Pelt offered. The special assistant to the president for national security affairs was well known to Arbatov. Jeffrey Pelt was an academic from the Georgetown University's Center for Strategic and International Studies—an enemy, but a well-mannered, *kulturny* enemy. Arbatov had a fondness for the niceties of formal behavior. Today, Pelt was standing at his boss's side, unwilling to come too close to the Russian bear. Arbatov did not get himself any coffee.

"Mr. Ambassador," Pelt began, "we have noted a troubling increase in Soviet naval activity in the North Atlantic."

"Oh?" Arbatov's eyebrows shot up in a display of surprise that fooled no one, and he knew it. "I have no knowledge of this. As you know, I have never been a sailor."

"Shall we dispense with the bullshit, Mr. Ambassador?" the president said. Arbatov did not permit himself to be surprised by the vulgarity. It made the American president seem very Russian, and like Soviet officials he seemed to need a professional like Pelt around to smooth the edges. "You certainly have nearly a hundred naval vessels operating in the North Atlantic or heading in that direction. Chairman Narmonov and my predecessor agreed years ago that no such operation would take place without prior notification. The purpose of this agreement, as you know, was to prevent acts that might appear to be unduly provocative to one side or the other. This agreement has been kept—until now.

"Now, my military advisers tell me that what is going on looks very much like a war exercise, indeed, could be the precursor to a war. How are we to tell the difference? Your ships are now passing east of Iceland, and will soon be in a position from which they can threaten our trade routes to Europe. This situation is at the least unsettling, and at the most a grave and wholly unwarranted provocation. The scope of this action has not yet been made public. That will change, and when it does, Alex, the American people will demand action on my part." The president paused, expecting a response but getting only a nod.

Pelt went on for him. "Mr. Ambassador, your country has seen fit to cast aside an agreement which for years has been a model of East-West cooperation. How can you expect us to regard this as anything other than a provocation?"

"Mr. President, Dr. Pelt, truly I have no knowledge of this." Arbatov lied with the utmost sincerity. "I will contact Moscow at once to ascertain the facts. Is there any message you wish me to pass along?"

"Yes. As you and your superiors in Moscow will understand," the president said, "we will deploy our ships and aircraft to observe yours. Prudence requires this. We have no wish to interfere with whatever legitimate operations your forces may be engaged in. It is not our intention to make a provocation of our own, but under the terms of our agreement we have the right to know what is going on, Mr. Ambassador. Until we do, we are unable to issue the proper orders to our men. It would be well for your government to consider that having so many of your ships and our ships, your aircraft and our aircraft in close proximity is an inherently dangerous situation. Accidents can happen. An action by one side or the other which at another time would seem harmless might seem to be something else entirely. Wars have begun in this way, Mr. Ambassador." The president leaned back to let that thought hang in the air for a moment. When he went on, he spoke more gently. "Of course, I regard this possibility as remote, but is it not irresponsible to take such chances?"

"Mr. President, you make your point well, as always, but as you know, the sea is free for the passage of all, and—"

"Mr. Ambassador," Pelt interrupted, "consider a simple analogy. Your next-door neighbor begins to patrol his front yard with a loaded shotgun while your children are at play in your own front yard. In this country such action would be technically legal. Even so, would it not be a matter of concern?"

"So it would, Dr. Pelt, but the situation you describe is very different—"

Now the president interrupted. "Indeed it is. The situation at hand is far more dangerous. It is the breach of an agreement, and I find that especially disquieting. I had hoped that we were entering a new era of Soviet-American relations. We have settled our trade differences. We have just concluded a new grain agreement. You had a major part in that. We have been moving forward, Mr. Ambassador—is this at an end?" The president shook his head emphatically. "I hope not, but the choice is yours. The relationship between our countries can only be based on trust.

"Mr. Ambassador, I trust that I have not alarmed you. As you know, it is my habit to speak plainly. I personally dislike the greasy dissimulation of diplomacy. At times like this, we must communicate quickly and clearly. We have a dangerous situation before us, and we must work together, rapidly, to resolve it. My military commanders are greatly concerned, and I need to know—today—what your naval forces are up to. I expect a reply by seven this evening. Failing that I will be on the direct line to Moscow to demand one."

Arbatov stood. "Mr. President, I will transmit your message within the hour. Please keep in mind, however, the time differential between Washington and Moscow—"

"I know that a weekend has just begun, and that the Soviet Union is a worker's paradise, but I expect that some of your country's managers may still be at work. In any case, I will detain you no further. Good day."

Pelt led Arbatov out, then came back and sat down.

"Maybe I was just a little tough on him," the president said.

"Yes, sir." Pelt thought that he had been too damned tough. He had little affection for the Russian but he too liked the niceties of diplomatic exchange. "I think we can say that you succeeded in getting your message across."

"He knows."

"He knows. But he doesn't know we know."

"We think," the president grimaced. "What a crazy goddamned game this is! And to think I had a nice, safe career going for me putting mafiosi in jail . . . Do you think he'll snap at the bait I offered?"

" 'Legitimate operations?' Did you see his hands twitch at that? He'll go after it like a marlin after a squid." Pelt walked over to pour himself half a cup of coffee. It pleased him that the china service was gold trimmed. "I wonder what they'll call it? Legitimate operations . . . probably a rescue mission. If they call it a fleet exercise they admit to violating the notification protocol. A rescue operation justifies the level of activity, the speed with which it was laid on, and the lack of publicity. Their press never reports this sort of thing. As a guess, I'd say they'll call it a rescue, say a submarine is missing, maybe even to the point of calling it a missile sub."

"No, they won't go that far. We also have that agreement about keeping our missile subs five hundred miles offshore. Arbatov probably has his instructions on what to tell us already, but he'll play for all the time he can. It's also vaguely possible that he's in the dark. We know how they compartmentalize information. You suppose we're reading too much into this talent for obfuscation?"

"I think not, sir. It is a principle of diplomacy," Pelt observed, "that one must know something of the truth in order to lie convincingly."

The president smiled. "Well, they've had enough time to play this game. I hope my belated reaction will not disappoint them."

"No, sir. Alex must have half expected you to kick him out the door."

"The thought's occurred to me more than once. His diplomatic charm has always been lost on me. That's the one thing about the Russians—they remind me so much of the mafia chieftains I used to prosecute. The same smattering of culture and good manners, and the same absence of morality." The president shook his head. He was talking like a hawk again. "Stay close, Jeff. I have George Farmer coming in here in a few minutes, but I want you around when our friend comes back."

Pelt walked back to his office pondering the president's remark. It was, he admitted to himself, crudely accurate. The most wounding insult to an educated Russian was to be called *nekulturny*, uncultured—the term didn't translate adequately—

yet the same men who sat in the gilt boxes at the Moscow State Opera weeping at the end of a performance of *Boris Gudunov* could immediately turn around and order the execution or imprisonment of a hundred men without blinking. A strange people, made more strange by their political philosophy. But the president had too many sharp edges, and Pelt wished he'd learn to soften them. A speech in front of the American Legion was one thing, a discussion with the ambassador of a foreign power was something else.

CIA Headquarters

"CARDINAL's in trouble, Judge." Ritter sat down.

"No surprise there." Moore removed his glasses and rubbed his eyes. Something Ryan had not seen was the cover note from the station chief in Moscow saying that to get his latest signal out, CARDINAL had bypassed half the courier chain that ran from the Kremlin to the U.S. embassy. The agent was getting bold in his old age. "What does the station chief say exactly?"

"CARDINAL's supposed to be in the hospital with pneumonia. Maybe it's true, but..."

"He's getting old, and it is winter over there, but who believes in coincidences?" Moore looked down at his desk. "What do you suppose they'd do if they've turned him?"

"He'd die quietly. Depends on who turned him. If it was the KGB, they might want to make something out of it, especially since our friend Andropov took a lot of their prestige with him when he left. But I don't think so. Given who his sponsor is, it would raise too much of a ruckus. Same thing if the GRU turns him. No, they'd grill him for a few weeks, then quietly do away with him. A public trial would be too counterproductive."

Judge Moore frowned. They sounded like doctors discussing a terminally ill patient. He didn't even know what CARDINAL looked like. There was a photograph somewhere in the file, but he had never seen it. It was easier that way. As an appellate court judge he had never had to look a defendant in the eye; he'd just reviewed the law in a detached way. He tried to keep his stewardship of the CIA the same way. Moore knew that this might be perceived as cowardly, and was very different from what people expect of a DCI—but even spies got old, and old men developed consciences and doubts that rarely troubled the young. It was time to leave the "Company." Nearly three years, it was enough. He'd accomplished what he was supposed to do.

"Tell the station chief to lay off. No inquiries of any kind directed at CARDINAL. If he's really sick, we'll be hearing from him again. If not, we'll know that soon enough, too."

"Right."

Ritter had succeeded in confirming CARDINAL's reports. One agent had reported that the fleet was sailing with additional political officers, another that the surface force was commanded by an academic sailor and crony of Gorshkov, who had flown to Severomorsk and boarded the *Kirov* minutes before the fleet had sailed. The naval architect who was believed to have designed the *Red October* was supposed to have gone with him. A British agent had reported that detonators for the various weapons carried by the surface ships had been hastily taken aboard from their usual storage depots ashore. Finally, there was an unconfirmed report that Admiral Korov, commander of the Northern Fleet, was not at his command post; his whereabouts were unknown. Together the information was enough to confirm the WILLOW report, and more was still coming in.

The U.S. Naval Academy

"Skip?"

"Oh, howdy, Admiral. Will you join me?" Tyler waved to a vacant chair across the table.

"I got a message from the Pentagon for you." The superintendent of the Naval Academy, a former submarine officer, sat down. "You have an appointment tonight at 1930 hours. That's all they said."

"Great!" Tyler was just finishing his lunch. He'd been working on the simulation program nearly around the clock since Monday. The appointment meant that he would have access to the air force's Cray-2 tonight. His program was just about ready.

"What's this all about anyway?"

"Sorry, sir, I can't say. You know how it is."

The White House

The Soviet ambassador was back at four in the afternoon. To avoid press notice he had been taken into the Treasury building across the street from the White House and brought through a connecting tunnel which few knew existed. The president hoped that he had found this unsettling. Pelt hustled in to be there when Arbatov arrived.

"Mr. President," Arbatov reported, standing at attention. The president had not known that he had any military experience. "I am instructed to convey to you the regrets of my government that there has not been time to inform you of this. One of our nuclear submarines is missing and presumed lost. We are conducting an emergency rescue operation."

The president nodded soberly, motioning the ambassador to a chair. Pelt sat next to him.

"This is somewhat embarrassing, Mr. President. You see, in our navy as in yours, duty on a nuclear submarine is a posting of the greatest importance, and consequently those selected for it are among our best educated and trusted men. In this particular case several members of the crew—the officers, that is—are sons of high Party officials. One is even the son of a Central Committee member—I cannot say which, of course. The Soviet Navy's great effort to find her sons is understandable, though I admit a bit undisciplined." Arbatov feigned embarrassment beautifully, speaking as though he were confiding a great family secret. "Therefore, this has developed into what your people call an 'all hands' operation. As you undoubtedly know, it was undertaken virtually overnight."

"I see," the president said sympathetically. "That makes me feel a little better, Alex. Jeff, I think it's late enough in the day. How about you fix us all a drink. Bourbon, Alex?"

"Yes, thank you, sir."

Pelt walked over to a rosewood cabinet against the wall. The ornate antique contained a small bar, complete with an ice bucket which was stocked every afternoon. The president often liked to have a drink or two before dinner, something else that reminded Arbatov of his countrymen. Dr. Pelt had had ample experience playing presidential bartender. In a few minutes he came back with three glasses in his hands.

"To tell you the truth, we rather suspected this was a rescue operation," Pelt said.

"I don't know how we get our young men to do this sort of work." The president sipped at his drink. Arbatov worked hard on his. He had said frequently at local cocktail parties that he preferred American bourbon to his native vodka. Maybe it was true. "We've lost a pair of nuclear boats, I believe. How many does this make for you, three, four?"

"I don't know, Mr. President. I expect your information on this is better than my own." The president noted that he had just told the truth for the first time today. "Certainly I can agree with you that such duty is both dangerous and demanding."

"How many men aboard, Alex?" the president asked.

"I have no idea. A hundred more or less, I suppose. I've never been aboard a naval vessel."

"Mostly kids, probably, just like our crews. It is indeed a sad commentary on both our countries that our mutual suspicions must condemn so many of our best young men to such hazards, when we know that some won't be coming back. But—how can it be otherwise?" The president paused, turning to look out the windows. The snow was melting on the South Lawn. It was time for his next line.

"Perhaps we can help," the president offered speculatively. "Yes, perhaps we can use this tragedy as an opportunity to reduce those suspicions by some small amount. Perhaps we can make something good come from this to demonstrate that our relations really have improved."

Pelt turned away, fumbling for his pipe. In their many years of friendship he could never understand how the president got away with so much. Pelt had met him at Washington University, when he was majoring in political science, the president in prelaw. Back then the chief executive had been president of the dramatics society. Certainly amateur theatrics had helped his legal career. It was said that at least one Mafia don had been sent up the river by sheer rhetoric. The president referred to it as his sincere act.

"Mr. Ambassador, I offer you the assistance and the resources of the United States in the search for your missing countrymen."

"That is most kind of you, Mr. President, but—"

The president held his hand up. "No buts, Alex. If we cannot cooperate in something like this, how can we hope to cooperate in more serious matters? If memory serves, last year when one of our navy patrol aircraft crashed off the Aleutians, one of your fishing vessels"—it had been an intelligence trawler—"picked up the crew, saved their lives. Alex, we owe you a debt for that, a debt of honor, and the United States will not be said to be ungrateful." He paused for effect. "They're probably all dead, you know. I don't suppose there's more chance of surviving a sub accident than of surviving a plane crash. But at least the crew's families will know. Jeff, don't we have some specialized submarine rescue equipment?"

"With all the money we give the navy? We damned well ought to. I'll call Foster about it."

"Good," the president said. "Alex, it is too much to expect that your mutual suspicions will be allayed by something so small as this. Your history and ours conspire against us. But let's make a small beginning with this. If we can shake hands in space or over a conference table in Vienna, maybe we can do it here also. I will give the necessary instructions to my commanders as soon as we're finished here."

"Thank you, Mr. President." Arbatov concealed his uneasiness.

"And please convey my respects to Chairman Narmonov and my sympathy for the families of your missing men. I appreciate his effort, and yours, in getting this information to us."

"Yes. Mr. President." Arbatov rose. He left after shaking hands. What were the Americans really up to? He'd warned Moscow: call it a rescue mission and they'd demand to help. It was their stupid Christmas season, and Americans were addicted to happy endings. It was madness not to call it something else—to hell with the protocol.

At the same time he was forced to admire the American president. A strange man, very open, yet full of guile. A friendly man most of the time, yet always ready to seize the advantage. He remembered stories his grandmother had told, about how the gypsies switched babies. The American president was very Russian.

"Well," the president said after the doors closed, "now we can keep a nice close eye on them, and they can't complain. They're lying and we know it—but they don't know we know.

And we're lying, and they certainly suspect it, but not why we're lying. Gawd! and I told him this morning that not knowing was dangerous! Jeff, I've been thinking about this. I do not like the fact that so much of their navy is operating off our coast. Ryan was right, the Atlantic is our ocean. I want the air force and the navy to cover them like a goddamned blanket! That's our ocean, and I damned well want them to know it." The president finished off his drink. "On the question of the sub, I want our people to have a good look at it, and whoever of the crew wants to defect, we take care of. Quietly, of course."

"Of course. As a practical matter, having the officers is as great a coup as having the submarine."

"But the navy still want to keep it."

"I just don't see how we can do that, not without eliminating the crewmen, and we can't do that."

"Agreed." The president buzzed his secretary. "Get me General Hilton."

The Pentagon

The air force's computer center was in a subbasement of the Pentagon. The room temperature was well below seventy degrees. It was enough to make Tyler's leg ache where it met the metal-plastic prosthesis. He was used to that.

Tyler was sitting at a control console. He had just finished a trial run of his program, named MORAY after the vicious eel that inhabited oceanic reefs. Skip Tyler was proud of his programming ability. He'd taken the old dinosaur program from the files of the Taylor Lab, adapted it to the common Defense Department computer language, ADA—named for Lady Ada Lovelace, daughter of Lord Byron—and then tightened it up. For most people this would have been a month's work. He'd done it in four days, working almost around the clock not only because the money was an attractive incentive but also because the project was a professional challenge. He ended the job quietly satisfied that he could still meet an impossible deadline with time to spare. It was eight in the evening. MORAY had just run through a one-variable-value test and not crashed. He was ready.

He'd never seen the Cray-2 before, except in photographs, and he was pleased to have a chance to use it. The -2 was five units of raw electrical power, each one roughly pentagonal in shape, about six feet high and four across. The largest unit was the main-frame processor bank; the other four were memory banks, arrayed around it in a cruciform configuration. Tyler typed in the command to load his variable sets. For each of the *Red October*'s main dimensions—length, beam, height—he input ten discrete numerical values. Then came six subtly different values for her hull form block and prismatic coefficients. There were five sets of tunnel dimensions. This aggregated to over thirty thousand possible permutations. Next he keyed in eighteen power variables to cover the range of possible engine systems. The Cray-2 absorbed this information and placed each number in its proper slot. It was ready to run.

"Okay," he announced to the system operator, an air force master sergeant.

"Roge." The sergeant typed "XQT" into his terminal. The Cray-2 went to work.

Tyler walked over to the sergeant's console.

"That's a right lengthy program you've input, sir." The sergeant laid a ten-dollar bill on the top of the console. "Betcha my baby can run it in ten minutes."

"Not a chance." Tyler laid his own bill next to the sergeant's. "Fifteen minutes, easy."

"Split the difference?"

"Alright. Where's the head around here?"

"Out the door, sir, turn right, go down the hall and it's on the left."

Tyler moved towards the door. It annoyed him that he could not walk gracefully, but after four years the inconvenience was a minor one. He was alive—that's what counted. The accident had occurred on a cold, clear night in Groton, Connecticut, only a block from the shipyard's main gate. On Friday at three in the morning he was driving home after a twenty-hour day getting his new command ready for sea. The civilian yard worker had had a long day also, stopping off at a favorite watering hole for a few too many, as the police established afterwards. He got into his car, started it, and ran a red light, ramming Tyler's Pontiac broadside at fifty miles per hour. For him the accident was fatal. Skip was luckier. It was at an intersection, and he had the green light; when he saw the front end of the Ford not a foot from his left-side door, it was far too late. He did not remember going through a pawnshop window, and the next week, when he hovered near death at the Yale–New Haven hospital, was a complete blank. His most vivid memory was of waking up, eight days later he was to learn, to see his wife, Jean, holding his hand. His marriage up to that point had been a troubled one, not an uncommon problem for nuclear submarine officers. His first sight of her was not a complimentary one—her eyes were bloodshot, her hair was tousled—but she had never looked quite so good. He had never appreciated just how important she was. A lot more important than half a leg.

"Skip? Skip Tyler!"

The former submariner turned awkwardly to see a naval officer running towards him.

"Johnnie Coleman! How the hell are you!"

It was Captain Coleman now, Tyler noted. They had served together twice, a year on the *Tecumseh*, another on the *Shark*. Coleman, a weapons expert, had commanded a pair of nuclear subs.

"How's the family, Skip?"

"Jean's fine. Five kids now, and another on the way."

"Damn!" they shook hands with enthusiasm. "You always were a randy bugger. I hear you're teaching at Annapolis."

"Yeah, and a little engineering stuff on the side."

"What are you doing here?"

"I'm running a program on the air force computer. Checking a new ship configuration for Sea Systems Command." It was an accurate enough cover story. "What do they have you doing?"

"OP-02's office. I'm chief of staff for Admiral Dodge."

"Indeed?" Tyler was impressed. Vice Admiral Sam Dodge was the current OP-02. The office of the deputy chief of naval operations for submarine warfare had administrative control of all aspects of submarine operations. "Keeping you busy?"

"You know it! The crap's really hit the fan."

"What do you mean?" Tyler hadn't seen the news or read a paper since Monday.

"You kidding?"

"I've been working on this computer program twenty hours a day since Monday, and I don't get ops dispatches anymore." Tyler frowned. He had heard something the other day at the Academy but not paid any attention to it. He was the sort who could focus his whole mind on a single problem.

Coleman looked up and down the corridor. It was late on a Friday evening, and they had it entirely to themselves. "Guess I can tell you. Our Russian friends have some sort of major exercise laid on. Their whole Northern Fleet's at sea, or damned near. They have subs all over the place."

"Doing what?"

"We're not sure. Looks like they might have a major search and rescue operation. The question is, after what? They have four *Alfa*s doing a max speed run for our coast right now, with a gaggle of *Victor*s and *Charlie*s charging in behind them. At first we were worried that they wanted to block the trade routes, but they blitzed right past those. They're definitely heading for our coast, and whatever they're up to, we're getting tons of information."

"What do they have moving?" Tyler asked.

"Fifty-eight nuclear subs, and thirty or so surface ships."

"Gawd! CINCLANT must be going ape!"

"You know it, Skip. The fleet's at sea, all of it. Every nuke we have is scrambling for a redeployment. Every P-3 Lockheed ever made is either over the Atlantic or heading that way." Coleman paused. "You're still cleared, right?"

"Sure, for the work I do for the Crystal City gang. I had a piece of the evaluation of the new *Kirov*."

"I thought that sounded like your work. You always were a pretty good engineer. You know, the old man still talks about that job you did for him on the old *Tecumseh*. Maybe I can get you in to see what's happening. Yeah, I'll ask him."

Tyler's first cruise after graduating from nuc school in Idaho had been with Dodge. He'd done a tricky repair job on some ancillary reactor equipment two weeks earlier than estimated with a little creative effort and some back-channel procurement of spare parts. This had earned him and Dodge a flowery letter of commendation.

"I bet the old man would love to see you. When will you be finished down here?"

"Maybe half an hour."

"You know where to find me?"

"Have they moved OP-02?"

"Same place. Call me when you're finished. My extension is 78730. Okay? I gotta get back."

"Right." Tyler watched his old friend disappear down the

corridor, then proceeded on his way to the men's room, wondering what the Russians were up to. Whatever it was, it was enough to keep a three-star admiral and his four-striped captain working on a Friday night in Christmas season.

"Eleven minutes, 53.18 seconds, sir," the sergeant reported, pocketing both bills.

The computer printout was over two hundred pages of data. The cover sheet plotted a rough-looking bell curve of speed solutions, and below it was the noise prediction curve. The case-by-case solutions were printed individually on the remaining sheets. The curves were predictably messy. The speed curve showed the majority of solutions in the ten- to twelve-knot range, the total range going from seven to eighteen knots. The noise curve was surprisingly low.

"Sergeant, that's one hell of a machine you have here."

"Believe it, sir. And reliable. We haven't had an electronic fault all month."

"Can I use a phone?"

"Sure, take your pick, sir."

"Okay, Sarge." Tyler picked up the nearest phone. "Oh, and dump the program."

"Okay." He typed in some instructions. "MORAY is . . . gone. Hope you kept a copy, sir."

Tyler nodded and dialed the phone.

"OP-02A, Captain Coleman."

"Johnnie, this is Skip."

"Great! Hey, the old man wants to see you. Come right up."

Tyler placed the printout in his briefcase and locked it. He thanked the sergeant one more time before hobbling out the door, giving the Cray-2 one last look. He'd have to get in here again.

He could not find an operating elevator and had to struggle up a gently sloped ramp. Five minutes later he found a marine guarding the corridor.

"You Commander Tyler, sir?" the guard asked. "Can I see some ID, please?"

Tyler showed the corporal his Pentagon pass, wondering how many one-legged former submarine officers there might be.

"Thank you, Commander. Please go down the corridor. You know the room, sir?"

"Sure. Thanks, Corporal."

Vice Admiral Dodge was sitting on the corner of a desk reading over some message flimsies. Dodge was a small, combative man who'd made his mark commanding three separate boats, then pushing the *Los Angeles*–class attack submarines through their lengthy development program. Now he was "Grand Dolphin," the senior admiral who fought all the battles with Congress.

"Skip Tyler! You're looking good, laddy." Dodge gave Tyler's leg a furtive glance as he came over to take his hand. "I hear you're doing a great job at the Academy."

"It's all right, sir. They even let me scout the occasional ballgame."

"Hmph, shame they didn't let you scout Army."

Tyler hung his head theatrically. "I did scout Army, sir. They were just too tough this year. You heard about their middle linebacker, didn't you?"

"No, what about him?" Dodge asked.

"He picked armor as his duty assignment, and they gave him an early trip to Fort Knox—not to learn about tanks. To *be* a tank."

"Ha!" Dodge laughed. "Johnnie says you have a bunch of new kids."

"Number six is due the end of February," Tyler said proudly.

"Six? You're not a Catholic or a Mormon, are you? What's with all this bird hatching?"

Tyler gave his former boss a wry look. He'd never understood that prejudice in the nuclear navy. It came from Rickover, who had invented the disparaging term *bird hatching* for fathering more than one child. What the hell was wrong with having kids?

"Admiral, since I'm not a nuc anymore, I have to do *something* on nights and weekends." Tyler arched his eyebrows lecherously. "I hear the Russkies are playing games."

Dodge was instantly serious. "They sure are. Fifty-eight attack boats—every nuclear boat in the Northern Fleet—heading this way with a big surface group, and most of their service forces tagging along."

"Doing what?"

"Maybe you can tell me. Come on back to my inner sanctum." Dodge led Tyler into a room where he saw another new gadget, a projection screen that displayed the North Atlantic from the Tropic of Cancer to the polar ice pack. Hundreds of ships were represented. The merchantmen were white, with flags to identify their nationality; the Soviet ships were red, and their shapes depicted their ship type; the American and allied ships were blue. The ocean was getting crowded.

"Christ."

"You got that one right, lad," Tyler nodded grimly. "How are you cleared?"

"Top secret and some special things, sir. I see everything we have on their hardware, and I do a lot of work with Sea Systems on the side."

"Johnnie said you did the evaluation of the new *Kirov* they just sent out to the Pacific—not bad, by the way."

"These two *Alfa*s heading for Norfolk?"

"Looks like it. And they're burning a lot of neutrons doing it." Dodge pointed. "That one's heading to Long Island Sound as though to block the entrance to New London and that one's heading to Boston, I think. These *Victor*s are not far behind. They already have most of the British ports staked out. By Monday they'll have two or more subs off every major port we have."

"I don't like the looks of this, sir."

"Neither do I. As you see, we're nearly a hundred percent at sea ourselves. The interesting thing, though—what they're doing just doesn't figure. I—" Captain Coleman came in.

"I see you let the prodigal son in, sir," Coleman said.

"Be nice to him, Johnnie. I seem to remember when he was a right fair sub driver. Anyway, at first it looked like they were going to block the SLOCs, but they went right past. What with these *Alfa*s, they might be trying to blockade our coast."

"What about out west?"

"Nothing. Nothing at all, just routine activity."

"That doesn't make any sense," Tyler objected. "You don't ignore half the fleet. Of course, if you're going to war you don't announce it by kicking every boat to max power either."

"The Russians are a funny bunch, Skip," Coleman pointed out.

"Admiral, if we start shooting at them—"

"We hurt 'em," Dodge said. "With all the noise they're

making we have good locations on near all of 'em. They have to know that, too. That's the one thing that makes me believe they're not up to anything really bad. They're smart enough not to be that obvious—unless that's what they want us to think."

"Have they said anything?" Tyler asked.

"Their ambassador says they've lost a boat, and since it has a bunch of big shots' kids aboard, they laid on an all-hands rescue mission. For what that's worth."

Tyler set his briefcase down and walked closer to the screen. "I can see the pattern for a search and rescue, but why blockade our ports?" He paused, thinking rapidly as his eyes scanned the top of the display. "Sir, I don't see any boomers up here."

"They're in port—all of 'em, on both oceans. The last *Delta* tied up a few hours ago. That's funny, too," Dodge said, looking at the screen again.

"All of them, sir?" Tyler asked as offhandedly as he could. Something had just occurred to him. The display screen showed the *Bremerton* in the Barents Sea but not her supposed quarry. He waited a few seconds for an answer. Getting none, he turned to see the two officers observing him closely.

"Why do you ask, son?" Dodge said quietly. In Sam Dodge, gentleness could be a real warning flag.

Tyler thought this one over for a few seconds. He'd given Ryan his word. Could he phrase his answer without compromising it and still find out what he wanted? Yes, he decided. There was an investigative side to Skip Tyler's character, and once he was onto something, his psyche compelled him to run it down.

"Admiral, do they have a missile sub at sea, a brand new one?"

Dodge stood very straight. Even so he still had to look up at the younger man. When he spoke, his voice was glacial. "Exactly where did you get that information, Commander?"

Tyler shook his head. "Admiral, I'm sorry, but I can't say. It's compartmented, sir. I think this is something you ought to know, and I'll try to get it to you."

Dodge backed off to try a different tack. "You used to work for me, Skip." The admiral was unhappy. He'd bent a rule to show something to his former subordinate because he knew him well and was sorry that he had not received the command he had worked so hard for. Tyler was technically a civilian, even though his suits were still navy blue. What made it really bad was that he knew something himself. Dodge had given him some information, and Tyler wasn't giving any back.

"Sir, I gave my word," Skip apologized. "I will try to get this to you. That's a promise, sir. May I use a phone?"

"Outer office," Dodge said flatly. There were four telephones within sight.

Tyler went out and sat at a secretary's desk. He took his notebook from a coat pocket and dialed the number on the card Ryan had left him.

"Acres," a female voice answered.

"Could I speak to Dr. Ryan, please?"

"Dr. Ryan is not here at the moment."

"Then . . . give me Admiral Greer, please."

"One moment, please."

"James Greer?" Dodge was behind him. "Is that who you're working for?"

"This is Greer. Your name Skip Tyler?"

"Yes, sir."

"You have that information for me?"

"Yes, sir, I do."

"Where are you?"

"In the Pentagon, sir."

"Okay, I want you to drive right up here. You know how to find the place? The guards at the main gate will be waiting for you. Get moving, son." Greer hung up.

"You're working for the CIA?" Dodge asked.

"Sir—I can't say. If you will excuse me, sir, I have some information to deliver."

"Mine?" the admiral demanded.

"No, sir. I already had it when I came in here. That's the truth, Admiral. And I will try to get this back to you."

"Call me," Dodge ordered. "We'll be here all night."

CIA Headquarters

The drive up the George Washington Parkway was easier than he expected. The decrepit old highway was crowded with shoppers but moved along at a steady crawl. He got off at the right exit and presently found himself at the guard post for the main highway entrance to the CIA. The barrier was down.

"Your name Tyler, Oliver W.?" the guard asked. "ID please." Tyler handed him his Pentagon pass.

"Okay, Commander. Pull your car right to the main entrance. Somebody will be there to meet you."

It was another two minutes to the main entrance through mostly empty parking lots glazed with ice from yesterday's melted snow. The armed guard who was waiting for him tried to help him out of the car. Tyler didn't like to be helped. He shrugged him off. Another man was waiting for him under the canopied main entrance. They were waved right through to the elevator.

He found Admiral Greer sitting in front of his office fireplace, seemingly half asleep. Skip didn't know that the DDI had only returned from England a few hours earlier. The admiral came to and ordered his plain-clothes security officer to withdraw. "You must be Skip Tyler. Come on over and sit down."

"That's quite a fire you have going there, sir."

"I shouldn't bother. Looking at a fire makes me go to sleep. Of course, I could use a little sleep right now. So, what do you have for me?"

"May I ask where Jack is?"

"You may ask. He's away."

"Oh." Tyler unlocked his briefcase and removed the printout. "Sir, I ran the performance model for this Russian sub. May I ask her name?"

Greer chuckled. "Okay, you've earned that much. Her name is *Red October*. You'll have to excuse me, son. I've had a busy couple of days, and being tired makes me forget my manners. Jack says you're pretty sharp. So does your personnel file. Now, you tell me. What'll she do?"

"Well, Admiral, we have a wide choice of data here, and—"

"The short version, Commander. I don't play with computers. I have people who do that for me."

"From seven to eighteen knots, the best bet is ten to twelve. With that speed range, you can figure a radiated noise level about the same as that of a *Yankee* doing six knots, but you'd have to factor reactor plant noise into that also. Moreover, the character of the noise will be different from what we're used to. These multiple impeller models don't put out normal propulsion noises. They seem to generate an irregular harmonic rumble. Did Jack tell you about this? It results from a backpressure wave in the tunnels. This fights the water flow, and that makes the rumble. Evidently there's no way around it. Our guys spent two years trying to find one. What they got was a new principle of hydrodynamics. The water almost acts like air in a jet engine at idle or low speed, except that water doesn't compress like air does. So, our guys will be able to detect something, but it will be different. They're going to have to get used to a wholly new acoustical signature. Add to that the lower signal intensity, and you have a boat that will be harder to detect than anything they have at this time."

"So that's what all this says." Greer riffled through the pages.

"Yes, sir. You'll want to have your own people look through it. The model—the program, that is—could stand a little improvement. I didn't have much time. Jack said you wanted this in a hurry. May I ask a question, sir?"

"You can try." Greer leaned back, rubbing his eyes.

"Is, ah, *Red October* at sea? That's it, isn't it? They're trying to locate her right now?" Tyler asked innocently.

"Uh huh, something like that. We couldn't figure what these doors meant. Ryan said you might be able to, and I suppose he was right. You've earned your money, Commander. This data might just enable us to find her."

"Admiral, I think *Red October* is up to something, maybe even trying to defect to the United States."

Greer's head came around. "Whatever makes you think that?"

"The Russkies have a major fleet operation in progress. They have subs all over the Atlantic, and it looks like they're trying to blockade our coast. The story is a rescue job for a lost boat. Okay, but Jack shows up Monday with pictures of a new missile boat—and today I hear that all of their other missile boats have been recalled to port." Tyler smiled. "That's kind of an odd set of coincidences, sir."

Greer turned and stared at the fire. He had just joined the DIA when the army and air force had pulled off the daring raid on the Song Tay prison camp twenty miles west of Hanoi. The raid had been a failure because the North Vietnamese had removed all of the captured pilots a few weeks before, something that aerial photographs could not determine. But everything else had gone perfectly. After penetrating hundreds of miles into hostile territory, the raiding force appeared entirely by surprise and caught many of the camp guards literally with their pants down. The Green Berets did a letter-perfect job of getting in and out. In the process they killed several hundred enemy troops, themselves sustaining a single casualty, a broken ankle. The most impressive part of the mission, however, was its secrecy. Operation KINGPIN had been rehearsed for months, and despite this its nature and objective had not been guessed by friend or enemy—until the day of the raid itself. On that day a young air force captain of intelligence went into his general's office to ask if a deep-penetration raid into North Vietnam had been laid on for the Song Tay prisoner-of-war camp. His astonished commander proceeded to grill the captain at length, only to learn that the bright young officer had seen enough disjointed bits and pieces to construct a clear picture of what was about to happen. Events like this gave security officers peptic ulcers.

"*Red October*'s going to defect, isn't she?" Tyler persisted.

If the admiral had had more sleep he might have bluffed it out. As it was, his response was a mistake. "Did Ryan tell you this?"

"Sir, I haven't spoken with Jack since Monday. That's the truth, sir."

"Then where did you get this other information?" Greer snapped.

"Admiral, I used to wear the blue suit. Most of my friends still do. I hear things," Tyler evaded. "The whole picture dropped into place an hour ago. The Russkies have never recalled all of their boomers at once. I know, I used to hunt them."

Greer sighed. "Jack thinks the same as you. He's out with the fleet right now. Commander, if you tell that to anyone, I'll have your other leg mounted overtop that fireplace. Do you understand me?"

"Aye aye, sir. What are we going to do with her?" Tyler smiled to himself, thinking that as a senior consultant to Sea Systems Command, he'd sure as hell get a chance to look at a for-real Russian submarine.

"Give her back. After we've had a chance to look her over,

of course. But there's a lot of things that could happen to prevent our ever seeing her."

It took Skip a moment to grasp what he'd just been told. "Give her back! Why, for Christ's sake?"

"Commander, just how likely do you think this scenario is? Do you think the whole crew of a submarine has decided to come over to us all at once?" Greer shook his head. "Smart money is that it's only the officers, maybe not all of them, and that they're trying to get over here without the crew's knowing what they're up to."

"Oh." Tyler considered that. "I suppose that does make sense—but why give her back? This isn't Japan. If somebody landed a MiG-25 here we wouldn't give it back."

"This is not like holding onto a stray fighter plane. The boat is worth a billion dollars, more if you throw in the missiles and warheads. And legally, the president says, it's their property. So if they find out we have her, they'll ask for her back, and we'll have to give her back. Okay, how will they know we have her? Those crew members who don't want to defect will ask to go home. Whoever asks, we send."

"You know, sir, that whoever does want to go back will be in a whole shitload of trouble—excuse me, sir."

"A shitload and a half." Tyler hadn't known that Greer was a mustang and could swear like a real sailor. "Some will want to stay, but most won't. They have families. Next you'll ask me if we might arrange for the crew to disappear."

"The thought has occurred to me," Tyler said.

"It's occurred to us, too. But we won't. Murder a hundred men? Even if we wanted to, there's no way we could conceal it in this day and age. Hell, I doubt even the Soviets could. Besides that, this simply is not the sort of thing you do in peacetime. That's one difference between us and them. You can take those reasons in any order you want."

"So, except for the crew, we'd keep her..."

"Yes, if we could hide her. And if a pig had wings, it could fly."

"Lots of places to hide her, Admiral. I can think of a few right here on the Chesapeake, and if we could get her round the Horn, there's a million little atolls we could use, and they all belong to us."

"But the crew will know, and when we send them home,

they'll tell their bosses," Greer explained patiently. "And Moscow will ask for her back. Oh, sure, we'll have a week or so to conduct, uh, safety and quarantine inspections, to make sure they weren't trying to smuggle cocaine into the country." The admiral laughed. "A British admiral suggested we invoke the old slave-trading treaty. Somebody did that back in World War II, to put the grab on a German blockade runner right before we got into it. So, we'll get a ton of intelligence regardless."

"Better to keep her, and run her, and take her apart . . ." Tyler said quietly, staring into the orange-white flames on the oak logs. How do we keep her? he wondered. An idea began to rattle around in his head. "Admiral, what if we could get the crew off without them knowing that we have the submarine?"

"Your full name is Oliver Wendell Tyler? Well, son, if you were named after Harry Houdini instead of a justice of the Supreme Court, I—" Greer looked into the engineer's face. "What do you have in mind?"

While Tyler explained Greer listened intently.

"To do this, sir, we'll have to get the navy in on it right quick. Specifically, we'll need the cooperation of Admiral Dodge, and if my speed figures for this boat are anything like accurate, we'll have to move smartly."

Greer rose and walked around the couch a few times to get his circulation going. "Interesting. The timing would be almost impossible, though."

"I didn't say it would be easy, sir, just that we *could* do it."

"Call home, Tyler. Tell your wife you won't be making it home. If I don't get any sleep tonight, neither do you. There's coffee behind my desk. First I have to call the judge, then we'll talk to Sam Dodge."

The USS Pogy

"*Pogy,* this is Black Gull 4. We're getting low on fuel. Have to return to the barn," the Orion's tactical coordinator reported, stretching after ten hours at his control console. "Anything you want us to get you? Over."

"Yeah, have a couple cases of beer sent out," Commander Wood replied. It was the current joke between P-3C and submarine crews. "Thanks for the data. We'll take it from here. Out."

Overhead, the Lockheed Orion increased power and turned southwest. The crewmen aboard would each hoist an extra beer or two at dinner, saying it was for their friends on the submarine.

"Mr. Dyson, take her two hundred feet. One-third speed."

The officer of the deck gave the proper orders as Commander Wood moved over to the plot.

The USS *Pogy* was three hundred miles northeast of Norfolk, awaiting the arrival of two Soviet *Alfa*-class submarines which several relays of antisubmarine patrol aircraft had tracked all the way from Iceland. The *Pogy* was named for a distinguished World War II fleet submarine, named in turn for an undistinguished game fish. She had been at sea for eighteen hours, and was fresh from an extended overhaul at the Newport News shipyard. Nearly everything aboard was either straight from manufacturers' crates or had been completely worked over by the skilled shipfitters on the James River. This was not to say that everything worked properly. Many items had failed in one way or another on the post-overhaul shakedown the previous week, a fact less unusual than lamentable, Commander Wood thought. The *Pogy*'s crew was new, too. Wood was on his first deployment as a commanding officer after a year of desk duty in Washington, and too many of the enlisted men were green, just out of sub school at New London, still getting accustomed to their first cruise on a submarine. It takes time for men used to blue skies and fresh air to learn the regime inside a thirty-two-foot-diameter steel pipe. Even the experienced men were making adjustments to their new boat and officers.

The *Pogy* had met her top speed of thirty-three knots on post-overhaul trials. This was fast for a ship but slower than the speed of the *Alfa*s she was listening to. Like all American submarines, her long suit was stealth. The *Alfa*s had no way of knowing she was there and that they would be easy targets for her weapons, the more so since the patrolling Orion had fed the *Pogy* exact range information, something that ordinarily takes time to deduce from a passive sonar plot.

Lieutenant Commander Tom Reynolds, the executive officer

and fire control coordinator, stood casually over the tactical plot. "Thirty-six miles to the near one, and forty on the far one." On the display they were labeled Pogy-Bait 1 and 2. Everyone found the use of this service epithet amusing.

"Speed forty-two?" Wood asked.

"Yes, Captain." Reynolds had handled the radio exchange until Black Gull 4 had announced its intention to return to base. "They're driving those boats for all they're worth. Right for us. We have hard solutions on both . . . zap! What do you suppose they're up to?"

"The word from CINCLANT is that their ambassador says they're on a SAR mission for a lost boat." His voice indicated what he thought of that.

"Search and rescue, eh?" Reynolds shrugged. "Well, maybe they think they lost a boat off Point Comfort, 'cause if they don't slow down real fast, that's where they'll end up. I've never heard of *Alfa*s operating this close to our coast. Have you, sir?"

"Nope." Wood frowned. The thing about the *Alfa*s was that they were fast and noisy. Soviet tactical doctrine seemed to call for them mainly in defensive roles: as "interceptor submarines" they could protect their own missile subs, and with their high speed they could engage American attack submarines, then evade counterattack. Wood didn't think the doctrine was sound, but that was all right with him.

"Maybe they want to blockade Norfolk," Reynolds suggested.

"You might have a point there," Wood said. "Well, in any case, we'll just sit tight and let them burn right past us. They'll have to slow as they cross the continental shelf line, and we'll tag along behind them, nice and quiet."

"Aye," Reynolds said.

If they had to shoot, both men reflected, they'd find out just how tough the *Alfa* really was. There had been much talk about the strength of the titanium used for her hull, whether it really would withstand the force of several hundred pounds of high explosive in direct contact. A new shaped-charge warhead for the Mark 48 torpedo had been developed for just this purpose and for handling the equally tough *Typhoon* hull. Both officers set this thought aside. Their assigned mission was to track and shadow.

The E. S. Politovskiy

Pogy-Bait 2 was known to the Soviet Navy as the *E. S. Politovskiy*. This *Alfa*-class attack sub was named for the chief engineering officer of the Russian fleet who had sailed all the way around the world to meet his appointment with destiny in the Tsushima Straits. Evgeni Sigismondavich Politovskiy had served the czar's navy with skill and a devotion to duty equal to that of any officer in history, but in his diary, which was discovered years later in Leningrad, the brilliant officer had decried in the most violent terms the corruption and excesses of the czarist regime, giving a grim counterpoint to the selfless patriotism he had shown as he sailed knowingly to his death. This made him a genuine hero for Soviet seamen to emulate, and the State had named its greatest engineering achievement in his memory. Unfortunately the *Politovskiy* had enjoyed no better luck than he had enjoyed in the face of Togo's guns.

The *Politovskiy*'s acoustical signature was labeled *Alfa 3* by the Americans. This was incorrect; she had been the first of the *Alfas*. The small, spindle-shaped attack submarine had reached forty-three knots three hours into her initial builder's trials. Those trials had been cut short only a minute later by an incredible mishap: a fifty-ton right whale had somehow blundered in her path, and the *Politovskiy* had rammed the unfortunate creature broadside. The impact had smashed ten square meters of bow plating, annihilated the sonar dome, knocked a torpedo tube askew, and nearly flooded the torpedo room. This did not count shock damage to nearly every interior system from electronic equipment to the galley stove, and it was said that if anyone but the famous Vilnius headmaster had been in command, the submarine would surely have been lost. A two-meter segment of the whale's rib was now a permanent fixture at the officer's club in Severomorsk, dramatic testament to the strength of Soviet submarines; in fact the damage had taken over a year to repair, and by the time the *Politovskiy* sailed again there were already two other *Alfas* in service. Two days after sailing on her next shakedown, she suffered another major casualty, the total failure of her high-pressure turbine. This had taken six months to replace. There had been three

more minor incidents since, and the submarine was forever
marked as a bad luck ship.

Chief Engineer Vladimir Petchukocov was a loyal Party
member and a committed atheist, but he was also a sailor and
therefore profoundly superstitious. In the old days, his ship
would have been blessed on launching and thereafter every
time she sailed. It would have been an impressive ceremony,
· with a bearded priest, clouds of incense, and evocative hymns.
He had sailed without any of that and found himself wishing
otherwise. He needed some luck. Petchukocov was having
trouble with his reactor.

The *Alfa* reactor plant was small. It had to fit into a relatively
small hull. It was also powerful for its size, and this one had
been running at one hundred percent rated power for just over
four days. They were racing for the American coast at 42.3
knots, as fast as the eight-year-old plant would permit. The
Politovskiy was due for a comprehensive overhaul: new sonar,
new computers, and a redesigned reactor control suite were all
planned for the coming months. Petchukocov thought it irresponsible—reckless—to push his submarine so hard, even if
everything were functioning properly. No *Alfa* plant on a submarine had ever been pushed this hard, not even a new one.
And on this one, things were beginning to come apart.

The primary high-pressure reactor coolant pump was beginning to vibrate ominously. This was particularly worrying
to the engineer. There was a backup, but the secondary pump
had a lower rated power, and using it meant losing eight knots
of speed. The *Alfa* plant achieved its high power not with a
sodium-cooled system—as the Americans thought—but by
running at a far higher pressure than any reactor system afloat
and using a revolutionary heat exchange system that boosted
the plant's overall thermal efficiency to forty-one percent, well
in excess of that for any other submarine. But the price of this
was a reactor that at full power was red-lined on every monitor
gauge—and in this case the red lines were not mere symbolism.
They signified genuine danger.

This fact, added to the vibrating pump, had Petchukocov
seriously concerned; an hour earlier he had pleaded with the
captain to reduce power for a few hours so that his skilled crew
of engineers could make repairs. It was probably only a bad

bearing, after all, and they had spares. The pump had been designed so that it would be easy to fix. The captain had wavered, wanting to grant the request, but the political officer had intervened, pointing out that their orders were both urgent and explicit: they had to be on station as quickly as possible; to do otherwise would be "politically unsound." And that was that.

Petchukocov bitterly remembered the look in his captain's eyes. What was the purpose of a commanding officer if his every order had to be approved by a political flunky? Petchukocov had been a faithful Communist since joining the Octobrists as a boy—but damn it! what was the point of having specialists and engineers? Did the Party really think that physical laws could be overturned by the whim of some apparatchik with a heavy desk and a dacha in the Moscow suburbs? The engineer swore to himself.

He stood alone at the master control board. This was located in the engine room, aft of the compartment that held the reactor and the heat exchanger/steam generator, the latter placed right at the submarine's center of gravity. The reactor was pressurized to twenty kilograms per square centimeter, about twenty-eight hundred pounds per square inch. Only a fraction of this pressure came from the pump. The higher pressure caused a higher boiling point for the coolant. In this case, the water was heated to over 900° Celsius, a temperature sufficient to generate steam, which gathered at the top of the reactor vessel; the steam bubble applied pressure to the water beneath, preventing the generation of more steam. The steam and water regulated one another in a delicate balance. The water was dangerously radioactive as a result of the fission reaction taking place within the uranium fuel rods. The function of the control rods was to regulate the reaction. Again, the control was delicate. At most the rods could absorb just less than one percent of the neutron flux, but this was enough either to permit the reaction or to prevent it.

Petchukocov could recite all this data in his sleep. He could draw a wholly accurate schematic diagram of the entire engine plant from memory and could instantly grasp the significance of the slightest change in his instrument readings. He stood perfectly straight over the control board, his eyes tracing the myriad dials and gauges in a regular pattern, one hand poised over the SCRAM switch, the other over the emergency cooling controls.

He could hear the vibration. It had to be a bad bearing getting worse as it wore more and more unevenly. If the crankshaft bearings went bad, the pump would seize, and they'd have to stop. This would be an emergency, though not really a dangerous one. It would mean that repairing the pump—if they could repair it at all—would take days instead of hours, eating up valuable time and spare parts. That was bad enough. What was worse, and what Petchukocov did not know, was that the vibration was generating pressure waves in the coolant.

To make use of the newly developed heat exchanger, the *Alfa* plant had to move water rapidly through its many loops and baffles. This required a high-pressure pump which accounted for one hundred fifty pounds of the total system pressure—almost ten times what was considered safe in Western reactors. With the pump so powerful, the whole engine room complex, normally very noisy at high speed, was like a boiler factory, and the pump's vibration was disturbing the performance of the monitor instruments. It was making the needles on his gauges waver, Petchukocov noted. He was right, and wrong. The pressure gauges were really wavering because of the thirty-pound overpressure waves pulsing through the system. The chief engineer did not recognize this for what it was. He had been on duty too many hours.

Within the reactor vessel, these pressure waves were approaching the frequency at which a piece of equipment resonated. Roughly halfway down the interior surface of the vessel was a titanium fitting, part of the backup cooling system. In the event of a coolant loss, and *after* a successful SCRAM, valves inside and outside the vessel would open, cooling the reactor either with a mixture of water and barium or, as a last measure, with seawater which could be vented in and out of the vessel—at the cost of ruining the entire reactor. This had been done once, and though it had been costly, the action of a junior engineer had prevented the loss of a *Victor*-class attack sub by catastrophic meltdown.

Today the inside valve was closed, along with the corresponding through-hull fitting. The valves were made of titanium because they had to function reliably after prolonged exposure to high temperature, and also because titanium was very corrosion-resistant—high-temperature water was murderously corrosive. What had not been fully considered was that the metal was also exposed to intense nuclear radiation, and this particular titanium alloy was not completely stable under extended neutron bombardment. The metal had become brittle over the years. The minute waves of hydraulic pressure were beating against the clapper in the valve. As the pump's frequency of vibration changed it began to approach the frequency at which the clapper vibrated. This caused the clapper to snap harder and harder against its retaining ring. The metal at its edges began to crack.

A *michman* at the forward end of the compartment heard it first, a low buzz coming through the bulkhead. At first he thought it was feedback noise from the PA speaker, and he waited too long to check it. The clapper broke free and dropped out of the valve nozzle. It was not very large, only ten centimeters in diameter and five millimeters thick. This type of fitting is called a butterfly valve, and the clapper looked just like a butterfly, suspended and twirling in the water flow. If it had been made of stainless steel it would have been heavy enough to fall to the bottom of the vessel. But it was made of titanium, which was both stronger than steel and very much lighter. The coolant flow moved it up, towards the exhaust pipe.

The outward-moving water carried the clapper into the pipe, which had a fifteen-centimeter inside diameter. The pipe was made of stainless steel, two-meter sections welded together for easy replacement in the cramped quarters. The clapper was borne along rapidly towards the heat exchanger. Here the pipe took a forty-five-degree downward turn and the clapper jammed momentarily. This blocked half of the pipe's channel, and before the surge of pressure could dislodge the clapper too many things happened. The moving water had its own momentum. On being blocked, it generated a back-pressure wave within the pipe. Total pressure jumped momentarily to thirty-four hundred pounds. This caused the pipe to flex a few millimeters. The increased pressure, lateral displacement of a weld joint, and cumulative effect of years of high-temperature erosion of the steel damaged the joint. A hole the size of a pencil point opened. The escaping water flashed instantly into steam, setting off alarms in the reactor compartment and neighboring spaces. It ate at the remainder of the weld, rapidly expanding the failure until reactor coolant was erupting as though from a horizontal fountain. One jet of steam demolished the adjacent reactor-control wiring conduits.

What had just begun was a catastrophic loss-of-coolant accident.

The reactor was fully depressurized within three seconds. Its many gallons of coolant exploded into steam, seeking release into the surrounding compartment. A dozen alarms sounded at once on the master control board, and in the blink of an eye Vladimir Petchukocov faced his ultimate nightmare. The engineer's automatic trained reaction was to jam his finger on the SCRAM switch, but the steam in the reactor vessel had disabled the rod control system, and there wasn't time to solve the problem. In an instant, Petchukocov knew that his ship was doomed. Next he opened the emergency coolant controls, admitting seawater into the reactor vessel. This automatically set off alarms throughout the hull.

In the control room forward, the captain grasped the nature of the emergency at once. The *Politovskiy* was running at one hundred fifty meters. He had to get her to the surface immediately, and he shouted orders to blow all ballast and make full rise on the diving planes.

The reactor emergency was regulated by physical laws. With no reactor coolant to absorb the heat of the uranium rods, the nuclear reaction actually stopped—there was no water to attenuate the neutron flux. This was no solution, however, since the residual decay heat was sufficient to melt everything in the compartment. The cold water admitted into the vessel drew off the heat but also slowed down too many neutrons, keeping them in the reactor core. This caused a runaway reaction that generated even more heat, more than any amount of coolant could control. What had started as a loss-of-coolant accident became something worse: a cold-water accident. It was now only a matter of minutes before the entire core melted, and the *Politovskiy* had that long to get to the surface.

Petchukocov stayed at his post in the engine room, doing what he could. His own life, he knew, was almost certainly lost. He had to give his captain time to surface the boat. There was a drill for this sort of emergency, and he barked orders to implement it. It only made things worse.

His duty electrician moved along the electrical control panels switching from main power to emergency, since residual steam power in the turboalternators would die in a few more seconds. In a moment the submarine's power completely depended on standby batteries.

In the control room power was lost to the electrically controlled trim tabs on the trailing edge of the diving planes, which automatically switched back to electrohydraulic control. This powered not just the small trim tabs but the diving planes as well. The control assemblies moved instantly to a fifteen-degree up-angle—and she was still moving at thirty-nine knots. With all her ballast tanks now blasted free of water by compressed air, the submarine was very light, and she rose like a climbing aircraft. In seconds the astonished control room crew felt their boat rise to an up-angle that was forty-five degrees and getting worse. A moment later they were too busy trying to stand to come to grips with the problem. Now the *Alfa* was climbing almost vertically at thirty miles per hour. Every man and unsecured item aboard fell sternward.

In the motor control room aft, a crewman crashed against the main electrical switchboard, short-circuiting it with his body, and all power aboard was lost. A cook who had been inventorying survival gear in the torpedo room forward struggled into the escape trunk as he fought his way into an exposure suit. Even with only a year's experience, he was quick to understand the meaning of the hooting alarms and unprecedented actions of his boat. He yanked the hatch shut and began to work the escape controls as he had been taught in submarine school.

The *Politovskiy* soared through the surface of the Atlantic like a broaching whale, coming three quarters of her length out of the water before crashing back.

The USS Pogy

"Conn, sonar."

"Conn, aye, Captain speaking."

"Skipper, you better hear this. Something just went crazy on Bait 2," *Pogy*'s chief reported. Wood was in the sonar room

in seconds, putting on earphones plugged into a tape recorder
which had a two-minute offset. Commander Wood heard a
whooshing sound. The engine noises stopped. A few seconds
later there was an explosion of compressed air, and a staccato
of hull popping noises as a submarine changed depth rapidly.

"What's going on?" Wood asked quickly.

The E. S. Politovskiy

In the *Politovskiy*'s reactor, the runaway fission reaction had
virtually annihilated both the incoming seawater and the uranium fuel rods. Their debris settled on the after wall of the
reactor vessel. In a minute there was a meter-wide puddle of
radioactive slag, enough to form its own critical mass. The
reaction continued unabated, this time directly attacking the
tough stainless steel of the vessel. Nothing man made could
long withstand five thousand degrees of direct heat. In ten
seconds the vessel wall failed. The uranium mass dropped free,
against the aft bulkhead.

Petchukocov knew he was dead. He saw the paint on the
forward bulkhead turn black, and his last impression was of a
dark mass surrounded with the blue glow. The engineer's body
vaporized an instant later, and the mass of slag dropped to the
next bulkhead aft.

Forward, the submarine's nearly vertical angle in the water
eased. The high-pressure air in the ballast tanks spilled out of
the bottom floods and the tanks filled with water, dropping the
angle of the boat and submerging her. In the forward part of
the submarine men were screaming. The captain struggled to
his feet, ignoring his broken leg, trying to get control, to get
his men organized and out of the submarine before it was too
late, but the luck of Evgeni Sigismondavich Politovskiy would
plague his namesake one last time. Only one man escaped. The
cook opened the escape trunk hatch and got out. Following
what he had learned during the drill, he began to seal the hatch
so that men behind him could use it, but a wave slapped him
off the hull as the sub slid backwards.

In the engine room, the changing angle dropped the melted
core to the deck. The hot mass attacked the steel deck first,
burning through that, then the titanium of the hull. Five seconds
later the engine room was vented to the sea. The *Politovskiy*'s

largest compartment filled rapidly with water. This destroyed what little reserve buoyancy the ship had, and the acute down-angle returned. The *Alfa* began her last dive.

The stern dropped just as the captain began to get his control room crew to react to orders again. His head struck an instrument console. What slim hopes his crew had died with him. The *Politovskiy* was falling backwards, her propeller windmilling the wrong way as she slid to the bottom of the sea.

The Pogy

"Skipper, I was on the *Chopper* back in sixty-nine," the *Pogy*'s chief said, referring to a horrifying accident on a diesel-powered submarine.

"That's what it sounds like," his captain said. He was now listening to direct sonar input. There was no mistaking it. The submarine was flooding. They had heard the ballast tanks refill; this could only mean interior compartments were filling with water. If they had been closer, they might have heard the screams of men in that doomed hull. Wood was just as happy he couldn't. The continuing rush of water was dreadful enough. Men were dying. Russians, his enemy, but men not unlike himself, and there was not a thing that could be done about it.

Bait 1, he saw, was proceeding, unmindful of what had happened to her trailing sister.

The E. S. Politovskiy

It took nine minutes for the *Politovskiy* to fall the two thousand feet to the ocean floor. She impacted savagely on the hard sand bottom at the edge of the continental shelf. It was a tribute to her builders that her interior bulkheads held. All the compartments from the reactor room aft were flooded and half the crew killed in them, but the forward compartments were dry. Even this was more curse than blessing. With the aft air storage banks unusable and only emergency battery power to run the complex environmental control systems, the forty men had only a limited supply of air. They were spared a rapid death from the crushing North Atlantic only to face a slower one from asphyxiation.

THE NINTH DAY

SATURDAY, 11 DECEMBER

The Pentagon

A female yeoman first class held the door open for Tyler. He walked in to find General Harris standing alone over the large chart table pondering the placement of tiny ship models.

"You must be Skip Tyler." Harris looked up.

"Yes, sir." Tyler was standing as rigidly at attention as his prosthetic leg allowed. Harris came over quickly to shake hands.

"Greer says you used to play ball."

"Yes, General, I played right tackle at Annapolis. Those were good years." Tyler smiled, flexing his fingers. Harris looked like an iron-pumper.

"Okay, if you used to play ball, you can call me Ed." Harris poked him in the chest. "Your number was seventy-eight, and you made All American, right?"

"Second string, sir. Nice to know somebody remembers."

"I was on temporary duty at the Academy for a few months back then, and I caught a couple games. I never forget a good offensive lineman. I made All Conference at Montana—long time ago. What happened to the leg?"

"Drunk driver clipped me. I was the lucky one. The drunk didn't make it."

"Serves the bastard right."

Tyler nodded agreement, but remembered that the drunken shipfitter had had his own wife and family, according to the police. "Where is everybody?"

"The chiefs are at their normal—well, normal for a week-day, not a Saturday—intelligence briefing. They ought to be down in a few minutes. So, you're teaching engineering at Annapolis now, eh?"

"Yes, sir. I got a doctorate in that along the way."

"Name's Ed, Skip. And this morning you're going to tell us how we can hold onto that maverick Russian sub?"

"Yes, sir—Ed."

"Tell me about it, but let's get some coffee first." The two men went to a table in the corner with coffee and donuts. Harris listened to the younger man for five minutes, sipping his coffee and devouring a couple of jelly donuts. It took a lot of food to support his frame.

"Son of a gun," the J-3 observed when Tyler finished. He walked over to the chart. "That's interesting. Your idea depends a lot on sleight of hand. We'd have to keep them away from where we're pulling this off. About here, you say?" He tapped the chart.

"Yes, General. The thing is, the way they seem to be op-erating we can do this to seaward of them—"

"And do a double shuffle. I like it. Yeah, I like it, but Dan Foster won't like losing one of our own boats."

"I'd say it's worth the trade."

"So would I," Harris agreed. "But they're not my boats. After we do this, where do we hide her—if we get her?"

"General, there are some nice places right here on the Ches-apeake Bay. There's a deep spot on the York River and another on the Patuxent, both owned by the navy, both marked Keep Out on the charts. Nice thing about subs, they're supposed to be invisible. You just find a deep enough spot and flood your tanks. That's temporary, of course. For a more permanent spot, maybe Truk or Kwajalein in the Pacific. Nice and far from any place."

"And the Soviets would never notice the presence of a sub tender and three hundred submarine technicians there all of a sudden? Besides, those islands don't really belong to us anymore, remember?"

Tyler hadn't expected this man to be a dummy. "So, what if they do find out in a few months? What will they do, announce it to the whole world? I don't think so. By that time we'll have all the information we want, and we can always produce the defecting officers in a nice news conference. How would that look for them? Anyway, it figures that after we've had her for a while, we'll break her up. The reactor'll go to Idaho for tests. The missiles and warheads will get taken off. The electronics gear will be taken to California for testing, and the CIA, NSA, and navy will have gunfights over the crypto gear. The stripped hulk will be taken to a nice deep spot and scuttled. No evidence. We don't have to keep this a secret forever, just for a few months."

Harris set his cup down. "You'll have to forgive me for playing devil's advocate. I see you've thought this out. Fine, I think it's worth a hard look. It means coordinating a lot of hardware, but it doesn't really interfere with what we're already doing. Okay, you have my vote."

The Joint Chiefs arrived three minutes later. Tyler had never seen so many stars in one room.

"You wanted to see all of us, Eddie?" Hilton asked.

"Yes, General. This is Dr. Skip Tyler."

Admiral Foster came over first to take his hand. "You got us that performance data on *Red October* that we were just briefed on. Good work, Commander."

"Dr. Tyler thinks we should hold onto her if we get her," Harris said deadpan. "And he thinks he has a way we can do it."

"We already thought of killing the crew," Commandant Maxwell said. "The president won't let us."

"Gentlemen, what if I told you that there was a way to send the crewmen home without them knowing that we have her? That's the issue, right? We have to send the crewmen back to Mother Russia. I say there's a way to do that, and the remaining question is where to hide her."

"We're listening," Hilton said suspiciously.

"Well, sir, we'll have to move quickly to get everything in

place. We'll need *Avalon* from the West Coast. *Mystic* is already aboard the *Pigeon* in Charleston. We need both of them, and we need an old boomer of our own that we can afford to do without. That's the hardware. The real trick, however, is the timing—and we have to find her. That may be the hardest part."

"Maybe not," Foster said. "Admiral Gallery reported this morning that *Dallas* may be onto her. Her report dovetails nicely with your engineering model. We'll know more in a few days. Go on."

Tyler explained. It took ten minutes since he had to answer questions and use the chart to diagram time and space constraints. When he was finished, General Barnes was at the phone calling the commander of the Military Airlift Command. Foster left the room to call Norfolk, and Hilton was on his way to the White House.

The Red October

Except for those on watch, every officer was in the wardroom. Several pots of tea were on the table, all untouched, and again the door was locked.

"Comrades," Petrov reported, "the second set of badges was contaminated, worse than the first."

Ramius noted that Petrov was rattled. It wasn't the first set of badges, or the second. It was the third and fourth since sailing. He had chosen his ship's doctor well.

"Bad badges," Melekhin growled. "Some bastard of a trickster in Severomorsk—or perhaps an imperialist spy playing a typical enemy trick on us. When they catch the son of a bitch I will shoot him myself—whoever he is! This sort of thing is treasonous!"

"Regulations require that I report this," Petrov noted. "Even though the instruments show safe levels."

"Your adherence to the rules is noted, Comrade Doctor. You have acted correctly," Ramius said. "And now regulations stipulate that we make yet another check. Melekhin, I want you and Borodin to do it personally. First check the radiation instruments themselves. If they are working properly, we will be certain that the badges are defective—or have been tampered with. If so, my report on this incident will demand someone's

head." It was not unknown for drunken shipyard workers to
be sent to the gulag. "Comrades, in my opinion there is nothing
at all to concern us. If there were a leak, Comrade Melekhin
would have discovered it days ago. So. We all have work to
do."

They were all back in the wardroom half an hour later.
Passing crewmen noticed this, and already the whispering
started.

"Comrades," Melekhin announced, "we have a major problem."

The officers, especially the younger ones, looked a little
pale. On the table was a Geiger counter stripped into a score
of small parts. Next to it was a radiation detector taken off the
reactor room bulkhead, its inspection cover removed.

"Sabotage," Melekhin hissed. It was a word fearsome enough
to make any Soviet citizen shudder. The room went deathly
still, and Ramius noted that Svyadov was holding his face under
rigid control.

"Comrades, mechanically speaking these instruments are
quite simple. As you know, this counter has ten different settings. We can choose from ten sensitivity ranges, using the
same instrument to detect a minor leak or to quantify a major
one. We do that by dialing this selector, which engages one of
ten electrical resistors of increasing value. A child could design
this, or maintain and repair it." The chief enginer tapped the
underside of the selector dial. "In this case the proper resistors
have been clipped off, and new ones soldered on. Settings one
to eight have the same impedance value. All of our counters
were inspected by the same dockyard technician three days
before we sailed. Here is his inspection sheet." Melekhin tossed
it on the table contemptuously.

"Either he or another spy sabotaged this and all the other
counters I've looked at. It would have taken a skilled man no
more than an hour. In the case of this instrument." The engineer
turned the fixed detector over. "You see that the electrical parts
have been disconnected, except for the test circuit, which was
rewired. Borodin and I removed this from the forward bulkhead. This is skilled work; whoever did this is no amateur. I
believe that an imperialist agent has sabotaged our ship. First
he disabled our radiation monitor instruments, then he probably
arranged a low-level leak in our hot piping. It would appear,

comrades, that Comrade Petrov was correct. We may have a
leak. My apologies, Doctor."

Petrov nodded jerkily. Compliments like this he could easily
forego.

"Total exposure, Comrade Petrov?" Ramius asked.

"The greatest is for the enginemen, of course. The maximum
is fifty rads for Comrades Melekhin and Svyadov. The other
engine crewmen run from twenty to forty-five rads, and the
cumulative exposure drops rapidly as one moves forward. The
torpedomen have only five rads or so, mostly less. The officers
exclusive of engineers run from ten to twenty-five." Petrov
paused, telling himself to be more positive. "Comrades, these
are not lethal doses. In fact, one can tolerate a dose of up to
a hundred rads without any near-term physiological effects,
and one can survive several hundred. We do face a serious
problem here, but it is not yet a life-threatening emergency."

"Melekhin?" the captain asked.

"It is my engine plant, and my responsibility. We do not yet
know that we have a leak. The badges could still be defective
or sabotaged. This could all be a vicious psychological trick
played on us by the main enemy to damage our morale. Borodin
will assist me. We will personally repair these and conduct a
thorough inspection of all reactor systems. I am too old to have
children. For the moment, I suggest that we deactivate the
reactor and proceed on battery. The inspection will take us four
hours at most. I also recommend that we reduce reactor watches
to two hours. Agreed, Captain?"

"Certainly, Comrade. I know that there is nothing you cannot
repair."

"Excuse me, Comrade Captain," Ivanov spoke up. "Should
we report this to fleet headquarters?"

"Our orders are not to break radio silence," Ramius said.

"If the imperialists were able to sabotage our instruments
. . . What if they knew our orders beforehand and are attempting
to make us use the radio so they can locate us?" Borodin asked.

"A possibility," Ramius replied. "First we will determine if
we have a problem, then its severity. Comrades, we have a
fine crew and the best officers in the fleet. We will see to our
own problems, conquer them, and continue our mission. We
all have a date in Cuba that I intend to meet—to hell with
imperialist plots!"

"Well said," Melekhin concurred.

"Comrades, we will keep this secret. There is no reason to excite the crew over what may be nothing, and at most is something we can handle on our own." Ramius ended the meeting.

Petrov was less sure, and Svyadov was trying very hard not to shake. He had a sweetheart at home and wanted one day to have children. The young lieutenant had been painstakingly trained to understand everything that went on in the reactor systems and to know what to do if things went awry. And it was some consolation to know that most of the solutions to reactor problems to be found in the book had been written by some of the men in this room. Even so, something that could neither be seen nor felt was invading his body, and no rational person would be happy with that.

The meeting adjourned. Melekhin and Borodin went aft to the engineering stores. A *michman* electrician came with them to get the proper parts. He noted that they were reading from the maintenance manual for a radiation detector. When he went off duty an hour later, the whole crew knew that the reactor had been shut down yet again. The electrician conferred with his bunkmate, a missile maintenance technician. Together they discussed the reason for working on a half dozen Geiger counters and other instruments, and their conclusion was an obvious one.

The submarine's bosun overheard the discussion and pondered the conclusion himself. He had been on nuclear submarines for ten years. Despite this he was not an educated man and regarded any activity in the reactor spaces as something to the left of witchcraft. It worked the ship, how he did not know, though he was certain that there was something unholy about it. Now he began to wonder if the devils he never saw inside that steel drum—were coming loose? Within two hours the entire crew knew that something was wrong and that their officers had not yet figured out a way to deal with it.

The cooks bringing food forward from the galley to the crew spaces were seen to linger in the bow as long as they could. Men standing watch in the control room shifted on their feet more than usual, Ramius noted, hurrying forward at the change of watch.

The USS New Jersey

It took some getting used to, Commodore Zachary Eaton reflected. When his flagship was built, he was sailing boats in a bathtub. Back then the Russians were allies, but allies of convenience, who shared a common enemy instead of a common goal. Like the Chinese today, he judged. The enemy then had been the Germans and the Japanese. In his twenty-six-year career, he had been to both countries many times, and his first command, a destroyer, had been home-ported at Yokoshuka. It was a strange world.

There were several nice things about his flagship. Big as she was, her movement on the ten-foot seas was just enough to remind him that he was at sea, not at a desk. Visibility was about ten miles, and somewhere out there, about eight hundred miles away, was the Russian fleet. His battleship was going to meet them just like in the old old days, as if the aircraft carrier had never come along. The destroyers *Caron* and *Stump* were in sight, five miles off either bow. Further forward, the cruisers *Biddle* and *Wainwright* were doing radar picket duty. The surface action group was marking time instead of proceeding forward as he would have preferred. Off the New Jersey coast, the helicopter assault ship *Tarawa* and two frigates were racing to join up, bringing ten AV-8B Harrier attack fighters and fourteen ASW helicopters to supplement his air strength. This was useful, but not of critical concern to Eaton. The *Saratoga*'s air wing was now operating out of Maine, along with a goodly collection of air force birds working hard to learn the maritime strike business. HMS *Invincible* was two hundred miles to his east, conducting aggressive ASW patrols, and eight hundred miles east of that force was the *Kennedy*, hiding under a weather front off the Azores. It slightly irked the commodore that the Brits were helping out. Since when did the U.S. Navy need help defending the American coast? Not that they didn't owe us the favor, though.

The Russians had split into three groups, with the carrier *Kiev* easternmost to face the *Kennedy*'s battle group. His expected responsibility was the *Moskva* group, with the *Invincible* handling the *Kirov*'s. Data on all three was being fed to him continuously and digested by his operations staff down in flag plot. What were the Soviets up to? he wondered.

He knew the story that they were searching for a lost sub, but Eaton believed that as much as if they'd explained that they had a bridge they wanted to sell. Probably, he thought, they want to demonstrate that they can trail their coats down our coast whenever they want, to show that they have a seagoing fleet and to establish a precedent for doing this again.

Eaton did not like that.

He did not much care for his assigned mission either. He had two tasks that were not fully compatible. Keeping an eye on their submarine activity would be difficult enough. The *Saratoga*'s Vikings were not working his area, despite his request, and most of the Orions were working farther out, closer to the *Invincible*. His own ASW assets were barely adequate for local defense, much less active sub hunting. The *Tarawa* would change that, but also change his screening requirements. His other mission was to establish and maintain sensor contact with the *Moskva* group and to report at once any unusual activity to CINCLANTFLT, the commander in chief of the Atlantic Fleet. This made sense, sort of. If their surface ships did anything untoward, Eaton had the means to deal with them. It was being decided now how closely he should shadow them.

The problem was whether he should be nearby or far away. Near meant twenty miles—gun range. The *Moskva* had ten escorts, none of which could possibly survive more than two of his sixteen-inch projectiles. At twenty miles he had the choice of using full-sized or subcaliber rounds, the latter guided to their targets by a laser designator installed atop the main director tower. Tests the previous year had determined that he could maintain a steady firing rate of one round every twenty seconds, with the laser shifting fire from one target to another until there were no more. But this would expose the *New Jersey* and her escorts to torpedo and missile fire from the Russian ships.

Backing farther off, he could still fire sabot rounds from fifty miles, and they could be directed to the target by a laser designator aboard the battlewagon's helicopter. This would expose the chopper to surface-to-air missile fire and to Soviet helicopters suspected of having air-to-air missile capability. To help out with this, the *Tarawa* was bringing a pair of Apache attack helicopters, which carried lasers, air-to-air missiles, and their own air-to-surface missiles; they were antitank weapons expected to work well against small warships.

His ships would be exposed to missile fire, but he didn't fear for his flagship. Unless the Russians were carrying nuclear warheads, their antiship missiles would not be able to damage his ship gravely—the *New Jersey* had upwards of a foot of class B armor plate. They would, however, play hell with his radar and communications gear, and worse, they would be lethal to his thin-hulled escorts. His ships carried their own antiship missiles, Harpoons and Tomahawks, though not as many as he would have liked.

And what about a Russian sub hunting them? Eaton had been told of none, but you never knew where one might be hiding. Oh well—he couldn't worry about everything. A submarine could sink the *New Jersey,* but she would have to work at it. If the Russians were really up to something nasty, they'd get the first shot, but Eaton would have enough warning to launch his own missiles and get off a few rounds of gunfire while calling for air support—none of which would happen, he was sure.

He decided that the Russians were on some sort of fishing expedition. His job was to show them that the fish in these waters were dangerous.

Naval Air Station, North Island, California

The oversized tractor-trailer crept at two miles per hour into the cargo bay of the C-5A Galaxy transport under the watchful eyes of the aircraft's loadmaster, two flight officers, and six naval officers. Oddly, only the latter, none of whom wore aviator's wings, were fully versed in the procedure. The vehicle's center of gravity was precisely marked, and they watched the mark approach a particular number engraved on the cargo bay floor. The work had to be done exactly. Any mistake could fatally impair the aircraft's trim and imperil the lives of the flight crew and passengers.

"Okay, freeze it right there," the senior officer called. The driver was only too glad to stop. He left the keys in the ignition, set all the brakes, and put the truck in gear before getting out. Someone else would drive it out of the aircraft on the other side of the country. The loadmaster and six airmen immediately went to work, snaking steel cables to eyebolts on the truck and trailer to secure the heavy load. Shifting cargo was something else an aircraft rarely survived, and the C-5A did not have ejection seats.

The loadmaster saw to it that his ground crewmen were properly at work before walking over to the pilot. He was a twenty-five-year sergeant who loved the C-5s despite their blemished history.

"Cap'n, what the hell is this thing?"

"It's called a DSRV, Sarge, deep submergence rescue vehicle."

"Says *Avalon* on the back, sir," the sergeant pointed out.

"Yeah, so it has a name. It's a sort of a lifeboat for submarines. Goes down to get the crew out if something screws up."

"Oh." The sergeant considered that. He'd flown tanks, helicopters, general cargo, once a whole battalion of troops on his—he thought of the aircraft as his—Galaxy before. This was the first time he had ever flown a ship. If it had a name, he reasoned, it was a ship. Damn, the Galaxy could do anything! "Where we takin' it, sir?"

"Norfolk Naval Air Station, and I've never been there either." The pilot watched the securing process closely. Already a dozen cables were attached. When a dozen more were in place, they'd put tension on the cables to prevent the minutest shift. "We figure a trip of five hours, forty minutes, all on internal fuel. We got the jet stream on our side today. Weather's supposed to be okay until we hit the coast. We lay over for a day, then come back Monday morning."

"Your boys work pretty fast," said the senior naval officer, Lieutenant Ames, coming over.

"Yes, Lieutenant, another twenty minutes." The pilot checked his watch. "We ought to be taking off on the hour."

"No hurry, Captain. If this thing shifts in flight, I guess it would ruin our whole day. Where do I send my people?"

"Upper deck forward. There's room for fifteen or so just aft of the flight deck." Lieutenant Ames knew this but didn't say so. He'd flown with his DSRV across the Atlantic several times and across the Pacific once, every time on a different C-5.

"May I ask what the big deal is?" the pilot inquired.

"I don't know," Ames said. "They want me and my baby in Norfolk."

"You really take that little bitty thing underwater, sir?" the loadmaster asked.

"That's what they pay me for. I've had her down to forty-eight hundred feet, almost a mile." Ames regarded his vessel with affection.

"A mile *under* water, sir? Jesus—uh, pardon me, sir, but I mean, isn't that a little hairy—the water pressure, I mean?"

"Not really. I've been down to twenty thousand aboard *Trieste*. It's really pretty interesting down there. You see all kinds of strange fish." Though a fully qualified submariner, Ames' first love was research. He had a degree in oceanography and had commanded or served in all of the navy's deep-submergence vehicles except the nuclear-powered *NR-1*. "Of course, the water pressure would do bad things to you if anything went wrong, but it would be so fast you'd never know it. If you fellows want a check ride, I could probably arrange it. It's a different world down there."

"That's okay, sir." The sergeant went back to swearing at his men.

"You weren't serious," the pilot observed.

"Why not? It's no big deal. We take civilians down all the time, and believe me, it's a lot less hairy than riding this damned white whale during a midair refueling."

"Uh-huh," the pilot noted dubiously. He'd done hundreds of those. It was entirely routine, and he was surprised that anyone would find it dangerous. You had to be careful, of course, but, hell, you had to be careful driving every morning. He was sure that an accident on this pocket submarine wouldn't leave enough of a man to make a decent meal for a shrimp. It takes all kinds, he decided. "You don't go to sea by yourself in that, do you?"

"No, ordinarily we work off a submarine rescue ship, *Pigeon* or *Ortolan*. We can also operate off a regular submarine. That gadget you see there on the trailer is our mating collar. We can nest on the back of a sub at the after escape trunk, and the sub takes us where we need to go."

"Does this have to do with the flap on the East Coast?"

"That's a good bet, but nobody's said anything official to us. The papers say the Russians have lost a sub. If so, we might go down to look at her, maybe rescue any survivors. We can take off twenty or twenty-five men at a time, and our mating collar is designed to fit Russian subs as well as our own."

"Same size?"

"Close enough." Ames cocked an eyebrow. "We plan for all kinds of contingencies."

"Interesting."

The North Atlantic

The YAK-36 Forger had left the *Kiev* half an hour before, guided first by gyro compass and now by the ESM pod on the fighter's stubby rudder fin. Senior Lieutenant Viktor Shavrov's mission was not an easy one. He was to approach the American E-3A Sentry radar surveillance aircraft, one of which had been shadowing his fleet for three days now. The AWACS (airborne warning and control system) aircraft had been careful to circle well beyond SAM range, but had stayed close enough to maintain constant coverage of the Soviet fleet, reporting every maneuver and radio transmission to their command base. It was like having a burglar watching one's apartment and being unable to do anything about it.

Shavrov's mission was to do something about it. He couldn't shoot, of course. His orders from Admiral Stralbo on the *Kirov* had been explicit about that. But he was carrying a pair of Atoll heat-seeking missiles which he would be sure to show the imperialists. He and his admiral expected that this would teach them a lesson: the Soviet Navy did not like having imperialist snoopers about, and accidents had been known to happen. It was a mission worthy of the effort it took.

This effort was considerable. To avoid detection by the airborne radar Shavrov had to fly as low and slow as his fighter could operate, a bare twenty meters above the rough Atlantic; this way he would get lost in the sea return. His speed was two hundred knots. This made for excellent fuel economy, though his mission was at the ragged edge of his fuel load. It also made for very rough flying as his fighter bounced through the roiled air at the wave tops. There was a low-hanging mist that cut visibility to a few kilometers. So much the better, he thought. The nature of the mission had chosen him, rather than the other way around. He was one of the few Soviet pilots experienced in low-level flying. Shavrov had not become a sailor-pilot by himself. He'd started flying attack helicopters for frontal aviation in Afghanistan, graduating to fixed-wing aircraft after a year's bloody apprenticeship. Shavrov was an expert in nap-of-the-earth flying, having learned it by necessity, hunting the bandits and counterrevolutionaries that hid in the towering mountains like hydrophobic rats. This skill had made him attractive to the fleet, which had transferred him to sea duty without his having had much say in the matter. After a few months he had no complaints, his perqs and extra pay being more attractive than his former frontal aviation base on the Chinese border. Being one of the few hundred carrier-qualified Soviet airmen had softened the blow of missing his chance to fly the new MiG-27, though with luck, if the new full-sized carrier were ever finished, he'd have the chance to fly the naval version of that wonderful bird. Shavrov could wait for that, and with a few successful missions like this one he might have his squadron command.

He stopped daydreaming—the mission was too demanding for that. This was real flying. He'd never flown against Americans, only against the weapons they gave to the Afghan bandits. He had lost friends to those weapons, some of whom had survived their crashes only to be done to death by the Afghan savages in ways that would have made even a German puke. It would be good to teach the imperialists a lesson personally.

The radar signal was growing stronger. Beneath his ejection seat a tape recorder was making a continuous record of the signal characteristics of the American aircraft so that the scientific people would be able to devise a means of jamming and foiling the vaunted American flying eye. The aircraft was only a converted 707, a glorified passenger plane, hardly a worthy opponent for a crack fighter pilot! Shavrov checked his chart. He'd have to find it soon. Next he checked his fuel. He'd dropped his last external tank a few minutes earlier, and all he had now was his internal fuel. The turbofan was guzzling fuel, something he had to keep an eye on. He planned to have only five or ten minutes of fuel left when he returned to his ship.

This did not trouble him. He already had over a hundred carrier landings.

There! His hawk's eyes caught the glint of sun off metal at one o'clock high. Shavrov eased back on his stick and increased power gently, bringing his Forger into a climb. A minute later he was at two thousand meters. He could see the Sentry now, its blue paint blending neatly into the darkening sky. He was coming up beneath its tail, and with luck the empennage would shield him from the rotating radar antenna. Perfect! He'd blaze by her a few times, letting the flight crew see his Atolls, and—

It took Shavrov a moment to realize that he had a wingman.

Two wingmen.

Fifty meters to his left and right, a pair of American F-15 Eagle fighters. The visored face of one pilot was staring at him.

"YAK-106, YAK-106, please acknowledge." The voice on the SSB (single side band) radio circuit spoke flawless Russian. Shavrov did not acknowledge. They had read the number off his engine intake housing before he had known they were there.

"106, 106, this is the Sentry aircraft you are now approaching. Please identify yourself and your intentions. We get a little anxious when a stray fighter comes our way, so we've had three following you for the past hundred kilometers."

Three? Shavrov turned his head around. A third Eagle with four sparrow missiles was hanging fifty meters from his tail, his "six."

"Our men compliment you on your ability to fly low and slow, 106."

Lieutenant Shavrov was shaking with rage as he passed four thousand meters, still eight thousand from the American AWACS. He had checked his six every thirty seconds on the way in. The Americans must have been riding back there, hidden in the mist, and vectored in on him by instructions from the Sentry. He swore to himself and held course. He'd teach that AWACS a lesson!

"Break off, 106." It was a cool voice, without emotion except perhaps a trace of irony. "106, if you do not break off, we will consider your mission to be hostile. Think about it, 106. You are beyond radar coverage of your own ships, and you are not yet within missile range of us."

Shavrov looked to his right. The Eagle was breaking off—
so was the one to the left. Was it a gesture, taking the heat off
of him and expecting some courtesy in return? Or were they
clearing the way for the one behind him—he checked, still
there—to shoot? There was no telling what these imperialist
criminals would do; he was at least a minute from the fringe
of their missile range. Shavrov was anything but a coward.
Neither was he a fool. He moved his stick, curving his fighter
a few degrees to the right.

"Thank you, 106," the voice acknowledged. "You see, we
have some trainee operators aboard. Two of them are women,
and we don't want them to get rattled their first time out."
Suddenly it was too much. Shavrov thumbed the radio switch
on his stick.

"Shall I tell you what you can do with your women, Yankee?"

"You are *nekulturny*, 106," the voice replied softly. "Perhaps
the long overwater flight has made you nervous. You must be
about at the limit of your internal fuel. Bastard of a day to fly,
what with all these crazy, shifting winds. Do you need a position
check, over?"

"Negative, Yankee!"

"Course back to *Kiev* is one-eight-five, true. Have to be
careful using a magnetic compass this far north, you know.
Distance to *Kiev* is 318.6 kilometers. Warning—there is a
rapidly moving cold front moving in from the southwest. That's
going to make flying a little rough in a few hours. Do you
require an escort back to *Kiev?*"

"Pig!" Shavrov swore to himself. He switched his radio off,
cursing himself for his lack of discipline. He had allowed the
Americans to wound his pride. Like most fighter pilots, he had
a surfeit of that.

"106, we did not copy your last transmission. Two of my
Eagles are heading that way. They will form up on you and
see that you get home safely. Have a happy day, Comrade.
Sentry-November, out."

The American lieutenant turned to his colonel. He couldn't
keep a straight face any longer. "God, I thought I'd strangle
talking like that!" He sipped some Coke from a plastic cup.
"He really thought he'd sneak up on us."

"In case you didn't notice, he did get within a mile of Atoll range, and we don't have authorization to shoot at him until he flips one at us—which might wreck our day," the colonel grumped. "Nice job of twisting his tail, Lieutenant."

"A pleasure, Colonel." The operator looked at his screen. "Well, he's heading back to momma, with Cobras 3 and 4 on his six. He's going to be one unhappy Russkie when he gets home. If he gets home. Even with those drop tanks, he must be near his range limit." He thought for a moment. "Colonel, if they do this again, how 'bout we offer to take the guy home with us?"

"Get a Forger—what for? I suppose the navy'd like to have one to play with, they don't get much of Ivan's hardware, but the Forger's a piece of junk."

Shavrov was tempted to firewall his engine but restrained himself. He'd already shown enough personal weakness for one day. Besides, his YAK could only break Mach 1 in a dive. Those Eagles could do it straight up, and they had plenty of fuel. He saw that they both carried FAST-pack comformal fuel cells. They could cross whole oceans with those. Damn the Americans and their arrogance! Damn his own intelligence officer for telling him he could sneak up on the Sentry! Let the air-to-air armed Backfires go after them. They could handle that famed overbred passenger bus, could get to it faster than its fighter guardians could react.

The Americans, he saw, were not lying about the weather front. A line of cold weather squawls racing northeast was just on the horizon as he approached the *Kiev*. The Eagles backed off as he approached the formation. One American pilot pulled alongside briefly to wave goodbye. His head bobbed at Shavrov's return gesture. The Eagles paired up and turned back north.

Five minutes later he was aboard the *Kiev*, still pale with rage. As soon as the wheels were choked he jumped to the carrier deck, stomping off to see his squadron commander.

The Kremlin

The city of Moscow was justly famous for its subway system. For a pittance, people could ride nearly anywhere they wanted

on a modern, safe, garishly decorated electric railway system.
In case of war, the underground tunnels could serve as a bomb
shelter for the citizens of Moscow. This secondary use was the
result of the efforts of Nikita Khrushchev, who when construction was begun in the mid-thirties had suggested to Stalin that the
system be driven deep. Stalin had approved. The shelter con-
sideration had been decades ahead of its time; nuclear fission
had then only been a theory, fusion hardly thought of at all.

On a spur of the line running from Sverdlov Square to the
old airport, which ran near the Kremlin, workers bored a tunnel
that was later closed off with a ten-meter-thick steel and concrete plug. The hundred-meter-long space was connected to
the Kremlin by a pair of elevator shafts, and over time it had
been converted to an emergency command center from which
the Politburo could control the entire Soviet empire. The tunnel
was also a convenient means of going unseen from the city to
a small airport from which Politburo members could be flown
to their ultimate redoubt, beneath the granite monolith at Zhiguli. Neither command post was a secret to the West—both
had existed far too long for that—but the KGB confidently
reported that nothing in the Western arsenals could smash through
the hundreds of feet of rock which in both places separated the
Politburo from the surface.

This fact was of little comfort to Admiral Yuri Ilych Padorin.
He found himself seated at the far end of a ten-meter-long
conference table looking at the grim faces of the ten Politburo
members, the inner circle that alone made the strategic decisions affecting the fate of his country. None of them were
officers. Those in uniform reported to these men. Up the table
to his left was Admiral Sergey Gorshkov, who had disassociated
himself from this affair with consummate skill, even producing
a letter in which he had opposed Ramius' appointment to command the *Red October*. Padorin, as chief of the Main Political
Administration, had successfully blocked Ramius' transfer,
pointing out that Gorshkov's candidate for command was occasionally late in paying his Party dues and did not speak up
at the regular meetings often enough for an officer of his rank.
The truth was that Gorshkov's candidate was not so proficient
an officer as Ramius, whom Gorshkov had wanted for his own
operations staff, a post that Ramius had successfully evaded
for years.

Party General Secretary and President of the Union of Soviet Socialist Republics Andre Narmonov shifted his gaze to Padorin. His face gave nothing away. It never did, unless he wished it to—which was rare enough. Narmonov had succeeded Andropov when the latter had suffered a heart attack. There were rumors about that, but in the Soviet Union there are always rumors. Not since the days of Laventri Beria had the security chieftain come so close to power, and senior Party officials had allowed themselves to forget that. It would not be forgotten again. Bringing the KGB to heel had taken a year, a necessary measure to secure the privileges of the Party elite from the supposed reforms of the Andropov clique.

Narmonov was the apparatchik par excellence. He had first gained prominence as a factory manager, an engineer with a reputation for fulfilling his quota early, a man who produced results. He had risen steadily by using his own talents and those of others, rewarding those he had to, ignoring those he could. His position as general secretary of the Communist Party was not entirely secure. It was still early in his stewardship of the Party, and he depended on a loose coalition of colleagues— not friends, these men did not make friends. His succession to this chair had resulted more from ties within the Party structure than from personal ability, and his position would depend on consensus rule for years, until such time as his will could dictate policy.

Narmonov's dark eyes, Padorin could see, were red from tobacco smoke. The ventilation system down here had never worked properly. The general secretary squinted at Padorin from the other end of the table as he decided what to say, what would please the members of this cabal, these ten old, passionless men.

"Comrade Admiral," he began coldly, "we have heard from Comrade Gorshkov what the chances are of finding and destroying this rebellious submarine before it can complete its unimaginable crime. We are not pleased. Nor are we pleased with the fantastic error in judgment that gave command of our most valuable ship to this slug. What I want to know from you, Comrade, is what happened to the *zampolit* aboard, and what security measures were taken by your office to prevent this infamy from taking place!"

There was no fear in Narmonov's voice, but Padorin knew

it had to be there. This "fantastic error" could ultimately be laid at the chairman's feet by members who wanted another in that chair—unless he were able somehow to separate himself from it. If this meant Padorin's skin, that was the admiral's problem. Narmonov had had men flayed before.

Padorin had prepared himself for this over several days. He was a man who had lived through months of intensive combat operations and had several boats sunk from under him. If his body was softer now, his mind was not. Whatever his fate might be, Padorin was determined to meet it with dignity. *If they remember me as a fool,* he thought, *it will be as a courageous fool.* He had little left to live for in any case. "Comrade General Secretary," he began, "the political officer aboard *Red October* was Captain Ivan Yurievich Putin, a stalwart and faithful Party member. I cannot imagine—"

"Comrade Padorin," Defense Minister Ustinov interrupted, "we presume that you also could not imagine the unbelievable treachery of this Ramius. You now expect us to trust your judgment on this man also?"

"The most disturbing thing of all," added Mikhail Alexandrov, the Party theoretician who had replaced the dead Mikhail Suslov and was even more determined than the departed ideologue to be simon-pure on Party doctrine, "is how tolerant the Main Political Administration has been toward this renegade. It is amazing, particularly in view of his obvious efforts to construct his own personality cult throughout the submarine service, even in the political arm, it would seem. Your criminal willingness to overlook this—this *obvious* aberration from Party policy—does not make your judgment appear very sound."

"Comrades, you are correct in judging that I erred badly in approving Ramius for command, and also that we allowed him to select most of *Red October*'s senior officers. At the same time, we chose some years ago to do things in this way, to keep officers associated with a single ship for many years, and to give the captain great sway over their careers. This is an operational question, not a political one."

"We have already considered that," Narmonov replied. "It is true that in this case there is enough blame for more than one man." Gorshkov didn't move, but the message was explicit: his effort to separate himself from this scandal had failed.

Narmonov didn't care how many heads it took to prop up his chair.

"Comrade Chairman," Gorshkov objected, "the efficiency of the fleet—"

"Efficiency?" Alexandrov said. "Efficiency. This Lithuanian half-breed is *efficiently* making fools of our fleet with his chosen officers while our remaining ships blunder about like newly castrated cattle." Alexandrov alluded to his first job on a state farm. A fitting beginning, it was generally thought, for the man who held the position of chief ideologue was as popular in Moscow as the plague, but the Politburo had to have him or one like him. The ideological chieftain was always the kingmaker. Whose side was he on now—in addition to his own?

"The most likely explanation is that Putin was murdered," Padorin continued. "He alone of the officers left behind a wife and family."

"That's another question, Comrade Admiral." Narmonov seized this issue. "Why is it that none of these men are married? Didn't that tell you something? Must we of the Politburo supervise everything? Can't you think for yourselves?"

As if you want us to, Padorin thought. "Comrade General Secretary, most of our submarine commanders prefer young, unmarried officers in their wardrooms. Duty at sea is demanding, and single men have fewer distractions. Moreover, each of the senior officers aboard is a Party member in good standing with a praiseworthy record. Ramius has been treacherous, there is no denying that, and I would gladly kill the son of a bitch with my own hands—but he has deceived more good men than there are in this room."

"Indeed," Alexandrov observed. "And now that we are in this mess, how do we get out of it?"

Padorin took a deep breath. He'd been waiting for this. "Comrades, we have another man aboard *Red October*, unknown to either Putin or Captain Ramius, an agent of the Main Political Administration."

"What?" Gorshkov said. "And why did I not know of this?"

Alexandrov smiled. "That's the first intelligent thing we've heard today. Go on."

"This individual is covered as an enlisted man. He reports

directly to our office, bypassing all operational and political channels. His name is Igor Loginov. He is twenty-four, a—"

"*Twenty-four!*" Narmonov shouted. "You trust a child with this responsibility?"

"Comrade, Loginov's mission is to blend in with the conscripted crewmen, to listen in on conversations, to identify likely traitors, spies, and saboteurs. In truth he looks younger still. He serves alongside young men, and he must be young himself. He is, in fact, a graduate of the higher naval school for political officers at Kiev and the GRU intelligence academy. He is the son of Arkady Ivanovich Loginov, chief of the Lenin Steel Plant at Kazan. Many of you here know his father." Narmonov was among those who nodded, a flickering of interest in his eyes. "Only an elite few are chosen for this duty. I have met and interviewed this boy myself. His record is clear, he is a Soviet patriot without question."

"I know his father," Narmonov confirmed. "Arkady Ivanovich is an honorable man who has raised several good sons. What are this boy's orders?"

"As I said, Comrade General Secretary, his ordinary duties are to observe the crewmen and report on what he sees. He's been doing this for two years, and he is good at it. He does not report to the *zampolit* aboard, but only to Moscow or to one of my representatives. In a genuine emergency, his orders are to report to the *zampolit*. If Putin is alive—and I do not believe this, comrades—he would be part of the conspiracy, and Loginov would know not to do this. In a true emergency, therefore, his orders are to destroy the ship and make his escape."

"This is possible?" Narmonov asked. "Gorshkov?"

"Comrades, all of our ships carry powerful scuttling charges, submarines especially."

"Unfortunately," Padorin said, "these are generally not armed, and only the captain can activate them. Ever since the incident on *Storozhevoy*, we in the Main Political Administration have had to consider that an incident such as this one was indeed a possibility, and that its most damaging manifestation would involve a missile-carrying submarine."

"Ah," Narmonov observed, "he is a missile mechanic."

"No, Comrade, he is a ship's cook," Padorin replied.

"Wonderful! He spends all his day boiling potatoes!" Narmonov's hands flew up in the air, his hopeful demeanor gone in an instant, replaced with palpable wrath. "You wish your bullet now, Padorin?"

"Comrade Chairman, this is a better cover assignment than you may imagine." Padorin did not flinch, wanting to show these men what he was made of. "On *Red October* the officers' accommodations and galley are aft. The crew's quarters are forward—the crew eat there since they do not have a separate messroom—with the missile room in between. As a cook he must travel back and forth many times each day, and his presence in any particular area will not be thought unusual. The food freezer is located adjacent to the lower missile deck forward. It is not our plan that he should activate the scuttling charges. We have allowed for the possibility that the captain could disarm them. Comrades, these measures have been carefully thought out."

"Go on," Narmonov grunted.

"As Comrade Gorshkov explained earlier, *Red October* carries twenty-six Seahawk missiles. These are solid-fuel rockets, and one has a range-safety package installed."

"Range safety?" Narmonov was puzzled.

Up to this point the other military officers at the meeting, none of them Politburo members, had kept their peace. Padorin was surprised when General V.M. Vishenkov, commander of the Strategic Rocket Forces, spoke up. "Comrades, these details were worked out through my office some years ago. As you know, when we test our missiles, we have safety packages aboard to explode them if they go off course. Otherwise they might land on one of our own cities. Our operational missiles do not ordinarily carry them—for the obvious reason, the imperialists might learn a way to explode them in flight."

"So, our young GRU comrade will blow up the missile. What of the warheads?" Narmonov asked. An engineer by training, he could always be distracted by technical discourse, always impressed by a clever one.

"Comrade," Vishenkov went on, "the missile warheads are armed by accelerometers. Thus they cannot be armed until the missile reaches its full programmed speed. The Americans use the same system, and for the same reason, to prevent sabotage. These safety systems are absolutely reliable. You could drop one of the reentry vehicles from the top of the Moscow television transmitter onto a steel plate and it would not fire." The general referred to the massive TV tower whose construction Narmonov had personally supervised while head of the Central Communications Directorate. Vishenkov was a skilled political operator.

"In the case of a solid-fuel rocket," Padorin continued, recognizing his debt to Vishenkov, wondering what he'd ask for in return, and hoping he'd live long enough to deliver, "a safety package ignites all of the missile's three stages simultaneously."

"So the missile just takes off?" Alexandrov asked.

"No, Comrade Academician. The upper stage might, if it could break through the missile tube hatch, and this would flood the missile room, sinking the submarine. But even if it did not, there is sufficient thermal energy in either of the first two stages to reduce the entire submarine to a puddle of molten iron, twenty times what is necessary to sink it. Loginov has been trained to bypass the alarm system on the missile tube hatch, to activate the safety package, set a timer, and escape."

"Not just to destroy the ship?" Narmonov asked.

"Comrade General Secretary," Padorin said, "it is too much to ask a young man to do his duty, knowing that it means certain death. We would be unrealistic to expect this. He must have at least the possibility of escape, otherwise human weakness might lead to failure."

"This is reasonable," Alexandrov said. "Young men are motivated by hope, not fear. In this case, young Loginov would hope for a considerable reward."

"And get it," Narmonov said. "We will make every effort to save this young man, Gorshkov."

"If he is truly reliable," Alexandrov noted.

"I know that my life depends on this, Comrade Academician," Padorin said, his back still straight. He did not get a verbal answer, only nods from half the heads at the table. He had faced death before and was at the age where it remains the last thing a man need face.

The White House

Arbatov came into the Oval Office at 4:50 P.M. He found the president and Dr. Pelt sitting in easy chairs across from the chief executive's desk.

"Come on over, Alex. Coffee?" The president pointed to a tray on the corner of his desk. He was not drinking today, Arbatov noted.

"No, thank you, Mr. President. May I ask—"

"We think we found your sub, Alex," Pelt answered. "They just brought these dispatches over, and we're checking them now." The adviser held up a ring binder of message forms.

"Where is it, may I ask?" The ambassador's face was deadpan.

"Roughly three hundred miles northeast of Norfolk. We have not located it exactly. One of our ships noted an underwater explosion in the area—no, that's not right. It was recorded on a ship, and when the tapes were checked a few hours later, they thought they heard a submarine explode and sink. Sorry, Alex," Pelt said. "I should have known better than to read through all this stuff without an interpreter. Does your navy talk in its own language, too?"

"Officers do not like for civilians to understand them," Arbatov smiled. "This has doubtless been true since the first man picked up a stone."

"Anyway, we have ships and aircraft searching the area now."

The president looked up. "Alex, I talked to the chief of naval operations, Dan Foster, a few minutes ago. He said not to expect any survivors. The water there's over a thousand feet deep, and you know what the weather is like. They said it's right on the edge of the continental shelf."

"The Norfolk Canyon, sir," Pelt added.

"We are conducting a thorough search," the president continued. "The navy is bringing in some specialized rescue equipment, search gear, all that sort of thing. If the submarine is located, we'll get somebody down to them on the chance there might be survivors. From what the CNO tells me it is just possible that there might be if the interior partitions—bulkheads, I think he called them—are intact. The other question is their air supply, he said. Time is very much against us, I'm afraid. All this fantastically expensive equipment we buy them, and they can't locate one damned object right off our coast."

Arbatov made a mental record of these words. It would make a worthwhile intelligence report. The president occasionally let—

"By the way, Mr. Ambassador, what exactly was your submarine doing there?"

"I have no idea, Dr. Pelt."

"I trust it was not a missile sub," Pelt said. "We have an agreement to keep those five hundred miles offshore. The wreck will of course be inspected by our rescue craft. Were we to learn that it is indeed a missile sub..."

"Your point is noted. Still, those are international waters."

The president turned and spoke softly. "So is the Gulf of Finland, Alex, and, I believe, the Black Sea." He let this observation hang in the air for a moment. "I sincerely hope that we are not heading back to that kind of situation. Are we talking about a missile submarine, Alex?"

"Truly, Mr. President, I have no idea. Certainly I should hope not."

The president could see how carefully the lie was phrased. He wondered if the Russians would admit that there was a captain out there who had disregarded his orders. No, they would probably claim a navigation error.

"Very well. In any case, we will be conducting our own search and rescue operation. We'll know soon enough what sort of vessel we're talking about." The president looked suddenly uneasy. "One more thing Foster talked about. If we find bodies—pardon the crudity on a Saturday afternoon—I expect that you will want them returned to your country."

"I have had no instructions on this," the ambassador answered truthfully, caught off guard.

"It was explained to me in too much detail what a death like this does to a man. In simple terms, they're crushed by the water pressure, not a very pretty thing to see, they tell me. But they were men, and they deserve some dignity even in death."

Arbatov conceded the point. "If this is possible, then, I believe that the Soviet people would appreciate this humanitarian gesture."

"We'll do our best."

And the American best, Arbatov remembered, included a ship named the *Glomar Explorer*. This notorious exploration ship had been built by the CIA for the specific purpose of recovering a Soviet *Golf*-class missile submarine from the floor of the Pacific Ocean. She had been placed in storage, no doubt to await the next such opportunity. There would be nothing the Soviet Union could do to prevent the operation, a few hundred miles off the American coast, three hundred miles from the United States' largest naval base.

"I trust that the precepts of international law will be observed, gentlemen. That is, with respect to the vessel's remains and the crew's bodies."

"Of-course, Alex." The president smiled, gesturing to a memorandum on his desk. Arbatov struggled for control. He'd been led down this path like a schoolboy, forgetting that the American president had been a skilled courtroom tactician—not something that life in the Soviet Union prepares a man for—and knew all about legal tricks. Why was this bastard so easy to underestimate?

The president was also struggling to control himself. It was not often that he saw Alex flustered. This was a clever opponent, not easily caught off balance. Laughing would spoil it.

The memorandum from the attorney general had arrived only that morning. It read:

Mr. President,

Pursuant to your request, I have asked the chief of our admiralty law department to review the question of international law regarding the ownership of sunken or derelict vessels, and the law of salvage pertaining to such vessels. There is a good deal of case law on the subject. One simple example is *Dalmas v Stathos* (84FSuff. 828, 1949 A.M.C. 770 [S.D.N.Y. 1949]):

No problem of foreign law is here involved, for it is well settled that "salvage is a question arising out of the *jus gentium* and does not ordinarily depend on the municipal law of particular countries."

The international basis for this is the Salvage Convention of 1910 (Brussels), which codified the transnational nature of admiralty and salvage law. This was ratified by the United States in the Salvage Act of

1912, 37 Stat. 242, (1912), 46 U.S.C.A. §§ 727-731;
and also in 37 Stat. 1658 (1913).

"International law will be observed, Alex," the president
promised. "In all particulars." And whatever we get, he thought,
will be taken to the nearest port, Norfolk, where it will be
turned over to the receiver of wrecks, an overworked federal
official. If the Soviets want anything back, they can bring action
in admiralty court, which means the federal district court sitting
in Norfolk, where, if the suit were successful—*after* the value
of the salvaged property was determined, and *after* the U.S.
Navy was paid a proper fee for its salvage effort, also determined by the court—the wreck would be returned to its rightful
owners. Of course, the federal district court in question had,
at last check, an eleven-month backlog of cases.

Arbatov would cable Moscow on this. For what good it
would do. He was certain the president would take perverse
pleasure in manipulating the grotesque American legal system
to his own advantage, all the time pointing out that, as president, he was constitutionally unable to interfere with the working of the courts.

Pelt looked at his watch. It was about time for the next
surprise. He had to admire the president. For a man with only
limited knowledge of international affairs only a few years
earlier, he'd learned fast. This outwardly simple, quiet-talking
man was at his best in face to face situations, and after a
lifetime's experience as a prosecutor, he still loved to play the
game of negotiation and tactical exchange. He seemed able to
manipulate people with frighteningly casual skill. The phone
rang and Pelt got it, right on cue.

"This is Dr. Pelt speaking. Yes, Admiral—where? When?
Just one? I see . . . Norfolk? Thank you, Admiral, that is very
good news. I will inform the president immediately. Please
keep us advised." Pelt turned around. "We got one, alive, by
God!"

"A survivor off the lost sub?" The president stood.

"Well, he's a Russian sailor. A helicopter picked him up an
hour ago, and they're flying him to the Norfolk base hospital.
They picked him up 290 miles northeast of Norfolk, so I guess
that makes it fit. The men on the ship say he's in pretty bad
shape, but the hospital is ready for him."

The president walked to his desk and lifted the phone. "Grace, ring me Dan Foster right now . . . Admiral, this is the president. The man they picked up, how soon to Norfolk? Another two hours?" He grimaced. "Admiral, you get on the phone to the naval hospital, and you tell them that *I* say they are to do everything they can for that man. I want him treated like he was my own son, is that clear? Good. I want hourly reports on his condition. I want the best people we have in on this, the very best. Thank you, Admiral." He hung up. "All right!"

"Maybe we were too pessimistic, Alex," Pelt chirped up.

"Certainly," the president answered. "You have a doctor at the embassy, don't you?"

"Yes, we do, Mr. President."

"Take him down, too. He'll be extended every courtesy. I'll see to that. Jeff, are they searching for other survivors?"

"Yes, Mr. President. There's a dozen aircraft in the area right now, and two more ships on the way."

"Good!" The president clapped his hands together, enthusiastic as a kid in a toystore. "Now, if we can find some more survivors, maybe we can give your country a meaningful Christmas present, Alex. We will do everything we can, you have my word on that."

"That is very kind of you, Mr. President. I will communicate this happy news to my country at once."

"Not so fast, Alex." The chief executive held his hand up. "I'd say this calls for a drink."

THE TENTH DAY

SUNDAY, 12 DECEMBER

SOSUS Control

At SOSUS Control in Norfolk, the picture was becoming increasingly difficult. The United States simply did not have the technology to keep track of submarines in the deep ocean basins. The SOSUS receptors were principally laid at shallow-water choke points, on the bottom of undersea ridges and highlands. The strategy of the NATO countries was a direct consequence of this technological limitation. In a major war with the Soviets, NATO would use the Greenland–Iceland–United Kingdom SOSUS barrier as a huge tripwire, a burglar alarm system. Allied submarines and ASW patrol aircraft would try to seek out, attack, and destroy Soviet submarines as they approached it, before they could cross the lines.

The barrier had never been expected to halt more than half of the attacking submarines, however, and those that succeeded in slipping through would have to be handled differently. The deep ocean basins were simply too wide and too deep—the

average depth was over two miles—to be littered with sensors
as the shallow choke points were. This was a fact that cut both
ways. The NATO mission would be to maintain the Atlantic
Bridge and continue transoceanic trade, and the obvious Soviet
mission would be to interdict this trade. Submarines would
have to spread out over the vast ocean to cover the many
possible convoy routes. NATO strategy behind the SOSUS
barriers, then, was to assemble large convoys, each ringed with
destroyers, helicopters, and fixed-wing aircraft. The escorts
would try to establish a protective bubble about a hundred miles
across. Enemy submarines would not be able to exist within
that bubble; if in it they would be hunted down and killed—
or merely driven off long enough for the convoy to speed past.
Thus while SOSUS was designed to neutralize a huge, fixed ex-
panse of sea, deep-basin strategy was founded on mobility, a
moving zone of protection for the vital North Atlantic shipping.

This was an altogether sensible strategy, but one that could
not be tested under realistic conditions, and, unfortunately, one
that was largely useless at the moment. With all of the Soviet
*Alfa*s and *Victor*s already on the coast, and the last of the
*Charlie*s, *Echoe*s, and *November*s just arriving on their stations,
the master screen Commander Quentin was staring at was no
longer filled with discrete little red dots but rather with large
circles. Each dot or circle designated the position of a Soviet
submarine. A circle respresented an estimated position, calculated from the speed with which a sub could move without
giving off enough noise to be localized by the many sensors
being employed. Some circles were ten miles across, some as
much as fifty; an area anywhere from seventy-eight to two
thousand square miles had to be searched if the submarine were
again to be pinned down. And there were just too damned
many of the boats.

Hunting the submarines was principally the job of the P-3C
Orion. Each Orion carried sonobuoys, air-deployable active
and passive sonar sets that were dropped from the belly of the
aircraft. On detecting something, a sonobuoy reported to its
mother aircraft and then automatically sank lest it fall into
unfriendly hands. The sonobuoys had limited electrical power
and thus limited range. Worse, their supply was finite. The
sonobuoy inventory was already being depleted alarmingly, and
soon they would have to cut back on expenditures. Additionally,

each P-3C carried FLIRs, forward-looking infrared scanners, to identify the heat signature of a nuclear sub, and MADs, magnetic anomaly detectors that located the disturbance in the earth's magnetic field caused by a large chunk of ferrous metal like a submarine. MAD gear could only detect a magnetic disturbance six hundred yards to the left and right of an aircraft's course track, and to do this the aircraft had to fly low, consuming fuel and limiting the crew's visual search range. FLIR had roughly the same limitation.

Thus the technology used to localize a target first detected by SOSUS, or to "delouse" a discrete piece of ocean preparatory to the passage of a convoy, simply was not up to a random search of the deep ocean.

Quentin leaned forward. A circle had just changed to a dot. A P-3C had just dropped an explosive sounding charge and localized an *Echo*-class attack sub five hundred miles south of the Grand Banks. For an hour they had a near-certain shooting solution on that *Echo;* her name was written on the Orion's Mark 46 ASW torpedoes.

Quentin sipped at his coffee. His stomach rebelled at the additional caffeine, remembering the abuse of four months of hellish chemotherapy. If there were to be a war, this was one way it might start. All at once, their submarines would stop, perhaps just like this. Not sneaking to kill convoys in midocean but attacking them closer to shore, the way the Germans had done . . . and all the American sensors would be in the wrong place. Once stopped the dots would grow to circles, ever wider, making the task of finding the subs all the more difficult. Their engines quiet, the boats would be invisible traps for the passing merchant vessels and warships racing to bring life-saving supplies to the men in Europe. Submarines were like cancer. Just like the disease that he had only barely defeated. The invisible, malignant vessels would find a place, stop to infect it, and on his screen the malignancies would grow until they were attacked by the aircraft he controlled from this room. But he could not attack them now. Only watch.

"PK EST 1 HOUR—RUN," he typed into his computer console.

"23," the computer answered at once.

Quentin grunted. Twenty-four hours earlier the PK, probability of a kill, had been forty—forty probable kills in the

first hour after getting a shooting authorization. Now it was
barely half that, and this number had to be taken with a large
grain of salt, since it assumed that everything would work, a
happy state of affairs found only in fiction. Soon, he judged,
the number would be under ten. This did not include kills from
friendly submarines that were trailing the Russians under strict
orders not to reveal their positions. His sometime allies in the
*Sturgeon*s, *Permit*s, and *Los Angeles*es were playing their own
ASW game by their own set of rules. A different breed. He
tried to think of them as friends, but it never quite worked. In
his twenty years of naval service submarines had always been
the enemy. In war they would be useful enemies, but in a war
it was widely recognized that there was no such thing as a
friendly submarine.

A B-52

The bomber crew knew exactly where the Russians were. Navy
Orions and air force Sentries had been shadowing them for
days now, and the day before, he'd been told, the Soviets had
sent an armed fighter from the *Kiev* to the nearest Sentry.
Possibly an attack mission, probably not, it had in any case
been a provocation.

Four hours earlier the squadron of fourteen had flown out
of Plattsburg, New York, at 0330, leaving behind black trails
of exhaust smoke hidden in the predawn gloom. Each aircraft
carried a full load of fuel and twelve missiles whose total weight
was far less than the -52's design bombload. This made for
good, long range.

Which was exactly what they needed. Knowing where the
Russians were was only half the battle. Hitting them was the
other. The mission profile was simple in concept, rather more
difficult in execution. As had been learned in missions over
Hanoi—in which the B-52 had participated and sustained SAM
(surface-to-air missile) damage—the best method of attacking
a heavily defended target was to converge from all points of
the compass at once, "like the enveloping arms of an angry
bear," the squadron commander had put it at the briefing, in-
dulging his poetic nature. This gave half the squadron relatively
direct courses to their target; the other half had to curve around,

careful to keep well beyond effective radar coverage; all had to turn exactly on cue.

The B-52s had turned ten minutes earlier, on command from the Sentry quarterbacking the mission. The pilot had added a twist. His course to the Soviet formation took his bomber right down a commercial air route. On making his turn, he had switched his IFF transponder from its normal setting to international. He was fifty miles behind a commercial 747, thirty miles ahead of another, and on Soviet radar all three Boeing products would look exactly alike—harmless.

It was still dark down on the surface. There was no indication that the Russians were alerted yet. Their fighters were only supposed to be VFR (visual flight rules) capable, and the pilot imagined that taking off and landing on a carrier in the dark was pretty risky business, doubly so in bad weather.

"Skipper," the electronic warfare officer called on the intercom, "we're getting L- and S-band emissions. They're right where they're supposed to be."

"Roger. Enough for a return off us?"

"That's affirm, but they probably think we're flying Pan Am. No fire control stuff yet, just routine air search."

"Range to target?"

"One-three-zero miles."

It was almost time. The mission profile was such that all would hit the 125-mile circle at the same moment.

"Everything ready?"

"That's a roge."

The pilot relaxed for another minute, waiting for the signal from the entry.

"FLASHLIGHT, FLASHLIGHT, FLASHLIGHT." The signal came over the digital radio channel.

"That's it! Let 'em know we're here," the aircraft commander ordered.

"Right." The electronic warfare officer flipped the clear plastic cover off his set of toggle switches and dials controlling the aircraft's jamming systems. First he powered up his systems. This took a few seconds. The -52's electronics were all old seventies-vintage equipment, else the squadron would not be part of the junior varsity. Good learning tools, though, and the lieutenant was hoping to move up to the new B-1Bs now beginning to come off the Rockwell assembly line in California. For the past ten minutes the ESM pods on the bomber's nose and wingtips had been recording the Soviet radar signals, classifying their exact frequencies, pulse repetition rates, power, and the individual signature characteristics of the transmitters. The lieutenant was brand new to this game. He was a recent graduate of electronic warfare school, first in his class. He considered what he should do first, then selected a jamming mode, not his best, from a range of memorized options.

The Nikolayev

One hundred twenty-five miles away on the *Kara*-class cruiser *Nikolayev,* a radar *michman* was examining some blips that seemed to be in a circle around his formation. In an instant his screen was covered with twenty ghostly splotches tracing crazily in various directions. He shouted the alarm, echoed a second later by a brother operator. The officer of the watch hurried over to check the screen.

By the time he got there the jamming mode had changed and six lines like the spokes of a wheel were rotating slowly around a central axis.

"Plot the strobes," the officer ordered.

Now there were blotches, lines, and sparkles.

"More than one aircraft, Comrade." The *michman* tried flipping through his frequency settings.

"Attack warning!" another *michman* shouted. His ESM receiver had just reported the signals of aircraft search-radar sets of the type used to acquire targets for air-to-surface missiles.

The B-52

"We got hard targets," the weapons officer on the -52 reported. "I got a lock on the first three birds."

"Roger that," the pilot acknowledged. "Hold for ten more seconds."

"Ten seconds," the officer replied. "Cutting switches ... *now.*"

"Okay, kill the jamming."

"ECM systems off."

The Nikolayev

"Missile acquisition radars have ceased," the combat information center officer reported to the cruiser's captain, just now arrived from the bridge. Around them the *Nikolayev*'s crew was racing to battle stations. "Jamming has also ceased."

"What is out there?" the captain asked. Out of a clear sky his beautiful clipper-bowed cruiser had been threatened—and now all was well?

"At least eight enemy aircraft in a circle around us."

The captain examined the now normal S-band air search screen. There were numerous blips, mainly civilian aircraft. The half circle of others had to be hostile, though.

"Could they have fired missiles?"

"No, Comrade Captain, we would have detected it. They jammed our search radars for thirty seconds and illuminated us with their own search systems for twenty. Then everything stopped."

"So, they provoke us and now pretend nothing has happened?" the captain growled. "When will they be within SAM range?"

"This one and these two will be within range in four minutes if they do not change course."

"Illuminate them with our missile control systems. Teach the bastards a lesson."

The officer gave the necessary instructions, wondering who was being taught what. Two thousand feet above one of the B-52's was an EC-135 whose computerized electronic sensors were recording all signals from the Soviet cruiser and taking them apart, the better to know how to jam them. It was the first good look at the new SA-N-8 missile system.

Two F-14 Tomcats

The double-zero code number on its fuselage marked the Tomcat as the squadron commander's personal bird; the black ace of spades on the twin-rudder tail indicated his squadron, Fighting 41, "The Black Aces." The pilot was Commander Robby Jackson, and his radio call sign was Spade 1.

Jackson was leading a two-plane section under the direction

of one of the *Kennedy*'s E-2C Hawkeyes, the navy's more diminutive version of the air force's AWACS and close brother to the COD, a twin-prop aircraft whose radome makes it look like an airplane being terrorized by a UFO. The weather was bad—depressingly normal for the North Atlantic in December—but was supposed to improve as they headed west. Jackson and his wingman, Lieutenant (j.g.) Bud Sanchez, were flying through nearly solid clouds, and they had eased their formation out somewhat. In the limited visibility both remembered that each Tomcat had a crew of two and a price of over thirty million dollars.

They were doing what the Tomcat does best. An all-weather interceptor, the F-14 has transoceanic range, Mach 2 speed, and a radar computer fire control system that can lock onto and attack six separate targets with long-range Phoenix air-to-air missiles. Each fighter was now carrying two of those along with a pair each of AIM-9M Sidewinder heat-seekers. Their prey was a flight of YAK-36 Forgers, the bastard V/STOL fighters that operated from the carrier *Kiev*. After harassing the Sentry the previous day, Ivan had decided to close with the *Kennedy* force, no doubt guided in with data from a reconnaissance satellite. The Soviet aircraft had come up short, their range being fifty miles less than they needed to sight the *Kennedy*. Washington decided that Ivan was getting a little too obnoxious on this side of the ocean. Admiral Painter had been given permission to return the favor, in a friendly sort of way.

Jackson figured that he and Sanchez could handle this, even outnumbered. No Soviet aircraft, least of all the Forger, was equal to the Tomcat—certainly not while I'm flying it, Jackson thought.

"Spade 1, your target is at your twelve o'clock and level, distance now twenty miles," reported the voice of Hummer 1, the Hawkeye a hundred miles aft. Jackson did not acknowledge.

"Got anything, Chris?" he asked his radar intercept officer, Lieutenant Commander Christiansen.

"An occasional flash, but nothing I can use." They were tracking the Forgers with passive systems only, in this case an infrared sensor.

Jackson considered illuminating their targets with his powerful fire control radar. The Forgers' ESM pods would sense this at once, reporting to their pilots that their death warrant had been written but not yet signed. "How about *Kiev?*"

"Nothing. The *Kiev* group is under total EMCON."

"Cute," Jackson commented. He guessed that the SAC raid on the *Kirov-Nikolayev* group had taught them to be more careful. It was not generally known that warships often made no use whatever of their radar systems, a protective measure called EMCON, for emission control. The reason was that a radar beam could be detected at several times the distance at which it generated a return signal to its transmitter and could thus tell an enemy more than it told its operators. "You suppose these guys can find their way home without help?"

"If they don't, you know who's gonna get blamed." Christiansen chuckled.

"That's a roge," Jackson agreed.

"Okay, I got infrared acquisition. Clouds must be thinning out some." Christiansen was concentrating on his instruments, oblivious of the view out of the canopy.

"Spade 1, this is Hummer 1, your target is twelve o'clock, at your level, range now ten miles." The report came over the secure radio circuit.

Not bad, picking up the Forgers' heat signature through this slop, Jackson thought, especially since they had small, inefficient engines.

"Radar coming on, Skipper," Christiansen advised. "*Kiev* has an S-band air search just come on. They have us for sure."

"Right." Jackson thumbed his mike switch. "Spade 2, illuminate targets—now."

"Roger, lead," Sanchez acknowledged. No point hiding now.

Both fighters activated their powerful AN/AWG-9 radars. It was now two minutes to intercept.

The radar signals, received by the ESM threat-receivers on the Forgers' tail fins, set off a musical tone in the pilot headsets which had to be turned off manually, and lit up a red warning light on each control panel.

The Kingfisher Flight

"Kingfisher flight, this is *Kiev,*" called the carrier's air operations officer. "We show two American fighters closing you at high speed from the rear."

"Acknowledged." The Russian flight leader checked his mirror. He'd hoped to avoid this, though he hadn't expected to. His orders were to take no action unless fired upon. They had just broken into the clear. Too bad, he'd have felt safer in the clouds.

The pilot of Kingfisher 3, Lieutenant Shavrov, reached down to arm his four Atolls. Not this time, Yankee, he thought.

The Tomcats

"One minute, Spade 1, you ought to have visual any time," Hummer 1 called in.

"Roger . . . Tallyho!" Jackson and Sanchez broke into the clear. The Forgers were a few miles ahead, and the Tomcats' 250-knot speed advantage was eating that distance up rapidly. *The Russian pilots are keeping a nice, tight formation,* Jackson thought, *but anybody can drive a bus.*

"Spade 2, let's go to burners on my mark. Three, two, one—mark!"

Both pilots advanced their engine controls and engaged their afterburners, which dumped raw fuel into the tail pipes of their new F-110 engines. The fighters lept forward with a sudden double thrust and went quickly through Mach 1.

The Kingfisher Flight

"Kingfisher, warning, warning, the *Amerikantsi* have increased speed," *Kiev* cautioned.

Kingfisher 4 turned in his seat. He saw the Tomcats a mile aft, twin dart-like shapes racing before trails of black smoke. Sunlight glinted off one canopy, and it almost looked like the flashes of a—

"They're attacking!"

"What?" The flight leader checked his mirror again. "Negative, negative—hold formation!"

The Tomcats screeched fifty feet overhead, the sonic booms they trailed sounding just like explosions. Shavrov acted entirely on his combat-trained instincts. He jerked back on his stick and triggered his four missiles at the departing American fighters.

"Three, what did you do?" the Russian flight leader demanded.

"They were attacking us, didn't you hear?" Shavrov protested.

The Tomcats

"Oh shit! Spade Flight, you have four Atolls after you," the voice of the Hawkeye's controller said.

"Two, break right," Jackson ordered. "Chris, activate countermeasures." Jackson threw his fighter into a violent evasive turn to the left. Sanchez broke the other way.

In the seat behind Jackson's, the radar intercept officer flipped switches to activate the aircraft's defense systems. As the Tomcat twisted in midair, a series of flares and balloons was ejected from the tail section, each an infrared or radar lure for the pursuing missiles. All four were targeted on Jackson's fighter.

"Spade 2 is clear, Spade 2 is clear. Spade 1, you still have four birds in pursuit," the voice from the Hawkeye said.

"Roger." Jackson was surprised at how calmly he took it. The Tomcat was doing over eight hundred miles per hour and accelerating. He wondered how much range the Atoll had. His rearward-looking-radar warning light flicked on.

"Two, get after them!" Jackson ordered.

"Roger, lead." Sanchez swept into a climbing turn, fell off into a hammerhead, and dove at the retreating Soviet fighters.

When Jackson turned, two of the missiles lost lock and kept going straight into open air. A third, decoyed into hitting a flare, exploded harmlessly. The fourth kept its infrared seeker head on Spade 1's glowing tail pipes and bored right in. The missile struck the Spade 1 at the base of its starboard rudder fin.

The impact tossed the fighter completely out of control. Most of the explosive force was spent as the missile blasted through the boron surface into open air. The fin was blown completely off, along with the right-side stabilizer. The left fin was badly holed by fragments, which smashed through the back of the fighter's canopy, hitting Christiansen's helmet. The right engine's fire warning lights came on at once.

Jackson heard the *oomph* over his intercom. He killed every

engine switch on the right side and activated the in-frame fire
extinguisher. Next he chopped power to his port engine, still
on afterburner. By this time the Tomcat was in an inverted spin.
The variable-geometry wings angled out to low-speed configuration. This gave Jackson aileron control, and he worked
quickly to get back to normal attitude. His altitude was four
thousand feet. There wasn't much time.

"Okay, baby," he coaxed. A quick burst of power gave him
back aerodynamic control, and the former test pilot snapped
his fighter over—too hard. It went through two complete rolls
before he could catch it in level flight. "Gotcha! You with me,
Chris?"

Nothing. There was no way he could look around, and there
were still four hostile fighters behind him.

"Spade 2, this is lead."

"Roger, lead." Sanchez had the four Fighters bore-sighted.
They had just fired at his commander.

Hummer 1

On Hummer 1, the controller was thinking fast. The Forgers
were holding formation, and there was a lot of Russian chatter
on the radio circuit.

"Spade 2, this is Hummer 1, break off, I say again, break
off, do not, repeat do not fire. Acknowledge. Spade 2, Spade
1 is at your nine o'clock, two thousand feet below you." The
officer swore and looked at one of the enlisted men he worked
with.

"That was too fast, sir, just too fuckin' fast. We got tapes
of the Russkies. I can't understand it, but it sounds like *Kiev*
is right pissed."

"They're not the only ones," the controller said, wondering
if he had done the right thing calling Spade 2 off. It sure as
hell didn't feel that way.

The Tomcats

Sanchez' head jerked in surprise. "Roger, breaking off." His
thumb came off the switch. "Goddammit!" He pulled his stick

back, throwing the Tomcat into a savage loop. "Where are you, lead?"

Sanchez brought his fighter under Jackson's and did a slow circle to survey the visible damage.

"Fire's out, Skipper. Right side rudder and stabilizer are gone. Left side fin—shit, I can see through it, but it looks like it oughta hold together. Wait a minute. Chris is slumped over, Skipper. Can you talk to him?"

"Negative, I've tried. Let's go back home."

Nothing would have pleased Sanchez more than to blast the Forgers right out of the sky, and with his four missiles he could have done this easily. But like most pilots, he was highly disciplined.

"Roger, lead."

"Spade 1, this is Hummer 1, advise your condition, over."

"Hummer 1, we'll make it unless something else falls off. Tell them to have docs standing by. Chris is hurt. I don't know how bad."

It took an hour to get to the *Kennedy*. Jackson's fighter flew badly, would not hold course in any specific attitude. He had to adjust trim constantly. Sanchez reported some movement in the aft cockpit. Maybe it was just the intercom shot out, Jackson thought hopefully.

Sanchez was ordered to land first so that the deck would be cleared for Commander Jackson. On the final approach the Tomcat started to handle badly. The pilot struggled with his fighter, planting it hard on the deck and catching the number one wire. The right-side landing gear collapsed at once, and the thirty-million-dollar fighter slid sideways into the barrier that had been erected. A hundred men with fire-fighting gear raced toward it from all directions.

The canopy went up on emergency hydraulic power. After unbuckling himself Jackson fought his way around and tried to grab for his backseater. They had been friends for many years.

Chris was alive. It looked like a quart of blood had poured down the front of his flight suit, and when the first corpsman took the helmet off, he saw that it was still pumping out. The second corpsman pushed Jackson out of the way and attached a cervical collar to the wounded airman. Christiansen was lifted gently and lowered onto a stretcher whose bearers ran towards the island. Jackson hesitated a moment before following it.

Norfolk Naval Medical Center

Captain Randall Tait of the Navy Medical Corps walked down the corridor to meet with the Russians. He looked younger than his forty-five years because his full head of black hair showed not the first sign of gray. Tait was a Mormon, educated at Brigham Young University and Stanford Medical School, who had joined the navy because he had wanted to see more of the world than one could from an office at the foot of the Wasatch Mountains. He had accomplished that much, and until today had also avoided anything resembling diplomatic duty. As the new chief of the Department of Medicine at Bethesda Naval Medical Center he knew that couldn't last. He had flown down to Norfolk only a few hours earlier to handle the case. The Russians had driven down, and taken their time doing it.

"Good morning, gentlemen. I'm Dr. Tait." They shook hands all around, and the lieutenant who had brought them up walked back to the elevator.

"Dr. Ivanov," the shortest one said. "I am physician to the embassy."

"Captain Smirnov." Tait knew him to be assistant naval attaché, a career intelligence officer. The doctor had been briefed on the helicopter trip down by a Pentagon intelligence officer who was now drinking coffee in the hospital commissary.

"Vasily Petchkin, Doctor. I am second secretary to the embassy." This one was a senior KGB officer, a "legal" spy with a diplomatic cover. "May we see our man?"

"Certainly. Will you follow me please?" Tait led them back down the corridor. He'd been on the go for twenty hours. This was part of the territory as chief of service at Bethesda. He got all the hard calls. One of the first things a doctor learns is how not to sleep.

The whole floor was set up for intensive care, Norfolk Naval Medical Center having been built with war casualties in mind. Intensive Care Unit Number Three was a room twenty-five feet square. The only windows were on the corridor wall, and the curtains had been drawn back. There were four beds, only one occupied. The young man in it was almost totally concealed. The only thing not hidden by the oxygen mask covering his face was an unruly clump of wheat-colored hair. The rest of his body was fully draped. An IV stand was next to the bed, its two bottles of fluid merging in a single line that led under the covers. A nurse dressed like Tait in surgical greens was standing at the foot of the bed, her green eyes locked on the electrocardiograph readout over the patient's head, dropping momentarily to make a notation on his chart. On the far side of the bed was a machine whose function was not immediately obvious. The patient was unconscious.

"His condition?" Ivanov asked.

"Critical," Tait replied. "It's a miracle he got here alive at all. He was in the water for at least twelve hours, probably more like twenty. Even accounting for the fact that he was wearing a rubber exposure suit, given the ambient air and water temperatures there's just no way he ought to have been alive. On admission his core temperature was 23.8°C." Tait shook his head. "I've read about worse hypothermia cases in the literature, but this is by far the worst I've ever seen."

"Prognosis?" Ivanov looked into the room.

Tait shrugged. "Hard to say. Maybe as good as fifty-fifty, maybe not. He's still extremely shocky. He's a fundamentally healthy person. You can't see it from here, but he's in superb physical shape, like a track and field man. He has a particularly strong heart; that's probably what kept him alive long enough to get here. We have the hypothermia pretty much under control now. The problem is, with hypothermia so many things go wrong at once. We have to fight a number of separate but connected battles against different systemic enemies to keep them from overwhelming his natural defenses. If anything's going to kill him, it'll be the shock. We're treating that with electrolytes, the normal routine, but he's going to be on the edge for several days at least I—"

Tait looked up. Another man was pacing down the hall. Younger than Tait, and taller, he had a white lab coat over his greens. He carried a metal chart.

"Gentlemen, this is Doctor—Lieutenant—Jameson. He's the physician of record on the case. He admitted your man. What do you have, Jamie?"

"The sputum sample showed pneumonia. Bad news. Worse, his blood chemistry isn't getting any better, and his white count is *dropping*."

"Great." Tait leaned against the window frame and swore to himself.

"Here's the printout from the blood analyzer." Jameson handed the chart over.

"May I see this, please?" Ivanov came around.

"Sure." Tait flipped the metal cloud chart open and held it so that everyone could see it. Ivanov had never worked with a computerized blood analyzer, and it took several seconds for him to orient himself.

"This is not good."

"Not at all," Tait agreed.

"We're going to have to jump on that pneumonia, hard," Jameson said. "This kid's got too many things going wrong. If the pneumonia really takes hold . . ." He shook his head.

"Keflin?" Tait asked.

"Yeah." Jameson pulled a vial from his pocket. "As much as he'll handle. I'm guessing that he had a mild case before he got dumped in the water, and I hear that some penicillin-resistant strains have been cropping up in Russia. You use mostly penicillin over there, right?" Jameson looked down at Ivanov.

"Correct. What is this keflin?"

"It's a big gun, a synthetic antibiotic, and it works well on resistant strains."

"Right now, Jamie," Tait ordered.

Jameson walked around the corner to enter the room. He injected the antibiotic into a 100cc piggyback IV bottle and hung it on a stand.

"He's so young," Ivanov noted. "He treated our man initially?"

"His name's Albert Jameson. We call him Jamie. He's twenty-nine, graduated Harvard third in his class, and he's been with us ever since. He's board-certified in internal medicine and virology. He's as good as they come." Tait suddenly realized how uncomfortable he was dealing with the Russians. His education and years of naval service taught him that these men were the enemy. That didn't matter. Years before he had sworn

an oath to treat patients without regard to outside considerations. Would they believe or did they think he'd let their man
die because he was a Russian? "Gentlemen, I want you to
understand this: we're giving your man the very best care we
can. We're not holding anything back. If there's a way to give
him back to you alive, we'll find it. But I can't make any
promises."

The Soviets could see that. While waiting for instructions
from Moscow, Petchkin had checked up on Tait and found him
to be, though a religious fanatic, an efficient and honorable
physician, one of the best in government service.

"Has he said anything?" Petchkin asked, casually.

"Not since I've been here. Jamie said that right after they
started warming him up he was semiconscious and babbled for
a few minutes. We taped it, of course, and had a Russian-
speaking officer listen to it. Something about a girl with brown
eyes, didn't make any sense. Probably his sweetheart—he's a
good-looking kid, he probably has a girl at home. It was totally
incoherent, though. A patient in his condition has no idea what's
going on."

"Can we listen to the tape?" Petchkin said.

"Certainly. I'll have it sent up."

Jameson came around the corner. "Done. A gram of keflin
every six hours. Hope it works."

"How about his hands and feet?" Smirnov asked. The captain knew something about frostbite.

"We're not even bothering about that," Jameson answered.
"We have cotton around the digits to prevent maceration. If he
survives the next few days, we'll get blebs and maybe have
some tissue loss, but that's the least of our problems. You guys
know what his name is?" Petchkin's head snapped around. "He
wasn't wearing any dogtags when he arrived. His clothes didn't
have the ship's name. No wallet, no identification, not even
any coins in the pockets. It doesn't matter very much for his
initial treatment, but I'd feel better if you could pull his medical
records. It would be good to know if he has any allergies or
underlying medical conditions. We don't want him to go into
shock from an allergic reaction to drug treatment."

"What was he wearing?" Smirnov asked.

"A rubber exposure suit," Jameson answered. "The guys

who found him left it on him, thank God. I cut it off him when he arrived. Under that, shirt, pants, handerchief. Don't you guys wear dogtags?"

"Yes," Smirnov responded. "How did you find him?"

"From what I hear, it was pure luck. A helicopter off a frigate was patrolling and spotted him in the water. They didn't have any rescue gear aboard, so they marked the spot with a dye marker and went back to their ship. A bosun volunteered to go in after him. They loaded him and a raft cannister into the chopper and flew him back, with the frigate hustling down south. The bosun kicked out the raft, jumped in after it—and landed on it. Bad luck. He broke both his legs, but he did get your sailor into the raft. The tin can picked them up an hour later and they were both flown directly here."

"How is your man?"

"He'll be all right. The left leg wasn't too bad, but the right tibia was badly splintered," Jameson went on. "He'll recover in a few months. Won't be doing much dancing for a while, though."

The Russians thought the Americans had deliberately removed their man's identification. Jameson and Tait suspected that the man had disposed of his tags, possibly hoping to defect. There was a red mark on the neck that indicated forcible removal.

"If it is permitted," Smirnov said, "I would like to see your man, to thank him."

"Permission granted, Captain," Tait nodded. "That would be kind of you."

"He must be a brave man."

"A sailor doing his job. Your people would do the same thing." Tait wondered if this were true. "We have our differences, gentlemen, but the sea doesn't care about that. The sea—well, she tries to kill us all regardless what flag we fly."

Petchkin was back looking through the window, trying to make out the patient's face.

"Could we see his clothing and personal effects?" he asked.

"Sure, but it won't tell you much. He's a cook. That's all we know," Jameson said.

"A cook?" Petchkin turned around.

"The officer who listened in on the tape—obviously he was

an intelligence officer, right? He looked at the number on his shirt and said it made him a cook." The three-digit number indicated that the patient had been a member of the port watch, and that his battle station was damage control. Jameson wondered why the Russians numbered all their enlisted men. To be sure they didn't trespass? Petchkin's head, he noticed, was almost touching the glass pane.

"Dr. Ivanov, do you wish to attend the case?" Tait asked.

"Is this permitted?"

"It is."

"When will he be released?" Petchkin inquired. "When may we speak with him?"

"Released?" Jameson snapped. "Sir, the only way he'll be out of here in less than a month will be in a box. So far as consciousness is concerned, that's anyone's guess. That's one very sick kid you have in there."

"But we must speak to him!" the KGB agent protested.

Tait had to look up at the man. "Mr. Petchkin, I understand your desire to communicate with your man—but he is my patient now. We will do nothing, repeat *nothing*, that might interfere with his treatment and recovery. I got orders to fly down here to handle this. They tell me those orders came from the White House. Fine. Doctors Jameson and Ivanov will assist me, but that patient is now my responsibility, and my job is to see to it that he walks out of this hospital alive and well. Everything else is secondary to that objective. You will be extended every courtesy. But I make the rules here." Tait paused. Diplomacy was not something he was good at. "Tell you what, you want to sit in there yourselves in relays, that's fine with me. But you have to follow the rules. That means you scrub, change into sterile clothing, and follow the instructions of the duty nurse. Fair enough?"

Petchkin nodded. American doctors think they are gods, he said to himself.

Jameson, busy reexamining the blood analyzer printout, had ignored the sermon. "Can you gentlemen tell us what kind of sub he was on?"

"No," Petchkin said at once.

"What are you thinking, Jamie?"

"The dropping white count and some of these other indicators are consistent with radiation exposure. The gross symptoms would have been masked by the overlying hypothermia." Suddenly Jameson looked at the Soviets. "Gentlemen, we have to know this, was he on a nuclear sub?"

"Yes," Smirnov answered, "he was on a nuclear-powered submarine."

"Jamie, take his clothing to radiology. Have them check the buttons, zipper, anything metal for evidence of contamination."

"Right." Jameson went to collect the patient's effects.

"May we be involved in this?" Smirnov asked.

"Yes, sir," Tait responded, wondering what sort of people these were. The guy had to come off a nuclear submarine, didn't he? Why hadn't they told him at once? Didn't they want him to recover?

Petchkin pondered the significance of this. Didn't they know he had come off a nuclear-powered sub? Of course—he was trying to get Smirnov to blurt out that the man was off a missile submarine. They were trying to cloud the issue with this story about contamination. Nothing that would harm the patient, but something to confuse their class enemies. Clever. He'd always thought the Americans were clever. And he was supposed to report to the embassy in an hour—report what? How was he supposed to know who the sailor was?

Norfolk Naval Shipyard

The USS *Ethan Allen* was about at the end of her string. Commissioned in 1961, she had served her crews and her country for over twenty years, carrying Polaris sea-launched ballistic missiles in endless patrols through sunless seas. Now she was old enough to vote, and this was very old for a submarine. Her missile tubes had been filled with ballast and sealed months before. She had only a token maintenance crew while the Pentagon bureaucrats debated her future. There had been talk of a complicated cruise missile system to make her into a SSGN like the new Russian *Oscar*s. This was judged too expensive. *Ethan Allen*'s was generation-old technology. Her S5W reactor was too dated for much more use. Nuclear radiation had bombarded the metal vessel and its internal fittings with many billions of neutrons. As recent examination of test strips had revealed, over time the character of the metal had changed, becoming dangerously brittle. The system had at most another three years of useful life. A new reactor would be too expensive. The *Ethan Allen* was doomed by her senescence.

The maintenance crew was made up of members of her last operational team, mainly old-timers looking forward to retirement, with a leavening of kids who needed education in repair skills. The *Ethan Allen* could still serve as a school, especially a repair school since so much of her equipment was worn out.

Admiral Gallery had come aboard early that morning. The chiefs had regarded that as particularly ominous. He had been her first skipper many years before, and admirals always seemed to visit their early commands—right before they were scrapped. He'd recognized some of the senior chiefs and asked them if the old girl had any life left in her. To a man, the chiefs said yes. A ship becomes more than a machine to her crew. Each of a hundred ships, built by the same men at the same yard to the same plans, will have her own special characteristics— most of them bad, really, but after her crew becomes accustomed to them they are spoken of affectionately, particularly in retrospect. The admiral had toured the entire length of the *Ethan Allen*'s hull, pausing to run his gnarled, arthritic hands over the periscope he had used to make certain that there really was a world outside the steel hull, to plan the rare "attack" against a ship hunting his sub—or a passing tanker, just for practice. He'd commanded the *Ethan Allen* for three years, alternating his gold crew with another officer's blue crew, working out of Holy Loch, Scotland. Those were good years, he told himself, a damned sight better than sitting at a desk with a lot of vapid aides running around. It was the old navy game, up or out: just when you got something that you were really good at, something you really liked, it was gone. It made good organizational sense. You had to make room for the youngsters coming up—but, God! to be young again, to command one of the new ones that now he only had the opportunity to ride a few hours at a time, a courtesy to the skinny old bastard in Norfolk.

She'd do it, Gallery knew. She'd do fine. It was not the end he would have preferred for *his* fighting ship, but when you came down to it, a decent end for a fighting ship was something rare. Nelson's *Victory,* the *Constitution* in Boston harbor, the odd battleship kept mummified by her namesake state—they'd had honorable treatment. Most warships were sunk as targets or broken up for razor blades. The *Ethan Allen* would die for a purpose. A crazy purpose, perhaps crazy enough to work, he said to himself as he returned to COMSUBLANT headquarters.

Two hours later a truck arrived at the dock where the *Ethan Allen* lay dormant. The chief quartermaster on deck at the time noted that the truck came from Oceana Naval Air Station. Curious, he thought. More curiously, the officer who got out was wearing neither dolphins nor wings. He saluted the quarterdeck first, then the chief who had the deck while *Ethan Allen*'s remaining two officers supervised a repair job on the engine spaces. The officer from the naval air station made arrangements for a work gang to load the sub with four bullet-shaped objects, which went through the deck hatches. They were large, barely able to fit through the torpedo and capsule loading hatches, and it took some handling to get them emplaced. Next came plastic pallets to set them on and metal straps to secure them. They look like bombs, the chief electrician thought as the younger men did the donkey work. But they couldn't be that; they were too light, obviously made of ordinary sheet metal. An hour later a truck with a pressurized tank on its loadbed arrived. The submarine was cleared of her personnel and carefully ventilated. Then three men snaked a hose to each of the four objects. Finished, they ventilated the hull again, leaving gas detectors near each object. By this time, the crew noted, their dock and the one next to it were being guarded by armed marines so that no one could come over and see what was happening to the *Ethan Allen.*

When the loading, or filling, or whatever, was finished, a chief went below to examine the metal shells more carefully. He wrote down the stenciled acronym PPB76A/J6713 on a pad. A chief yeoman looked the designation up in a catalog and did not like what he found—Pave Pat Blue 76. Pave Pat Blue 76 was a bomb, and the *Ethan Allen* had four of them aboard. Nothing nearly so powerful as the missile warheads she had once carried, but a lot more ominous, the crew agreed. The smoking lamp was out by mutual accord before anyone made an order of it.

Gallery came back soon thereafter and spoke with all of the senior men individually. The youngsters were sent ashore with their personal gear and an admonition that they had not seen, felt, heard, or otherwise noticed anything unusual on the *Ethan Allen*. She was going to be scuttled at sea. That was all. Some political decision in Washington—and if you tell *that* to anyone, start thinking about a twenty-year tour at McMurdo Sound, as one man put it.

It was a tribute to Vincent Gallery that each of the old chiefs stayed aboard. Partly it was a chance for one last cruise on the old girl, a chance to say goodbye to a friend. Mostly it was because Gallery said it was important, and the old-timers remembered that his word had been good once.

The officers showed up at sundown. The lowest-ranking among them was a lieutenant commander. Two four-striped captains would be working the reactor, along with three senior chiefs. Two more four-stripers would handle the navigation, a pair of commanders the electronics. The rest would be spread around to handle the plethora of specialized tasks necessary to the operation of a complex warship. The total complement, not even a quarter the size of a normal crew, might have caused some adverse comment on the part of the senior chiefs, who didn't consider just how much experience these officers had.

One officer would be working the diving planes, the chief quartermaster was scandalized to learn. The chief electrician he discussed this with took it in stride. After all, he noted, the real fun was driving the boats, and officers only got to do that at New London. After that all they got to do was walk around and look important. True, the quartermaster agreed, but could they handle it? If not, the electrician decided, they would take care of things—what else were chiefs for but to protect officers from their mistakes? After that they argued good-naturedly over who would be chief of the boat. Both men had nearly identical experience and time in rate.

The USS *Ethan Allen* sailed for the last time at 2345 hours. No tug helped her away from the dock. The skipper eased her deftly away from the dock with gentle engine commands and strains on his lines that his quartermaster could only admire. He'd served with the skipper before, on the *Skipjack* and the *Will Rogers*. "No tugs, no nothin'," he reported to his bunkmate later. "The old man knows his shit." In an hour they were past the Virginia Capes and ready to dive. Ten minutes later they were gone from sight. Below, on a course of one-one-zero, the small crew of officers and chiefs settled into the demanding routine of running their old boomer shorthanded. The *Ethan Allen* responded like a champ, steaming at twelve knots, her old machinery hardly making any noise at all.

THE ELEVENTH DAY

MONDAY, 13 DECEMBER

An A-10 Thunderbolt

It was a lot more fun than flying DC-9s. Major Andy Richardson had over ten thousand hours in those and only six hundred or so in his A-10 Thunderbolt II strike fighter, but he much preferred the smaller of the twin-engine aircraft. Richardson belonged to the 175th Tactical Fighter Group of the Maryland Air National Guard. Ordinarily his squadron flew out of a small military airfield east of Baltimore. But two days earlier, when his outfit had been activated, the 175th and six other national guard and reserve air groups had crowded the already active SAC base at Loring Air Force Base in Maine. They had taken off at midnight and had refueled in midair only half an hour earlier, a thousand miles out over the North Atlantic. Now Richardson and his flight of four were skimming a hundred feet over the black waters at four hundred knots.

A hundred miles behind the four fighters, ninety aircraft were following at thirty thousand feet in what would look very

much to the Soviets like an alpha strike, a weighted attack
mission of armed tactical fighters. It was exactly that—and
also a feint. The real mission belonged to the low-level team
of four.

Richardson loved the A-10. She was called with backhanded
affection the Warthog or just plain Hog by the men who flew
her. Nearly all tactical aircraft had pleasing lines conferred on
them by the need in combat for speed and maneuverability.
Not the Hog, which was perhaps the ugliest bird ever built for
the U.S. Air Force. Her twin turbofan engines hung like af-
terthoughts at the twin-rudder tail, itself a throwback to the
thirties. Her slablike wings had not a whit of sweepback and
were bent in the middle to accommodate the clumsy landing
gear. The undersides of the wings were studded with many
hard points so ordance could be carried, and the fuselage was
built around the aircraft's primary weapon, the GAU-8 thirty-
millimeter rotary cannon designed specifically to smash Soviet
tanks.

For tonight's mission, Richardson's flight had a full load of
depleted uranium slugs for their Avenger cannons and a pair
of Rockeye cluster bomb cannisters, additional antitank weapons. Directly beneath the fuselage was a LANTIRN (low-
altitude navigation and targeting infrared for night) pod; all the
other ordance stations save one were occupied by fuel tanks.

The 175th had been the first national guard squadron to
receive LANTIRN. It was a small collection of electronic and
optical systems that enabled the Hog to see at night while flying
at minimum altitude searching for targets. The systems projected a heads-up display (HUD) on the fighter's windshield,
in effect turning night to day and making this mission profile
marginally less hazardous. Beside each LANTIRN pod was a
smaller object which, unlike the cannon shells and Rockeyes,
was intended for use tonight.

Richardson didn't mind—indeed, he relished—the hazards
of the mission. Two of his three comrades were, like him,
airline pilots, the third a crop duster, all experienced men with
plenty of practice in low-level tactics. And their mission was
a good one.

The briefing, conducted by a naval officer, had taken over
an hour. They were paying a visit to the Soviet Navy. Rich-

ardson had read in the papers that the Russians were up to something, and when he had heard at the briefing that they were sending their fleet to trail its coat this close to the American coast, he had been shocked by their boldness. It had angered him to learn that one of their crummy little day fighters had back-shot a navy Tomcat the day before, nearly killing one of its officers. He wondered why the navy was being cut out of the response. Most of the *Saratoga*'s air group was visible on the concrete pads at Loring, sitting alongside the B-52s, A-6E Intruders, and F-18 Hornets with their ordnance carts a few feet away. He guessed that his mission was only the first act, the delicate part. While Soviet eyes were locked on the alpha strike hovering at the edge of their SAM range, his flight of four would dash in under radar cover to the fleet flagship, the nuclear-powered battle cruiser *Kirov*. To deliver a message.

It was surprising that guardsmen had been selected for this mission. Nearly a thousand tactical aircraft were now mobilized on the East Coast, about a third of them reservists of one kind or another, and Richardson guessed that that was part of the message. A very difficult tactical operation was being run by second-line airmen, while the regular squadrons sat ready on the runways of Loring, and McGuire, and Dover, and Pease, and several other bases from Virginia to Maine, fueled, briefed, and ready. Nearly a thousand aircraft! Richardson smiled. There wouldn't be enough targets to go around.

"Linebacker Lead, this is Sentry-Delta. Target bearing zero-four-eight, range fifty miles. Course is one-eight-five, speed twenty."

Richardson did not acknowledge the transmission over the encrypted radio link. The flight was under EMCON. Any electronic noise might alert the Soviets. Even his targeting radar was switched off, and only passive infrared and low-light television sensors were operating. He look quickly left and right. Second-line flyers, hell! he said to himself. Every man in the flight had at least four thousand hours, more than most regular pilots would ever have, more than most of the astronauts, and their birds were maintained by people who tinkered with airplanes because they liked to. The fact of the matter was that his squadron had better aircraft-availability than any regular squadron and had had fewer accidents than the wet-nosed hotdogs who flew the warthogs in England and Korea. They'd show the Russkies that.

He smiled to himself. This sure beat flying his DC-9 from Washington to Providence and Hartford and back every day for U.S. Air! Richardson, who had been an air force fighter pilot, had left the service eight years earlier because he craved the higher pay and flashy lifestyle of a commercial airline pilot. He'd missed Vietnam, and commercial flying did not require anything like this degree of skill; it lacked the *rush* of skimming at treetop level.

So far as he knew, the Hog had never been used for maritime strike missions—another part of the message. It was no surprise that she'd be good at it. Her antitank munitions would be effective against ships. Her cannon slugs and Rockeye clusters were designed to shred armored battle tanks, and he had no doubts what they would do to thin-hulled warships. Too bad this wasn't for real. It was about time somebody taught Ivan a lesson.

A radar sensor light blinked on his threat receiver; S-band radar, it was probably meant for surface search, and was not powerful enough for a return yet. The Soviets did not have any aerial radar platforms, and their ship-carried sets were limited by the earth's curvature. The beam was just over his head; he was getting the fuzzy edge of it. They would have avoided detection better still by flying at fifty feet instead of a hundred, but orders were not to.

"Linebacker flight, this is Sentry-Delta. Scatter and head in," the AWACS commanded.

The A-10s separated from their interval of only a few feet to an extended attack formation that left miles between aircraft. The orders were for them to scatter at thirty miles' distance. About four minutes. Richardson checked his digital clock; the Linebacker flight was right on time. Behind them, the Phantoms and Corsairs in the alpha strike would be turning toward the Soviets, just to get their attention. He ought to be seeing them soon . . .

The HUD showed small bumps on the projected horizon— the outer screen of destroyers, the *Udaloys* and *Sovremennys*. The briefing officer had shown them silhouettes and photos of the warships.

Beep! his threat receiver chirped. An X-band missile guidance radar had just swept over his aircraft and lost it, and was now trying to regain contact. Richardson flipped on his ECM (electronic countermeasures) jamming systems. The destroyers were only five miles away now. Forty seconds. Stay dumb, comrades, he thought.

He began to maneuver his aircraft radically, jinking up, down, left, right, in no particular pattern. It was only a game, but there was no sense in giving Ivan an easy time. If this had been for real, his Hogs would be blazing in behind a swarm of antiradar missiles and would be accompanied by Wild Weasel aircraft trying to scramble and kill Soviet missile control systems. Things were moving very fast now. A screening destroyer loomed in his path, and he nudged his rudder to pass clear of her by a quarter mile. Two miles to the *Kirov*—eighteen seconds.

The HUD system painted an intensified image. The *Kirov*'s pyramidal mast-stack-radar structure was filling his windshield. He could see blinking signal lights all around the battle cruiser. Richardson gave more right rudder. They were supposed to pass within three hundred yards of the ship, no more, no less. His Hog would blaze past the bow, the others past the stern and either beam. He didn't want to cut it too close. The major checked to be certain that his bomb and cannon controls were locked in the safe position. No sense getting carried away. About now in a real attack he'd trigger his cannon and a stream of solid slugs would lance the light armor of the *Kirov*'s forward missile magazines, exploding the SAM and cruise missiles in a huge fireball and slicing through the superstructure as if it were thin as newsprint.

At five hundred yards, the captain reached down to arm the flare pod, attached next to the LANTIRN.

Now! He flipped the switch, which deployed half a dozen high-intensity magnesium parachute flares. All four Linebacker aircraft acted within seconds. Suddenly the *Kirov* was inside a box of blue-white magnesium light. Richardson pulled back on his stick, banking into a climbing turn past the battle cruiser. The brilliant light dazzled him, but he could see the graceful lines of the Soviet warship as she was turning hard on the choppy seas, her men running along the deck like ants.

If we were serious, you'd all be dead now—get the message?

Richardson thumbed his radio switch. "Linebacker Lead to Sentry-Delta," he said in the clear. "Robin Hood, repeat, Robin Hood. Linebacker flight, this is lead, form up on me. Let's go home!"

"Linebacker flight, this is Sentry-Delta. Outstanding!" the controller responded. "Be advised that *Kiev* has a pair of Forgers in the air, thirty miles east, heading your way. They'll have to hustle to catch up. Will advise. Out."

Richardson did some fast arithmetic in his head. They probably could not catch up, and even if they did, twelve Phantoms from the 107th Fighter Interceptor Group were ready for it.

"Hot damn, lead!" Linebacker 4, the crop duster, moved gingerly into his slot. "Did you see those turkeys pointing up at us? God damn, did we rattle their cage!"

"Heads up for Forgers," Richardson cautioned, grinning ear to ear inside his oxygen mask. *Second-line flyers, hell!*

"Let 'em come," Linebacker 4 replied. "Any of those bastards closes me and my thirty, it'll be the last mistake he ever makes!" Four was a little too aggressive for Richardson's liking, but the man did know how to drive his Hog.

"Linebacker flight, this is Sentry-Delta. The Forgers have turned back. You're in the clear. Out."

"Roger that, out. Okay, flight, let's settle down and head home. I guess we've earned our pay for the month." Richardson looked to make sure he was on an open frequency. "Ladies and gentlemen, this is Captain Barry Friendly," he said, using the in-house U.S. Air public relations joke that had become a tradition in the 175th. "I hope you have enjoyed your flight, and thank you for flying Warthog Air."

The *Kirov*

On the *Kirov*, Admiral Stralbo raced from the combat information center to the flag bridge, too late. They had acquired the low-level raiders only a minute from the outer screen. The box of flares was already behind the battle cruiser, several still burning in the water. The bridge crew, he saw, was rattled.

"Sixty to seventy seconds before they were on us, Comrade

Admiral," the flag captain reported, "we were tracking the orbiting attack force and these four—we think, four—racing in under our radar coverage. We had missile lock on two of them despite their jamming."

Stralbo frowned. That performance was not nearly good enough. If the strike had been real, the *Kirov* would have been badly damaged at least. The Americans would gladly trade a pair of fighters for a nuclear powered cruiser. If all American aircraft attacked like this...

"The arrogance of the Americans is fantastic!" The fleet *zampolit* swore.

"It was foolish to provoke them," Stralbo observed sourly. "I knew that something like that would happen, but I expected it from *Kennedy.*"

"That was a mistake, a pilot error," the political officer replied.

"Indeed, Vasily. And *this* was no mistake! They just sent us a message, telling us that we are fifteen hundred kilometers from their shore without useful air cover, and that they have over five hundred fighters waiting to pounce on us from the west. In the meantime *Kennedy* is stalking us to the east like a rabid wolf. We are not in an attractive position."

"The Americans would not be so brash."

"Are you sure of that, Comrade Political Officer? Sure? What if one of their aircraft commits a 'pilot error'? And sinks one of our destroyers? And what if the American president gets a direct link to Moscow to apologize before we can ever report it? They swear it was an accident and promise to punish the stupid pilot—then what? You think the imperialists are so predictable this close to their own coastline? I do not. I think they are praying for the smallest excuse to pounce on us. Come to my cabin. We must consider this."

The two men went aft. Stralbo's cabin was a spartan affair. The only decoration on the wall was a print of Lenin speaking to Red Guards.

"What is our mission, Vasily?" Stralbo asked.

"To support our submarines, help them to conduct the search—"

"Exactly. Our mission is to support, not to conduct offensive operations. The Americans do not want us here. Objectively,

I can understand this. With all our missiles we are a threat to them."

"But our orders are not to threaten them," the *zampolit* protested. "Why would we want to strike their home-land?"

"And, of course, the imperialists recognize that we are peaceful socialists! Come now, Vasily, these are our enemies! Of course they do not trust us. Of *course* they wish to attack us, given the smallest excuse. They are already interfering with our search, pretending to help. They do not want us here— and in allowing ourselves to be provoked by their aggressive actions, we fall into their trap." The admiral stared down at his desk. "Well, we shall change that. I will order the fleet to discontinue anything that may appear the least bit aggressive. We will end all air operations beyond normal local patrolling. We will not harass their nearby fleet units. We will use only normal navigational radars."

"And?"

"And we will swallow our pride and be as meek as mice. Whatever provocation they make, we will not react to it."

"Some will call this cowardice, Comrade Admiral," the *zampolit* warned.

Stralbo had expected that. "Vasily, don't you see? In pre-tending to attack us they have already victimized us. They force us to activate our newest and most secret defense systems so they can gather intelligence on our radars and fire control systems. They examine the performance of our fighters and helicopters, the maneuverability of our ships, and most of all, our command and control. We shall put an end to that. Our primary mission is too important. If they continue to provoke us, we will act as though our mission is indeed peaceful— which it is as far as they are concerned—and protest our in-nocence. And we make them the aggressors. If they continue to provoke us, we shall watch to see what their tactics are, and give them nothing in return. Or would you prefer that they prevent us from carrying out our mission?"

The *zampolit* mumbled his consent. If they failed in their mission, the charge of cowardice would be a small matter indeed. If they found the renegade submarine, they'd be heroes regardless of what else happened.

The Dallas

How long had he been on duty? Jones wondered. He could have checked easily enough by punching the button on his digital watch, but the sonarman didn't want to. It would be too depressing. Me and my big mouth—*you bet, Skipper,* my ass! he swore to himself. He'd detected the sub at a range of about twenty miles, maybe, had just barely gotten her—and the fuckin' Atlantic Ocean was three thousand miles across, at least sixty footprint diameters. He'd need more than luck now.

Well, he did get a Hollywood shower out of it. Ordinarily a shower on a freshwater-poor ship meant a few seconds of wetting down and a minute or so of lathering, followed by a few more seconds of rinsing the suds off. It got you clean but was not very satisfying. This was an improvement over the old days, the oldtimers liked to say. But back then, Jones often responded, the sailors had to pull oars—or run off diesel and batteries, which amounted to the same thing. A Hollywood shower is something a sailor starts thinking about after a few days at sea. You leave the water running, a long, continuous stream of wonderfully warm water. Commander Mancuso was given to awarding this sensuous pastime in return for above-average performance. It gave people something tangible to work for. You couldn't spend extra money on a sub, and there was no beer or women.

Old movies—they were making an effort on that score. The boat's library wasn't bad, when you had time to sort through the jumble. And the *Dallas* had a pair of Apple computers and a few dozen game programs for amusement. Jones was the boat champion at Choplifter and Zork. The computers were also used for training purposes, of course, for practice exams and programmed learning tests that ate up most of the use time.

The *Dallas* was quartering an area east of the Grand Banks. Any boat transiting Route One tended to come through here. They were moving at five knots, trailing out the BQR-15 towed-array sonar. They'd had all kinds of contacts. First, half the submarines in the Russian Navy had whipped by at high speed, many trailed by American boats. An *Alfa* had burned past them at over forty knots, not three thousand yards away. It would have been so easy, Jones had thought at the time. The *Alfa* had been making so much noise that one could have heard it with a glass against the hull, and he'd had to turn his amplifiers down to minimums to keep the noise from ruining his ears. A pity they couldn't have fired. The setup had been so simple, the firing solution so easy that a kid with an old-fashioned sliderule could have done it. That *Alfa* had been meat on the table. The *Victor*s came running next, and the *Charlie*s and *November*s last of all. Jones had been listening to surface ships a ways to the west, a lot of them doing twenty knots or so, making all kinds of noise as they pounded through the waves. They were way far off, and not his concern.

They had been trying to acquire this particular target for over two days, and Jones had had only an odd hour of sleep here and there. Well, that's what they pay me for, he reflected bleakly. This was not unprecedented, he'd done it before, but he'd be happy when the labor ended.

The large-aperture towed array was at the end of a thousand-foot cable. Jones referred to the use of it as trolling for whales. In addition to being their most sensitive sonar rig, it protected the *Dallas* against intruders shadowing her. Ordinarily a submarine's sonar will work in any direction except aft—an area called the cone of silence, or the baffles. The BQR-15 changed that. Jones had heard all sorts of things on it, subs and surface ships all the time, low-flying aircraft on occasion. Once, during an exercise off Florida, it had been the noise of diving pelicans that he could not figure out until the skipper had raised the periscope for a look. Then off Bermuda they had encountered mating humpbacks, and a very impressive noise that was. Jones had a personal copy of the tape of them for use on the beach; some women had found it interesting, in a kinky sort of way. He smiled to himself.

There was a considerable amount of surface noise. The signal processors filtered most of it out, and every few minutes Jones switched them off his channel, getting the sound unimpeded to make sure that they weren't filtering too much out. Machines were dumb; Jones wondered if SAPS might be letting some of that anomalous signal get lost inside the computer chips. That was a problem with computers, really a problem with programming: you'd tell the machine to do something, and it would go do it to the wrong thing. Jones often amused himself working up programs. He knew a few people from college who drew up game programs for personal computers; one of them was making good money with Sierra On-Line Systems . . .

Daydreaming again, Jonesy, he chided himself. It wasn't easy listening to nothing for hours on end. It would have been a good idea, he thought, to let sonarmen read on duty. He had better sense than to suggest it. Mr. Thompson might go along, but the skipper and all the senior officers were ex-reactor types with the usual rule of iron: You shall watch every instrument with absolute concentration all the time. Jones didn't think this was very smart. It was different with sonarmen. They burned out too easily. To combat this Jones had his music tapes and his games. He could lose himself in any sort of diversion, especially Choplifter. A man had to have something, he reasoned, to lose his mind in, at least once a day. And something on duty in some cases. Even truck drivers, hardly the most intellectual of people, had radios and tape players to keep from becoming mesmerized. But sailors on a nuclear sub costing the best part of a billion . . .

Jones leaned forward, pressing the headphones tight against his head. He tore a page of doodles from his scratch pad and noted the time on a fresh sheet. Next he made some adjustments on his gain controls, already near the top of the scale, and flipped off the processors again. The cacophony of surface noise nearly took his head off. Jones tolerated this for a minute, working the manual muting controls to filter out the worst of the high-frequency noise. Aha! Jones said to himself. Maybe SAPS is messing me up a little—too soon to tell for sure.

When Jones had first been checked out on this gear in sonar school he'd had a burning desire to show it to his brother, who had a masters in electrical engineering and worked as a consultant in the recording industry. He had eleven patents to his name. The stuff on the *Dallas* would have knocked his eyes out. The navy's systems for digitalizing sound were years ahead of any commercial technique. Too bad it was all classified right alongside nuclear stuff . . .

"Mr. Thompson," Jones said quietly, not looking around, "can you ask the skipper if maybe we can swing more easterly and drop down a knot or two?"

"Skipper," Thompson went out into the passageway to relay

the request. New course and engine orders were given in fifteen seconds. Mancuso was in sonar ten seconds after that.

The skipper had been sweating this. It had been obvious two days ago that their erstwhile contact had not acted as expected, had not run the route, or had never slowed down. Commander Mancuso had guessed wrong on something—had he also guessed wrong on their visitor's course? And what did it mean if their friend had not run the route? Jones had figured that one out long before. It made her a boomer. Boomer skippers never go fast.

Jones was sitting as usual, hunched over his table, his left hand up commanding quiet as the towed array came around to a precise east-west azimuth at the end of its cable. His cigarette burned away unnoticed in the ashtray. A reel-to-reel tape recorder was operating continuously in the sonar room, its tapes changed hourly and kept for later analysis on shore. Next to it was another whose recordings were used aboard the *Dallas* for reexamination of contacts. He reached up and switched it on, then turned to see his captain looking down at him. Jones' face broke into a thin, tired smile.

"Yeah," he whispered.

Mancuso pointed to the speaker. Jones shook his head. "Too faint, Cap'n. I just barely got it now. Roughly north, I think, but I need some time on that." Mancuso looked at the intensity needle Jones was tapping. It was down to zero—almost. Every fifty seconds or so it twitched, just a little. Jones was making furious notes. "The goddamned SAPS filters are blanking part of this out!!!!! We need smoother amplifiers and better manual filter controls!!" he wrote.

Mancuso told himself that this was faintly ridiculous. He was watching Jones as he had watched his wife when she'd had Dominic and he was timing the twitches on a needle as he had timed his wife's contractions. But there was no thrill to match this. The comparison he used to explain it to his father was the thrill you got on the first day of hunting season, when you hear the leaves rustle and you know it's not a man making the noise. But it was better than that. He was hunting men, men like himself in a vessel like his own...

"Getting louder, Skipper." Jones leaned back and lit a cigarette. "He's heading our way. I make him three-five-zero, maybe more like three-five-three. Still real faint, but that's our boy. We got him." Jones decided to risk an impertinence. He'd earned a little tolerance. "We wait or we chase, sir?"

"We wait. No sense spooking him. We let him come in nice and close while we do our famous imitation of a hole in the water, then we tag along behind him to wax his tail for a while. I want another tape of this set up, and I want the BC-10 to run a SAPS scan. Use the instruction to bypass the processing algorithms. I want this contact analyzed, not interpreted. Run it every two minutes. I want his signature recorded, digitalized, folded, spindled, and mutilated. I want to know everything there is about him, his propulsion noises, his plant signature, the works. I want to know exactly who he is."

"He's a Russkie, sir," Jones observed.

"But which Russkie?" Mancuso smiled.

"Aye, Cap'n." Jones understood. He'd be on duty another two hours, but the end was in sight. Almost. Mancuso sat down and lifted a spare set of headphones, stealing one of Jones' cigarettes. He'd been trying to break the habit for a month. He'd have a better chance on the beach.

HMS Invincible

Ryan was now wearing a Royal Naval uniform. This was temporary. Another mark of how fast this job had been laid on was that he had only the one uniform and two shirts. All of his wardrobe was now being cleaned and in the interim he had on a pair of English-made trousers and a sweater. Typical, he thought—nobody even knows I'm here. They had forgotten him. No messages from the president—not that he'd ever expected one—and Painter and Davenport were only too glad to forget that he was ever on the *Kennedy*. Greer and the judge were probably going over some damned fool thing or another, maybe chuckling to themselves about Jack Ryan having a pleasure cruise at government expense.

It was not a pleasure cruise. Jack had rediscovered his vulnerability to seasickness. The *Invincible* was off Massachusetts, waiting for the Russian surface force and hunting vigorously after the red subs in the area. They were steaming in circles on an ocean that would not settle down. Everyone was busy—

except him. The pilots were up twice a day or more, exercising
with their U.S. Air Force and Navy counterparts working from
shore bases. The ships were practicing surface warfare tactics.
As Admiral White had said at breakfast, it had developed into
a jolly good extension of NIFTY DOLPHIN. Ryan didn't like
being a supernumerary. Everyone was polite, of course. Indeed,
the hospitality was nearly overpowering. He had access to the
command center, and when he watched to see how the Brits
hunted subs down, everything was explained to him in sufficient detail that he actually understood about half of it.

At the moment he was reading alone in White's sea cabin,
which had become his permanent home aboard. Ritter had
thoughtfully tucked a CIA staff study into his duffle bag. Entitled "Lost Children: A Psychological Profile of East Bloc
Defectors," the three-hundred-page document had been drafted
by a committee of psychologists and psychiatrists who worked
with the CIA and other intelligence agencies helping defectors
settle into American life—and, he was sure, helping spot security risks in the CIA. Not that there were many of those, but
there were two sides to everything the Company did.

Ryan admitted to himself that this was pretty interesting
stuff. He had never really thought about what makes a defector,
figuring that there were enough things happening on the other
side of the Iron Curtain to make any rational person want to
take whatever chance he got to run west. But it was not that
simple, he read, not that simple at all. Everyone who came
over was a fairly unique individual. While one might recognize
the inequities of life under Communism and yearn for justice,
religious freedom, a chance to develop as an individual, another
might simply want to get rich, having read about how greedy
capitalists exploit the masses and decided that being an exploiter
has its good points. Ryan found this interesting if cynical.

Another defector type was the fake, the imposter, someone
planted on the CIA as a living piece of disinformation. But this
kind of character could cut both ways. He might ultimately
turn out to be a genuine defector. America, Ryan smiled, could
be pretty seductive to someone used to the gray life in the
Soviet Union. Most of the plants, however, were dangerous
enemies. For this reason a defector was never trusted. Never.
A man who had changed countries once could do it again. Even

the idealists had doubts, great pangs of conscience at having deserted their motherland. In a footnote a doctor commented that the most wounding punishment for Aleksander Solzhenitsyn was exile. As a patriot, being alive far from his home was more of a torment than living in a gulag. Ryan found that curious, but enough so to be true.

The rest of the document addressed the problem of getting them settled. Not a few Soviet defectors had committed suicide after a few years. Some had simply been unable to cope with freedom, the way that long-term prison inmates often fail to function without highly structured control over their lives and commit new crimes hoping to return to their safe environment. Over the years the CIA had developed a protocol for dealing with this problem, and a graph in an appendix showed that the severe maladjustment cases were trending dramatically down. Ryan took his time reading. While getting his doctorate in history at Georgetown University he had used a little free time to audit some psychology classes. He had come away with the gut suspicion that shrinks didn't really know much of anything, that they got together and agreed on random ideas they could all use . . . He shook his head. His wife occasionally said that, too. A clinical instructor in ophthalmic surgery on an exchange program at St. Guy's Hospital in London, Caroline Ryan regarded everything as cut and dried. If someone had eye trouble, she would either fix it or not fix it. A mind was different, Jack decided after reading through the document a second time, and each defector had to be treated as an individual, handled carefully by a sympathetic case officer who had both the time and inclination to look after him properly. He wondered if he'd be good at it.

Admiral White walked in. "Bored, Jack?"

"Not exactly, Admiral. When do we make contact with the Soviets?"

"This evening. Your chaps have given them a very rough time over that Tomcat incident."

"Good. Maybe people will wake up before something really bad happens."

"You think it will?" White sat down.

"Well, Admiral, if they really are hunting a missing sub, yes. If not, then they're here for another purpose entirely, and

I've guessed wrong. Worse than that, I'll have to live with that misjudgment—or die with it."

Norfolk Naval Medical Center

Tait was feeling better. Dr. Jameson had taken over for several hours, allowing him to curl up on a couch in the doctor's lounge for five hours. That was the most sleep he ever seemed to get in one shot, but it was sufficient to make him look indecently chipper to the rest of the floor staff. He made a quick phone call and some milk was sent up. As a Mormon, Tait avoided everything with caffeine—coffee, tea, even cola drinks—and though this type of self-discipline was unusual for a physician, to say nothing of a uniformed officer, he scarcely thought about it except on rare occasions when he pointed out its longevity benefits to his brother practitioners. Tait drank his milk and shaved in the restroom, emerging ready to face another day.

"Any word on the radiation exposure, Jamie?"

The radiology lab had struck out. "They brought a nucleonics officer over from a sub tender, and he scanned the clothes. There was a possible twenty-rad contamination, not enough for frank physiological effects. I think what it might have been was that the nurse took the sample from the back of his hand. The extremities might still have been suffering from the vascular shutdown. That could explain the depleted white count. Maybe."

"How is he otherwise?"

"Better. Not much, but better. I think maybe the keflin's taking hold." The doctor flipped open the chart. "White count is coming back. I put a unit of whole blood into him two hours ago. The blood chemistry is approaching normal limits. Blood pressure is one hundred over sixty-five, heart rate is ninety-four. Temperature ten minutes ago was 100.8—it's been fluctuating for several hours.

"His heart looks pretty good. In fact, I think he's going to make it, unless something unexpected crops up." Jameson reminded himself that in extreme hypothermia cases the unexpected can take a month or more to appear.

Tait examined the chart, remembering what he had been like years ago. A bright young doc, just like Jamie, certain that he could cure the world. It was a good feeling. A pity that experience—in his case, two years at Danang—beat that out of you. Jamie was right, though; there was enough improvement here to make the patient's chances appear measurably better.

"What are the Russians doing?" Tait asked.

"Petchkin has the watch at the moment. When it came his turn, and he changed into scrubs—you know he has that Captain Smirnov holding onto his clothes, like he expected us to steal them or something?"

Tait explained that Petchkin was a KGB agent.

"No kidding? Maybe he has a gun tucked away." Jameson chuckled. "If he does, he'd better watch it. We got three marines up here with us."

"Marines. What for?"

"Forgot to tell you. Some reporter found out we had a Russkie up here and tried to bluff his way onto the floor. A nurse stopped him. Admiral Blackburn found out and went ape. The whole floor's sealed off. What's the big secret, anyway?"

"Beats me, but that's the way it is. What do you think of this Petchkin guy?"

"I don't know. I've never met any Russians before. They don't smile a whole lot. The way they're taking turns watching the patient, you'd think they expect us to make off with him."

"Or maybe that he'll say something they don't want us to hear?" Tait wondered. "Did you get the feeling that they might not want him to make it? I mean, when they didn't want to tell us about what his sub was?"

Jameson thought about that. "No. The Russians are supposed to make a secret of everything, aren't they? Anyway, Smirnov did come through with it."

"Get some sleep, Jamie."

"Aye, Cap'n." Jameson walked off toward the lounge.

We asked them what kind of a sub, the captain thought, meaning whether it was a nuke or not. What if they thought we were asking if it was a missile sub? That makes sense, doesn't it? Yeah. A missile sub right off our coast, and all this activity in the North Atlantic. Christmas season. Dear God! If they were going to do it, they'd do it right now, wouldn't they? He walked down the hall. A nurse came out of the room with a blood sample to be taken down to the lab. This was being done hourly, and it left Petchkin alone with the patient for a few minutes.

Tait walked around the corner and saw Petchkin through the window, sitting in a chair at the corner of the bed and watching his countryman, who was still unconscious. He had on green scrubs. Made to put on in a hurry, these were reversible, with a pocket on both sides so a surgeon didn't have to waste a second to see if they were inside out. As Tait watched, Petchkin reached for something through the low collar.

"Oh, God!" Tait raced around the corner and shot through the swinging door. Petchkin's look of surprise changed to amazement as the doctor batted a cigarette and lighter from his hand, then to outrage as he was lifted from his chair and flung towards the door. Tait was the smaller of the two, but his sudden burst of energy was sufficient to eject the man from the room. "Security!" Tait screamed.

"What is the meaning of this?" Petchkin demanded. Tait was holding him in a bearhug. Immediately he heard feet racing down the hall from the lobby.

"What is it, sir?" A breathless marine lance corporal with a .45 Colt in his right hand skidded to a halt on the tile floor.

"This man just tried to kill my patient!"

"What!" Petchkin's face was crimson.

"Corporal, your post is now at that door. If this man tries to get into that room, you will stop him any way you have to. Understood?"

"Aye aye, sir!" the corporal looked at the Russian. "Sir, would you please step away from the door?"

"What is the meaning of this outrage!"

"Sir, you will step away from the door, right now." The marine holstered his pistol.

"What is going on here?" It was Ivanov, who had sense enough to ask this question in a quiet voice from ten feet away.

"Doctor, do you want your sailor to survive or not?" Tait asked, trying to calm himself.

"What—of course we wish him to survive. How can you ask this?"

"Then why did Comrade Petchkin just try to kill him?"

"I did not do such a thing!" Petchkin shouted.

"What did he do, exactly?" Ivanov asked.

Before Tait could answer, Petchkin spoke rapidly in Russian, then switched to English. "I was reaching for a smoke, that is all. I have no weapon. I wish to kill no one. I only wish to have a cigarette."

"We have No Smoking signs all over the floor, except in the lobby—you didn't see them? You were in a room in intensive care, with a patient on hundred-percent oxygen, the air and bedclothes saturated with oxygen, and you were going to flick your goddamned Bic!" The doctor rarely used profanity. "Oh sure, you'd get burned some, and it would look like an accident—and that kid would be dead! I know what you are, Petchkin, and I don't think you're that stupid. Get off my floor!"

The nurse, who had been watching this, went into the patient's room. She came back out with a pack of cigarettes, two loose ones, a plastic butane lighter, and a curious look on her face.

Petchkin was ashen. "Dr. Tait, I assure you that I had no such intention. What are you saying would happen?"

"Comrade Petchkin," Ivanov said slowly in English, "there would be an explosion and fire. You cannot have a flame near oxygen."

"Nichevo!" Petchkin finally realized what he had done. He had waited for the nurse to leave—medical people never let you smoke when you ask. He didn't know the first thing about hospitals, and as a KGB agent he was accustomed to doing whatever he wanted. He started speaking to Ivanov in Russian. The Soviet doctor looked like a parent listening to a child's explanation for a broken glass. His response was spirited.

For his part, Tait began to wonder if he hadn't overreacted—anyone who smoked was an idiot to begin with.

"Dr. Tait," Petchkin said finally, "I swear to you that I had no idea of this oxygen business. Perhaps I am a fool."

"Nurse," Tait turned, "we will not leave this patient unattended by our personnel at any time—never. Have a corpsman come to pick up the blood samples and anything else. If you have to go to the head, get relief first."

"Yes, Doctor."

"No more screwing around, Mr. Petchkin. Break the rules

again, sir, and you're off the floor again. Do you understand?"

"It will be as you say, Doctor, and allow me, please, to apologize."

"You stay put," Tait said to the marine. He walked away shaking his head angrily, mad at the Russians, embarrassed with himself, wishing he were back at Bethesda where he belonged, and wishing he knew how to swear coherently. He took the service elevator down to the first floor and spent five minutes looking for the intelligence officer who had flown down with him. Ultimately he found him in a game room playing Pac Man. They conferred in the hospital administrator's vacant office.

"You really thought he was trying to kill the guy?" the commander asked incredulously.

"What was I supposed to think?" Tait demanded. "What do you think?"

"I think he just screwed up. They want that kid alive—no, first they want him talking—more than you do."

"How do you know that?"

"Petchkin calls their embassy every hour. We have the phones tapped, of course. How do you think?"

"What if it's a trick?"

"If he's that good an actor he belongs in the movies. You keep that kid alive, Doctor, and leave the rest to us. Good idea to have the marine close, though. That'll rattle 'em a bit. Never pass up a chance to rattle 'em. So, when will he be conscious?"

"No telling. He's still feverish, and very weak. Why do they want him to talk?" Tait asked.

"To find out what sub he was on. Petchkin's KGB contact blurted that out on the phone—sloppy! *Very* sloppy! They must be real excited about this."

"Do we know what sub it was?"

"Sure," the intelligence officer said mischievously.

"Then what's going on, for Lord's sake!"

"Can't say, Doc." The commander smiled as if he knew, though he was as much in the dark as anyone.

Norfolk Naval Shipyard

The USS *Scamp* sat at the dock while a large overhead crane settled the *Avalon* in its support rack. The captain watched impatiently from atop the sail. He and his boat had been called in from hunting a pair of *Victors*, and he did not like it one bit. The attack boat skipper had only run a DSRV exercise a few weeks before, and right now he had better things to do than play mother whale to this damned useless toy. Besides, having the minisub perched on his after escape trunk would knock ten knots off his top speed. And there'd be four more men to bunk and feed. The *Scamp* was not all that large.

At least they'd get good food out of this. The *Scamp* had been out five weeks when the recall order arrived. Their supply of fresh vegetables was exhausted, and they availed themselves of the opportunity to have fresh food trucked down to the dock. A man tires quickly of three-bean salad. Tonight they'd have real lettuce, tomatoes, fresh corn instead of canned. But that didn't make up for the fact that there were Russians out there to worry about.

"All secure?" the captain called down to the curved after deck.

"Yes, Captain. We're ready when you are," Lieutenant Ames answered.

"Engine room," the captain called down on intercom. "I want you ready to answer bells in ten minutes."

"Ready now, Skipper."

A harbor tug was standing by to help maneuver them from the dock. Ames had their orders, something else that the captain didn't like. Surely they would not be doing any more hunting, not with that damned *Avalon* strapped on.

The Red October

"Look here, Svyadov," Melekhin pointed, "I will show you how a saboteur thinks."

The lieutenant came over and looked. The chief engineer was pointing at an inspection valve on the heat exchanger. Before he got an explanation, Melekhin went to the bulkhead phone.

"Comrade Captain, this is Melekhin. I have found it. I require the reactor to be stopped for an hour. We can operate the caterpillar on batteries, no?"

"Of course, Comrade Chief Engineer," Ramius said, "proceed."

Melekhin turned to the assistant engineering officer. "You will shut the reactor down and connect the batteries to the caterpillar motors."

"At once, Comrade." The officer began to work the controls.

The time taken to find the leak had been a burden on everyone. Once they had discovered that the Geiger counters were sabotaged and Melekhin and Borodin had repaired them, they had begun a complete check of the reactor spaces, a devilishly tricky task. There had never been a question of a major steam leak, else Svyadov would have gone looking for it with a broomstick—even a tiny leak could easily shave off an arm. They reasoned that it had to be a small leak in the low-pressure part of the system. Didn't it? It was the not knowing that had troubled everyone.

The check made by the chief engineer and executive officer had lasted no less than eight hours, during which the reactor had again been shut down. This cut all electricity off throughout the ship except for emergency lights and the caterpillar motors. Even the air systems had been curtailed. That had set the crew muttering to themselves.

The problem was, Melekhin could still not find the leak, and when the badges had been developed a day earlier, there was nothing on them! How was this possible?

"Come, Svyadov, tell me what you see." Melekhin came back over and pointed.

"The water test valve." Opened only in port, when the reactor was cold, it was used to flush the cooling system and to check for unusual water contamination. The thing was grossly unremarkable, a heavy-duty valve with a large wheel. The spout underneath it, below the pressurized part of the pipe, was threaded rather than welded.

"A large wrench, if you please, Lieutenant." Melekhin was drawing the lesson out, Svyadov thought. He was the slowest of teachers when he was trying to communicate something important. Svyadov returned with a meter-long pipe wrench. The chief engineer waited until the plant was closed down, then double-checked a gauge to make sure the pipes were depressurized. He was a careful man. The wrench was set on the fitting, and he turned it. It came off easily.

"You see, Comrade Lieutenant, the threads on the pipe actually go up onto the valve casing. Why is this permitted?"

"The threads are on the outside of the pipe, Comrade. The valve itself bears the pressure. The fitting which is screwed on is merely a directional spigot. The nature of the union does not compromise the pressure loop."

"Correct. A screw fitting is not strong enough for the plant's total pressure." Melekhin worked the fitting all the way off with his hands. It was perfectly machined, the threads still bright from the original engine work. "And there is the sabotage."

"I don't understand."

"Someone thought this one over very carefully, Comrade Lieutenant." Melekhin's voice was half admiration, half rage. "At normal operating pressure, cruising speed, that is, the system is pressurized to eight kilograms per square centimeter, correct?"

"Yes, Comrade, and at full power the pressure is ninety percent higher." Svyadov knew all this by heart.

"But we rarely go to full power. What we have here is a dead-end section of the steam loop. Now, here a small hole has been drilled, not even a millimeter. Look." Melekhin bent over to examine it himself. Svyadov was happy to keep his distance. "Not even a millimeter. The saboteur took the fitting off, drilled the hole, and put it back. The tiny hole permits a minuscule amount of steam to escape, but only very slowly. The steam cannot go up, because the fitting sits against this flange. Look at this machine work! It is perfect, you see, perfect! The steam, therefore, cannot escape upward. It can only force its way down the threads around and around, ultimately escaping inside the spout. Just enough. Just enough to contaminate this compartment by a tiny amount." Melekhin looked up. "Someone was a very clever man. Clever enough to know exactly how this system works. When we reduced power to check for the leak before, there was not enough pressure remaining in the loop to force the steam down the threads, and we could not find the leak. There is only enough pressure at normal power levels—but if you suspect a leak, you power-down the system. And if we had gone to maximum power, who can say what might have happened?" Melekhin shook his head in admiration. "Someone was very, very clever.

I hope I meet him. Oh, I hope I meet this clever man. For when I do, I will take a pair of large steel pliers—," Melekhin's voice lowered to a whisper, "—and I will crush his balls! Get me the small electric welding set, Comrade. I can fix this myself in a few minutes."

Captain First Rank Melekhin was as good as his word. He wouldn't let anyone near the job. It was his plant, and his responsibility. Svyadov was just as happy for that. A tiny bead of stainless steel was worked into the fault, and Melekhin filed it down with jeweler's tools to protect the threads. Then he brushed rubber-based sealant onto the threads and worked the fitting back into place. The whole procedure took twenty-eight minutes by Svyadov's watch. As they had told him in Leningrad, Melekhin was the best engineer in submarines.

"A static pressure test, eight kilograms," he ordered the assistant engineer officer.

The reactor was reactivated. Five minutes later the pressure went all the way to normal power. Melekhin held a counter under the spout for ten minutes—and got nothing, even on the number two setting. He walked to the phone to tell the captain the leak was fixed.

Melekhin had the enlisted men let back into the compartment to return the tools to their places.

"You see how it is done, Lieutenant?"

"Yes, Comrade. Was that one leak sufficient to cause all of our contamination?"

"Obviously."

Svyadov wondered about this. The reactor spaces were nothing but a collection of pipes and fittings, and this bit of sabotage could not have taken long. What if other such time bombs were hidden in the system?

"Perhaps you worry too much, Comrade," Melekhin said. "Yes, I have considered this. When we get to Cuba, I will have a full-power static test made to check the whole system, but for the moment I do not think this is a good idea. We will continue the two-hour watch cycle. There is the possibility that one of our own crewmen is the saboteur. If so, I will not have people in these spaces long enough to commit more mischief. You will watch the crew closely."

THE TWELFTH DAY

TUESDAY, 14 DECEMBER

The Dallas

"Crazy Ivan!" Jones shouted loudly enough to be heard in the attack center. "Turning to starboard!"

"Skipper!" Thompson repeated the warning.

"All stop!" Mancuso ordered quickly. "Rig ship for ultra-quiet!"

A thousand yards ahead of the *Dallas,* her contact had just begun a radical turn to the right. She had been doing so about every two hours since they had regained contact, though not regularly enough for the *Dallas* to settle into a comfortable pattern. Whoever is driving that boomer knows his business, Mancuso thought. The Soviet missile submarine was making a complete circle so her bow-mounted sonar could check for anyone hiding in her baffles.

Countering this maneuver was more than just tricky—it was dangerous, especially the way Mancuso did it. When the *Red*

October changed course, her stern, like those of all ships, moved in the direction opposite the turn. She was a steel barrier directly in the *Dallas'* path for as long as it took her to move through the first part of the turn, and the 7,000-ton attack submarine took a lot of space to stop.

The exact number of collisions that had occurred between Soviet and American submarines was a closely guarded secret; that there had been such collisions was not. One characteristically Russian tactic for forcing Americans to keep their distance was a stylized turn called the Crazy Ivan in the U.S. Navy.

The first few hours they had trailed this contact, Mancuso had been careful to keep his distance. He had learned that the submarine was not turning quickly. She was, rather, maneuvering in a leisurely manner, and seemed to ascend fifty to eighty feet as she turned, banking almost like an aircraft. He suspected that the Russian skipper was not using his full maneuverability—an intelligent thing for a captain to do, keeping some of his performance in reserve as a surprise. These facts allowed the *Dallas* to trail very closely indeed and gave Mancuso a chance to chop his speed and drift forward so that he barely avoided the Russian's stern. He was getting good at it— a little too good, his officers were whispering. The last time they had not missed the Russian's screws by more than a hundred fifty yards. The contact's large turning circle was taking her completely around the *Dallas* as the latter sniffed at her prey's trail.

Avoiding collision was the most dangerous part of the maneuver, but not the only part. The *Dallas* also had to remain invisible to her quarry's passive sonar systems. For her to do so the engineers had to cut power in their S6G reactor to a tiny fraction of its total output. Fortunately the reactor was able to run on such low power without the use of a coolant pump, since coolant could be transferred by normal convection circulation. In addition, a strict silent ship routine was enforced. No activity on the *Dallas* that might generate noise was permitted, and the crew took it seriously enough that even ordinary conversations in the mess were muted.

"Speed coming down," Lieutenant Goodman reported. Mancuso decided that the *Dallas* would not be part of a ramming this time and went aft to sonar.

"Target is still turning right," Jones reported quietly. "Ought to be clear now. Distance to the stern, maybe two hundred yards, maybe a shade less . . . Yeah, we're clear now, bearing is changing more rapidly. Speed and engine noises are constant. A slow turn to the right." Jones caught the captain out of the corner of his eye and turned to hazard an observation. "Skipper, this guy is real confident in himself. I mean, *real* confident."

"Explain," Mancuso said, figuring he knew the answer.

"Cap'n, he's not chopping speed the way we do, and we turn a lot sharper than this. It's almost like—like he's doing this out of habit, y'know? Like he's in a hurry to get some-where, and really doesn't think anybody can track—wait . . . Yeah, okay, he's just about reversed course now, bearing off the starboard bow, say half a mile . . . Still doing the slow turn. He'll go right around us again. Sir, if he knows anybody's back here, he's playing it awful cool. What do you think, Frenchie?"

Chief Sonarman Laval shook his head. "He don't know we're here." The chief didn't want to say anything else. He thought Mancuso's close tailing was reckless. The man had balls, playing with a 688 like this, but one little screw-up and he'd find himself with a pail and shovel, on the beach.

"Passing down the starboard side. No pinging." Jones took out his calculator and punched in some numbers. "Sir, this angular turn rate at this speed makes the range about a thousand yards. You suppose his funny drive system goofs up his rudders any?"

"Maybe." Mancuso took a spare set of phones and plugged them in to listen.

The noise was the same. A swish, and every forty or fifty seconds an odd, low-frequency rumble. This close they could also hear the gurgling and throbbing of the reactor pump. There was a sharp sound, maybe a cook moving a pan on a metal grate. No silent ship drill on this boat. Mancuso smiled to himself. It was like being a cat burglar, hanging this close to an enemy submarine—no, not an enemy, not exactly—hearing everything. In better acoustical conditions they could have heard conversations. Not well enough to understand them, of course, but as if they were at a dinner party listening to the gabble of a dozen couples at once.

"Passing aft and still circling. His turning radius must be a good thousand yards," Mancuso observed.

"Yes, Cap'n, about that," Jones agreed.

"He just can't be using all his rudder, and you're right, Jonesy, he is very damned casual about this. Hmph, the Russians are all supposed to be paranoid—not this boy." So much the better, Mancuso thought.

If he were going to hear the *Dallas* it would be now, with the bow-mounted sonar pointed almost directly at them. Mancuso took off his headphones to listen to his boat. The *Dallas* was a tomb. The words *Crazy Ivan* had been passed, and within seconds his crew had responded. How do you reward a whole crew? Mancuso wondered. He knew he worked them hard, sometimes too hard—but damn! Did they deliver!

"Port beam," Jones said. "Exactly abeam now, speed unchanged, traveling a little straighter, maybe, distance about eleven hundred, I think." The sonarman took a handkerchief from his back pocket and used it to wipe his hands.

There's tension all right, but you'd never know it listening to the kid, the captain thought. Everyone in his crew was acting like a professional.

"He's passed us. On the port bow, and I think the turn has stopped. Betcha he's settled back down on one-nine-zero." Jones looked up with a grin. "We did it again, Skipper."

"Okay. Good work, you men." Mancuso went back to the attack center. Everyone was waiting expectantly. The *Dallas* was dead in the water, drifting slowly downward with her slight negative trim.

"Let's get the engines turned back on. Build her up slowly to thirteen knots." A few seconds later an almost imperceptible noise began as the reactor plant increased power. A moment after that the speed gauge twitched upward. The *Dallas* was moving again.

"Attention, this is the captain speaking," Mancuso said into the sound-powered communications system. The electrically powered speakers were turned off, and his word would be relayed by watchstanders in all compartments. "They circled us again without picking us up. Well done, everybody. We can all breathe again." He placed the handset back in its holder. "Mr. Goodman, let's get back on her tail."

"Aye, Skipper. Left five degrees rudder, helm."

"Left five degrees rudder, aye." The helmsman acknowledged the order, turning his wheel as he did so. Ten minutes
later the *Dallas* was back astern of her contact.

A constant fire control solution was set up on the attack
director. The Mark 48 torpedoes would barely have sufficient
distance to arm themselves before striking the target in twenty-
nine seconds.

Ministry of Defense, Moscow

"And how are you feeling, Misha?"

Mikhail Semyonovich Filitov looked up from a large pile
of documents. He looked flushed and feverish still. Dmitri
Ustinov, the defense minister, worried about his old friend. He
should have stayed in the hospital another few days as the
doctors had advised. But Misha had never been one to take
advice, only orders.

"I feel good, Dmitri. Any time you walk out of a hospital
you feel good—even if you are dead," Filitov smiled.

"You still look sick," Ustinov observed.

"Ah! At our age you always look sick. A drink, Comrade
Defense Minister?" Filitov hoisted a bottle of Stolychnaya vodka
from a desk drawer.

"You drink too much, my friend," Ustinov chided.

"I do not drink enough. A bit more antifreeze and I would
not have caught cold last week." He poured two tumblers half
full and held one out to his guest. "Here, Dmitri, it is cold
outside."

Both men tipped their glasses, took a gulp of the clear liquid,
and expelled their breath with an explosive *pah*.

"I feel better already." Filitov's laugh was hoarse. "Tell me,
what became of that Lithuanian renegade?"

"We're not sure," Ustinov said.

"Still? Can you tell me now what his letter said?"

Ustinov took another swallow before explaining. When he
finished the story Filitov was leaning forward at his desk,
shocked.

"Mother of God! And he has still not been found? How
many heads?"

"Admiral Korov is dead. He was arrested by the KGB, of

course, and died of a brain hemorrhage soon thereafter."

"A nine-millimeter hemorrhage, I trust," Filitov observed coldly. "How many times have I said it? What goddamned use is a navy? Can we use it against the Chinese? Or the NATO armies that threaten us—no! How many rubles does it cost to build and fuel those pretty barges for Gorshkov, and what do we get for it—nothing! Now he loses one submarine and the whole fucking fleet cannot find it. It is a good thing that Stalin is not alive."

Ustinov agreed. He was old enough to remember what happened then to anyone who reported results short of total success. "In any case, Padorin may have saved his skin. There is one extra element of control on the submarine."

"Padorin!" Filitov took another gulp of his drink. "That eunuch! I've only met him, what, three times. A cold fish, even for a commissar. He never laughs, even when he drinks. Some Russian he is. Why is it, Dmitri, that Gorshkov keeps so many old farts like that around?"

Ustinov smiled into his drink. "The same reason I do, Misha." Both men laughed.

"So, how will Comrade Padorin save our secrets and keep his skin? Invent a time machine?"

Ustinov explained to his old friend. There weren't many men whom the defense minister could speak to and feel comfortable with. Filitov drew the pension of a full colonel of tanks and still wore the uniform proudly. He had faced combat for the first time on the fourth day of the Great Patriotic War, as the Fascist invaders were driving east. Lieutenant Filitov had met them southeast of Brest Litovsk with a troop of T-34/76 tanks. A good officer, he had survived his first encounter with Guderian's panzers, retreated in good order, and fought a constant mobile action for days before being caught in the great encirclement at Minsk. He had fought his way out of that trap, and later another at Vyasma, and had commanded a battalion spearheading Zhukov's counterblow from the suburbs of Moscow. In 1942 Filitov had taken part in the disastrous counteroffensive toward Kharkov but again escaped, this time on foot, leading the battered remains of regiment from that dreadful cauldron on the Dnieper River. With another regiment later that year he had led the drive that shattered the Italian Army on the flank of Stalingrad and encircled the Germans. He'd been wounded twice in that campaign. Filitov had acquired the reputation of a commander who was both good and lucky. That luck had run out at Kursk, where he had battled the troopers of SS division *Das Reich*. Leading his men into a furious tank battle, Filitov and his vehicle had run straight into an ambush of eighty-eight-millimeter guns. That he had survived at all was a miracle. His chest still bore the scars from the burning tank, and his right arm was next to useless. This was enough to retire a charging tactical commander who had won the old star of the Hero of the Soviet Union no less than three times, and a dozen other decorations.

After months of being shuttled from one hospital to another, he had become a representative of the Red Army in the armament factories that had been moved to the Urals east of Moscow. The drive that made him a premiere combat soldier would come to serve the State even better behind the lines. A born organizer, Filitov learned to run roughshod over factory bosses to streamline production, and he cajoled design engineers to make the small but often crucial changes in their products that would save crews and win battles.

It was in these factories that Filitov and Ustinov first met, the scarred combat veteran and the gruff apparatchik detailed by Stalin to produce enough tools to drive the hated invaders back. After a few clashes, the young Ustinov came to recognize that Filitov was totally fearless and would not be bullied on a question involving quality control or fighting efficiency. In the midst of one disagreement, Filitov had practically dragged Ustinov into the turret of a tank and taken it through a combat training course to make his point. Ustinov was the sort who only had to be shown something once, and they soon became fast friends. He could not fail to admire the courage of a soldier who could say no to the people's commissar of armaments. By mid-1944 Filitov was a permanent part of his staff, a special inspector—in short, a hatchet man. When there was a problem at a factory, Filitov saw that it was settled, quickly. The three gold stars and the crippling injuries were usually enough to persuade the factory bosses to mend their ways—and if not, Misha had the booming voice and vocabulary to make a sergeant major wince.

Never a high Party official, Filitov gave his boss valuable input from people in the field. He still worked closely with the tank design and production teams, often taking a prototype or randomly chosen production model through a test course with a team of picked veterans to see for himself how well things worked. Crippled arm or not, it was said that Filitov was among the best gunners in the Soviet Union. And he was a humble man. In 1965 Ustinov thought to surprise his friend with general's stars and was somewhat angered by Filitov's reaction—he had not earned them on the field of battle, and that was the only way a man could earn stars. A rather impolitic remark, as Ustinov wore the uniform of a marshal of the Soviet Union, earned for his Party work and industrial management, it nevertheless demonstrated that Filitov was a true New Soviet Man, proud of what he was and mindful of his limitations.

It is unfortunate, Ustinov thought, that Misha has been so unlucky otherwise. He had been married to a lovely woman, Elena Filitov, who had been a minor dancer with the Kirov when the youthful officer had met her. Ustinov remembered her with a trace of envy; she had been the perfect soldier's wife. She had given the State two fine sons. Both were now dead. The elder had died in 1956, still a boy, an officer cadet sent to Hungary because of his political reliability and killed by counterrevolutionaries before his seventeenth birthday. He was a soldier who had taken a soldier's chance. But the younger had been killed in a training accident, blown to pieces by a faulty breech mechanism in a brand-new T-55 tank in 1959. That had been a disgrace. And Elena had died soon thereafter, of grief more than anything else. Too bad.

Filitov had not changed all that much. He drank too much, like many soldiers, but he was a quiet drunk. In 1961 or so, Ustinov remembered, he had taken to cross-country skiing. It made him healthier and tired him out, which was probably what he really wanted, along with the solitude. He was still a fine listener. When Ustinov had a new idea to float before the Politburo, he usually tried it out on Filitov first to get his reaction. Not a sophisticated man, Filitov was an uncommonly shrewd one who had a soldier's instinct for finding weaknesses and exploiting strengths. His value as a liaison officer was unsurpassed. Few men living had three gold stars won on the field of battle. That got him attention, and it still made officers far his senior listen to him.

"So, Dmitri Fedorovich, do you think this would work? Can one man destroy a submarine?" Filitov asked. "You know rockets, I don't."

"Certainly. It's merely a question of mathematics. There is enough energy in a rocket to melt the submarine."

"And what of our man?" Filitov asked. Always the combat soldier, he would be the type to worry about a brave man alone in enemy territory.

"We will do our best, of course, but there is not much hope."

"He must be rescued, Dmitri! Must! You forget, young men like that have a value beyond their deeds, they are not mere machines who perform their duties. They are symbols for our other young officers, and alive they are worth a hundred new tanks or ships. Combat is like that, Comrade. We have forgotten this—and look what has happened in Afghanistan!"

"You are correct, my friend, but—only a few hundred kilometers from the American coast, if that much?"

"Gorshkov talks so much about what his navy can do, let him do this!" Filitov poured another glass. "One more, I think."

"You are not going skiing again, Misha." Ustinov noted that he often fortified himself before driving his car to the woods east of Moscow. "I will not permit it."

"Not today, Dmitri, I promise—though I think it would do me good. Today I will go to the *banya* to take steam and sweat the rest of the poisons from this old carcass. Will you join me?"

"I have to work late."

"The *banya* is good for you," Filitov persisted. It was a waste of time, and both knew it. Ustinov was a member of the "nobility" and would not mingle in the public steam baths. Misha had no such pretentions.

The Dallas

Exactly twenty-four hours after reacquiring the *Red October*, Mancuso called a conference of his senior officers in the wardroom. Things had settled down somewhat. Mancuso had even managed to squeeze in a couple of four-hour naps and was feeling vaguely human again. They now had time to build an accurate sonar picture of the quarry, and the computer was refining a signature classification that would be out to the other fleet attack boats in a matter of weeks. From trailing they had a very accurate model of the propulsion system's noise characteristics, and from the bihourly circling they had also built a picture of the boat's size and power plant specifications.

The executive officer, Wally Chambers, twirled a pencil in his fingers like a baton. "Jonesy's right. It's the same power plant that the *Oscar*s and *Typhoon*s have. They've quieted it down, but the gross signature characteristics are virtually identical. Question is, what's it turning? It sounds like the propellers are ducted somehow, or shrouded. A directional prop with a collar around it, maybe, or some sort of tunnel drive. Didn't we try that once?"

"Long time ago," Lieutenant Butler, the engineering officer, said. "I heard a story about it while I was at Arco. It didn't work out, but I don't remember why. Whatever it is, it's really knocked down on the propulsion noises. That rumble though . . . It's some sort of harmonic all right—but a harmonic of what? You know, except for that we'd never have picked it up in the first place."

"Maybe," Mancuso said. "Jonesy says that the signal processors have tended to filter this noise out, almost as though the Soviets know what SAPS does and have tailored a system to beat it. But that's hard to believe." There was general agreement on this point. Everyone knew the principles on which SAPS operated, but there were probably not fifty men in the country who could really explain the nuts and bolts details.

"We're agreed she's a boomer?" Mancuso asked.

Butler nodded. "No way you could fit that power plant into an attack hull. More important, she acts like a boomer."

"Could be an *Oscar*," Chambers suggested.

"No. Why send an *Oscar* this far south? *Oscar*'s an antiship platform. Uh-uh, this guy's driving a boomer. He ran the route at the speed he's running now—and that's acting like a missile boat," Lieutenant Mannion noted. "What are they up to with all this other activity? That's the real question. Maybe trying to sneak up on our coast—just to see if they can do it. It's been done before, and all this other activity makes for a hell of a diversion."

They all considered that. The trick had been tried before by both sides. Most recently, in 1978, a Soviet *Yankee*-class missile sub had closed to the edge of the continental shelf off the coast of New England. The evident objective had been to see if the United States could detect it or not. The navy had succeeded, and then the question had been whether or not to react and let the Soviets know.

"Well, I think we can leave the grand strategy to the folks on the beach. Let's phone this one in. Lieutenant Mannion, tell the OOD to get us to periscope depth in twenty minutes. We'll try to slip away and back without his noticing." Mancuso frowned. This was never easy.

A half an hour later the *Dallas* radioed her message.

Z140925ZDEC

TOP SECRET THEO

FR: USS DALLAS

TO: COMSUBLANT

INFO: CINCLANTFLT

A. USS DALLAS Z090414ZDEC

1. ANOMALOUS CONTACT REACQUIRED 0538Z 13DEC. CURRENT POSITION LAT 42° 35′ LONG 49° 12′. COURSE 194 SPEED 13 DEPTH 600. HAVE TRACKED 24 HOURS WITHOUT COUNTERDETECTION. CONTACT EVALUATED AS REDFLEET SSBN GROSS SIZE, ENGINE CHARACTERISTICS INDICATIVE TYPHOON CLASS. HOWEVER CONTACT USING NEW DRIVE SYSTEM NOT REPEAT NOT PROPELLERS. HAVE ESTABLISHED DETAILED SIGNATURE PROFILE.
2. RETURNING TO TRACKING OPERATIONS. REQUEST ADDITIONAL OPAREA ASSIGNMENTS. AWAIT REPLY 1030Z.

COMSUBLANT Operations

"Bingo!" Gallery said to himself. He walked back to his office, careful to close the door before lifting the scrambled line to Washington.

"Sam, this is Vince. Listen up: *Dallas* reports she is tracking a Russian boomer with a new kind of quiet drive system, about six hundred miles southwest of the Grand Banks, course one-nine-four, speed thirteen knots."

"All right! That's Mancuso?" Dodge said.

"Bartolomeo Vito Mancuso, my favorite Guinea," Gallery confirmed. Getting him this command had not been easy because of his age. Gallery had gone the distance for him. "I told you the kid was good, Sam."

"Jesus, you see how close they are to the *Kiev* group?" Dodge was looking at his tactical display.

"They are cutting it close," Gallery agreed. *"Invincible's* not too far away, though, and I have *Pogy* out there, too. We moved her off the shelf when we called *Scamp* back in. I figure *Dallas* will need help. The question is how obvious do we want to be."

"Not very. Look, Vince, I have to talk to Dan Foster about this."

"Okay. I have to reply to *Dallas* in, hell, in fifty-five minutes. You know the score. He has to break contact to reach us, then sneak back. Hustle, Sam."

"Right, Vince." Dodge switched buttons on his phone. "This is Admiral Dodge. I need to talk to Admiral Foster right now."

The Pentagon

"Ouch. Between *Kiev* and *Kirov*. Nice." Lieutenant General Harris took a marker from his pocket to represent the *Red October*. It was a sub-shaped piece of wood with a Jolly Roger attached. Harris had an odd sense of humor. "The president says we can try and keep her?" he asked.

"If we can get her to the place we want at the time we want," General Hilton said. "Can *Dallas* signal her?"

"Good trick, General." Foster shook his head. "First things first. Let's get *Pogy* and *Invincible* there for starters, then we figure out how to warn him. From this course track, Christ, he's heading right for Norfolk. You believe the balls on this guy? If worse comes to worse, we can always try to escort him in."

"Then we'd have to give the boat back," Admiral Dodge objected.

"We have to have a fall-back position, Sam. If we can't warn him off, we can try and run a bunch of ships through with him to keep Ivan from shooting."

"The law of the sea is your bailiwick, not mine," General Barnes, the air force chief of staff, commented. "But from where I sit doing that could be called anything from piracy to an overt act of war. Isn't this exercise complicated enough already?"

"Good point, General," Foster said.

"Gentlemen, I think we need time to consider this. Okay, we still have time, but right now let's tell *Dallas* to sit tight and track the bugger," Harris said. "And report any changes in course or speed. I figure we have about fifteen minutes to do that. Next we can get *Pogy* and *Invincible* staked out on their path."

"Right, Eddie." Hilton turned to Admiral Foster. "If you agree, let's do that right now."

"Send the message, Sam," Foster ordered.

"Aye aye." Dodge went to the phone and ordered Admiral Gallery to send the reply.

Z141030ZDEC

TOP SECRET

FR: COMSUBLANT

TO: USS DALLAS

A. USS DALLAS Z140925ZDEC

1. CONTINUE TRACKING. REPORT ANY CHANGES IN COURSE OR SPEED. HELP ON THE WAY.
2. ELF TRANSMISSION "G" DESIGNATES FLASH OPS DIRECTIVE READY FOR YOU.
3. YOUR OPAREA UNRESTRICTED BRAVO ZULU DALLAS KEEP IT UP. VADM GALLERY SENDS.

"Okay, let's look at this," Harris said. "What the Russians are up to never has figured, has it?"

"What do you mean, Eddie?" Hilton asked.

"Their force composition for one thing. Half these surface platforms are antiair and antisurface, not primary ASW assets. And why bring *Kirov* along at all? Granted she makes a nice force flag, but they could do the same thing with *Kiev*."

"We talked about that already," Foster observed. "They ran down the list of what they had that could travel this far at a high speed of advance and took everything that would steam. Same with the subs they sent, half of them are antisurface SSGNs with limited utility against submarines. The reason, Eddie, is that Gorshkov wants every platform here he can get. A half-capable ship is better than nothing. Even one of the old *Echo*es might get lucky, and Sergey is probably hitting the knees every night praying for luck."

"Even so, they've split their surface groups into three forces, each with antiair and antisurface elements, and they're kind of thin on ASW hulls. Nor have they sent their ASW aircraft to stage out of Cuba. Now that is curious," Harris pointed out.

"It would blow their cover story. You don't look for a dead sub with aircraft—well, they might, but if they started using a wing of Bears out of Cuba, the president would go ape," Foster said. "We'd harass them so much they'd never accomplish anything. For us this would be a technical operation, but they factor politics into everything they do."

"Fine, but that still doesn't explain it. What ASW ships and choppers they do have are pinging away like mad. You might look for a dead sub that way, but *October* ain't dead, is she?"

"I don't understand, Eddie," Hilton said.

"How would you look for a stray sub, given these circumstances?" Harris asked Foster.

"Not like this," Foster said after a moment. "Using surface, active sonar would warn the boat off long before they could get a hard contact. Boomers are fat on passive sonar. She'd hear them coming and skedaddle out of the way. You're right, Eddie. It's a sham."

"So what the hell are their surface ships up to?" Barnes asked, puzzled.

"Soviet naval doctrine is to use surface ships to support submarine operations," Harris explained. "Gorshkov is a decent tactical theoretician, and occasionally a very innovative gent.

He said years ago that for submarines to operate effectively they have to have outside help, air or surface assets in direct or proximate support. They can't use air this far from home without staging out of Cuba, and at best finding a boat in open ocean that doesn't want to be found would be a difficult assignment.

"On the other hand, they know where she's heading, a limited number of discrete areas, and those are staked out with fifty-eight submarines. The purpose of the surface forces, therefore, is not to participate in the hunt itself—though if they got lucky, they wouldn't mind. The purpose of the surface forces is to keep us from interfering with their submarines. They can do that by staking out the areas we're likely to be with their surface assets and watching what we're doing." Harris paused for a moment. "That's smart. We have to cover them, right? And since they're on a 'rescue' mission, we have to do more or less what they're doing, so we ping away also, and they can use our own ASW expertise against us for their own purposes. We play right into their hands."

"Why?" Barnes asked again.

"We're committed to helping in the search. If we find their boat, they're close enough to find out, acquire, localize, and shoot—and what can we do about it? Not a thing.

"Like I said, they figure to locate and shoot with their submarines. A surface acquisition would be pure luck, and you don't plan for luck. So, the primary objective of the surface fleet is to ride shotgun for, and draw our forces away from, their subs. Secondarily they can act as beaters, driving the game to the shooters—and again, since we're pinging, we're helping them. We're providing an additional stalking horse." Harris shook his head in grudging admiration. "Not too shabby, is it? If *Red October* hears them coming, she runs a little harder for whatever port the skipper wants, right into a nice, tight trap. Dan, what are the chances they can bag her coming into Norfolk, say?"

Foster looked down at the chart. Russian submarines were staked out on every port from Maine to Florida. "They have more subs than we have ports. Now we know that this guy can be picked up, and there's only so much area to cover off each port, even outside the territorial limit . . . You're right, Eddie.

They have too good a chance of making the kill. Our surface groups are too far away to do anything about it. Our subs don't know what's happening, we have orders not to tell them, and even if we could, how could they interfere? Fire at the Russian subs before they could shoot—and start a war?" Foster let out a long breath. "We gotta warn him off."

"How?" Hilton asked.

"Sonar, a gertrude message maybe," Harris suggested.

Admiral Dodge shook his head. "You can hear that through the hull. If we continue to assume that only the officers are in on this, well, the crew might figure out what's happening, and there's no predicting the consequences. Think we can use *Nimitz* and *America* to force them off the coast? They'll be close enough to enter the operation soon. Damn! I don't want this guy to get this close, then get blown away right off our coast."

"Not a chance," Harris said. "Ever since the raid on *Kirov* they've been acting too docile. That's pretty cute, too. I bet they had that figured out. They know that having so many of their ships operating off our coast is bound to provoke us, so they make the first move, we up the ante, and they just plain fold—so now if we keep leaning on them, we're the bad guys. They're just doing a rescue operation, not threatening anybody. The *Post* reported this morning that we have a Russian survivor in the Norfolk naval hospital. Anyway, the good news is that they've miscalculated *October*'s speed. These two groups will pass her left and right, and with their seven-knot speed advantage they'll just pass her by."

"Disregard the surface groups entirely?" Maxwell asked.

"No," Hilton said, "that tells them we are no longer buying the cover story. They'd wonder why—and we still have to cover their surface groups. They're a threat whether they're acting like honest merchants or not."

"What we can do is pretend to release *Invincible*. With *Nimitz* and *America* ready to enter the game, we can send her home. As they pass *October* we can use that to our advantage. We put *Invincible* to seaward of their surface groups as though she's heading home and interpose her on *October*'s course. We still have to figure out a way to communicate with her, though. I can see how to get the assets in place, but that hurdle remains, gentlemen. For the moment, are we agreed to position *Invincible* and *Pogy* for the intercept?"

The Invincible

"How far is she from us?" Ryan asked.

"Two hundred miles. We can be there in ten hours." Captain Hunter marked the position on the chart. "USS *Pogy* is coming east, and she ought to be able to rendezvous with *Dallas* an hour or so after we do. This will put us about a hundred miles east of this surface group when *October* arrives. Bloody hell, *Kiev* and *Kirov* are a hundred miles east and west of her."

"You suppose her captain knows it?" Ryan looked at the chart, measuring the distances with his eyes.

"Unlikely. He's deep, and their passive sonars are not as good as ours. Sea conditions are against it also. A twenty-knot surface wind can play havoc with sonar, even that deep."

"We have to warn him off." Admiral White looked at the ops dispatch. "'Without using acoustical devices.'"

"How the hell do you do that? You can't reach down that far with a radio," Ryan noted. "Even I know that. My God, this guy's come four thousand miles, and he's going to get killed within sight of his objective."

"How to communicate with a submarine?"

Commander Barclay straightened up. "Gentlemen, we are not trying to communicate with a submarine, we are trying to communicate with a man."

"What are you thinking?" Hunter asked.

"What do we know about Marko Ramius?" Barclay's eyes narrowed.

"He's a cowboy, typical submarine commander, thinks he can walk on water," Captain Carstairs said.

"Who spent most of his time in attack submarines," Barclay added. "Marko's bet his life that he could sneak into an American port undetected by anyone. We have to shake that confidence to warn him off."

"We have to talk to him first," Ryan said sharply.

"And so we shall," Barclay smiled, the thought now fully formed in his mind. "He's a former *attack* submarine commander. He'll still be thinking about how to attack his enemies, and how does a sub commander do that?"

"Well?" Ryan demanded.

Barclay's answer was the obvious one. They discussed his

idea for another hour, then Ryan transmitted it to Washington for approval. A rapid exchange of technical information followed. The *Invincible* would have to make the rendezvous in daylight, and there was not time for that. The operation was set back twelve hours. The *Pogy* joined formation with the *Invincible,* standing as sonar sentry twenty miles to her east. An hour before midnight, the ELF transmitter in northern Michigan transmitted a message: "G." Twenty minutes later, the *Dallas* approached the surface to get her orders.

THE THIRTEENTH DAY

WEDNESDAY, 15 DECEMBER

The Dallas

"Crazy Ivan," Jones called out again, "turning to port!"

"Okay, all stop," Mancuso ordered, holding a dispatch in his hand which he had been rereading for hours. He was not pleased with it.

"All stop, sir," the helmsman responded.

"All back full."

"All back full, sir." The helmsman dialed in the command and turned, his face a question.

Throughout the *Dallas* the crew heard noise, too much noise as poppet valves opened to vent steam onto the reverse turbine blades, trying to spin the propeller the wrong way. It made for instant vibration and cavitation noises aft.

"Right full rudder."

"Right full rudder, aye."

"Conn, sonar, we are cavitating," Jones spoke over the intercom.

"Very well, sonar!" Mancuso answered sharply. He did not understand his new orders, and things he didn't understand made him angry.

"Speed down to four knots," Lieutenant Goodman reported.

"Rudder amidships, all stop."

"Rudder amidships aye, all stop aye," the helmsman responded at once. He didn't want the captain barking at him. "Sir, my rudder is amidships."

"Jesus!" Jones said in the sonar room. "What's the skipper doin'?"

Mancuso was in sonar a second later.

"Still doing the turn to port, Cap'n. He's astern of us 'cause of the turn we made," Jones observed as neutrally as he could. It was close to an accusation, Mancuso noticed.

"Flushing the game, Jonesy," Mancuso said coolly.

You're the boss, Jones thought, smart enough not to say anything else. The captain looked as though he was going to snap somebody's head off, and Jones had just used up a month's worth of tolerance. He switched his phones to the towed array plug.

"Engine noises diminishing, sir. He's slowing down." Jones paused. He had to report the next part. "Sir, it's a fair guess he heard us."

"He was supposed to," Mancuso said.

The Red October

"Captain, an enemy submarine," the *michman* said urgently.

"Enemy?" Ramius asked.

"American. He must have been trailing us, and he had to back down to avoid a collision when we turned. Definitely an American, broad on the port bow, range under a kilometer, I think." He handed Ramius his phones.

"688," Ramius said to Borodin. "Damn! He must have stumbled across us in the past two hours. Bad luck."

The Dallas

"Okay, Jonesy, yankee-search him." Mancuso gave the order for an active sonar search personally. The *Dallas* had slewed farther around before coming to a near halt.

Jones hesitated for a moment, still reading the reactor plant noise on his passive systems. Reaching, he powered up the active transducers in the BQQ-5's main sphere at the bow.

Ping! A wave front of sound energy was directed at the target.

Pong! The wave was reflected back off the hard steel hull and returned to the *Dallas.*

"Range to target 1,050 yards," Jones said. The returning pulse was processed through the BC-10 computer and showed some rough details. "Target configuration is consistent with a *Typhoon*-class boomer. Angle on the bow seventy or so. No doppler. He's stopped." Six more pings confirmed this.

"Secure pinging," Mancuso said. There was some small satisfaction in learning that he had elevated the contact correctly. But not much.

Jones killed power to the system. What the hell did I have to do that for? he wondered. He'd already done everything but read the number off her stern.

The Red October

Every man on the *October* knew now that they had been found. The lash of the sonar waves had resounded through the hull. It was not a sound a submariner liked to hear. Certainly not on top of a troublesome reactor, Ramius thought. Perhaps he could make use of this . . .

The Dallas

"Somebody on the surface," Jones said suddenly. "Where the hell did they come from? Skipper, there was nothing, *nothing,* a minute ago, and now I'm getting engine sounds. Two, maybe more—make that two 'cans . . . and something bigger. Like they were sitting up there waiting for us. A minute ago they were sitting still. Damn! I didn't hear a *thing.*"

The Invincible

"We timed that rather nicely," Admiral White said.

"Lucky," Ryan observed.

"Luck is part of the game, Jack."

HMS *Bristol* was the first to pick up the sound of the two

submarines and of the turn the *Red October* had made. Even
at five miles the subs were barely readable. The Crazy Ivan
maneuver had terminated three miles away, and the surface
ships had been able to get good position fixes by reading off
the *Dallas'* active sonar emissions.

"Two helicopters en route, sir," Captain Hunter reported.
"They'll be on station in another minute."

"Signal *Bristol* and *Fife* to stay to windward of us. I want
Invincible between them and the contact."

"Aye aye, sir." Hunter relayed the order to the communications room. The destroyermen on the escorts would find that
order peculiar, using a carrier to screen destroyers.

A few seconds later a pair of Sea King helicopters stopped
and hovered fifty feet over the surface, letting down dipping
sonars at the end of a cable as they struggled to hold position.
These sonars were far less powerful than ship-carried sonars
and had distinctive characteristics. The data they developed
was transmitted by digital link to the *Invincible*'s command
center.

The Dallas

"Limeys," Jones said at once. "That's a helicopter set, the 195,
I think. That means the big ship off to the south is one of their
baby carriers, sir, with a two-can escort."

Mancuso nodded. "HMS *Invincible*. She was over our side
of the lake for NIFTY DOLPHIN. That means the Brit varsity,
their best ASW operators."

"The big one's moving this way, sir. Turns indicate ten
knots. The choppers—two of them—have both of us. No other
subs around that I hear."

The Invincible

"Positive sonar contact," said the metal speaker. "Two submarines, range two miles from *Invincible*, bearing zero-two-
zero."

"Now for the hard part," Admiral White said.

Ryan and the four Royal Navy officers who were privy to
the mission were on the flag bridge, with the fleet ASW officer
in the command center below, as the *Invincible* steamed slowly
north, slightly to the left of the direct course to the contacts.

All five swept the contact area with powerful binoculars.

"Come on, Captain Ramius," Ryan said quietly. "You're supposed to be a hotshot. Prove it."

The Red October

Ramius was back in his control room scowling at his chart. A stray American *Los Angeles* stumbling onto him was one thing, but he had run into a small task force. English ships, at that. Why? Probably an exercise. The Americans and the English often work together, and pure accident had walked *October* right into them. Well. He'd have to evade before he could get on with what he wanted to do. It was that simple. Or was it? A hunter submarine, a carrier, and two destroyers after him. What else? He would have to find out if he were going to lose them all. This would take the best part of a day. But now he'd have to see what he was up against. Besides, it would show them that he was confident, that he could hunt *them* if he wished.

"Borodin, bring the ship to periscope depth. Battle stations."

The Invincible

"Come up, Marko," Barclay urged. "We have a message for you, old boy."

"Helicopter three reports contact is coming up," the speaker said.

"All right!" Ryan pounded his hand on the rail.

White lifted a phone. "Recall one of the helicopters."

The distance to the *Red October* was down to a mile and a half. One of the Sea Kings lifted up and circled around, reeling in its sonar transducer.

"Contact depth is five hundred feet, coming up slowly."

The Red October

Borodin was pumping water slowly from the *October*'s trim tanks. The missile submarine increased speed to four knots, and most of the force required to change her depth came from the diving planes. The *starpom* was careful to bring her up slowly, and Ramius had her heading directly towards the *Invincible*.

The Invincible

"Hunter, are you up on your Morse?" Admiral White inquired.

"I believe so, Admiral," Hunter answered. Everyone was getting excited. What a chance this was!

Ryan swallowed hard. In the past few hours, while the *Invincible* had been lying still on the rolling sea, his stomach had really gone bad. The pills the ship's doctor had given him helped, but now the excitement was making it worse. There was an eighty-foot sheer drop from the flag bridge to the sea. Well, he thought, if I have to puke, there's nothing in the way. Screw it.

The Dallas

"Hull popping noises, sir," Jones said. "Think he's heading up."

"Up?" Mancuso wondered for a second. "Yeah, that fits. He's a cowboy. He wants to see what he's up against before he tries to evade. That fits. I bet he doesn't know where we've been the past few days." The captain went forward to the attack center.

"Looks like he's going up, Skipper," Mannion said, watching the attack director. "Dumb." Mannion had his own opinion of submarine captains depending on their periscopes. Too many of them spent too much time looking out at the world. He wondered how much of this was an implicit reaction to the enforced confinement of submarining, something just to make sure that there really was a world up there, to make sure the instruments were correct. Entirely human, Mannion thought, but it could make you vulnerable...

"We go up, too, Skipper?"

"Yeah, slow and easy."

The Invincible

The sky was half-filled with white, fleecy clouds, their undersides gray with the threat of rain. A twenty-knot wind was blowing from the southwest, and a six-foot sea was running, its dark waves streaked with whitecaps. Ryan saw the *Bristol* and *Fife* holding station to windward. Their captains, no doubt, were muttering a few choice words at this disposition. The American escorts, which had been detached the previous day, were now sailing to rendezvous with the USS *New Jersey.*

White was talking into the phone again. "Commander, I want to know the instant we get a radar return from the target area. Train every set aboard onto that patch of ocean. I also want to know of any, repeat any, sonar signals from the area ... That is correct. Depth of target? Very well. Recall the second helicopter, I want both on station to windward."

They had agreed that the best method of passing the message would be to use a blinker light. Only someone placed in the direct line of sight would be able to read the signal. Hunter moved to the light, holding a sheet of paper Ryan had given him. The yeomen and signalmen normally stationed here were gone.

The Red October

"Thirty meters, Comrade Captain," Borodin reported. The battle watch was set in the control center.

"Periscope," Ramius said calmly. The oiled metal tube hissed upward on hydraulic pressure. The captain handed his cap to the junior officer of the watch as he bent to look into the eyepiece. "So, we have here three imperialist ships. HMS *Invincible.* Such a name for a ship!" He scoffed for his audience. "Two escorts, *Bristol,* and a County-class cruiser."

The Invincible

"Periscope, starboard bow!" the speaker announced.

"I see it!" Barclay's hand shot out to point. "There it is!"

Ryan strained to find it. "I got it." It was like a small broomstick sitting vertically in the water, about a mile away. As the waves rolled past, the bottommost visible part of the periscope flared out.

"Hunter," White said quietly. To Ryan's left the captain began jerking his hand on the lever that controlled the light shutters.

The Red October

Ramius didn't see it at first. He was making a complete circle of the horizon, checking for any other ships or aircraft. When he finished the circuit, the flashing light caught his eye. Quickly he tried to interpret the signal. It took him a moment to realize it was pointed right at him.

> AAA AAA AAA RED OCTOBER RED OCTOBER
> CAN YOU READ THIS CAN YOU READ THIS
> PLEASE PING US ONE TIME ON ACTIVE SONAR
> IF YOU CAN READ THIS PLEASE PING US ONE
> TIME ON ACTIVE SONAR IF YOU CAN READ THIS
> AAA AAA AAA RED OCTOBER RED OCTOBER
> CAN YOU READ THIS CAN YOU READ THIS

The message kept repeating. The signal was jerky and awkward. Ramius didn't notice this. He translated the English signal in his head, at first thinking it was a signal to the American submarine. His knuckles went white on the periscope hand grips as he translated the message in his mind.

"Borodin," he said finally, after reading the message a fourth time, "we set up a practice firing solution on *Invincible*. Damn, the periscope rangefinder is sticking. A single ping, Comrade. Just one, for range."

Ping!

The Invincible

"One ping from the contact area, sir, sounds Soviet," the speaker reported.

White lifted his phone. "Thank you. Keep us informed." He set it back down. "Well, gentlemen..."

"He did it!" Ryan sang out. "Send the rest, for Christ's sake!"

"At once." Hunter grinned like a madman.

> RED OCTOBER RED OCTOBER YOUR WHOLE
> FLEET IS CHASING AFTER YOU YOUR WHOLE
> FLEET IS CHASING AFTER YOU YOUR PATH IS

BLOCKED BY NUMEROUS VESSELS NUMEROUS
ATTACK SUBMARINES ARE WAITING TO ATTACK
YOU REPEAT NUMEROUS ATTACK SUBMARINES
ARE WAITING TO ATTACK YOU PROCEED TO
RENDEZVOUS 33N 75W WE HAVE SHIPS THERE
WAITING FOR YOU REPEAT PROCEED TO REN-
DEZVOUS 33N 75W WE HAVE SHIPS THERE WAIT-
ING FOR YOU IF YOU UNDERSTAND AND AGREE
PLEASE PING US AGAIN ONE TIME

The Red October

"Distance to target, Borodin?" Ramius asked, wishing he had
more time as the message was repeated again and again.

"Two thousand meters, Comrade Captain. A nice, fat target
for us if we . . ." The *starpom*'s voice trailed off as he saw the
look on his commander's face.

They know our name, Ramius was thinking, *they know our
name! How can this be? They knew where to find us—exactly!
How? What can the Americans have? How long has the* Los
Angeles *been trailing us? Decide—you must decide!*

"Comrade, one more ping on the target, just one."

The Invincible

"One more ping, Admiral."

"Thank you." White looked at Ryan. "Well, Jack, it would
seem that your intelligence estimate was indeed correct. Jolly
good."

"Jolly good my ass, my Lord Earl! I was right. Son of a
bitch!" Ryan's hands flew up in the air, his seasickness forgotten. He calmed down. The occasion called for more decorum. "Excuse me, Admiral. We have some things to do."

The Dallas

Whole fleet is chasing after you . . . Proceed to 33N 75W. What
the hell was going on? Mancuso wondered, catching the end
of the second signal.

"Conn, sonar. Getting hull popping noises from the target.
His depth is changing. Engine noise increasing."

"Down scope." Mancuso lifted the phone. "Very well, sonar. Anything else, Jones?"

"No, sir. The helicopters are gone, and there aren't any emissions from the surface ships. What gives, sir?"

"Beats me." Mancuso shook his head as Mannion brought the *Dallas* back in pursuit of the *Red October*. What the hell was happening here? the captain wondered. Why was a Brit carrier signaling to a Russian submarine, and why were they sending her to a rendezvous off the Carolinas? *Whose* subs were blocking her path? It couldn't be. No way. It just couldn't be . . .

The Invincible

Ryan was in the *Invincible*'s communications room. "MAGI TO OLYMPUS," he typed into the special encoding device the CIA had sent out with him, "PLAYED MY MANDOLIN TODAY. SOUNDED PRETTY GOOD. I'M PLANNING A LITTLE CONCERT, AT THE USUAL PLACE. EXPECT GOOD CRITICAL REVIEWS. AWAITING INSTRUCTIONS." Ryan had laughed before at the code words he was supposed to use for this. He was laughing now, for a different reason.

The White House

"So," Pelt observed, "Ryan expects the mission will be successful. Everything's going according to plan, but he didn't use the code group for certain success."

The president leaned back comfortably. "He's honest. Things can always go wrong. You have to admit, though, things do look good."

"This plan the chiefs came up with is crazy, sir."

"Perhaps, but you've been trying to poke a hole in it for several days now, and you haven't succeeded. The pieces will all fall in place shortly."

The president was being clever, Pelt saw. The man liked being clever.

The Invincible

"OLYMPUS TO MAGI. I LIKE OLD-FASHIONED MANDOLIN MUSIC. CONCERT APPROVED," the message said.

Ryan sat back comfortably, sipping at his brandy. "Well, that's good. I wonder what the next part of the plan is."

"I expect that Washington will let us know. For the moment," Admiral White said, "we'll have to move back west to interpose ourselves between *October* and the Soviet fleet."

The Avalon

Lieutenant Ames surveyed the scene through the tiny port on the *Avalon*'s bow. The *Alfa* lay on her port side. She had obviously hit stern first, and hard. One blade was snapped off the propeller, and the lower rudder fin was smashed. The whole stern might have been knocked off true; it was hard to tell in the low visibility.

"Moving forward slowly," he said, adjusting the controls. Behind him an ensign and a senior petty officer were monitoring instruments and preparing to deploy the manipulator arm, attached before they sailed, which carried a television camera and floodlights. These gave them a slightly wider field of view than the navigation ports permitted. The DSRV crept forward at one knot. Visibility was under twenty yards, despite the million candles of illumination from the bow lights.

The sea floor at this point was a treacherous slope of alluvial silt dotted with boulders. It appeared that the only thing that had prevented the *Alfa* from sliding farther down was her sail, driven like a wedge into the bottom.

"Holy gawd!" The petty officer saw it first. There was a crack in the *Alfa*'s hull—or was there?

"Reactor accident," Ames said, his voice detached and clinical. "Something burned through the hull. Lord, and that's *titanium!* Burned right through, from the inside out. There's another one, two burn-throughs. This one's bigger, looks like a good yard across. No mystery what killed her, guys. That's two compartments open to the sea." Ames looked over to the depth gauge: 1,880 feet. "Getting all this on tape?"

"Aye, Skipper," the electrician first class answered. "Crummy way to die. Poor bastards."

"Yeah, depending on what they were up to." Ames maneuvered the *Avalon* around the *Alfa*'s bow, working the directional propeller carefully and adjusting trim to cruise down the other side, actually the top of the dead sub. "See any evidence of a hull fracture?"

"No," the ensign answered, "just the two burn-throughs. I wonder what went wrong?"

"A for-real China Syndrome. It finally happened to somebody." Ames shook his head. If there was anything the navy preached about reactors, it was safety. "Get the transducer against the hull. We'll see if anybody's alive in there."

"Aye." The electrician worked the waldo controls as Ames tried to keep the *Avalon* dead still. Neither task was easy. The DSRV was hovering, nearly resting on the sail. If there were survivors, they had to be in the control room or forward. There could be no life aft.

"Okay, I got contact."

All three men listened intently, hoping for something. Their job was search and rescue, and as submariners themselves they took it seriously.

"Maybe they're asleep." The ensign switched on the locater sonar. The high-frequency waves resonated through both vessels. It was a sound fit to wake the dead, but there was no response. The air supply in the *Politovskiy* had run out a day before.

"That's that," Ames said quietly. He maneuvered upward as the electrician rigged in the manipulator arm, looking for a spot to drop a sonar transponder. They would be back again when the topside weather was better. The navy would not pass up this chance to inspect an *Alfa*, and the *Glomar Explorer* was sitting unused somewhere on the West Coast. Would she be activated? Ames would not bet against that.

"*Avalon, Avalon*, this is *Scamp*—" the voice on the gertrude was distorted but readable, "—return at once. Acknowledge."

"*Scamp*, this is *Avalon*. On the way."

The *Scamp* had just received an ELF message and gone briefly to periscope depth for a FLASH operational order. "PROCEED AT BEST SPEED TO 33N 75W." The message didn't say why.

CIA Headquarters

"CARDINAL is still with us," Moore told Ritter.

"Thank God for that." Ritter sat down.

"There's a signal en route. This time he didn't try to kill himself getting it to us. Maybe being in the hospital scared him a little. I'm extending another offer to extract him."

"Again?"

"Bob, we have to make the offer."

"I know. I had one sent myself a few years back, you know. The old bastard just doesn't want to quit. You know how it goes, some people thrive on the action. Or maybe he hasn't worked out his rage yet . . . I just got a call from Senator Donaldson." Donaldson was the chairman of the Select Committee on Intelligence.

"Oh?"

"He wants to know what we know about what's going on. He doesn't buy the cover story about a rescue mission, and thinks we know something different."

Judge Moore leaned back. "I wonder who planted that idea in his head?"

"Yeah. I have a little idea we might try. I think it's time, and this is a dandy opportunity."

The two senior executives discussed this for an hour. Before Ritter left for the Hill, they cleared it with the president.

Washington, D.C.

Donaldson kept Ritter waiting in his outer office for fifteen minutes while he read the paper. He wanted Ritter to know his place. Some of the DDO's remarks about leaks from the Hill had touched a sore spot with the senator from Connecticut, and it was important for appointed and civil service officials to understand the difference between themselves and the elected representatives of the people.

"Sorry to keep you waiting, Mr. Ritter." Donaldson did not rise, nor did he offer to shake hands.

"Quite all right, sir. Took the chance to read a magazine. Don't get to do that much, what with the schedule I work." They fenced with each other from the first moment.

"So, what are the Soviets up to?"

"Senator, before I address that subject, I must say this: I had to clear this meeting with the president. This information is for you alone, no one else may hear it, sir. No one. That comes from the White House."

"There are other men on my committee, Mr. Ritter."

"Sir, if I do not have your word, as a gentleman," Ritter added with a smile, "I will not reveal this information. Those are my orders. I work for the executive branch, Senator. I take my orders from the president." Ritter hoped his recording device was getting all of this.

"Agreed," Donaldson said reluctantly. He was angry because of the foolish restrictions, but pleased that he was getting to hear this. "Go on."

"Frankly, sir, we're not sure exactly what's going on," Ritter said.

"Oh, so you've sworn me to secrecy so that I can't tell anyone that, again, the CIA doesn't know what the hell is going on?"

"I said we don't know exactly what's happening. We do know a few things. Our information comes mainly from the Israelis, and some from the French. From both channels we have learned that something has gone very wrong with the Soviet Navy."

"I gathered that. They've lost a sub."

"At least one, but that's not what's going on. Someone, we think, has played a trick on the operations directorate of the Soviet Northern Fleet. I can't say for sure, but I think it was the Poles."

"Why the Poles?"

"I don't know for sure that it is, but both the French and Israelis are well connected with the Poles, *and* the Poles have a long-standing beef with the Soviets. I do know—at least I think I know—that whatever this is did not come from a Western intelligence agency."

"So, what's happening?" Donaldson demanded.

"Our best guess is that someone has committed at least one forgery, possibly as many as three, all aimed at raising hell in the Soviet Navy—but whatever it was, it's gotten far out of hand. A lot of people are working hard to cover their asses, the Israelis say. As a guess, I think they managed to alter a submarine's operational orders, then forged a letter from her skipper threatening to fire his missiles. The amazing thing is that the Soviets went for it." Ritter frowned. "We may have it all backwards, though. All we really know for sure is that somebody, probably the Poles, has played a fantastic dirty trick on the Russians."

"Not us?" Donaldson asked pointedly.

"No, sir, absolutely not! If we tried something like that—even if we succeeded, which isn't likely—they might try the same thing with us. You could start a war that way, and you know the president would never authorize it."

"But someone at the CIA might not care what the president thinks."

"Not in my department! It would be my head. Do you really think we could run an operation like this and then successfully conceal it? Hell, Senator, I *wish* we could."

"Why the Poles, and why are they able to do it?"

"We've been hearing for some time about a dissident faction inside their intelligence community, one that does not especially love the Soviets. You can pick any number of reasons why. There's the fundamental historical enmity, and the Russians seem to forget that the Poles are Polish first, Communists second. My own guess is that it's this business with the pope, even more than the martial law thing. We know that our old friend Andropov initiated a replay of the Henry II/Becket business. The pope has given Poland a great deal of prestige, done things for the country that even Party members feel good about. Ivan went and spit on their whole country when he did that—you wonder that they're mad? As to their ability, people seem to overlook just what a class act their intelligence service always has been. They're the ones who made the Enigma breakthrough in 1939, not the Brits. They're damned effective, and for the same reason as the Israelis. They have enemies to the east and the west. That sort of thing breeds good agents. We know for certain that they have a lot of people inside Russia, guest workers paying Narmonov off for the economic supports given to their country. We also know that a lot of Polish engineers are working in Soviet shipyards. I admit it's funny, neither country has much of a maritime tradition, but the Poles build a lot of Soviet merchant hulls. Their yards are more efficient than the Russian ones, and lately they've been giving technical help, mainly in quality control, to the naval building yards."

"So, the Polish intelligence service has played a trick on

the Soviets," Donaldson summarized. "Gorshkov is one of the guys who took a hard line on intervention, wasn't he?"

"True, but he's probably just a target of opportunity. The real aim of this has to be to embarrass Moscow. The fact that this operation attacks the Soviet Navy has no significance in itself. The objective is to raise hell in their senior military channels, and they all come together in Moscow. God, I wish I knew what was really happening! From the five percent we do know, this operation has to be a real masterpiece, the sort of thing legends are made of. We're working on it, trying to find out. So are the Brits, and the French, and the Israelis—Benny Herzog of the Mossad is supposed to be going ape. The Israelis *do* pull this kind of trick on their neighbors, regularly. They say officially that they don't know anything beyond what they've told us. Maybe so. Or maybe they gave the Poles some technical help—hard to say. It's certain that the Soviet Navy is a strategic threat to Israel. But we need more time on that. The Israeli connection looks a little too pat at this point."

"But you don't know what's happening, just the how and why."

"Senator, it's not that easy. Give us some time. At the moment we may not even want to know. To summarize, somebody has laid a colossal piece of disinformation on the Soviet Navy. It was probably aimed at merely shaking them up, but it has clearly gotten out of hand. How or why it happened, we do not know. You can bet, however, that whoever initiated this operation is working very hard to cover his tracks." Ritter wanted the senator to get this right. "If the Soviets find out who did it, their reaction will be nasty—depend on it. In a few weeks we might know more. The Israelis owe us for a few things, and eventually they'll let us in on it."

"For a couple more F-15s and a company of tanks," Donaldson observed.

"Cheap at the price."

"But if we're not involved in this, why the secrecy?"

"You gave me your word, Senator," Ritter reminded him. "For one thing, if word leaked out, would the Soviets believe we're not involved? Not likely! We're trying to civilize the intelligence game. I mean, we're still enemies, but having the various intelligence services in conflict uses up too many assets, and it's dangerous to both sides. For another, well, if we ever do find out how all this happened, we just might want to make use of it ourselves."

"Those reasons are contradictory."

Ritter smiled. "The intelligence game is like that. If we find out who did this, we can use that information to our advantage. In any case, Senator, you gave me your word, and I will report that to the president on my return to Langley."

"Very well." Donaldson rose. The interview was at an end. "I trust you will keep us informed of future developments."

"That's what we have to do, sir." Ritter stood.

"Indeed. Thank you for coming down." They did not shake hands this time either.

Ritter walked into the hall without passing through the anteroom. He stopped to look down into the atrium of the Hart building. It reminded him of the local Hyatt. Uncharacteristically, he took the stairs instead of the elevator down to the first floor. With luck he had just settled a major score. His car was waiting for him outside, and he told the driver to head for the FBI building.

"Not a CIA operation?" Peter Henderson, the senator's chief aide, asked.

"No, I believe him," Donaldson said. "He's not smart enough to pull something like that."

"I don't know why the president doesn't get rid of him," Henderson commented. "Of course, the kind of person he is, maybe it's better that he's incompetent." The senator agreed.

When he returned to his office, Henderson adjusted the venetian blinds on his window, though the sun was on the other side of the building. An hour later the driver of a passing Black & White taxicab looked up at the window and made a mental note.

Henderson worked late that night. The Hart building was nearly empty with most of the senators out of town. Donaldson was there only because of personal business and to keep an eye on things. As chairman of the Select Committee on Intelligence, he had more duties than he would have liked at this time of year. Henderson took the elevator down to the main lobby, looking every inch the senior congressional aide—a three-piece gray suit, an expensive leather attaché case, his hair

310 Tom Clancy

just so, and his stride jaunty as he left the building. A Black
& White cab came around the corner and stopped to let out a
fare. Henderson got in.

"Watergate," he said. Not until the taxi had driven a few
blocks did he speak again.

Henderson had a modest one-bedroom condo in the Watergate complex, an irony that he himself had considered many
times. When he got to his destination he did not tip the driver.
A woman got in as he walked to the main entrance. Taxis in
Washington are very busy in the early evening.

"Georgetown University, please," she said, a pretty young
woman with auburn hair and an armload of books.

"Night school?" the driver asked, checking the mirror.

"Exams," the girl said, her voice a trace uneasy. "Psych."

"Best thing to do with exams is relax," the driver advised.

Special Agent Hazel Loomis fumbled with her books. Her
purse dropped to the floor. "Oh, damn." She bent over to pick
it up, and while doing so retrieved a miniature tape recorder
that another agent had left under the driver's seat.

It took fifteen minutes to get to the university. The fare was
$3.85. Loomis gave the driver a five and told him to keep the
change. She walked across the campus and entered a Ford
which drove straight to the J. Edgar Hoover Building. A lot
of work had gone into this—and it had been so easy!

"Always is, when the bear walks into your sight." The
inspector who had been running the case turned left onto Pennsylvania Avenue. "The problem is finding the damned bear in
the first place."

The Pentagon

"Gentlemen, you have been asked here because each of you is
a career intelligence officer with a working knowledge of submarines and Russian," Davenport said to the four officers seated
in his office. "I have need of officers with your qualifications.
This is a volunteer assignment. It could involve a considerable
element of danger—we cannot be sure at this point. The only
other thing I can say is that this will be a dream job for an
intelligence officer—but the sort of dream that you'll never be
able to tell anyone about. We're all used to that, aren't we?"

Davenport ventured a rare smile. "As they say in the movies, if you want in, fine; if not, you may leave at this point, and nothing will ever be said. It is asking a lot to expect men to walk into a potentially dangerous assignment blindfolded."

Of course nobody left; the men who had been called here were not quitters. Besides, something would be said, and Davenport had a good memory. These were professional officers. One of the compensations for wearing a uniform and earning less money than an equally talented man can make in the real world is the off chance of being killed.

"Thank you, gentlemen. I think you will find this worth your while." Davenport stood and handed each man a manila envelope. "You will soon have the chance to examine a Soviet missile submarine—from the inside." Four pairs of eyes blinked in unison.

33N 75W

The USS *Ethan Allen* had been on station now for more than thirty hours. She was cruising in a five-mile circle at a depth of two hundred feet. There was no hurry. The submarine was making just enough speed to maintain steerage way, her reactor producing only ten percent of rated power. The chief quartermaster was assisting in the galley.

"First time I've ever done this in a sub," one of the *Allen*'s officers who was acting as ship's cook noted, stirring an omelette.

The quartermaster sighed imperceptibly. They ought to have sailed with a proper cook, but theirs had been a kid, and every enlisted man aboard now had over twenty years of service. The chiefs were all technicians, except the quartermaster, who could handle a toaster on a good day.

"You cook much at home, sir?"

"Some. My parents used to have a restaurant down at Pass Christian. This is my mama's special Cajun omelette. Shame we don't have any bass. I can do some nice things with bass and a little lemon. You fish much, Chief?"

"No, sir." The small complement of officers and senior chiefs was working in an informal atmosphere, and the quartermaster was a man accustomed to discipline and status boundaries. "Commander, can I ask what the hell we're doing?"

"Wish I knew, Chief. Mostly we're waiting for something."

"But what, sir?"

"Damned if I know. You want to hand me those ham cubes? And could you check the bread in the oven? Ought to be about done."

The New Jersey

Commander Eaton was perplexed. His battle group was holding twenty miles south of the Russians. If it hadn't been dark he could have seen the *Kirov*'s towering superstructure on the horizon from his perch on the flat bridge. Her escorts were in a single broad line ahead of the battle cruiser, pinging away in the search for a submarine.

Since the air force had staged its mock attack the Soviets had been acting like sheep. This was out of character to say the least. The *New Jersey* and her escorts were keeping the Russian formation under constant observation, and a pair of Sentry aircraft were watching for good measure. The Russian redeployment had switched Eaton's responsibility to the *Kirov* group. This suited him. His main battery turrets were trained in, but the guns were loaded with eight-inch guided rounds and the fire control stations were fully manned. The *Tarawa* was thirty miles south, her armed strike force of Harriers sitting ready to move at five-minute notice. The Soviets had to know this, even though their ASW helicopters had not come within five miles of an American ship for two days. The Bear and Backfire bombers which were passing overhead in shuttle rounds to Cuba—only a few, and those returning to Russia as quickly as they could be turned around—could not fail to report what they saw. The American vessels were in extended attack formation, the missiles on the *New Jersey* and her escorts being fed continuous information from the ships' sensors. And the Russians were ignoring them. Their only electronic emissions were routine navigation radars. Strange.

The *Nimitz* was now within air range after a five-thousand-mile dash from the South Atlantic; the carrier and her nuclear-powered escorts, the *California, Bainbridge,* and *Truxton,* were now only four hundred miles to the south, with the *America* battle group half a day behind them. The *Kennedy* was five hundred miles to the east. The Soviets would have to consider the danger of three carrier air wings at their backs and hundreds of land-based air force birds gradually shifting south from one base to another. Perhaps this explained their docility.

The Backfire bombers were being escorted in relays all the way from Iceland, first by navy Tomcats from the *Saratoga*'s air wing, then by air force Phantoms operating in Maine, which handed the Soviet aircraft off to Eagles and Fighting Falcons as they worked down the coast almost as far south as Cuba. There was not much doubt how seriously the United States was taking this, though American units were no longer actively harassing the Russians. Eaton was glad they weren't. There was nothing more to be gained from harassment, and anyway, if it had to, his battle group could switch from a peace to a war footing in about two minutes.

The Watergate Apartments

"Excuse me. I just moved in down the hall, and my phone isn't hooked up yet. Would you mind if I made a call?"

Henderson arrived at that decision quickly enough. Five three or so, auburn hair, gray eyes, adequate figure, a dazzling smile, and fashionably dressed. "Sure, welcome to the Watergate. Come on in."

"Thank you. I'm Hazel Loomis. My friends call me Sissy." She held out her hand.

"Peter Henderson. The phone's in the kitchen. I'll show you." Things were looking up. He'd just ended a lengthy relationship with one of the senator's secretaries. It had been hard on both of them.

"I'm not disturbing anything, am I? You don't have anyone here, do you?"

"No, just me and the TV. Are you new to D.C.? The night life isn't all it's cracked up to be. At least, not when you have to go to work the next day. Who do you work for—I take it you're single?"

"That's right. I work for DARPA, as a computer programmer. I'm afraid I can't talk about it very much."

All sorts of good news, Henderson thought. "Here's the phone."

Loomis looked around quickly as though evaluating the job

the decorator had done. She reached into her purse and took out a dime, handing it to Henderson. He laughed.

"The first call is free, and believe me, you can use my phone whenever you want."

"I just knew," she said, punching the buttons, "that this would be nicer than living in Laurel. Hello, Kathy? Sissy. I just got moved in, haven't even got my phone hooked up yet . . . Oh, a guy down the hall was kind enough to let me use his phone . . . Okay, see you tomorrow for lunch. Bye, Kathy."

Loomis looked around. "Who decorated for you?"

"Did it myself. I minored in art at Harvard, and I know some nice shops in Georgetown. You can find some good bargains if you know where to look."

"Oh, I'd just *love* to have my place look like this! Could you show me around?"

"Sure, the bedroom first?" Henderson laughed to show that he had no untoward intentions—which of course he did, though he was a patient man in such matters. The tour, which lasted several minutes, assured Loomis that the condo was indeed empty. A minute later there was a knock at the door. Henderson grumbled good-naturedly as he went to answer it.

"Pete Henderson?" The man asking the question was dressed in a business suit. Henderson had on jeans and a sport shirt.

"Yes?" Henderson backed up, knowing what this had to be. What came next, though, surprised him.

"You're under arrest, Mr. Henderson," Sissy Loomis said, holding up her ID card. "The charge is espionage. You have the right to remain silent, you have the right to speak with an attorney. If you give up the right to remain silent, everything you say will be recorded and may be used against you. If you do not have an attorney or cannot afford one, we will see to it that an attorney is appointed to represent you. Do you understand these rights, Mr. Henderson?" It was Sissy Loomis' first espionage case. For five years she had specialized in bank robbery stakeouts, often working as a teller with a .357 magnum revolver in her cash drawer. "Do you wish to waive these rights?"

"No, I do not." Henderson's voice was raspy.

"Oh, you will," the inspector observed. "You will." He turned to the three agents who accompanied him. "Take this

place apart. Neatly, gentlemen, and quietly. We don't want to
wake anyone. You, Mr. Henderson, will come with us. You
can change first. We can do this the easy way or the hard way.
If you promise to cooperate, no cuffs. But if you try to run—
you don't want to do that, believe me." The inspector had been
in the FBI for twenty years and had never even drawn his
service revolver in anger, while Loomis had already shot and
killed two men. He was old-time FBI, and couldn't help but
wonder what Mr. Hoover would think of that, not to mention
the new Jewish director.

The Red October

Ramius and Kamarov conferred over the chart for several minutes, tracing alternate course tracks before agreeing on one.
The enlisted men ignored this. They had never been encouraged
to know about charts. The captain walked to the aft bulkhead
and lifted the phone.

"Comrade Melekhin," he ordered, waiting a few seconds.
"Comrade, this is the captain. Any further difficulties with the
reactor systems?"

"No, Comrade Captain."

"Excellent. Hold things together another two days." Ramius
hung up. It was thirty minutes to the turn of the next watch.

Melekhin and Kirill Surzpoi, the assistant engineer, had the
duty in the engine room. Melekhin monitored the turbines and
Surzpoi handled the reactor systems. Each had a *michman* and
three enlisted men in attendance. The engineers had had a very
busy cruise. Every gauge and monitor in the engine spaces, it
seemed, had been inspected, and many had been entirely rebuilt
by the two senior officers, who had been helped by Valintin
Bugayev, the electronics officer and on-board genius who was
also handling the political awareness classes for the crewmen.
The engine room crewmen were the most rattled on the vessel.
The supposed contamination was common knowledge—there
are no long-lived secrets on a submarine. To ease their loads
ordinary seamen were supplementing the engine watches. The
captain called this a good chance for the cross-training he believed in. The crew thought it was a good way to get poisoned.
Discipline was being maintained, of course. This was owing

partly to the trust the men had in their commanding officer,
partly to their training, but mostly to their knowledge of what
would happen if they failed to carry out their orders immediately
and enthusiastically.

"Comrade Melekhin," Surzpoi called, "I am showing pressure fluctuation on the main loop, number six gauge."

"Coming." Melekhin hurried over and shoved the *michman*
out of the way when he got to the master control panel. "More
bad instruments! The others show normal. Nothing important,"
the chief engineer said blandly, making sure everyone could
hear. The whole compartment watch saw the chief engineer
whisper something to his assistant. The younger one shook
his head slowly, while two sets of hands worked the controls.

A loud two-phase buzzer and a rotating red alarm light went
off.

"SCRAM the pile!" Melekhin ordered.

"SCRAMing." Surzpoi stabbed his finger on the master
shutdown button.

"You men, get forward!" Melekhin ordered next. There was
no hesitation. "No, you, connect battery power to the caterpillar
motors, quickly!"

The warrant officer raced back to throw the proper switches,
cursing his change of orders. It took forty seconds.

"Done, Comrade!"

"*Go!*"

The warrant officer was the last man out of the compartment.
He made certain that the hatches were dogged down tight before
running to the control room.

"What is the problem?" Ramius asked calmly.

"Radiation alarm in the heat-exchange room!"

"Very well, go forward and shower with the rest of your
watch. Get control of yourself." Ramius patted the *michman*
on the arm. "We have had these problems before. You are a
trained man. The crewmen look to you for leadership."

Ramius lifted the phone. It was a moment before the other
end was picked up. "What has happened, Comrade?" The control room crew watched their captain listen to the answer. They
could not help but admire his calm. Radiation alarms had sounded
throughout the hull. "Very well. We do not have too many
hours of battery power left, Comrade. We must go to snorkling

depth. Stand by to activate the diesel. Yes." He hung up.

"Comrades, you will listen to me." Ramius' voice was under total control. "There has been a minor failure in the reactor control systems. The alarm you heard was not a major radiation leak, but rather a failure of the reactor rod control systems. Comrades Melekhin and Surzpoi successfully executed an emergency reactor shutdown, but we cannot operate the reactor properly without the primary controls. We will, therefore, complete our cruise on diesel power. To ensure against any *possible* radiation contamination, the reactor spaces have been isolated, and all compartments, engineering spaces first, will be vented with surface air when we snorkle. Kamarov, you will go aft to work the environmental controls. I will take the conn."

"Aye, Comrade Captain!" Kamarov went aft.

Ramius lifted the microphone to give this news to the crew. Everyone was waiting for something. Forward, some crewmen muttered among themselves that *minor* was a word suffering from overuse, that nuclear submarines did not run on diesel and ventilate with surface air for the hell of it.

Finished with his terse announcement, Ramius ordered the submarine to approach the surface.

The Dallas

"Beats me, Skipper." Jones shook his head. "Reactor noises have stopped, pumps are cut way back, but he's running at the same speed, just like before. On battery, I guess."

"Must be a hell of a battery system to drive something that big this fast," Mancuso observed.

"I did some computations on that a few hours ago." Jones held up his pad. "This is based on the *Typhoon* hull, with a nice slick hull coefficient, so it's probably conservative."

"Where did you learn to do this, Jonesy?"

"Mr. Thompson looked up the hydrodynamic stuff for me. The electrical end is fairly simple. He might have something exotic—fuel cells, maybe. If not, if he's running ordinary batteries, he has enough raw electrical power to crank every car in L.A."

Mancuso shook his head. "Can't last forever."

Jones held up his hand. "Hull creaking . . . Sounds like he's going up some."

The Red October

"Raise snorkle," Ramius said. Looking through the periscope he verified that the snorkle was up. "Well, no other ships in view. That is good news. I think we have lost our imperialist hunters. Raise the ESM antenna. Let's be sure no enemy aircraft are lurking about with their radars."

"Clear, Comrade Captain." Bugayev was manning the ESM board. "Nothing at all, not even airline sets."

"So, we have indeed lost our rat pack." Ramius lifted the phone again. "Melekhin, you may open the main induction and vent the engine spaces, then start the diesel." A minute later everyone aboard felt the vibration as the *October*'s massive diesel engine cranked on battery power. This sucked up all the air from the reactor spaces, replacing it with air drawn through the snorkle and ejecting the "contaminated" air into the sea.

The engine continued to crank two minutes, and throughout the hull men waited for the rumble that would mean the engine had caught and could generate power to run the electric motors. It didn't catch. After another thirty seconds the cranking stopped. The control room phone buzzed. Ramius lifted it.

"What is wrong with the diesel, Comrade Chief Engineer?" the captain asked sharply. "I see. I'll send men back—oh. Stand by." Ramius looked around, his mouth a thin, bloodless smile. The junior engineering officer, Svyadov, was standing at the back of the compartment. "I need a man who knows diesel engines to help Comrade Melekhin."

"I grew up on a State farm," Bugayev said. "I started playing with tractor engines as a boy."

"There is an additional problem . . ."

Bugayev nodded knowingly. "So I gather, Comrade Captain, but we need the diesel, do we not?"

"I will not forget this, Comrade," Ramius said quietly.

"Then you can buy me some rum in Cuba, Comrade." Bugayev smiled courageously. "I wish to meet a Cuban comrade, preferably one with long hair."

"May I accompany you, Comrade?" Svyadov asked anxiously. He had just been going on watch, approaching the reactor room hatch, when he'd been knocked aside by escaping crewmen.

"Let us assess the nature of the problem first," Bugayev said, looking at Ramius for confirmation.

"Yes, there is plenty of time. Bugayev, report to me yourself in ten minutes."

"Aye aye, Comrade Captain."

"Svyadov, take charge of the lieutenant's station." Ramius pointed to the ESM board. "Use the opportunity to learn some new skills."

The lieutenant did as he was ordered. The captain seemed very preoccupied. Svyadov had never seen him like this before.

THE FOURTEENTH DAY

THURSDAY, 16 DECEMBER

A Super Stallion

They were traveling at one hundred fifty knots, two thousand feet over the darkened sea. The Super Stallion helicopter was old. Built towards the end of the Vietnam War, she had first seen service clearing mines off Haiphong harbor. That had been her primary duty, pulling a sea sled and acting as a flying minesweeper. Now, the big Sikorski was used for other purposes, mainly long-range heavy-lift missions. The three turbine engines perched atop the fuselage packed a considerable amount of power and could carry a platoon of armed combat troops a great distance.

Tonight, in addition to her normal flight crew of three, she was carrying four passengers and a heavy load of fuel in the outrigger tanks. The passengers were clustered in the aft corner of the cargo area, chatting among themselves or trying to over the racket of the engines. Their conversation was animated. The intelligence officers had dismissed the danger implicit in

their mission—no sense dwelling on that—and were speculating on what they might find aboard an honest-to-God Russian
submarine. Each man considered the stories that would result,
and decided it was a shame that they would never be able to
tell them. None voiced this thought, however. At most a handful
of people would ever know the entire story; the others would
only see disjointed fragments that later might be thought parts
of any number of other operations. Any Soviet agent trying to
determine what this mission had been would find himself in a
maze with dozens of blank walls.

The mission profile was a tight one. The helicopter was
flying on a specific track to HMS *Invincible,* from which they
would fly to the USS *Pigeon* aboard a Royal Navy Sea King.
The Stallion's disappearance from Oceana Naval Air Station
for only a few hours would be viewed merely as a matter of
routine.

The helicopter's turboshaft engines, running at maximum
cruising power, were gulping down fuel. The aircraft was now
four hundred miles off the U.S. coast and had another eighty
miles to go. Their flight to the *Invincible* was not direct; it was
a dogleg course intended to fool whoever might have noticed
their departure on radar. The pilots were tired. Four hours is
a long time to sit in a cramped cockpit, and military aircraft
are not known for their creature comforts. The flight instruments glowed a dull red. Both men were especially careful to
watch their artificial horizon; a solid overcast denied them a
fixed reference point aloft, and flying over water at night was
mesmerizing. It was by no means an unusual mission, however.
The pilots had done this many times, and their concern was
not unlike that of an experienced driver on a slick road. The
dangers were real, but routine.

"Juliet 6, your target is bearing zero-eight-zero, range seventy-five miles," the Sentry called in.

"Thinks we're lost?" Commander John Marcks wondered
over the intercom.

"Air force," his copilot replied. "They don't know much
about flying over water. They think you get lost without roads
to follow."

"Uh-huh," Marcks chuckled. "Who do you like in the Eagles
game tonight?"

"Oilers by three and a half."

"Six and a half. Philly's fullback is still hurt."

"Five."

"Okay, five bucks. I'll go easy on you." Marcks grinned. He loved to gamble. The day after Argentina had attacked the Falklands, he'd asked if anyone in the squadron wanted to take Argentina and seven points.

A few feet above their heads and a few feet aft, the engines were racing at thousands of RPM, turning gears to drive the seven-bladed main rotor. They had no way of knowing that a fracture was developing in the transmission casing, near the fluid test port.

"Juliet 6, your target has just launched a fighter to escort you in. Will rendezvous in eight minutes. Approaching you at eleven o'clock, angels three."

"Nice of them," Marcks said.

Harrier 2-0

Lieutenant Parker was flying the Harrier that would escort the Super Stallion. A sublieutenant sat in the back seat of the Royal Navy aircraft. Its purpose was not actually to escort the chopper to the *Invincible;* it was to make a last check for any Soviet submarines that might notice the Super Stallion in flight and wonder what it was doing.

"Any activity on the water?" Parker asked.

"Not a glimmer." The sublieutenant was working the FLIR package, which was sweeping left and right over their course track. Neither man knew what was going on, though both had speculated at length, incorrectly, on what it was that was chasing their carrier all over the bloody ocean.

"Try looking for the helicopter," Parker said.

"One moment . . . There. Just south of our track." The sublieutenant pressed a button and the display came up on the pilot's screen. The thermal image was mainly of the engines clustered atop the aircraft inside the fainter, dull-green glow of the hot rotor tips.

"Harrier 2-0, this is Sentry Echo. Your target is at your one o'clock, distance twenty miles, over."

"Roger, we have him on our IR box. Thank you, out,"

Parker said. "Bloody useful things, those Sentries."

"The Sikorski's running for all she's worth. Look at that engine signature."

The Super Stallion

At this moment the transmission casing fractured. Instantly the gallons of lubricating oil became a greasy cloud behind the rotor hub, and the delicate gears began to tear at one another. An alarm light flashed on the control panels. Marcks and the copilot instantly reached down to cut power to all three engines. There was not enough time. The transmission tried to freeze, but the power of the three engines tore it apart. What happened was the next thing to an explosion. Jagged pieces burst through the safety housing and ripped the forward part of the aircraft. The rotor's momentum twisted the Stallion savagely around, and it dropped rapidly. Two of the men in the back, who had loosened their seatbelts, jerked out of their seats and rolled forward.

"MAYDAY MAYDAY MAYDAY, this is Juliet 6," the copilot called. Commander Marcks' body slumped over the controls, a dark stain at the back of his neck. "We're goin' in, we're goin' in. MAYDAY MAYDAY MAYDAY."

The copilot was trying to do something. The main rotor was windmilling slowly—too slowly. The automatic decoupler that was supposed to allow it to autorotate and give him a vestige of control had failed. His controls were nearly useless, and he was riding the point of a blunt lance towards a black ocean. It was twenty seconds before they hit. He fought with his airfoil controls and tail rotor in order to jerk the aircraft around. He succeeded, but it was too late.

Harrier 2-0

It was not the first time Parker had seen men die. He had taken a life himself after sending a Sidewinder missile up the tailpipe of an Argentine Dagger fighter. That had not been pleasant. This was worse. As he watched, the Super Stallion's hump-backed engine cluster blew apart in a shower of sparks. There was no fire as such, for what good it did them. He watched and tried to will the nose to come up—and it did, but not enough. The Stallion hit the water hard. The fuselage snapped apart in the middle. The front end sank in an instant, but the after part wallowed for a few seconds like a bathtub before beginning to fill with water. According to the picture supplied by the FLIR package, no one got clear before it sank.

"Sentry, Sentry, did you see that, over?"

"Roger that, Harrier. We're calling a SAR mission right now. Can you orbit?"

"Roger, we can loiter here." Parker checked his fuel. "Nine-zero minutes. I—stand by." Parker nosed his fighter down and flicked on his landing lights. This lit up the low-light TV system. "Did you see that, Ian?" he asked his backseater.

"I think it moved."

"Sentry, Sentry, we have a possible survivor in the water. Tell *Invincible* to get a Sea King down here straightaway. I'm going down to investigate. Will advise."

"Roger that, Harrier 2-0. Your captain reports a helo spooling up right now. Out."

The Royal Navy Sea King was there in twenty-five minutes. A rubber-suited paramedic jumped in the water to get a collar on the one survivor. There were no others, and no wreckage, only a slick of jet fuel evaporating slowly into the cold air. A second helicopter continued the search as the first raced back to the carrier.

The Invincible

Ryan watched from the bridge as the medics carried the stretcher into the island. Another crewman appeared a moment later with a briefcase.

"He had this, sir. He's a lieutenant commander, name of Dwyer, one leg and several ribs broken. He's in a bad way, Admiral."

"Thank you." White took the case. "Any possibility of other survivors?"

The sailor shook his head. "Not a good one, sir. The Sikorski must have sunk like a stone." He looked at Ryan. "Sorry, sir."

Ryan nodded. "Thanks."

"Norfolk on the radio, Admiral," a communications officer said.

"Let's go, Jack." Admiral White handed him the briefcase and led him to the communications room.

"The chopper went in. We have one survivor being worked on right now," Ryan said over the radio. It was silent for a moment.

"Who is it?"

"Name's Dwyer. They took him right to sick bay, Admiral. He's out of action. Tell Washington. Whatever this operation is supposed to be, we have to rethink it."

"Roger. Out," Admiral Blackburn said.

"Whatever we decide to do," Admiral White observed, "it will have to be fast. We must get our helo off to the *Pigeon* in two hours to have her back before dawn."

Ryan knew exactly what that would mean. There were only four men at sea who both knew what was going on and were close enough to do anything. He was the only American among them. The *Kennedy* was too far away. The *Nimitz* was close enough, but using her would mean getting the data to her by radio, and Washington was not enthusiastic about that. The only other alternative was to assemble and dispatch another intelligence team. There just wasn't enough time.

"Let's get this case open, Admiral. I need to see what this plan is." They picked up a machinist's mate on the way to White's cabin. He proved to be an excellent locksmith.

"Dear God!" Ryan breathed, reading the contents of the case. "You better see this."

"Well," White said a few minutes later, "that is clever."

"It's cute, all right," Ryan said. "I wonder what genius thought it up. I know I'm going to be stuck with this. I'll ask Washington for permission to take a few officers along with me."

Ten minutes later they were back in communications. White had the compartment cleared. Then Jack spoke over the encrypted voice channel. Both hoped the scrambling device worked.

"I hear you fine, Mr. President. You know what happened to the helicopter."

"Yes, Jack, most unfortunate. I need you to pinch-hit for us."

"Yes, sir, I anticipated that."

"I can't order you, but you know what the stakes are. Will you do it?"

Ryan closed his eyes. "Affirmative."

"I appreciate it, Jack."

Sure you do. "Sir, I need your authorization to take some help with me, a few British officers."

"One," the president said.

"Sir, I need more than that."

"One."

"Understood, sir. We'll be moving in an hour."

"You know what's supposed to happen?"

"Yes, sir. The survivor had the ops orders with him. I've already read them over."

"Good luck, Jack."

"Thank you, sir. Out." Ryan flipped off the satellite channel and turned to Admiral White. "Volunteer once, just one time, and see what happens."

"Frightened?" White did not appear amused.

"Damned right I am. Can I borrow an officer? A guy who speaks Russian if possible. You know what this may involve."

"We'll see. Come on."

Five minutes later they were back in White's cabin awaiting the arrival of four officers. All turned out to be lieutenants, all under thirty.

"Gentlemen," the admiral began, "this is Commander Ryan. He needs an officer to accompany him on a voluntary basis for a mission of some importance. Its nature is secret and most unusual, and there may be some danger involved. You four have been asked here because of your knowledge of Russian. That is all I can say."

"Going to talk to a Sov submarine?" the oldest of them chirped up. "I'm your man. I have a degree in the language, and my first posting was aboard HMS *Dreadnought*."

Ryan weighed the ethics of accepting the man before telling him what was involved. He nodded, and White dismissed the others.

"I'm Jack Ryan." He extended his hand.

"Owen Williams. So, what are we up to?"

"The submarine is named *Red October*—"

"Krazny Oktyabr." Williams smiled.

"And she's attempting to defect to the United States."

"Indeed? So that's what we've been mucking about for. Jolly decent of her CO. Just how certain are we of this?"

Ryan took several minutes to detail the intelligence information. "We blinkered instructions to him, and he seems to have played along. But we won't know for sure until we get aboard. Defectors have been known to change their minds, it happens a lot more often than you might imagine. Still want to come along?"

"Miss a chance like this? Exactly how do we get aboard, Commander?"

"The name's Jack. I'm CIA, not navy." He went on to explain the plan.

"Excellent. Do I have time to pack some things?"

"Be back here in ten minutes," White said.

"Aye aye, sir." Williams drew to attention and left.

White was on the phone. "Send Lieutenant Sinclair to see me." The admiral explained that he was the commander of the *Invincible's* marine detachment. "Perhaps you might need another friend along."

The other friend was an FN nine-millimeter automatic pistol with a spare clip and a shoulder holster that disappeared nicely under his jacket. The mission orders were shredded and burned before they left.

Admiral White accompanied Ryan and Williams to the flight deck. They stood at the hatch, looking at the Sea King as its engines screeched into life.

"Good luck, Owen." White shook hands with the youngster, who saluted and moved off.

"My regards to your wife, Admiral." Ryan took his hand.

"Five and a half days to England. You'll probably see her before I do. Be careful, Jack."

Ryan smiled crookedly. "It's my intelligence estimate, isn't it? If I'm right, it'll just be a pleasure cruise—assuming the helicopter doesn't crash on me."

"The uniform looks good on you, Jack."

Ryan hadn't expected that. He drew himself to attention and saluted as he'd been taught at Quantico. "Thank you, Admiral. Be seeing you."

White watched him enter the chopper. The crew chief slid the door shut, and a moment later the Sea King's engines increased power. The helicopter lifted unevenly for a few feet before its nose dipped to port and began a climbing turn to the south. Without flying lights the dark shape was lost to sight in less than a minute.

33N 75W

The *Scamp* rendezvoused with the *Ethan Allen* a few minutes after midnight. The attack sub took up station a thousand yards astern of the old missile boat, and both cruised in an easy circle as their sonar operators listened to the approach of a diesel-powered vessel, the USS *Pigeon*. Three of the pieces were now in place. Three more were to come.

The Red October

"There is no choice," Melekhin said. "I must continue to work on the diesel."

"Let us help you," Svyadov said.

"And what do you know of diesel fuel pumps?" Melekhin asked in a tired but kind voice. "No, Comrade. Surzpoi, Bugayev, and I can handle it alone. There is no reason to expose you also. I will report back in an hour."

"Thank you, Comrade." Ramius clicked the speaker off. "This cruise has been a troublesome one. Sabotage. Never in my career has something like this happened! If we cannot fix the diesel . . . We have only a few hours more of battery power, and the reactor requires a total overhaul and safety inspection. I swear to you, Comrades, if we find the bastard who did this to us . . ."

"Shouldn't we call for help?" Ivanov asked.

"This close to the American coast, and perhaps an imperialist submarine still on our tail? What sort of 'help' might we get, eh? Comrades, perhaps our problem is no accident, have you considered that? Perhaps we have become pawns in a murderous game." He shook his head. "No, we cannot risk this. The Americans must not get their hands on this submarine!"

CIA Headquarters

"Thank you for coming on such short notice, Senator. I apologize for getting you up so early." Judge Moore met Donaldson at the door and led him into his capacious office. "You know Director Jacobs, don't you?"

"Of course, and what brings the heads of the FBI and CIA together at dawn?" Donaldson asked with a smile. This had to be good. Heading the Select Committee was more than a job, it was fun, real fun to be one of the few people who were really in the know.

The third person in the room, Ritter, helped a fourth person out of a high-backed chair that had blocked him from view. It was Peter Henderson, Donaldson saw to his surprise. His aide's suit was rumpled as though he'd been up all night. Suddenly it wasn't fun anymore.

Judge Moore waxed solicitous. "You know Mr. Henderson, of course."

"What is the meaning of this?" Donaldson asked, his voice more subdued than anyone expected.

"You lied to me, Senator," Ritter said. "You promised that you would not reveal what I told you yesterday, knowing all the time you'd tell this man—"

"I did no such thing."

"—who then told a fellow KGB agent," Ritter went on. "Emil?"

Jacobs set his coffee down. "We've been onto Mr. Henderson for some time. It was his contact that had us stumped. Some things are just too obvious. A lot of people in D.C. have regular cab pickup. Henderson's contact was a cab driver. We finally got it right."

"The way we found out about Henderson was through you, Senator." Moore explained: "We had a very good agent in Moscow a few years ago, a colonel in their Strategic Rocket Forces. He'd been giving us good information for five years, and we were about to get him and his family out. We try to do that, you know; you can't run agents forever, and we really owed this man. But I made the mistake of revealing his name to your committee. One week later, he was gone—vanished.

He was eventually shot, of course. His wife and three daughters were sent to Siberia. Our information is that they live in a lumber settlement east of the Urals. Typical sort of place, no plumbing, lousy food, no medical facilities available, and since they're the family of a convicted traitor, you can probably imagine what sort of hell they must endure. A good man dead, and a family destroyed. Try thinking about that, Senator. This is a true story, and these are real people.

"We didn't know at first who had leaked it. It had to be you, or one of two others, so we began to leak information to individual committee members. It took six months, but your name came up three times. After that we had Director Jacobs check out all of your staffers. Emil?"

"When Henderson was an assistant editor of the Harvard *Crimson,* in 1970, he was sent to Kent State to do a piece on the shooting. You remember, the 'Days of Rage' thing after the Cambodian incursion and that awful screw-up with the national guard. I was in on that, too, as luck would have it. Evidently it turned Henderson's stomach. Understandable. But not his reaction. When he graduated and joined your staff he started talking with his old activist friends about his job. This led to a contract from the Russians, and they asked for some information. That was during the Christmas bombing—he really didn't like that. He delivered. It was low-level stuff at first, nothing they couldn't have gotten a few days later from the *Post.* That's how it works. They offered the hook, and he nibbled at it. A few years later, of course, they struck the hook nice and hard and he couldn't get away. We all know how the game works.

"Yesterday we planted a tape recorder in his taxi. You'd be amazed how easy it was. Agents get lazy, too, just like the rest of us. To make a long story short, we have you on tape promising not to reveal the information to anyone, and we have Henderson here spilling that data not three hours later to a known KGB agent, also on tape. You have violated no laws, Senator, but Mr. Henderson has. He was arrested at nine last night. The charge is espionage, and we have the evidence to make it stick."

"I had no knowledge whatever of this," Donaldson said.

"We hadn't the slightest thought that you might," Ritter said.

Donaldson faced his aide. "What do you have to say for yourself?"

Henderson didn't say anything. He thought about saying how sorry he was, but how to explain his emotions? The dirty feeling of being an agent for a foreign power, juxtaposed with the thrill of fooling a whole legion of government spooks. When he was caught these emotions changed to fear at what would happen to him, and relief that it was all over.

"Mr. Henderson has agreed to work for us," Jacobs said helpfully. "As soon as you leave the Senate, that is."

"What does that mean?" Donaldson asked.

"You've been in the Senate, what? Thirteen years, isn't it? You were originally appointed to fill out an unexpired term, if memory serves," Moore said.

"You might try asking my reaction to blackmail," the senator observed.

"Blackmail?" Moore held his hands out. "Good Lord, Senator, Director Jacobs has already told you that you have broken no laws, and you have my word that the CIA will not leak a word of this. Now, whether or not the Justice Department decides to prosecute Mr. Henderson is not in our hands. 'Senate Aide Convicted of Treason: Senator Donaldson Professes No Knowledge of Aide's Action.'"

Jacobs went on, "Senator, the University of Connecticut has offered you the chair in their school of government for some years now. Why not take it?"

"Or Henderson goes to prison. You put that on my conscience?"

"Obviously he cannot go on working for you, and it should be equally obvious that if he is fired after so many years of exemplary service in your office, it will be noticed. If, on the other hand, you decide to leave public life, it would not be too surprising if he were not able to get a job of equivalent stature with another senator. So, he will get a nice job in the General Accounting Office, where he will still have access to all sorts of secrets. Only from now on," Ritter said, "we decide which secrets he passes along."

"No statute of limitations on espionage," Jacobs pointed out.

"If the Soviets find out," Donaldson said, and stopped. He

didn't really care, did he? Not about Henderson, not about the fictitious Russian. He had an image to save, losses to cut.

"You win, Judge."

"I thought you'd see it our way. I'll tell the president. Thanks for coming in, Senator. Mr. Henderson will be a little late to the office this morning. Don't feel too badly about him, Senator. If he plays ball with us, in a few years we might let him off the hook. It's happened before, but he'll have to earn it. Good morning, sir."

Henderson would play along. His alternative was life in a maximum security penitentiary. After listening to the tape of his conversation in the cab, he'd made his confession in front of a court stenographer and a television camera.

The Pigeon

The ride to the *Pigeon* had been mercifully uneventful. The catamaran-hull rescue ship had a small helicopter platform aft, and the Royal Navy helicopter had hovered two feet above it, allowing Ryan and Williams to jump down. They were taken immediately to the bridge as the helicopter buzzed back northeast to her home.

"Welcome aboard, gentlemen," the captain said agreeably. "Washington says you have orders for me. Coffee?"

"Do you have tea?" Williams asked.

"We can probably find some."

"Let's go someplace we can talk in private," Ryan said.

The Dallas

The *Dallas* was now in on the plan. Alerted by another ELF transmission, Mancuso had brought her to antenna depth briefly during the night. The lengthy EYES ONLY message had been decrypted by hand in his cabin. Decryption was not Mancuso's strong point. It took him an hour as Chambers conned the *Dallas* back to trail her contact. A crewman passing the captain's cabin heard a muted *damn* through the door. When Mancuso reappeared, his mouth couldn't keep from twitching into a smile. He was not a good card player either.

The Pigeon

The *Pigeon* was one of the navy's two modern submarine rescue
ships designed to locate and reach a sunken nuclear sub quickly
enough to save her crew. She was outfitted with a variety of
sophisticated equipment, chief among them the DSRV. This
vessel, the *Mystic*, was hanging on its rack between the *Pigeon*'s twin catamaran hulls. There was also a 3-d sonar operating at low power, mainly as a beacon, while the *Pigeon*
cruised in slow circles a few miles south of the *Scamp* and
Ethan Allen. Two *Perry*-class frigates were twenty miles north,
operating in conjunction with three Orions to sanitize the area.

"*Pigeon*, this is *Dallas*, radio check, over."

"*Dallas*, this is *Pigeon*. Read you loud and clear, over,"
the rescue ship's captain replied on the secure radio channel.

"The package is here. Out."

"Captain, on *Invincible* we had an officer send the message
with a blinker light. Can you handle the blinker light?" Ryan
asked.

"To be part of this? Are you kidding?"

The plan was simple enough, just a little too cute. It was
clear that the *Red October* wanted to defect. It was even possible that everyone aboard wanted to come over—but hardly
likely. They were going to get everyone off the *Red October*
who might want to return to Russia, then pretend to blow up
the ship with one of the powerful scuttling charges Russian
ships are known to carry. The remaining crewmen would then
take their boat northwest into Pamlico Sound to wait for the
Soviet fleet to return home, sure that the *Red October* had been
sunk and with the crew to prove it. What could possibly go
wrong? A thousand things.

The Red October

Ramius looked through his periscope. The only ship in view
was the USS *Pigeon*, though his ESM antenna reported surface
radar activity to the north, a pair of frigates standing guard
over the horizon. So, this was the plan. He watched the blinker
light, translating the message in his mind.

Norfolk Naval Medical Center

"Thanks for coming down, Doc." The intelligence officer had taken over the office of assistant hospital administrator. "I understand our patient woke up."

"About an hour ago," Tait confirmed. "He was conscious for about twenty minutes. He's asleep now."

"Does that mean he'll make it?"

"It's a positive sign. He was reasonably coherent, so there's no evident brain damage. I was a little worried about that. I'd have to say the odds are in his favor now, but these hypothermia cases have a way of souring on you in a hurry. He's a sick kid, that hasn't changed." Tait paused. "I have a question for you, Commander: Why aren't the Russians happy?"

"What makes you think that?"

"Kind of hard to miss. Besides, Jamie found a doctor on staff who understands Russian, and we have him attending the case."

"Why didn't you let me know about that?"

"The Russians don't know either. That was a medical judgment, Commander. Having a physician around who speaks the patient's language is simply good medical practice." Tait smiled, pleased with himself for having thought up his own intelligence ploy while at the same time adhering to proper medical ethics and naval regulations. He took a file card from his pocket. "Anyway, the patient's name is Andre Katyskin. He's a cook, like we thought, from Leningrad. The name of his ship was the *Politovskiy*."

"My compliments, Doctor." The intelligence officer acknowledged Tait's maneuver, though he wondered why it was that amateurs had to be so damned clever when they butted into things that didn't concern them.

"So why are the Russians unhappy?" Tait did not get an answer. "And why don't *you* have a guy up there? You knew all along, didn't you? You knew what ship he escaped from, and you knew why she sank . . . So, if they wanted most of all to know what ship he came from, and if they don't like the news they got—does that mean they have *another* missing sub out there?"

CIA Headquarters

Moore lifted his phone. "James, you and Bob get in here right now!"

"What is it, Arthur?" Greer asked a minute later.

"The latest from CARDINAL." Moore handed xeroxed copies of a message to both men. "How quick can we get word out?"

"That far out? Means a helicopter, a couple of hours at least. We have to get this out quicker than that," Greer urged.

"We can't endanger CARDINAL, period. Draw up a message and get the navy or air force to relay it by hand." Moore didn't like it, but he had no choice.

"It'll take too long!" Greer objected loudly.

"I like the boy, too, James. Talking about it doesn't help. Get moving."

Greer left the room cursing like the fifty-year sailor he was.

The Red October

"Comrades. Officers and men of *Red October,* this is the captain speaking." Ramius' voice was subdued, the crewmen noticed. The incipient panic that had started a few hours earlier had driven them to the brittle edge of riot. "Efforts to repair our engines have failed. Our batteries are nearly flat. We are too far from Cuba for help, and we cannot expect help from the *Rodina.* We do not have enough electrical power even to operate our environmental control systems for more than a few hours. We have no choice, we must abandon ship.

"It is no accident that an American ship is now close to us, offering what they call assistance. I will tell you what has happened, comrades. An imperialist spy has sabotaged our ship, and somehow they knew what our orders were. They were waiting for us, comrades, waiting and hoping to get their dirty hands on our ship. They will not. The crew will be taken off. They will not get our *Red October!* The senior officers and I will remain behind to set off the scuttling charges. The water here is five thousand meters deep. They will not have our ship. All crewmen except those on duty will assemble in their quarters. That is all." Ramius looked around the control room. "We have lost, comrades. Bugayev, make the necessary signals to Moscow and to the American ship. We will then dive to a hundred meters. We will take no chance that they will seize our ship. I take full responsibility for this—disgrace! Mark this well, comrades. The fault is mine alone."

The Pigeon

"Signal received: 'SSS,'" the radioman reported.

"Ever been on a submarine before, Ryan?" Cook asked.

"Nope, I hope it's safer 'n flying." Ryan tried to make a joke of it. He was deeply frightened.

"Well, let's get you down to *Mystic*."

The Mystic

The DSRV was nothing more than three metal spheres welded together with a propeller on the back and some boiler plating all around to protect the pressure-bearing parts of the hull. Ryan was first through the hatch, then Williams. They found seats and waited. A crew of three was already at work.

The *Mystic* was ready for operation. On command, the *Pigeon*'s winches lowered her to the calm water below. She dived at once, her electric motors hardly making any noise. Her low-power sonar system immediately acquired the Russian submarine, half a mile away, at a depth of three hundred feet. The operating crew had been told that this was a straightforward rescue mission. They were experts. The *Mystic* was hovering over the missile sub's forward escape trunk within ten minutes.

The directional propellers worked them carefully into place and a petty officer made certain that the mating skirt was securely fastened. The water in the skirt between *Mystic* and *Red October* was explosively vented into a low-pressure chamber on the DSRV. This established a firm seal between the two vessels, and the residual water was pumped out.

"Your ball now, I guess." The lieutenant motioned Ryan to the hatch in the floor of the middle segment.

"I guess." Ryan knelt by the hatch and banged a few times with his hand. No response. Next he tried a wrench. A moment later three clangs echoed back, and Ryan turned the locking wheel in the center of the hatch. When he pulled the hatch up, he found another that had already been opened from below. The lower perpendicular hatch was shut. Ryan took a deep breath and climbed down the ladder of the white painted cylinder, followed by Williams. After reaching the bottom Ryan knocked on the lower hatch.

The Red October

It opened at once.

"Gentlemen, I am Commander Ryan, United States Navy. Can we be of assistance?"

The man he spoke to was shorter and heavier than himself. He wore three stars on his shoulder boards, an extensive set of ribbons on his breast, and a broad gold stripe on his sleeve. So, this was Marko Ramius . . .

"Do you speak Russian?"

"No sir, I do not. What is the nature of your emergency, sir?"

"We have a major leak in our reactor system. The ship is contaminated aft of the control room. We must evacuate."

At the words *leak* and *reactor* Ryan felt his skin crawl. He remembered how positive he had been that his scenario was correct. On land, nine hundred miles away, in a nice, warm office, surrounded by friends—well, not enemies. The looks he was getting from the twenty men in this compartment were lethal.

"Dear God! Okay, let's get moving then. We can take off twenty-five men at a time, sir."

"Not so fast, Commander Ryan. What will become of my men?" Ramius asked loudly.

"They will be treated as our guests, of course. If they need medical attention, they will get it. They will be returned to the Soviet Union as quickly as we can arrange it. Did you think we'd put them in prison?"

Ramius grunted and turned to speak with the others in Russian. On the flight from the *Invincible* Ryan and Williams had decided to keep the latter's knowledge of Russian secret for a while, and Williams was now dressed in an American uniform. Neither thought a Russian would notice the different accent.

"Dr. Petrov," Ramius said, "you will take the first group of twenty-five. Keep control of the men, Comrade Doctor! Do not let the Americans speak to them as individuals, and let no man wander off alone. You will behave correctly, no more, no less."

"Understood, Comrade Captain."

Ryan watched Petrov count the men off as they passed through the hatch and up the ladder. When they were finished, Williams secured first the *Mystic*'s hatch and then the one on the *October*'s escape truck. Ramius had a *michman* check it. They heard the DSRV disengage and motor off.

The silence that ensued was as long as it was awkward. Ryan and Williams stood in one corner of the compartment, Ramius and his men opposite them. It made Ryan think back to high school dances where boys and girls gathered in separate groups and there was a no-man's-land in the middle. When an officer fished out a cigarette, he tried breaking the ice.

"May I have a cigarette, sir?"

Borodin jerked the pack, and a cigarette came part way out. Ryan took it, and Borodin lit it with a paper match.

"Thanks. I gave it up, but underwater in a sub with a bad reactor, I don't think it's too dangerous, do you?" Ryan's first experience with a Russian cigarette was not a happy one. The black coarse tobacco made him dizzy, and it added an acrid smell to the air around them, which was already thick with the odor of sweat, machine oil, and cabbage.

"How did you come to be here?" Ramius asked.

"We were heading towards the coast of Virginia, Captain. A Soviet submarine sank there last week."

"Oh?" Ramius admired the cover story. "A Soviet submarine?"

"Yes, Captain. The boat was what we call an *Alfa*. That's all I know for sure. They picked up a survivor, and he's in the Norfolk naval hospital. May I ask your name, sir?"

"Marko Aleksandrovich Ramius."

"Jack Ryan."

"Owen Williams." They shook hands all around.

"You have a family, Commander Ryan?" Ramius asked.

"Yes, sir. A wife, a son, and a daughter. You, sir?"

"No, no family." He turned and addressed a junior officer in Russian. "Take the next group. You heard my instructions to the doctor?"

"Yes, Comrade Captain!" the young man said.

They heard the *Mystic*'s electric motors overhead. A moment later came the metallic clang of the mating collar gripping the escape trunk. It had taken forty minutes, but it had seemed like a week. God, what if the reactor really was bad? Ryan thought.

The Scamp

Two miles away, the *Scamp* had halted a few hundred yards from the *Ethan Allen*. Both submarines were exchanging messages on their gertrudes. The *Scamp* sonarmen had noted the passage of the three submarines an hour earlier. The *Pogy* and *Dallas* were now between the *Red October* and the other two American subs, their sonar operators listening intently for any interference, any vessel that might come their way. The transfer area was far enough offshore to miss the coastal traffic of commercial freighters and tankers, but that might not keep them from meeting a stray vessel from another port.

The Red October

When the third set of crewmen left under the control of Lieutenant Svyadov, a cook at the end of the line broke away, explaining that he wanted to retrieve his cassette tape machine, something he had saved months for. No one noticed when he didn't return, not even Ramius. His crewmen, even the experienced *michmanyy*, jostled one another to get out of their submarine. There was only one more group to go.

The Pigeon

On the *Pigeon*, the Soviet crewmen were taken to the crew's mess. The American sailors were observing their Russian counterparts closely, but no words passed. The Russians found the tables set with a meal of coffee, bacon, eggs, and toast. Petrov was happy for that. It was no problem keeping control of the men when they ate like wolves. With a junior officer acting as interpreter, they asked for and got plenty of additional bacon. The cooks had orders to stuff the Russians with all the food they could eat. It kept everyone busy as a helicopter landed from shore with twenty new men, one of whom raced to the bridge.

The Red October

"Last group," Ryan murmured to himself. The *Mystic* mated again. The last round trip had taken an hour. When the pair of hatches was opened, the lieutenant from the DSRV came down.

"Next trip will be delayed, gentlemen. Our batteries have about had it. It'll take ninety minutes to recharge. Any problem?"

"It will be as you say," Ramius replied. He translated for his men and then ordered Ivanov to take the next group. "The senior officers will stay behind. We have work to do." Ramius took the young officer's hand. "If something happens, tell them in Moscow that we have done our duty."

"I will do that, Comrade Captain." Ivanov nearly choked on his answer.

Ryan watched the sailors leave. The *Red October*'s escape trunk hatch was closed, then the *Mystic*'s. One minute later there was a clanging sound as the minisub lifted free. He heard the electric motors whirring off, fading rapidly away, and felt the green-painted bulkheads closing in on him. Being on an airplane was frightening, but at least the air didn't threaten to crush you. Here he was, underwater, three hundred miles from shore in the world's largest submarine, with only ten men aboard who knew how to run her.

"Commander Ryan," Ramius said, drawing himself to attention, "my officers and I request political asylum in the United States—and we bring you this small present." Ramius gestured toward the steel bulkheads.

Ryan had already framed his reply. "Captain, on behalf of the president of the United States, it is my honor to grant your request. Welcome to freedom, gentlemen."

No one knew that the intercom system in the compartment had been switched on. The indicator light had been unplugged hours before. Two compartments forward the cook listened, telling himself that he had been right to stay behind, wishing he had been wrong. Now what will I do? he wondered. His duty. That sounded easy enough—but would he remember how to carry it out?

"I don't know what to say about you guys." Ryan shook

everyone's hand again. "You pulled it off. You really pulled it off!"

"Excuse me, Commander," Kamarov said. "Do you speak Russian?"

"Sorry, Lieutenant Williams here does, but I do not. A group of Russian-speaking officers was supposed to be here in my place, but their helicopter crashed at sea last night." Williams translated this. Four of the officers had no knowledge of English.

"And what happens now?"

"In a few minutes, a missile submarine will explode two miles from here. One of ours, an old one. I presume that you told your men you were going to scuttle—Jesus, I hope you didn't say what you were really doing?"

"And have a war aboard my ship?" Ramius laughed. "No, Ryan. Then what?"

"When everybody thinks *Red October* has sunk, we'll head northwest to the Ocracoke Inlet and wait. USS *Dallas* and *Pogy* will be escorting us. Can these few men operate the ship?"

"These men can operate any ship in the world!" Ramius said it in Russian first. His men grinned. "So, you think that our men will not know what has become of us?"

"Correct. *Pigeon* will see an underwater explosion. They have no way of knowing it's in the wrong place, do they? You know that your navy has many ships operating off our coast right now? When they leave, well, then we'll figure out where to keep this present permanently. I don't know where that will be. You men, of course, will be our guests. A lot of our people will want to talk with you. For the moment, you can be sure that you will be treated very well—better than you can imagine." Ryan was sure that the CIA would give each a considerable sum of money. He didn't say so, not wanting to insult this kind of bravery. It had surprised him to learn that defectors rarely expect to receive money, almost never ask for any.

"What about political education?" Kamarov asked.

Ryan laughed. "Lieutenant, somewhere along the line somebody will take you aside to explain how our country works. That will take about two hours. After that you can immediately start telling us what we do wrong—everybody else in the world does, why shouldn't you? But I can't do that now. Believe this, you will love it, probably more than I do. I have never lived in a country that was not free, and maybe I don't appreciate my home as much as I should. For the moment, I suppose you have work to do."

"Correct," Ramius said. "Come, my new comrades, we will put you to work also."

Ramius led Ryan aft through a series of watertight doors. In a few minutes he was in the missile room, a vast compartment with twenty-six dark-green tubes towering through two decks. The business end of a boomer, with two-hundred-plus thermonuclear warheads. The menace in this room was enough to make hair bristle at the back of Ryan's neck. These were not academic abstractions, these were real. The upper deck he walked on was a grating. The lower deck, he could see, was solid. After passing through this and another compartment they were in the control room. The interior of the submarine was ghostly quiet; Ryan sensed why sailors are superstitious.

"You will sit here." Ramius pointed Ryan to the helmsman's station on the port side of the compartment. There was an aircraft-style wheel and a gang of instruments.

"What do I do?" Ryan asked, sitting.

"You will steer the ship, Commander. Have you never done this before?"

"No, sir. I've never been on a submarine before."

"But you are a naval officer."

Ryan shook his head. "No, captain. I work for the CIA."

"CIA?" Ramius hissed the acronym as if it were poisonous.

"I know, I know." Ryan dropped his head on the wheel. "They call us the Dark Forces. Captain, this is one Dark Force who's probably going to wet his pants before we're finished here. I work at a desk, and believe me on this if nothing else—there's nothing I'd like better than to be home with my wife and kids right now. If I had half a brain, I would have stayed in Annapolis and kept writing my books."

"Books? What do you mean?"

"I'm an historian, Captain. I was asked to join the CIA a few years ago as an analyst. Do you know what that is? Agents bring in their data, and I figure out what it means. I got into this mess by mistake—shit, you don't believe me, but it's true. Anyway, I used to write books on naval history."

"Tell me your books," Ramius ordered.

"*Options and Decisions, Doomed Eagles,* and a new one coming out next year, *Fighting Sailor,* a biography of Admiral Halsey. My first one was about the Battle of Leyte Gulf. It was reviewed in *Morskoi Sbornik,* I understand. It dealt with the nature of tactical decisions made under combat conditions. There's supposed to be a dozen copies at the Frunze library."

Ramius was quiet for a moment. "Ah, I know this book. Yes, I read parts of it. You were wrong, Ryan. Halsey acted stupidly."

"You will do well in my country, Captain Ramius. You are already a book critic. Captain Borodin, can I trouble you for a cigarette?" Borodin tossed him a full pack and matches. Ryan lit one. It was terrible.

The Avalon

The *Mystic*'s fourth return was the signal for the *Ethan Allen* and *Scamp* to act. The *Avalon* lifted off her bed and motored the few hundred yards to the old missile boat. Her captain was already assembling his men in the torpedo room. Every hatch, door, manhole, and drawer had been opened all over the boat. One of the officers was coming forward to join the others. Behind him trailed a black wire that led to each of the bombs aboard. This he connected to a timing device.

"All ready, Captain."

The Red October

Ryan watched Ramius order his men to their posts. Most went aft to run the engines. Ramius had the good manners to speak in English, repeating himself in Russian for those who did not understand their new language.

"Kamarov and Williams, will you go forward and secure all hatches." Ramius explained for Ryan's benefit. "If something goes wrong—it won't, but if it does—we do not have enough men to make repairs. So, we seal the entire ship."

It made sense to Ryan. He set an empty cup on the control pedestal to serve as an ashtray. He and Ramius were alone in the control room.

"When are we to leave?" Ramius asked.

"Whenever you are ready, sir. We have to get to Ocracoke Inlet at high tide, about eight minutes after midnight. Can we make it?"

Ramius consulted his chart. "Easily."

Kamarov led Williams through the communications room forward of control. They left the watertight door there open, then went forward to the missile room. Here they climbed down a ladder and walked forward on the lower missile deck to the forward missile room bulkhead. They proceeded through the door into the stores compartments, checking each hatch as they went. Near the bow they went up another ladder into the torpedo room, dogging the hatch down behind them, and proceeded aft through the torpedo storage and crew spaces. Both men sensed how strange it was to be aboard a ship with no crew, and they took their time, Williams twisting his head to look at everything and asking Kamarov questions. The lieutenant was happy to answer them in his mother language. Both men were competent officers, sharing a romantic attachment to their profession. For his part, Williams was greatly impressed by the *Red October* and said as much several times. A great deal of attention had been paid to small details. The deck was tiled. The hatches were lined with thick rubber gaskets. They hardly made any noise at all as they moved about checking watertight integrity, and it was obvious that more than mere lip service had been paid to making this submarine a quiet one.

Williams was translating a favorite sea story into Russian as they opened the hatch to the missile room's upper deck. When he stepped through the hatch behind Kamarov, he remembered that the missile room's bright overhead lights had been left on. Hadn't they?

Ryan was trying to relax and failing at it. The seat was uncomfortable, and he recalled the Russian joke about how they were shaping the New Soviet Man—with airliner seats that contorted an individual into all kinds of impossible shapes. Aft, the engine room crew had begun powering up the reactor. Ramius was speaking over the intercom phone with his chief engineer, just before the sound of moving reactor coolant increased to generate steam for the turboalternators.

Ryan's head went up. It was as though he felt the sound before hearing it. A chill ran up the back of his neck before his brain told him what the sound had to be.

"What was that?" he said automatically, knowing already what it was.

"What?" Ramius was ten feet aft, and the caterpillar engines were now turning. A strange rumble reverberated through the hull.

"I heard a shot—no, several shots."

Ramius looked amused as he came a few steps forward. "I think you hear the sounds of the caterpillar engines, and I think it is your first time on a submarine boat, as you said. The first time is always difficult. It was so even for me."

Ryan stood up. "That may be, Captain, but I know a shot when I hear it." He unbottoned his jacket and pulled out the pistol.

"You will give me that." Ramius held out his hand. "You may not have a pistol on my submarine!"

"Where are Williams and Kamarov?" Ryan wavered.

Ramius shrugged. "They are late, yes, but this is a big ship."

"I'm going forward to check."

"You will stay at your post!" Ramius ordered. "You will do as I say!"

"Captain, I just heard something that sounded like gunshots, and I am going forward to check it out. Have you ever been shot at? I have. I have the scars on my shoulder to prove it. You'd better take the wheel, sir."

Ramius picked up a phone and punched a button. He spoke in Russian for a few seconds and hung up. "I will go to show you that my submarine has no souls—ghosts, yes? Ghosts, no ghosts." He gestured to the pistol. "And you are no spy, eh?"

"Captain, believe what you want to believe, okay? It's a long story, and I'll tell it to you someday." Ryan waited for the relief that Ramius had evidently called for. The rumble of the tunnel drive made the sub sound like the inside of a drum.

An officer whose name he did not remember came into the control room. Ramius said something that drew a laugh—which stopped when the officer saw Ryan's pistol. It was obvious that neither Russian was happy he had one.

"With your permission, Captain?" Ryan gestured forward.

"Go on, Ryan."

The watertight door between control and the next space had been left open. Ryan entered the radio room slowly, eyes tracing left and right. It was clear. He went forward to the missile room door, which was dogged tight. The door, four feet or so high and about two across, was locked in place with a central wheel. Ryan turned the wheel with one hand. It was well oiled. So were the hinges. He pulled the door open slowly and peered around the hatch coaming.

"Oh, shit," Ryan breathed, waving the captain forward. The missile compartment was a good two hundred feet long, lit only by six or eight small glow lights. Hadn't it been brightly lit before? At the far end was a splash of bright light, and the far hatch had two shapes sprawled on the gratings next to it. Neither moved. The light Ryan saw them by was flickering next to a missile tube.

"Ghosts, Captain?" he whispered.

"It is Kamarov." Ramius said something else under his breath in Russian.

Ryan pulled the slide back on his FN automatic to make sure a round was in the chamber. Then he stepped out of his shoes.

"Better let me handle this. Once upon a time I was a lieutenant in the marines." And my training at Quantico, he thought to himself, had damned little to do with this. Ryan entered the compartment.

The missile room was almost a third of the submarine's length and two decks high. The lower deck was solid metal. The upper one was made of metal grates. Sherwood Forest, this place was called on American missile boats. The term was apt enough. The missile tubes, a good nine feet in diameter and painted a darker green than the rest of the room, looked like the trunks of enormous trees. He pulled the hatch shut behind him and moved to his right.

The light seemed to be coming from the farthest missile tube on the starboard side of the upper missile deck. Ryan stopped to listen. Something was happening there. He could hear a low rustling sound, and the light was moving as though it came from a hand-held work lamp. The sound was traveling down the smooth sides of the interior hull plating.

"Why me?" he whispered to himself. He'd have to get past thirteen missile tubes to get to the source of that light, cross over two hundred feet of open deck.

He moved around the first one, pistol in his right hand at waist level, his left hand tracing the cold metal of the tube. Already he was sweating into the checkered hard-rubber pistol grips. That, he told himself, is why they're checkered. He got between the first and second tubes, looked to port to make sure nobody was there, and got ready to move forward. Twelve to go.

The deck grating was welded out of eighth-inch metal bars. Already his feet hurt from walking on it. Moving slowly and carefully around the next circular tube, he felt like an astronaut orbiting the moon and crossing a continuous horizon. Except on the moon there wasn't anybody waiting to shoot you.

A hand came down on his shoulder. Ryan jumped and whirled around. Ramius. He had something to say, but Ryan put his fingertips on the man's lips and shook his head. Ryan's heart was beating so loudly that he could have used it for sending Morse code, and he could hear his own breathing—so why the hell hadn't he heard Ramius?

Ryan gestured his intention to go around the outboard side of each missile. Ramius indicated that he would go around the inboard sides. Ryan nodded. He decided to button his jacket and turn the collar up. It would make him a harder target. Better a dark shape than one with a white triangle on it. Next tube.

Ryan saw that words were painted on the tubes, with other inscriptions forged onto the metal itself. The letters were in Cyrillic and probably said No Smoking or Lenin Lives or something similarly useless. He saw and heard everything with great acuity, as though someone had taken sandpaper to all his senses to make him fantastically alert. He edged around the next tube, his fingers flexing nervously on the pistol grip, wanting to wipe the sweat from his eyes. There was nothing here; the port side was okay. Next one . . .

It took five minutes to get halfway down the compartment, between the sixth and seventh tubes. The noise from the forward end of the compartment was more pronounced now. The light was definitely moving. Not by much, but the shadow of the number one tube was jittering ever so slightly. It had to be a work light plugged into a wall socket or whatever they called that on a ship. What was he doing? Working on a missile? Was there more than one man? Why didn't Ramius do a head count getting his crew into the DSRV?

Why didn't *I?* Ryan swore to himself. Six more to go.

As he went around the next tube he indicated to Ramius that there was probably one man all the way at the far end. Ramius nodded curtly, having already reached that conclusion. For the first time he noticed that Ryan's shoes were off, and, thinking that was a good idea, he lifted his left foot to take off a shoe. His fingers, which felt awkward and stiff, fumbled with the shoe. It fell on a loose piece of grating with a clatter. Ryan was caught in the open. He froze. The light at the far end shifted, then went dead still. Ryan darted to his left and peered around the edge of the tube. Five more to go. He saw part of a face—and a flash.

He heard the shot and cringed as the bullet hit the after bulkhead with a *clang*. Then he drew back for cover.

"I will cross to the other side," Ramius whispered.

"Wait till I say." Ryan grabbed Ramius' upper arm and went back to the starboard side of the tube, pistol in front. He saw the face and this time he fired first, knowing he'd miss. At the same moment he pushed Ramius left. The captain raced to the other side and crouched behind a missile tube.

"We have you," Ryan said aloud.

"You have nothing." It was a young voice, young and very scared.

"What are you doing?" Ryan asked.

"What do you think, Yankee?" This time the taunt was more effective.

Probably figuring a way to set off a warhead, Ryan decided. A happy thought.

"Then you will die too," Ryan said. Didn't the police try to reason with barricaded suspects? Didn't a New York cop say on TV once, "We try to bore them to death?" But those were criminals. What was Ryan dealing with? A sailor who stayed behind? One of Ramius' own officers who'd had second thoughts? A KGB agent? A GRU agent covered as a crewman?

"Then I will die," the voice agreed. The light moved. Whatever he was doing, he was trying to get back to it.

Ryan fired twice as he went around the tube. Four to go. His bullets clanged uselessly as they hit the forward bulkhead. There was a remote chance that a carom shot—no . . . He looked left and saw that Ramius was still with him, shading to the port side of the tubes. He had no gun. Why hadn't he gotten himself one?

Ryan took a deep breath and leaped around the next tube. The guy was waiting for this. Ryan dove to the deck, and the bullet missed him.

"Who are you?" Ryan asked, raising himself on his knees and leaning against the tube to catch his breath.

"A Soviet patriot! You are the enemy of my country, and you shall not have this ship!"

He was talking too much, Ryan thought. Good. Probably. "You have a name?"

"My name is of no account."

"How about a family?" Ryan asked.

"My parents will be proud of me."

A GRU agent. Ryan was certain. Not the political officer. His English was too good. Probably some kind of backup for the political officer. He was up against a trained field officer. Wonderful. A trained agent, and just like he said, a patriot. Not a fanatic, a man trying to do his duty. He was scared, but he'd do it.

And blow this whole fucking ship up, with me on it.

Still, Ryan knew he had an edge. The other guy had something he had to do. Ryan only had to stop him or delay him long enough. He went to the starboard side of the tube and looked around the edge with just his right eye. There was no light at his end of the compartment—another edge. Ryan could see him more easily than he could see Ryan.

"You don't have to die, my friend. If you just set the gun down . . ." And *what?* End up in a federal prison? More likely just disappear. Moscow could not learn that the Americans had their sub.

"And CIA will not kill me, eh?" the voice sneered, quavering. "I am no fool. If I am to die, it will be to my purpose, my friend!"

Then the light clicked off. Ryan had wondered how long that would take. Did it mean that he was finished whatever the hell he was doing? If so, in an instant they'd be all gone. Or maybe the guy just realized how vulnerable the light made him. Trained field officer or not, he was a kid, a frightened kid, and probably had as much to lose as Ryan had. Like hell, Ryan thought, I have a wife and two kids, and if I don't get to him fast, I'll sure as hell lose them.

Merry Christmas, kids, your daddy just got blown up. Sorry there's no body to bury, but you see . . . It occurred to Ryan to pray briefly—but for what? For help in killing another man? *It's like this, Lord . . .*

"Still with me, Captain?" he called out.

"Da."

That would give the GRU agent something to worry about. Ryan hoped the captain's presence would force the man to shade more to the port side of his tube. Ryan ducked and rushed around the port side of his. Three to go. Ramius followed suit on his side. He drew a shot, but Ryan heard it miss.

He had to stop, to rest. He was hyperventilating. It was the wrong time for that. He had been a marine lieutenant—for three whole months before the chopper crashed—and he was supposed to know what to do! He had *led* men. But it was a whole lot easier to lead forty men with rifles than it was to fight all by himself.

Think!

"Maybe we can make a deal," Ryan suggested.

"Ah, yes, we can decide which ear the shot comes in."

"Maybe you'd like being an American."

"And my parents, Yankee, what of them?"

"Maybe we can get them out," Ryan said from the starboard side of his tube, moving left as he waited for a reply. He jumped again. Now there were two missile tubes separating him from his friend in the GRU, who was probably trying to crosswire the warheads and make half a cubic mile of ocean turn to plasma.

"Come, Yankee, we will die together. Now only one *pus-katel* separates us."

Ryan thought quickly. He couldn't remember how many times he'd fired, but the pistol held thirteen rounds. He'd have enough. The extra clip was useless. He could toss it one way and move the other, creating a diversion. Would it work? Shit! It worked in the movies. It was for damned sure that doing nothing wasn't going to work.

Ryan took the gun in his left hand and fished in his coat pocket for the spare clip with his right. He put the clip in his

mouth while he switched the gun back. A poor highwayman's
shift . . . He took the clip in his left hand. Okay. He had to toss
the clip right and move left. Would it work? Right or wrong,
he didn't have a hell of a lot of time.

At Quantico he was taught to read maps, evaluate terrain,
call in air and artillery strikes, maneuver his squads and fire
teams with skill—and here he was, stuck in a goddamned steel
pipe three hundred feet under water, shooting it out with pistols
in a room with two hundred hydrogen bombs!

It was time to do something. He knew what that had to
be—but Ramius moved first. Out the corner of his eye he
caught the shape of the captain running toward the forward
bulkhead. Ramius leaped at the bulkhead and flicked a light
switch on as the enemy fired at him. Ryan tossed the clip to
the right and ran forward. The agent turned to his left to see
what the noise was, sure that a cooperative move had been
planned.

As Ryan covered the distance between the last two missile
tubes he saw Ramius go down. Ryan dove past the number
one missile tube. He landed on his left side, ignoring the pain
that set his arm on fire as he rolled to line up his target. The
man was turning as Ryan jerked off six shots. Ryan didn't hear
himself screaming. Two rounds connected. The agent was lifted
off the deck and twisted halfway around from the impact. His
pistol dropped from his hand as he fell limp to the deck.

Ryan was shaking too badly to get up at once. The pistol,
still tight in his hand, was aimed at his victim's chest. He was
breathing hard and his heart was racing. Ryan closed his mouth
and tried to swallow a few times; his mouth was as dry as
cotton. He got slowly to his knees. The agent was still alive,
lying on his back, eyes open and still breathing. Ryan had to
use his hand to stand up.

He'd been hit twice, Ryan saw, once in the upper left chest
and once lower down, about where the liver and spleen are.
The lower wound was a wet red circle which the man's hands
clutched. He was in his early twenties, if that, and his clear
blue eyes were staring at the overhead while he tried to say
something. His face was rigid with pain as he mouthed words,
but all that came out was an unintelligible gurgle.

"Captain," Ryan called, "you okay?"

"I am wounded, but I think I shall live, Ryan. Who is it?"

"How the hell should I know?"

The blue eyes fixed on Jack's face. Whoever he was, he knew death was coming to him. The pain on the face was replaced by something else. Sadness, an infinite sadness... He was still trying to speak. A pink froth gathered at the corners of his mouth. Lung shot. Ryan moved closer, kicking the gun clear and kneeling down beside him.

"We could have made a deal," he said quietly.

The agent tried to say something, but Ryan couldn't understand it. A curse, a call for his mother, something heroic? Jack would never know. The eyes went wide with pain one last time. The last breath hissed out through the bubbles and the hands on the belly went limp. Ryan checked for a pulse at the neck. There was none.

"I'm sorry." Ryan reached down to close his victim's eyes. He was sorry—why? Tiny beads of sweat broke out all over his forehead, and the strength he had drawn up in the shootout deserted him. A sudden wave of nausea overpowered him. "Oh, Jesus, I'm—" He dropped to all fours and threw up violently, his vomit spilling through the grates onto the lower deck ten feet below. For a whole minute his stomach heaved, well past the time he was dry. He had to spit several times to get the worst of the taste from his mouth before standing.

Dizzy from the stress and the quart of adrenalin that had been pumped into his system, he shook his head a few times, still looking at the dead man at his feet. It was time to come back to reality.

Ramius had been hit in the upper leg. It was bleeding. Both his hands, covered with blood, were placed on the wound, but it didn't look that bad. If the femoral artery had been cut, the captain would already have been dead.

Lieutenant Williams had been hit in the head and chest. He was still breathing but unconscious. The head wound was only a crease. The chest wound, close to the heart, made a sucking noise. Kamarov was not so lucky. A single shot had gone straight through the top of his nose, and the back of his head was a bloody wreckage.

"Jesus, why didn't somebody come and help us!" Ryan said when the thought hit him.

"The bulkhead doors are closed, Ryan. There is the—how do you say it?"

Ryan looked where the captain pointed. It was the intercom system. "Which button?" The captain held up two fingers. "Control room, this is Ryan. I need help here, your captain has been shot."

The reply came in excited Russian, and Ramius responded loudly to make himself heard. Ryan looked at the missile tube. The agent had been using a work light, just like an American one, a lightbulb in a metal holder with wire across the front. A door into the missile tube was open. Beyond it a smaller hatch, evidently leading into the missile itself, was also open.

"What was he doing, trying to explode the warheads?"

"Impossible," Ramius said, in obvious pain. "The rocket warheads—we call this special safe. The warheads cannot—not fire."

"So what was he doing?" Ryan went over to the missile tube. A sort of rubber bladder was lying on the deck. "What's this?" He hefted the gadget in his hand. It was made of rubber or rubberized fabric with a metal or plastic frame inside, a metal nipple on one corner, and a mouthpiece.

"He was doing something to the missile, but he had an escape device to get off the sub," Ryan said. "Oh, Christ! A timing device." He bent down to pick up the work light and switched it on, then stood back and peered into the missile compartment. "Captain, what's in here?"

"That is—the guidance compartment. It has a computer that tells the rocket how to fly. The door—," Ramius' breaths were coming hard, "—is a hatch for the officer."

Ryan peered into the hatch. He found a mass of multicolored wires and circuit boards connected in a way he'd never seen before. He poked through the wires half expecting to find a ticking alarm clock wired to some dynamite sticks. He didn't.

Now what should he do? The agent had been up to something—but what? Did he finish? How could Ryan tell? He couldn't. One part of his brain screamed at him to do something, the other part said that he'd be crazy to try.

Ryan put the rubber-coated handle to the light between his teeth and reached into the compartment with both hands. He grabbed a double handful of wires and yanked back. Only a few broke loose. He released one bunch and concentrated on the other. A clump of plastic and copper spaghetti came loose. He did it again for the other bunch. "Aaah!" he gasped, receiving an electric shock. An eternal moment followed while he waited to be blown up. It passed. There were more wires to pull. In under a minute he'd ripped out every wire he could see along with a half-dozen small breadboards. Next he smashed the light against everything he thought might break until the compartment looked like his son's toybox—full of useless fragments.

He heard people running into the compartment. Borodin was in front. Ramius motioned him over to Ryan and the dead agent.

"Sudets?" Borodin said. "Sudets?" He looked at Ryan. "This is cook."

Ryan took the pistol from the deck. "Here's his recipe file. I think he was a GRU agent. He was trying to blow us up. Captain Ramius, how about we launch this missile—just jettison the goddamned thing, okay?"

"A good idea, I think." Ramius' voice had become a hoarse whisper. "First close the inspection hatch, then we—can fire from the control room."

Ryan used his hand to sweep the fragments away from the missile hatch, and the door slid neatly back into place. The tube hatch was different. It was a pressure-bearing one and much heavier, held in place by two spring-loaded latches. Ryan slammed it three times. Twice it rebounded, but the third time it stuck.

Borodin and another officer were already carrying Williams aft. Someone had set a belt on Ramius' leg wound. Ryan got him to his feet and helped him walk. Ramius grunted in pain every time he had to move his left leg.

"You took a foolish chance, Captain," Ryan observed.

"This is my ship—and I do not like the dark. It was my fault! We should have made a careful counting as the crew left."

They arrived at the watertight door. "Okay, I'll go through first." Ryan stepped through and helped Ramius through backward. The belt had loosened, and the wound was bleeding again.

"Close the hatch and lock it," Ramius ordered.

It closed easily. Ryan turned the wheel three times, then got under the captain's arm again. Another twenty feet and they were in the control room. The lieutenant at the wheel was ashen.

Ryan sat the captain in a chair on the port side. "You have a knife, sir?"

Ramius reached in his pocket and came out with a folding knife and something else. "Here, take this. It's the key for the rocket warheads. They cannot fire unless this is used. You keep it." He tried to laugh. It had been Putin's, after all.

Ryan flipped it around his neck, opened the knife, and cut the captain's pants all the way up. The bullet had gone clean through the meaty part of the thigh. He took a clean handkerchief from his pocket and held it against the entrance wound. Ramius handed him another handkerchief. Ryan placed this against the half-inch exit wound. Next he set the belt across both, drawing it as tight as he could.

"My wife might not approve, but that will have to do."

"Your wife?" Ramius asked.

"She's a doc, an eye surgeon to be exact. The day I got shot she did this for me." Ramius' lower leg was growing pale. The belt was too tight, but Ryan didn't want to loosen it just yet. "Now, what about the missile?"

Ramius gave an order to the lieutenant at the wheel, who relayed it through the intercom. Two minutes later three officers entered the control room. Speed was cut to five knots, which took several minutes. Ryan worried about the missile and whether or not he had destroyed whatever boobytrap the agent had installed. Each of the three newly arrived officers took a key from around his neck. Ramius did the same, giving his second key to Ryan. He pointed to the starboard side of the compartment.

"Rocket control."

Ryan should have guessed as much. Arrayed throughout the control room were five panels, each with three rows of twenty-six lights and a key slot under each set.

"Put your key in number one, Ryan." Jack did, and the others inserted their keys. The red light came on and a buzzer sounded.

The missile officer's panel was the most elaborate. He turned a switch to flood the missile tube and open the number one hatch. The red panel lights began to blink.

"Turn your key, Ryan," Ramius said.

"Does this fire the missile?" Christ, what if that happens? Ryan wondered.

"No no. The rocket must be armed by the rocket officer. This key explodes the gas charge."

Could Ryan believe him? Sure he was a good guy and all that, but how could Ryan know he was telling the truth?

"Now!" Ramius ordered. Ryan turned his key at the same instant as the others. The amber light over the red light blinked on. The one under the green cover stayed off.

The *Red October* shuddered as the number one SS-N-20 was ejected upward by the gas charge. The sound was like a truck's air brake. The three officers withdrew their keys. Immediately the missile officer shut the tube hatch.

The Dallas

"What?" Jones said. "Conn, sonar, the target just flooded a tube—a missile tube? God almighty!" On his own, Jones powered up the under-ice sonar and began high-frequency pinging.

"What the hell are you doing?" Thompson demanded. Mancuso was there a second later.

"What's going on?" the captain snapped. Jones pointed at his display.

"The sub just launched a missile, sir. Look, Cap'n, two targets. But it's just hangin' there, no missile ignition. God!"

The Red October

Will it float? Ryan wondered.

It didn't. The Seahawk missile was pushed upward and to starboard by the gas charge. It stopped fifty feet over her deck as the *October* cruised past. The guidance hatch that Ryan had closed was not fully sealed. Water filled the compartment and flooded the warhead bus. The missile in any case had a sizable negative bouyancy, and the added mass in the nose tipped it over. The nose-heavy trim gave it an eccentric path, and it spiraled down like a seedpod from a tree. At ten thousand feet water pressure crushed the seal over the missile blast cones, but the Seahawk, otherwise undamaged, retained its shape all the way to the bottom.

The Ethan Allen

The only thing still operating was the timer. It had been set for thirty minutes, which had allowed the crew plenty of time to board the *Scamp*, now leaving the area at ten knots. The old reactor had been completely shut down. It was stone cold. Only a few emergency lights remained on from residual battery power. The timer had three redundant firing circuits, and all went off within a millisecond of one another, sending a signal down the detonator wires.

They had put four Pave Pat Blue bombs on the *Ethan Allen*. The Pave Pat Blue was a FAE (fuel-air explosive) bomb. Its blast efficiency was roughly five times that of an ordinary chemical explosive. Each bomb had a pair of gas-release valves, and only one of the eight valves failed. When they burst open, the pressurized propane in the bomb casings expanded violently outward. In an instant the atmospheric pressure in the old submarine tripled as her every part was saturated with an explosive air-gas mixture. The four bombs filled the *Ethan Allen* with the equivalent of twenty-five tons of TNT evenly distributed throughout the hull.

The squibs fired almost simultaneously, and the results were catastrophic: the *Ethan Allen*'s strong steel hull burst as if it were a balloon. The only item not totally destroyed was the reactor vessel, which fell free of the shredded wreckage and dropped rapidly to the ocean floor. The hull itself was blasted into a dozen pieces, all bent into surreal shapes by the explosion. Interior equipment formed a metallic cloud within the shattered hull, and everything fluttered downward, expanding over a wide area during the three-mile descent to the hard sand bottom.

The Dallas

"Holy shit!" Jones slapped the headphones off and yawned to clear his ears. Automatic relays within the sonar system protected his ears from the full force of the explosion, but what had been transmitted was enough to make him feel as though his head had been hammered flat. The explosion was heard through the hull by everyone aboard.

"Attention all hands, this is the captain speaking. What you just heard is nothing to worry about. That's all I can say."

"Gawd, Skipper!" Mannion said.

"Yeah, let's get back on the contact."

"Aye, Cap'n." Mannion gave his commander a curious look.

The White House

"Did you get the word to him in time?" the president asked.

"No, sir." Moore slumped into his chair. "The helicopter arrived a few minutes too late. It may be nothing to worry about. You'd expect that the captain would know enough to get everyone off except for his own people. We're concerned, of course, but there isn't anything we can do."

"I asked him personally to do this, Judge. Me."

Welcome to the real world, Mr. President, Moore thought. The chief executive had been lucky—he'd never had to send men to their deaths. Moore reflected that it was something easy to consider beforehand, less easy to get used to. He had affirmed death sentences from his seat on an appellate bench, and that had not been easy—even for men who had richly deserved their fates.

"Well, we'll just have to wait and see, Mr. President. The source this data comes from is more important than any one operation."

"Very well. What about Senator Donaldson?"

"He agreed to our suggestion. This aspect of the operation has worked out very well indeed."

"Do you really expect the Russians to buy it?" Pelt asked.

"We've left some nice bait, and we'll jerk the line a little to get their attention. In a day or two we'll see if they nibble at it. Henderson is one of their all-stars—his code name is Cassius—and their reaction to this will tell us just what sort of disinformation we can pass through him. He could turn out to be very useful, but we'll have to watch out for him. Our KGB colleagues have a very direct method for dealing with doubles."

"We don't let him off the hook unless he earns it," the president said coldly.

Moore smiled. "Oh, he'll earn it. We own Mr. Henderson."

THE FIFTEENTH DAY

FRIDAY, 17 DECEMBER

Ocracoke Inlet

There was no moon. The three-ship procession entered the inlet
at five knots, just after midnight to take advantage of the extra-
high spring tide. The *Pogy* led the formation since she had the
shallowest draft, and the *Dallas* trailed the *Red October*. The
coast guard stations on either side of the inlet were occupied
by naval officers who had relieved the "coasties."

Ryan had been allowed atop the sail, a humanitarian gesture
from Ramius that he much appreciated. After eighteen hours
inside the *Red October* Jack had felt confined, and it was good
to see the world—even if it was nothing but dark empty space.
The *Pogy* showed only a dim red light that disappeared if it
was looked at for more than a few seconds. He could see the
water's feathery wisps of foam and the stars playing hide-and-
seek through the clouds. The west wind was a harsh twenty
knots coming off the water.

Borodin was giving terse, monosyllabic orders as he conned

the submarine up a channel that had to be dredged every few months despite the enormous jetty which had been built to the north. The ride was an easy one, the two or three feet of chop not mattering a whit to the missile sub's 30,000-ton bulk. Ryan was thankful for this. The black water calmed, and when they entered sheltered waters a Zodiac-type rubber boat zoomed towards them.

"Ahoy *Red October!*" a voice called in the darkness. Ryan could barely make out the gray lozenge shape of the Zodiac. It was ahead of a tiny patch of foam formed by the sputtering outboard motor.

"May I answer, Captain Borodin?" Ryan asked, getting a nod. "This is Ryan. We have two casualties aboard. One's in bad shape. We need a doctor and a surgical team right away! Do you understand?"

"Two casualties, and you need a doc, right." Ryan thought he saw a man holding something to his face, and thought he heard the faint crackle of a radio. It was hard to tell in the wind. "Okay. We'll have a doc flown down right away, *October*. *Dallas* and *Pogy* both have medical corpsmen aboard. You want 'em?"

"Damn straight!" Ryan replied at once.

"Okay. Follow *Pogy* two more miles and stand by." The Zodiac sped forward, reversed course, and disappeared in the darkness.

"Thank God for that," Ryan breathed.

"You are be—believer?" Borodin asked.

"Yeah, sure." Ryan should not have been surprised by the question. "Hell, you gotta believe in something."

"And why is that, Commander Ryan?" Borodin was ex-a.nining the *Pogy* through oversized night glasses.

Ryan wondered how to answer. "Well, because if you don't, what's the point of life? That would mean Sartre and Camus and all those characters were right—all is chaos, life has no meaning. I refuse to believe that. If you want a better answer, I know a couple priests who'd be glad to talk to you."

Borodin did not respond. He spoke an order into the bridge microphone, and they altered course a few degrees to starboard.

The Dallas

A half mile aft, Mancuso was holding a light-amplifying night scope to his eyes. Mannion was at his shoulder, struggling to see.

"Jesus Christ," Mancuso whispered.

"You got that one right, Skipper," Mannion said, shivering in his jacket. "I'm not sure I believe it either. Here comes the Zodiac." Mannion handed his commander the portable radio used for docking.

"Do you read?"

"This is Mancuso."

"When our friend stops, I want you to transfer ten men to her, including your corpsman. They report two casualties who need medical attention. Pick good men, Commander, they'll need help running the boat—just make damned sure they're men who don't talk."

"Acknowledged. Ten men including the medic. Out." Mancuso watched the raft speed off to the *Pogy.* "Want to come along, Pat?"

"Bet your ass, uh, sir. You planning to go?" Mannion asked.

Mancuso was judicious. "I think Chambers is up to handling *Dallas* for a day or so, don't you?"

On shore, a naval officer was on the phone to Norfolk. The coast guard station was crowded, almost entirely with officers. A fiberglass box sat next to the phone so that they could communicate with CINCLANT in secrecy. They had been here only two hours and would soon leave. Nothing could appear out of the ordinary. Outside, an admiral and a pair of captains watched the dark shapes through starlight scopes. They were as solemn as men in a church.

Cherry Point, North Carolina

Commander Ed Noyes was resting in the doctor's lounge of the naval hospital at the U.S. Marine Corps Air Station, Cherry Point, North Carolina. A qualified flight surgeon, he had the duty for the next three nights so that he'd have four days off over Christmas. It had been a quiet night. This was about to change.

"Doc?"

Noyes looked up to see a marine captain in MP livery. The doctor knew him. Military police delivered a lot of accident cases. He set down his *New England Journal of Medicine*.

"Hi, Jerry. Something coming in?"

"Doc, I got orders to tell you to pack everything you need for emergency surgery. You got two minutes, then I take you to the airfield."

"What for? What kind of surgery?" Noyes stood.

"They didn't say, sir, just that you fly out somewheres, alone. The orders come from topside, that's all I know."

"Damn it, Jerry, I have to know what sort of surgery it is so I know what to take!"

"So take everything, sir. I gotta get you to the chopper."

Noyes swore and went into the trauma receiving room. Two more marines were waiting there. He handed them four sterile sets, prepackaged instrument trays. He wondered if he'd need some drugs and decided to grab an armful, along with two units of plasma. The captain helped him on with his coat, and they moved out the door to a waiting jeep. Five minutes later they pulled up to a Sea Stallion whose engines were already screaming.

"What gives?" Noyes asked the colonel of intelligence inside, wondering where the crew chief was.

"We're heading out over the sound," the colonel explained. "We have to let you down on a sub that has some casualties aboard. There's a pair of corpsmen to assist you, and that's all I know, okay?" It had to be okay. There was no choice in the matter.

The Stallion lifted off at once. Noyes had flown in them often enough. He had two hundred hours piloting helicopters, another three hundred in fixed-wing aircraft. Noyes was the kind of doctor who'd discovered too late that flying was as attractive a calling as medicine. He went up at every opportunity, often giving pilots special medical care for their dependents to get backseat time in an F-4 Phantom. The Sea Stallion, he noted, was not cruising. It was running flat out.

Pamlico Sound

The *Pogy* came to a halt about the time the helicopter left Cherry Point. The *October* altered course to starboard again and halted even with her to the north. The *Dallas* followed suit. A minute after that the Zodiac reappeared at the *Dallas*' side, then approached the *Red October* slowly, almost wallowing with her cargo of men.

"Ahoy *Red October!*"

This time Borodin answered. He had an accent but his English was understandable. "Identify."

"This is Bart Mancuso, commanding officer of USS *Dallas*. I have our ship's medical representative aboard and some other men. Request permission to come aboard, sir."

Ryan saw the *starpom* grimace. For the first time Borodin really had to face up to what was happening, and he would have been less than human to accept it without some kind of struggle.

"Permission is—yes."

The Zodiac edged right up to the curve of the hull. A man leaped aboard with a line to secure the raft. Ten men clambered off, one breaking away to climb up the submarine's sail.

"Captain? I'm Bart Mancuso. I understand you have some hurt men aboard."

"Yes," Borodin nodded, "the captain and a British officer, both shot."

"Shot?" Mancuso was surprised.

"Worry about that later," Ryan said sharply. "Let's get your doc working on them, okay?"

"Sure, where's the hatch?"

Borodin spoke into the bridge mike, and a few seconds later a circle of light appeared on deck at the foot of the sail.

"We haven't got a physician, we have an independent duty corpsman. He's pretty good, and *Pogy*'s man will be here in another couple minutes. Who are you, by the way?"

"He is a spy," Borodin said with palpable irony.

"Jack Ryan."

"And you, sir?"

"Captain Second Rank Vasily Borodin. I am—first officer, yes? Come over into the station, Commander. Please excuse me, we are all very tired."

"You're not the only ones." There wasn't that much room. Mancuso perched himself on the coaming. "Captain, I want you to know we had a bastard of a time tracking you. You are to be complimented for your professional skill."

The compliment did not elicit the anticipated response from Borodin. "You were able to track us. How?"

"I brought him along, you can meet him."

"And what are we to do?"

"Orders from shore are to wait for the doc to arrive and dive. Then we sit tight until we get orders to move. Maybe a day, maybe two. I think we could all use the rest. After that, we get you to a nice safe place, and I will personally buy you the best damned Italian dinner you ever had." Mancuso grinned.

"You get Italian food in Russia?"

"No, and if you are accustomed to good food, you may find *Krazny Oktyabr* not to your liking."

"Maybe I can fix that. How many men aboard?"

"Twelve. Ten Soviet, the Englishman, and the spy." Borodin glanced at Ryan with a thin smile.

"Okay." Mancuso reached into his coat and came out with a radio. "This is Mancuso."

"We're here, Skipper," Chambers replied.

"Get some food together for our friends. Six meals for twenty-five men. Send a cook over with it. Wally, I want to show these men some good chow. Got it?"

"Aye aye, Skipper. Out."

"I got some good cooks, Captain. Shame this wasn't last week. We had lasagna, just like momma used to make. All that was missing was the Chianti."

"They have vodka," Ryan observed.

"Only for spies," Borodin said. Two hours after the shootout Ryan had had the shakes badly, and Borodin had sent him a drink from the medical stores. "We are told that your submarine men are greatly pampered."

"Maybe so," Mancuso nodded. "But we stay out sixty or seventy days at a time. That's hard enough, don't you think?"

"How about we go below?" Ryan suggested. Everyone agreed. It was getting cold.

Borodin, Ryan and Mancuso went below to find the Americans on one side of the control room and the Soviets on the other, just like before. The American captain broke the ice.

"Captain Borodin, this is the man who found you. Come here, Jonesy."

"It wasn't very easy, sir," Jones said. "Can I get to work?

Can I see your sonar room?"

"Bugayev." Borodin waved the ship's electronics officer over. The captain-lieutenant led the sonarman aft.

Jones took one look at the equipment and muttered, "Kludge." The face plates all had louvers on them to let out the heat. God, did they use vacuum tubes? Jones wondered. He pulled a screwdriver from his pocket to find out.

"You speak English, sir?"

"Yes, a little."

"Can I see the circuit diagrams for these, please?"

Bugayev blinked. No enlisted man, and only one of his *michmanyy,* had ever asked for it. Then he took the binder of schematics from its shelf on the forward bulkhead.

Jones matched the code number of the set he was checking with the right section of the binder. Unfolding the diagram, he noted with relief that ohms were ohms, all over the world. He began tracing his finger along the page, then pulled the cover panel off to look inside the set.

"Kludge, megakludge to the max!" Jones was shocked enough to lapse into Valspeak.

"Excuse me, what is this 'kludge'?"

"Oh, pardon me, sir. That's an expression we use in the navy. I don't know how to say it in Russian. Sorry." Jones stifled a grin as he went back to the schematic. "Sir, this one here's a low-powered high-frequency set, right? You use this for mines and stuff?"

It was Bugayev's turn to be shocked. "You have been trained in Soviet equipment?"

"No, sir, but I've sure heard a lot of it." Wasn't this obvious? Jones wondered. "Sir, this is a high-frequency set, but it doesn't draw a lot of power. What else is it good for? A low-power FM set you use for mines, for work under ice, and for docking, right?"

"Correct."

"You have a gertrude, sir?"

"Gertrude?"

"Underwater telephone, sir, for talking to other subs." Didn't this guy know anything?

"Ah, yes, but it is located in control, and it is broken."

"Uh-huh." Jones looked over the diagram again. "I think I

can rig a modulator on this baby, then, and make it into a gertrude for ya. Might be useful. You think your skipper would want that, sir?"

"I will ask." He expected Jones to stay put, but the young sonarman was right behind him when he went to control. Bugayev explained the suggestion to Borodin while Jones talked to Mancuso.

"They got a little FM set that looks just like the old gertrudes in sonar school. We have a spare modulator in stores, and I can probably rig it up in thirty minutes, no sweat," the sonarman said.

"Captain Borodin, do you agree?" Mancuso asked.

Borodin felt as if he were being pushed too fast, even though the suggestion made perfectly good sense. "Yes, have your man do it."

"Skipper, how long we gonna be here?" Jones asked.

"A day or two, why?"

"Sir, this boat looks kinda thin on creature comforts, you know? How 'bout I grab a TV and a tape machine? Give 'em something to look at, you know, sort of give 'em a quick look at the USA?"

Mancuso laughed. They wanted to learn everything they could about this boat, but they had plenty of time for that, and Jones' idea looked like a good way to ease the tension. On the other hand, he didn't want to incite a mutiny on his own sub. "Okay, take the one from the wardroom."

"Right, Skipper."

The Zodiac delivered the *Pogy*'s corpsman a few minutes later, and Jones took the boat back to the *Dallas*. Gradually the officers were beginning to engage in conversation. Two Russians were trying to talk to Mannion and were looking at his hair. They had never met a black man before.

"Captain Borodin, I have orders to take something out of the control room that will identify—I mean, something that comes from this boat." Mancuso pointed. "Can I take that depth gauge? I can have one of my men rig a substitute." The gauge, he saw, had a number.

"For what reason?"

"Beats me, but those are my orders."

"Yes," Borodin replied.

Mancuso ordered one of his chiefs to perform the job. The

chief pulled a crescent wrench from his pocket and removed
the nut holding the needle and dial in place.

"This is a little bigger than ours, Skipper, but not by much.
I think we have a spare. I can flip it backwards and scribe in
the markings, okay?"

Mancuso handed his radio over. "Call it in and have Jonesy
bring the spare back with him."

"Aye, Cap'n." The chief put the needle back in place after
setting the dial on the deck.

The Sea Stallion did not attempt to land, though the pilot
was tempted. The deck was almost large enough to try. As it
was, the helicopter hovered a few feet over the missile deck,
and the doctor leaped into the arms of two seamen. His supplies
were tossed down a moment later. The colonel remained in the
back of the chopper and slid the door shut. The bird turned
slowly to move back southwest, its massive rotor raising spray
from the waters of Pamlico Sound.

"Was that what I think it was?" the pilot asked over the
intercom.

"Wasn't it backwards? I thought missile subs had the missiles aft of the sail. Those were in front of the sail, weren't
they? I mean, wasn't that the rudder sticking up behind the
sail?" the copilot responded quizzically.

"It was a Russian sub!" the pilot said.

"*What?*" It was too late to see, they were already two miles
away. "Those were our guys on the deck. They weren't Russians."

"*Son of a bitch!*" the major swore wonderingly. And he
couldn't say a thing. The colonel of division intelligence had
been damned specific about that: "You don't see nothin', you
don't hear nothin', you don't think nothin', and you goddamned
well don't ever say nothin'."

"I'm Doctor Noyes," the commander said to Mancuso
in the control room. He had never been on a submarine before, and when he looked around he saw a compartment
full of instruments all in a foreign language. "What ship is
this?"

"*Krazny Oktyabr,*" Borodin said, coming over. In the centerpiece of his cap there was a gleaming red star.

"What the hell is going on here?" Noyes demanded.

"Doc," Ryan took him by the arm, "you have two patients aft. Why not let's worry about them?"

Noyes followed him aft to sick bay. "What's going on here?" he persisted more quietly.

"The Russians just lost a submarine," Ryan explained, "and now she belongs to us. And if you tell anybody—"

"I read you, but I don't believe you."

"You don't have to believe me. What kind of cutter are you?"

"Thoracic."

"Good," Ryan turned into sick bay, "you have a gunshot wound victim who needs you bad."

Williams was lying naked on the table. A sailor came in with an armful of medical supplies and set them on Petrov's desk. The *October*'s medical locker had a supply of frozen plasma, and the two corpsmen already had two units running into the lieutenant. A chest tube was in, draining into a vacuum bottle.

"We got a nine-millimeter in this man's chest," one of the corpsmen said after introducing himself and his partner. "He's had a chest tube in the last ten hours, they tell me. The head looks worse than it is. Right pupil is a little blown, but no big deal. The chest is bad, sir. You'd better take a listen."

"Vitals?" Noyes fished in his bag for a stethoscope.

"Heart is 110 and thready. Blood pressure's eighty over forty."

Noyes moved his stethoscope around Williams' chest, frowning. "Heart's in the wrong place. We have a left tension pneumothorax. There must be a quart of fluid in there, and it sounds like he's heading for congestive failure." Noyes turned to Ryan. "You get out of here. I've got a chest to crack."

"Take care of him, Doc. He's a good man."

"Aren't they all," Noyes observed, stripping off his jacket. "Let's get scrubbed, people."

Ryan wondered if a prayer would help. Noyes looked and talked like a surgeon. Ryan hoped he was. He went aft to the captain's cabin, where Ramius was sleeping with the drugs he'd been given. The leg had stopped bleeding, and evidently one of the corpsmen had checked on it. Noyes could work on him next. Ryan went forward.

Borodin felt he had lost control and didn't like it, though it was something of a relief. Two weeks of constant tension plus the nerve-wrenching change in plans had shaken the officer more than he would have believed. The situation now was unpleasant—the Americans were trying to be kind, but they were so damned overpowering! At least the *Red October*'s officers were not in danger.

Twenty minutes later the Zodiac was back again. Two sailors went topside to unload a few hundred pounds of frozen food, then helped Jones with his electronic gear. It took several minutes to get everything squared away, and the seamen who took the food forward came back shaken after finding two stiff bodies and a third frozen solid. There had not been time to move the two recent casualties.

"Got everything, Skipper," Jones reported. He handed the depth gauge dial to the chief.

"What is all of this?" Borodin asked.

"Captain, I got the modulator to make the gertrude." Jones held up a small box. "This other stuff is a little color TV, a video cassette recorder, and some movie tapes. The skipper thought you gentlemen might want something to relax with, to get to know us a little, you know?"

"Movies?" Borodin shook his head. "Cinema movies?"

"Sure," Mancuso chuckled. "What did you bring, Jonesy?"

"Well, sir, I got *E.T.*, *Star Wars*, *Big Jake*, and *Hondo*." Clearly Jones wanted to be careful what parts of America he introduced the Russians to.

"My apologies, Captain. My crewman has limited taste in movies."

At the moment Borodin would have settled for *The Battleship Potemkin*. The fatigue was really hitting him hard.

The cook bustled aft with an armload of groceries. "I'll have coffee in a few minutes, sir," he said to Borodin on his way to the galley.

"I would like something to eat. None of us has eaten in a day," Borodin said.

"Food!" Mancuso called aft.

"Aye, Skipper. Let me figure this galley out."

Mannion checked his watch. "Twenty minutes, sir."

"We have everything we need aboard?"

"Yes, sir."

Jones bypassed the pulse control on the sonar amplifier and wired in the modulator. It was even easier than he'd expected. He had taken a radio microphone from the *Dallas* along with everything else and now connected it to the sonar set before powering the system up. He had to wait for the set to warm up. Jones hadn't seen this many tubes since he'd gone out on TV repair jobs with his father, and that had been a long time ago.

"*Dallas,* this is Jonesy, do you copy?"

"Aye." The reply was scratchy, like a taxicab radio.

"Thanks. Out." He switched off. "It works. That was pretty easy, wasn't it?"

Enlisted man, hell! And not even trained on Soviet equipment! the *October*'s electronics officer thought. It never occurred to him that this piece of equipment was a near copy of an obsolete American FM system. "How long have you been a sonarman?"

"Three and a half years, sir. Since I dropped out of college."

"You learn all this in three years?" the officer asked sharply.

Jones shrugged. "What's the big deal, sir? I've been foolin' with radios and stuff since I was a kid. You mind if I play some music, sir?"

Jones had decided to be especially nice. He had only one tape of a Russian composer, the Nutcracker Suite, and had brought that along with four Bachs. Jones liked to hear music while he prayed over circuit diagrams. The young sonarman was in Hog Heaven. All the Russian sets he had listened to for three years—now he had their schematics, their hardware, and the time to figure them all out. Bugayev continued to watch in amazement as Jones' fingers did their ballet through the manual pages to the music of Tchaikovsky.

"Time to dive, sir," Mannion said in control.

"Very well. With your permission, Captain Borodin, I will assist with the vents. All hatches and openings are . . . shut." The diving board used the same light-array system as American boats, Mancuso noticed.

Mancuso took stock of the situation one last time. Butler and his four most senior petty officers were already tending to the nuclear tea kettle aft. The situation looked pretty good, considering. The only thing that could really go badly wrong would be for the *October*'s officers to change their minds. The

Dallas would be keeping the missile sub under constant sonar observation. If she moved, the *Dallas* had a ten-knot speed advantage with which to block the channel.

"The way I see it, Captain, we are rigged for dive," Mancuso said.

Borodin nodded and sounded the diving alarm. It was a buzzer, just like on American boats. Mancuso, Mannion, and the Russian officer worked the complex vent controls. The *Red October* began her slow descent. In five minutes she was resting on the bottom, with seventy feet of water over the top of her sail.

The White House

Pelt was on the phone to the Soviet embassy at three in the morning. "Alex, this is Jeffrey Pelt."

"How are you, Dr. Pelt? I must offer my thanks and that of the Soviet people for your action to save our sailor. I was informed a few minutes ago that he is now conscious, and that he is expected to recover fully."

"Yes, I just learned that myself. What's his name, by the way?" Pelt wondered if he had awakened Arbatov. It didn't sound like it.

"Andre Katyskin, a cook petty officer from Leningrad."

"Good, Alex, I am informed that USS *Pigeon* has rescued nearly the entire crew of another Soviet submarine off the Carolinas. Her name, evidently, was *Red October*. That's the good news, Alex. The bad news is that the vessel exploded and sank before we could get them all off. Most of the officers, and two of our officers, were lost."

"When was this?"

"Very early yesterday morning. Sorry about the delay, but *Pigeon* had trouble with the radio, as a result of the underwater explosion, they say. You know how that sort of thing can happen."

"Indeed." Pelt had to admire the response, not a trace of irony. "Where are they now?"

"The *Pigeon* is sailing to Charleston, South Carolina. We'll have your crewmen flown directly to Washington from there."

"And this submarine exploded? You are sure?"

"Yeah, one of the crewmen said they had a major reactor

accident. It was just good luck that *Pigeon* was there. She was
heading to the Virginia coast to look at the other one you lost.
I think your navy needs a little work, Alex," Pelt observed.

"I will pass that along to Moscow, Doctor," Arbatov responded dryly. "Can you tell us where this happened?"

"I can do better than that. We have a ship taking a deep-
diving research sub down to look for the wreckage. If you
want, you can have your navy fly a man to Norfolk, and we'll
fly him out to check it for you. Fair enough?"

"You say you lost two officers?" Arbatov played for time,
surprised at the offer.

"Yes, both rescue people. We did get a hundred men off,
Alex," Pelt said defensively. "That's something."

"Indeed it is, Dr. Pelt. I must cable Moscow for instructions.
I will be back to you. You are at your office?"

"Correct. Bye, Alex." He hung up and looked at the president. "Do I pass, boss?"

"Work a little bit on the sincerity, Jeff." The president was
sprawled in a leather chair, a robe over his pajamas. "They'll
bite?"

"They'll bite. They sure as hell want to confirm the destruction of the sub. Question is, can we fool 'em?"

"Foster seems to think so. It sounds plausible enough."

"Hmph. Well, we have her, don't we?" Pelt observed.

"Yep, I guess that story about the GRU agent was wrong,
or else they kicked him off with everybody else. I want to see
that Captain Ramius. Jeez! Pulling a reactor scare, no wonder
he got everybody off the ship!"

The Pentagon

Skip Tyler was in the CNO's office trying to relax in a chair.
The coast guard station on the inlet had had a low-light tele-
vision, the tape from which had been flown by helicopter to
Cherry Point and from there by Phantom jet fighter to Andrews.
Now it was in the hands of a courier whose automobile was
just pulling up at the Pentagon's main entrance.

"I have a package to hand deliver to Admiral Foster," an
ensign announced a few minutes later. Foster's flag secretary
pointed him to the door.

"Good morning, sir! This is for you, sir." The ensign handed
Foster the wrapped cassette.

"Thank you. Dismissed."

Foster inserted the cassette in the tape player atop his office television. The set was already on, and the picture appeared in several seconds.

Tyler was standing beside the CNO as it focused. "Yep."

"Yep," Foster agreed.

The picture was lousy—no other word for it. The low-light television system did not give a very sharp picture since it amplified all of the ambient light equally. This tended to wash out many details. But what they saw was enough: a very large missile submarine whose sail was much farther aft than the sails on anything a Western country made. She dwarfed the *Dallas* and *Pogy*. They watched the screen without a word for the next fifteen minutes. Except for the wobbly camera, the picture was about as lively as a test pattern.

"Well," Foster said as the tape ended, "we got us a Russian boomer."

"How 'bout that?" Tyler grinned.

"Skip, you were up for command of *Los Angeles*, right?"

"Yes, sir."

"We owe you for this, Commander, we owe you a lot. I did some checking the other day. An officer injured in the line of duty does not necessarily have to retire unless he is demonstrably unfit for duty. An accident while returning from working on your boat is line of duty, I think, and we've had a few ship commanders who were short a leg. I'll go to the president myself on this, son. It will mean a year's work getting back in the groove, but if you still want your command, by God, I'll get it for you."

Tyler sat down for that. It would mean being fitted for a new leg, something he'd been considering for months, and a few weeks getting used to it. Then a year—a good year—relearning everything he needed to know before he could go to sea . . . He shook his head. "Thank you, Admiral. You don't know what that means to me—but, no. I'm past that now. I have a different life, and different responsibilities now, and I'd just be taking someone else's slot. Tell you what, you let me get a look at that boomer, and we're even."

"That I can guarantee." Foster had hoped he'd respond that way, had been nearly sure of it. It was too bad, though. Tyler, he thought, would have been a good candidate for his own flag except for the leg. Well, nobody ever said the world was fair.

The Red October

"You guys seem to have things under control," Ryan observed. "Does anybody mind if I flake out somewhere?"

"Flake out?" Borodin asked.

"Sleep."

"Ah, take Dr. Petrov's cabin, across from the medical office."

On his way aft Ryan looked in Borodin's cabin and found the vodka bottle that had been liberated. It didn't have much taste, but it was smooth enough. Petrov's bunk was not very wide or very soft. Ryan was past caring. He took a long swallow and lay down in his uniform, which was already so greasy and dirty as to be beyond hope. He was asleep in five minutes.

The Sea Cliff

The air-purifier system was not working properly, Lieutenant Sven Johnsen thought. If his sinus cold had lasted a few more days he might not have noticed. The *Sea Cliff* was just passing ten thousand feet, and they couldn't tinker with the system until they surfaced. It was not dangerous—the environmental control systems had as many built-in redundancies as the Space Shuttle—just a nuisance.

"I've never been so deep," Captain Igor Kaganovich said conversationally. Getting him here had been complicated. It had required a Helix helicopter from the *Kiev* to the *Tarawa*, then a U.S. Navy Sea King to Norfolk. Another helicopter had taken him to the USS *Austin*, which was heading for 33N 75W at twenty knots. The *Austin* was a landing ship dock, a large vessel whose aft end was a covered well. She was usually used for landing craft, but today she carried the *Sea Cliff*, a three-man submarine that had been flown down from Woods Hole, Massachusetts.

"Does take some getting used to," Johnsen agreed, "but when you get down to it, five hundred feet, ten thousand feet, doesn't make much difference. A hull fracture would kill you just as fast, just down here there'd be less residue for the next boat to try and recover."

"Keep thinking those happy thoughts, sir," Machinist's Mate First Class Jesse Overton said. "Still clear on sonar?"

"Right, Jess." Johnsen had been working with the machinist's mate for two years. The *Sea Cliff* was their baby, a small, rugged research submarine used mainly for oceanographic tasks, including the emplacement or repair of SOSUS sensors. On the three-man sub there was little place for bridge discipline. Overton was not well educated or very articulate—at least not politely articulate. His skill at maneuvering the minisub was unsurpassed, however, and Johnsen was just as happy to leave that job to him. It was the lieutenant's task to manage the mission at hand.

"Air system needs some work," Johnsen observed.

"Yeah, the filters are about due for replacement. I was going to do that next week. Coulda' done it this morning, but I figured the backup control wiring was more important."

"Guess I have to go along with you on that. Handling okay?"

"Like a virgin." Overton's smile was reflected in the thick Lexan view port in front of the control seat. The *Sea Cliff*'s awkward design made her clumsy to maneuver. It was as though she knew what she wanted to do, just not quite how she wanted to do it. "How wide's the target area?"

"Pretty wide. *Pigeon* says after the explosion the pieces spread from hell to breakfast."

"I believe it. Three miles down, and a current to spread it around."

"The boat's name is *Red October*, Captain? A *Victor*-class attack submarine, you said?"

"That is your name for the class," Kaganovich said.

"What do you call them?" Johnsen asked. He got no reply. What was the big deal? he wondered. What did the name of the class matter to anybody?

"Switching on locater sonar." Johnsen activated several systems, and the *Sea Cliff* pulsed with the sound of the high-frequency sonar mounted on her belly. "There's the bottom." The yellow screen showed bottom contours in white.

"Anything sticking up, sir?" Overton asked.

"Not today, Jess."

A year before they had been operating a few miles from this spot and nearly been impaled on a Liberty ship, sunk around 1942 by a German U-boat. The hulk had been sitting up at an angle, propped up by a massive boulder. That near collision would surely have been fatal, and it had taught both men caution.

"Okay, I'm starting to get some hard returns. Directly ahead, spread out like a fan. Another five hundred feet to the bottom."

"Right."

"Hmph. There's one big piece, 'bout thirty feet long, maybe nine or ten across, eleven o'clock, three hundred yards. We'll go for that one first."

"Coming left, lights coming on now."

A half-dozen high-intensity floodlights came on, at once surrounding the submersible in a globe of light. It did not penetrate more than ten yards in the water, which ate up the light energy.

"There's the bottom, just where you said, Mr. Johnsen," Overton said. He halted the powered descent and checked for buoyancy. Almost exactly neutral, good. "This current's going to be tough on battery power."

"How strong is it?"

"Knot an' a half, maybe more like two, depending on bottom contours. Same as last year. I figure we can maneuver an hour, hour an' a half, tops."

Johnsen agreed. Oceanographers were still puzzling over this deep current, which seemed to change direction from time to time in no particular pattern. Odd. There were a lot of odd things in the ocean. That's why Johnsen got his oceanography degree, to figure some of the buggers out. It sure beat working for a living. Being three miles down wasn't work, not to Johnsen.

"I see somethin', a flash off the bottom right in front of us. Want I should grab it?"

"If you can."

They couldn't see it yet on any of the *Sea Cliff*'s three TV monitors, which looked straight ahead, forty-five degrees left and right of the bow.

"Okay." Overton put his right hand on the waldo control. This was what he was really best at.

"Can you see what it is?" Johnsen asked, fiddling with the TV.

"Some kinda instrument. Can you kill the number one flood, sir? It's dazzlin' me."

"Wait one." Johnsen leaned forward to kill the proper switch. The number one floodlight provided illumination for the bow camera, which went immediately blank.

"Okay, baby, now let's just hold steady . . ." The machinist's mate's left hand worked the directional propeller controls; his right was poised in the waldo glove. Now he was the only one who could see the target. Overton's reflection was grinning at itself. His right hand moved rapidly.

"Gotcha!" he said. The waldo took the depth-gauge dial a diver had magnetically affixed to the *Sea Cliff*'s bow prior to setting out from the *Austin*'s dock bay. "You can hit the light again, sir."

Johnsen flicked it on, and Overton maneuvered his catch in front of the bow camera. "Can ya see what it is?"

"Looks like a depth gauge. Not one of ours, though," Johnsen observed. "Can you make it out, Captain?"

"*Da*," Kaganovich said at once. He let out a long breath, trying to sound unhappy. "It is one of ours. I cannot read the number, but it is Soviet."

"Put it in the basket, Jess," Johnsen said.

"Right." He maneuvered the waldo, placing the dial in a basket welded on the bow, then getting the manipulator arm back to its rest position. "Getting some silt. Let's pick up a little."

As the *Sea Cliff* got too close to the bottom the wash from her propellers stirred up the fine alluvial silt. Overton increased power to get back to a twenty-foot height.

"That's better. See what the current is doin', Mr. Johnsen? Good two knots. Gonna cut our bottom time." The current was wafting the cloud to port, rather quickly. "Where's the big target?"

"Dead ahead, hundred yards. Let's make sure we see what that is."

"Right. Going forward . . . There's something, looks like a butcher knife. We want it?"

"No, let's keep going."

"Okay, range?"

"Sixty yards. Ought to be seeing it soon."

The two officers saw it on TV the same time Overton did. Just a spectral image at first, it faded like an afterimage in one's eye. Then it came back.

Overton was the first to react. "Damn!"

It was more than thirty feet long and appeared perfectly round. They approached from its rear and saw the main circle and within it four smaller cones that stuck out a foot or so.

"That's a missile, Skipper, a whole fuckin' Russkie nuclear missile!"

"Hold position, Jess."

"Aye aye." He backed off on the power controls.

"You said she was a *Victor*," Johnsen said to the Soviet.

"I was mistaken." Kaganovich's mouth twitched.

"Let's take a closer look, Jess."

The *Sea Cliff* moved forward, up the side of the rocket body. The Cyrillic lettering was unmistakable, though they were too far off to make out the serial numbers. There was a new treasure for Davey Jones, an SS-N-20 Seahawk, with its eight five-hundred-kiloton MIRVs.

Kaganovich was careful to note the markings on the missile body. He'd been briefed on the Seahawk immediately before flying from the *Kiev*. As an intelligence officer, he ordinarily knew more about American weapons than their Soviet counterparts.

How convenient, he thought. The Americans had allowed him to ride in one of their most advanced research vessels whose internal arrangements he had already memorized, and they had accomplished his mission for him. The *Red October* was dead. All he had to do was get that information to Admiral Stralbo on the *Kirov* and the fleet could leave the American coast. Let them come to the Norwegian Sea to play their nasty games! See who would win them up there!

"Position check, Jess. Mark the sucker."

"Aye." Overton pressed a button to deploy a sonar transponder that would respond only to a coded American sonar signal. This would guide them back to the missile. They would return later with their heavy-lift rig to put a line on the missile and haul it to the surface.

"That is the property of the Soviet Union," Kaganovich pointed out. "It is in—under international waters. It belongs to my country."

"Then you can fuckin' come and get it!" snapped the American seaman. He must be an officer in disguise, Kaganovich thought. "Beg pardon, Mr. Johnsen."

"We'll be back for it," Johnsen said.

"You'll never lift it. It is too heavy," Kaganovich objected.

"I suppose you're right." Johnsen smiled.

Kaganovich allowed the Americans their small victory. It

could have been worse. Much worse. "Shall we continue to search for more wreckage?"

"No, I think we'll go back up," Johnsen decided.

"But your orders—"

"My orders, Captain Kaganovich, were to search for the remains of a *Victor*-class attack submarine. We found the grave of a boomer. You lied to us, Captain, and our courtesy to you ends at this point. You got what you wanted, I guess. Later we'll be back for what we want." Johnsen reached up and pulled the release handle for the iron ballast. The metal slab dropped free. This gave the *Sea Cliff* a thousand pounds of positive buoyancy. There was no way to stay down now, even if they wanted to.

"Home, Jess."

"Aye aye, Skipper."

The ride back to the surface was a silent one.

The USS Austin

An hour later, Kaganovich climbed to the *Austin*'s bridge and requested permission to send a message to the *Kirov*. This had been agreed upon beforehand, else the *Austin*'s commanding officer would have refused. Word on the dead sub's identity had spread fast. The Soviet officer broadcast a series of code words, accompanied by the serial number from the depth-gauge dial. These were acknowledged at once.

Overton and Johnsen watched the Russian board the helicopter, carrying the depth-gauge dial.

"I didn't like him much, Mr. Johnsen. *Keptin Kaganobitch*. The name sounds like a terminal studder. We snookered him, didn't we?"

"Remind me never to play cards with you, Jess."

The Red October

Ryan woke up after six hours to music that seemed dreamily familiar. He lay in his bunk for a minute trying to place it, then slipped his feet into his shoes and went forward to the wardroom.

It was *E.T.* Ryan arrived just in time to see the credits scrolling up the thirteen-inch TV set sitting on the forward end of the wardroom table. Most of the Russian officers and three

Americans had been watching it. The Russians were all dabbing their eyes. Jack got a cup of coffee and sat at the end of the table.

"You liked it?"

"It was magnificent!" Borodin proclaimed.

Lieutenant Mannion chuckled. "Second time we ran it."

One of the Russians started speaking rapidly in his native language. Borodin translated for him. "He asks if all American children act with such—Bugayev, *svobodno?*"

"Free," Bugayev translated, incorrectly but close enough.

Ryan laughed. "I never did, but the movie was set in California—people out there are a little crazy. The truth is, no, kids don't act like that—at least I've never seen it, and I have two. At the same time, we do raise our kids to be a lot more independent than Soviet parents do."

Borodin translated, and then gave the Russian response. "So, all American children are not such hooligans?"

"Some are. America is not perfect, gentlemen. We make lots of mistakes." Ryan had decided to tell the truth insofar as he could.

Borodin translated again. The reactions around the table were a little dubious.

"I have told them this movie is a child's story and should not be taken too seriously. This is so?"

"Yes, sir," Mancuso, who had just come in, said. "It's a kid's story, but I've seen it five times. Welcome back, Ryan."

"Thank you, Commander. I take it you have things under control."

"Yep. I guess we all needed the chance to unwind. I'll have to write Jonesy another commendation letter. This really was a good idea." He waved at the television. "We have lots of time to be serious."

Noyes came in. "How's Williams?" Ryan asked.

"He'll make it." Noyes filled his cup. "I had him open for three and a half hours. The head wound was superficial—bloody as hell, but head wounds are like that. The chest was a close one, though. The bullet missed the pericardium by a whisker. Captain Borodin, who gave that man first aid?"

The *starpom* pointed to a lieutenant. "He does not speak English."

"Tell him that Williams owes him his life. Putting that chest tube in was the difference. He would have died without it."

"You're sure he'll make it?" Ryan persisted.

"Of course he'll make it, Ryan. That's what I do for a living. He'll be a sick boy for a while, and I'd feel better if we had him in a real hospital, but everything's under control."

"And Captain Ramius?" Borodin asked.

"No problem. He's still sleeping. I took my time sewing it up. Ask him where he got his first aid training."

Borodin did. "He said he likes to read medical books."

"How old is he?"

"Twenty-four."

"Tell him if he ever wants to study medicine, I'll tell him how to get started. If he knows how to do the right thing at the right time, he might just be good enough to do it for a living."

The young officer was pleased by this comment and asked how much money a doctor could make in America.

"I'm in the service, so I don't make very much. Forty-eight thousand a year, counting flight pay. I could do a lot better on the outside."

"In the Soviet Union," Borodin pointed out, "doctors are paid about the same as factory workers."

"Maybe that explains why your docs are no good," Noyes observed.

"When will the captain be able to resume command?" Borodin asked.

"I'm going to keep him down all day," Noyes said. "I don't want him to start bleeding again. He can start moving around tomorrow. Carefully. I don't want him on that leg too much. He'll be fine, gentlemen. A little weak from the blood loss, but he'll recover fully." Noyes made his pronouncements as though he were quoting physical laws.

"We thank you, Doctor," Borodin said.

Noyes shrugged. "It's what they pay me for. Now can I ask a question? What the hell is going on here?"

Borodin laughed, translating the question for his comrades. "We will all become American citizens."

"And you're bringing a sub along with you, eh? Son of a gun. For a while there I thought this was some sort of—I don't know, something. This is quite a story. Guess I can't tell it to anybody, though."

"Correct, Doctor." Ryan smiled.

"Too bad," Noyes muttered as he headed back to sick bay.

Moscow

"So, Comrade Admiral, you report success to us?" Narmonov asked.

"Yes, Comrade General Secretary," Gorshkov nodded, surveying the conference table in the underground command center. All of the inner circle were here, along with the military chiefs and the head of the KGB. "Admiral Stralbo's fleet intelligence officer, Captain Kaganovich, was permitted by the Americans to view the wreckage from aboard one of their deep-submergence research vessels. The craft recovered a fragment of wreckage, a depth-gauge dial. These objects are numbered, and the number was immediately relayed to Moscow. It was positively from *Red October*. Kaganovich also inspected a missile blasted loose from the submarine. It was definitely a Seahawk. *Red October* is dead. Our mission is accomplished."

"By chance, Comrade Admiral, not by design," Mikhail Alexandrov pointed out. "Your fleet failed in its mission to *locate* and destroy the submarine. I think Comrade Gerasimov has some information for us."

Nikolay Gerasimov was the new KGB chief. He had already given his report to the political members of this group and was eager to release it to these strutting peacocks in uniform. He wanted to see their reactions. The KGB had scores to settle with these men. Gerasimov summarized the report he had from agent Cassius.

"Impossible!" Gorshkov snapped.

"Perhaps," Gerasimov conceded politely. "There is a strong probability that this is a very clever piece of disinformation. It is now being investigated by our agents in the field. There are, however, some interesting details which support this hypothesis. Permit me to review them, Comrade Admiral.

"First, why did the Americans allow our man aboard one of their most advanced research submarines? Second, why did they cooperate with us at all, saving our sailor from the *Politovskiy* and *telling* us about it? They let us see our man immediately. Why? Why not keep our man, use him, and dispose of him? Sentimentality? I think not. Third, at the same time they picked this man up their air and fleet units were harassing our fleet in the most blatant and aggressive manner. This suddenly stopped, and a day later they were tripping over their own feet in their efforts to assist in our 'search and rescue.'"

"Because Stralbo wisely and courageously decided to refrain from reacting to their provocations," Gorshkov replied.

Gerasimov nodded politely again. "Perhaps so. That was an intelligent decision on the admiral's part. It cannot be easy for a uniformed officer to swallow his pride so. On the other hand, I speculate that it is also possible that about this time the Americans received this information which Cassius passed on to us. I further speculate that the Americans were fearful of our reaction were we to suspect that they had perpetrated this entire affair as a CIA operation. We know now that several imperialist intelligence services are inquiring as to the reason for this fleet operation.

"Over the past two days we have been doing some fast checking of our own. We find," Gerasimov consulted his notes, "that there are twenty-nine Polish engineers at the Polyarnyy submarine yard, mainly in quality control and inspection posts, that mail and message-handling procedures are very lax, and the Captain Ramius did not, as he supposedly threatened in his letter to Comrade Padorin, sail his submarine into New York harbor, but was rather in a position a thousand kilometers south when the submarine was destroyed."

"That was an obvious piece of disinformation on Ramius' part," Gorshkov objected. "Ramius was both baiting us and deliberately misleading us. For that reason we deployed our fleet at all of the American ports."

"And never did find him," Alexandrov noted quietly. "Go on, Comrade."

Gerasimov continued. "Whatever port he was supposedly heading for, he was over five hundred kilometers from any of them, and we are certain that he could have reached any of them on a direct course. In fact, Comrade Admiral, as you reported in your initial briefing, he could have reached the American coast within seven days of leaving port."

"To do that, as I explained at length last week, would have meant traveling at maximum speed. Missile submarine commanders prefer not to do this," Gorshkov said.

"I can understand it," Alexandrov observed, "in view of the fate of the *Politovskiy*. But you would expect a traitor to the *Rodina* to run like a thief."

"Into the trap we set," Gorshkov replied.

"Which failed," Narmonov commented.

"I do not claim that this story is true, nor do I claim it is even a likely one at this point," Gerasimov said, keeping his voice detached and clinical, "but there is sufficient circumstantial evidence supporting it that I must recommend an in-depth investigation by the Committee for State Security touching on all aspects of this affair."

"Security in my yards is a naval and GRU matter," Gorshkov said.

"No longer." Narmonov announced the decision reached two hours earlier. "The KGB will investigate this shameful business along two lines. One group will investigate the information from our agent in Washington. The other will proceed on the assumption that the letter from—allegedly from—Captain Ramius was genuine. If this was a traitorous conspiracy, it could only have been possible because Ramius was able under current regulations and practices to choose his own officers. The Committee for State Security will report to us on the desirability of continuing this practice, on the current degree of control ship captains have over the careers of their officers, and over Party control of the fleet. I think we will begin our reforms by allowing officers to transfer from one ship to another with greater frequency. If officers stay in one place too long, obviously they may develop confusion in their loyalties."

"What you suggest will destroy the efficiency of my fleet!" Gorshkov pounded on the table. It was a mistake.

"The People's fleet, Comrade Admiral," Alexandrov corrected. "The Party's fleet." Gorshkov knew where that idea came from. Narmonov still had Alexandrov's support. That made the comrade general secretary's position secure, and that meant the positions of other men around this table were not. Which men?

Padorin's mind revolted at the suggestion from the KGB. What did those bastard spies know about the navy? Or the Party? They were all corrupt opportunists. Andropov had proven that, and the Politburo was now letting this whelp Gerasimov attack the armed services, which safeguarded the nation against the imperialists, had saved it from Andropov's clique, and had never been anything but the stalwart servants of the Party. But it does all fit, doesn't it? he thought. Just as Khrushchev had deposed Zhukov, the man who made his succession possible when Beria was done away with, so these bastards would now play the KGB against the uniformed men who had made their positions safe in the first place...

"As for you, Comrade Padorin," Alexandrov went on.

"Yes, Comrade Academician." For Padorin there was no apparent escape. The Main Political Administration had passed final approval on Ramius' appointment. If Ramius were indeed a traitor, then Padorin stood condemned for gross misjudgment, but if Ramius had been an unknowing pawn, then Padorin along with Gorshkov had been duped into precipitous action.

Narmonov took his cue from Alexandrov. "Comrade Admiral, we find that your secret provisions to safeguard the security of the submarine *Red October* were successfully implemented—unless, that is, Captain Ramius was blameless and scuttled the ship himself along with his officers and the Americans who were doubtless trying to steal it. In either case, pending the KGB's inspection of the parts recovered from the wreck, it would appear that the submarine did not fall into enemy hands."

Padorin blinked several times. His heart was beating fast, and he could feel a twinge of pain in his left chest. Was he being let off? Why? It took him a second to understand. He was the political officer, after all. If the Party was seeking to reestablish political control over the fleet—no, to reassert what never had been lost—then the Politburo could not afford to depose the Party's representative in high command. This would make him the vassal of these men, Alexandrov especially. Padorin decided that he could live with that.

And it made Gorshkov's position extremely vulnerable. Though it would take some months, Padorin was sure that the Russian fleet would have a new chief, one whose personal power would not be sufficient to make policy without Politburo approval. Gorshkov had become too big, too powerful, and the Party chieftains did not wish to have a man with so much personal prestige in high command.

I have my head, Padorin thought to himself, amazed at his good fortune.

"Comrade Gerasimov," Narmonov went on, "will be working with the political security section of your office to review your procedures and to offer suggestions for improvements."

So, now he became the KGB's spy in high command? Well, he had his head, his office, his dacha, and his pension in two years. It was a small price to pay. Padorin was more than content.

THE SIXTEENTH DAY

SATURDAY, 18 DECEMBER

The East Coast

The USS *Pigeon* arrived at her dock in Charleston at four in the morning. The Soviet crewmen, quartered in the crew's mess, had become a handful for everyone. As much as the Russian officers had worked to limit contact between their charges and their American rescuers, this had never really been possible. To state it simply, they had been unable to block the call of nature. The *Pigeon* had stuffed her visitors with good navy chow, and the nearest head was a few yards aft. On the way to and from the facilities, the *Red October*'s crewmen met with American sailors, some of whom were Russian-speaking officers disguised as enlisted men, others of whom were Russian language specialists in the enlisted rates flown out just as the last load of Soviets had arrived aboard. The fact that they were aboard a putatively hostile vessel and had found friendly Russian-speaking men had been overpowering for many of the young conscripts. Their remarks had been recorded on hidden tape machines for later examination in Washington. Petrov and the three junior officers had been slow to catch on, but when they did they took to escorting the men to the toilet in relays, like protective parents. What they were not able to prevent was an intelligence officer in a bosun's uniform making an offer of asylum: anyone who wished to remain in the United States would be permitted to do so. It took ten minutes for the information to spread throughout the crew.

When it came time for the American crewmen to eat, the Russian officers could hardly prohibit contact, and it turned out that the officers themselves got very little to eat, so busy were they patrolling the mess tables. To the bemused surprise of their American counterparts, they were forced to decline repeated invitations to the *Pigeon*'s wardroom.

The *Pigeon* docked carefully. There was no hurry. As the gangway was set in place, the band on the dock played a selection of Soviet and American airs to mark the cooperative nature of the rescue mission. The Soviets had expected that their arrival would be a quiet one given the time of day. They were mistaken in this. When the first Soviet officer was halfway down the gangway, he was dazzled by fifty high-intensity television lights and the shouted questions of television reporters routed out of bed to meet the rescue ship and so have a bright piece of Christmas season news for the morning network broadcasts. The Russians had never encountered anything like Western newsmen before, and the resulting cultural collision was total chaos. Reporters singled out the officers, blocking their paths to the consternation of marines trying to keep control of things. To a man the officers pretended not to know a word of English, only to find that an enterprising reporter had brought along a Russian language professor from the University of South Carolina in Columbia. Petrov found himself stumbling through politically acceptable platitudes in front of a half-dozen cameras and wishing the entire affair were the bad dream it seemed to be. It took an hour to get every Russian sailor aboard the three buses chartered for the purpose and off to the airport. Along the way cars and vans filled with news crews raced alongside the buses, continuing to annoy the Russians with camera lights and further shouted questions that no one could understand. The scene at the airport was not much different. The air force had sent down a VC-135 transport, but before the Russians could board it they again had to jostle their way through a sea of reporters. Ivanov found himself confronted with a Slavic language expert whose Russian was marred by a horrendous accent. Boarding took another half hour.

A dozen air force officers got everyone seated and passed out cigarettes and liquor miniatures. By the time the VIP transport reached twenty thousand feet, it was a very happy flight. An officer spoke to them over the intercom system, explaining what was to happen. Medical checks would be made of everyone. The Soviet Union would be sending a plane for them the next day, but everyone hoped their stay might be extended a day or two so that they might experience American hospitality in full. The flight crew outdid itself, telling their passengers the history of every landmark, town, village, interstate highway, and truck stop on the flight route, proclaiming through the interpreter the wish of all Americans for peaceful, friendly relations with the Soviet Union, expressing the professional admiration of the U.S. Air Force for the courage of the Soviet seamen, and mourning the deaths of the officers who had courageously lingered behind, allowing their men to go first. The whole affair was a masterpiece of duplicity aimed at overwhelming them, and it began to succeed.

The aircraft flew low over the Washington suburbs while approaching Andrews Air Force Base. The interpreter explained that they were flying over middle-class homes that belonged to ordinary workers in government and local industry. Three more buses awaited them on the ground, and instead of driving on the beltway around Washington, D.C., the buses drove directly through town. American officers on each bus apologized for the traffic jams, telling the passengers that nearly every American family has one car, many two or more, and that people only use public transportation to avoid the nuisance of driving. The *nuisance* of driving one's own car, the Soviet seaman thought in amazement. Their political officers might later tell them that this was a total lie, but who could deny the thousands of cars on the road? Surely this could not all be a sham staged for the benefit of a few sailors on an hour's notice? Driving through southeast D.C. they noted that black people owned cars—scarcely had room to park them all! The bus continued down the Mall, with the interpreters voicing the hope that they would be allowed to see the many museums open to everyone. The Air and Space Museum, it was mentioned, had a moon rock brought back by the Apollo astronauts . . . The Soviets saw the joggers in the Mall and the thousands of people casually strolling around. They jabbered among themselves as the buses turned north to Bethesda through the nicer sections of northwest Washington.

At Bethesda they were met by television crews broadcasting live over all three networks and by friendly, smiling U.S. Navy doctors and corpsmen who led them into the hospital for medical checks.

Ten embassy officials were there, wondering how to control the group but politically unable to protest the attention given their men in the spirit of détente. Doctors had been brought in from Walter Reed and other government hospitals to give each man a quick and thorough medical examination, particularly to check for radiation poisoning. Along the way each man found himself alone with a U.S. Navy officer who asked politely if that individual might wish to stay in the United States, pointing out that each man making this decision would be required to make his intentions known in person to a representative of the Soviet embassy—but that if he wished to do so, he would be permitted to stay. To the fury of the embassy officials, four men made this decision, one recanting after a confrontation with the naval attaché. The Americans had been careful to have each meeting videotaped so that later accusations of intimidation could be refuted at once.

When the medical checks were completed—thankfully, radiation exposure levels had been slight—the men were again fed and bedded down.

Washington, D.C.

"Good morning, Mr. Ambassador," the president said. Arbatov noted that again Dr. Pelt was standing at his master's side behind the large antique desk. He had not expected this meeting to be a pleasant one.

"Mr. President, I am here to protest the attempted kidnapping of our seamen by the United States government."

"Mr. Ambassador," the president responded sharply, "in the eyes of a former district attorney, kidnapping is a vile and loathsome crime, and the government of the United States of

America will not be accused of such a thing—certainly not in this office! We have not, do not, and never will kidnap people. Is that clear to you, sir?"

"Besides which, Alex," Pelt said less forcefully, "the men to whom you refer would not be alive were it not for us. We lost two good men rescuing your servicemen. You might at least express some appreciation for our efforts to save your crew, and perhaps make a gesture of sympathy for the Americans who lost their lives in the process."

"My government notes the heroic effort of your two officers, and does wish to express its appreciation and that of the Soviet people for the rescue. Even so, gentlemen, deliberate efforts have been made to entice some of those men to betray their country."

"Mr. Ambassador, when your trawler rescued the crew of our patrol plane last year, officers of the Soviet armed forces offered money, women, and other enticements to our crewmen if they would give out information or agree to stay behind in Vladivostok, correct? Don't tell me that you have no knowledge of this. You know that's how the game is played. At the time we did not object to this, did we? No, we were sufficiently grateful that those six men were still alive, and now, of course, all of them are back at work. We remain grateful for your country's humanitarian concern for the lives of ordinary American citizens. In this case, each officer and enlisted man was told that he could stay if he wished to do so. No force of any kind was used. Each man wishing to remain here was required by us to meet with an official of your embassy so as to give you a fair chance to explain to him the error of his ways. Surely this is fair, Mr. Ambassador. We made no offers of money or women. We do not buy people, and we damned well do not— ever—kidnap people. Kidnappers are people I put in jail. I even managed to have one executed. Don't you ever accuse me of that again," the president concluded righteously.

"My government insists that all of our men be returned to their homeland," Arbatov persisted.

"Mr. Ambassador, any person in the United States, regardless of his nationality or the manner of his arrival, is entitled to the full protection of our law. Our courts have ruled on this many times, and under our law no man or woman may be compelled to do something against his will without due process.

The subject is closed. Now, I have a question for you. What
was a ballistic missile submarine doing three hundred miles
from the American coast?"

"A missile submarine, Mr. President?"

Pelt lifted a photograph from the president's desk and handed
it to Arbatov. Taken from the tape recorder on the *Sea Cliff*,
it showed the SS-N-20 sea-launched ballistic missile.

"The name of the submarine is—was *Red October*," Pelt
said. "It exploded and sank three hundred miles from the coast
of South Carolina. Alex, we have an agreement between our
two countries that no such vessel will approach either country
to within five hundred miles—eight hundred kilometers. We
want to know what that submarine was doing there. Don't try
to tell us that this missile is some kind of fabrication—even
if we had wanted to do such a foolish thing, we wouldn't have
had the time. That's one of your missiles, Mr. Ambassador,
and the submarine carried nineteen more just like it." Pelt
deliberately misstated the number. "And the government of the
United States asks the government of the Soviet Union how it
came to be there, in violation of our agreement, while so many
other of your ships are so close to our Atlantic coast."

"That must be the lost submarine," Arbatov offered.

"Mr. Ambassador," the president said softly, "the submarine
was not lost until Thursday, seven days after you told us about
it. In short, Mr. Ambassador, your explanation of last Friday
does not coincide with the facts we have physically established."

"What accusation are you making?" Arbatov bristled.

"Why, none, Alex," the president said. "If that agreement
is no longer operative, then it is no longer operative. I believe
we discussed that possibility last week also. The American
people will know later today what the facts are. You are sufficiently familiar with our country to imagine their reaction. I
will have an explanation. For the moment, I see no further
reason for your fleet to be off our coast. The 'rescue' has been
successfully concluded, and the further presence of the Soviet
fleet can only be a provocation. I want you and your government to consider what my military commanders are telling me
right now—or if you prefer, what your commanders would be
telling General Secretary Narmonov if the situation were reversed. I will have an explanation. Without one I can reach

one of only a few conclusions—and those are conclusions I would prefer not to choose from. Send that message to your government, and tell them that since some of your men have opted to stay here, we'll probably find out what was really happening in short order. Good day."

Arbatov left the office, turning left to leave by the west entrance. A marine guard held the door open, a polite gesture that stopped short of his eyes. The ambassador's driver, waiting outside in a Cadillac limousine, held the door open for him. The driver was chief of the KGB's political intelligence section at that organization's Washington station.

"So," he said, checking traffic on Pennsylvania Avenue before making a left turn.

"So, the meeting went exactly as I had predicted, and now we can be absolutely certain why they are kidnapping our men," Arbatov replied.

"And that is, Comrade Ambassador?" the driver prompted. He did not let his irritation show. Only a few years before this Party hack would not have dared temporize with a senior KGB officer. It was a disgrace, what had happened to the Committee for State Security since the death of Comrade Andropov. But things would be set right again. He was certain of that.

"The president all but accused us of sending the submarine deliberately to their shore in violation of our secret 1979 protocol. They are holding our men to interrogate them, to take their heads apart so that they can learn what the submarine's orders were. How long will that take the CIA? A day? Two?" Arbatov shook his head angrily. "They may know already—a few drugs, a woman, perhaps, to loosen their tongues. The president also invited Moscow to imagine what the Pentagon hotheads are telling him to think! And telling him to do. No mystery there, is there? They will say we were rehearsing a surprise nuclear attack—perhaps even executing one! As if we were not working harder than they to achieve peaceful co-existence! Suspicious fools, they are fearful about what has happened, and even more angry."

"Can you blame them, Comrade?" the driver asked, taking all of this in, filing, analyzing, composing his independent report to Moscow Center.

"And he said that there was no further reason for our fleet to be off their coast."

"How did he say this? Was it a demand?"

"His words were soft. Softer than I expected. This concerns me. They are planning something, I think. Rattling a saber makes noise, drawing it does not. He demands an explanation for this entire affair. What do I tell him? What *was* happening?"

"I suspect that we will never know." The senior agent did know—the original story, that is, incredible as it was. That the navy and the GRU could allow such a fantastic error to take place had amazed him. The story from agent Cassius was scarcely less mad. The driver had passed it on to Moscow himself. Was it possible that the United States and the Soviet Union were both victims of a third party? An operation gone awry, and the Americans trying to find out who was responsible and how it was done so that they might try to do it themselves? That part of the story made sense, but did the rest? He frowned at the traffic. He had orders from Moscow Center: if this was a CIA operation, he was supposed to find out immediately. He didn't believe it was. If so the CIA was being unusually effective in covering it. Was it possible to cover such a complex operation? He didn't think so. Regardless, he and his colleagues would be working for several weeks to penetrate any cover there was, to find out what was being said in Langley and in the field, while other KGB sections did the same throughout the world. If the CIA had penetrated the Northern Fleet's high command he'd find out. Of that he was confident. He could almost wish they had done so. The GRU would be responsible for the disaster, and would be disgraced after profiting from the KGB's loss of prestige a few years back. If he was reading the situation correctly, the Politburo was turning the KGB loose on the GRU and the military, allowing Moscow Center to initiate its own independent investigation of the affair. Regardless of what was found, the KGB would come out ahead and deflate the armed services. One way or another, his organization would discover what had taken place, and if it was damaging to his rivals, so much the better . . .

When the door closed behind the Soviet ambassador, Dr. Pelt opened a side door to the Oval Office. Judge Moore came in.

"Mr. President, it's been a while since I've had to do things like hide in closets."

"You really expect this to work?" Pelt said.

"Yes, I do now," Moore settled comfortably into a leather chair.

"Isn't this a little shaky, Judge?" Pelt asked. "I mean, running an operation this complex?"

"That's the beauty of it, Doctor, we're not running anything. The Soviets will be doing that for us. Oh, sure, we'll have a lot of our people prowling around Eastern Europe asking a lot of questions. So will Sir Basil's fellows. The French and the Israelis already are, because we've asked them if they know what's happening with the stray missile sub. The KGB will find out quickly enough and wonder why the four main Western intelligence agencies are all asking the same questions—instead of pulling into their shells like they'd expect them to if this were our operation.

"You have to appreciate the dilemma the Soviets face, a choice between two equally unattractive scenarios. On the one hand, they can choose to believe that one of their most trusted professional officers has committed high treason on an unprecedented scale. You've seen our file on Captain Ramius. He's the Communist version of an eagle scout, a genuine New Soviet Man. Add to that the fact that a defection conspiracy necessarily involves a number of equally trusted officers. The Soviets have a mind block against believing that individuals of this type will ever leave the Workers' Paradise. That seems paradoxical, I admit, given the strenuous efforts they expend to keep people from leaving their country, but it's true. Losing a ballet dancer or a KGB agent is one thing—losing the son of a Politburo member, an officer with nearly thirty years of unblemished service, is quite another. Moreover, a naval captain has a lot of privileges; you might call his defection the equivalent of a self-made millionaire leaving New York to live in Moscow. They simply will not believe it.

"On the other hand, they can believe the story we planted through Henderson, which is also unattractive but is supported by a good deal of circumstantial evidence, especially our efforts to entice their crewmen to defect. You saw how furious they are about that. The way they think, this is a gross violation of the rules of civilized behavior. The president's forceful reaction to our discovery that this was a missile submarine is also evidence that favors Henderson's story."

"So what side will they come down on?" the president asked.

"That, sir, is a question of psychology more than anything
else, and Soviet psychology is very hard for us to read. Given
the choice between the collective treason of ten men and an
outside conspiracy, my opinion is that they will prefer the latter.
For them to believe that this really was defection—well, it
would force them to reexamine their own beliefs. Who likes
to do that?" Moore gestured grandly. "The latter alternative
means that their security has been violated by outsiders, but
being a victim is more palatable than having to recognize the
intrinsic contradictions of their own governing philosophy. On
top of that we have the fact that the KGB will be running the
investigation."

"Why?" Pelt asked, caught up in the judge's plot.

"In either case, a defection or a penetration of naval operational security, the GRU would have been responsible. Security of the naval and military forces is their bailiwick, the
more so with the damage done to the KGB after the departure
of our friend Andropov. The Soviets can't have an organization
investigating itself—not in their intelligence community! So,
the KGB will be looking to take its rival service apart. From
the KGB's perspective, outside instigation is the far more attractive alternative; it makes for a bigger operation. If they
confirm Henderson's story and convince everyone that it's true—
and they will, of course—it makes them look all that much
better for having uncovered it."

"They will confirm the story?"

"Of course they will! In the intelligence business if you look
hard enough for something, you find it, whether it's really there
or not. Lord, we owe this Ramius fellow more than he will
ever know. An opportunity like this doesn't come along once
in a generation. We simply can't lose."

"But the KGB will emerge stronger," Pelt observed. "Is that
a good thing?"

Moore shrugged. "Bound to happen eventually. Unseating
and possibly killing Andropov gave the military services too
much prestige, just like with Beria back in the fifties. The
Soviets depend on political control of their military as much
as we do—more. Having the KGB take their high command
apart gets the dirty work done for them. It had to happen

anyway, so it's just as well that we can profit by it. There's only a few more things we have to do."

"Such as?" the president asked.

"Our friend Henderson will leak information in a month or so saying that we had a submarine tracking *Red October* all the way from Iceland."

"But why?" Pelt objected. "Then they'll know that we were lying, that all the excitement over the missile sub was a lie."

"Not exactly, Doctor," Moore said. "Having a missile sub this close to our coast remains a violation of the agreement, and from their point of view we have no way of knowing why she was there—until we interrogate the crewmen remaining behind, who will probably tell us little of value. The Soviets will expect that we have not been completely truthful with them on this affair. The fact that we were trailing their sub and were ready to destroy it at any time gives them the evidence of our duplicity that they'll be looking for. We'll also say that *Dallas* monitored the reactor incident on sonar, and that will explain the proximity of our rescue ship. They know, well, they certainly suspect, that we have concealed something. This will mislead them about what it was we really concealed. The Russians have a saying for this. They call it wolf meat. And they will launch an extensive operation to penetrate our operation, whatever it is. But they will find nothing. The only people in the CIA who know what is really going on are Greer, Ritter, and myself. Our operations people have orders to *find out* what was going on, and that's all that can leak out."

"What about Henderson, and how many of our people know about the submarine?" the president asked.

"If Henderson spills anything to them he'll be signing his own death warrant. The KGB deals severely with double agents, and would not believe that we tricked him into delivering false information. He knows it, and we'll be keeping a close eye on him in any case. How many of our people know about the sub? A hundred perhaps, and the number will increase somewhat— but remember that they think we now have two dead Soviet subs off our coast, and they have every reason to believe that whatever Soviet sub equipment turns up in our labs has been recovered from the ocean floor. We will, of course, be reactivating the *Glomar Explorer* for just that purpose. They'd be suspicious if we didn't. Why disappoint them? Sooner or later they just might figure the whole story out, but by that time the stripped hulk will be at the bottom of the sea."

"So, we can't keep this a secret forever?" Pelt asked.

"Forever's a long time. We have a plan for the possibility. For the immediate future the secret should be fairly safe, what with only a hundred people in on it. In a year, minimum, more likely two or three, they may have accumulated enough data to suspect what has happened, but by that time there won't be much physical evidence to point to. Moreover, if the KGB discovers the truth, will they *want* to report it? Were the GRU to find out, they certainly would, and the resulting chaos within their intelligence community would also work to our benefit." Moore took a cigar from a leather holder. "As I said, Ramius has given us a fantastic opportunity on several levels. And the beauty of it is that we don't have to do much of anything. The Russians will be doing all the legwork, looking for something that isn't there."

"What about the defectors, Judge?" the president asked.

"They, Mr. President, will be taken care of. We know how to do this, and we rarely have a complaint about the CIA's hospitality. We'll take some months to debrief them, and at the same time we'll be preparing them for life in America. They'll get new identities, reeducation, cosmetic surgery if necessary, and they'll never have to work another day as long as they live—but they will want to work. Almost all of them do. I expect the navy will find places for them, paid consultants for their submarine warfare department, that sort of thing."

"I want to meet them," the president said impulsively.

"That can be arranged, sir, but it will have to be discreet," Moore cautioned.

"Camp David, that ought to be secure enough. And Ryan, Judge, I want him taken care of."

"Understood, sir. We're bringing him along rather quickly already. He has a big future with us."

Tyuratam, USSR

The reason *Red October* had been ordered to dive long before dawn was orbiting the earth at a height of eight hundred kilometers. The size of a Greyhound bus, Albatross 8 had been sent aloft eleven months earlier by a heavy-lift booster from the Cosmodrome at Tyuratam. The massive satellite, called a RORSAT, for radar ocean reconnaissance satellite, was specifically designed for maritime surveillance.

Albatross 8 passed over Pamlico Sound at 1131 local time. Its on-board programming was designed to trace thermal receptors over the entire visible horizon, interrogating everything in sight and locking on any signature that fit its acquisition parameters. As it continued on its orbit and passed over elements of the U.S. fleet, the *New Jersey*'s jammers were aimed upward to scramble its signal. The satellite's tape systems dutifully recorded this. The jamming would tell the operators something about American electronic warfare systems. As Albatross 8 crossed the pole, the parabolic dish on its front tracked in on the carrier signal of another bird, the *Iskra* communications satellite.

When the reconnaissance satellite located its higher flying cousin, a laser side-link transmitted the contents of the Albatross' tape bank. The *Iskra* immediately relayed this to the ground station at Tyuratam. The signal was also received by a fifteen-meter dish located in western China which was operated by the U.S. National Security Agency in cooperation with the Chinese, who used the data received for their own purposes. The Americans transmitted it via their own communications satellite to NSA headquarters at Fort Meade, Maryland. At almost the same time the digital signal was examined by two teams of experts five thousand miles apart.

"Clear weather," a technician moaned. *"Now* we get clear weather!"

"Enjoy it while you can, Comrade." His neighbor at the next console was watching data from a geosynchronous weather satellite that monitored the Western Hemisphere. Knowing the weather over a hostile country can have great strategic value. "There's another cold front approaching their coast. Their winter has been like ours. I hope they are enjoying it."

"Our men at sea will not." The technician mentally shuddered at the thought of being at sea in a major storm. He'd taken a Black Sea cruise the previous summer and become hopelessly seasick. "Aha! What is this? Colonel!"

"Yes, Comrade?" The colonel supervising the watch came over quickly.

"See here, Comrade Colonel." The technician traced a finger on the TV screen. "This is Pamlico Sound, on the central coast of the United States. Look here, Comrade." The thermal image of the water on the screen was black, but as the technician adjusted the display it changed to green with two white patches, one larger than the other. Twice the large one split into two segments. The image was of the surface of the water, and some of the water was half a degree warmer than it should have been. The differential was not constant, but it did return enough to prove that something was adding heat to the water.

"Sunlight, perhaps?" the colonel asked.

"No, Comrade, the clear sky gives even sunlight to the entire area," the technician said quietly. He was always quiet when he thought he was on to something. "Two submarines, perhaps three, thirty meters under the water."

"You are certain?"

The technician flipped on a switch to display the radar picture, which showed only the corduroy pattern of small waves.

"There is nothing *on* the water to generate this heat, Comrade Colonel. Therefore it must be something *under* the water. The time of year is wrong for mating whales. It can only be nuclear submarines, probably two, perhaps three. I speculate, Colonel, that the Americans have been sufficiently frightened by the deployment of our fleet to seek shelter for their missile submarines. Their missile sub base is only a few hundred kilometers south. Perhaps one of their *Ohio*-class boats have taken shelter here and is being protected by a hunter sub, as ours are."

"Then he will soon move out. Our fleet is being recalled."

"Too bad, it would be good to track him. This is a rare opportunity, Comrade Colonel."

"Indeed. Well done, Comrade Academician." Ten minutes later the data had been transmitted to Moscow.

Soviet Naval High Command, Moscow

"We will make use of this opportunity, Comrade," Gorshkov said. "We are now recalling our fleet, and we will allow several submarines to remain behind to gather electronic intelligence. The Americans will probably lose several in the shuffle."

"Quite likely," the chief of fleet operations said.

"The *Ohio* will go south, probably to their submarine base at Charleston or Kings Bay. Or north to Norfolk. We have *Konovalov* at Norfolk, and *Shabilikov* off Charleston. Both will stay in place for several days, I think. We must do something right to show the politicians that we have a real navy. Being able to track on an *Ohio* would be a beginning."

"I'll have the orders out in fifteen minutes, Comrade." The chief of operations thought this was a good idea. He had not liked the report of the Politburo meeting that he'd gotten from Gorshkov—though if Sergey were on his way out, he would be in a good place to take over the job . . .

The New Jersey

The RED ROCKET message had arrived in Eaton's hand only moments before: Moscow had just transmitted a lengthy operational letter via satellite to the Soviet fleet. Now the Russians were in a real fix, the commodore thought. Around them were three carrier battle groups—the *Kennedy, America,* and *Nimitz*—all under Josh Painter's command. Eaton had them in sight, and had operational control of the *Tarawa* to augment his own surface action group. The commodore turned his binoculars on the *Kirov.*

"Commander, bring the group to battle stations."

"Aye." The group operations officer lifted the tactical radio mike. "Blue Boys, this is Blue King. Amber Light, Amber Light, execute. Out."

Eaton waited four seconds for the *New Jersey*'s general quarters alarm to sound. The crew raced to their guns.

"Range to *Kirov?*"

"Thirty-seven thousand six hundred yards, sir. We've been sneaking in a laser range every few minutes. We're dialed in, sir," the group operations officer reported. "Main battery turrets are still loaded with sabots, and gunnery's been updating the solution every thirty seconds."

A phone buzzed next to Eaton's command chair on the flag bridge.

"Eaton."

"All stations manned and ready, Commodore," the battleship's captain reported. Eaton looked at his stopwatch.

"Well done, Captain. We've got the men drilled very well indeed."

In the *New Jersey*'s combat information center the numerical displays showed the exact range to the *Kirov*'s mainmast. The logical first target is always the enemy flagship. The only question was how much punishment the *Kirov* could absorb— and what would kill her first, the gun rounds or the Tomahawk missiles. The important part, the gunnery officer had been saying for days, was to kill the *Kirov* before any aircraft could interfere. The *New Jersey* had never sunk a ship all on her own. Forty years was a long time to wait.

"They're turning," the group operations officer said.

"Yep, let's see how far."

The *Kirov*'s formation had been on a westerly course when the signal arrived. Every ship in the circular array turned to starboard, all together. Their turns stopped when they reached a heading of zero-four-four-zero.

Eaton set his glasses down in the holder. "They're going home. Let's inform Washington and keep the men at stations for a while."

Dulles International Airport

The Soviets outdid themselves getting their men away from the United States. An Aeroflot Illyushin IL-62 was taken out of regular international service and sent directly from Moscow to Dulles. It landed at sunset. A near copy of the British VC-10, the four-engine aircraft taxied to the remotest service area for refueling. Along with some other passengers who did not de-plane to stretch their legs, a spare flight crew was brought along so that the plane could immediately return home. A pair of mobile lounges drove from the terminal building two miles to the waiting aircraft. Inside them the crewmen of the *Red October* looked out at the snow-dusted countryside, knowing this was their final look at America. They were quiet, having been roused from bed in Bethesda and taken by bus to Dulles only an hour earlier. This time no reporters harassed them.

The four officers, nine *michmanyy,* and the remaining en-listed crew were split into distinct groups as they boarded. Each group was taken to a separate part of the aircraft. Each officer and *michman* had his own KGB interrogator, and the debriefing began as the aircraft started its takeoff roll. By the time the Illyushin reached cruising altitude most of the crewmen were asking themselves why they had not opted to remain behind with their traitorous countrymen. These interviews were decidedly unpleasant.

"Did Captain Ramius act strangely?" a KGB major asked Petrov.

"Certainly not!" Petrov answered quickly, defensively. "Didn't you know our submarine was sabotaged? We were lucky to escape with our lives!"

"Sabotaged? How?"

"The reactor systems. I am the wrong one to ask on this, I am not an engineer, but it was I who detected the leaks. You see, the radiation film badges showed contamination, but the engine room instruments did not. Not only was the reactor tampered with, but all of the radiation-sensing instruments were disabled. I saw this myself. Chief Engineer Melekhin had to rebuild several to locate the leaking reactor piping. Svyadov can tell this better. He saw it himself."

The KGB officer was scribbling notes. "And what was your submarine doing so close to the American coast?"

"What do you mean? Don't you know what our orders were?"

"What were your orders, Comrade Doctor?" The KGB officer stared hard into Petrov's eyes.

The doctor explained, concluding, "I saw the orders. They were posted for all to see, as is normal."

"Signed by whom?"

"Admiral Korov. Who else?"

"Did you not find those orders a little strange?" the major asked angrily.

"Do you question your orders, Comrade Major?" Petrov summoned up some spine. "*I* do not."

"What happened to your political officer?"

In another space Ivanov was explaining how the *Red October* had been detected by American and British ships. "But Captain Ramius evaded them brilliantly! We would have made it except for that damned reactor accident. You must find who did that to us, Comrade Captain. I wish to see him die myself!"

The KGB officer was unmoved. "And what was the last thing the captain said to you?"

"He ordered me to keep control of my men, not to let them speak with Americans any more than necessary, and he said that the Americans would never get their hands on our ship." Ivanov's eyes teared at the thought of his captain and his ship, both lost. He was a proud and privileged young Soviet man, the son of a Party academician. "Comrade, you and your people must find the bastards who did this to us."

"It was very clever," Svyadov was recounting a few feet away. "Even Comrade Melekhin only found it on his third attempt, and he swore vengeance on the men who did it. I saw it myself," the lieutenant said, forgetting that he never had, really. He explained in detail, to the point of drawing a diagram of how it had been done. "I don't know about the final accident. I was just coming on duty then. Melekhin, Surzpoi, and Bugayev worked for hours attempting to engage our auxiliary power systems." He shook his head. "I tried to join them, but Captain Ramius forbade it. I tried again, against orders, but Comrade Petrov prevented me."

Two hours over the Atlantic the senior KGB interrogators met aft to compare notes.

"So, if this captain was acting, he was devilishly good at it," the colonel in charge of the initial interrogations summarized. "His orders to his men were impeccable. The mission orders were announced and posted as is normal—"

"But who among these men knows Korov's signature? And we can't very well ask Korov, can we?" a major said. The commander of the Northern Fleet had died of a cerebral hemorrhage two hours into his first interrogation in the Lubyanka, much to everyone's disappointment. "It could have been forged in any case. Do we have a secret submarine base in Cuba? And what of the death of the *zampolit?*"

"The doctor is sure it was an accident," another major answered. "The captain thought he had struck his head, but he had actually broken his neck. I feel they should have radioed for instructions, though."

"A radio silence order," the colonel said. "I checked. This is entirely normal for missile submarines. Was this Captain Ramius skilled in unarmed combat? Might he have murdered the *zampolit?*"

"A possibility," mused the major who had questioned Petrov. "He was not trained in such things, but it is not hard to do."

The colonel did not know whether to agree. "Do we have any evidence that the crew thought a defection was being attempted?" All heads shook negatively. "Was the submarine's operational routine otherwise normal?"

"Yes, Comrade Colonel," a young captain said. "The surviving navigation officer, Ivanov, says that the evasion of imperialist surface and sub forces was effected perfectly—exactly in accordance with established procedures, but executed brilliantly by this Ramius fellow over a period of twelve hours. I have not even suggested that treason might be involved. Yet." Everyone knew that these sailors would be spending time in the Lubyanka until each head had been picked clean.

"Very well," the colonel said, "up to this point we have no indication of treason by the officers of the submarine? I thought not. Comrades, you will continue your interrogations in a gentler fashion until we arrive in Moscow. Allow your charges to relax."

The atmosphere on the aircraft gradually became more pleasant. Snacks were served, and vodka to loosen the tongues and encourage comradely good fellowship with the KGB officers, who were drinking water. The men all knew that they would be imprisoned for some time, and this fate was accepted with what to a Westerner would be surprising fatalism. The KGB would be working for weeks to reconstruct every event on the submarine from the time the last line was cast off at Polyarnyy to the moment the last man entered the *Mystic*. Other teams of agents were already working worldwide to learn if what happened to the *Red October* was a CIA plot or the plot of some other intelligence service. The KGB would find its answer, but the colonel in charge of the case was beginning to think the answer did not lie with these seamen.

The Red October

Noyes allowed Ramius to walk the fifteen feet from sick bay to the wardroom under supervision. The patient did not look very good, but this was largely because he needed a wash and a shave, like everyone else aboard. Borodin and Mancuso assisted him into his seat at the head of the table.

"So, Ryan, how are you today?"

"Good, thank you, Captain Ramius." Ryan smiled over his

coffee. In fact he was hugely relieved, having for the past several hours been able to leave the question of running the sub to the men who actually knew something about it. Though he was counting the hours until he could get out of the *Red October,* for the first time in two weeks he was neither seasick nor terrified. "How is your leg, sir?"

"Painful. I must learn not to be shot again. I do not remember saying to you that I owe you my life, as all of us do."

"It was my life, too," Ryan replied, a little embarrassed.

"Good morning, sir!" It was the cook. "May I fix you some breakfast, Captain Ramius?"

"Yes, I am very hungry."

"Good! One U.S. Navy breakfast. Let me get some fresh coffee, too." He disappeared into the passageway. Thirty seconds later he was back with fresh coffee and a place setting for Ramius. "Ten minutes on the breakfast, sir."

Ramius poured a cup of coffee. There was a small envelope in the saucer. "What is this?"

"Coffee Mate," Mancuso chuckled. "Cream for your coffee, Captain."

Ramius tore open the packet, staring suspiciously inside before dumping the contents into the cup and stirring.

"When do we leave?"

"Sometime tomorrow," Mancuso answered. The *Dallas* was going to periscope depth periodically to receive operational orders and relaying them to the *October* by gertrude. "We learned a few hours ago that the Soviet fleet is heading back northeast. We'll know for sure by sundown. Our guys are keeping a close eye on them."

"Where do we go?" Ramius asked.

"Where did you tell them you were going?" Ryan wanted to know. "What exactly did your letter say?"

"You know about the letter—how?"

"We know—that is, I know about the letter, but that's all I can say, sir."

"I told Uncle Yuri that we were sailing to New York to make a present of this ship to the president of the United States."

"But you didn't head for New York," Mancuso objected.

"Certainly not. I wished to enter Norfolk. Why go to a civilian port when a naval base is so close? You say I should tell Padorin the truth?" Ramius shook his head. "Why? Your coast is so large."

Dear Admiral Padorin, I'm sailing for New York... No wonder they went ape! Ryan thought.

"We go to Norfolk or Charleston?" Ramius asked.

"Norfolk, I think," Mancuso said.

"Didn't you know they'd send the whole fleet after you?" Ryan snapped. "Why send the letter at all?"

"So they will know," Ramius answered. "So they will know. I did not expect that anyone would locate us. There you surprised us."

The American skipper tried to smile. "We detected you off the coast of Iceland. You were luckier than you imagine. If we'd sailed from England on schedule, we'd have been fifteen miles closer in shore, and we would have had you cold. Sorry, Captain, but our sonars and sonar operators are very good. You can meet the man who first tracked you later. He's working with your man Bugayev at the moment."

"*Starshina*," Borodin said.

"Not an officer?" Ramius asked.

"No, just a very good operator," Mancuso said, surprised. Why would anyone want an officer to stand watch on sonar gear?

The cook came back in. His idea of the standard U.S. Navy breakfast was a large platter with a slab of ham, two eggs over easy, a pile of hash browns, and four slices of toast, with a container of apple jelly.

"Let me know if you want more, sir," the cook said.

"This is a normal breakfast?" Ramius asked Mancuso.

"Nothing unusual about it. I prefer waffles myself. Americans eat big breakfasts." Ramius was already attacking his. After two days without a normal meal and all the blood loss from his leg wound, his body was screaming for food.

"Tell me, Ryan," Borodin was lighting a cigarette, "what is it in America that we will find most amazing?"

Jack motioned to the captain's plate. "Food stores."

"Food stores?" Mancuso asked.

"While I was sitting on *Invincible* I read over a CIA report on people who come over to our side." Ryan didn't want to say *defectors*. Somehow the word sounded demeaning. "Supposedly the first thing that surprises people, people from your part of the world, is going through a supermarket."

"Tell me about them," Borodin ordered.

"A building about the size of a football field—well, maybe a little smaller than that. You go in the front door and get a shopping cart. The fresh fruits and vegetables are on the right, and you gradually work your way left through the other departments. I've been doing that since I was a kid."

"You say fresh fruits and vegetables? What about now, in winter?"

"What about winter?" Mancuso said. "Maybe they cost a little more, but you can always get fresh produce. That's the one thing we miss on the boats. Our supply of fresh produce and milk only lasts us about a week."

"And meat?" Ramius asked.

"Anything you want," Ryan answered. "Beef, pork, lamb, turkey, chicken. American farmers are very efficient. The United States feeds itself and has plenty left over. You know that, the Soviet Union buys our grain. Hell, we pay farmers not to grow things, just to keep the surplus under control." The four Russians were doubtful.

"What else?" Borodin asked.

"What else will surprise you? Nearly everyone has a car. Most people own their own homes. If you have money, you can buy nearly anything you want. The average family in America makes something like twenty thousand dollars a year, I guess. These officers all make more than that. The fact of the matter is that in our country if you have some brains—and all of you men do—and you are willing to work—and all of you men are—you will live a comfortable life even without any help. Besides, you can be sure that the CIA will take good care of you. We wouldn't want anybody to complain about our hospitality."

"And what will become of my men?" Ramius asked.

"I can't say exactly, sir, since I've never been involved in this sort of thing myself. I would guess that you will be taken to a safe place to relax and unwind. People from the CIA and the navy will want to talk to you at length. That's no surprise, right? I told you this before. A year from now you will be doing whatever you choose to do."

"And anybody who wants to take a cruise with us is welcome to," Mancuso added.

Ryan wondered how true this was. The navy would not want to let any of these men on a 688-class boat. It might give one of them information valuable enough to enable him to return home and keep his head.

"How does a friendly man become a CIA spy?" Borodin asked.

"I am not a spy, sir," Ryan said again. He couldn't blame them for not believing them. "Going through graduate school I got to know a guy who mentioned my name to a friend of his in the CIA, Admiral James Greer. Back a few years ago I was asked to join a team of academics that was called in to check up on some of the CIA's intelligence estimates. At the time I was happily engaged writing books on naval history. At Langley—I was there for two months during the summer—I did a paper on international terrorism. Greer liked it, and two years ago he asked me to go to work there full time. I accepted. It was a mistake," Ryan said, not really meaning it. Or did he? "A year ago I was transferred to London to work on a joint intelligence evaluation team with the British Secret Service. My normal job is to sit at a desk and figure out the stuff that field agents send in. I got myself roped into this because I figured out what you were up to, Captain Ramius."

"Was your father a spy?" Borodin asked.

"No, my dad was a police officer in Baltimore. He and my mother were killed in a plane crash ten years ago."

Borodin expressed his sympathy. "And you, Captain Mancuso, what made you a sailor?"

"I wanted to be a sailor since I was a kid. My dad's a barber. I decided on submarines at Annapolis because I thought it looked interesting."

Ryan was watching something he had never seen before, men from two different places and two very different cultures trying to find common ground. Both sides were reaching out, seeking similarities of character and experience, building a foundation for understanding. This was more than interesting. It was touching. Ryan wondered how difficult it was for the Soviets. Probably harder than anything he had ever done—their bridges were burned. They had cast themselves away from everything they had known, trusting that what they found would be better. Ryan hoped they would succeed and make their transition from Communism to freedom. In the past two days he had come to realize what courage it took for men to defect. Facing a gun in a missile room was a small matter compared with walking away from one's whole life. It was strange how easily Americans put on their freedoms. How difficult would it be for these men who had risked their lives to adapt to something that men like Ryan so rarely appreciated? It was people like these who had built the American Dream, and people like these who were needed to maintain it. It was odd that such men should come from the Soviet Union. Or perhaps not so odd, Ryan thought, listening to the conversation going back and forth in front of him.

THE SEVENTEENTH DAY

SUNDAY, 19 DECEMBER

The Red October

"Eight more hours," Ryan whispered to himself. That's what they had told him. An eight-hour run to Norfolk. He was back at the rudder diving-plane controls by his own request. Operating them was the only thing he knew how to do, and he had to do something. The *October* was still badly shorthanded. Nearly all of the Americans were helping out in the reactor and engine spaces aft. Only Mancuso, Ramius, and himself were in control. Bugayev, with the help of Jones, was monitoring the sonar equipment a few feet away, and the medical people were still worrying over Williams in sick bay. The cook was shuttling back and forth with sandwiches and coffee, which Ryan found disappointing, probably because he had been spoiled by Greer's.

Ramius was half sitting on the rail that surrounded the periscope pedestal. The leg wound was not bleeding, but it had to be hurting more than the man admitted since he was letting Mancuso check the instruments and handle the navigation.

"Rudder amidships," Mancuso ordered.

"Midships," Ryan turned the wheel back to the right to center it, checking his rudder angle indicator. "Rudder is amidships, steady on course one-two-zero."

Mancuso frowned at his chart, nervous at being forced to pilot the massive submarine in so cavalier a manner. "You have to be careful around here. The sandbar keeps building up from the southerly littoral drift, and they have to dredge it every few months. The storms this area's been having can't have helped much." Mancuso went back to look through the periscope.

"I am told this is a dangerous area," Ramius said.

"The graveyard of the Atlantic," Mancuso confirmed. "A lot of ships have died along the Outer Banks. Weather and current conditions are bad enough. The Germans are supposed to have had a hell of a time here during the war. Your charts don't show it, but there's hundreds of wrecks spotted on the bottom." He went back to the chart table. "Anyway, we give this place a nice wide berth, and we don't turn north till about here." He traced a line on the chart.

"These are your waters," Ramius agreed.

They were in a loose three-boat formation. The *Dallas* was leading them out to sea, the *Pogy* was trailing. All three boats were traveling flooded-down, their decks nearly awash, with no one on their bridge stations. All visual navigation was being done by periscope. No radar sets were operating. None of the three boats was making any electronic noise. Ryan glanced casually at the chart table. They were beyond the inlet proper, but the chart was marked with sandbars for several more miles.

Nor were they using the *Red October*'s caterpillar drive system. It had turned out to be almost exactly what Skip Tyler had predicted. There were two sets of tunnel impellers, a pair about a third of the way back from the bow and three more just aft of midships. Mancuso and his engineers had examined the plans with great interest, then commented at length on the quality of the caterpillar design.

For his part, Ramius had not wanted to believe that he had been detected so early on. Mancuso had ultimately produced Jones with his personal map to show the *October*'s estimated course off Iceland. Though a few miles off the ship's log, it was too close to have been a coincidence.

"Your sonar must be better than we expected," Ramius

grumbled a few feet from Ryan's control station.

"It is pretty good," Mancuso allowed. "Better yet, there's Jonesy—he's the best sonarman I've ever had."

"So young, and so smart."

"We get a lot of them that way," Mancuso smiled. "Never as many as we'd like, of course, but our kids are all volunteers. They know what they're getting into. We're picky about who we take, and then we train the hell out of 'em."

"Conn, sonar." It was Jones' voice. "*Dallas* is diving, sir."

"Very well." Mancuso lit a cigarette as he went to the intercom phone. He punched the button for engineering. "Tell Mannion we need him forward. We'll be diving in a few minutes. Yeah." He hung up and went back to the chart.

"You have them for more than three years, then?" Ramius asked.

"Oh, yeah. Hell, otherwise we'd be letting them go right after they're fully trained, right?"

Why couldn't the Soviet Navy get and retain people like this? Ramius thought. He knew the answer all too well. The Americans fed their men decently, gave them a proper mess room, paid them decently, gave them trust—all the things he had fought twenty years for.

"You need me to work the vents?" Mannion said, coming in.

"Yeah, Pat, we'll dive in another two or three minutes."

Mannion gave the chart a quick look on his way to the vent manifold.

Ramius hobbled to the chart. "They tell us that your officers are chosen from the bourgeois classes to control ordinary sailors from the working class."

Mannion ran his hands over the vent controls. There sure were enough of them. He'd spent two hours the previous day figuring the complex system out. "That's true, sir. Our officers do come from the ruling class. Just look at me," he said deadpan. Mannion's skin was about the color of coffee grounds, his accent pure South Bronx.

"But you are a black man," Ramius objected, missing the jibe.

"Sure, we're a real ethnic boat." Mancuso looked through the periscope again. "A Guinea skipper, a black navigator, and a crazy sonarman."

"I heard that, sir!" Jones called out rather than use the intercom speaker. "Gertrude message from *Dallas*. Everything looks okay. They're waiting for us. Last gertrude message for a while."

"Conn, aye. We're clear, finally. We can dive whenever you wish, Captain Ramius," Mancuso said.

"Comrade Mannion, vent the ballast tanks," Ramius said. The *October* had never actually surfaced and was still rigged for dive.

"Aye aye, sir." The lieutenant turned the topmost rank of master switches on the hydraulic controls.

Ryan winced. The sound made him think of a million toilets being flushed at once.

"Five degrees down on the planes, Ryan," Ramius said.

"Five degrees down, aye." Ryan pushed forward on the yoke. "Planes five degrees down."

"She's slow going down," Mannion observed, watching the handpainted depth-gauge replacement. "So durn big."

"Yeah," Mancuso said. The needle passed twenty meters.

"Planes to zero," Ramius said.

"Planes to zero angle, aye." Ryan pulled back on the control. It took thirty seconds for the submarine to settle. She seemed very slow to respond to the controls. Ryan had thought that submarines were as responsive as aircraft.

"Make her a little light, Pat. Enough that it takes a degree of down to hold her level," Mancuso said.

"Uh-huh." Mannion frowned, checking the depth gauge. The ballast tanks were now fully flooded, and the balancing act would have to be done with the much smaller trim tanks. It took him five minutes to get the balance exactly right.

"Sorry, gentlemen. I'm afraid she's too big to dial in quick," he said, embarrassed with himself.

Ramius was impressed but too annoyed to show it. He had expected the American captain to take longer than this to do it himself. Trimming a strange sub so expertly on his first try . . .

"Okay, now we can come around north," Mancuso said. They were two miles past the last charted bar. "Recommend new course zero-zero-eight, Captain."

"Ryan, rudder left ten degrees," Ramius ordered. "Come to zero-zero-eight."

"Okay, rudder left ten degrees," Ryan responded, keeping

one eye on the rudder indicator, the other on the gyro compass repeater. "Come to oh-oh-eight."

"Caution, Ryan. He turns slowly, but once turning you must use much backward—"

"Opposite," Mancuso corrected politely.

"Yes, opposite rudder to stop him on proper course."

"Right."

"Captain, do you have rudder problems?" Mancuso asked. "From tracking you it seemed that your turning circle was rather large."

"With the caterpillar it is. The flow from the tunnels strikes the rudder very hard, and it flutters if you use too much rudder. On our first sea trials, we had damage from this. It comes from—how do you say—the come-together of the two caterpillar tunnels."

"Does this affect operations with the propellers?" Mannion asked.

"No, only with the caterpillar."

Mancuso didn't like that. It didn't really matter. The plan was a simple, direct one. The three boats would make a straight dash to Norfolk. The two American attack boats would leapfrog forward at thirty knots to sniff out the areas ahead while the *October* plodded along at a constant twenty.

Ryan began to ease his rudder as the bow came around. He waited too long. Despite five degrees of right rudder, the bow swung right past the intended course, and the gyro repeater clicked accusingly on every third degree until it stopped at zero-zero-one. It took another two minutes to get back on the proper course.

"Sorry about that. Steady on zero-zero-eight," he finally reported.

Ramius was forgiving. "You learn fast, Ryan. Perhaps one day you will be a true sailor."

"No thanks! The one thing I've learned on this trip is that you guys earn every nickel you get."

"Don't like subs?" Mannion chuckled.

"No place to jog."

"True. Unless you still need me, Captain, I'm ready to go aft. The engine room's awful shorthanded," Mannion said.

Ramius nodded. Was he from the ruling class? the captain wondered.

The V. K. Konovalov

Tupolev was heading back west. The fleet order had instructed everyone but his *Alfa* and one other to return home at twenty knots. Tupolev was to move west for two and half hours. Now he was on a reciprocal heading at five knots, about the top speed the *Alfa* could travel without making much noise. The idea was that his sub would be lost in the shuffle. So, an *Ohio* was heading for Norfolk—or Charleston more probably. In any case, Tupolev would circle quietly and observe. The *Red October* was destroyed. That much he knew from the ops order. Tupolev shook his head. How could Marko have done such a thing? Whatever the answer, he had paid for his treason with his life.

The Pentagon

"I'd feel better if we had some more air cover," Admiral Foster said, leaning against the wall.

"Agreed, sir, but we can't be so obvious, can we?" General Harris asked.

A pair of P-3Bs was now sweeping the track from Hatteras to the Virginia Capes as though on a routine training mission. Most of the other Orions were far out at sea. The Soviet fleet was already four hundred miles offshore. The three surface groups had rejoined and were now ringed by their submarines. The *Kennedy, America,* and *Nimitz* were five hundred miles to their east, and the *New Jersey* was dropping back. The Russians would be watched all the way home. The carrier battle groups would be following them all the way to Iceland, keeping a discreet distance and maintaining air groups at the fringe of their radar coverage continuously, just to let them know that the United States still cared. Aircraft based in Iceland would track them the rest of the way home.

HMS *Invincible* was now out of operation and about halfway home. American attack subs were returning to normal patrol patterns, and all Soviet subs were reported to be off the coast, though this data was sketchy. They were traveling in loose packs and the noise generated made tracking difficult for the patrolling Orions, which were short of sonobuoys. Still and all, the operation was about over, the J-3 judged.

"You heading for Norfolk, Admiral?" Harris asked.

"Thought I might get together with CINCLANT, a post-action conference, you understand," Foster said.

"Aye aye, sir," Harris said.

The New Jersey

She was traveling at twelve knots, with a destroyer fueling on either beam. Commodore Eaton was in the flag plot. It was all over and nothing had happened, thank God. The Soviets were now a hundred miles ahead, within Tomahawk range but well beyond everything else. All in all, he was satisfied. His force had operated successfully with the *Tarawa,* which was now headed south to Mayport, Florida. He hoped they'd be able to do this again soon. It had been a long time since a flag officer on a battleship had had a carrier respond to his command. They had kept the *Kirov* force under continuous surveillance. If there had been a battle, Eaton was convinced that they'd have handled Ivan. More importantly, he was certain that Ivan knew it. All they awaited now was the order to return to Norfolk. It would be nice to be back home for Christmas. He figured his men had earned it. Many of the battleship's men were oldtimers, and nearly everyone had a family.

The Red October

Ping. Jones noted the time on his pad and called out, "Captain, just got a ping from *Pogy*."

The *Pogy* was now ten miles ahead of the *October* and *Dallas*. The idea was that after she got ahead and listened for ten minutes, a single ping from her active sonar would signal that the ten miles to the *Pogy* and the twenty or more miles beyond her were clear. The *Pogy* would drift slowly to confirm this, and a mile to the *October*'s east the *Dallas* went to full speed to leapfrog ten miles beyond the other attack sub.

Jones was experimenting with the Russian sonar. The active gear, he'd found, was not too bad. The passive systems he didn't want to think about. When the *Red October* had been lying still in Pamlico Sound, he'd been unable to track in on the American subs. They had also been still, with their reactors only turning generators, but they had been no more than a mile away. He was disappointed that he'd not been able to locate them.

The officer with him, Bugayev, was a friendly enough guy. At first he'd been a little standoffish—as if he were a lord and I were a serf, Jones thought—until he'd seen how the skipper treated him. This surprised Jones. From what little he knew of Communism, he had expected everyone to be fairly equal. Well, he decided, that's what I get from reading *Das Kapital* in a freshman poli-sci course. It made a lot more sense to look at what Communism built. Garbage, mostly. The enlisted men didn't even have their own mess room. Wasn't that some crap! Eating your meals in your bunk rooms!

Jones had taken an hour—when he was supposed to be sleeping—to explore the submarine. Mr. Mannion had joined him. They started in the bunkroom. The individual footlockers didn't lock—probably so that officers could rifle through them. Jones and Mannion did just that. There was nothing of interest. Even the sailor porn was junk. The poses were just plain dumb, and the women—well, Jones had grown up in California. Garbage. It was not at all hard for him to understand why the Russians wanted to defect.

The missile had been interesting. He and Mannion opened an inspection hatch to examine the inside of the missile. Not too shabby, they thought. There was a little too much loose wiring, but that probably made testing easier. The missile seemed awfully big. So, he thought, that's what the bastards have been aiming at us. He wondered if the navy would hold onto a few. If it was ever necessary to flip some at old Ivan, might as well include a couple of his own. *Dumb* idea, Jonesy, he said to himself. He didn't ever want those goddamned things to fly. One thing was for sure: everything on this bucket would be stripped off, tested, taken apart, tested again—and he was the navy's number one expert on Russian sonar. Maybe he'd be present during the analysis . . . It might be worth staying in the navy a few extra months for.

Jones lit a cigarette. "Want one of mine, Mr. Bugayev?" He held his pack out to the electronics officer.

"Thank you, Jones. You were in university?" The lieutenant took the American cigarette that he'd wanted but been too proud to ask for. It was dawning on him slowly that this enlisted man was his technical equal. Though not a qualified watch officer, Jones could operate and maintain sonar gear as well as anyone he'd known.

"Yes, sir." It never hurt to call officers sir, Jones knew. Especially the dumb ones. "California Institute of Technology. Five semesters completed. A average. I didn't finish."

"Why did you leave?"

Jones smiled. "Well, sir, you gotta understand that Cal Tech is, well, kinda a funny place. I played a little trick on one of my professors. He was working with strobe lights for high-speed photography, and I rigged a little switch to work the room lights off the strobe. Unfortunately there was a short in the switch, and it started this little electrical fire." Which had burned out a lab, destroying three months of data and fifteen thousand dollars of equipment. "That broke the rules."

"What did you study?"

"I was headin' for a degree in electrical engineering, with a strong minor in cybernetics. Three semesters to go. I'll get it, then my masters, then my doctorate, and then I'll go back to work for the navy as a civilian."

"Why are you a sonar operator?" Bugayev sat down. He had never spoken like this with an enlisted man.

"Hell, sir, it's fun! When something's going on—you know, a war game, tracking another sub, like that—*I* am the skipper. All the captain does is react to the data I give him."

"And you like your commander?"

"Sure thing! He's the best I've had—I've had three. My skipper's a good guy. You do your job okay, and he doesn't hassle you. You got something to say to him, and he listens."

"You say you will go back to college. How do you pay for it? They tell us that only the ruling class sons go to university."

"That's crap, sir. In California if you're smart enough to go, you go. In my case, I've been saving my money—you don't spend much on a sub, right?—and the navy pitches in, too. I got enough to see me all the way through my masters. What's your degree in?"

"I attended a higher naval school. Like your Annapolis. I would like to get a proper degree in electronics," Bugayev said, voicing his own dream.

"No sweat. I can help you out. If you're good enough for Cal Tech, I can tell you who to talk to. You'd like California. That is the place to live."

"And I wish to work on a real computer," Bugayev went on, wishful.

Jones laughed quietly. "So, buy yourself one."

"Buy a computer?"

"Sure, we got a couple of little ones, Apples, on *Dallas*. Cost you about, oh, two thousand for a nice system. That's a lot less than what a car goes for."

"A computer for two thousand dollars?" Bugayev went from wishful to suspicious, certain that Jones was leading him on.

"Or less. For three grand you can get a really nice rig. Hell, you tell Apple who you are, and they'll probably give it to you for free, or the navy will. If you don't want an Apple, there's the Commodore, TRS-80, Atari. All kinds. Depends on what you want to use it for. Look, just one company, Apple, has sold over a million of 'em. They're little, sure, but they're real computers."

"I have never heard of this—Apple?"

"Yeah, Apple. Two guys started the company back when I was in junior high. Since then they've sold a million or so, like I said—and they are some kinda rich! I don't have one myself—no room on a sub—but my brother has his own computer, an IBM-PC. You still don't believe me, do you?"

"A working man with his own computer? It is hard to believe." He stabbed out the cigarette. American tobacco was a little bland, he thought.

"Well, sir, then you can ask somebody else. Like I said, *Dallas* has a couple of Apples, just for the crew to use. There's other stuff for fire control, navigation, and sonar, of course. We use the Apples for games—you'll *love* computer games, for sure. You've never had fun till you've tried Choplifter— and other things, education programs, stuff like that. Honest, Mr. Bugayev, you can walk into most any shopping center and find a place to buy a computer. You'll see."

"How do you use a computer with your sonar?"

"That would take a while to explain, sir, and I'd probably have to get permission from the skipper." Jones reminded himself that this guy was still the enemy, sort of.

The V. K. Konovalov

The *Alfa* drifted slowly at the edge of the continental shelf, about fifty miles southeast of Norfolk. Tupolev ordered the reactor plant chopped back to about five percent of total output, enough to operate the electrical systems and little else. It also made his submarine almost totally quiet. Orders were passed by word of mouth. The *Konovalov* was on a strict silent ship routine. Even ordinary cooking was forbidden. Cooking meant moving metal pots on metal grates. Until further notice, the crew was on a diet of cheese sandwiches. They spoke in whispers when they spoke at all. Anyone who made noise would attract the attention of the captain, and everyone aboard knew what that meant.

SOSUS Control

Quentin was reviewing data sent by digital link from the two Orions. A crippled missile boat, the USS *Georgia,* was heading into Norfolk after a partial turbine failure, escorted by a pair of attack boats. They had been keeping her out, the admiral had said, because of all the Russian activity on the coast, and the idea now was to get her in, fixed, and out as quickly as possible. The *Georgia* carried twenty-four Trident missiles, a noteworthy fraction of the country's total deterrent force. Repairing her would be a high priority item now that the Russians were gone. It was safe to bring her in, but they wanted the Orions first to check and see if any Soviet submarines had lingered behind in the general confusion.

A P-3B was cruising at nine hundred feet about fifty miles southeast of Norfolk. The FLIR showed nothing, no heat signature on the surface, and the MAD gear detected no measurable disturbance in the earth's magnetic field, though one aircraft's flight path took her within a hundred yards of the *Alfa*'s position. The *Konovalov*'s hull was made of non-magnetic titanium. A sonobuoy dropped seven miles to the south of her position also failed to pick up the sound of her reactor plant. Data was being transmitted continuously to Norfolk, where Quentin's operations staff entered it into his computer. The problem was, not all of the Soviet subs had been accounted for.

Well, the commander thought, that figures. Some of the boats had taken the opportunity to creep away from their charted loci. There was the odd chance, he had reported, that one or two strays were still out there, but there was no evidence of this. He wondered what CINCLANT had working. Certainly he had seemed awfully pleased with something, almost euphoric. The operation against the Soviet fleet had been handled pretty well, what he'd seen of it, and there was that dead *Alfa* out there. How long until the *Glomar Explorer* came out of mothballs to go and get that? He wondered if he'd get a chance to look the wreck over. What an opportunity!

Nobody was taking the current operation all that seriously. It made sense. If the *Georgia* were indeed coming in with a sick engine she'd be coming slow, and a slow *Ohio* made about as much noise as a virgin whale determined to retain her status. And if CINCLANTFLT were all that concerned about it, he would not have detailed the delousing operation to a pair of P-3s piloted by reservists. Quentin lifted the phone and dialed CINCLANTFLT Operations to tell them again that there was no indication of hostile activity.

The Red October

Ryan checked his watch. It had been five hours already. A long time to sit in one chair, and from a quick glance at the chart it appeared that the eight-hour estimate had been optimistic— or he'd misunderstood them. The *Red October* was tracing up the shelf line and would soon begin to angle west for the Virginia Capes. Maybe it would take another four hours. It couldn't be too soon. Ramius and Mancuso looked pretty tired. Everybody was tired. Probably the engine room people most of all—no, the cook. He was ferrying coffee and sandwiches to everyone. The Russians seemed especially hungry.

The Dallas/The Pogy

The Dallas passed the *Pogy* at thirty-two knots, leapfrogging again, with the *October* a few miles aft. Lieutenant Commander Wally Chambers, who had the conn, did not like being blind on the speed run of thirty-five minutes despite word from the *Pogy* that everything was clear.

The *Pogy* noted her passage and turned to allow her lateral array to track on the *Red October*.

"Noisy enough at twenty knots," the *Pogy*'s sonar chief said to his companions. "*Dallas* doesn't make that much at thirty."

The V. K. Konovalov

"Some noise to the south," the *michman* said.

"What, exactly?" Tupolev had been hovering at the door for hours, making life unpleasant for the sonarmen.

"Too soon to say, Comrade Captain. Bearing is not changing, however. It is heading this way."

Tupolev went back to the control room. He ordered power reduced further in the reactor systems. He considered killing the plant entirely, but reactors took time to start up and there was no telling yet how distant the contact might be. The captain smoked three cigarettes before going back to sonar. It would not do at all to make the *michman* nervous. The man was his best operator.

"One propeller, Comrade Captain, an American, probably a *Los Angeles,* doing thirty-five knots. Bearing has changed only two degrees in fifteen minutes. He will pass close aboard, and—wait . . . His engines have stopped." The forty-year-old warrant officer pressed the headphones against his ears. He could hear the cavitation sounds diminish, then stop entirely as the contact faded away to nothing. "He has stopped to listen, Comrade Captain."

Tupolev smiled. "He will not hear us, Comrade. Racing and stopping. Can you hear anything else? Might he be escorting something?"

The *michman* listened to the headphones again and made some adjustments on his panel. "Perhaps . . . there is a good deal of surface noise, Comrade, and I—wait. There seems to be some noise. Our last target bearing was one-seven-one, and this new noise is . . . one-seven-five. Very faint, Comrade Captain—a ping, a single ping on active sonar."

"So." Tupolev leaned against the bulkhead. "Good work, Comrade. Now we must be patient."

The Dallas

Chief Laval pronounced the area clear. The BQQ-5's sensitive receptors revealed nothing, even after the SAPS system had been used. Chambers maneuvered the bow around so that the single ping would go out to the *Pogy,* which in turn fired off her own ping to the *Red October* to make sure the signal was received. It was clear for another ten miles. The *Pogy* moved out at thirty knots, followed by the U.S. Navy's newest boomer.

The V. K. Konovalov

"Two more submarines. One single screw, the other twin screw, I think. Still faint. The single-screw submarine is turning much more rapidly. Do the Americans have twin-screw submarines, Comrade Captain?"

"Yes, I believe so." Tupolev wondered about this. The difference in signature characteristics was not all that pronounced. They'd see in any case. The *Konovalov* was creeping along at two knots, one hundred fifty meters beneath the surface. Whatever was coming seemed to be coming right for them. Well, he'd teach the imperialists something after all.

The Red October

"Can anybody spell me at the wheel?" Ryan asked.

"Need a stretch?" Mancuso asked, coming over.

"Yeah. I could stand a trip to the head, too. The coffee's about to bust my kidneys."

"I relieve you, sir." The American captain moved into Ryan's seat. Jack headed aft to the nearest head. Two minutes later he was feeling much better. Back in the control room, he did some knee bends to get circulation back in his legs, then looked briefly at the chart. It seemed strange, almost sinister, to see the U.S. coast marked in Russian.

"Thank you, Commander."

"Sure." Mancuso stood.

"It is certain that you are no sailor, Ryan." Ramius had been watching him without a word.

"I have never claimed to be one, Captain," Ryan said agreeably. "How long to Norfolk?"

"Oh, another four hours, tops," Mancuso said. "The idea's to arrive after dark. They have something to get us in unseen, but I don't know what."

"We left the sound in daylight. What if somebody saw us then?" Ryan asked.

"I didn't see anything, but if anybody was there, all he'd have seen was three sub conning towers with no numbers on them." They had left in daylight to take advantage of a "window" in Soviet satellite coverage.

Ryan lit another cigarette. His wife would give him hell for this, but he was tense from being on the submarine. Sitting at the helmsman's station left him with nothing to do but stare at the handful of instruments. The sub was easier to hold level than he had expected, and the only radical turn he had attempted showed how eager the sub was to change course in any direction. Thirty-some-thousand tons of steel, he thought—no wonder.

The Pogy/The Red October

The *Pogy* stormed past the *Dallas* at thirty knots and continued for twenty minutes, stopping eleven miles beyond her—and three miles from the *Konovalov,* whose crew was scarcely breathing now. The *Pogy*'s sonar, though lacking the new BC-10/SAPS signal-processing system, was otherwise state of the art, but it was impossible to hear something that made no noise at all, and the *Konovalov* was silent.

The *Red October* passed the *Dallas* at 1500 hours after receiving the latest all-clear signal. Her crew was tired and looking forward to arriving at Norfolk two hours after sundown. Ryan wondered how quickly he could fly back to London. He was afraid that the CIA would want to debrief him at length. Mancuso and the crewmen of the *Dallas* wondered if they'd get to see their families. They weren't counting on it.

The V. K. Konovalov

"Whatever it is, it is big, very big, I think. His course will take him within five kilometers of us."

"An *Ohio,* as Moscow said," Tupolev commented.

"It sounds like a twin-screw submarine, Comrade Captain," the *michman* said.

"The *Ohio* has one propeller. You know that."

"Yes, Comrade. In any case, he will be with us in twenty minutes. The other attack submarine is moving at thirty-plus knots. If the pattern holds, he will proceed fifteen kilometers beyond us."

"And the other American?"

"A few kilometers seaward, drifting slowly, like us. I do not have an exact range. I could raise him on active sonar, but that—"

"I am aware of the consequences," Tupolev snapped. He went back to the control room.

"Tell the engineers to be ready to answer bells. All men at battle stations?"

"Yes, Comrade Captain," the *starpom* replied. "We have an excellent firing solution on the American hunter sub—the one moving, that is. The way he runs at full speed makes it easy for us. The other we can localize in seconds."

"Good, for a change," Tupolev smiled. "You see what we can do when circumstances favor us?"

"And what shall we do?"

"When the big one passes us, we will close and ream his asshole. They have played their games. Now we shall play ours. Have the engineers increase power. We will need full power shortly."

"It will make noise, Comrade," the *starpom* cautioned.

"True, but we have no choice. Ten percent power. The *Ohio* cannot possibly hear that, and perhaps the near hunter sub won't either."

The Pogy

"Where did that come from?" The sonar chief made some adjustments on his board. "Conn, sonar, I got a contact, bearing two-three-zero."

"Conn, aye," Commander Wood answered at once. "Can you classify?"

"No, sir. It just came up. Reactor plant and steam noises, real faint, sir. I can't quite read the plant signature . . ." He flipped the gain controls to maximum. "Not one of ours. Skipper, I think maybe we got us an *Alfa* here."

"Oh, great! Signal *Dallas* right now!"

The chief tried, but the *Dallas,* running at thirty-two knots, missed the five rapid pings. The *Red October* was now eight miles away.

The Red October

Jones' eyes suddenly screwed shut. "Mr. Bugayev, tell the skipper I just heard a couple of pings."

"Couple?"

"More 'n one, but I didn't get a count."

The Pogy

Commander Wood made his decision. The idea had been to send the sonar signals on a highly directional, low-power basis so as to minimize the chance of revealing his own position. But the *Dallas* hadn't picked that up.

"Max power, Chief. Hit *Dallas* with everything."

"Aye aye." The chief flipped his power controls to full. It took several seconds until the system was ready to send a hundred-kilowatt blast of energy.

Ping ping ping ping ping!

The Dallas

"Wow!" Chief Laval exclaimed. "Conn, sonar, danger signal from *Pogy!*"

"All stop!" Chambers ordered. "Quiet ship."

"All stop." Lieutenant Goodman relayed the orders a second later. Aft, the reactor watch reduced steam demand, increasing the temperature in the reactor. This allowed neutrons to escape out of the pile, rapidly slowing the fission reaction.

"When speed gets to four knots, go to one-third speed," Chambers told the officer of the deck as he went aft to the sonar room. "Frenchie, I need data in a hurry."

"Still going too fast, sir," Laval said.

The Red October

"Captain Ramius, I think we should slow down," Mancuso said judiciously.

"The signal was not repeated," Ramius disagreed. The second directional signal had missed them, and the *Dallas* had not relayed the danger signal yet because she was still traveling too fast to locate the *October* and pass it along.

The Pogy

"Okay, sir, *Dallas* has killed power."

Wood chewed on his lower lip. "All right, let's find the bastard. Yankee search, Chief, max power." He went back to control. "Man battle stations." An alarm went off two seconds later. The *Pogy* had already been at increased readiness, and within forty seconds all stations were manned, with the executive officer, Lieutenant Commander Tom Reynolds, as fire control coordinator. His team of officers and technicians were waiting for data to feed into the Mark 117 fire control computer.

The sonar dome in the *Pogy*'s bow was blasting sound energy into the water. Fifteen seconds after it started the first return signal appeared on Chief Palmer's screen.

"Conn, sonar, we have a positive contact, bearing two-three-four, range six thousand yards. Classify probable *Alfa* class from his plant signature," Palmer said.

"Get me a solution!" Wood said urgently.

"Aye." Reynolds watched the data input as another team of officers was making a paper and pencil plot on the chart table. Computer or not, there had to be a backup. The data paraded across the screen. The *Pogy*'s four torpedo tubes contained a pair of Harpoon antiship missiles and two Mark 48 torpedoes. Only the torpedoes were useful at the moment. The Mark 48 was the most powerful torpedo in the inventory; wire-guided—and able to home in with its own active sonar—it ran at over fifty knots and carried a half-ton warhead. "Skipper, we got a solution for both fish. Running time four minutes, thirty-five seconds."

"Sonar, secure pinging," Wood said.

"Aye aye. Pinging secured, sir." Palmer killed power to the active systems. "Target elevation-depression angle is near zero, sir. He's about at our depth."

"Very well, sonar. Keep on him." Wood now had his target's position. Further pinging would only give it a better idea of his own.

The Dallas

"*Pogy* was pinging something. They got a return, bearing one-nine-one, about," Chief Laval said. "There's another sub out there. I don't know what. I can read some plant and steam noises, but not enough for a signature."

The Pogy

"The boomer's still movin', sir," Chief Palmer reported.

"Skipper," Reynolds looked up from the paper tracks, "her course takes her between us and the target."

"Terrific. All ahead one-third, left twenty degrees rudder." Wood moved to the sonar room while his orders were carried out. "Chief, power up and stand by to ping the boomer hard."

"Aye aye, sir." Palmer worked his controls. "Ready, sir."

"Hit him straight on. I don't want him to miss this time."

Wood watched the heading indicator on the sonar plot swing. The *Pogy* was turning rapidly, but not rapidly enough to suit him. The *Red October*—only he and Reynolds knew that she was Russian, though the crew was speculating like mad—was coming in too fast.

"Ready, sir."

"Hit it."

Palmer punched the impulse control.

Ping ping ping ping ping!

The Red October

"Skipper," Jones yelled. "Danger signal!"

Mancuso jumped to the annunciator without waiting for Ramius to react. He twisted the dial to All Stop. When this was done he looked at Ramius. "Sorry, sir."

"All right." Ramius scowled at the chart. The phone buzzed a moment later. He took it and spoke in Russian for several seconds before hanging up. "I told them that we have a problem but we do not know what it is."

"True enough." Mancuso joined Ramius at the chart. Engine noises were diminishing, though not quickly enough to suit the American. The *October* was quiet for a Russian sub, but this was still too noisy for him.

"See if your sonarman can locate anything," Ramius suggested.

"Right." Mancuso took a few steps aft. "Jonesy, find what's out there."

"Aye, Skipper, but it won't be easy on this gear." He already had the sensor arrays working in the direction of the two escorting attack subs. Jones adjusted the fit of his headphones and started working on the amplifier controls. No signal processors, no SAPS, and the transducers weren't worth a damn! But this wasn't the time to get excited. The Soviet systems had to be manipulated electromechanically, unlike the computer-controlled ones he was used to. Slowly and carefully, he altered the directional receptor gangs in the sonar dome forward, his right hand twirling a cigarette pack, his eyes shut tight. He didn't notice Bugayev sitting next to him, listening to the same input.

The Dallas

"What do we know, Chief?" Chambers asked.

"I got a bearing and nothing else. *Pogy's* got him all dialed in, but our friend powered back his engine right after he got lashed, and he faded out on me. *Pogy* got a big return off him. He's probably pretty close, sir."

Chambers had only moved up to his executive officer's posting four months earlier. He was a bright, experienced officer and a likely candidate for his own command, but he was only thirty-three years old and had only been back in submarines for those four months. The year and a half prior to that he'd been a reactor instructor in Idaho. The gruffness that was part of his job as Mancuso's principal on-board disciplinarian also shielded more insecurity than he would have cared to admit. Now his career was on the line. He knew exactly how important this mission was. His future would ride on the decisions he was about to make.

"Can you localize with one ping?"

The sonar chief considered this for a second. "Not enough for a shooting solution, but it'll give us something."

"One ping, do it."

"Aye." Laval worked on his board briefly, triggering the active elements.

The V. K. Konovalov

Tupolev winced. He had acted too soon. He should have waited until they were past—but then if he had waited that long, he would have had to move, and now he had all three of them hovering nearby, almost still.

The four submarines were moving only fast enough for depth control. The Russian *Alfa* was pointed southeast, and all four were arrayed in a roughly trapezoidal fashion, open end seaward. The *Pogy* and the *Dallas* were to the north of the *Konovalov,* the *Red October* was southeast of her.

The Red October

"Somebody just pinged her," Jones said quietly. "Bearing is roughly northwest, but she isn't making enough noise for us to read her. Sir, if I had to make a bet, I'd say she was pretty close."

"How do you know that?" Mancuso asked.

"I heard the pulse direct—just one ping to get a range, I think. It was from a BQQ-5. Then we heard the echo off the target. The math works out a couple of different ways, but smart money is he's between us and our guys, and a little west. I know it's shaky, sir, but it's the best we got."

"Range ten kilometers, perhaps less," Bugayev commented.

"That's kinda shaky, too, but it's as good a starting place as any. Not a whole lot of data. Sorry, Skipper. Best we can do," Jones said.

Mancuso nodded and returned to control.

"What gives?" Ryan asked. The plane controls were pushed all the way forward to maintain depth. He had not grasped the significance of what was going on.

"There's a hostile submarine out there."

"What information do we have?" Ramius asked.

"Not much. There's a contact northwest, range unknown, but probably not very far. I know for sure it's not one of ours. Norfolk said this area was cleared. That leaves one possibility. We drift?"

"We drift," Ramius echoed, lifting the phone. He spoke a few orders.

The *October*'s engines were providing the power to move

the submarine at a fraction over two knots, barely enough to maintain steerage way and not enough to maintain depth. With her slight positive buoyancy, the *October* was drifting upward a few feet per minute despite the plane setting.

The Dallas

"Let's move back south. I don't like the idea of having that *Alfa* closer to our friend than we are. Come right to one-eight-five, two-thirds," Chambers said finally.

"Aye aye," Goodman said. "Helm, right fifteen degrees rudder, come to new course one-eight-five. All ahead two thirds."

"Right fifteen degrees rudder, aye." The helmsman turned the wheel. "Sir, my rudder is right fifteen degrees, coming to new course one-eight-five."

The *Dallas'* four torpedo tubes were loaded with three Mark 48s and a decoy, an expensive MOSS (mobile submarine simulator). One of her torpedoes was targeted on the *Alfa*, but the firing solution was vague. The "fish" would have to do some of the tracking by itself. The *Pogy's* two torpedoes were almost perfectly dialed in.

The problem was that neither boat had authority to shoot. Both attack submarines were operating under the normal rules of engagement. They could fire in self-defense only and defend the *Red October* only by bluff and guile. The question was whether the *Alfa* knew what the *Red October* was.

The V. K. Konovalov

"Steer for the *Ohio*," Tupolev ordered. "Bring speed to three knots. We must be patient, comrades. Now that the Americans know where we are they will not ping us again. We will move from our place quietly."

The *Konovalov's* bronze propeller turned more quickly. By shutting down some nonessential electrical systems, the engineers were able to increase speed without increasing reactor output.

The Pogy

On the *Pogy*, the nearest attack boat, the contact faded, degrading the directional bearing somewhat. Commander Wood debated whether or not to get another bearing with active sonar but decided against it. If he used active sonar his position would be like that of a policeman looking for a burglar in a dark building with a flashlight. Sonar pings could well tell his target more than they told him. Using passive sonar was the normal routine in such a case.

Chief Palmer reported the passage of the *Dallas* down their port side. Both Wood and Chambers decided not to use their underwater telephones to communicate. They could not afford to make any noise now.

The Red October

They had been creeping along for a half hour now. Ryan was chain-smoking at his station, and his palms were sweating as he struggled to maintain his composure. This was not the sort of combat he had been trained for, being trapped inside a steel pipe, unable to see or hear anything. He knew that there was a Soviet submarine out there, and he knew what her orders were. If her captain realized who they were—then what? The two captains, he thought, were amazingly cool.

"Can your submarines protect us?" Ramius asked.

"Shoot at a Russian sub?" Mancuso shook his head. "Only if he shoots first—at them. Under the normal rules, we don't count."

"What?" Ryan was stunned.

"You want to start a war?" Mancuso smiled, as though he found this situation amusing. "That's what happens when warships from two countries start exchanging shots. We have to smart our way out of this."

"Be calm, Ryan," Ramius said. "This is our usual game. The hunter submarine tries to find us, and we try not to be found. Tell me, Captain Mancuso, at what range did you hear us off Iceland?"

"I haven't examined your chart closely, Captain," Mancuso mused. "Maybe twenty miles, thirty or so kilometers."

"And then we were traveling at thirteen knots—noise increases faster than speed. I think we can move east, slowly, without being detected. We use the caterpillar, move at six knots. As you know, Soviet sonar is not so efficient as American. Do you agree, Captain?"

Mancuso nodded. "She's your boat, sir. May I suggest northeast? That ought to put us behind our attack boats inside an hour, maybe less."

"Yes." Ramius hobbled over to the control board to open the tunnel hatches, then went back to the phone. He gave the necessary orders. In a minute the caterpillar motors were engaged and speed was increasing slowly.

"Rudder right ten, Ryan," Ramius said. "And ease the plane controls."

"Rudder right ten, sir, easing the planes, sir." Ryan carried the orders out, glad that they were doing something.

"Your course is zero-four-zero, Ryan," Mancuso said from the chart table.

"Zero-four-zero, coming right through three-five-zero." From the helmsman's seat he could hear the water swishing down the portside tunnel. Every minute or so there was an odd rumble that lasted three or four seconds. The speed gauge in front of him passed through four knots.

"You are frightened, Ryan?" Ramius chuckled.

Jack swore to himself. His voice had wavered. "I'm a little tired, too."

"I know it is difficult for you. You do well for a new man with no training. We will be late to Norfolk, but we shall get there, you will see. Have you been on a missile boat, Mancuso?"

"Oh, sure. Relax, Ryan. This is what boomers do. Somebody comes lookin' for us, we just disappear." The American commander looked up from the chart. He had set coins at the estimated positions of the three other subs. He considered marking it up more but decided not to. There were some very interesting notations on this coastal chart—like programmed missile-firing positions. Fleet intelligence would go ape over this sort of information.

The *Red October* was moving northeast at six knots now. The *Konovalov* was coming southeast at three. The *Pogy* was heading south at two, and the *Dallas* south at fifteen. All four submarines were now within a six-mile-diameter circle, all converging on about the same point.

The V. K. Konovalov

Tupolev was enjoying himself. For whatever reason, the Americans had chosen to play a conservative game that he had not expected. The smart thing, he thought, would have been for one of the attack boats to close in and harrass him, allowing the missile sub to pass clear with the other escort. Well, at sea nothing was ever quite the same twice. He sipped at a cup of tea as he selected a sandwich.

His sonar *michman* noted an odd sound in his sonar set. It only lasted a few seconds, then was gone. Some far-off seismic rumble, he thought at first.

The Red October

They had risen because of the *Red October*'s positive trim, and now Ryan had five degrees of down-angle on the diving planes to get back down to a hundred meters. He heard the captains discussing the absence of a thermocline. Mancuso explained that it was not unusual for the area, particularly after violent storms. They agreed that it was unfortunate. A thermal layer would have helped their evasion.

Jones was at the aft entrance of the control room, rubbing his ears. The Russian phones were not very comfortable. "Skipper, I'm getting something to the north, comes and goes. I haven't gotten a bearing lock on it."

"Whose?" Mancuso asked.

"Can't say, sir. The active sonar isn't too bad, but the passive stuff just isn't up to the drill, Skipper. We're not blind, but close to it."

"Okay, if you hear something, sing out."

"Aye aye, Captain. You got some coffee out here? Mr. Bugayev sent me for some."

"I'll have a pot sent in."

"Right." Jones went back to work.

The V. K. Konovalov

"Comrade Captain, I have a contact, but I do not know what it is," the *michman* said over the phone.

Tupolev came back, munching on his sandwich. *Ohio*s had

been acquired so rarely by the Russians—three times to be exact, and in each case the quarry had been lost within minutes—that no one had a feel for the characteristics of the class.

The *michman* handed the captain a spare set of phones. "It may take a few minutes, Comrade. It comes and goes."

The water off the American coast, though nearly isothermal, was not entirely perfect for sonar systems. Minor currents and eddies set up moving walls that reflected and channeled sound energy on a nearly random basis. Tupolev sat down and listened patiently. It took five minutes for the signal to come back.

The *michman*'s hand waved. "Now, Comrade Captain."

His commanding officer looked pale.

"Bearing?"

"Too faint, and too short to lock in—but three degrees on either bow, one-three-six to one-four-two."

Tupolev tossed the headphones on the table and went forward. He grabbed the political officer by the arm and led him quickly to the wardroom.

"It's *Red October!*"

"Impossible. Fleet Command said that his destruction was confirmed by visual inspection of the wreckage." The *zampolit* shook his head emphatically.

"We have been tricked. The caterpillar acoustical signature is unique, Comrade. The Americans have him, and he is out there. We must destroy him!"

"No. We must contact Moscow and ask for instructions."

The *zampolit* was a good Communist, but he was a surface ship officer who didn't belong on submarines, Tupolev thought.

"Comrade Zampolit, it will take several minutes to approach the surface, perhaps ten or fifteen to get a message to Moscow, thirty more for Moscow to respond at all—and then they will request *confirmation!* An hour in all, two, three? By that time *Red October* will be gone. Our original orders are operative, and there is no time to contact Moscow."

"But what if you are wrong?"

"I am not wrong, Comrade!" the captain hissed. "I will enter my contact report in the log, and my recommendations. If you forbid this, I will log that also! I am right, Comrade. It will be your head, not mine. Decide!"

"You are certain?"

"Certain!"

"Very well." The *zampolit* seemed to deflate. "How will you do this?"

"As quickly as possible, before the Americans have a chance to destroy us. Go to your station, Comrade." The two men went back to the control room. The *Konovalov*'s six bow torpedo tubes were loaded with Mark C 533-millimeter wire-guided torpedoes. All they needed was to be told where to go.

"Sonar, search forward on all active systems!" the captain ordered.

The *michman* pushed the button.

The Red October

"Ouch." Jones' head jerked around. "Skipper, we're being pinged. Port side, midships, maybe a little forward. Not one of ours, sir."

The Pogy

"Conn, sonar, the *Alfa*'s got the boomer! The *Alfa* bearing is one-nine-two."

"All ahead two-thirds," Wood ordered immediately.

"All ahead two-thirds, aye."

The *Pogy*'s engines exploded into life, and soon her propeller was thrashing the black water.

The V. K. Konovalov

"Range seven thousand, six hundred meters. Elevation angle zero," the *michman* reported. So, this was the submarine they had been sent to hunt, he thought. He had just donned a headset that allowed him to report directly to the captain and fire control officer.

The *starpom* was the chief fire control supervisor. He quickly entered the data into the computer. It was a simple problem of target geometry. "We have a solution for torpedoes one and two."

"Prepare to fire."

"Flooding tubes." The *starpom* flipped the switches himself, reaching past the petty officer. "Outer torpedo tube doors are open."

"Recheck firing solution!" Tupolev said.

The Pogy

The *Pogy*'s sonar chief was the only man to hear the transient noise.

"Conn, sonar, *Alfa* contact—she just flooded tubes, sir! Target bearing is one-seven-nine."

The V. K. Konovalov

"Solution confirmed, Comrade Captain," the *starpom* said.

"Fire one and two," Tupolev ordered.

"Firing one . . . Firing two." The *Konovalov* shuddered twice as compressed air charges ejected the electrically powered torpedoes.

The Red October

Jones heard it first. "High-speed screws port side!" he said loudly and clearly. "Torpedoes in the water port side!"

"Ryl nalyeva!" Ramius ordered automatically.

"What?" Ryan asked.

"Left, rudder left!" Ramius pounded his fist on the rail.

"Left full, do it!" Mancuso said.

"Left full rudder, aye." Ryan turned the wheel all the way and held it down. Ramius was spinning the annunciator to flank speed.

The Pogy

"Two fish running," Palmer said. "Bearing is changing right to left. I say again, torpedo bearing changing right to left rapidly on both fish. They're targeted on the boomer."

The Dallas

The *Dallas* heard them, too. Chambers ordered flank speed and a turn to port. With torpedoes running his options were limited, and he was doing what American practice taught, heading someplace else—very fast.

The Red October

"I need a course!" Ryan said.

"Jonesy, give me a bearing!" Mancuso shouted.

"Three-two-zero, sir. Two fish heading in," Jones responded at once, working his controls to nail the bearing down. This was no time to screw up.

"Steer three-two-zero, Ryan," Ramius ordered, "if we can turn so fast."

Thanks a lot, Ryan thought angrily, watching the gyrocompass click through three-five-seven. The rudder was hard over, and with the sudden increase in power from the caterpillar motors, he could feel feedback flutter through the wheel.

"Two fish heading in, bearing is three-two-zero, I say again bearing is constant," Jones reported, much cooler than he felt. "Here we go, guys..."

The Pogy

Her tactical plot showed the *October,* the *Alfa,* and the two torpedoes. The *Pogy* was four miles north of the action.

"Can we shoot?" the exec asked.

"At the *Alfa?*" Wood shook his head emphatically. "No, dammit. It wouldn't make a difference anyway."

The V. K. Konovalov

The two Mark C torpedoes were charging at forty-one knots, a slow speed for this range, so that they could be more easily guided by the *Konovalov*'s sonar system. They had a projected six-minute run, with one minute already completed.

The Red October

"Okay, coming through three-four-five, easing the rudder off," Ryan said.

Mancuso kept quiet now. Ramius was using a tactic that he didn't particularly agree with, turning into the fish. It offered a minimum target profile, but it gave them a simpler geometric intercept solution. Presumably Ramius knew what Russian fish could do. Mancuso hoped so.

"Steady on three-two-zero, Captain," Ryan said, eyes locked

on the gyro repeater as though it mattered. A small voice in his brain congratulated him for going to the head an hour earlier.

"Ryan, down, maximum down on the diving planes."

"All the way down." Ryan pushed the yoke to the stops. He was terrified, but even more frightened of fouling up. He had to assume that both commanders knew what they were about. There was no choice for him. Well, he thought, he did know one thing. Guided torpedoes can be tricked. Like radar signals that are aimed at the ground, sonar pulses can be obscured, especially when the sub they are trying to locate is near the bottom or the surface, areas where the pulses tend to be reflected. If the *October* dove she could lose herself in an opaque field—presuming she got there fast enough.

The V. K. Konovalov

"Target aspect has changed, Comrade Captain. Target is now smaller," the *michman* said.

Tupolev considered this. He knew everything there was on Soviet combat doctrine—and knew that Ramius had written a good deal of it. Marko would do what he taught all of us to do, Tupolev thought. Turn into the oncoming weapons to minimize target cross-section and dive for the bottom to become lost in the confused echoes. "Target will be attempting to dive into the bottom-capture field. Be alert."

"Aye, Comrade. Can he reach the bottom quickly enough?" the *starpom* asked.

Tupolev racked his brain for the *October*'s handling characteristics. "No, he cannot dive that deep in so short a time. We have him." Sorry, my old friend, but I have no choice, he thought.

The Red October

Ryan cringed each time the sonar lash echoed through the double hull. "Can't you jam that or something?" he demanded.

"Patience, Ryan," Ramius said. He had never faced live warheads before but had exercised this problem a hundred times in his career. "Let him know he has us first."

"Do you carry decoys?" Mancuso asked.

"Four of them, in the torpedo room, forward—but we have no torpedomen."

Both captains were playing the cool game, Ryan noted bitterly from inside his terrified little world. Neither was willing to show fright before his peer. But they were both trained for this.

"Skipper," Jones called, "two fish, bearing constant at three-two-zero—they just went active. I say again, the fish are now active—shit! they sound just like 48s. Skipper, they sound like Mark 48 fish."

Ramius had been waiting for this. "Yes, we stole the torpedo sonar from you five years ago, but not your torpedo engines. *Bugayev!*"

In the sonar room, Bugayev had powered up the acoustical jamming gear as soon as the fish were launched. Now he carefully timed his jamming pulses to coincide with those from the approaching torpedoes. The pulses were dialed into the same carrier frequency and pulse repetition rate. The timing had to be precise. By sending out slightly distorted return echoes, he could create ghost targets. Not too many, nor too far away. Just a few, close by, and he might be able to confuse the fire control operators on the attacking *Alfa*. He thumbed the trigger switch carefully, chewing on an American cigarette.

The V. K. Konovalov

"Damn! He's jamming us." The *michman*, noting a pair of new pips, showed his first trace of emotion. The fading pip from the true contact was now bordered with two new ones, one north and closer, the other south and farther away. "Captain, the target is using Soviet jamming equipment."

"You see?" Tupolev said to the *zampolit*. "Use caution now," he ordered his *starpom*.

The Red October

"Ryan, all up on planes!" Ramius shouted.

"All the way up." Ryan yanked back, pulling the yoke hard against his belly and hoping that Ramius knew what the hell he was doing.

"Jones, give us time and range."

"Aye." The jamming gave them a sonar picture plotted on the main scopes. "Two fish, bearing three-two-zero. Range to number one is 2,000 yards, to number two is 2,300—I got a depression angle on number one! Number one fish is heading down a little, sir." Maybe Bugayev wasn't so dumb after all, Jones thought. But they had two fish to sweat...

The Pogy

The *Pogy*'s skipper was enraged. The goddamned rules of engagement prevented him from doing a goddamned thing, except, maybe—

"Sonar, ping the sonuvabitch! Max power, blast the sucker!"

The *Pogy*'s BQQ-5 sent timed wave fronts of energy lashing at the *Alfa*. The *Pogy* couldn't shoot, but maybe the Russian didn't know that, and maybe this lashing would interfere with their targeting sonar.

The Red October

"Any time now—one of the fish has capture, sir. I don't know which." Jones moved the phones off one ear, his hand poised to slap the other off. The homing sonar on one torpedo was now tracking them. Bad news. If these were like Mark 48s ... Jones knew all too well that those things didn't miss much. He heard the change in the Doppler shift of the propellers as they passed beneath the *Red October*. "One missed, sir. Number one missed under us. Number two is heading in, ping interval is shortening." He reached over and patted Bugayev on the shoulder. Maybe he really was the on-board genius that the Russians said he was.

The V. K. Konovalov

The second Mark C torpedo was cutting through the water at forty-one knots. This made the torpedo-target closing speed about fifty-five. The guidance and decision loop was a complex one. Unable to mimic the computer homing system on the American Mark 48, the Soviets had the torpedo's targeting sonar report back to the launching vessel through an insulated wire. The *starpom* had a choice of sonar data with which to guide the torpedoes, that from the sub-mounted sonar or that from the torpedoes themselves. The first fish had been duped by the ghost images that the jamming had duplicated on the torpedo sonar frequency. For the second, the *starpom* was using the lower-frequency bow sonar. The first one had missed low, he knew now. That meant that the target was the middle pip. A quick frequency change by the *michman* cleared the sonar picture for few seconds before the jamming mode was altered. Coolly and expertly, the *starpom* commanded the second torpedo to select the center target. It ran straight and true.

The five-hundred-pound warhead struck the target a glancing blow aft of midships, just forward of the control room. It exploded a millisecond later.

The Red October

The force of the explosion hurled Ryan from his chair, and his head hit the deck. He came to from a moment's unconsciousness with his ears ringing in the dark. The shock of the explosion had shorted out a dozen electrical switchboards, and it was several seconds before the red battle lights clicked on. Aft, Jones had flipped his headphones off just in time, but Bugayev, trying to the last second to spoof the incoming torpedo, had not. He was rolling in agony on the deck, one eardrum ruptured, totally deafened. In the engine spaces men were scrambling back to their feet. Here the lights had stayed on, and Melekhin's first action was to look at the damage-control status board.

The explosion had occurred on the outer hull, a skin of light steel. Inside it was a water-filled ballast tank, a beehive of cellular baffles seven feet across. Located beyond the tank were high-pressure air flasks. Then came the *October*'s battery and the inner pressure hull. The torpedo had impacted in the center of a steel plate on the outer hull, several feet from any weld joints. The force of the explosion had torn a hole twelve feet across, shredded the interior ballast tank baffles, and ruptured a half-dozen air flasks, but already much of its force had been dissipated. The final damage was done to thirty of the large nickle-cadmium battery cells. Soviet engineers had placed these here deliberately. They had known that such a placement would make them difficult to service, difficult to recharge, and worst of all expose them to seawater contamination. All this had been accepted in light of their secondary purpose as additional armor for the hull. The *October*'s batteries saved her. Had it not been for them, the force of the explosion would have been spent on the pressure hull. Instead it was greatly reduced by the layered

defensive system which had no Western counterpart. A crack
had developed at the weld joint on the inner hull, and water
was spraying into the radio room as though from a high-pressure
hose, but the hull was otherwise secure.

In control, Ryan was soon back in his seat trying to determine if his instruments still worked. He could hear water splashing into the next compartment forward. He didn't know what
to do. He did know it would be a bad time to panic, much as
his brain screamed for the release.

"What do I do?"

"Still with us?" Mancuso's face looked satanic in the red
lights.

"No goddammit, I'm dead—what do I do?"

"Ramius?" Mancuso saw the captain holding a flashlight
taken from a bracket on the aft bulkhead.

"Down, dive for bottom." Ramius took the phone and called
engineering to order the engines stopped. Melekhin had already
given the order.

Ryan pushed his controls forward. In a goddamned submarine that's got a goddamned hole punched in it, they tell
you to go *down!* he thought.

The V. K. Konovalov

"A solid hit, Comrade Captain," the *michman* reported. "His
engines stopped. I hear hull creaking noises, his depth is changing." He tried some additional pings but got nothing. The
explosion had greatly disturbed the water. There were rumbling
echoes of the initial explosion reverberating through the sea.
Trillions of bubbles had formed, creating an "ensonified zone"
around the target that rapidly obscured it. His active pings were
reflected back by the cloud of bubbles, and his passive listening
ability was greatly reduced by the recurring rumbles. All he
knew for sure was that one torpedo had hit, probably the second. He was an experienced man trying to decide what was
noise and what was signal, and he had reconstructed most of
the events correctly.

The Dallas

"Score one for the bad guys," the sonar chief said. The *Dallas*
was running too fast to make proper use of her sonar, but the

explosion was impossible to miss. The whole crew heard it through the hull.

In the attack center Chambers plotted their position two miles from where the *October* had been. The others in the compartment looked at their instruments without emotion. Ten of their shipmates had just been hit, and the enemy was on the other side of the wall of noise.

"Slow to one-third," Chambers ordered.

"All ahead one-third," the officer of the deck repeated.

"Sonar, get me some data," Chambers said.

"Working on it, sir." Chief Laval strained to make sense of what he heard. It took a few minutes as the *Dallas* slowed to under ten knots. "Conn, sonar, the boomer took one hit. I don't hear her engines . . . but there ain't no breakup noises. I say again, sir, no breakup noises."

"Can you hear the *Alfa?*"

"No, sir, too much crud in the water."

Chamber's face screwed into a grimace. You're an officer, he told himself, they pay you to think. First, what's happening? Second, what do you do about it? Think it through, then act.

"Estimated distance to target?"

"Something like nine thousand yards, sir," Lieutenant Goodman said, reading the last solution off the fire control computer. "She'll be on the far side of the ensonified zone."

"Make your depth six hundred feet." The diving officer passed this on to the helmsman. Chambers considered the situation and decided on his course of action. He wished Mancuso and Mannion were here. The captain and navigator were the other two members of what passed for the *Dallas'* tactical management committee. He needed to exchange some ideas with other experienced officers—but there weren't any.

"Listen up. We're going down. The disturbance from the explosion will stay fairly steady. If it moves at all, it'll go up. Okay, we'll go under it. First we want to locate the boomer. If she isn't there, then she's on the bottom. It's only nine hundred feet here, so she could be on the bottom with a live crew. Whether or not she's on the bottom, we gotta get between her and the *Alfa.*" And, he thought on, if the *Alfa* shoots then, I kill the fucker, and rules of engagement be damned. They had to trick this guy. But how? And where was the *Red October?*

The Red October

She was diving more quickly than expected. The explosion had also ruptured a trim tank, causing more negative buoyancy than they had at first allowed for.

The leak in the radio room was bad, but Melekhin had noted the flooding on his damage control board and reacted immediately. Each compartment had its own electrically powered pump. The radio room pump, supplemented by a master-zone pump that he had also activated, was managing, barely, to keep up with the flooding. The radios were already destroyed, but no one was planning to send any messages.

"Ryan, all the way up, and come right full rudder," Ramius said.

"Right full rudder, all the way up on the planes," Ryan said. "We going to hit the bottom?"

"Try not to," Mancuso said. "It might spring the leak worse."

"Great," Ryan growled back.

The *October* slowed her descent, arcing east below the ensonified zone. Ramius wanted it between himself and the *Alfa*. Mancuso thought that they might just survive after all. In that case he'd have to give this boat's plans a closer look.

The Dallas

"Sonar, give me two low-powered pings for the boomer. I don't want anybody else to hear this, Chief."

"Aye." Chief Laval made the proper adjustments and sent the signals out. "All right! Conn, sonar, I got her! Bearing two-zero-three, range two thousand yards. She is not, repeat *not,* on the bottom, sir."

"Left fifteen degrees rudder, come to two-zero-three," Chambers ordered.

"Left fifteen degrees rudder, aye!" the helmsman sang out. "New course two-zero-three. Sir, my rudder is left fifteen degrees."

"Frenchie, tell me about the boomer!"

"Sir, I got . . . pump noises, I think . . . and she's moving a little, bearing is now two-zero-one. I can track her on passive, sir."

"Thompson, plot the boomer's course. Mr. Goodman, we

still have that MOSS ready for launch?"

"Aye aye," responded the torpedo officer.

The V. K. Konovalov

"Did we kill him?" the *zampolit* asked.

"Probably," Tupolev answered, wondering if he had or not. "We must close to be certain. Ahead slow."

"Ahead slow."

The Pogy

The *Pogy* was now within two thousand yards of the *Konovalov*, still pinging her mercilessly.

"He's moving, sir. Enough that I can read passive," Sonar Chief Palmer said.

"Very well, secure pinging," Wood said.

"Aye, pinging secured."

"We got a solution?"

"Locked in tight," Reynolds answered. "Running time is one minute eighteen seconds. Both fish are ready."

"All ahead one-third."

"All ahead one-third, aye." The *Pogy* slowed. Her commanding officer wondered what excuse he might find for shooting.

The Red October

"Skipper, that was one of our sonars that pinged us, off north-north-east. Low-power ping, sir, must be close."

"Think you can raise her on gertrude?"

"Yes sir!"

"Captain?" Mancuso asked. "Permission to communicate with my ship?"

"Yes."

"Jones, raise her right now."

"Aye. This is Jonesy calling Frenchie, do you copy?" The sonarman frowned at the speaker. "Frenchie, answer me."

The Dallas

"Conn, sonar, I got Jonesy on the gertrude."

Chambers lifted the control room gertrude phone. "Jones,

this is Chambers. What is your condition?"

Mancuso took the mike away from his man. "Wally, this is Bart," he said. "We took one midships, but she's holding together. Can you run interference for us?"

"Aye aye! Starting right now, out." Chambers replaced the phone. "Goodman, flood the MOSS tube. Okay, we'll go in behind the MOSS. If the *Alfa* shoots at it, we take her out. Set it to run straight for two thousand yards, then turn south."

"Done. Outer door open, sir."

"Launch."

"MOSS away, sir."

The decoy ran forward at twenty knots for two minutes to clear the *Dallas*, then slowed. It had a torpedo body whose forward portion carried a powerful sonar transducer that ran off a tape recorder and broadcast the recorded sounds of a 688-class submarine. Every four minutes it changed over from loud operation to silent. The *Dallas* trailed a thousand yards behind the decoy, dropping several hundred feet below its course track.

The *Konovalov* approached the wall of bubbles carefully, with the *Pogy* trailing to the north.

"Shoot at the decoy, you son of a bitch," Chambers said quietly. The attack center crew heard him and nodded grim agreement.

The Red October

Ramius judged that the ensonified zone was now between him and the *Alfa*. He ordered the engines turned back on, and the *Red October* proceeded on a north-easterly course.

The V. K. Konovalov

"Left ten degrees rudder," Tupolev ordered quietly. "We'll come around the dead zone to the north and see if he is still alive when we turn back. First we must clear the noise."

"Still nothing," the *michman* reported. "No bottom impact, no collapse noises . . . New contact, bearing one-seven-zero . . . Different sound, Comrade Captain, one propeller . . . Sounds like an American."

"What heading?"

"South, I think. Yes, south . . . The sound's changing. It is American."

"An American sub is decoying. We ignore it."

"Ignore it?" the *zampolit* said.

"Comrade, if you were heading north and were torpedoed,
would you then head south? Yes, you would—but not Marko.
It is too obvious. This American is decoying to try to take us
away from him. Not too clever, this one. Marko would do
better. And he would go north. I know him, I know how he
thinks. He is now heading north, perhaps northeast. They would
not decoy if he was dead. Now we know that he is alive but
crippled. We will find him, and finish him," Tupolev said
calmly, fully caught up in the hunt for *Red October*, remembering all he had been taught. He would prove now that he
was the new master. His conscience was still. Tupolev was
fulfilling his destiny.

"But the Americans—"

"Will not shoot, Comrade," the captain said with a thin
smile. "If they could shoot, we would already be dead from
the one to the north. They cannot shoot without permission.
They must *ask* for permission, as we must—but we already
have the permission, and the advantage. We are now where
the torpedo struck him, and when we clear the disturbance we
will find him again. Then we will have him."

The Red October

They couldn't use the caterpillar. One side was smashed by
the torpedo hit. The *October* was moving at six knots, driven
by her propellers, which made more noise than the other system. This was much like the normal drill of protecting a boomer.
But the exercise always presupposed that the escorting attack
boats could shoot to make the bad guy go away . . .

"Left rudder, reverse course," Ramius ordered.

"What?" Mancuso was astounded.

"Think, Mancuso," Ramius said, looking to be sure that
Ryan carried out the order. Ryan did, not knowing why.

"Think, Commander Mancuso," Ramius repeated. "What
has happened? Moskva ordered a hunter sub to remain behind,
probably a *Politovskiy*-class boat, the *Alfa* you call him. I know
all their captains. All young, all, ah, aggressive? Yes, aggressive. He must know we are not dead. If he knows this, he will
pursue us. So, we go back like a fox and let him pass."

Mancuso didn't like this. Ryan could tell without looking.

"We cannot shoot. Your men cannot shoot. We cannot run from him—he is faster. We cannot hide—his sonar is better. He will move east, use his speed to contain us and his sonar to locate us. By moving west, we have the best chance to escape. This he will not expect."

Mancuso still didn't like it, but he had to admit it was clever. Too damned clever. He looked back down at the chart. It wasn't his boat.

The Dallas

"The bastard went right past. Either ignored the decoy or flat didn't hear it. He's abeam of us, we'll be in his baffles soon," Chief Laval reported.

Chambers swore quietly. "So much for that idea. Right fifteen degrees rudder." At least the *Dallas* had not been heard. The submarine responded rapidly to the controls. "Let's get behind him."

The Pogy

The *Pogy* was now a mile off the *Alfa*'s port quarter. She had the *Dallas* on sonar and noted her change of course. Commander Wood simply did not know what to do next. The easiest solution was to shoot, but he couldn't. He contemplated shooting on his own. His every instinct told him to do just this. The *Alfa* was hunting Americans . . . But he couldn't give in to his instinct. Duty came first.

There was nothing worse than overconfidence, he reflected bitterly. The assumption behind this operation had been that there wouldn't be anybody around, and even if there were the attack subs would be able to warn the boomer off well in advance. There was a lesson in this, but Wood didn't care to think about it just now.

The V. K. Konovalov

"Contact," the *michman* said into the microphone. "Ahead, almost dead ahead. Using propellers and going at slow speed. Bearing zero-four-four, range unknown."

"Is it *Red October*?" Tupolev asked.

"I cannot say, Comrade Captain. It could be an American. He's coming this way, I think."

"Damn!" Tupolev looked around the control room. Could they have passed the *Red October?* Might they already have killed him?

The Dallas

"Does he know we're here, Frenchie?" Chambers asked, back in sonar.

"No way, sir." Laval shook his head. "We're directly behind him. Wait a minute . . ." The chief frowned. "Another contact, far side of the *Alfa.* That's gotta be our friend, sir. Jesus! I think he's heading this way. Using his wheels, not that funny thing."

"Range to the *Alfa?*"

"Under three thousand yards, sir."

"All ahead two thirds! Come left ten degrees!" Chambers ordered. "Frenchie, ping, but use the under-ice sonar. He may not know what that is. Make him think we're the boomer."

"Aye aye, sir!"

The V. K. Konovalov

"High-frequency pinging aft!" the *michman* called out. "Does not sound like an American sonar, Comrade."

Tupolev was suddenly puzzled. Was it an American to seaward? The other one on his port quarter was certainly American. It had to be the *October.* Marko was still the fox. He had lain still, letting them go past, so that he could shoot at them!

"All ahead full, left full rudder!"

The Red October

"Contact!" Jones sang out. "Dead ahead. Wait . . . It's an *Alfa!* She's close! Seems to be turning. Somebody pinging her on the other side. Christ, she's *real* close. Skipper, the *Alfa* is not a point source. I got signal separation between the engine and the screw."

"Captain," Mancuso said. The two commanders looked at one another and communicated a single thought as if by telepathy. Ramius nodded.

"Get us range."

"Jonesy, ping the sucker!" Mancuso ran aft.

"Aye." The systems were fully powered. Jones loosed a single ranging ping. "Range fifteen hundred yards. Zero elevation angle, sir. We're level with her."

"Mancuso, have your man give us range and bearing!" Ramius twisted the annunciator handle savagely.

"Okay, Jonesy, you're our fire control. Track the mother."

The V. K. Konovalov

"One active sonar ping to starboard, distance unknown, bearing zero-four-zero. The seaward target just ranged on us," the *michman* said.

"Give me a range," Tupolev ordered.

"Too far aft of the beam, Comrade. I am losing him aft."

One of them was the *October*—but which? Could he risk shooting at an American sub? No!

"Solution to the forward target?"

"Not a good one," the *starpom* replied. "He's maneuvering and increasing speed."

The *michman* concentrated on the western target. "Captain, contact forward is not, repeat not Soviet. Forward contact is American."

"*Which* one?" Tupolev screamed.

"West and northwest are both American. East target unknown."

"Keep the rudder at full."

"Rudder is full," the helmsman responded, holding the wheel over.

"The target is behind us. We must lock on and shoot as we turn. Damn, we are going too fast. Slow to one-third speed."

The *Konovalov* was normally quick to turn, but the power reduction made her propeller act like a brake, slowing the maneuver. Still, Tupolev was doing the right thing. He had to point his torpedo tubes near the bearing of the target, and he had to slow rapidly enough for his sonar to give him accurate firing information.

The Red October

"Okay, the *Alfa* is continuing her turn, now heading right to left . . . Propulsion sounds are down some. She just chopped power," Jones said, watching the screen. His mind was working furiously computing course, speed, and distance. "Range is now twelve hundred yards. She's still turning. We doin' what I think?"

"Looks that way."

Jones set the active sonar on automatic pinging. "Have to see what this turn does, sir. If she's smart she'll burn off south and get clear first."

"Then pray she ain't smart," Mancuso said from the passageway. "Steady as she goes!"

"Steady as she goes," Ryan said, wondering if the next torpedo would kill them.

"Her turn is continuing. We're on her port beam now, maybe her port bow." Jones looked up. "She's going to get around first. Here come the pings."

The *Red October* accelerated to eighteen knots.

The V. K. Konovalov

"I have him," the *michman* said. "Range one thousand meters, bearing zero-four-five. Angle zero."

"Set it up," Tupolev ordered his exec.

"It will have to be a zero-angle shot. We're swinging too rapidly," the *starpom* said. He set it up as quickly as he could. The submarines were now closing at over forty knots. "Ready for tube five only! Tube flooded, door—open. Ready!"

"Shoot!"

"Fire five!" The *starpom*'s finger stabbed the button.

The Red October

"Range down to nine hundred—high-speed screws dead ahead! We have one torpedo in the water dead ahead. One fish, heading right in!"

"Forget it, track the *Alfa!*"

"Aye, okay, the *Alfa*'s bearing two-two-five, steadying down. We need to come left a little, sir."

"Ryan, come left five degrees, your course is two-two-five."

"Left five rudder, coming to two-two-five."

"The fish is closing rapidly, sir," Jones said.

"Screw it! Track the *Alfa.*"

"Aye. Bearing is still two-two-five. Same as the fish."

The combined speed ate up the distance between the submarines rapidly. The torpedo was closing the *October* faster still, but it had a safety device built in. To prevent them from blowing up their own launch platform, torpedoes could not arm until they were five hundred to a thousand yards from the boat that launched them. If the *October* closed the *Alfa* fast enough, she could not be hurt.

The *October* was now passing twenty knots.

"Range to the *Alfa* is seven hundred fifty yards, bearing two-two-five. The torpedo is close, sir, a few more seconds." Jones cringed, staring at the screen.

Klonk!

The torpedo struck the *Red October* dead center in her hemispherical bow. The safety lock still had another hundred meters to run. The impact broke it into three pieces, which were batted aside by the accelerating missile submarine.

"A dud!" Jones laughed. "Thank you, God! Target still bearing two-two-five, range is seven hundred yards."

The V. K. Konovalov

"No explosion?" Tupolev wondered.

"The safety locks!" The *starpom* swore. He'd had to set it up too fast.

"Where is the target?"

"Bearing zero-four-five, Comrade. Bearing is constant," the *michman* replied, "closing rapidly."

Tupolev blanched. "Left full rudder, all ahead flank!"

The Red October

"Turning, turning left to right," Jones said. "Bearing is now two-three-zero, spreading out a little. Need a little right rudder, sir."

"Ryan, come right five degrees."

"Rudder is right five," Jack answered.

"No, rudder ten right!" Ramius countermanded his order. He had been keeping a track with pencil and paper. And he knew the *Alfa*.

"Right ten degrees," Ryan said.

"Near-field effect, range down to four hundred yards, bearing is two-two-five to the center of the target. Target is spreading out left and right, mostly left," Jones said rapidly. "Range . . . three hundred yards. Elevation angle is zero, we are level with the target. Range two hundred fifty, bearing two-two-five to target center. We can't miss, Skipper."

"We're gonna hit!" Mancuso called out.

Tupolev should have changed depth. As it was he depended on the *Alfa*'s acceleration and maneuverability, forgetting that Ramius knew exactly what these were.

"Contact spread way the hell out—instantaneous return, sir!"

"Brace for impact!"

Ramius had forgotten the collision alarm. He yanked at it only seconds before impact.

The *Red October* rammed the *Konovalov* just aft of midships at a thirty-degree angle. The force of the collision ruptured the *Konovalov*'s titanium pressure hull and crumpled the *October*'s bow as if it were a beer can.

Ryan had not braced hard enough. He was thrown forward, and his face struck the instrument panel. Aft, Williams was catapulted from his bed and caught by Noyes before his head hit the deck. Jones' sonar systems were wiped out. The missile submarine bounded up and over the top of the *Alfa,* her keel grating across the upper deck of the smaller vessel as the momentum carried her forward and upward.

The V. K. Konovalov

The *Konovalov* had had full watertight integrity set. It did not make a difference. Two compartments were instantly vented to the sea, and the bulkhead between the control room and the after compartments failed a moment later from hull deformation. The last thing that Tupolev saw was a curtain of white foam coming from the starboard side. The *Alfa* rolled to port, turned by the friction of the *October*'s keel. In a few seconds the submarine was upside down. Throughout her length men and gear tumbled about like dice. Half the crew were already drowning. Contact with the *October* ended at this point, when the *Konovalov*'s flooded compartments made her drop stern first toward the bottom. The political officer's last conscious act was to yank at the disaster beacon handle, but it was to no avail: the sub was inverted, and the cable fouled on the sail. The only marker on the *Konovalov*'s grave was a mass of bubbles.

The Red October

"We still alive?" Ryan's face was bleeding profusely.

"Up, up on the planes!" Ramius shouted.

"All the way up." Ryan pulled back with his left hand, holding his right over the cuts.

"Damage report," Ramius said in Russian.

"Reactor system is intact," Melekhin answered at once. "The damage control board shows flooding in the torpedo room—I think. I have vented high-pressure air into it, and the pump is activated. Recommend we surface to assess damage."

"Da!" Ramius hobbled to the air manifold and blew all tanks.

The Dallas

"Jesus," the sonar chief said, "somebody hit somebody. I got breakup noises going down and hull-popping noises going up. Can't tell which is which, sir. Both engines are dead."

"Get us up to periscope depth quick!" Chambers ordered.

The Red October

It was 1654 local time when the *Red October* broke the surface of the Atlantic Ocean for the first time, forty-seven miles southeast of Norfolk. There was no other ship in sight.

"Sonar is wiped out, Skipper." Jones was switching off his boxes. "Gone, crunched. We got some piddly-ass lateral hydrophones. No active stuff, not even the gertrude."

"Go forward, Jonesy. Nice work."

Jones took the last cigarette from his pack. "Any time, sir—but I'm gettin' out next summer, depend on it."

Bugayev followed him forward, still deafened and stunned from the torpedo hit.

The *October* was sitting still on the surface, down by the bow and listing twenty degrees to port from the vented ballast tanks.

The Dallas

"How about that," Chambers said. He lifted the microphone. "This is Commander Chambers. They killed the *Alfa!* Our guys are safe. Surfacing the boat now. Stand by the fire and rescue party!"

The Red October

"You okay, Commander Ryan?" Jones turned his head carefully. "Looks like you broke some glass the hard way, sir."

"You don't worry till it stops bleeding," Ryan said drunkenly.

"Guess so." Jones held his handkerchief over the cuts. "But I sure hope you don't always drive this bad, sir."

"Captain Ramius, permission to lay to the bridge and communicate with my ship?" Mancuso asked.

"Go, we may need help with the damage."

Mancuso got into his jacket, checking to make sure his small docking radio was still in the pocket where he had left it. Thirty seconds later he was atop the sail. The *Dallas* was surfacing as he made his first check of the horizon. The sky had never looked so good.

He couldn't recognize the face four hundred yards away, but it had to be Chambers.

"Dallas, this is Mancuso."

"Skipper, this is Chambers. You guys okay?"

"Yes! But we may need some hands. The bow's all stove in and we took a torpedo midships."

"I can see it, Bart. Look down."

"Jesus!" The jagged hole was awash, half out of the water, and the submarine was heavily down by the bow. Mancuso wondered how she could float at all, but it wasn't the time to question why.

"Come over here, Wally, and get the raft out."

"On the way. Fire and rescue is standing by, I—there's our other friend," Chambers said.

The *Pogy* surfaced three hundred yards directly ahead of the *October.*

"Pogy says the area's clear. Nobody here but us. Heard that

one before?" Chambers laughed mirthlessly. "How about we radio in?"

"No, let's see if we can handle it first." The *Dallas* approached the *October*. Within minutes Mancuso's command submarine was seventy yards to port, and ten men on a raft were struggling across the chop. Up to this time only a handful of men aboard the *Dallas* had known what was going on. Now everyone knew. He could see his men pointing and talking. What a story they had.

Damage was not as bad as they had feared. The torpedo room had not flooded—a sensor damaged by the impact had given a false reading. The forward ballast tanks were permanently vented to the sea, but the submarine was so big and her ballast tanks so subdivided that she was only eight feet down at the bow. The list to port was only a nuisance. In two hours the radio room leak had been plugged, and after a lengthy discussion among Ramius, Melekhin, and Mancuso it was decided that they could dive again if they kept their speed down and did not go below thirty meters. They'd be late getting to Norfolk.

THE EIGHTEENTH DAY

MONDAY, 20 DECEMBER

The Red October

Ryan again found himself atop the sail thanks to Ramius, who said that he had earned it. In return for the favor, Jack had helped the captain up the ladder to the bridge station. Mancuso was with them. There was now an American crew below in the control room, and the engine room complement had been supplemented so that there was something approaching a normal steaming watch. The leak in the radio room had not been fully contained, but it was above the waterline. The compartment had been pumped out, and the *October*'s list had eased to fifteen degrees. She was still down by the bow, which was partially compensated for when the intact ballast tanks were blown dry. The crumpled bow gave the submarine a decidedly asymmetrical wake, barely visible in the moonless, cloud-laden sky. The *Dallas* and the *Pogy* were still submerged, somewhere aft, sniffing for additional interference as they neared Capes Henry and Charles.

Somewhere farther aft an LNG (liquified natural gas) carrier was approaching the passage, which the coast guard had closed to all normal traffic in order to allow the floating bomb to travel without interference all the way to the LNG terminal at Cove Point, Maryland—or so the story went. Ryan wondered how the navy had persuaded the ship's skipper to fake engine trouble or somehow delay his arrival. They were six hours late. The navy must have been nervous as all hell until they had finally surfaced forty minutes earlier and been spotted immediately by a circling Orion.

The red and green buoy lights winked at them, dancing on the chop. Forward he could see the lights of the Chesapeake Bay Bridge-Tunnel, but there were no moving automobile lights. The CIA had probably staged a messy wreck to shut it down, maybe a tractor-trailer or two full of eggs or gasoline. Something creative.

"You've never been to America before," Ryan said, just to make conversation.

"No, never to a Western country. Cuba once, many years ago."

Ryan looked north and south. He figured they were inside the capes now. "Well, welcome home, Captain Ramius. Speaking for myself, sir, I'm damned glad you're here."

"And happier that you are here," Ramius observed.

Ryan laughed out loud. "You can bet your ass on that. Thanks again for letting me up here."

"You have earned it, Ryan."

"The name's Jack, sir."

"Short for John, is it?" Ramius asked. "John is the same as Ivan, no?"

"Yes, sir, I believe it is." Ryan didn't understand why Ramius' face broke into a smile.

"Tug approaching." Mancuso pointed.

The American captain had superb eyesight. Ryan didn't see the boat through his binoculars for another minute. It was a shadow, darker than the night, perhaps a mile away.

"*Sceptre,* this is tug *Paducah*. Do you read? Over."

Mancuso took the docking radio from his pocket. "*Paducah* this is *Sceptre*. Good morning, sir." He was speaking in an English accent.

"Please form up on me, Captain, and follow us in."

"Jolly good, *Paducah*. Will do. Out."

HMS *Sceptre* was the name of an English attack submarine. She must be somewhere remote, Ryan thought, patrolling the Falklands or some other faraway location so that her arrival at Norfolk would be just another routine occurrence, not unusual and difficult to disprove. Evidently they were thinking about some agent's being suspicious of a strange sub's arrival.

The tug approached to within a few hundred yards, then turned to lead them in at five knots. A single red tuck light showed.

"I hope we don't run into any civilian traffic," Mancuso said.

"But you said the harbor entrance was closed," Ramius said.

"Might be some guy in a little sailboat out there. The public has free passage through the yard to the Dismal Swamp Canal, and they're damned near invisible on radar. They slip through all the time."

"This is crazy."

"It's a free country, Captain," Ryan said softly. "It will take you some time to understand what free really means. The word is often misused, but in time you will see just how wise your decision was."

"Do you live here, Captain Mancuso?" Ramius asked.

"Yes, my squadron is based in Norfolk. My home is in Virginia Beach, down that way. I probably won't get there anytime soon. They're going to send us right back out. Only thing they can do. So, I miss another Christmas at home. Part of the job."

"You have a family?"

"Yes, Captain. A wife and two sons. Michael, eight, and Dominic, four. They're used to having daddy away."

"And you, Ryan?"

"Boy and a girl. Guess I will be home for Christmas. Sorry, Commander. You see, for a while there I had my doubts. After things get settled down some I'd like to get this whole bunch together for something special."

"Big dinner bill," Mancuso chuckled.

"I'll charge it to the CIA."

"And what will the CIA do with us?" Ramius asked.

"As I told you, Captain, a year from now you will be living your own lives, wherever you wish to live, doing whatever you wish to do."

"Just so?"

"Just so. We take pride in our hospitality, sir, and if I ever get transferred back from London, you and your men are welcome in my home at any time."

"Tug's turning to port." Mancuso pointed. The conversation was taking too maudlin a turn for him.

"Give the order, Captain," Ramius said. It was, after all, Mancuso's harbor.

"Left five degrees rudder," Mancuso said into the microphone.

"Left five degrees rudder, aye," the helmsman responded. "Sir, my rudder is left five degrees."

"Very well."

The *Paducah* turned into the main channel, past the *Saratoga,* which was sitting under a massive crane, and headed towards a mile-long line of piers in the Norfolk Naval Shipyard. The channel was totally empty, just the *October* and the tug. Ryan wondered if the *Paducah* had a normal complement of enlisted men or a crew made entirely of admirals. He would not have given odds either way.

Norfolk, Virginia

Twenty minutes later they were at their destination. The Eight-Ten Dock was a new dry dock built to service the *Ohio*-class fleet ballistic missile submarines, a huge concrete box over eight hundred feet long, larger than it had to be, covered with a steel roof so that spy satellites could not see if it were occupied or not. It was in the maximum security section of the base, and one had to pass several security barriers of armed guards—marines, not the usual civilian guards—to get near the dock, much less into it.

"All stop," Mancuso ordered.

"All stop, aye."

The *Red October* had been slowing for several minutes, and it was another two hundred yards before she came to a complete halt. The *Paducah* curved around to starboard to push her bow round. Both captains would have preferred to power their own way in, but the damaged bow made maneuvering tricky. The diesel-powered tug took five minutes to line the bow up properly, headed directly into the water-filled box. Ramius gave the engine command himself, the last for this submarine. She eased forward through the black water, passing slowly under the wide roof. Mancuso ordered his men topside to handle the lines tossed them by a handful of sailors on the rim of the dock, and the submarine came to a halt exactly in its center. Already the gate they had passed through was closing, and a canvas cover the size of a clipper's mainsail was being drawn across it. Only when cover was securely in place were the overhead lights switched on. Suddenly a group of thirty or so officers began screaming like fans at a ballgame. The only thing left out was the band.

"Finished with the engines," Ramius said in Russian to the crew in the maneuvering room, then switched to English with a trace of sadness in his voice. "So. We are here."

The overhead traveling crane moved down toward them and stopped to pick up the brow, which it brought around and laid carefully on the missile deck forward of the sail. The brow was hardly in place when a pair of officers with gold braid nearly to their elbows walked—ran—across it. Ryan recognized the one in front. It was Dan Foster.

The chief of naval operations saluted the quarterdeck as he got to the edge of the gangway, then looked up at the sail. "Request permission to come aboard, sir."

"Permission is—"

"Granted," Mancuso prompted.

"Permission is granted," Ramius said loudly.

Foster jumped aboard and hurried up the exterior ladder on the sail. It wasn't easy, since the ship still had a sizable list to port. Foster was puffing as he reached the control station.

"Captain Ramius, I'm Dan Foster." Mancuso helped the CNO over the bridge coaming. The control station was suddenly crowded. The American admiral and the Russian captain shook hands, then Foster shook Mancuso's. Jack came last.

"Looks like the uniform needs a little work, Ryan. So does the face."

"Yeah, well, we ran into some trouble."

"So I see. What happened?"

Ryan didn't wait for the explanation. He went below without

excusing himself. It wasn't his fraternity. In the control room
the men were standing around exchanging grins, but they were
quiet, as if they feared the magic of the moment would evaporate all too quickly. For Ryan it already had. He looked for
the deck hatch and climbed up through it, taking with him
everything he'd brought aboard. He walked up the gangway
against traffic. No one seemed to notice him. Two hospital
corpsmen were carrying a stretcher, and Ryan decided to wait
on the dock for Williams to be brought out. The British officer
had missed everything, having only been fully conscious for
the past three hours. As Ryan waited he smoked his last Russian
cigarette. The stretcher, with Williams tied onto it, was man-
handled out. Noyes and the medical corpsmen from the subs
tagged along.

"How are you feeling?" Ryan walked alongside the stretcher
toward the ambulance.

"Alive," Williams said, looking pale and thin. "And you?"

"What I feel under my feet is solid concrete. Thank God
for that!"

"And what he's going to feel is a hospital bed. Nice meeting
you, Ryan," the doctor said briskly. "Let's move it, people."
The corpsmen loaded the stretcher into an ambulance parked
just inside the oversized doors. A minute later it was gone.

"You Commander Ryan, sir?" a marine sergeant asked after
saluting.

Ryan returned the salute. "Yes."

"I have a car waiting for you, sir. Will you follow me,
please?"

"Lead on, Sergeant."

The car was a gray navy Chevy that took him directly to
the Norfolk Naval Air Station. Here Ryan boarded a helicopter.
By now he was too tired to care if it were a sleigh with reindeer
attached. During the thirty-five-minute trip to Andrews Air
Force Base Ryan sat alone in the back, staring into space. He
was met by another car at the base and driven straight to Langley.

CIA Headquarters

It was four in the morning when Ryan finally entered Greer's
office. The admiral was there, along with Moore and Ritter.

The admiral handed him something to drink. Not coffee, Wild Turkey bourbon whiskey. All three senior executives took his hand.

"Sit down, boy," Moore said.

"Damned well done." Greer smiled.

"Thank you." Ryan took a long pull on the drink. "Now what?"

"Now we debrief you," Greer answered.

"No, sir. Now I fly the hell home."

Greer's eyes twinkled as he pulled a folder from a coat pocket and tossed it in Ryan's lap. "You're booked out of Dulles at 7:05 A.M. First flight to London. And you really should wash up, change your clothes, and collect your Skiing Barbie."

Ryan tossed the rest of the drink off. The sudden slug of whiskey made his eyes water, but he was able to refrain from coughing.

"Looks like that uniform got some hard use," Ritter observed.

"So did the rest of me." Jack reached inside the jacket and pulled out the automatic pistol. "This got some use, too."

"The GRU agent? He wasn't taken off with the rest of the crew?" Moore asked.

"You *knew* about him? You knew and you didn't get word to me, for Christ's sake!"

"Settle down, son," Moore said. "We missed connections by half an hour. Bad luck, but you made it. That's what counts."

Ryan was too tired to scream, too tired to do much of anything. Greer took out a tape recorder and a yellow pad full of questions.

"Williams, the British officer, is in a bad way," Ryan said, two hours later. "The doc says he'll make it, though. The sub isn't going anywhere. Bow's all crunched in, and there's a pretty nice hole where the torpedo got us. They were right about the *Typhoon*, Admiral, the Russians built that baby strong, thank God. You know, there may be people left alive on that *Alfa* . . ."

"Too bad," Moore said.

Ryan nodded slowly. "I figured that. I don't know that I like it, sir, leaving men to die like that."

"Nor do we," Judge Moore said, "nor do we, but if we were to rescue someone from her, well, then everything we've—

everything you've been through would be for nothing. Would you want that?"

"It's a chance in a thousand anyway," Greer said.

"I don't know," Ryan said, finishing off his third drink and feeling it. He had expected Moore to be uninterested in checking the *Alfa* for signs of life. Greer had surprised him. So, the old seaman had been corrupted by this affair—or just by being at the CIA—into forgetting the seaman's code. And what did this say about Ryan? "I just don't know."

"It's a war, Jack," Ritter said, more kindly than usual, "a real war. You did well, boy."

"In a war you do well to come home alive," Ryan stood, "and that, gentlemen, is what I plan to do, right now."

"Your things are in the head." Greer checked his watch. "You have time to shave if you want."

"Oh, almost forgot." Ryan reached inside his collar to pull out the key. He handed it to Greer. "Doesn't look like much, does it? You can kill fifty million people with that. 'My name is Ozymandias, king of kings! Look on my works, ye mighty, and despair!'" Ryan headed for the washroom, knowing he had to be drunk to quote Shelley.

They watched him disappear. Greer switched off the tape machine, looking at the key in his hand. "Still want to take him to see the president?"

"No, not a good idea," Moore said. "Boy's half smashed, not that I blame him a bit. Get him on the plane, James. We'll send a team to London tomorrow or the next day to finish the debriefing."

"Good." Greer looked into his empty glass. "Kind of early in the day for this, isn't it?"

Moore finished off his third. "I suppose. But then it's been a fairly good day, and the sun's not even up yet. Let's go, Bob. We have an operation of sorts to run."

Norfolk Naval Shipyard

Mancuso and his men boarded the *Paducah* before dawn and were ferried back to the *Dallas*. The 688-class attack submarine sailed immediately and was back underwater before the sun rose. The *Pogy,* which had never entered port, would complete her deployment without her corpsman aboard. Both submarines had orders to stay out thirty more days, during which their crewmen would be encouraged to forget everything they had seen, heard, or wondered about.

The *Red October* sat alone with the dry dock draining around her, guarded by twenty armed marines. This was not unusual in the Eight-Ten Dock. Already a select group of engineers and technicians was inspecting her. The first items taken off were her cipher books and machines. They would be in National Security Agency headquarters at Fort Meade before noon.

Ramius, his officers, and their personal gear were taken by bus to the same airfield Ryan had used. An hour later they were in a CIA safe house in the rolling hills south of Charlottesville, Virginia. They went immediately to bed except for two men, who stayed awake watching cable television, already amazed at what they saw of life in the United States.

Dulles International Airport

Ryan missed the dawn. He boarded a TWA 747 that left Dulles on time, at 7:05 A.M. The sky was overcast, and when the aircraft burst through the cloud layer into sunlight, Ryan did something he had never done before. For the first time in his life, Jack Ryan fell asleep on an airplane.

ABOUT THE AUTHOR

He has had a private chat with the President of the United States who proclaimed himself to be an avid fan of *The Hunt for Red October*. He has lunched with the White House staff. His novel has been a top seller at the Pentagon. Yet the author in question is neither a former intelligence nor naval officer. Rather, Tom Clancy is an insurance broker from a small town in Maryland whose only previously published writing was a letter to the editor and a three-page article about the MX missile. Clancy always wanted to write a suspense novel, and a newspaper article about a mutiny on a Soviet frigate gave him the initial idea for *Red October*. He did extensive research about Soviet–American naval strategies and submarine technology. Then, in the time he could spare from his insurance business, Clancy sat down at his typewriter and wrote. The rest is history ... and now Clancy is at work on a major new novel.

"*The Witches of Eastwick* is John Updike with his shoes off.... vastly enjoyable...Updike captures the tone of women of a certain age and frame of mind—their crushing directness, their cynical optimism—with the lack of sentimentality that betokens a deep and honest love."

New York Magazine

"As he approaches his middle period as a writer, John Updike keeps giving evidence that it is possible to simply get better and better.... Updike is the most genial of writers.... His intelligence delights in ambiguities and his wit angles always toward irony and paradox and the joys of parody.... this is his best in years."

Ron Hansen
San Francisco Chronicle Review

"At the heart of the fantasy, with its Latin-American brand of baroque whimsy (the witches' victims spit feathers and bugs), is native New England sorcery and the seven deadly sins. It is an excess of one virtue—sympathy—that gets Eastwick's witches off the ground, if also into trouble. Mr. Updike's sympathy for them may be the closest some of us ever come to flying."

The New Yorker

THE WITCHES OF EASTWICK

John Updike

FAWCETT CREST • NEW YORK

A Fawcett Crest Book
Published by Ballantine Books
Copyright © 1984 by John Updike

Library of Congress Catalog Card Number: 83-49048

ISBN 0-449-20647-5

This edition published by arrangement with Alfred A. Knopf, Inc.

A signed first edition of this book has been privately printed by The Franklin
Library.

Manufactured in the United States of America

First Ballantine Books Edition: July 1985

Chapters

i. The Coven

"He was a meikle blak roch man, werie cold."
—*Isobel Gowdie, in 1662*

"Now efter that the deuell had endit his admonitions, he cam down out of the pulpit, and caused all the company to com and kiss his ers, quhilk they said was cauld lyk yce; his body was hard lyk yrn, as they thocht that handled him."
—*Agnes Sampson, in 1590*

"AND OH YES," Jane Smart said in her hasty yet purposeful way; each *s* seemed the black tip of a just-extinguished match held in playful hurt, as children do, against the skin. "Sukie said a man has bought the Lenox mansion."

"A man?" Alexandra Spofford asked, feeling off-center, her peaceful aura that morning splayed by the assertive word.

"From New York," Jane hurried on, the last syllable almost barked, its *r* dropped in Massachusetts style. "No wife and family, evidently."

"Oh. One of those." Hearing Jane's northern voice bring her this rumor of a homosexual come up from Manhattan to invade them, Alexandra felt intersected where she was, in this mysterious crabbed state of

1

Rhode Island. She had been born in the West, where white and violet mountains lift in pursuit of the delicate tall clouds, and tumbleweed rolls in pursuit of the horizon.

"Sukie wasn't so sure," Jane said swiftly, her *s*'s chastening. "He appeared quite burly. She was struck by how hairy the backs of his hands were. He told the people at Perley Realty he needed all that space because he was an inventor with a lab. And he owns a number of pianos."

Alexandra giggled; the noise, little changed since her Colorado girlhood, seemed produced not out of her throat but by a birdlike familiar perched on her shoulder. In fact the telephone was aching at her ear. And her forearm tingled, going numb. "How many pianos can a man have?"

This seemed to offend Jane. Her voice bristled like a black cat's fur, iridescent. She said defensively, "Well Sukie's only going by what Marge Perley told her at last night's meeting of the Horse Trough Committee." This committee supervised the planting and, after vandalism, the replanting of a big blue marble trough for watering horses that historically stood at the center of Eastwick, where the two main streets met; the town was shaped like an L, fitted around its ragged bit of Narragansett Bay. Dock Street held the downtown businesses, and Oak Street at right angles to it was where the lovely big old homes were. Marge Perley, whose horrid canary-yellow For Sale signs leaped up and down on trees and fences as on the tides of economics and fashion (Eastwick had for decades been semi-depressed and semi-fashionable) people moved in and out of the town, was a heavily made-up, go-getting woman who, if one at all, was a witch on a different wavelength from Jane, Alexandra, and Sukie. There was a husband, a tiny fussy Homer Perley always trimming their forsythia hedge back to stubble, and this made a difference. "The papers were passed in Providence," Jane explained, pressing the *nce* hard into Alexandra's ear.

"And with hairy backs to his hands," Alexandra mused. Near her face floated the faintly scratched and flecked and often repainted blankness of a wooden kitchen-cabinet door; she was conscious of the atomic fury spinning and skidding beneath such a surface, like an eddy of weary eyesight. As if in a crystal ball she saw that she would meet and fall in love with this man and that little good would come of it. "Didn't he have a name?" she asked.

"That's the stupidest thing," Jane Smart said. "Marge told Sukie and Sukie told me but something's scared it right out of my head. One of those names with a 'van' or a 'von' or a 'de' in it."

"How very swell," Alexandra answered, already dilating, diffusing herself to be invaded. A tall dark European, ousted from his ancient heraldic inheritance, travelling under a curse... "When is he supposed to move in?"

"She said he said soon. He could be in there now!" Jane sounded alarmed. Alexandra pictured the other woman's rather too full (for the rest of her pinched face) eyebrows lifting to make half-circles above her dark resentful eyes, whose brown was always a shade paler than one's memory of it. If Alexandra was the large, drifting style of witch, always spreading herself thin to invite impressions and merge with the landscape, and in her heart rather lazy and entropically cool, Jane was hot, short, concentrated like a pencil point, and Sukie Rougemont, busy downtown all day long gathering news and smiling hello, had an oscillating essence. So Alexandra reflected, hanging up. Things fall into threes. And magic occurs all around us as nature seeks and finds the inevitable forms, things crystalline and organic falling together at angles of sixty degrees, the equilateral triangle being the mother of structure.

She returned to putting up Mason jars of spaghetti sauce, sauce for more spaghetti than she and her children could consume even if bewitched for a hundred years in an Italian fairy tale, jar upon jar lifted steaming from the white-speckled blue boiler on the trembling, singing round wire rack. It was, she dimly perceived, some kind of ridiculous tribute to her present lover, a plumber of Italian ancestry. Her recipe called for no onions, two cloves of garlic minced and sautéed for three minutes (no more, no less; that was the magic) in heated oil, plenty of sugar to counteract acidity, a single grated carrot, more pepper than salt; but the teaspoon of crumbled basil is what catered to virility, and the dash of belladonna provided the release without which virility is merely a murderous congestion. All this must be added to her own tomatoes, picked and stored on every window sill these weeks past and now sliced and fed to the blender: ever since, two summers ago, Joe Marino had begun to come into her bed, a preposterous fecundity had overtaken the staked plants, out in the side garden where the southwestern sun slanted in through the line of willows each long afternoon. The crooked little tomato branches, pulpy and pale as if made of cheap green paper, broke under the weight of so much fruit; there was something frantic in such fertility, a crying-out like that of children frantic to please. Of plants tomatoes seemed the most human, eager and fragile and prone to rot. Picking the watery orange-red orbs, Alexandra felt she was cupping a giant lover's testicles in her hand. She recognized as she labored in her kitchen the something sadly menstrual in all this, the bloodlike sauce to be ladled upon the white spaghetti. The fat white strings would become her own white fat. This female struggle of hers against her own weight: at the age of thirty-eight she found it increasingly unnatural. In order to attract love must she deny her own body, like a neurotic saint of old? Nature is the index and context of all health and if we have an appetite it is there to be satisfied, satisfying thereby the cosmic order. Yet she sometimes despised herself as lazy, in taking a lover of a race so notoriously tolerant of corpulence.

Alexandra's lovers in the handful of years since her divorce had tended to be odd husbands let stray by the women who owned them. Her own former husband, Oswald Spofford, rested on a high kitchen shelf in a jar, reduced to multi-colored dust, the cap screwed on tight. Thus she had reduced him as her powers unfolded after their move to Eastwick from Norwich, Connecticut. Ozzie had known all about chrome and had transferred from a fixture factory in that hilly city with its too many peeling white churches to a rival manufacturer in a half-mile-long cinder-block plant south of Providence, amid the strange industrial vastness of this small state. They had moved seven years ago. Here in Rhode Island her powers had expanded like gas in a vacuum and she had reduced dear Ozzie as he made his daily trek to work and back along Route 4 first to the size of a mere man, the armor of patriarchal protector falling from him in the corrosive salt air of Eastwick's maternal beauty, and then to the size of a child as his chronic needs and equally chronic acceptance of her solutions to them made him appear pitiful, manipulable. He quite lost touch with the expanding universe within her. He had become much involved with their sons' Little League activities, and with the fixture company's bowling team. As Alexandra accepted first one and then several lovers, her cuckolded husband shrank to the dimensions and dryness of a doll, lying beside her in her great wide receptive bed at night like a painted log picked up at a roadside stand, or a stuffed baby alligator. By the time of their actual divorce her former lord and master had become mere dirt—matter in the wrong place, as her mother had briskly defined it long ago—some polychrome dust she swept up and kept in a jar as a souvenir.

The other witches had experienced similar transformations in their marriages; Jane Smart's ex, Sam, hung in the cellar of her ranch house among the dried herbs and simples and was occasionally sprinkled, a pinch at a time, into a philtre, for piquancy; and Sukie Rougemont had permanized hers in plastic and used him as a place mat. This last had happened rather recently; Alexandra could still picture Monty standing at cocktail parties in his Madras jacket and parsley-green slacks, braying out the details of the day's golf round and inveighing against the slow feminine foursome that had held them up all day and never invited them to play through. He had hated uppity women— female governors, hysterical war protesters, "lady" doctors, Lady Bird Johnson, even Lynda Bird and Luci Baines. He had thought them all butch. Monty had had wonderful teeth when he brayed, long and very even but not false, and, undressed, rather touching, thin bluish legs, much less muscular than his brown golfer's forearms. And with that puckered droop to his buttocks common to the softening flesh of middle-aged women. He had been one of Alexandra's first lovers. Now, it felt queer and queerly satisfying to set a mug of Sukie's tarry coffee upon a glossy plastic Madras, leaving a gritty ring.

This air of Eastwick empowered women. Alexan-

dra had never tasted anything like it, except perhaps
a corner of Wyoming she had driven through with
her parents when she was about eleven. They had let
her out of the car to pee beside some sagebrush and
she had thought, seeing the altitudinous dry earth for
the moment dampened in a dark splotch, *It doesn't
matter. It will evaporate.* Nature absorbs all. This girlhood perception had stayed forever with her, along
with the sweet sage taste of that roadside moment.
Eastwick in its turn was at every moment kissed by
the sea. Dock Street, its trendy shops with their per-
fumed candles and stained-glass shade-pulls aimed at
the summer tourists and its old-style aluminum diner
next to a bakery and its barber's next to a framer's
and its little clattering newspaper office and long dark
hardware store run by Armenians, was intertwined
with saltwater as it slipped and slapped and slopped
against the culverts and pilings the street in part
was built upon, so that an unsteady veiny aqua sea-
glare shimmered and shuddered on the faces of the
local matrons as they carried orange juice and low-fat
milk, luncheon meat and whole-wheat bread and filtered cigarettes out of the Bay Superette. The real
supermarket, where one did a week's shopping, lay
inland, in the part of Eastwick that had been farm-
land; here, in the eighteenth century, aristocratic
planters, rich in slaves and cattle, had paid social calls
on horseback, a slave galloping ahead of them to open
the fence gates one after the other. Now, above the
asphalted acres of the shopping-mall parking lot,
exhaust fumes dyed with leaden vapors air within
memory oxygenated by fields of cabbages and potatoes. Where corn, that remarkable agricultural artifact
of the Indians, had flourished for generations, windowless little plants with names like Dataprobe and
Computech manufactured mysteries, components so

fine the workers wore plastic caps to keep dandruff
from falling into the tiny electro-mechanical works.

Rhode Island, though famously the smallest of the
fifty states, yet contains odd American vastnesses, tracts
scarcely explored amid industrial sprawl, abandoned
homesteads and forsaken mansions, vacant hinter-
lands hastily traversed by straight black roads, heath-
like marshes and desolate shores on either side of the
Bay, that great wedge of water driven like a stake clean
to the state's heart, its trustfully named capital. "The
fag end of creation" and "the sewer of New England,"
Cotton Mather called the region. Never meant to be
a separate polity, settled by outcasts like the bewitch-
ing, soon-to-die Anne Hutchinson, this land holds
manifold warps and wrinkles. Its favorite road sign is
a pair of arrows pointing either way. Swampy poor
in spots, elsewhere it became a playground of the
exceedingly rich. Refuge of Quakers and antinomians, those final distillates of Puritanism, it is run
by Catholics, whose ruddy Victorian churches loom
like freighters in the sea of bastard architecture.
There is a kind of metallic green stain, bitten deep
into Depression-era shingles, that exists nowhere else.
Once you cross the state line, whether at Pawtucket
or Westerly, a subtle change occurs, a cheerful di-
shevelment, a contempt for appearances, a chimerical
uncaring. Beyond the clapboard slums yawn lunar
stretches where only an abandoned roadside stand
offering the ghost of last summer's CUKES betrays the
yearning, disruptive presence of man.

Through such a stretch Alexandra now drove to
steal a new look at the old Lenox mansion. She took
with her, in her pumpkin-colored Subaru station
wagon, her black Labrador, Coal. She had left the last
of the sterilized jars of sauce to cool on the kitchen
counter and with a magnet shaped like Snoopy had

pinned a note to the refrigerator door for her four children to find: MILK IN FRIG, OREOS IN BREADBOX, BACK IN ONE HOUR, LOVE.

The Lenox family in the days when Roger Williams was still alive had cozened the sachems of the Narragansett tribe out of land enough to form a European barony, and though a certain Major Lenox had heroically fallen in the Great Swamp Fight in King Philip's War, and his great-great-great-grandson Emory had eloquently urged New England's secession from the Union at the Hartford Convention of 1815, the family had taken a generally downward trend. By the time of Alexandra's arrival in Eastwick there was not a Lenox left in South County save one old widow, Abigail, in the stagnant quaint village of Old Wick; she went about the lanes muttering and cringing from the pebbles thrown at her by children who, called to account by the local constable, claimed they were defending themselves against her evil eye. The vast Lenox lands had long been broken up. The last of the effective male Lenoxes had caused to be built on an island the family still owned, in the tracts of salt marsh behind East Beach, a brick mansion in diminished but locally striking imitation of the palatial summer "cottages" being erected in Newport during this gilded age. Though a causeway had been constructed and repeatedly raised by fresh importation of gravel, the mansion always suffered the inconvenience of being cut off when the tide was high, and had been occupied fitfully by a succession of owners since 1920, and had been allowed by them to slide into disrepair. The great roof slates, some reddish and some a bluish gray, came crashing unobserved in the winter storms and lay like nameless tombstones in summer's lank tangle of uncut grass; the cunningly fashioned copper gutters and flashing turned green and rotten; the

ornate octagonal cupola with a view to all points of
the compass developed a list to the west; the massive
end chimneys, articulated like bundles of organ pipes
or thickly muscled throats, needed mortar and were
dropping bricks. Yet the silhouette the mansion presented from afar was still rather chasteningly grand,
Alexandra thought. She had parked on the shoulder
of the beach road to gaze across the quarter-mile of
marsh.

This was September, season of full tides; the marsh
between here and the island this afternoon was a sheet
of skyey water flecked by the tips of salt hay turning
golden. It would be an hour or two before the causeway in and out became passable. The time now was
after four; there was a stillness, and a clothy weight
to the sky that hid the sun. Once the mansion would
have been masked by an *allée* of elms continuing the
causeway upward toward the front entrance, but the
elms had died of Dutch elm disease and remained as
tall stumps lopped of their wide-arching branches,
standing like men in shrouds, leaning like that armless
statue of Balzac by Rodin. The house had a forbidding, symmetrical face, with many windows that
seemed slightly small—especially the third-story row,
which went straight across beneath the roof without
variation: the servants' floor. Alexandra had been in
the building years ago, when, still trying to do the
right wifely things, she had gone with Ozzie to a benefit concert held in its ballroom. She could remember
little but room after room, scantly furnished and
smelling of salt air and mildew and vanished plea-
sures. The slates of its neglected roof merged in tint
with a darkness gathering in the north—no, more
than clouds troubled the atmosphere. Thin white
smoke was lifting from the left-hand chimney. Someone was inside.

That man with hairy backs to his hands.

Alexandra's future lover.

More likely, she decided, a workman or watchman he had hired. Her eyes smarted from trying to see so far, so intensely. Her insides like the sky had gathered to a certain darkness, a sense of herself as a pathetic onlooker. Female yearning was in all the papers and magazines now; the sexual equation had become reversed as girls of good family flung themselves toward brutish rock stars, callow unshaven guitarists from the slums of Liverpool or Memphis somehow granted indecent power, dark suns turning these children of sheltered upbringing into suicidal orgiasts. Alexandra thought of her tomatoes, the juice of violence beneath the plump complacent skin. She thought of her own older daughter, alone in her room with those Monkees and Beatles...one thing for Marcy, another for her mother to be mooning so, straining her eyes.

She shut her eyes tight, trying to snap out of it. She got back into the car with Coal and drove the half-mile of straight black road to the beach.

After season, if no one was about, you could walk with a dog unleashed. But the day was warm, and old cars and VW vans with curtained windows and psychedelic stripes filled the narrow parking lot; beyond the bathhouses and the pizza shack many young people wearing bathing suits lay supine on the sand with their radios as if summer and youth would never end. Alexandra kept a length of clothesline on the back-seat floor in deference to beach regulations. Coal shivered in distaste as she passed the loop through his studded collar. All muscle and eagerness, he pulled her along through the resisting sand. She halted to tug off her beige espadrilles and the dog gagged; she dropped the shoes behind a tuft of beach grass near the end of the boardwalk. The boardwalk had been scattered into its six-foot segments by a recent high tide, which had also left above the flat sand beside the sea a wrack of Clorox bottles and tampon sleeves and beer cans so long afloat their painted labels had been eaten away; these unlabelled cans looked frightening—blank like the bombs terrorists make and then leave in public places to bring the system down and thus halt the war. Coal pulled her on, past a heap of barnacled square-cut rocks that had been part of a jetty built when this beach was the toy of rich men and not an overused public playground. The rocks were a black-freckled pale granite and one of the largest held a bolted bracket rusted by the years to the fragility of a Giacometti. The emissions of the young people's radios, rock of an airier sort, washed around her as she walked along, conscious of her heaviness, of the witchy figure she must cut with her bare feet and men's baggy denims and worn-out green brocaded jacket, something from Algeria she and Ozzie had bought in Paris on their honeymoon seventeen years ago. Though she turned a gypsyish olive in summer, Alexandra was of northern blood; her maiden name had been Sorensen. Her mother had recited to her the superstition about changing your initial when you marry, but Alexandra had been a scoffer at magic then and on fire to make babies. Marcy had been conceived in Paris, on an iron bed.

Alexandra wore her hair in a single thick braid down her back; sometimes she pinned the braid up like a kind of spine to the back of her head. Her hair had never been a true clarion Viking blond but of a muddy pallor now further dirtied by gray. Most of the gray hair had sprouted in front; the nape was still as finespun as those of the girls that lay here basking. The smooth young legs she walked past were caramel in color, with white fuzz, and aligned as if in solidarity. One girl's bikini bottom gleamed, taut and simple as a drum in the flat light.

Coal plunged on, snorting, imagining some scent, some dissolving animal vein within the kelpy scent of the oceanside. The beach population thinned. A young couple lay intertwined in a space they had hollowed in the pocked sand; the boy murmured into the base of the girl's throat as if into a microphone. An over-muscled male trio, their long hair flinging as they grunted and lunged, were playing Frisbee, and only when Alexandra purposefully let the powerful black Labrador pull her through this game's wide triangle did they halt their insolent tossing and yelping. She thought she heard the word "hag" or "bag" at her back after she had passed through, but it might have been an acoustic trick, a mistaken syllable of sea-slap. She was drawing near to where a wall of eroded concrete topped by a helix of rusted barbed wire marked the end of public beach; still there were knots of youth and seekers of youth and she did not feel free to set loose poor Coal, though he repeatedly gagged at the restraint of his collar. His desire to run burned the rope in her hand. The sea seemed unnaturally still—tranced, marked by milky streaks far out, where a single small launch buzzed on the sounding board of its level surface. On Alexandra's other side, nearer to hand, beach pea and woolly hudsonia crept down from the dunes; the beach narrowed here and became intimate, as you could see from the nests of cans and bottles and burnt driftwood and the bits of shattered Styrofoam cooler and the condoms like small dried jellyfish corpses. The cement wall had been spray-painted with linked names. Everywhere, desecration had set its hand and only footsteps were eased away by the ocean.

The dunes at one point were low enough to permit a glimpse of the Lenox mansion, from another angle and farther away; its two end chimneys stuck up like hunched buzzard's wings on either side of the cupola. Alexandra felt irritated and vengeful. Her insides felt bruised; she resented the overheard insult "hag" and the general vast insult of all this heedless youth prohibiting her from letting her dog, her friend and familiar, run free. She decided to clear the beach for herself and Coal by willing a thunderstorm. One's inner weather always bore a relation to the outer; it was simply a question of reversing the current, which occurred rather easily once power had been assigned to the primary pole, oneself as a woman. So many of Alexandra's remarkable powers had flowed from this mere reappropriation of her assigned self, achieved not until midlife. Not until midlife did she truly believe that she had a right to exist, that the forces of nature had created her not as an afterthought and companion—a bent rib, as the infamous *Malleus Maleficarum* had it—but as the mainstay of the continuing Creation, as the daughter of a daughter and a woman whose daughters in turn would bear daughters. Alexandra closed her eyes while Coal shivered and whimpered in fright and she willed this vast interior of herself—this continuum reaching back through the generations of humanity and the parenting primates and beyond them through the lizards and the fish to the algae that cooked up the raw planet's first DNA in their microscopic tepid innards, a continuum that in the other direction arched to the end of all life, through form after form, pulsing, bleeding, adapting to the cold, to the ultraviolet rays, to the bloating, weakening sun—she willed these so pregnant depths of herself to darken, to condense, to generate an interface of lightning between tall walls of air. And the sky

in the north did rumble, so faintly only Coal could
hear. His ears stiffened and swivelled, their roots in
his scalp come alive. *Mertalia, Musalia, Dophalia:* in
loud unspoken syllables she invoked the forbidden
names. *Onemalia, Zitanseia, Goldaphaira, Dedulsaira.*
Invisibly Alexandra grew huge, in a kind of maternal
wrath gathering all the sheaves of this becalmed September world to herself, and the lids of her eyes flew
open as if at a command. A blast of cold air hit from
the north, the approach of a front that whipped the
desultory pennants on the distant bathhouse straight
out from their staffs. Down at that end, where the
youthful naked crowd was thickest, a collective sigh
of surprise arose, and then titters of excitement as the
wind stiffened, and the sky toward Providence stood
revealed as possessing the density of some translucent,
empurpled rock. *Gheminaiea, Gegropheira, Cedani, Gil-
thar, Godieb.* At the base of this cliff of atmosphere
cumulus clouds, moments ago as innocuous as flowers
afloat in a pond, had begun to boil, their edges brilliant as marble against the blackening air. The very
medium of seeing was altered, so that the seaside
grasses and creeping glassworts near Alexandra's fat
bare toes, corned and bent by years in shoes shaped
by men's desires and cruel notions of beauty, seemed
traced in negative upon the sand, whose tracked and
pitted surface, suddenly tinted lavender, appeared to
rise like the skin of a bladder being inflated under
the stress of the atmospheric change. The offending
youths had seen their Frisbee sail away from their
hands like a kite and were hurrying to gather up their
portable radios and their six-packs, their sneakers and
jeans and tie-dyed tank tops. Of the couple who had
made a hollow for themselves, the girl could not be
comforted; she was sobbing while the boy with fumbling haste tried to relatch the hooks of her loosened

bikini bra. Coal barked at nothing, in one direction
and then the other, as the drop in barometric pressure
maddened his ears.

Now the immense and impervious ocean, so recently
tranquil all the way to Block Island, sensed the change.
Its surface rippled and corrugated where sweeping
cloud shadows touched it—these patches shrivelling,
almost, like something burned. The motor of the
launch buzzed more sharply. The sails at sea had
melted and the air vibrated with the merged roar of
auxiliary engines churning toward harbor. A hush
caught in the throat of the wind, and then the rain
began, great icy drops that hurt like hailstones. Footsteps pounded past Alexandra as honey-colored lovers raced toward cars parked at the far end, by the
bathhouses. Thunder rumbled, at the top of the cliff
of dark air, along whose face small scuds of paler gray,
in the shape of geese, of gesticulating orators, of
unravelling skeins of yarn, were travelling rapidly.
The large hurtful drops broke up into a finer, thicker
rain, which whitened in streaks where the wind like
a harpist's fingers strummed it. Alexandra stood still
while cold water glazed her; she recited in her inner
spaces, *Ezoill, Musil, Puri, Tamen*. Coal at her feet
whimpered; he had wrapped her legs around with
clothesline. His body, its hair licked flat against the
muscles, glistened and trembled. Through veils of
rain she saw that the beach was empty. She undid the
rope leash and set the dog free.

But Coal stayed huddled by her ankles, alarmed as
lightning flashed once, and then again, double. Alexandra counted the seconds until thunder: five. By
rough rule this made the storm she had conjured up
two miles in diameter, if these strokes were at the
heart. Blunderingly thunder rumbled and cursed.
Tiny speckled sand crabs were emerging now from

their holes by the dozen and scurrying sideways toward the frothing sea. The color of their shells was so sandy they appeared transparent. Alexandra steeled herself and crunched one beneath the sole of her bare foot. Sacrifice. There must always be sacrifice. It was one of nature's rules. She danced from crab to crab, crushing them. Her face from hairline to chin streamed and all the colors of the rainbow were in this liquid film, because of the agitation of her aura. Lightning kept taking her photograph. She had a cleft in her chin and a smaller, scarcely perceptible one in the tip of her nose; her handsomeness derived from the candor of her broad brow beneath the gray-edged wings of hair swept symmetrically back to form her braid, and from the clairvoyance of her slightly protuberant eyes, the gun-metal gray of whose irises was pushed to the rims as if each utterly black pupil were an anti-magnet. Her mouth had a grave plumpness and deep corners that lent the appearance of a smile. She had attained her height of five-eight by the age of fourteen and had weighed one-twenty at the age of twenty; she was somewhere around one hundred sixty pounds now. One of the liberations of becoming a witch had been that she had ceased constantly weighing herself.

As the little sand crabs were transparent on the speckled sand, so Alexandra, wet through and through, felt transparent to the rain, one with it, its temperature and that of her blood brought into concord. The sky over the sea had now composed itself into horizontal fuzzy strips; the thunder was subsiding to a mutter and the rain to a warm drizzle. This downpour would never make the weather maps. The crab she had first crushed was still moving its claws, like tiny pale feathers touched by a breeze. Coal, his terror slipped at last, ran in circles, wider and wider, adding the quadruple gouges of his claws to the triangular

designs of gull feet, the daintier scratches of the sand-
pipers, and the dotted lines of crab scrabble. These
clues to other realms of being—to be a crab, moving
sideways on tiptoe with eyes on stems! to be a barnacle,
standing on your head in a little folding bucket kicking
food toward your mouth!—had been cratered over
by raindrops. The sand was soaked to the color of
cement. Her clothes even to her underwear had been
plastered against her skin so that she felt to herself
like a statue by Segal, pure white, all the sinuous tubes
and bones of her licked by a kind of mist. Alexandra
strode to the end of the purged public beach, to the
wire-topped wall, and back. She reached the parking
lot and picked up her sodden espadrilles where she
had left them, behind a tuft of *Ammophila breviligulata*.
Its long arrowlike blades glistened, having relaxed
their edges in the rain.

She opened the door of her Subaru and turned to
call loudly for Coal, who had vanished into the dunes.
"Come, doggie!" this stately plump woman sang out.
"Come, baby! Come, angel!" To the eyes of the young
people huddled with their sodden gritty towels and
ignominious goosebumps inside the gray-shingled
bathhouse and underneath the pizza shack's awning
(striped the colors of tomato and cheese), Alexandra
appeared miraculously dry, not a hair of her massive
braid out of place, not a patch of her brocaded green
jacket damp. It was such unverifiable impressions that
spread among us in Eastwick the rumor of witchcraft.

Alexandra was an artist. Using few tools other than
toothpicks and a stainless-steel butter knife, she
pinched and pressed into shape little lying or sitting
figurines, always of women in gaudy costumes painted
over naked contours; they sold for fifteen or twenty
dollars in two local boutiques called the Yapping Fox

and the Hungry Sheep. Alexandra had no clear idea of who bought them, or why, or exactly why she made them, or who was directing her hand. The gift of sculpture had descended with her other powers, in the period when Ozzie turned into colored dust. The impulse had visited her one morning as she sat at the kitchen table, the children off at school, the dishes done. That first morning, she had used one of her children's Play-Doh, but she came to depend for clay upon an extraordinarily pure kaolin she dug herself from a little pit near Coventry, a slippery exposed bank of greasy white earth in an old widow's back yard, behind the mossy wreck of an outhouse and the chassis of a prewar Buick just like, by uncanny coincidence, one that Alexandra's father used to drive, to Salt Lake City and Denver and Albuquerque and the lonely towns between. He had sold work clothes, overalls and blue jeans before they became fashionable— before they became the world's garb, the costume that sheds the past. You took your own burlap sacks to Coventry, and you paid the widow twelve dollars a bag. If the sacks were too heavy she helped you lift them; like Alexandra she was strong. Though at least sixty-five, she dyed her hair a glittering brass color and wore pants suits of turquoise or magenta so tight the flesh below her belt was bunched in sausagey rolls. This was nice. Alexandra read a message for herself here: Getting old could be jolly, if you stayed strong. The widow sported a high horselaugh and big gold loop earrings her brassy hair was always pulled back to display. A rooster or two performed its hesitant, preening walk in the tall grass of this unkempt yard; the back of the woman's lean clapboard house had peeled down to the bare gray wood, though the front was painted white. Alexandra, with the back of her Subaru sagging under the weight of the widow's clay, always returned from these trips heartened and exhilarated, full of the belief that a conspiracy of women upholds the world.

Her figurines were in a sense primitive. Sukie or was it Jane had dubbed them her "bubbies"—chunky female bodies four or five inches long, often faceless and without feet, coiled or bent in recumbent positions and heavier than expected when held in the hand. People seemed to find them comforting and took them away from the shops, in a steady, sneaking trickle that intensified in the summer but was there even in January. Alexandra sculpted their naked forms, stabbing with the toothpick for a navel and never failing to provide a nicked hint of the vulval cleft, in protest against the false smoothness there of the dolls she had played with as a girl; then she painted clothes on them, sometimes pastel bathing suits, sometimes impossibly clinging gowns patterned in polka dots or asterisks or wavy cartoon-ocean stripes. No two were quite alike, though all were sisters. Her procedure was dictated by the feeling that as clothes were put on each morning over our nakedness, so they should be painted upon rather than carved onto these primal bodies of rounded soft clay. She baked them two dozen at a time in a little electric Swedish kiln kept in a workroom off her kitchen, an unfinished room but with a wood floor, unlike the next room, a dirt-floored storage space where old flowerpots and lawn rakes, hoes and Wellington boots and pruning shears were kept. Self-taught, Alexandra had been at sculpture for five years—since before the divorce, to which it, like most manifestations of her blossoming selfhood, had contributed. Her children, especially Marcy, but Ben and little Eric too, hated the bubbies, thought them indecent, and once in their agony of embarrassment had shattered a batch that was cool-

ing; but now they were reconciled, as if to defective
siblings. Children are of a clay that to an extent remains
soft, though irremediable twists show up in their
mouths and a glaze of avoidance hardens in their eyes.

Jane Smart, too, was artistically inclined—a musician. She gave piano lessons to make ends meet, and
substituted as choir director in local churches sometimes, but her love was the cello; its vibratory melancholy tones, pregnant with the sadness of wood
grain and the shadowy largeness of trees, would at
odd moonlit hours on warm nights come sweeping
out of the screened windows of her low little ranch
house where it huddled amid many like it on the
curved roads of the Fifties development called Cove
Homes. Her neighbors on their quarter-acre lots, husband and wife, child and dog, would move about,
awakened, and discuss whether or not to call the police.
They rarely did, abashed and, it may be, intimidated
by the something naked, a splendor and grief, in Jane's
playing. It seemed easier to fall back to sleep, lulled
by the double-stopped scales, first in thirds, then in
sixths, of Popper's études, or, over and over, the four
measures of tied sixteenth-notes (where the cello
speaks almost alone) of the second andante of Beethoven's Quartet No. 15, in A Minor. Jane was no
gardener, and the neglected tangle of rhododendron,
hydrangea, arborvitae, barberry, and box around her
foundations helped muffle the outpour from her windows. This was an era of many proclaimed rights, and
of blatant public music, when every supermarket
played its Muzak version of "Satisfaction" and "I Got
You, Babe" and wherever two or three teen-agers
gathered together the spirit of Woodstock was proclaimed. Not the volume but the timbre of Jane's passion, the notes often fumbled at but resumed at the
same somber and undivertible pitch, caught at the

attention bothersomely. Alexandra associated the dark
notes with Jane's dark eyebrows, and with that burning insistence in her voice that an answer be provided
forthwith, that a formula be produced with which to
wedge life into place, to nail its secret down, rather
than drifting as Alexandra did in the faith that the
secret was ubiquitous, an aromaless element in the air
that the birds and blowing weeds fed upon.

Sukie had nothing of what she would call an artistic
talent but she loved social existence and had been
driven by the reduced circumstances that attend
divorce to write for the local weekly, the Eastwick
Word. As she marched with her bright lithe stride up
and down Dock Street listening for gossip and speculating upon the fortunes of the shops, Alexandra's
gaudy figurines in the window of the Yapping Fox,
or a poster in the window of the Armenians' hardware
store advertising a chamber-music concert to be held
in the Unitarian Church and including *Jane Smart,
cello* thrilled her like a glint of beach glass in the sand
or a quarter found shining on the dirty sidewalk—a
bit of code buried in the garble of daily experience,
a stab of communication between the inner and outer
world. She loved her two friends, and they her. Today,
after typing up her account of last night's meetings
at Town Hall of the Board of Assessors (dull: the same
old land-poor widows begging for an abatement) and
the Planning Board (no quorum: Herbie Prinz was in
Bermuda), Sukie looked forward hungrily to Alexandra's and Jane's coming over to her house for a
drink. They usually convened Thursdays, in one of
their three houses. Sukie lived in the middle of town,
which was convenient for her work, though the house,
a virtually miniature 1760 saltbox on a kind of curved
little alley off Oak called Hemlock Lane, was a great
step down from the sprawling farmhouse—six bed-

rooms, thirty acres, a station wagon, a sports car, a Jeep, four dogs—that she and Monty had shared. But her girlfriends made it seem fun, a kind of pretense or interlude of enchantment; they usually affected some odd and colorful bit of costume for their gatherings. In a gold-threaded Parsi shawl Alexandra entered, stooping, at the side door to the kitchen; in her hands, like dumbbells or bloody evidence, were two jars of her peppery, basil-flavored tomato sauce.

The witches kissed, cheek to cheek. "Here sweetie, I know you like nutty dry things best *but*," Alexandra said, in that thrilling contralto that dipped deep into her throat like a Russian woman saying "*byelo.*" Sukie took the twin gifts into her own, more slender hands, their papery backs stippled with fading freckles. "The tomatoes came on like a plague this year for some reason," Alexandra continued. "I put about a hundred jars of this up and then the other night I went out in the garden in the dark and shouted, 'Fuck you, the rest of you can all rot!'"

"I remember one year with the zucchini," Sukie responded, setting the jars dutifully on a cupboard shelf from which she would never take them down. As Alexandra said, Sukie loved dry nutty things— celery, cashews, pilaf, pretzel sticks, tiny little nibbles such as kept her monkey ancestors going in the trees. When alone, she never sat down to eat, just dipped into some yoghurt with a Wheat Thin while standing at the kitchen sink or carrying a 79¢ bag of onion-flavored crinkle chips into her TV den with a stiff bourbon. "I did *ev*erything," she said to Alexandra, relishing exaggeration, her active hands flickering in the edges of her own vision. "Zucchini bread, zucchini soup, salad, frittata, zucchini stuffed with hamburger and baked, cut into slices and fried, cut into sticks to use with a dip, it was *wild*. I even threw a lot into the blender and told the children to put it on their bread instead of peanut butter. Monty was desperate; he said even his shit smelled of zucchini."

Though this reminiscence had referred, implicitly and pleasurably, to her married days and their plenty, mention of an old husband was a slight breach of decorum and snatched away Alexandra's intention to laugh. Sukie was the most recently divorced and the youngest of the three. She was a slender redhead, her hair down her back in a sheaf trimmed straight across and her long arms laden with these freckles the cedar color of pencil shavings. She wore copper bracelets and a pentagram on a cheap thin chain around her throat. What Alexandra, with her heavily Hellenic, twice-cleft features, loved about Sukie's looks was the cheerful simian thrust: Sukie's big teeth pushed her profile below the brief nose out in a curve, a protrusion especially of her upper lip, which was longer and more complex in shape than her lower, with a plumpness on either side of the center that made even her silences seem puckish, as if she were tasting amusement all the time. Her eyes were hazel and round and rather close together. Sukie moved nimbly in her little comedown of a kitchen, everything crowded together and the sink stained and miniature, and beneath it a smell of poverty lingering from all the Eastwick generations who had lived here and had imposed their patchy renovations in the centuries when old hand-hewn houses like this were not considered charming. Sukie pulled a can of Planter's Beer Nuts, wickedly sugary, from a cupboard shelf with one hand and with the other took from the rubber-coated wire drainer on the sink a little paisley-patterned brass-rimmed dish to hold them. Boxes crackling, she strewed an array of crackers on a platter around a wedge of red-coated Gouda cheese and some supermarket pâté still

in the flat tin showing a laughing goose. The platter
was coarse tan earthenware gouged and glazed with
the semblance of a crab. Cancer. Alexandra feared it,
and saw its emblem everywhere in nature—in clusters
of blueberries in the neglected places by rocks and
bogs, in the grapes ripening on the sagging rotten
arbor outside her kitchen windows, in the ants bringing up conical granular hills in the cracks in her asphalt
driveway, in all blind and irresistible multiplications.
"Your usual?" Sukie asked, a shade tenderly, for Alexandra, as if older than she was, had with a sigh dropped
her body, without removing her shawl, into the kitch-
en's one welcoming concavity, an old blue easy chair
too disgraceful to have elsewhere; it was losing stuffing at its seams and at the corners of its arms a polished gray stain had been left where many wrists had
rubbed.

"I guess it's still tonic time," Alexandra decided, for
the coolness that had come in with the thunderstorm
some days ago had stayed. "How's your vodka supply?" Someone had once told her that not only was
vodka less fattening but it irritated the lining of your
stomach less than gin. Irritation, psychic as well as
physical, was the source of cancer. Those get it who
leave themselves open to the idea of it; all it takes is
one single cell gone crazy. Nature is always waiting,
watching for you to lose faith so she can insert her
fatal stitch.

Sukie smiled, broader. "I knew you were coming."
She displayed a brand-new Gordon's bottle, with its
severed boar's head staring with a round orange eye
and its red tongue caught between teeth and a curling
tusk.

Alexandra smiled to see this friendly monster.
"Plenty of tonic, puh-*leese*. The calories!"

The tonic bottle fizzed in Sukie's fingers as if scolding. Perhaps cancer cells were more like bubbles of carbonation, percolating through the bloodstream, Alexandra thought. She must stop thinking about it. "Where's Jane?" she asked.

"She said she'd be a little late. She's rehearsing for that concert at the Unitarians'."

"With that awful Neff," Alexandra said.

"With that awful Neff," Sukie echoed, licking quinine water from her fingers and looking in her bare refrigerator for a lime. Raymond Neff taught music at the high school, a pudgy effeminate man who yet had fathered five children upon his slovenly, sallow, steel-bespectacled, German-born wife. Like most good schoolteachers he was a tyrant, unctuous and insistent; in his dank way he wanted to sleep with everybody. Jane was sleeping with him these days. Alexandra had succumbed a few times in the past but the episode had moved her so little Sukie was perhaps unaware of its vibrations, its afterimage. Sukie herself appeared to be chaste vis-à-vis Neff, but then she had been available least long. Being a divorcee in a small town is a little like playing Monopoly; eventually you land on all the properties. The two friends wanted to rescue Jane, who in a kind of indignant hurry was always selling herself short. It was the hideous wife, with her strawy dull hair cut short as if with grass clippers and her carefully pronounced malapropisms and her goggle-eyed intent way of listening to every word, whom they disapproved of. When you sleep with a married man you in a sense sleep with the wife as well, so she should not be an utter embarrassment.

"Jane has such *beauti*ful possibilities," Sukie said a bit automatically, as she scrabbled with a furious monkey-motion in the refrigerator's icemaker to loosen some more cubes. A witch can freeze water at a glance but sometimes unfreezing it is the problem. Of the

four dogs she and Monty had supported in their hey-
day, two had been loping silvery-brown Weimaraners,
and she had kept one, called Hank; he was now leaning on her legs in the hope that she was struggling in
the refrigerator on his behalf.

"But she *wastes* herself," Alexandra said, complet-
ing the sentence. "Wastes in the old-fashioned sense,"
she added, since this was during the Vietnam War
and the war had given the word an awkward new
meaning. "If she's serious about her music she should
go somewhere serious with it, a city. It's a terrible
waste, a conservatory graduate playing fiddle for a
bunch of deaf old biddies in a dilapidated church."

"She feels safe here," Sukie said, as if they didn't.

"She doesn't even wash herself, have you ever
noticed her smell?" Alexandra asked, not about Jane
but about Greta Neff, by a train of association Sukie
had no trouble following, their hearts were so aligned
on one wavelength.

"And those granny glasses!" Sukie agreed. "She
looks like John Lennon." She made a kind of solemn
sad-eyed thin-lipped John Lennon face. "I sink sen
we can drink ouur—*sprechen Sie wass?*—bev-er-aitches
neeoauu." There was an awful un-American diph-
thong that came out of Greta Neff's mouth, a kind
of twisting of the vowel up against her palate.

Cackling, they took their drinks into the "den," a
little room with peeling wallpaper in a splashy faded
pattern of vines and fruit baskets and a bellied plaster
ceiling at a strange sharp slant because the room was
half tucked under the stairs that went up to the attic-
like second floor. The room's one window, too high
for a woman not standing on a stool to peer out of,
had lozenge panes of leaded glass, thick glass bubbled
and warped like bottle bottoms.

"A cabbagy smell," Alexandra amplified, lowering

herself and her tall silvery drink onto a love seat covered in a crewelwork of flamboyant tattered swirls, stylized vines unravelling. "He carries it on his clothes," she said, thinking simultaneously that this was a little like Monty and the zucchini and that she was evidently inviting Sukie with this intimate detail to guess that she had slept with Neff. Why? It was nothing to brag about. And yet, it was. How he had sweated! For that matter she had slept with Monty, too; and had never smelled zucchini. One fascinating aspect of sleeping with husbands was the angle they gave you on their wives: they saw them as nobody else did. Neff saw poor dreadful Greta as a kind of quaint beribboned Heidi, a sweet bit of edelweiss he had fetched from a perilous romantic height (they had met in a Frankfurt beer hall while he was stationed in West Germany instead of fighting in Korea), and Monty... Alexandra squinted at Sukie, trying to remember what Monty had said of her. He had said little, being such a would-be gentleman. But once he had let slip, having come to Alexandra's bed from some awkward consultation at the bank, and being still preoccupied, the words "She's a lovely girl, but bad luck, somehow. Bad luck for others, I mean. I think she's fairly good luck for herself." And it was true, Monty had lost a great deal of his family's money while married to Sukie, which everyone had blamed simply on his own calm stupidity. *He* had never sweated. He had suffered from that hormonal deficiency of the wellborn, an inability to relate himself to the possibility of hard labor. His body had been almost hairless, with that feminine soft bottom.

"Greta must be great in the sack," Sukie was saying. "All those *Kinder*. *Fünf*, yet."

Neff had allowed to Alexandra that Greta was ardent but strenuous, very slow to come but deter-

mined to do so. She would make a grim witch: those
murderous Germans. "We must be nice to her," Alexandra said, back to the subject of Jane. "Speaking to
her on the phone yesterday, I was struck by how angry
she sounded. That lady is burning up."

Sukie glanced over at her friend, since this seemed
a slightly false note. Some intrigue had begun for
Alexandra, some new man. In the split-second of
Sukie's glance, Hank with his lolling gray Weimaraner
tongue swept two Wheat Thins off the crab platter,
which she had set down on a much-marred pine sea
chest refinished by an antique dealer to be used as a
coffee table. Sukie loved her shabby old things; there
was a kind of blazonry in them, a costume of rags
affected by the soprano in the second act of the opera.
Hank's tongue was coming back for the cheese when
Sukie caught the motion in the corner of her eye and
slapped his muzzle; it was rubbery, in the hard way
of automobile tires, so the slap hurt her own fingers.
"Ow, you bastard," she said to the dog, and to her
friend, "Angrier than anybody else?," meaning themselves. She took a rasping sip of neat bourbon. She
drank whiskey summer and winter and the reason,
which she had forgotten, was that a boyfriend at Cor-
nell had once told her that it brought out the gold
flecks in her green eyes. For the same vain reason she
tended to dress in shades of brown and in suede with
its animal shimmer.

"Oh yes. We're in lovely shape," the bigger, older
woman answered, her mind drifting from this irony
toward the subject of that conversation with Jane—
the new man in town, in the Lenox mansion. But even
as it drifted, her mind, like a passenger in an airplane
who amidst the life-imperilling sensations of lifting
off looks down to marvel at the enamelled precision
and glory of the Earth (the houses with their roofs

and chimneys so sharp, so finely made, and the lakes truly mirrors as in the Christmas yards our parents had arranged while we were sleeping; it was all true, and even maps are true!), took note of how lovely Sukie was, bad luck or not, with her vivid hair dishevelled and even her eyelashes looking a little mussed after her hard day of typing and looking for the right word under the harsh lights, her figure in its milky-green sweater and dark suede skirt so erect and trim, her stomach flat and her breasts perky and high and her bottom firm, and that big broad-lipped mouth on her monkeyish face so mischievous and giving and brave.

"Oh I *know* about him!" she exclaimed, having read Alexandra's mind. "I have such *tons* to tell, but I wanted to wait until Jane got here."

"I can wait," Alexandra said, suddenly resenting now, as if suddenly feeling a cool draft, this man and his place in her mind. "Is that a new skirt?" She wanted to touch it, to stroke it, its doelike texture, the firm lean thigh underneath.

"Resurrected for the fall," Sukie said. "It's really too long, the way skirts are going."

The kitchen doorbell rang: a tittering, ragged sound. "That connection's going to burn the house down some day," Sukie prophesied, darting from the den. Jane had let herself in already. She looked pale, her pinched hot-eyed face overburdened by a floppy furry tam-o'-shanter whose loud plaid fussily matched that of her scarf. Also she was wearing ribbed knee-socks. Jane was not physically radiant like Sukie and was afflicted all over her body with small patches of asymmetry, yet an appeal shone from her as light from a twisted filament. Her hair was dark and her mouth small, prim, and certain. She came from Bos-

ton originally and that gave her something there was
no unknowing.

"That Neff is such a bitch," she began, clearing a
frog from her throat. "He had us do the Haydn over
and over. He said my intonation was prissy. *Prissy.* I
burst into tears and told him he was a disgusting male
chauv." She heard herself and couldn't resist a pun.
"I should have told him to chauv it."

"They can't help it," Sukie said lightly. "It's just
their way of asking for more love. Lexa's having her
usual diet drink, a v-and-t. *Moi,* I'm ever deeper into
the bourbon."

"I shouldn't be doing this, but I'm so fucking hurt
I'm going to be a bad girl for once and ask for a
martini."

"Oh, baby. I don't think I have any dry vermouth."

"No sweat, pet. Just put the gin on the rocks in a
wine glass. You don't by any chance have a bit of
lemon peel?"

Sukie's refrigerator, rich in ice, yoghurt, and celery,
was barren of much else. She had her lunches at
Nemo's Diner downtown, three doors away from the
newspaper offices, past the framer's and the barber's
and the Christian Science reading room, and had taken
to having her evening meals there too, because of the
gossip she heard in Nemo's, the mutter of Eastwick
life all around her. The old-timers congregated there,
the police and the highway crew, the out-of-season
fishermen and the momentarily bankrupt business-
men. "Don't seem to have any oranges either," she
said, tugging at the two produce drawers of sticky
green metal. "I did buy some peaches at that roadside
stand over on 4."

"Do I dare to eat a peach?" Jane quoted. "I shall
wear white flannel trousers, and walk upon the beach."
Sukie winced, watching the other woman's agitated

hands—one tendony and long, from fingering the strings, and the other squarish and slack, from holding the bow—dig with a rusty dull carrot grater into the blushing cheek, the rosiest part, of the yellow pulpy peach. Jane dropped the rosy sliver in; a sacred hush, the spell of any recipe, amplified the tiny *plip*. "I can't start drinking utterly raw gin this early in life," Jane announced with puritanical satisfaction, looking nevertheless haggard and impatient. She moved toward the den with that rapid stiff walk of hers.

Alexandra guiltily reached over and snapped off the TV, where the President, a lugubrious gray-jawed man with pained dishonest eyes, had been making an announcement of great importance to the nation.

"Hi there, you gorgeous creature," Jane called, a bit loudly in this small slant space. "Don't get up, I can see you're all settled. Tell me, though—was that thunderstorm the other day yours?"

The peach skin in the inverted cone of her drink looked like a bit of brightly diseased flesh preserved in alcohol.

"I went to the beach," Alexandra confessed, "after talking to you. I wanted to see if this man was in the Lenox place yet."

"I *thought* I'd upset you, poor chicken," said Jane. "And was he?"

"There was smoke from the chimney. I didn't drive up."

"You should have driven up and said you were from the Wetlands Commission," Sukie told her. "The noise around town is that he wants to build a dock and fill in enough on the back of the island there to have a tennis court."

"That'll never get by," Alexandra told Sukie lazily. "That's where the snowy egrets nest."

"Don't be too sure" was the answer. "That property

hasn't paid any taxes to the town for ten years. For somebody who'll put it back on the rolls the selectmen can evict a lot of egrets."

"Oh, isn't this *cozy!*" Jane exclaimed, rather desperately, feeling ignored. Their four eyes upon her then, she had to improvise. "Greta came into the church," she said, "right after he called my Haydn prissy, and laughed."

Sukie did a German laugh: "Hö hö hö."

"Do they still fuck, I wonder?" asked Alexandra idly, amid this ease with her friends letting her mind wander and gather images from nature. "How could he stand it? It must be like excited sauerkraut."

"No," Jane said firmly. "It's like—what's that pale white stuff they like so?—sauerbraten."

"They marinate it," Alexandra said. "In vinegar, with garlic, onions, and bay leaves. And I think peppercorns."

"Is that what he tells you?" Sukie asked Jane mischievously.

"We never talk about it, even at our most intimate," Jane prissily said. "All he ever confided on the subject was that she had to have it once a week or she began to throw things."

"A poltergeist," Sukie said, delighted. "A polterfrau."

"Really," Jane said, not seeing the humor of it, "you're right. She is an impossibly awful woman. So pedantic; so smug; such a *Nazi.* Ray's the only one who doesn't see it, poor soul."

"I wonder how much she guesses," Alexandra mused.

"She doesn't *want* to guess," Jane said, pressing home the assertion so the last word hissed. "If she guessed she might have to do something about it."

"Like turn him loose," Sukie supplied.

"Then we'd all have to cope with him," Alexandra said, envisioning this plump dank man as a tornado, a voracious natural reservoir, of desire. Desire did come in containers out of all proportion.

"Hang on, Greta!" Jane chimed in, seeing the humor at last.

All three cackled.

The side door solemnly slammed, and footsteps slowly marched upstairs. It was not a poltergeist but one of Sukie's children, home from school, where extracurricular activities had kept him or her late. The upstairs television came on with its comforting humanoid rumble.

Greedily Sukie had crammed too big a handful of salted nuts into her mouth; she flattened her palm against her chin to keep morsels from falling. Still laughing, she sputtered crumbs. "Doesn't *any*body want to hear about this new man?"

"Not especially," Alexandra said. "Men aren't the answer, isn't that what we've decided?"

She was different, a little difficult, when Jane was present, Sukie had often noticed. Alone with Sukie she had not tried to conceal her interest in this new man. The two women had in common a certain happiness in their bodies, which had often been called beautiful, and Alexandra was enough older (six years) to establish when just they were gathered, a certain maternal fit: Sukie frisky and chatty, Lexa lazy and sybilline. Alexandra tended to dominate, when the three were together, by being somewhat sullen and inert, making the other two come to her.

"They're not the answer," Jane Smart said. "But maybe they're the question." Her gin was two-thirds gone. The bit of peach skin was a baby waiting to be thrust out dry into the world. Beyond the graying lozenge panes blackbirds were noisily packing the day away, into its travelling bag of dusk.

Sukie stood to make her announcement. "He's rich," she said, "and forty-two. Never married, and from New York, one of the old Dutch families. He was evidently a child prodigy at the piano, and invents things besides. The whole big room in the east wing, where the billiard table still is, and the laundry area under it are to be his laboratory, with all these stainless-steel sinks and distilling tubes and everything, and on the west side, where the Lenoxes had this greenhousy whatchamacallum, a conservatory, he wants to install a big sunken tub, with the walls wired for stereo." Her round eyes, quite green in the late light, shone with the madness of it. "Joe Marino has the plumbing contract and was talking about it last night after they couldn't get a quorum because Herbie Prinz went to Bermuda without telling anybody. Joe was really freaked out: no estimate asked for, everything the best, price be damned. A *teak* tub eight feet in diameter, and the man doesn't like the feel of tile under his feet so the whole floor is going to be some special fine-grained slate you have to order from Tennessee."

"He sounds pompous," Jane told them.

"Does this big spender have a name?" Alexandra asked, thinking what a romantic Sukie was as well as a gossip columnist and wondering if a second vodka-and-tonic would give her a headache later, when she was home alone in her rambling former farmhouse with only the steady breathing of her sleeping children and Coal's restless scratching and the baleful staring of the moon to keep her stark-awake spirit company. In the West a coyote would howl in the lavender distance and even farther away a transcontinental train would pull its slithering miles of cars and these sounds would lead her spirit out of the

window and dissolve its wakefulness in the delicate
star-blanched night. Here, in the crabbed, water-
logged East, everything was so close; night-sounds
surrounded her house like a bristling thicket. Even
these women, in Sukie's cozy little cubbyhole, loomed
close, so that each dark hair of Jane's faint mustache
and the upright amber down, sensitive to static, of
Sukie's long forearms made Alexandra's eyes itch. She
was jealous of this man, that the very shadow of him
should so excite her two friends, who on other Thursdays were excited simply by her, her regally lazy powers stretching there like a cat's power to cease purring
and kill. On those Thursdays the three friends would
conjure up the spectres of Eastwick's little lives and
set them buzzing and circling in the darkening air. In
the right mood and into their third drinks they could
erect a cone of power above them like a tent to the
zenith, and know at the base of their bellies who was
sick, who was sinking into debt, who was loved, who
was frantic, who was burning, who was asleep in a
remission of life's bad luck; but this wouldn't happen
today. They were disturbed.

"Isn't that funny about his name?" Sukie was saying, staring up at the day's light ebbing from the leaded
window. She could not see through the high wobbly
lozenge panes, but in her mind's eye clearly stood her
back yard's only tree, a slender young pear tree overburdened with pears, heavy yellow suspended shapes
like costume jewels hung on a child. Each day now
was redolent of hay and ripeness, the little pale late
asters glowing by the side of the roads like litter. "They
were all saying his name last night, and I heard it
before from Marge Perley, it's on the tip of my
tongue...."

"Mine too," Jane said. "*Damn.* It has one of those
little words in it."

"De, da, du," Alexandra prompted hopelessly.

The three witches fell silent, realizing that, tongue-tied, they were themselves under a spell, of a greater.

Darryl Van Horne came to the chamber-music concert in the Unitarian Church on Sunday night, a bearish dark man with greasy curly hair half-hiding his ears and clumped at the back so that his head from the side looked like a beer mug with a monstrously thick handle. He wore gray flannels bagged at the backs of his knees somehow and an elbow-patched jacket of Harris Tweed in a curious busy pattern of green and black. A pink Oxford button-down shirt of the type fashionable in the Fifties and, on his feet, incongruously small and pointy black loafers completed the costume. He was out to make an impression.

"So you're our local sculptress," he told Alexandra at the reception afterwards, which was held in the church parlor, for the players and their friends, and centered about an unspiked punch the color of antifreeze. The church was a pretty enough little Greek Revival, with a shallow Doric-columned porch and a squat octagonal tower, on Cocumscussoc Way, off of Elm behind Oak, which the Congregationalists had put up in 1823 but which a generation later had gone under to the Unitarian tide of the 1840s. In this hazy late age of declining doctrine its interior was decorated here and there with crosses anyway, and the social parlor bore on one wall a large felt banner, concocted by the Sunday school, of the Egyptian tau cross, the hieroglyph for "life," surrounded by the four triangular alchemic signs for the elements. The category of "players and their friends" included everyone except Van Horne, who pushed into the parlor anyway. People knew who he was; it added to the excitement. When he spoke, his voice resounded in a way that did not quite go with the movements of his mouth and jaw, and this impression of an artificial element somewhere in his speech apparatus was reinforced by the strange slipping, patched-together impression his features made and by the excess of spittle he produced when he talked, so that he occasionally paused to wipe his coat sleeve roughly across the corners of his mouth. Yet he had the confidence of the cultured and well-to-do, stooping low to achieve intimacy with Alexandra.

"They're just little things," Alexandra said, feeling abruptly petite and demure, confronted by this brooding dark bulk. It was that time of the month when she was especially sensitive to auras. This thrilling stranger's was the shiny black-brown of a wet beaver pelt and stood up stiff behind his head. "My friends call them my bubbies," she said, and fought a blush. Fighting it made her feel slightly faint, in this crowd. Crowds and new men were not what she was used to.

"Little things," Van Horne echoed. "But so *potent*," he said, wiping his lips. "So full of psychic juice, you know, when you pick one up. They knocked me out. I bought all they had at, what's that place?—the Noisy Sheep—"

"The Yapping Fox," she said, "or the Hungry Sheep, two doors the other side of the little barbershop, if you ever get a haircut."

"Never if I can help it. Saps my strength. My mother used to call me Samson. But yeah, one of those. I bought all they had to show to a pal of mine, a really relaxed terrific guy who runs a gallery in New York, right there on Fifty-seventh Street. It's not for me to promise you anything, Alexandra—O.K. if I call you that?—but if you could bring yourself to create on a bigger scale, I bet we could get you a show. Maybe you'll never be Marisol but you could sure as hell be another Niki de Saint-Phalle. You know, those 'Nanas.' Now *those* have scale. I mean, she's *really* let go, she's not just futzin' around."

With some relief Alexandra decided she quite disliked this man. He was pushy, coarse, and a blabbermouth. His buying her out at the Hungry Sheep felt like a rape, and she would have to run another batch through the kiln now earlier than she had planned. The pressure his personality set up had intensified her cramps, which she had woken with that morning, days ahead of schedule; that was one of the signs of cancer, irregularities in your cycle. Also, she had brought with her from the West a regrettable trace of the regional prejudice against Indians and Chicanos, and to her eyes Darryl Van Horne didn't look *washed*. You could almost see little specks of black in his skin, as if he were a halftone reproduction. He wiped his lips with the hairy back of a hand, and his lips twitched with impatience while she searched her heart for an honest but polite response. Dealing with men was work, a chore she had become lazy at. "I don't *want* to be another Niki de Saint-Phalle," she said. "I want to be me. The potency, as you put it, comes from their being small enough to hold in the hand." Hastening blood made the capillaries in her face burn; she smiled at herself for being excited, when intellectually she had decided the man was a fraud, an apparition. Except for his money; that had to be real.

His eyes were small and watery, and looked rubbed. "Yeah, Alexandra, but what *is* you? Think small, you'll wind up small. You're not giving you a chance, with this old-giftie-shoppie mentality. I couldn't believe how little they were charging—a lousy twenty bucks, when you should be thinking five figures."

He was New York vulgar, she perceived, and felt sorry for him, landed in this subtle province. She remembered the wisp of smoke, how fragile and brave it had looked. She asked him forgivingly, "How do you like your new house? Are you pretty well settled in?"

With enthusiasm, he said, "It's hell. I work late, my ideas come to me at night, and every morning around seven-fifteen these fucking workmen show up! With their fucking radios! Pardon my Latin."

He seemed aware of his need for forgiveness; the need surrounded him, and rippled out from every clumsy, too-urgent gesture.

"You *gotta* come over and see the place," he said. "I need advice all over the lot. All my life I've lived in apartments where they decide everything for you, and the contractor I've got's an asshole."

"Joe?"

"You know him?"

"Everybody knows him," Alexandra said; this stranger should be told that insulting local people was not the way to win friends in Eastwick.

But his loose tongue and mouth tumbled on unabashed. "Little funny hat all the time?"

She had to nod, but perhaps not to smile. She sometimes hallucinated that Joe was still wearing his hat while making love to her.

"He's out to lunch every meal of the day," Van Horne said. "All he wants to talk about is how the Red Sox pitching collapsed again and how the Pats still don't have any pass defense. Not that the old guy doing the floor is any wizard either; this priceless slate, practically marble, up from Tennessee, and he lays it half with the rough side up, where you can see the marks of the quarry saw. These butchers you call workmen up here wouldn't last one day on a union

job in Manhattan. No offense, I can see you're thinking, 'What a snob,' and I guess the hicks don't get
much practice, putting up chicken coops; but no wonder it's such a weird-looking state. Hey, Alexandra,
between us: I'm crazy about that huffy frozen look
you get on your face when you get defensive and can't
think what to say. And the tip of your nose is cute."
Astonishingly, he reached out and touched it, the little
cleft tip she was sensitive about, a touch so quick and
improper she wouldn't have believed it happened but
for the chilly tingle it left.

She didn't just dislike him, she hated him; yet still
she stood there smiling, feeling trapped and faint and
wondering what her irregular insides were trying to
tell her.

Jane Smart came up to them. For the performance
she had had to spread her legs and therefore was the
only woman at the gathering in a full-length gown, a
shimmering concoction of aqua silk and lace trim perhaps a touch too bridal. "Ah, *la artiste*," Van Horne
exclaimed, and he seized her hand not in a handshake
but like a manicurist inspecting, taking her hand upon
his wide palm and then rejecting it, since it was the
left he wanted, the tendony fingering hand with its
glazed calluses where she pressed the strings. The
man made a tender sandwich of it between his own
hairy two. "What intonation," he said. "What vibrato
and stretch. Really. You think I'm an obnoxious madman but I do know music. It's the one thing makes
me humble."

Jane's dark eyes lightened, indeed glowed. "Not
prissy, you think," she said. "Our leader keeps saying
my intonation is prissy."

"What an asshole," pronounced Van Horne, wiping spit from the corners of his mouth. "You have
precision but that's not prissy necessarily; precision is

where passion begins. Without precision, *beaucoup de rien,* huh? Even your thumb, on your thumb position: you really keep that pressure on, where a lot of men crump out, it hurts too much." He pulled her left hand closer to his face and caressed the side of her thumb. "See that?" he said to Alexandra, brandishing Jane's hand as if it were detached, a dead thing to be admired. "That is one beautiful callus."

Jane tugged her hand back, feeling eyes gathering upon them. The Unitarian minister, Ed Parsley, was taking notice of the scene. Van Horne perhaps relished an audience, for he dramatically let Jane's left hand drop and seized the unguarded right, as it hung at Jane's side, to shake it in her own astonished face. "It's *this* hand," he almost shouted. "It's this hand's the fly in the ointment. Your *bow*ing. God! Your *spiccato* sounds like *marcato,* your *legato* like *détaché.* Honey, *string* those phrases together, you're not playing just notes, one after the other, biddledy um-um-um, you're playing *phrases,* you're playing human *out*cries!"

As if in silent outcry Jane's prim thin mouth dropped open and Alexandra saw tears form second lenses upon her eyes, whose brown was always a little lighter in color than you remembered, a tortoiseshell color.

Reverend Parsley joined them. He was a youngish man with a slippery air of doom about him; his face was like a handsome face distorted in a slightly warped mirror—too long from sideburn to nostril, as if perpetually being tugged forward, and the too full and expressive lips caught in the relentless smile of one who knows he is in the wrong place, on the wrong platform of the bus station in a country where no known language is spoken. Though just into his thirties, he was too old to be a window-trashing LSD-imbibing soldier in the Movement and this added to his sense of displacement and inadequacy, though he was always organizing peace marches and vigils and read-ins and proposing to his parish of dryasdust dutiful souls that they let their pretty old church become a sanctuary, with cots and hot plates and chemical toilet facilities, for the hordes of draft evaders. Instead, tasteful cultural events were sheltered here, where the acoustics were accidentally marvellous; those old builders perhaps did have secrets. But Alexandra, having been raised in the stark land mined for a thousand cowboy movies, was inclined to think that the past is often romanticized, that when it was the present it had that same curious hollowness we all feel now.

Ed looked up—he was not tall; this was another of his disappointments—at Darryl Van Horne quizzically. Then he addressed Jane Smart with a sharp shouldering-aside note in his voice: "Beautiful, Jane. Just a damn beautiful job all four of you did. As I was saying to Clyde Gabriel just now, I wish there had been a better way to advertise, to get more of the Newport crowd over here, though I know his paper did all it could, he took it that I was criticizing; he seems a lot on edge lately." Sukie was sleeping with Ed, Alexandra knew, and perhaps Jane had slept with him in the past. There was a quality men's voices had when you had slept with them, even years ago: the grain came up, like that of unpainted wood left out in the weather. Ed's aura—Alexandra couldn't stop seeing auras, it went with menstrual cramps—emanated in sickly chartreuse waves of anxiety and narcissism from his hair, which was combed away from an inflexible part and was somehow colorless without being gray. Jane was still fighting back tears and in the awkwardness Alexandra had become the introducer, this strange outsider's sponsor.

"Reverend Parsley—"

"Come on, Alexandra. We're better friends than that. The name's Ed, *please*." Sukie must talk about her a little while sleeping with him, so he felt this familiarity. Everywhere you turn people know you better than you know them; there is all this human spying. Alexandra could not make herself say "Ed," his aura of doom was so repulsive to her.

"—this is Mr. Van Horne, who's just moved into the Lenox place, you've probably heard."

"Indeed I have heard, and it's a delightful surprise to have you here, sir. Nobody had said you were a music-lover."

"In a half-ass way, you could say that. My pleasure, Reverend." They shook hands and the minister flinched.

"No 'Reverend,' please. Everybody, friend or foe, calls me Ed."

"Ed, this is a swell old building you have here. It must cost you a bundle in fire insurance."

"The Lord is our carrier," Ed Parsley joked, and his sickly aura widened in pleasure at this blasphemy. "To be serious, you can't rebuild this kind of plant, and the older members complain about all the steps. We've had people drop out of the choir because they can't make it up into the loft. Also, to my mind, an opulent building like this, with all its traditional associations, gets in the way of the message the modern-day Unitarian-Universalists are trying to bring. What I'd like to see is us open a storefront church right down there on Dock Street; that's where the young people gather, that's where business and commerce do their dirty work."

"What's dirty about it?"

"I'm sorry, I didn't catch your first name."

"Darryl."

"Darryl, I see you like to pull people's legs. You're

a man of sophistication and know as well as I do that the connection between the present atrocities in Southeast Asia and that new little drive-in branch Old Stone Bank has next to the Superette is direct and immediate; I don't need to belabor the point."

"You're right, fella, you don't," Van Horne said.

"When Mammon talks, Uncle Sam jumps."

"Amen," said Van Horne.

How nice it was, Alexandra thought, when men talked to one another. All that aggression: the clash of shirt fronts. Eavesdropping, she felt herself thrilled as when on a walk in the Cove woods she came upon traces in some sandy patch of a flurry of claws, and a feather or two, signifying a murderous encounter. Ed Parsley had sized Van Horne up as a banker type, an implementer of the System, and was fighting dismissal in the bigger man's eyes as a shrill and ineffectual liberal, the feckless agent of a nonexistent God. Ed wanted to be the agent of another System, equally fierce and far-flung. As if to torment himself he wore a clergyman's collar, in which his neck looked both babyish and scrawny; for his denomination such a collar was so unusual as to be, in its way, a protest.

"Did I hear," he said now, his voice gravelly in its insinuating sonority, "you offering a critique of Jane's cello-playing?"

"Just her bowing," Van Horne said, suddenly a bashful shambles, his jaw slipping and drooling. "I said the rest of it was great, her bowing just seemed a little choppy. Christ, you have to watch yourself around here, stepping on everybody's toes. I mentioned to sweet old Alexandra here about my plumbing contractor being none too swift and it turns out he's her best friend."

"Not best friend, just a friend," she felt obliged to intercede. The man, Alexandra saw even amid the confusions of this encounter, had the brute gift of bringing a woman out, of getting her to say more than she had intended. Here he had insulted Jane and she was gazing up at him with the moist mute fascination of a whipped dog.

"The Beethoven was especially splendid, don't you agree?" Parsley was still after Van Horne, to wring some concession out of him, the start of a pact, a basis they could meet on next time.

"Beethoven," the big man said with bored authority, "sold his soul to write those last quartets; he was stone deaf. All those nineteenth-century types sold their souls. Liszt. Paganini. What they did wasn't human."

Jane found her voice. "I practiced till my fingers bled," she said, gazing straight up at Van Horne's lips, which he had just rubbed with his sleeve. "All those terrible sixteenth-notes in the second andante."

"You keep practicing, little Jane. It's five-sixths muscle memory, as you know. When muscle memory takes over, the heart can start to sing its song. Until then, you're stymied. You're just going through the motions. Listen. Whyncha come over some time to my place and we'll fool around with a bit of old Ludwig's piano and cello stuff? That Sonata in A is an absolute honey, if you don't panic on the legato. Or that E Minor of Brahms: *fabuloso. Quel schmaltz!* I think it's still in the old fingers." He wiggled them, his fingers, at all of their faces. Van Horne's hands were eerily white-skinned beneath the hair, like tight surgical gloves.

Ed Parsley coped with his unease by turning to Alexandra and saying in sickly conspiracy, "Your friend appears to know whereof he speaks."

"Don't look at me, I just met the gentleman," Alexandra said.

"He was a child *pro*digy," Jane Smart told them, become somehow angry and defensive. Her aura, usually a rather dull mauve, had undergone a streaked orchid surge, betokening arousal, though by which man was not clear. The whole parlor to Alexandra's eyes was clouded by merged and pulsating auras, sickening as cigarette smoke. She felt dizzy, disenchanted; she longed to be home with Coal and her quietly ticking kiln and the expectant cold wet plasticity of clay in its burlap sacks hauled from Coventry. She closed her eyes and wished that this particular nexus around her—of arousal, dislike, radical insecurity, and a sinister will to dominate emanating not only from the dark stranger—would dissolve.

Several elderly parishioners were nudging forward for their share of Reverend Parsley's attention, and he turned to flatter them. The white hair of the women was touched in the caves of the curls of their perms with the tenderest golds and blues. Raymond Neff, profusely sweating and aglow with the triumph of the concert, came up to them all and, enduring in the deafness of celebrity their simultaneous compliments, jollily bore away Jane, his mistress and comrade in musical battle. She, too, had been glazed, shoulders and neck, by the exertions of the performance. Alexandra noticed this and was touched. What did Jane see in Raymond Neff? For that matter what did Sukie see in Ed Parsley? The smells of the two men when they had stood close had been, to Alexandra's nostrils, rank—whereas Joe Marino's skin had a certain sweet sourness, like the stale-milk aroma that arises from a baby's pate when you settle your cheek against its fuzzy bony warmth. Suddenly she was alone with Van Horne again, and feared she would have to bear again upon her breast the imploring inchoate weight of his conversation; but Sukie, who feared nothing, all russet and crisp and glimmering in her reportorial role, edged through the crowd and conducted an interview.

"What brings you to this concert, Mr. Van Horne?" she asked, after Alexandra had shyly performed introductions.

"My TV set's on the blink" was his sullen answer. Alexandra saw that he preferred to make the approaches himself; but there was no denying Sukie in her interrogating mood, her little pushy monkey-face bright as a new penny.

"And what has brought you to this part of the world?" was her next question.

"Seems time I got out of Gotham," he said. "Too much mugging, rent going sky-high. The price up here seemed right. This going into some paper?"

Sukie licked her lips and admitted, "I might put a mention in a column I write for the *Word* called 'Eastwick Eyes and Ears.'"

"Jesus, don't do that," the big man said, in his baggy tweed coat. "I came up here to cool the publicity."

"What kind of publicity were you receiving, may I ask?"

"If I told you, that'd be more publicity, wouldn't it?"

"Could be."

Alexandra marvelled at her friend, so cheerfully bold. Sukie's brazen ochre aura merged with the sheen of her hair. She asked, as Van Horne made as if to turn away, "People are saying you're an inventor. What sort of thing do you invent?"

"Toots, even if I took all night to explain it to ya ya wouldn't understand. It mostly deals with chemicals."

"Try me," Sukie urged. "See if I understand."

"Put it in your 'Eyes and Ears' and I might as well write a circular letter to my competition."

"Nobody who doesn't live in Eastwick reads the *Word,* I promise. Even in Eastwick nobody reads it, they just look at the ads and for their own names."

"Listen, Miss—"

"Rougemont. Ms. I was married."

"What was he, a French Canuck?"

"Monty always said his ancestors were Swiss. He acted Swiss. Don't the Swiss have square heads, supposedly?"

"Beats me. I thought that was the Manchurians. They have skulls like cement blocks, that's how Genghis Khan could stack 'em up so neatly."

"Do you feel we've wandered rather far from the subject?"

"About the inventions, listen, I can't talk. I am *watched.*"

"How exciting! For all of us," Sukie said, and she let her smile push her upper lip, creasing deliciously, up so far her nose wrinkled and a band of healthy gum showed. "How about for my eyes and ears only? And Lexa's here. Isn't she gorgeous?"

Van Horne turned his big head stiffly as if to check; Alexandra saw herself through his bloodshot blinking eyes as if at the end of a reversed telescope, a figure frighteningly small, cleft here and there and with wisps of gray hair. He decided to answer Sukie's earlier question: "I've been doing a fair amount lately with protective coatings—a floor finish you can't scratch with even a steak knife after it hardens, a coating you can spray on the red-hot steel as it's cooling so it bonds with the carbon molecules; your car body'll get metal fatigue before oxidization sets in. Synthetic polymers—that's the name of your brave new world, honeybunch, and it's just getting rolling. Bakelite was invented around 1907, synthetic rubber in 1910, nylon around 1930. Better check those dates if you use any of this. The point is, this century's just the infancy; synthetic polymers're going to be with us to the year one million or until we blow ourselves up, whichever comes sooner, and the beauty of it is, you can *grow* the raw materials, and when you run out of land you can grow 'em in the ocean. Move over, Mother Nature, we've got you beat. Also I'm working on the Big Interface."

"What interface is that?" Sukie was not ashamed to ask. Alexandra would just have nodded as if she knew; she had a lot still to learn about overcoming acculturated female recessiveness.

"The interface between solar energy and electrical energy," Van Horne told Sukie. "There *has* to be one, and once we find the combination you can run every appliance in your house right off the roof and have enough left over to recharge your electric car in the night. Clean, abundant, and *free*. It's coming, honeybunch, it's coming!"

"Those panels look so ugly," Sukie said. "There's a hippie in town who's done over an old garage so he can heat his water, I have no idea why, he never takes a bath."

"I'm not talking about collectors," Van Horne said. "That's Model T stuff." He looked about him; his head turned like a barrel being rolled on its edge. "I'm talking about a *paint*."

"A paint?" Alexandra said, feeling she should make a contribution. At least this man was giving her something new to think about, beyond tomato sauce.

"A paint," he solemnly assured her. "A simple paint you brush on with a brush and that turns the entire epidermis of your lovely home into an enormous lowvoltaic cell."

"There's only one word for that," Sukie said.

"Yeah, what's that?"

"Electrifying."

Van Horne aped being offended. "Shit, if I'd known that's the kind of flirtatious featherheaded thing you like to say I wouldn't have wasted my time spilling my guts. You play tennis?"

Sukie stood up a little taller. Alexandra experienced a wish to stroke that long flat stretch from the other woman's breasts to below her waist, the way one longs to dart out a hand and stroke the belly a cat on its back elongates in stretching, the toes of its hind paws a-tremble in this moment of muscular ecstasy. Sukie was just so nicely *made*. "A bit," she said, her tongue peeking through her smile and adhering for a moment to her upper lip.

"You gotta come over in a couple weeks or so, I'm having a court put in."

Alexandra interrupted. "You can't fill wetlands," she said.

This big stranger wiped his lips and repulsively eyed her. "Once they're filled," he said in his imperfectly synchronized, slightly slurring voice, "they're not wet."

"The snowy egrets like to nest there, in the dead elms out back."

"T, O, U, F, F," Van Horne said. "Tough."

From the sudden stariness of his eyes she wondered if he was wearing contact lenses. His conversation did seem distracted by a constant slipshod effort to keep himself together. "Oh," she said, and what Alexandra noticed now gave her, already slightly dizzy, the sensation of looking down a deep hole. His aura was gone. He had absolutely none, like a dead man or a wooden idol, above his head of greasy hair.

Sukie laughed, pealingly; her dainty round belly

pumped under the waistband of her suede skirt in sympathy with her diaphragm. "I love that. May I quote you, Mr. Van Horne? Filled Wetlands No Longer Wet, Declares Intriguing New Citizen."

Disgusted by this mating dance, Alexandra turned away. The auras of all the others at the party were blinding now, like the peripheral lights along a highway as raindrops collect on the windshield. And very stupidly she felt within herself the obscuring moisture of an unwanted infatuation condensing. The big man was a bundle of needs; he was a chasm that sucked her heart out of her chest.

Old Mrs. Lovecraft, her aura the tawdry magenta of those who are well pleased with their lives and fully expect to go to Heaven, came up to Alexandra bleating, "Sandy dear, we *miss* you at the Garden Club. You *must*n't keep so to yourself."

"*Do* I keep to myself? I *feel* busy. I've been putting up tomatoes, it's just incredible the way they kept coming this fall."

"I *know* you've been gardening; Horace and I admire your house every time we drive down Orchard Road: that *cun*ning little bed you have by your doorway, chock-a-block full of button mums. I've several times said to him, 'Let's *do* drop in,' but then I think, No, she might be making her little *things,* and we don't want to dis*turb* her inspiration."

Making her little things or love with Joe Marino, Alexandra thought: that was what Franny Lovecraft was implying. In a town like Eastwick there were no secrets, just areas of avoidance. When she and Oz were still together and new in town they had spent a number of evenings in the company of sweet old bores like the Lovecrafts; now Alexandra felt infinitely fallen from the world of decent and dreary amusements they represented.

"I'll come to some meetings this winter, when there's nothing else to do," Alexandra said, relenting. "When I'm homesick for nature," she added, though knowing she would never go, she was far beyond such tame delights. "I like the slide shows on English gardens; are you having any of them?"

"You *must* come next Thursday," Franny Lovecraft insisted, overplaying her hand as people of minor distinction—vice-presidents of savings banks, granddaughters of clipper-ship captains—will. "Daisy Robeson's son Warwick has *just* got back from three years in Iran, where he and his lovely little family had *such* a nice time, he was working as an adviser there, it somehow has all to do with oil, he says the Shah is performing *mir*acles, all this splendid modern architecture right in their capital city—oh, what *is* its name, I want to say New Delhi...."

Alexandra offered no help though she knew the name Tehran; the devil was getting into her.

"At *any* rate, Wicky is going to give a slide show on Oriental rugs. You see, Sandy dear, in the Arab mind, the rug *is* a garden, it's an indoor garden in their tents and palaces in the middle of all that desert, and there's all manner of real flowers in the design, that to casual eyes looks so abstract. Now *does*n't that sound fascinating?"

"It does," Alexandra said. Mrs. Lovecraft had adorned her wrinkled throat, collapsed upon itself in folds and gulleys like those of an eroded roadside embankment, with a strand of artificial pearls of which the centerpiece was an antique mother-of-pearl egg in which a tiny gold cross had been tediously inlaid. With an irritated psychic effort, Alexandra willed the frayed old string to break; fake pearls slipped down the old lady's sunken front and cascaded in constellations to the floor.

The floor of the church parlor was covered with industrial carpeting the dull green of goose scat; it muffled the patter of pearls. The crowd was slow to detect the disaster, and at first only those in the immediate vicinity stooped to collect them. Mrs. Lovecraft, her face blanched with shock beneath the patches of rouge, was herself too arthritic and brittle to stoop. Alexandra, while kneeling at the old lady's dropsical feet, wickedly willed the narrow strained straps of her once-fashionable lizardskin shoes to come undone. Wickedness was like food: once you got started it was hard to stop; the gut expanded to take in more and more. Alexandra straightened up and set a half-dozen retrieved pearls in her victim's trembling, blue-knuckled, greedily cupped hand. Then she backed away, through the widening circle of squatting searchers. These bodies squatting seemed grotesque giant cabbages of muscle and avidity and cloth; their auras were all confused like watercolors running together to make gray. Her way to the door was blocked by Reverend Parsley, his handsome waxy face with that Peer Gynt tweak of doom to it. Like many a man who shaves in the morning, he sported a visible stubble by nighttime.

"*Alexandra*," he began, his voice deliberately forced into its most searching, low-pitched register. "I was *so* much hoping to see you here tonight." He wanted her. He was tired of fucking Sukie. In the nervousness of his overture he reached up to scratch his quaintly combed head, and his intended victim took the opportunity to snap the cheap expansion band of his important-looking gold-plated watch, an Omega. He felt it release and grabbed the expensive accessory where it was entangled in his shirt cuff before it had time to drop. This gave Alexandra a second to slip past the smear of his startled face—a pathetic smear,

as she was to remember it guiltily; as if by sleeping
with him she could have saved him—into the open
air, the grateful black air.

The night was moonless. The crickets stridulated
their everlasting monotonous meaningful note. Car
headlights swept by on Cocumscussoc Way, and the
bushes by the church door, nearly stripped of leaves,
sprang up sharp in the illumination like the complicated mandibles and jointed feelers and legs of insects
magnified. The air smelled faintly of apples making
cider by themselves, in their own skins where these
apples fell uncollected and rotting in the neglected
orchards that backed up onto the church property,
empty land waiting for its developer. The sheltering
humped shapes of cars waited in the gravel parking
lot. Her own little Subaru figured in her mind as a
pumpkin-colored tunnel at whose far end glowed the
silence of her rustic kitchen, Coal's tail-thumping welcome, the breathing of her children as they lay asleep
or feigning in their rooms, having turned off television the instant her headlights glared at the windows.
She would check them, their bodies each in its room
and bed, and then take twenty of her baked bubbies,
cunningly stacked so that no two had touched and
married, out of the Swedish kiln, which would still be
ticking, cooling, talking to her as of the events in the
house in the time in which she had been away—for
time flowed everywhere, not just in the rivulet of the
delta in which we have been drifting. Then, duty done
to her bubbies, and to her bladder, and to her teeth,
she would enter upon the spacious queendom of her
bed, a kingdom without a king, all hers. Alexandra
was reading an endless novel by a woman with three
names and an airbrushed photograph of herself on
the shiny jacket; a few pages of its interminable woolly
adventures among cliffs and castles served each night

to smooth the border-crossing into unconsciousness. In her dreams she ranged far and wide, above the housetops, visiting rooms carved confusedly from the jumble of her past but seemingly solid as her oneiric self stood in each one, a ghost brimming with obscure mourning as she picked up an apple-shaped pin-cushion from her mother's sewing basket or waited while staring out at the snow-capped mountains for a playmate long dead to telephone. In her dreams omens cavorted around her as gaudily as papier-mâché advertisements beckoning innocents this way and that at an amusement park. Yet we never look forward to dreams, any more than to the fabled adventures that follow death.

Gravel crackled at her back. A dark man touched the soft flesh above her elbow; his touch was icy, or perhaps she was feverish. She jumped, frightened. He was chuckling. "The damnedest thing happened back in there just now. The old dame whose pearls let loose a minute ago tripped over her own shoes in her excitement and everybody's scared she broke her hip."

"How sad," Alexandra said, sincerely but absent-mindedly, her spirit drifting, her heart still thumping from the scare he gave her.

Darryl Van Horne leaned close and thrust words into her ear. "Don't forget, sweetheart. Think bigger. I'll check into that gallery. We'll be in touch. Nitey-nite."

"You actually *went*?" Alexandra asked Jane with a dull thrill of pleasure, over the phone.

"Why not?" Jane said firmly. "He really did have the music for the Brahms Sonata in E Minor, and plays amazingly. Like Liberace, only without all that smiling. You wouldn't think it; his hands don't look like they could do anything, somehow."

"You were alone? I keep picturing that perfume ad." The one which showed a young male violinist seducing his accompanist in her low-cut gown.

"Don't be vulgar, Alexandra. He feels quite asexual to me. And there are all these workmen around, including your friend Joe Marino, all dressed up in his little checked hat with a feather in it. And there's this constant rumbling from the backhoes moving boulders for the tennis court. Evidently they've had to do a lot of blasting."

"How can he get away with that, it's wetlands."

"I don't know, sweet, but he has the permit tacked up right on a tree."

"The poor egrets."

"Oh Lexa, they have all the rest of Rhode Island to nest in. What's nature for if it's not adaptable?"

"It's adaptable up to a point. Then it gets hurt feelings."

October's crinkled gold hung in her kitchen window; the big ragged leaves on her grape arbor were turning brown, from the edges in. Off to the left, toward her bog, a little stand of birches released in a shiver of wind a handful as of bright spear-points, twinkling as they fell to the lawn. "How long did you stay?"

"Oh," Jane drawled, lying. "About an hour. Maybe an hour and a half. He really *does* have some feeling for music and his manner when you're alone with him isn't as clownish as it may have seemed at the concert. He said being in a church, even a Unitarian one, gave him the creeps. I think behind all that bluffing he's really rather shy."

"Darling. You never give up, do you?"

Alexandra felt Jane Smart's lips move an inch back

from the mouthpiece in indignation. Bakelite, the first of the synthetic polymers, that man had said. Jane was saying hissingly, "I don't see it's a question of giving up or not, it's a question of doing your thing. You do your thing moping around in your garden in men's pants and then cooking up your little figurines, but to make music you *must* have people. *Oth*er people."

"They're not figurines and I don't mope around."

Jane was going on, "You and Sukie are always poking fun of my being with Ray Neff ever and yet until this other man has shown up the only music I could make in town was with Ray."

Alexandra was going on, "They're *sculp*tures, just because they're not on a big scale like a Calder or Moore, you sound as vulgar as Whatsisname did, insinuating I should do something bigger so some expensive New York gallery can take fifty percent, even if they *were* to sell, which I very much doubt. Everything now is so trendy and violent."

"Is that what he said? So he had a proposition for you too."

"I wouldn't call it a proposition, just typical New York pushiness, sticking your nose in where it doesn't belong. They all have to be in on the action, any action."

"He's fascinated by us," Jane Smart asserted. "Why we all live up here wasting our sweetness on the desert air."

"Tell him Narragansett Bay has always taken oddballs in and what's he doing up here himself?"

"I wonder." In her flat Massachusetts Bay style Jane slighted the *r*. "He almost gives the impression that things got too hot for him where he was. And he does love all the space in the big house. He owns three pianos, honestly, though one of them is an upright that he keeps in his library; he has all these beautiful old books, with leather bindings and titles in Latin."

"Did he give you anything to drink?"

"Just tea. This manservant he has, that he talks Spanish to, brought it on a huge tray with a lot of liqueurs in funny old bottles that had that air, you know, of coming out of a cellar full of cobwebs."

"I thought you said you just had tea."

"Well really, Lexa, maybe I did have a sip of black-berry cordial or something Fidel was very enthusiastic about called mescal; if I'd known I was going to have to make such a complete report I'd have written the name down. You're worse than the CIA."

"I'm sorry, Jane. I'm very jealous, I suppose. And my *peri*od. It's lasted five days now, ever since the concert, and the ovary on the left side *hurts*. Do you think it could be menopause?"

"At thirty-eight? Honey, really."

"Well then it must be cancer."

"It couldn't be cancer."

"Why couldn't it be?"

"Because you're you. You have too much magic to have cancer."

"Some days I don't feel like I have any magic. Anyway, other people have magic too." She was thinking of Gina, Joe's wife. Gina must hate her. The Italian word for witch was *strega*. All over Sicily, Joe had told her, they give each other the evil eye. "Some days my insides feel all tied in knots."

"See Doc Pat, if you're seriously worried," said Jane, not quite unsympathetically. Dr. Henry Paterson, a plump pink man their age, with wounded wide watery eyes and a beautiful gentle firm touch when he palpated. His wife had left him years ago. He had never grasped why or remarried.

"He makes me feel strange," Alexandra said. "The

way he drapes you with a sheet and does everything under that."

"The poor man, what is he supposed to do?"

"Not be so sly. I have a body. He knows it. I know it. Why do we have to pretend with this sheet?"

"They all get sued," Jane said, "if there isn't any nurse in the room." Her voice had a double to it, like a television signal when a truck goes by. This wasn't what she had called to talk about. Something else was on her mind.

"What else did you learn at Van Horne's?" Alexandra asked.

"*Well*—promise you won't tell anybody."

"Not even Sukie?"

"Es*pe*cially not Sukie. It's about her. Darryl is really rather remarkable, he picks everything up. He stayed at the reception later than we did, I went off to have a beer with the rest of the quartet at the Bronze Barrel—"

"Greta along?"

"Oh God yes. She told us all about Hitler, how her parents couldn't stand him because his German was so uncouth. Apparently on the radio he didn't always end his sentences with the verb."

"How awful for them."

"—and I guess you faded into the night after playing that dreadful trick with poor Franny Lovecraft's pearls—"

"What pearls?"

"Don't pretend, Lexa. You were naughty. I know your style. And then the shoes, she's been in bed ever since but I guess she didn't break anything; they were worried about her hip. Do you know a woman's bones shrink to about half by the time she gets old? That's why everything snaps. She was lucky: just contusions."

"I don't know, looking at her made me wonder if

I was going to be so sweet and boring and bullying when I got to be that age, if I *do* get to be, which I doubt. It was like looking into a mirror at my own dreary future, and I'm sorry, it drove me *wild.*"

"All *right,* sweetie; it's no skin off my nose. As I was trying to say, Darryl hung around to help clean up and noticed while Brenda Parsley was in the church kitchen putting the plastic cups and paper plates into the Trashmaster Ed and Sukie had both disappeared! Leaving poor Brenda to put the best face on it she could—but imagine, the humiliation!"

"They really should be more discreet."

Jane paused, waiting for Alexandra to say something more; there was a point here she was supposed to grasp and express, but her mind was off, entertaining images of cancer spreading within her like the clouds of galaxies whirling softly out into the blackness, setting a deadly star here, there....

"He's such a wimp," Jane at last supplied, lamely, of Ed. "And why is she always implying to us that she's given him up?"

Now Alexandra's mind pursued the lovers into the night, Sukie's slim body like a twig stripped of bark, but with pliant and muscular bumps; she was one of those women just this side of boyishness, of maleness, but vibrant, so close to this edge, the femininity somehow steeped in the guiltless energy men have, their lives consecrated like arrows, flying in slender storms at the enemy, taught from their cruel boyhoods onward how to die. Why don't they teach women? Because it isn't true that if you have daughters you will never die. "Maybe a clinic," she said aloud, having rejected Doc Pat, "where they don't know me."

"Well I would think *something,*" Jane said, "rather than going on tormenting yourself. And being rather boring, if I do say so."

"I think part of Ed's appeal to Sukie," Alexandra offered, trying to get back on Jane's wavelength, "may be her professional need to feel in the local swim. At any rate what's interesting is not so much her still seeing him as this Van Horne character's bothering to notice so avidly, when he's just come to town. It's flattering, I suppose we're meant to think."

"Darling Alexandra, in some ways you're still awfully unliberated. A man can be just a person too, you know."

"I know that's the theory, but I've never met one who thought he was. They all turn out to be men, even the faggots."

"Remember when we were wondering if he was one? Now he's after all of us!"

"I thought he wasn't after you, you were both after Brahms."

"We were. We are. Really, Alexandra. Relax. You *are* sounding *aw*fully crampy."

"I'm a mess. I'll be better tomorrow. It's my turn to have it, remember."

"Oh my God yes. I nearly forgot. That's the other thing I was calling about. I can't make it."

"Can't make a Thursday? What's happening?"

"Well, you'll sniff. But it's Darryl again. He has some lovely little Webern bagatelles he wants to try me on, and when I suggested Friday he said he has some roving Japanese investors coming by to look at his undercoating. I was thinking of swinging by Orchard Road this afternoon if you'd like, one of the boys wanted me to go watch him play soccer after school but I could just produce my face for a minute on the sidelines—"

"No thanks dear," Alexandra said. "I have a guest coming."

"Oh." Jane's voice was ice, dark ice with ash in it such as freezes in the winter driveway.

"Possibly," Alexandra softened it to. "He or she wasn't sure they could make it."

"Darling, I quite understand. No need to say any more."

It made Alexandra angry, to be put on the defensive, when she was the one being snubbed. She told her friend, "I thought Thursdays were sacred."

"They are, usually," Jane began.

"But I suppose in a world where nothing else is there's no reason for Thursdays to be." Why was she so hurt? Her weekly rhythm depended on the infrangible triangle, the cone of power. But she mustn't let her voice drag on, betraying her this way.

Jane was apologizing, "Just this one time—"

"It's *fine*, sweetie. All the more devilled eggs for me." Jane Smart loved devilled eggs, chalky and sharp with paprika and a pinch of dry mustard, garnished with chopped chives or an anchovy laid across each stuffed white like the tongue of a toad.

"Were you really going to the trouble of devilled eggs?" she asked plaintively.

"Of course not, dear," Alexandra said. "Just the same old soggy Saltines and stale Velveeta. I must hang up."

An hour later, gazing abstracted past the furry bare shoulder (with its touching sour-sweet smell like a baby's pate) of Joe Marino as he with more rigor than inspiration pumped away at her, while her bed groaned and swayed beneath the unaccustomed double weight, Alexandra had a vision. She saw the Lenox mansion in her mind's eye, clear as a piece of calendar art, with the one wisp of smoke that she had observed that day, its pathetic strand of vapor confused with the poignance of Jane's describing Van Horne as shy and hence clownish. Disoriented, had been more Alexandra's impression: like a man peering through a mask, or listening with wool in his ears. "Focus, for Chrissake," Joe snarled in her own ear, and came, helplessly, excited by his own anger, his bare furry body—the work-hardened muscles gone slightly punky with prosperity—heaving once, twice, and the third time, ending in a little shiver like a car with carbon build-up shuddering after the ignition has been turned off. She tried to catch up but the contact was gone.

"Sorry," he growled. "I thought we were doing great but you wandered off." He had been generous, too, in forgiving her the tag end of her period, though there was hardly any blood.

"My fault," Alexandra said. "Absolutely. You were lovely. I was lousy." *Plays amazingly*, Jane had said.

The ceiling in the wake of her vision wore a sudden clarity, as if seen for the first time: its impassive dead square stretch, certain small flaws in its surface scarcely distinguishable from the specks in the vitreous humor of her eyes, except that when she moved her focus these latter drifted like animalcules in a pond, like cancer cells in our lymph. Joe's rounded shoulder and the side of his neck were as indifferent and pale as the ceiling, and as smoothly traversed by these optical impurities, which were not usually part of her universe but when they did intrude were hard to shake, hard not to see. A sign of old age. Like snowballs rolling downhill we accumulate grit.

She felt her front, breasts and belly, swimming in Joe's sweat and by this circuitous route her mind was returning to enjoyment of his body, its spongy texture and weight and confiding male aroma and rather miraculous, in a world of minor miracles, thereness. He was usually not there. Usually he was with Gina. He rolled off Alexandra with a wounded sigh. She

had wounded his Mediterranean vanity. He was tan
and bald on top, his shiny skull somewhat rippled,
like the pages of a book we have left out in the dew,
and it was part of his vanity to put back on, first
thing, his hat. He said he felt cold without it. Hat in
place, he showed a youngish profile, with the sharply
hooked nose we see in Bellini portraits and with liverish deep dents beneath his eyes. She had been attracted to that sluggish debauched look, that hint of
the leaden-eyed *barone* or doge or Mafioso who deals
life and death with a contemptuous snick of his tongue
and teeth. But Joe, whom she had seduced when he
come to repair a toilet that murmured all night, proved
to be toothless in this sense, a devout bourgeois honest
down to the last brass washer, an infatuated father of
five children under eleven, and an in-law to half the
state. Gina's family had packed this coast from New
Bedford to Bridgeport with kin. Joe was a glutton for
loyalties; his heart belonged to more sports teams—
Celtics, Bruins, Whalers, Red Sox, Pawtucket Sox, Pats,
Teamen, Lobsters, Minutemen—than she had
dreamed existed. Once a week he came and pumped
away at her with much that same faithfulness. Adul-
tery had been a step toward damnation for him, and
he was honoring one more obligation, a satanic one.
Also, it was something of a contraceptive measure;
his fertility had begun to be frightening to him, and
the more seed of his that Alexandra with her IUD
absorbed, the less there was for Gina to work with.
The affair was in its third summer and Alexandra
should be ending it, but she liked Joe's taste—salty-
sugary, like nougat—and the way the air shimmered
about an inch above the gentle ridges of his skull. His
aura had no malice or bad color to it; his thoughts,
like his plumber's hands, were always seeking a certain

fittingness. Fate had passed her from a maker of chrome fixtures to their installer.

To see the Lenox mansion as it had been in her vision, distinct in its bricks, its granite sills and quoins and Arguslike windows, so frontally, one would have to be hovering in midair above the marsh, flying. Rapidly the vision had diminished in size, as if receding in space, beckoning her. It became the size of a postage stamp and had she not closed her eyes it might have vanished like a pea down the drain. It was when her eyes were closed that he had come. Now she felt dazed, and splayed, as if the orgasm had been partly hers.

"Maybe I should cash it in with Gina and start up fresh somewhere with you," Joe was saying.

"Don't be silly. You don't want to do anything of the kind," Alexandra told him. High unseen in the windy day above her ceiling, geese in a V straggled south, honking to reassure one another: *I'm here, you're here.* "You're a good Roman Catholic with five *bambini* and a thriving business."

"Yeah, what am I doing here then?"

"You're bewitched. It's easy. I tore your picture out of the Eastwick *Word* when you'd been to a Planning Board meeting and smeared my menstrual fluid all over it."

"Jesus, you can be disgusting."

"You like that, don't you? Gina is never disgusting. Gina is as sweet as Our Lady. If you were any kind of a gentleman you'd finish me off with your tongue. There isn't much blood, it's the tag end."

Joe grimaced. "How's about I give you a rain check on that?" he said, and looked around for clothes to put on under his hat. Though growing pudgy, his body had a neatness; he had been a schoolboy athlete, deft with every ball, though too short to star. His buttocks were taut, even if his abdomen had developed a swag. A big butterfly of fine black hair rested on his back, the top edge of its wings along his shoulders and its feet feathering into the dimples flanking the low part of his spine. "I gotta check in at that Van Horne job," he said, tucking in a pink slice of testicle that had peeped through one leghole of his elasticized shorts. They were bikini-style and tinted purple, a new thing, to go with the new androgyny. Among Joe's loyalties was one to changes of male fashion. He had been one of the first men around Eastwick to wear a denim leisure suit, and to sense that hats were making a comeback.

"How's that going, by the way?" Alexandra asked lazily, not wanting him to go. A desolation had descended to her from the ceiling.

"We're still waiting on this silver-plated faucet unit that had to be ordered from West Germany, and I had to send up to Cranston for a copper sheet big enough to fit under the tub and not have a seam. I'll be glad when it's done. There's something not right about that set-up. The guy sleeps past noon usually, and sometimes you go and there's nobody there at all, just this long-haired cat rubbing around. I hate cats."

"They're disgusting," Alexandra said. "Like me."

"No, listen, Al. You're *mia vacca. Mia vacca bianca.* You're my big plate of ice cream. What else can a poor guy say? Every attempt I make to get serious you turn me off."

"Seriousness scares me," she said seriously. "Anyway in your case I know it's just a tease."

But it was she who teased him, by making the laces of his shoes, oxblood cordovans like college men wear, come loose as fast as he tied them in bows; finally Joe had to shuffle out, defeated in his vanity and tidiness, with the laces dragging. His steps diminished on the stairs, one within the other, smaller and smaller, and the slam of the door was like the solid little nub, a mere peg of painted wood, innermost in a set of nested Russian dolls. Starling song scraped at the windows toward the yard; wild blackberries drew them to the bog by the hundreds. Abandoned and unsatisfied in the middle of a bed suddenly huge again, Alexandra tried to recapture, by staring at the blank ceiling, that strangely sharp and architectural vision of the Lenox place; but she could only produce a ghostly after-image, a rectangle of extra pallor as on an envelope so long stored in the attic that the stamp has flaked off without being touched.

Inventor Musician, Art Fancier
Busy Renovating Old Lenox Manse

BY SUZANNE ROUGEMONT

Courtly, deep-voiced, handsome in a casual, bear-ish way, Mr. Darryl Van Horne, recently of Manhat-tan and now a contented Eastwick taxpayer, welcomed your reporter to his island.

Yes, his island, for the famous "Lenox Manse" that this newcomer has purchased sits surrounded by marsh and at high tide by sheer sheets of water!

Constructed circa 1895 in a brick English style, with a symmetrical façade and massive chimneys at either end, the new proprietor hopes to convert his acqui-sition to multiple usages—as laboratory for his fab-ulous experiments with chemistry and solar energy, as a concert hall containing no less than three pianos (which he plays expertly, believe me), and as a large gallery upon whose walls hang startling works by such contemporary masters as Robert Rauschenburg, Claus Oldenberg, Bob Indiana, and James Van Dine.

An elaborate solarium-cum-greenhouse, a Japa-nese bath that will be a luxurious vision of exposed copper piping and polished teakwood, and an AsPhlex composition tennis court are all under construction as the privately owned island rings with the sound of hammer and saw and the beautiful pale herons who customarily nest in the lee of the property seek temporary refuge elsewhere.

Progress has its price!

Van Horne, though a genial host, is modest about his many enterprises and hopes to enjoy seclusion and opportunity for meditation in his new residence.

"I was attracted," he told your inquiring reporter, "to Rhode Island by the kind of space and beauty it affords, rare along the Eastern Seaboard in these troubled and overpopulated times. I feel at home here already.

"This is one heck of a spot!" he added informally, standing with your reporter on the ruins of the old Lenox dock and gazing out upon the vista of marsh, drumlin, channel, low-lying shrubland, and distant ocean horizon visible from the second floor.

The house with its vast stretches of parqueted maple floor and high ceiling bearing chandelier rosettes of molded plaster plus dentil molding along the sides felt chilly on the day of our fall visit, with much of the new "master's" equipment and furniture still in its sturdy packing cases, but he assured your reporter that the coming winter held no terrors for our resourceful host.

Van Horne plans to install a number of solar panels over the slates of the great roof and furthermore feels close to the eventual perfection of a closely guarded process that will render consumption of fossil fuels needless in the near future. Speed the day!

The grounds now abandoned to sumac, ailanthus, chokecherry and other weed trees the new proprietor envisions as a semi-tropical paradise brimming with exotic vegetation sheltered for the winter in the Lenox mansion's elaborate solarium-cum-greenhouse. The period statuary adorning the once-Versailles-like mall, now unfortunately so eroded by years of weather that many figures lack noses and hands, the proud owner plans to restore indoors, substituting Fiberglas replicas along the stately mall (well remembered in its glory by elderly citizens of this area) in the manner of the celebrated caryatids at the Parthenon in Athens, Greece.

The causeway, Van Horne said with an expansive gesture so characteristic of the man, could be improved by the addition of anchored aluminum pontoon sections at the lowest portions.

"A dock would be a lot of fun," he volunteered in a possibly humorous vein. "You could run a Hovercraft over to Newport or up to Providence."

Van Horne shares his extensive residence with no more company than an assistant-cum-butler, Mr. Fidel Malaguer, and an adorable fluffy Angora kitten whimsically yclept Thumbkin, because the animal has extra thumbs on several paws.

A man of impressive vision and warmth, your reporter welcomed the newcomer to this fabled region of South County confident that she spoke on behalf of many neighbors.

The Lenox Manse has again become a place to keep an eye on!

"You went there!" Alexandra jealously accused Sukie, over the phone, having read the article in the *Word*.

"Sweetie, it was an assignment."

"And whose idea was the assignment?"

"Mine," Sukie admitted. "Clyde wasn't sure it was news. And sometimes in cases like this when you talk about what a lovely home et cetera the person gets robbed the next week and sues the newspaper." Clyde Gabriel, a stringy weary man with a disagreeable dogooding wife, edited the *Word*. Apologetically Sukie asked, "What did you think of the piece?"

"Well, honey, it had color, but you *do* run on a bit and honestly—now don't be offended—you *must* watch your participles. They dangle all over the place."

"If it's less than five paragraphs you don't get a byline. And he got me drunk. First it was rum in the tea and then it was rum without the tea. That creepy spic kept bringing it on this enormous silver tray. I never saw such a big tray; it was like a tabletop, all engraved and chased or whatever."

"What about *him*? How did he act? Darryl Van Horne."

"Well he talked a blue streak I must say. Giving me a saliva bath half the time. It was hard to know how seriously to take some of the things—the pontoon bridge, for instance. He said the canisters if that's what they are could be painted green and would blend right in with the marsh grass. The tennis court is going to be green, even the fencing. It's almost done and he wants us all to come play while the weather isn't too bad yet."

"All of who?"

"All of *us*, you and me and Jane. He seemed very interested, and I told him a little bit, just the part everybody knows, about our divorces and finding ourselves and so on. And what a comfort especially you are. I don't find Jane all that comforting lately, I think she's looking for a husband behind our backs. And I don't mean awful Neff, either. Greta has him too socked in with those children. God, don't children get in the way? I keep having the most terrible fights with mine. They say I'm never home and I try to explain to the little shits that I'm *earn*ing a *liv*ing."

Alexandra would not be distracted from the encounter she wanted to envision, between Sukie and this Van Horne man. "You told him the dirt about us?"

"Is there dirt? I just don't let gossip get to me, Lexa, frankly. Hold your head up and keep thinking, *Fuck you:* that's how I get down Dock Street every day. No, of course I didn't. I was very discreet as always. But he did seem so curious. I think it might be you he loves."

"Well I don't love him. I hate complexions that dark. And I can't stand New York chutzpah. And his face doesn't fit his mouth, or his voice, or something."

"I found that rather appealing," Sukie said. "His clumsiness."

"What did he do clumsy, spill rum all over your lap?"

"And then lick it up, no. Just the way he lurched from one thing to another, showing me his crazy paintings—there must be a fortune on those walls—and then his lab and playing the piano a little, 'Mood Indigo,' I think it was, done to waltz time as sort of a joke. Then he went running around outdoors so one of the backhoes nearly knocked him into a pit, and wanted to know if I wanted to see the view from the cupola."

"You *did*n't go into the cupola with him! Not on your first date."

"Baby, you make me keep *say*ing, It wasn't a date, it was an as*sign*ment. No. I thought I had enough and I knew I was drunk and had this deadline." She paused. Last night there had been a high wind and this morning, Alexandra saw through her kitchen window, the birches and the grape arbor had been stripped of so many leaves that a new kind of light was in the air, that naked gray short-lived light of winter that shows us the lay of the land and how close the houses of our neighbors sit. "He *did* seem," Sukie was saying, "I don't know, almost too eager for publicity. I mean, it's just a little local paper. It's as if—"

"Go on," said Alexandra, touching the chill windowpane with her forehead as if to let her thirsty brain drink the fresh wide light.

"I just wonder if this business of his is really doing so well, or is it just whistling in the dark? If he's really making these things, shouldn't there be a factory?"

"Good questions. What sort of questions did he ask about us? Or, rather, what sort of things did you choose to tell him?"

"I don't know why you sound so huffy about it."

"I don't either. I mean, I really don't."

"I mean, I don't have to tell you any of this."

"You're right. I'm being awful. Please don't stop." Alexandra did not want her ill humor to close the window on the outside world that Sukie's gossip gave her.

"Oh," Sukie answered tantalizingly. "How cozy we are. How much we've discovered we prefer women to men, and so on."

"Did that offend him?"

"No, he said he preferred women to men too. They were much the superior mechanism."

"He said 'mechanism.'"

"Some word like that. Listen, angel, I must run, honest. I'm supposed to be interviewing the committee heads about the Harvest Festival."

"Which church?"

In the pause, Alexandra shut her eyes and saw an iridescent zigzag, as if a diamond on an unseen hand were etching darkness in electric parallel with Sukie's darting thoughts. "You know, the Unitarian. All the others think it's too pagan."

"May I ask, how are you feeling toward Ed Parsley these days?"

"Oh, the usual. Benign but distant. Brenda is *such* an impossible prig."

"What is she being impossibly priggish about, does he say?"

A certain reserve concerning sexual specifics obtained among the witches, but Sukie, by way of making up, moved against this constraint and broke into confession: "She doesn't do *any*thing for him, Lexa. And before he went to divinity school he knocked about quite a bit, so he knows what he's missing. He keeps wanting to run away and join the Movement."

"He's too old. He's over thirty. The Movement doesn't want him."

"He *knows* that. He de*spis*es himself. I *can't* be rejecting to him every time, he's too pa*thet*ic," Sukie cried out in protest.

Healing belonged to their natures, and if the world accused them of coming between men and wives, of tying the disruptive ligature, of knotting the *aiguillette* that places the kink of impotence or emotional coldness in the entrails of a marriage seemingly secure in its snugly roofed and darkened house, and if the world not merely accused but burned them alive in the tongues of indignant opinion, that was the price they must pay. It was fundamental and instinctive, it was womanly, to want to heal—to apply the poultice of acquiescent flesh to the wound of a man's desire, to give his closeted spirit the exaltation of seeing a witch slip out of her clothes and go skyclad in a room of tawdry motel furniture. Alexandra released Sukie with no more implied rebuke of the younger woman's continuing to minister to Ed Parsley.

In the silence of her house, childless for two more hours, Alexandra battled depression, moving beneath its weight like a fish sluggish and misshapen at the bottom of the sea. She felt suffocated by her uselessness and the containing uselessness of this house, a mid-nineteenth-century farmhouse with musty small rooms and a smell of linoleum. She thought of eating, to cheer herself up. All things, even giant sea slugs, feed; feeding is their essence and teeth and hoofs and wings have all evolved from the millions of years of small bloody struggles. She made herself a sandwich of sliced turkey breast and lettuce on diet whole-wheat bread, all hauled from the Bay Superette this morning, with Comet and Calgonite and this week's issue of the *Word*. The many laborious steps lunch involved nearly overwhelmed her—taking the meat from the refrigerator and undoing its taped jacket of butcher paper, locating the mayonnaise on the shelf where it hid amid jars of jelly and salad oil, clawing loose from the head of lettuce its clinging crinkling skin of plastic wrap, arranging these ingredients on the counter with a plate, getting a knife from the drawer to spread the mayonnaise, finding a fork to fish a long spear of pickle from the squat jar where seeds clouded a thin green juice, and then making herself coffee to wash the taste of turkey and pickle away. Every time she returned to its place in the drawer the little plastic dip that measured the coffee grounds into the percolator, a few more grains of coffee accumulated there, in the cracks, out of reach: if she lived forever these grains would become a mountain, a range of dark brown Alps. All around her in this home was an inexorable silting of dirt: beneath the beds, behind the books, between the spines of the radiators. She put away all the ingredients and equipment her hunger had called forth. She went through some motions of housekeeping. Why was there nothing to sleep in but beds that had to be remade, nothing to eat from but dishes that had to be washed? Inca women had had it no worse. She was indeed as Van Horne had said a mechanism, a robot cruelly conscious of every chronic motion.

She had been a cherished daughter, in that high

western town, with its main street like a wide and dusty
football field, the drugstore and the tack shop and
the Woolworth's and the barbershop scattered over
the space like creosote bushes that poison the earth
around them. She had been the life of her family, a
marvel of amusing grace flanked by dull brothers,
boys yoked to the clattering cart of maleness, their
lives one team after another. Her father, returning
from his trips selling Levi's, had looked upon the
growing Alexandra as upon a plant that grew in little
leaps, displaying new petals and shoots at each re-
union. As she grew, little Sandy stole health and power
from her fading mother, as she had once sucked milk
from her breasts. She rode horses and broke her
hymen. She learned to ride on the long saddle-shaped
seats of motorcycles, clinging so tightly her cheek took
the imprint of the studs on the back of the boy's jacket.
Her mother died and her father sent her east to college; her high-school guidance counselor had fastened on something with the safe-sounding name of
Connecticut College for Women. There in New London, as field-hockey captain and fine-arts major, she
moved through the many brisk costumes of the East's
four picture-postcard seasons and in the June of her
junior year found herself one day all in white and the
next with the many uniforms of wife lined up limp
in her wardrobe. She had met Oz on a sailing day on
Long Island that others had arranged; holding drink
after drink steady in a fragile plastic glass, he had
seemed neither sick nor alarmed, when she had been
both, and this had impressed her. Ozzie had delighted
in her too—her full figure and her western, mannish
way of walking. The wind shifted, the sail flapped,
the boat yawed, his grin flashed reassuringly in the
sun-scorched gin-fed pink of his face; he had a one-
sided sheepish smile a little like her father's. It was a

fall into his arms, but by such fallings she dimly understood life to rise, from strength to strength. She shouldered motherhood, the garden club, car pools, and cocktail parties. She shared morning coffee with the cleaning lady and midnight cognac with her husband, mistaking drunken lust for reconciliation. Around her the world was growing—child after child leaped from between her legs, they built an addition onto the house, Oz's raises kept pace with inflation—and somehow she was feeding the world but no longer fed by it. Her depressions grew worse. Her doctor prescribed Tofranil, her psychotherapist analysis, her clergyman *Either/Or*. She and Oz lived at that time, in Norwich, within sound of church bells and as winter afternoon darkened and before school returned her children to her Alexandra would lie in her bed beaten flatter by every stroke, feeling as shapeless and ill-smelling as an old galosh or the pelt of a squirrel killed days before on the highway. As a girl she would lie on the bed in their innocent mountain town excited by her body, a visitor of sorts who had come out of nowhere to enclose her spirit; she had studied herself in the mirror, saw the cleft in her chin and the curious dent at the end of her nose, stood back to appraise the sloping wide shoulders and gourdlike breasts and the belly like a shallow inverted bowl glowing above the demure triangular bush and solid oval thighs, and decided to be friends with her body; she could have been dealt a worse. Lying on the bed, she would marvel at her own ankle, turning it in the window light— the taut glimmer of its bones and sinews, the veins of palest blue with their magical traffic of oxygen—or stroke her own forearms, downy and plump and tapered. Then in mid-marriage her own body disgusted her, and Ozzie's attempts to make love to it seemed an unkind gibe. It was the body outside, beyond the windows, that light-struck, water-riddled, foliate flesh of that other self the world to which beauty still clung; when divorce came it was as if she had flown through that window. The morning after the decree, she was up at four, pulling up dead pea plants and singing by moonlight, singing by the light of that hard white stone with the tilted sad unisex face—a celestial presence, and dawn in the east the gray of a cat. This other body too had a spirit.

Now the world poured through her, wasted, down the drain. A woman is a hole, Alexandra had once read in the memoirs of a prostitute. In truth it felt less like being a hole than being a sponge, a heavy squishy thing on this bed soaking out of the air all the futility and misery there is: wars nobody wins, diseases conquered so we can all die of cancer. Her children would be clamoring home, so awkward and needy, plucking, clinging, looking to her for nurture, and they would find not a mother but only a frightened fat child no longer cute, no longer amazing to a father whose ashes two years ago had been scattered from a crop-duster over his favorite mountain meadow, where the family used to go gathering wildflowers— alpine phlox and sky pilot with its skunky-smelling leaves, monkshood and shooting stars and avalanche lily that blooms in the moist places left as the snow line retreats. Her father had carried a flower guide; little Sandra would bring him fresh-plucked offerings to name, delicate blooms with shy pale petals and stems chilly, it seemed to the child, from being out all night in the mountainous cold.

The chintz curtains that Alexandra and Mavis Jessup, the decorator divorcee from the Yapping Fox, had hung at the bedroom windows bore a big splashy pattern of pink and white peonies. The folds of the draperies as they hung produced out of this pattern a distinct clown's face, an evil pink-and-white clown's face with a little slit of a mouth: the more Alexandra looked, the more such sinister clowns' faces there were, a chorus of them amid the superimpositions of the peonies. They were devils. They encouraged her depression. She thought of her little bubbies waiting to be conjured out of the clay and they were images of her—sodden, amorphous. A drink, a pill, might uplift and glaze her, but she knew the price: she would feel worse two hours later. Her wandering thoughts were drawn as if by the glamorous shuttle and syncopated clatter of machinery toward the old Lenox place and its resident, that dark prince who had taken her two sisters in as if in calculated insult to her. Even in his insult and vileness there was something to push against and give her spirit exercise. She yearned for rain, the relief of its stir beyond the blankness of the ceiling, but when she turned her eyes to the window, there was no change in the cruelly brilliant weather outside. The maple against her window coated the panes with gold, the last flare of outlived leaves. Alexandra lay on her bed helpless, weighed down by all the incessant uselessness there is in the world.

Good Coal came in to her, scenting her sorrow. His lustrous long body, glittering in its loose sack of dog-skin, loped across the oval rug of braided rags and heaved without effort up onto her swaying bed. He licked her face in worry, and her hands, and nuzzled where for comfort she had loosened the waist of her dirt-hardened Levi's. She tugged up her blouse to expose more of her milk-white belly and he found the supernumerary pap there, a hand's-breadth from her navel, a small pink rubbery bud that had appeared a few years ago and that Doc Pat had assured her was benign and not cancerous. He had offered to remove it but she was frightened of the knife. The pap had no feeling, but the flesh around it tingled while Coal nuzzled and lapped as at a teat. The dog's body radiated warmth and a faint perfume of carrion. Earth has in her all these shades of decay and excrement and Alexandra found them not offensive but in their way handsome, decomposition's deep-woven plaid.

Abruptly Coal was exhausted by his suckling. He collapsed into the curve her grief-drugged body made on the bed. The big dog, sleeping, snored with a noise like moisture in a straw. Alexandra stared at the ceiling, waiting for something to happen. The watery skins of her eyes felt hot, and dry as cactus skins. Her pupils were two black thorns turned inwards.

Sukie turned in her story of the Harvest Festival ("Rummage Sale, Duck-the-Clown / Part of Unitarian Plans") to Clyde Gabriel in his narrow office and discovered him, disconcertingly, slumped at his desk with his head in his arms. He heard the sheets of her copy rustle in his wire basket and looked up. His eyes were red-rimmed but whether from crying or sleep or hangover or last night's sleeplessness she could not tell. She knew from rumor that he not only was a drinker but owned a telescope he would sometimes sit at for hours on his back porch, examining the stars. His oak-pale hair, thin on top, was mussed; he had puffy blue welts below his eyes and the rest of his face was faintly gray like newsprint. "Sorry," she said, "I thought you'd want to pop this in."

Without much raising his head off the desk he squinted at her pages. "Pop, schnop," he said, embarrassed by being found slumped over. "This item doesn't deserve a two-line head. How about 'Peacenik Parson Plans Poppycock'?"

"I didn't talk to Ed; it was his committee chairpersons."

"Oops, pardon me. I forgot you think Parsley's a great man."

"That isn't altogether what I think," Sukie said, standing extra erect. These unhappy or unlucky men it was her fate to be attracted to were not above pulling you down with them if you allowed it and didn't stand tall. His nasty sardonic side, which made some others of the staff cringe and which had soured his reputation around town, Sukie saw as a masked apology, a plea turned upside down. At a point earlier in his life he must have been beautiful with promise, but his handsomeness—high square forehead, broad could-be passionate mouth, and eyes a most delicate icy blue and framed by starry long lashes—was caving in; he was getting that dried-out starving look of the persistent drinker.

Clyde was a little over fifty. On the pegboard wall behind his desk, along with a sampler of headline sizes and some framed citations awarded to the *Word* under earlier managements, he had hung photographs of his daughter and son but none of his wife, though he was not divorced. The daughter, pretty in an innocent, moon-faced way, was an unmarried X-ray technician at Michael Reese Hospital in Chicago, on her way perhaps to becoming what Monty would have laughingly called a "lady doctor." The Gabriel son, a college dropout interested in theatre, had spent the summer on the fringes of summer stock in Connecticut, and had his father's pale eyes and the pouty good looks of an archaic Greek statue. Felicia Gabriel, the wife left off the wall, must have been a perky bright handful once but had developed into a sharp-featured little woman who could not stop talking. She was in this day and age outraged by everything: by the government and by the protesters, by the war, by the drugs, by dirty songs played on WPRO, by *Playboy*'s being sold openly at the local drugstores, by the lethargic town government and its crowd of down-town loafers, by the summer people scandalous in both costume and deed, by nothing's being quite as it would be if she were running everything. "Felicia was just on the phone," Clyde volunteered, in oblique apology for the sad posture in which Sukie had found him, "furious about this Van Horne man's violation of the wetlands regulations. Also she says your story about him was altogether too flattering; she says she's heard rumors about his past in New York that are pretty unsavory."

"Who'd she hear them from?"

"She won't say. She's protecting her sources. Maybe she got the poop straight from J. Edgar Hoover." Such antiwifely irony added little animation to his face, he had been ironical at Felicia's expense so often before. Something had died behind those long-lashed eyes. The two adult children pictured on his wall had his ghostliness, Sukie had often thought: the daughter's round features like an empty outline in their perfec-tion and the boy also eerily passive, with his fleshy lips and curly hair and silvery long face. This color-lessness in Clyde's instance was stained by the brown aromas of morning whiskey and cigarette tobacco and a strange caustic whiff the back of his neck gave off. Sukie had never slept with Clyde. But she had this mothering sense that she could give him health. He seemed to be sinking, clutching his steel desk like an overturned rowboat.

"You look exhausted," she was forward enough to tell him.

"I am. Suzanne, I really am. Felicia gets on the phone every night to one or another of her causes and leaves me to drink too much. I used to go use the telescope but I really need a stronger power, it barely brings the rings of Saturn in."

"Take her to the movies," Sukie suggested.

"I did, some perfectly harmless thing with Barbra Streisand—God, what a voice that woman has, it goes through you like a knife!—and she got so sore at the violence in one of the previews she went back and spent half the movie complaining to the manager. Then she came back for the last half and got sore because she thought they showed too much of Streisand's tits when she bent over, in one of these turn-of-the-century gowns. I mean, this wasn't even a PG movie, it was a G! It was all people singing on old trolley cars!" Clyde tried to laugh but his lips had lost the habit and the resultant crimped hole in his face was pathetic to look at. Sukie had an impulse to peel up her cocoa-brown wool sweater and unfasten her bra and give this dying man her perky breasts to suck; but she already had Ed Parsley in her life and one wry intelligent sufferer at a time was enough. Every night she was shrinking Ed Parsley in her mind, so that when the call came she could travel sufficiently lightened across the flooded marsh to Darryl Van Horne's island. That's where the action was, not here in town, where oil-streaked harbor water lapped the pilings and placed a shudder of reflected light upon the haggard faces of the citizens of Eastwick as they plodded through their civic and Christian duties.

Still, Sukie's nipples had gone erect beneath her sweater in awareness of her healing powers, of being for any man a garden stocked with antidotes and palliatives. Her areolas tingled, as when once babies needed her milk or as when she and Jane and Lexa raised the cone of power and a chilly thrill, a kind of alarm going off, moved through her bones, even her finger and toe bones, as if they were slender pipes conveying streams of icy water. Clyde Gabriel bent his head to a piece of editing; touchingly, his colorless scalp showed between the long loose strands of oak-pale hair, an angle he never saw.

Sukie left the *Word* offices and stepped out onto Dock Street and walked to Nemo's for lunch; the perspective of sidewalks and glaring shopfronts pulled tight as a drawstring around her upright figure. The masts of sailboats moored beyond the pilings like a forest of slender varnished trees had thinned. At the south end of the street, at Landing Square, the huge old beeches around the little granite war memorial formed a fragile towering wall of yellow, losing leaves to every zephyr. The water as it turned toward winter cold became a steelier blue, against which the white clapboards of houses on the Bay side of the street looked dazzlingly chalky, every nail hole vivid. *Such beauty!* Sukie thought, and felt frightened that her own beauty and vitality would not always be part of it, that some day she would be gone like a lost odd-shaped piece from the center of a picture puzzle.

Jane Smart was practicing Bach's Second Suite for unaccompanied cello, in D Minor, the little black sixteenth-notes of the prelude going up and down and then up again with the sharps and flats like a man slightly raising his voice in conversation, old Bach setting his infallible tonal suspense engine in operation again, and abruptly Jane began to resent it, these notes, so black and certain and masculine, the fingering getting trickier with each sliding transposition of the theme and he not caring, this dead square-faced old Lutheran with his wig and his Lord and his genius and two wives and seventeen children, not caring how the tips of her fingers hurt, or how her obedient spirit was pushed back and forth, up and down, by these military notes just to give him a voice after death, a bully's immortality; abruptly she rebelled, put down the bow, poured herself a little dry vermouth, and went to the phone. Sukie would be back from work by now, throwing some peanut butter and jelly at her poor children before heading out to the evening's idiotic civic meeting.

"We *must* do something about getting Alexandra over to Darryl's place" was the burden of Jane's call. "I swung by late Wednesday even though she had told me not to because she seemed so hurt about our Thursday not working out, she has gotten much too dependent on Thursdays, and she looked just terribly down, *sick* with jealousy, first me and the Brahms and then your article, I must say your prose did somehow rub it in, and I couldn't get her to say a word about it and I didn't dare press the topic myself, why she hasn't been invited."

"But darling, she *has* been, as much as you and I were. When he was showing me his art works for the article he even pulled out an expensive-looking catalogue for a show this Niki Whatever had had in Paris and said he was saving it for Lexa to see."

"Well she won't go now until she's formally asked and I can tell it's eating the poor thing alive. I thought maybe you could say something."

"Sweetie, why me? You're the one who knows him better, you're over there all the time now with all this music."

"I've been there twice," Jane said, hissing the last word most positively. "You just have that way about you, you can get away with saying things to a man. I'm too definite somehow; it would come out as meaning too much."

"I'm not sure he even liked the article," Sukie fended. "He never called me about it."

"Why wouldn't he have liked it? It was lovely, and made him seem very romantic and dashing and impressive. Marge Perley has it up on her bulletin board and tells all her prospective clients that this was her sale."

At Sukie's end of the line a crying female child came up to her; her older brother, this child managed to explain between sobs while Jane's voice crackled on like static, wouldn't let her watch an educational special about lions mating instead of a rerun of *Hogan's Heroes* on a UHF channel that *he* wanted to see. Peanut butter and jelly flecked this little girl's lips; her fine hair was an uncombed tangle. Sukie wanted to slap the repulsive child's dirty face and knock a little sense into those TV-glazed eyes. Greed, that was all TV taught, turning our minds to total pap. Darryl Van Horne had explained to her how TV was responsible for all the riots and war resistance; the commercial interruptions and the constant switching back and forth between channels had broken down in young people's brains the synapses that make logical connections, so that Make Love Not War seemed to them an actual idea.

"I'll think about it," she promised Jane hastily, and hung up. She had to go out to an emergency session of the Highway Department; last February's unexpected blizzards had used up all this year's snow-removal and road-salting budget and the chairman, Ike Arsenault, was threatening to resign. Sukie hoped to be able to leave early for a tryst with Ed Parsley at Point Judith. First she had to settle the squabble in the TV den. The children had their own set upstairs but to be perverse preferred to use hers; the noise filled the tiny house, and their glasses of milk and cocoa cups left rings on the sea chest refinished as a coffee table, and she would find bread crusts turning green between the love-seat cushions. She flounced in a fury and assigned the rudest brat to put the supper dishes into the dishwasher. "And be sure to rinse the peanut-butter knife, rinse and *wipe* it; if you just throw it in the heat bakes the peanut butter so you can *never* get it off." Before leaving the kitchen Sukie chopped up an Alpo can of blood-colored horsemeat and set it on the floor, in the plastic dog dish a child with a Magic Marker had lettered HANK, for the ravenous Weimaraner to gobble. She crammed half a fistful of salted Spanish peanuts into her own mouth; bits of red skin stuck to her sumptuous lips.

She went upstairs. To get to Sukie's bedroom, you went up the narrow stair and turned left into a narrow slanted hall of unadorned boards and then right, through an authentic eighteenth-century door studded in a double X pattern of squarish cut nails. She shut this door and with a wrought-iron latch shaped like a claw locked herself in. The room was papered in an old pattern of vines growing straight up like bean plants on poles, and the cobwebbed ceiling sagged like the underside of a hammock. Large washers bolted at the worst cracks kept the plaster from falling down. A single geranium was dying on the sill of the room's one small window. Sukie slept in a sway-backed double bed that wore a threadbare coverlet of dotted Swiss. She had remembered there was a copy of last week's *Word* by her bedside; with a pair of curved nail scissors she carefully cut out her "Inventor, Musician, Art Fancier" article, breathing warmly upon it as her nearsighted eyes strained not to include a single adjacent letter of any item that did not concern Darryl Van Horne. This done, she wrapped the article face inwards around a heavy-hipped, tiny-footed naked bubby Alexandra had given Sukie for her thirtieth birthday two years ago but which for the purposes of magic

would represent the creatrix herself. With a special
string Sukie kept in a narrow cupboard beside the
walled-in fireplace, a furry pale green jute such as
gardeners used to tie up plants and whose properties
included therefore that of encouraging growth, she
tightly wound the package around until not a glint of
the crackling print-filled paper showed. She tied it
with a bow, then another, and a third, for magic. The
fetish weighed pleasantly in the hand, a phallic oblong
with the texture of a closely woven basket. Uncertain
what the proper spell might be, she touched it lightly
to her forehead, her two breasts, her navel that was
a single link in the infinite chain of women, and, lifting
her skirt but keeping her underpants on, her pu-
dendum. For good measure she gave the thing a kiss.
"Have fun, you two," she said, and, remembering a
word of her schoolgirl Latin, chanted in a whisper,
"*Copula, copula, copula.*" Then she kneeled and put
this hairy green charm underneath her bed, where
she spotted about a dozen dust mice and a pair of lost
pantyhose she was in too much of a hurry to retrieve.
Already her nipples had stiffened, foreseeing Ed
Parsley, his dark parked car, the sweeping accusatory
beam of the Point Judith lighthouse, the crummy dank
motel room he would have already paid eighteen dollars for, and the storms of his guilt she would have
to endure once he was sexually satisfied.

On this afternoon of cold low silver sky Alexandra
thought East Beach might be too windy and raw so
she stopped the Subaru on a shoulder of the beach
road not far from the Lenox causeway. Here was a
wide stretch of marsh, the grass now bleached and
pressed flat in patches by the action of the tides, where
Coal could have a run. Between the speckled boulders
that were the causeway's huge bones the sea deposited

dead gulls and empty crab shells the dog loved to sniff and rummage among. Here also stood what was left of an entrance gate: two brick pillars capped by cement bowls of fruit and holding the rusting pivot pins for an iron gate that had vanished. While she stood gazing in the direction of the glowering symmetrical house, its owner pulled up behind her silently in his Mercedes. The car was an off-white that looked dirty; one front fender had been dented and the other repaired and repainted in an ivory that did not quite match. Alexandra was wearing a red bandanna against the wind, so when she turned she saw her face in the smiling dark man's eye as a startled oval, framed in red against the silver streaks over the sea, her hair covered like a nun's.

His car window had slid smoothly down on a motor. "You've come at last," he called, less with that prying clownish edge of the post-concert party than as a simple factual declaration by a busy man. His seamed face grinned. Beside him on the front seat sat a shadowy conical shape—a collie, but one in whose tricolor hair the black was unusually dominant. This creature yapped mercilessly when loyal Coal rallied from his far-ranging carrion-sniffing to his mistress's side.

She gripped her pet's collar to restrain him as he bristled and gagged, and lifted her voice to make it heard above the dogs' din. "I was just parking here, I wasn't..." Her voice came out frailer and younger than her own; she had been caught.

"I know, I know," Van Horne said impatiently. "Come on over anyway and have a drink. You haven't had your tour yet."

"I have to get back in a minute. The children will be coming home from school." But even as she said it Alexandra was dragging Coal, suspicious and resist-

ing, toward her car. His run wasn't over, he wanted
to say.

"Better hop in my jalopy with me," the man shouted.
"The tide's coming in and you don't want to get
stranded."

I don't? she wondered, obeying like an automaton,
betraying her best friend by shutting Coal alone in
the Subaru. He had expected her to join him and
drive home. She cranked the driver's window down
an inch, for air, and punched the locks on the doors.
The dog's black face rumpled with incredulity. His
ears were thrust out as far from his skull as their
crimped inner folds would bear their floppy weight.
These velvety pink folds she had often fondled by the
fireside, examining them for ticks. She turned away.
"Really just a minute," she stammered to Van Horne,
torn, awkward, years fallen from her with their poise
and powers.

The collie, whom Sukie's article had not mentioned, shed all ferocity and slunk gracefully into the
back seat as she opened the Mercedes door. The car's
interior was red leather; the front seats had been
dressed in sheep hides, woolly side up. With an expensive punky sound the door closed at her side.

"Say howdy-do, Needlenose," Van Horne said,
twisting his big head, like an ill-fitting helmet, toward
the back seat. The dog did indeed have a very pointed
nose, which he pushed into Alexandra's palm when
she offered it. Pointed, moist, and shocking—the tip
of an icicle. She pulled her hand back quickly.

"The tide won't be in for hours," she said, trying
to return her voice to its womanly register. The causeway was dry and full of potholes. His renovations had
not extended this far.

"The bastard can fool you," he said. "How the hell've
you been, anyway? You look depressed."

"I do? How can you tell?"

"I can tell. Some people find fall depressing, others hate spring. I've always been a spring person myself. All that growth, you can feel Nature groaning, the old bitch; she doesn't want to do it, not again, no, anything but *that,* but she *has* to. It's a fucking torture rack, all that budding and pushing, the sap up the tree trunks, the weeds and the insects getting set to fight it out once again, the seeds trying to remember how the hell the DNA is supposed to go, all that competition for a little bit of nitrogen; Christ, it's cruel. Maybe I'm too sensitive. I bet you revel in it. Women aren't that sensitive to things like that."

She nodded, hypnotized by the bumpy road diminishing under her, growing at her back. Brick pillars twin to those at the far end stood at the entrance to the island, and these still had their gate, its iron wings flung wide for years and the rusted scrolls become a lattice for wild grapevines and poison ivy and even interpenetrated by young trees, swamp maples, their little leaves turning the tenderest red, almost a rose. One of the pillars had lost its crown of mock fruit.

"Women take pain in their stride pretty much," Van Horne was going on. "Me, I can't stand it. I can't even bring myself to swat a housefly. The poor thing'll be dead in a couple days anyway."

Alexandra shuddered, remembering houseflies landing on her lips as she slept, their feathery tiny feet, the electric touch of their energy, like touching a frayed cord while ironing. "I like May," she admitted lamely. "Except every year it does feel, as you say, more of an effort. For gardeners, anyway."

Joe Marino's green truck, to her relief, was not parked anywhere out front of the mansion. The heavy work on the tennis court seemed to have been done; instead of the golden earthmovers Sukie had described, a few shirtless young men were with dainty pinging noises fastening wide swatches of green plastic-coated fencing to upright metal posts all around what at the distance, as she looked down from a curve of the driveway to where the snowy egrets used to nest in the dead elms, seemed a big playing card in two flat colors imitating grass and earth; the grid of white lines looked sharp with signification, as compulsively precise as a Wiccan diagram. Van Horne had stopped the car so she could admire. "I looked into that HarTrue and even if you see your way past the initial expense the maintenance of any kind of clay is one hell of a headache. With this AsPhlex composition all you need do is sweep the leaves off it now and then and with any luck you can play right into December. Couple of days more it'll be ready to baptize; my thought was with you and your two buddies we might have a foursome."

"My goodness, are we up to such an honor? I'm really in no shape—" she began, meaning her game. Ozzie and she for a time had played a lot of doubles with other couples, but in the years since, though Sukie once or twice a summer got her out for some Saturday singles on the battered public courts toward Southwick, she had really played hardly at all.

"Then *get* in shape," Van Horne said, misunderstanding, spitting in his enthusiasm. "Move around, get rid of that flub. Hell, thirty-eight is *young*."

He knows my age, Alexandra thought, more relieved than offended. It was nice to have yourself known by a man; it was getting to be known that was embarrassing: all that self-conscious verbalization over too many drinks, and then the bodies revealed with the hidden marks and sags like disappointing presents at Christmastime. But how much of love, when you thought about it, was not of the other but of yourself naked in his eyes: of that rush, that little flight, of shedding your clothes, and being you at last. With this overbearing strange man she felt known, essentially, already. His being awful rather helped.

He put the car into motion and coasted around the crackling driveway circle and halted at the front door. Two steps led up to a paved, pillared porch holding in tesserae of green marble the inlaid initial *L*. The door itself, freshly painted black, was so massive Alexandra feared it would pull its hinges loose when the owner swung it open. Inside the foyer, a sulphurous chemical smell greeted her; Van Horne seemed oblivious of it, it was his element. He ushered her in, past a stuffed hollow elephant foot full of knobbed and curved canes and one umbrella. He was not wearing baggy tweed today but a dark three-piece suit as if he had been somewhere on business. He gestured right and left with excited stiff arms that returned to his sides like collapsed levers. "Lab's over there, past the pianos, used to be the ballroom, nothing in there but a ton of equipment half of it still in crates, we've hardly begun to roll yet, but when we do, boy, we're going to make dynamite look like firecrackers. Here on the other side, let's call it the study, half my books still in cartons in the basement, some of the old sets I don't want to put out in the light till I can get an air-control unit set up, these old bindings, you know, and even the threads hold 'em together turn into dust like mummies when you lift the lid . . . cute room, though, isn't it? The antlers were here, and the heads. I'm no hunter myself, get up at four in the morning go out and blast some big-eyed doe never did anybody any harm in the world in the face with a shotgun, crazy. People are crazy. People are really wicked, you have to believe it. Here's the dining room. The table's mahogany, six leaves if I want to give a banquet, myself

I prefer dinners on the intimate side, four, six people, give everybody a chance to shine, strut their stuff. You invite a mob and mob psychology takes over, a few leaders and a lot of sheep. I have some super candelabra still packed, eighteenth-century, expert I know says positively from the workshop of Robert Joseph Auguste though it doesn't have the hallmark, the French were never into hallmarks like the English, the de*tail* on it you wouldn't believe, imitation grape-vines down to the tiniest little curlicue tendril, you can even see a little bug or two on 'em, you can even see where insects chewed the leaves, everything done two-thirds scale; I hate to get it up here in plain view until I have a foolproof burglar alarm installed, though burglars generally don't like to tackle a place like this, only one way in and out, they like to have an escape hatch. Not that that's any insurance policy, they're getting bolder, the drugs make the bastards desper-ate, the drugs and the general breakdown in respect for any damn thing at all; I've heard of people gone for only half an hour and cleaned out, they keep track of your routines, your every move, you're watched, that's one thing you can be sure of in this society, baby: you are *watched*."

Of Alexandra's responses to this outpouring she had no consciousness: polite noises, no doubt, as she held herself a distance behind him in fear of being accidentally struck as the big man wheeled and ges-tured. She was aware of, beyond his excited dark shape as he lavishly bragged, a certain penetrating bareness: a shabbiness of empty corners and rugless scratched floors, of ceilings whose cracks and buckled patches had gone untouched for decades, of woodwork whose once-white paint had yellowed and chipped and of elegant hand-printed panoramic wallpapers drooping loose in the corners and along the dried-out seams;

vanished paintings and mirrors were remembered by
rectangular and oval ghosts of lesser discoloration.
For all his talk of glories still to be unpacked, the
rooms were badly underfurnished; Van Horne had
the robust instincts of a creator but with only, it seemed,
half the needed raw materials. Alexandra found this
touching and saw in him something of herself, her
monumental statues that could be held in the hand.

"*Now*," he announced, booming as if to drown out
these thoughts in her head, "here's the room I wanted
you to see. *La chambre de résistance.*" It was a long living
room, with a portentous fireplace pillared like the
façade of a temple—leafy Ionic pillars carved to support a mantel above which a great bevelled mirror
gave back the room a speckled version of its lordly
space. She looked at her own image and removed the
bandanna, shaking down her hair, not fixed in a braid
today but with a sticky twistiness still in it. As her voice
had come out of her startled mouth younger than she
was, so she looked younger in this antique, forgiving
mirror. It was slightly tipped; she looked up into it,
pleased that the flesh beneath her chin did not show.
In the bathroom mirror at home she looked terrible,
a hag with cracked lips and a dented nose and with
broken veins in her septum, and when, driving in the
Subaru, she stole a peek at herself in the rearview
mirror, she looked worse yet, corpselike in color, the
eyes quite wild and a single stray lash laid like a beetle
leg across one lower lid. As a tiny girl Alexandra had
imagined that behind every mirror a different person
waited to peek back out, a different soul. Like so much
of what we fear as a child, it turned out to be in a
sense true.

Van Horne had put around the fireplace some boxy
modern stuffed chairs and a curved four-cushioned
sofa, refugees from a New York apartment obviously,

and well worn; but the room was mostly furnished with works of art, including several that took up floor space. A giant hamburger of violently colored, semi-inflated vinyl. A white plaster woman at a real ironing board, with an actual dead cat from a taxidermist's rubbing at her ankles. A vertical stack of Brillo cartons that close inspection revealed to be not airy stamped cardboard but meticulously silk-screened sheets mounted on great cubes of something substantial and immovable. A neon rainbow, unplugged and needing a dusting.

The man slapped an especially ugly assemblage, a naked woman on her back with legs spread; she had been concocted of chicken wire, flattened beer cans, an old porcelain chamber pot for her belly, pieces of chrome car bumper, items of underwear stiffened with lacquer and glue. Her face, staring straight up at the sky or ceiling, was that of a plaster doll such as Alexandra used to play with, with china-blue eyes and cherubic pink cheeks, cut off and fixed to a block of wood that had been crayoned to represent hair. "Here's the genius of the bunch for my money," Van Horne said, wiping the corners of his mouth dry with a two-finger pinching motion. "Kienholz. A Marisol with guts. You know, the tactility; there's nothing monot-onous or pre-ordained about it. That's the kind of thing *you* should be setting your sights toward. The richness, the *Vielfältigkeit*, the, you know, the ambi-guity. No offense, friend Lexa, but you're a Johnny-one-note with those little poppets of yours."

"They're not poppets, and this statue is rude, a joke against women," she said languidly, feeling splayed and out of focus, in tune with the moment—a gliding sensation, the world passing through her or she mov-ing the world, a cosmic confusion such as when the train silently tugs away from the station and it seems the platform is sliding backwards. "My little bubbies aren't jokes, they're meant affectionately." Yet her hand wandered on the assemblage and found there the glossy yet resistant texture of life. On the walls of this long room, once perhaps hung with Lenox family portraits from eighteenth-century Newport, there now hung or protruded or dangled gaudy travesties of the ordinary—giant pay telephones in limp canvas, American flags duplicated in impasto, oversize dollar bills rendered with deadpan fidelity, plaster eyeglasses with not eyes but parted lips behind the lenses, relentless enlargements of our comic strips and advertising insignia, our movie stars and bottle caps, our candies and newspapers and traffic signs. All that we wish to use and discard with scarcely a glance was here held up bloated and bright: permanized garbage. Van Horne gloated, snorted, and repeatedly wiped his lips as he led Alexandra through his collection, down one wall and back the other; and in truth she saw that he had acquired of this mocking art specimens of good quality. He had money and needed a woman to help him spend it. Across his dark vest curved the gold chain of an antique watch fob; he was an inheritor, though ill at ease with his inheritance. A wife could put him at ease.

The tea with rum came, but formed a more sedate ceremony than she had imagined from Sukie's description. Fidel materialized with that ideal silence of servants, a tidy scar placed so flatteringly beneath one cheekbone it seemed appliquéd to his mocha skin, a deliberate fillip to his small slanting features. The long-haired cat called Thumbkin, with the deformed paws mentioned in the *Word*, leaped onto Alexandra's lap just as she lifted her cup to sip; its liquid content scarcely swayed. The horizon of sea visible through the Palladian windows from where she sat stayed level also: the world was in part a gently shuffled deck of horizontal liquids, it occurred to her, thinking of the cold dense stratum of the sea where only giant eyeless slugs moved beneath the pressure, and then of mist licking the autumnal surface of a woodland pond, and of the spheres of ever-thinner gas that our astronauts pierce without puncturing, so the sky's blue does not leak away. She felt at peace here, which she had not expected, here in these rooms virtually empty but for their overload of sardonic art, rooms eloquent of a bachelor's lacks. Her host seemed pleasanter too. The manner of a man who wants to sleep with you is slicing and aggressive, testing, foreshadowing his eventual anger if he succeeds, and there seemed little of that in Van Horne's manner today. He looked tired, slumped in his tatty boxy armchair covered in a mushroom-colored corduroy. She fantasized that the business appointment for which he had put on his solemn three-piece suit had been a disappointment, perhaps a petition for a bank loan that had been refused. With plain need he poured extra rum into his tea from the bottle of Mount Gay his butler had set at his elbow, on a Queen Anne piecrust table. "How did you come to acquire such a large and wonderful collection?" Alexandra asked him.

"My investment adviser" was his disappointing answer. "Smartest thing financially you can ever do except strike oil in your back yard is buy a name artist before he has the name. Think of those two Russkis who picked up all that Picasso and Matisse cheap in Paris just before the war and now it sits over there in Leningrad where nobody can lay their eyes on it. Think of the lucky fools who took an early Pollock off his hands for the price of a bottle of Scotch. Even hit or miss you'll average out better than the stock market.

One Jasper Johns makes up for an awful lot of junk. Anyway, I love the junk."

"I see you do," Alexandra said, trying to help him. How could she ever rouse this heavy rambling man to fall in love with her? He was like a house with too many rooms, and the rooms with too many doors.

He did lurch forward in his chair, spilling tea. He had done it so often, evidently, that by reflex he spread his legs and the tan liquid flipped between them to the carpet. "Greatest thing about Orientals," he said. "They don't show your sins." With the sole of one little pointy black shoe—his feet were almost monstrously small for his bulk—he rubbed the tea stain in. "I *hated*," he volunteered, "that abstract stuff they were trying to sell us in the Fifties; Christ, it all reminded me of Eisenhower, a big blah. I want art to *show* me something, to tell me where I'm at, even if it's Hell, right?"

"I guess so. I'm really very dilettantish," Alexandra said, less comfortable now that he did seem to be rousing. What underwear had she put on? When had she last had a bath?

"So when this Pop came along, I thought, Jesus, this is the stuff for me. So fucking cheerful, you know—going down but going down with a smile. Like the late Romans in a way. 'Djou ever read Petronius? *Fun*ny. Funny, God, you can look at that goat Rauschenberg put in the rubber tire and laugh until sundown. I was in this gallery years ago on Fifty-seventh Street—that's where I'd like to see you, as I guess I've been saying to the point where it's boring—and the dealer, this faggot called Mischa, they used to call him Mischa the Muff, hell of a knowledgeable guy though, showed me these two beer cans by Johns—Ballantine ale, actually—in bronze, but painted up so sweet, with that ever-so-exact but slightly free way Johns has, and one with a triangle in the top where a beer opener had been and the other virgin, unopened. Mischa says to me, 'Pick that one up.' 'Which one?' I say. 'Any one,' he says. I pick up the virgin one. It's heavy. 'Pick up the other one,' he says. 'Really?' I ask. 'Go ahead,' he says. I do. It's lighter! The beer had been drunk!! In terms of the art, that is. I nearly came in my pants, that was such a turn-on when I saw the light."

He had sensed that Alexandra did not mind his talking dirty. She in fact rather liked it; it had a secret sweetness, like the scent of carrion on Coal's coat. She must go. Her dog's big heart would break in that little locked car.

"I asked him what the price was for these beer cans and Mischa told me and I said, 'No way.' There are limits. How much cash can you tie up in two fake beer cans? Alexandra, no kidding, if I'd taken the plunge I would have quintupled my money by now, and that wasn't so many years ago. Those cans are worth more than their weight in pure gold. I honestly believe, when future ages look back on us, when you and I are just a pair of skeletons lying in those idiotic expensive boxes they make you buy, our hair and bones and fingernails pillowed on all this ridiculous satin these fat-cat funeral directors rip you off for, Jesus I'm getting carried away, they can just take my *corpus* and dump it on the dump would suit me fine, when you and I are dead is all I mean to say, those beer cans, ale cans I should be saying, are going to be our Mona Lisa. We were talking about Kienholz; you know there's this entire sawed-off Dodge car he did, with a couple inside fucking. The car sits on a mat of artificial turf and a little ways away from it he put a little other patch of Astroturf or whatever he used, about the size of a checkerboard, with a single empty beer bottle on it! To show they'd been drinking and chucked it out.

To give the lovers' lane ambience. That's genius. The little extra piece of mat, the apartness. Somebody else would have just put the beer bottle on the main mat. But having it separate is what makes it art. Maybe *that's* our Mona Lisa, that empty of Kienholz's. I mean, I was out there in L.A. looking at this crazy sawed-off Dodge and tears came to my eyes. I'm not shitting you, Sandy. Tears." And he held his unnaturally white, waxy-looking hands in front of his eyes as if to pluck these watery reddish orbs from his skull.

"You travel," she said.

"Less than I used to. I'm just as glad. You go everywhere but it's always you unpacks the bag. Same bag, same you. You girls up here have the right idea. Find a Nowheresville and make your own space. All the junk comes after you anyway, with the TV and the global village and all." He slumped in his mushroom chair, empty at last of phrases. Needlenose trotted into the room and curled at his master's feet, tucking his long nose under his tail.

"Speaking of travel," Alexandra said. "I must run. I locked my poor doggie in the car, and my children will be home from school by now." She set down her teacup—monogrammed with *N*, strangely, instead of any of Van Horne's initials—on his scratched and chipped Mies van der Rohe glass table and stood to her height. She was wearing her brocaded Algerian jacket over a silver-gray cotton turtleneck, with her slacks of forest-green serge. A pang of relief at her waist as she stood reminded her of how uncomfortably tight these slacks had become. She had vowed to lose weight; but winter was the worst time for it, one nibbled to keep warm, to keep the early dark at bay, and anyway in this bulky man's eyes, turned upwards appraising the jut of her breasts, she read no demand to change her shape. Joe called her in their privacy his cow, his woman-and-a-half. Ozzie used to say she was better at night than two more blankets. Sukie and Jane called her gorgeous. She brushed from the serge tightly covering her pelvis several long white hairs Thumbkin had deposited there. She retrieved her bandanna with a scarlet flick from the arm of the curved sofa.

"But you haven't seen the lab!" Van Horne protested. "Or the hot-tub room, we *fin*ally got the mother finished, all but some accessory wiring. Or the upstairs. My big Rauschenberg lithographs are all upstairs."

"Perhaps there will be another time," Alexandra said, her voice quite settled now into her womanly contralto. She was enjoying leaving. Seeing him frantic, she was confident again of her powers.

"You ought at least to see my bedroom," Van Horne pleaded, leaping up and barking his shin on a corner of the glass table so that pain slipped his features awry. "It's all in black, even the sheets," he told her; "it's damn hard to buy good black sheets, what they call black is really navy blue. And in the hall I've just got some very subtly raunchy oils by a newish painter called John Wesley, no relation to the crazy Methodist, he does what look like illustrations to children's animal books until you realize what they're showing. Squirrels fucking and stuff like that."

"Sounds fun," Alexandra said, and moved briskly in a wide arc, an old hockey-player's move, so the chair blocked him for a moment and he could only loudly follow as she sailed out of the room with its ugly art, on through the library, past the music room, into the hall with the elephant's foot, where the rotten-egg smell was strongest but the breath of the out-of-doors could be scented too. The black door had been left its natural two-toned oak on this side.

Fidel had appeared from nowhere to position himself with a hand on the great brass latch. To Alexandra he seemed to be looking past her face toward his master; they were going to trap her here. In her fantasy she would count to five and start to scream; but there must have been a nod, for the latch clicked on the count of three.

Van Horne said behind her, "I'd offer to give you a ride back to the road but the tide may be up too far." He sounded out of breath: emphysema from too many cigarettes or inhaling those Manhattan bus fumes. He did need a wife's care.

"But you promised it wouldn't be!"

"Listen, what the hell do I know? I'm more of a stranger here than you are. Let's walk down and have a gander."

Whereas the driveway curved around, the grass mall, lined with limestone statues the weather and vandals had robbed of hands and noses, led directly down to where the causeway met the edge of the island. An untidy shore of weeds—seaside goldenrod, beach clotbur with its huge loose leaves—and gravel and a rubble of old asphalt paving spread behind the vine-entangled gate. The weeds trembled in a chill wind off the flooded marsh. The sky had lowered its bacon stripes of gray; the most luminous thing in sight was a great egret, not a snowy, loitering in the direction of the beach road, its yellow bill close to the color of her abandoned Subaru. Between here and there a tarnished glare of water had overswept the causeway. The scratch of tears arose in Alexandra's throat. "How *could* this have happened, we haven't been an hour!"

"When you're having fun..." he murmured.

"It wasn't *that* much fun! I can't get back!"

"Listen," Van Horne said close to her ear, and lightly closed his fingers on her upper arm, so she just felt his touch through the cloth. "Come on back and phone your kids and we'll have Fidel whip up a light supper. He does a terrific chili."

"It's not the *kids*, it's the *dog*," she cried. "Coal will be frantic. How deep is it?"

"I don't know. A foot, maybe two toward the middle. I could try to splash through with the car but get stuck out there it's bye-bye to a lot of fine old German machinery. Get saltwater in your brakes and differential, a car never drives the same. Like having your cherry popped."

"I'll wade," Alexandra said, and shook her arm free of his fingers, but not before, as if he had read her mind, he gave her a sharp quick pinch.

"Your pants'll get soaked," he said. "That water's brutal this time of year."

"I'll take my slacks off," she said, leaning on him to pull off her sneakers and socks. The spot where he had pinched her burned but she refused to acknowledge this presumptuous injury. After he had seemed so boyish and befuddled, spilling his tea and confiding his love of art. He was in truth a monster. Gravel prodded her bare feet. If she was going to do this she mustn't hesitate. "Here goes," she said. "Don't look."

She undid the side zipper of her slacks and pushed down at the waistband and her thighs joined the egret for brightness in this scene of rust and gray. Afraid she might topple on the unsteady stones, she bent over and pushed the shiny green serge past her pink ankles and blue-veined feet, and stepped out. Startled air lapped her naked legs. She made a bundle of sneakers and slacks and walked away from Van Horne down the causeway. Not looking back, she felt his eyes on her, her heavy thighs, their vulnerable ripple and jiggle. No doubt he had been watching with his hot tired eyes when she bent over. Alexandra had forgotten what underpants she had put on this morning and was relieved, glancing down, to discover them a plain beige, not ridiculously flowered or indecently cut like most you had to buy in the stores these days, designed for slim young hippies or groupies, half your ass hanging out behind and the crotch narrow as a rope. The air, endlessly tall, was cool on her skin. She enjoyed her own nakedness usually, especially in the open, taking a sunbath after lunch in her back yard on a blanket those first warm days of April and May before the bugs come. And under the full moon, gathering herbs skyclad.

So little used these years since the Lenoxes left, the causeway had grown grassy; barefoot she trod the center mane like the top of a soft broad wall. Color had drained from its wands of *Spartina patens* and the stretches of marsh on either side had turned sere. Where water first overcrept the surface of the road the matted grass gently swung in the transparent inches. The tide, infiltrating, made chuckling, hissing noises. Behind her, Darryl Van Horne was shouting something, encouragement or warning or apology, but Alexandra was too intent on the shock of her toes' first immersion to hear. How serious, how stark, the cold of this water was! Another element, where her blood was an alien. Brown pebbles stared up at her refracted and meaninglessly vivid, like the letters of an alphabet one doesn't know. The marsh grass had become seaweed, indolent and adrift, streaming leftwards with the rising water. Her own feet looked small, refracted like the pebbles. She must wade through quickly, while still numb. The tide covered her ankles now, and the distance to dry road was great, farther than she could have thrown a pebble. A dozen more shocking strides, and the water was up to her knees, and she could feel the sideways suck of its mindless flow. The coldest thing about this pull was that it would be here whether she was or not. It had been here before she was born and would be here when she was dead. She did not think it could knock her down, but she felt herself leaning against its force. And her ankles had begun to cry out, the numbness eaten through, the ache unendurable except that it must be endured.

Alexandra could no longer see her own feet, and the nodding tips of marsh grass no longer kept her company. She began to try to run, splashing; the splashing drowned out the sound of her host still shouting gibberish at her back. The intensity of her gaze enlarged the Subaru. She could see Coal's hopeful silhouette in the driver's seat, his ears lifted as high as they would go as he sensed rescue approaching. The icy pull came high on her thighs and her underpants were getting splashed. Foolish, so foolish, so vain and falsely girlish, she deserved this for leaving her only friend, her true and uncomplicated friend. Dogs perch on the edge of understanding, their bright eyes polished by the yearning to comprehend; an hour no worse than a minute to them, they live in a world without time, without accusation, without acceptance because there was no foresight. The water with its deathgrip rose to her crotch; a noise was forced from her throat. She was close enough to alarm the egret, who with a halt uncertain motion, like that of an old man tentatively reaching to brace himself on the arms of his chair, beat the air with the inverted W of his wings and rose, dragging his black stick feet behind him. Him? Her? Turning her own head with its bedraggled hair, Alexandra did see in the opposite direction, toward the ashen sand-hills of the beach, another white hole in the day's gray, another great egret, this one's mate though acres separated them under this dirty striped sky.

At the first bird's lift-off, the murderous clamps of the ocean had loosened a little on her thighs, sliding down as she waded on upwards, breathless, weeping with the shock and comedy of it, to the dry stretch of causeway that led to her car. Where the tide had been deepest there had been a kind of exultation, and now this ebbed. Alexandra shivered like a dog and laughed at her own folly, in seeking love, in getting stranded. The spirit needs folly as the body needs food; she felt healthier for this. Visions of herself as drowned, tinted greenish and locked stiff in the twist of last agony like those two embracing women in that amazing painting *Undertow* by Winslow Homer, had not come true. Drying, her feet hurt as if stung by a hundred wasps.

Manners demanded that she turn and wave in derisive flirtatious triumph toward Van Horne. He, a little black Y between the brick uprights of his crumbling gate, waved back with both arms held straight out. He applauded, beating his hands together to make a noise that arrived across the intervening plane of water a fraction of a second delayed. He shouted something of which she only heard the words "You *can* fly!" She dried her beaded, goosebumped legs with the red bandanna and pulled herself into her slacks while Coal woofed and pounded his tail on the vinyl within the Subaru. His happiness was infectious. She smiled to herself, wondering whom she should call first to tell about this, Sukie or Jane. At last she too had been initiated. Where he had pinched, her upper arm still burned.

The little trees, the sapling sugar maples and the baby red oaks squatting close to the ground, were the first to turn, as if green were a feat of strength, and the smallest weaken first. Early in October the Virginia creeper had suddenly drenched in alizarin crimson the tumbled boulder wall at the back of her property, where the bog began; the drooping parallel daggers of the sumac then showed a red suffused with orange. Like the slow sound of a great gong, yellow overspread the woods, from the tan of beech and ash to the hickory's spotty gold and the flat butter color of the mitten-shaped leaves of the sassafras, mittens that can have a thumb or two or none. Alexandra had often noticed how adjacent trees of the same species, sprung from two seeds spinning down together the same windy day, yet have leaves notched in different rhythms, and one turns as if bleached, from dull to duller, while the other looks as if each leaf were hand-painted by a Fauvist in clashing patches of red and green. The ferns underfoot in fading declared an extravagant variety of forms. Each cried out, *I am, I was.* There was thus in fall a rebirth of identity out of summer's mob of verdure. The breadth of the event, from the beach plums and bayberries along Block Island Sound to the sycamores and horse-chestnut trees lining the venerable streets (Benefit, Benevolent) on Providence's College Hill, answered to something diffuse and gentle within Alexandra, her sense of merge, her passive ability to contemplate a tree and feel herself a rigid trunk with many arms running to their tips with sap, to become the oblong cloud oddly alone in the sky or the toad hopping from the mower's path into deeper damper grass—a wobbly bubble on leathery long legs, a spark of fear behind a warty broad forehead. She was that toad, and as well the cruel battered black blades attached to the motor's poisonous explosions. The panoramic ebb of chlorophyll from the swamps and hills of the Ocean State lifted Alexandra up like smoke, like the eye above a

map. Even the exotic imports of the Newport rich—
the English walnut, the Chinese smoke tree, the *Acer
japonicum*—were swept into this mass movement of
surrender. A natural principle was being demonstrated, that of divestment. We must lighten ourselves
to survive. We must not cling. Safety lies in lessening,
in becoming random and thin enough for the new to
enter. Only folly dares those leaps that give life. This
dark man on his island was possibility. He was the
new, the magnetic, and she relived their stilted teatime
together moment by moment, as a geologist lovingly
pulverizes a rock.

Some shapely young maples with the sun behind
them became blazing torches, a skeleton of shadow
within an incandescent halo. The gray of naked
branches more and more tinged the woods beside the
roads. The sullen conical evergreens lorded where
other substance had dissolved. October did its work
of undoing day by day and came to its last day still
fair, fair enough for outdoor tennis.

Jane Smart in her pristine whites tossed up the
tennis ball. It became in midair a bat, its wings circled
in small circumference at first and, next instant,
snapped open like an umbrella as the creature flicked
away with its pink blind face. Jane shrieked, dropped
her racket, and called across the net, "That was not
funny." The other witches laughed, and Van Horne,
who was their fourth, belatedly, halfheartedly enjoyed
the joke. He had powerful, educated strokes but did
seem to have trouble seeing the ball, in the slant late-
afternoon sun that beamed in rays through the sheltering stand of larches here at the back end of his
island; the larches were dropping their needles and
these had to be swept from the court. Jane's own eyes
were excellent, preternaturally sharp. Bats' faces

looked to her like flattened miniature versions of
children pressing their noses against a candy-store
window, and Van Horne, who played incongruously dressed in basketball sneakers and a Malcolm X
T-shirt and the trousers of an old dark suit, had something of this same childish greed on his bewildered,
glassy-eyed face. He coveted their wombs, was Jane's
belief. She prepared to toss and serve again, but even
as she weighed the ball in her hand it took on a liquid
heft and a squirming wartiness. Another transformation had been wrought. With a theatrical sigh of
patience, she set the toad down on the blood-red composition surface over by the bright green fence and
watched it wriggle through. Van Horne's feeble-
minded and wrynecked collie, Needlenose, raced
around the outside of the fence to inspect; but he lost
the toad in the tumble of earth and blasted rocks the
bulldozers had left here.

"Once more and I quit," Jane called across the net.
She and Alexandra had been pitted against Sukie and
their host. "The three of you can play Canadian doubles," she threatened. With the bespectacled gesturing
face on Van Horne's T-shirt it seemed there were five
of them present anyway. The next tennis ball in her
hand went through some rapid textural changes, first
slimy like a gizzard then prickly like a sea urchin, but
she resolutely refused to look at it, to cede it that
reality, and when it appeared against the blue sky
above her head it was a fuzzy yellow Wilson, which,
following instruction books she had read, she imagined as a clockface to be struck at two o'clock. She
brought the strings smartly through this phantom and
felt from the surge of follow-through that the serve
would be good. The ball kicked toward Sukie's throat
and she awkwardly defended her breasts with the
racket held in the backhand position. As if the strings

had become noodles, the ball plopped at her feet and
rolled to the sideline.

"Super," Alexandra muttered to Jane. Jane knew
her partner loved, in different erotic keys, both their
opponents, and their partnering, which Sukie had
arranged at the outset of the match with a suspect
twirl of her racket, must give Alexandra some jealous
pain. The other two were a mesmerizing team, Sukie
with her coppery hair tied in a bouncing ponytail and
her slender freckled limbs swinging from a little peach
tennis dress, and Van Horne with his machinelike
swiftness, animated as when playing the piano by a
kind of demon. His effectiveness was only limited by
moments of dim-sighted uncoördination in which he
missed the ball entirely. Also, his demon tended to
play at a constant *forte* that sent some of his shots,
when a subtle chop into a vacant space would have
won the point, skimming out just past the base line.

As Jane prepared to serve to him, Sukie called gaily,
"Foot fault!" Jane looked down to see not her sneaker
toe across the line but the line itself, though a painted
one, across the front of her sneaker and holding it
fast like a bear trap. She shook off the illusion and
served to Darryl Van Horne, who returned the ball
with a sharp forehand that Alexandra alertly poached,
directing the ball at Sukie's feet; Sukie managed to
scoop it on the short hop into a lob that Jane, having
come to the net at her partner's adroit and aggressive
poach, just reached in time to turn it into another lob,
which Van Horne, eyes flashing fire, set himself to
smash with a grunting overhead and which he would
have smashed, had not a magical small sparkling storm,
what they call in many parts of the world a dust devil,
arisen and caused him to snap a sheltering right hand
to his brow with a curse. He was left-handed and wore
contact lenses. The ball remained suspended at the

level of his waist while he blinked away the pain; then he stroked it with a forehand so firm the orb changed color from optical yellow to a chameleon green that Jane could hardly see against the background of green court and green fence. She swung where she sensed the ball to be and the contact felt sweet; Sukie had to scramble to make a weak return, which Alexandra volleyed down into the opponents' forecourt so vehemently it bounced impossibly high, higher than the setting sun. But Van Horne skittered back quicker than a crab underwater and tossed his metal racket toward the stratosphere, slowly twirling, silvery. The disembodied racket returned the ball without power but within the base lines, and the point continued, the players interlacing, round and round, now clockwise, now widdershins, the music of it all enthralling, Jane Smart felt: the counterpoint of their four bodies, eight eyes, and sixteen extended limbs scored upon the now nearly horizontal bars of sunset red filtered through the larches, whose falling needles pattered like distant applause. When the rally and with it the match was at last over, Sukie complained, "My racket kept feeling dead."

"You should use catgut instead of nylon," Alexandra suggested benignly, her side having won.

"It felt absolutely leaden; I kept having shooting pains in my forearm trying to lift it. Which one of you hussies was doing that? Absolutely no fair."

Van Horne also pleaded in defeat. "Damn contact lenses," he said. "Get even a speck of dust behind them it's like a fucking razor blade."

"It was lovely tennis," Jane pronounced with finality. Often she was cast, it seemed to her, in this role of peacemaking parent, of maiden aunt devoid of passion, when in fact she was seething.

The end of Daylight Savings Time had been

declared and darkness came swiftly as they filed up
the path to the many lit windows of the house. Inside,
the three women sat in a row on the curved sofa in
Van Horne's long, art-filled, yet somehow barren living room, drinking the potions he brought them. Their
host was a master of exotic drinks, drinks alchemically
concocted of tequila and grenadine and crème de cas-
sis and Triple Sec and Seltzer water and cranberry
juice and apple brandy and additives even more
arcane, all kept in a tall seventeenth-century Dutch
cabinet topped by two startled angel's heads, their
faces split, right through the blank eyeballs, by the
aging of the wood. The sea seen through his Palladian
windows was turning the color of wine, of dogwood
leaves before they fall. Between the Ionic pillars of
his fireplace, beneath the ponderous mantel, stretched
a ceramic frieze of fauns and nymphs, naked figures
white on blue. Fidel brought hors d'oeuvres, pastes
and dips of crushed sea creatures, *empanadillas, cala-
mares en su tinta* that were consumed with squeals of
disgust, with fingers that turned the same muddy sepia
as the blood of these succulent baby squids. Now and
then one of the witches would exclaim that she *must*
do something about the children, either go home to
make their suppers or at least phone the house to put
the oldest daughter officially in charge. Tonight was
already deranged: it was the night of trick-or-treat,
and some of the children would be at parties and
others out begging on the shadowy crooked streets of
downtown Eastwick. Toddling in rustling groups along
the fences and hedges would be little pirates and Cin-
derellas wearing masks with fixed grimaces and live
moist eyes darting in papery eyeholes; there would
be ghosts in pillow cases carrying shopping bags rattling with M & M's and Hershey Kisses. Doorbells
would be constantly ringing. A few days ago Alex-

andra had gone shopping with her baby, little Linda, in the Woolworth's at the mall, the lights of this trashy place brave against the darkness outside, the elderly overweight clerks weary amid their child-tempting gimcracks at the end of the day, and for a moment Alexandra had felt the old magic, seeing through this nine-year-old child's wide gaze the symbolic majesty of the cut-rate spectres, the authenticity of the packaged goblin—mask, costume, and plastic trick-or-treat sack all for $3.98. America teaches its children that every passion can be transmuted into an occasion to buy. Alexandra in a moment of empathy became her own child wandering aisles whose purchasable wonders were at eye level and scented each with its own potent essence of ink or rubber or sugary dough. But such motherly moments came to her ever more rarely as she took possession of her own self, a demigoddess greater and sterner than any of the uses others might have for her. Sukie next to her on the sofa arched her back inward, stretching in her scant peach dress so that her white frilled panties showed, and said with a yawn, "I really should go home. The poor darlings. That house right in the middle of town, it must be besieged."

Van Horne was sitting opposite her in his corduroy armchair; he had been perspiring glowingly and had put on an Irish knit sweater, of natural wool still smelling oilily of sheep, over the stencilled image of gesticulating, buck-toothed Malcolm X. "Don't go, my friend," he said. "Stay and have a bath. That's what I'm going to do. I stink."

"Bath?" Sukie said. "I can take one at home."

"Not in an eight-foot teak hot tub you can't," the man said, twisting his big head with such violent roguishness that bushy Thumbkin, alarmed, jumped off his lap. "While we're all having a good long soak

Fidel can cook up some paella or tamales or something."

"Tamale and tamale and tamale," Jane Smart said compulsively. She was sitting on the end of the sofa, beyond Sukie, and her profile had an angry precision, Alexandra thought. The smallest of them physically, she got the most drunk, trying to keep up. Jane sensed she was being thought about; her hot eyes locked onto Alexandra's. "What about you, Lexa? What's your thought?"

"Well," was the drifting answer, "I *do* feel dirty, and I ache. Three sets is too much for this old lady."

"You'll feel like a million after this experience," Van Horne assured her. "Tell you what," he said to Sukie. "Run on home, check on your brats, and come back here soon as you can."

"Swing by my house and check on mine too, could you sweetie?" in chimed Jane Smart.

"Well I'll see," Sukie said, stretching again. Her long freckled legs displayed at their tips dainty sneakerless feet in little tasselled Peds like lucky rabbit's-feet. "I may not be back at all. Clyde was hoping I could do a little Halloween color piece—just go downtown, interview a couple trick-or-treaters on Oak Street, ask at the police station if there's been any destruction of property, maybe get some of the old-timers hanging around Nemo's to talking about the bad old days when they used to soap windows and put buggies on the roof and things."

Van Horne exploded. "Why're you always mothering that sad-ass Clyde Gabriel? He scares me. The guy is sick."

"That's why," Sukie said, very quickly.

Alexandra perceived that Sukie and Ed Parsley were at last breaking up.

Van Horne picked up on it too. "Maybe I should invite him over here some time."

Sukie stood and pushed her hair back from her face haughtily. She said, "Don't do it on my account, I see him all day at work." There was no telling, from the way she snatched up her racket and flung her fawn sweater around her neck, whether she would return or not. They all heard her car, a pale gray Corvair convertible with front-wheel drive and her ex-husband's vanity plate ROUGE still on the back, start up and spin out and crackle away down the drive. The tide was low tonight, low under a full moon, so low ancient anchors and rotten dory ribs jutted into starlight where saltwater covered them for all but a few hours of each month.

Sukie's departure left the three remaining more comfortable with themselves, at ease in their relatively imperfect skins. Still in their sweaty tennis clothes, their fingers dyed by squid ink, their throats and stomachs invigorated by the peppery sauces of Fidel's tamales and enchiladas, they walked with fresh drinks into the music room, where the two musicians showed Alexandra how far they had proceeded with the Brahms E Minor. How the man's ten fingers did thunder on the helpless keys! As if he were playing with hands more than human, stronger, and wide as hay rakes, and never fumbling, folding trills and arpeggios into the rhythm, gobbling them up. Only his softer passages lacked something of expressiveness, as if there were no notch in his system low enough for the tender touch necessary. Dear stubby Jane, brows knitted, struggled to keep up, her face turning paler and paler as concentration drained it, the pain in her bowing arm evident, her other hand scuttling up and down, pressing the strings as if they were too hot to pause upon. It was Alexandra's motherly duty to

applaud when the tense and tumultuous performance
was over.

"It's not my cello, of course," Jane explained,
unsticking black hair from her brow.

"Just an old Strad I had lying around," Van Horne
joked and then, seeing that Alexandra would believe
him—for there was coming to be in her lovelorn state
nothing she did not believe within his powers and
possessions—amended this to: "Actually, it's a Ceruti.
He was Cremona too, but later. Still, an O.K. old
fiddlemaker. Ask the man who owns one." Suddenly
he shouted as loudly as he had made the harp of the
piano resound, so that the thin black windowpanes in
their seats of cracked putty vibrated in sympathy.
"Fidel!" he called into the emptiness of the vast house.
"Margaritas! *¡Tres!* Bring them into the bath! *¡Trái-
galas al baño! ¡Rápidamente!!*"

So the moment of divestment was at hand. To
embolden Jane, Alexandra rose and followed Van
Horne at once; but perhaps Jane needed no embold-
ening after her private musical sessions in this house.
It was the ambiguous essence of Alexandra's relation
with Jane and Sukie that she was the leader, the pro-
foundest witch of the three, and yet also the slowest,
a bit in the dark, a bit—yes—innocent. The other
two were younger and therefore slightly more modern and less beholden to nature with its massive
patience, its infinite care and imperious cruelty, its
ancient implication of a slow-grinding, anthropocen-
tric order.

The procession of three passed through the long
room of dusty modern art and then a small chamber
hastily crammed with stacked lawn furniture and unopened cardboard boxes. New double doors, the inner
side padded with black vinyl quilting, sealed off the
heat and damp of the rooms Van Horne had added

where the old copper-roofed conservatory used to be.
The bathing space was floored in Tennessee slate and
lit by overhead lights sunk in the ceiling, itself a dark
pegboardy substance. "Rheostatted," Van Horne
explained in his hollow, rasping voice. He twisted a
luminous knob inside the double doors so these upside-
down ribbed cups brimmed into a brightness photographs could have been taken by and then ebbed back
to the dimness of a developing room. These lights
were sunk above not in rows but scattered at random
like stars. He left them at dim, in deference perhaps
to their puckers and blemishes and the telltale false
teats that mark a witch. Beyond this darkness, behind
a wall of plate glass, vegetation was underlit green by
buried bulbs and lit from above by violet growing
lamps that fed spiky, exotic shapes—plants from afar,
selected and harbored for their poisons. A row of
dressing cubicles and two shower stalls, all black like
the boxes in a Nevelson sculpture, occupied another
wall of the space, which was dominated as by a massive
musky sleeping animal by the pool itself, a circle of
water with burnished teak rim, an element opposite
from that icy tide Alexandra had braved some weeks
ago: this water was so warm the very air in here started
sweat on her face. A small squat console with burning
red eyes at the tub's near edge contained, she supposed, the controls.

"Take a shower first if you feel so dirty," Van Horne
told her, but himself made no move in that direction.
Instead he went to a cabinet on another wall, a wall
like a Mondrian but devoid of color, cut up in doors
and panels that must all conceal a secret, and took out
a white box, not a box but a long white skull, perhaps
a goat's or a deer's, with a hinged silver lid. Out of
this he produced some shredded something and a
packet of old-fashioned cigarette papers at which he

began clumsily fiddling like a bear worrying a fragment of beehive.

Alexandra's eyes were adjusting to the gloom. She went into a cubicle and slipped out of her gritty clothes and, wrapping herself in a purple towel she found folded there, ducked into the shower. Tennis sweat, guilt about the children, a misplaced bridal timidity—all sluiced from her. She held her face up into the spray as if to wash it away, that face given to you at birth like a fingerprint or Social Security number. Her head felt luxuriously heavier as her hair got wet. Her heart felt light like a small motor skimming on an aluminum track toward its inevitable connection with her rough strange host. Drying herself, she noticed that the monogram stitched into the nap of the towel seemed to be an *M*, but perhaps it was *V* and *H* merged. She stepped back into the shadowy room with the towel wrapped around her. The slate presented a fine reptilian roughness to the soles of her feet. The caustic pungence of marijuana scraped her nose like a friendly fur. Van Horne and Jane Smart, shoulders gleaming, were already in the tub, sharing the joint. Alexandra walked to the tub edge, saw the water was about four feet deep, let her towel drop, and slipped in. Hot. Scalding. In the old days, before burning her completely at the stake they would pull pieces of flesh from a witch's flesh with red-hot tongs; this was a window into that, that furnace of suffering.

"Too hot?" Van Horne asked, his voice even hollower, more mock-manly, amid these sequestered, steamy acoustics.

"I'll get used," she said grimly, seeing that Jane had. Jane looked furious that Alexandra was here at all, making waves, gently though she had tried to lower herself into the agonizing water. Alexandra felt her breasts tug upwards, buoyant. She had slipped in up to her neck and so had no dry hand to accept the joint; Van Horne placed it between her lips. She drew deep and held in the smoke. Her submerged trachea burned. The water's temperature was becoming one with her skin and, looking down, she saw how they had all been dwindled, Jane's body distorted with wedge-shaped wavering legs and Van Horne's penis floating like a pale torpedo, uncircumcised and curiously smooth, like one of those vanilla plastic vibrators that have appeared in city drugstore display windows now that the revolution is on and the sky is the limit.

Alexandra reached up and behind her to the towel she had dropped and dried her hands and wrists enough to accept in her turn the little reefer, fragile as a chrysalis, as it was passed among the three of them. She had had pot before; her older boy, Ben, in fact grew it in their back yard, in a patch past the tomato plants, which it superficially resembled. But it had never been part of their Thursdays: alcohol, calorie-rich goodies, and gossip had been transporting enough. After several deep tokes amid this steam Alexandra imagined she felt herself changing, growing weightless in the water and in the tub of her skull. As when a sock comes through the wash turned inside out and needs to be briskly reached into and pulled, so the universe; she had been looking at it as at the back side of a tapestry. This dark room with its just barely discernible seams and wires was the other side of the tapestry, the consoling reverse to nature's sunny fierce weave. She felt clean of worry. Jane's face still expressed worry, but her mannish brows and that smudge of insistence in her voice no longer intimidated Alexandra, seeing their source in the thick black pubic bush which beneath the water seemed to sway back and forth almost like a penis.

"God," Darryl Van Horne announced aloud, "I'd love to be a woman."

"For heaven's sake, why?" Jane sensibly asked.

"Think what a female body can do—make a baby and then make milk to feed it."

"Well think of your own body," Jane said, "the way it can turn food into shit."

"*Jane,*" Alexandra scolded, shocked by the analogy, which seemed despairing, though shit too was a kind of miracle if you thought about it. To Van Horne she confirmed, "It *is* wonderful. At the moment of birth there's nothing left of your ego, you're just a channel for this effort that comes from beyond."

"Must be," he said, dragging, "a fantastic high."

"You're so drugged you don't notice," the other woman said, sourly.

"Jane, that isn't true. It wasn't true for me. Ozzie and I did the whole natural-childbirth thing, with him in the room giving me ice chips to suck, I got so dehydrated, and helping me breathe. With the last two babies we didn't even have a doctor, we had a monitrice."

"Do you know," Van Horne stated, going into that pedantic, ponderous squint that Lexa instinctively loved, as a glimpse of the shy clumsy boy he must have been, "the whole witchcraft scare was an attempt—successful, as it turned out—on the part of the newly arising male-dominated medical profession, beginning in the fourteenth century, to get the child-birth business out of the hands of midwives. That's what a lot of the women burned were—midwives. They had the ergot, and atropine, and probably a lot of right instincts even without germ theory. When the male doctors took over they worked blind, with a sheet around their necks, and brought all the diseases from the rest of their practice with them. The poor cunts died in droves."

"Typical," said Jane abrasively. She had evidently decided that being nasty would keep her in the forefront of Van Horne's attention. "If there's one thing that infuriates me more than male chauvs," she told him now, "it's creeps who take up feminism just to work their way into women's underpants."

But her voice, it seemed to Alexandra, was slowing, softening, as the water worked upon them from without and the cannabis from within. "But baby you're not even wearing underpants," Alexandra pointed out. It seemed an illumination of some merit. The room was growing brighter, with nobody touching a dial.

"I'm not kidding," Van Horne pursued, that myopic little boy-scholar still in him, worming to understand. His face was set on the water's surface as on a platter; his hair was long as John the Baptist's and merged with the curls licked flat on his shoulders. "It comes from the heart, can't you girls tell? I love women. My mother was a brick, smart and pretty, Christ. I used to watch her slave around the house all day and around six-thirty in wanders this little guy in a business suit and I think to myself, 'What's this wimp butting in for?' My old dad, the hard-working wimp. Tell me honest, how does it feel when the milk flows?"

"How does it feel," Jane asked irritably, "when you come?"

"Hey come on, let's not get ugly."

Alexandra perceived genuine alarm on the man's heavy, seamed face; for some reason coming was a tender area in his mind.

"I don't see what's ugly," Jane was saying. "You want to talk physiology, I'm just offering a physiological sensation that women can't have. I mean, we don't come that way. Quite. Don't you love that word they have for the clitoris, 'homologous'?"

Alexandra offered, apropos of giving milk, "It feels like when you have to go pee and can't and then suddenly you can."

"That's what I love about women," Van Horne said. "Their homely similes. There's no such word as 'ugly' in your vocabulary. Men, Christ, they're so squeamish about everything—blood, spiders, blow jobs. You know, in a lot of species the bitch or sow or whatever eats the afterbirth?"

"I don't think you realize," Jane said, striving for a dry tone, "what a chauvinistic thing that is to say." But her dryness took a strange turn as she stood on tiptoe in the tub, so her breasts lifted silvery from the water; one was a little higher and smaller than the other. She held them in her two hands and explained to a point in space between the man and the other woman, as if to the invisible witness of her life, a witness we all carry with us and seldom address aloud, "I always wanted my breasts to be bigger. Like Lexa's. She has lovely big boobs. Show him, sweet."

"Jane, *please*. You're making me blush. I don't think it's the size that matters so much to men, it's the, it's the *tilt*, and the way they go with the whole body. And what you yourself think of them. If you're pleased, others will be. Am I right or wrong?" she asked Van Horne.

But he would not be held to the role of male spokesman. He too stood up out of the water and cupped his hairy-backed palms over his vestigial male nipples, tiny warts surrounded by wet black snakes. "Think of *volv*ing all that," he beseeched. "The machinery, all that plumbing, of the body of one sex to make food, food more exactly suited to the baby than any formula you can cook up in a lab. Think of evolving sexual pleasure. Do squids have it? What about plankton? With them, they don't have to think, but we, we think. To keep us in the game, what a bait they had to rig up! There's more built into it than one of these crazy reconnaissance planes that costs the taxpayers a zillion before it gets shot down. Suppose they left it out, nobody would fuck anybody and the species would stop dead with everybody admiring sunsets and the Pythagorean theorem."

Alexandra liked the way his mind worked; she had no trouble following it. "I adore this room," she announced dreamily. "At first I didn't think I would. All the black, except for the nice copper tubing Joe put in. Joe can be sweet, when he takes off his hat."

"Who's Joe?" Van Horne asked.

"This conversation," Jane said, so the *s*'s in her words slightly burned, "seems to have descended to a rather primitive level."

"I could put on some music," Van Horne said, touchingly anxious that they not be bored. "We're all wired up for four-track stereo."

"*Shh,*" Jane said. "I heard a car on the driveway."

"Trick-or-treaters," Van Horne suggested. "Fidel'll give 'em some razor-blade apples we've been cooking up."

"Maybe Sukie's come back," Alexandra said. "I love you, Jane; you have such good ears."

"Aren't they nice?" the other woman agreed. "I *do* have pretty ears, even my father always said. Look." She held her hair back from one and then, turning her head, the other. "The only trouble is, one's a little higher than the other, so any glasses I wear sit cock-eyed on my nose."

"They're rather square," Alexandra said.

Taking it as a compliment, Jane added, "And nice

and flat to the skull. Sukie's are cupped out like a monkey's, have you ever noticed?"

"Often."

"Her eyes are too close together, too, and her over-bite should have been corrected when she was young. And her nose, just a little blob really. I honestly don't know how she makes it all work as well as she does."

"I don't think Sukie will be coming back," Van Horne said. "She's too tied up with these neurotic creeps that run this town."

"She is and she isn't," someone said; Alexandra thought it had to be Jane but it sounded like her own voice.

"Isn't this cozy and nice?" she said, to test her own voice. It sounded deep, a man's voice.

"Our home away from home," Jane said, sarcastically, Alexandra supposed. It was really by no means easy to attain etheric harmony with Jane.

The sound Jane had heard was not Sukie, it was Fidel, bringing margaritas, on the enormous engraved silver tray Sukie had once mentioned to Alexandra admiringly, each broad wineglass on its thin stem rimmed with chunky sea-salt. It looked odd to Alexandra, so at home in her nudity had she already become, that Fidel was not naked too, but wearing a pajamalike uniform the color of army chinos.

"Dig this, ladies," Van Horne called, boyish in his boasting and also in the look of his white behind, for he had gotten out of the water and was fiddling with some dials at the far black wall. There was a greased rumble and, overhead, the ceiling, not perforated here but of dull corrugated metal as in a tool shed, rolled back to disclose the inky sky and its thin splash of stars. Alexandra recognized the sticky web of the Pleiades and giant red Aldebaran. These preposter-ously far bodies and the unseasonably warm but still

sharp autumn air and the Nevelson intricacies of the
black walls and the surreal Arp shapes of her own
bulbous body all fitted around her sensory self exactly,
as tangible as the steaming bath and the chilled glass
stem pinched between her fingertips, so that she was
as it were interlocked with a multitude of ethereal
bodies. These stars condensed as tears and cupped
her warm eyes. Idly she turned the stem in her hand
to the stem of a fat yellow rose and inhaled its aroma.
It smelled of lime juice. Her lips came away loaded
with salt crystals fat as dewdrops. A thorn in the stem
had pricked one finger and she watched a single drop
of blood well up at the center of the whorl of a fingerprint. Darryl Van Horne was bending over to fuss
at some more of his controls and his white bottom
glowingly seemed the one part of him that was not
hairy or repellently sheathed by a kind of exoskeleton
but authentically his self, as we take in most people
the head to be their true self. She wanted to kiss it,
his glossy innocent unseeing ass. Jane passed her
something burning which she obediently put to her
lips. The burning inside Alexandra's trachea mingled
with the hot angry look of Jane's stare as under the
water her friend's hand fishlike nibbled and slid across
her belly, around those buoyant breasts she had said
she coveted.

"Hey don't leave me out," Van Horne begged, and
splashed back into the water, shattering the moment,
for Jane's little hand, with its callused fingertips like
fish teeth, floated away. They resumed their con-
versing, but the words drifted free of meaning, the
talk was like touching, and time fell in lazy loops
through the holes in Alexandra's caressed consciousness until Sukie did come back, bringing time back
with her.

In she hurried with autumn caught in the suede

skirt with its frontal ties of rawhide and her tweed jacket nipped at the waist and double-pleated at the back like a huntswoman's, her peach tennis dress left at home in a hamper. "Your kids are fine," she informed Jane Smart, and did not seem nonplussed to find them all in the tub, as if she knew this room already, with its slates, its bright serpents of copper, the jagged piece of illumined green jungle beyond, and the ceiling with its cold rectangle of sky and stars. With her wonderful matter-of-fact quickness, first setting down a leather pocketbook big as a saddlebag on a chair Alexandra had not noticed before—there was furniture in the room, chairs and mattresses, black so they blended in—Sukie undressed, first slipping off her low-heeled square-toed shoes, and then removing the hunting jacket, and then pushing the untied suede skirt down over her hips, and then unbuttoning the silk blouse of palest beige, the tint of an engraved invitation, and pushing down her half-slip, the pink-brown of a tea rose, and her white panties with it, and lastly uncoupling her bra and leaning forward with extended arms so the two emptied cups fell down her arms and into her hands, lightly; her exposed breasts swayed outward with this motion. Sukie's breasts were small enough to keep firm in air, rounded cones whose tips had been dipped in a deeper pink without there being any aggressive jut of buttonlike nipple. Her body seemed a flame, a flame of soft white fire to Alexandra, who watched as Sukie calmly stooped to pick her underthings up from the floor and drop them onto the chair that was like a shadow materialized and then matter-of-factly rummaged in her big loose-flapped pocketbook for some pins to put up her hair of that pale yet plangent color called red but that lies between apricot and the blush at the heart of yew wood. Her hair was this color wherever it was, and her pinning gesture bared the two tufts, double in shape like two moths alighted sideways, in her armpits. This was progressive of her; Alexandra and Jane had not yet broken with the patriarchal command to shave laid upon them when they were young and learning to be women. In the Biblical desert women had been made to scrape their armpits with flint; female hair challenged men, and Sukie as the youngest of the witches felt least obliged to trim and temper her natural flourishing. Her slim body, freckled the length of her forearms and shins, was yet ample enough for her outline to undulate as she walked toward them, into the sallow floor lights that guarded the rim of the tub, out of the black background of this place, its artificial dark monotone like that of a recording studio; the edge of the apparition of her naked beauty undulated as when in a movie a series of stills are successively imposed upon the viewer to give an effect of fluttering motion, disturbing and spectral, in silence. Then Sukie was close to them and restored to three dimensions, her so lovely long bare side marred endearingly by a pink wart and a livid bruise (Ed Parsley in a fit of radical guilt?) and not only her limbs freckled but her forehead too, and a band across her nose, and even, a distinct constellation, on the flat of her chin, a little triangular chin crinkled in determination as she sat on the tub edge and, taking a breath, with arched back and tensed buttocks eased herself into the smoking, healing water. "Holy Mo," Sukie said.

"You'll get used," Alexandra reassured her. "It's heavenly once you make your mind up."

"You kids think this is hot?" Darryl Van Horne bragged anxiously. "I set the thermostat twenty degrees higher when it's just me. For a hangover it's great. All those poisons, they bake right out."

"What were they doing?" Jane Smart asked. Her head and throat looked shrivelled, Alexandra's eyes having dwelt so long and fondly on Sukie.

"Oh," Sukie answered her, "the usual. Watching old movies on Channel Fifty-six and getting themselves sick on the candy they'd begged."

"You didn't by any chance swing by my house?" Alexandra asked, feeling shy, Sukie was so lovely and now beside her in the water; waves she made laved Alexandra's skin.

"Baby, Marcy is seventeen," Sukie said. "She's a big girl. She can cope. Wake up." And she touched Alexandra on the shoulder, a playful push. Reaching the little distance to give the push lifted one of Sukie's rose-tipped breasts out of the water; Alexandra wanted to suck it, even more than she had wanted to kiss Van Horne's bottom. She suffered a prevision of the experience, her face laid sideways in the water, her hair streaming loose and drifting into her lips as they shaped their receptive O. Her left cheek felt hot, and Sukie's green glance showed she was reading Alexandra's mind. The auras of the three witches merged beneath the skylight, pink and violet and tawny, with Van Horne's stiff brown collapsible thing over his head like a clumsy wooden halo on a saint in an impoverished Mexican church.

The girl Sukie had spoken of, Marcy, had been born when Alexandra was only twenty-one, having dropped out of college at Oz's entreaties to be his wife, and she was reminded now of her four babies, how as they came one by one it was the female infants suckling that tugged at her insides more poignantly, the boys already a bit like men, that aggressive vacuum, the hurt of the sudden suction, the oblong blue skulls bulging and bullying above the clusters of frowning muscles where their masculine eyebrows would some day sprout. The girls were daintier, even those first days, such hopeful thirsty sweet clinging sugar-sacks destined to become beauties and slaves. Babies: their dear rubbery bowlegs as if they were riding tiny horses in their sleep, the lovable swaddled crotch the diaper makes, their flexible violet feet, their skin everywhere fine as the skin of a penis, their grave indigo stares and their curly mouths so forthrightly drooling. The way they ride your left hip, clinging lightly as vines to a wall to your side, the side where your heart is. The ammonia of their diapers. Alexandra began to cry, thinking of her lost babies, babies swallowed by the children they had become, babies sliced into bits and fed to the days, the years. Tears slid warm and then by contrast to her hot face cool down the sides of her nose, finding the wrinkles hinged at her nostril wings, salting the corners of her mouth and dribbling down her chin, making a runnel of the little cleft there. Amid all these thoughts Jane's hands had never left her; Jane intensified her caresses, massaging now the back of Alexandra's neck, then the *musculus trapezius* and on to the deltoids and the pectorals, oh, that did ease sorrow, Jane's strong hand, that pressure now above, now below the water, below even the waist, the little red eyes of the thermal controls keeping poolside watch, the margarita and marijuana mixing their absolving poisons in the sensitive hungry black realm beneath her skin, her poor neglected children sacrificed so she could have her powers, her silly powers, and only Jane understanding, Jane and Sukie, Sukie lithe and young next to her, touching her, being touched, her body woven not of aching muscle but of a kind of osier, supple and gently speckled, the nape beneath her pinned-up hair of a whiteness that never sees the sun, a piece of pliant alabaster beneath the amber wisps. As Jane was doing to Alexandra Alexandra did to Sukie, caressed her. Sukie's body in her hands seemed silk, seemed heavy slick fruit, Alexandra so dissolved in melancholy triumphant affectionate feelings there was no telling the difference between caresses given and caresses received; shoulders and arms and breasts emergent, the three women drew closer to form, like graces in a print, a knot, while their hairy swarthy host, out of the water, scrabbled through his black cabinets. Sukie in a strange practical voice that Alexandra heard as if relayed from a great distance into this recording studio was discussing with this Van Horne man what music to put on his expensive and steam-resistant stereo system. He was naked and his swinging gabbling pallid genitals had the sweetness of a dog's tail curled tight above the harmless button of its anus.

Our town of Eastwick was to gossip that winter—for here as in Washington and Saigon there were leaks; Fidel made friends with a woman in town, a waitress at Nemo's, a sly black woman from Antigua called Rebecca—about the evil doings at the old Lenox place, but what struck Alexandra this first night and ever after was the amiable human awkwardness of it all, controlled as it was by the awkwardness of their eager and subtly ill-made host, who not only fed them and gave them shelter and music and darkly suitable furniture but provided the blessing without which courage of our contemporary sort fails and trickles away into ditches others have dug, those old ministers and naysayers and proponents of heroic constipation who sent lovely Anne Hutchinson, a woman ministering to women, off into the wilderness to be scalped by redmen in their way as fanatic and unforgiving as Puritan divines. Like all men Van Horne demanded the women call him king, but his system of taxation at least dealt in assets—bodies, personal liveliness—

they did have and not in spiritual goods laid up in some nonexistent Heaven. It was Van Horne's kindness to subsume their love for one another into a kind of love for himself. There was something a little abstract about his love for them and something therefore formal and merely courteous in the obeisances and favors they granted him—wearing the oddments of costume he provided, the catskin gloves and green leather garters, or binding him with the *cingulum*, the nine-foot cord of plaited red wool. He stood, often, as at that first night, above and beyond them, adjusting his elaborate and (his proud claims notwithstanding) moisture-sensitive equipment.

He pressed a button and the corrugated roof rumbled back across the section of night sky. He put on records—first Joplin, yelling and squawking herself hoarse on "Piece of My Heart" and "Get It While You Can" and "Summertime" and "Down on Me," the very voice of joyful defiant female despair, and then Tiny Tim, tiptoeing through the tulips with a thrilling androgynous warbling that Van Horne couldn't get enough of, returning the needle to the beginning grooves over and over, until the witches clamorously demanded Joplin again. On his acoustical system the music surrounded them, arising in all four corners of the room; they danced, the four clad in only their auras and hair, with shy and minimal motions, keeping within the music, often turning their backs, letting the titanic ghostly presences of the singers soak them through and through. When Joplin croaked "Summertime" at that broken tempo, remembering the words in impassioned spasms as if repeatedly getting up off the canvas in some internal drug-hazed prizefight, Sukie and Alexandra swayed in each other's arms without their feet moving, their fallen hair stringy and tangled with tears, their breasts touching, nuzzling, fumbling in pale pillow fight lubricated by drops of sweat worn on their chests like the broad bead necklaces of ancient Egypt. And when Joplin with that deceptively light-voiced opening drifted into the whirlpool of "Me and Bobby McGee," Van Horne, his empurpled penis rendered hideously erect by a service Jane had performed for him on her knees, pantomimed with his uncanny hands—encased it seemed in white rubber gloves with wigs of hair and wide at the tips like the digits of a tree toad or lemur—in the dark above her bobbing head the tumultuous solo provided by the inspired pianist of the Full Tilt Boogie band.

On the black velour mattresses Van Horne had provided, the three women played with him together, using the parts of his body as a vocabulary with which to speak to one another; he showed supernatural control, and when he did come his semen, all agreed later, was marvellously cold. Dressing after midnight, in the first hour of November, Alexandra felt as if she were filling her clothes—she played tennis in slacks, to hide somewhat her heavy legs—with a weightless gas, her flesh had been so rarefied by its long immersion and assimilated poisons. Driving home in her Subaru, whose interior smelled of dog, she saw the full moon with its blotchy mournful face in the top of her tinted windshield and irrationally thought for a second that astronauts had landed and in an act of imperial atrocity had spray-painted that vast sere surface green.

ii. Malefica

> "I will not be other than I am; I find too much content
> in my condition; I am always caressed."
> — *a young French witch, c. 1660*

"HE HAS?" Alexandra asked over the phone. At her kitchen windows the Puritan hues of November prevailed, the arbor a tangle of peeling vines, the birdfeeder hung up and filled now that the first frosts had shrivelled the berries of the woods and bog.

"That's what Sukie says," said Jane, her *s*'s burning. "She says she saw it long coming but didn't want to say anything to betray him. Not that telling just us would be betraying anybody, if you ask me."

"But how long has Ed known the girl?" A row of Alexandra's teacups, hung on brass hooks beneath a pantry shelf, swayed as if an invisible hand had caressed them in the manner of a harpist.

"Some months. Sukie thought he seemed different with her. He just wanted mostly to talk, to use her as a sounding board. She's glad: think of the venereal diseases she might have gotten. All these flower children have crabs at the least, you know."

The Reverend Ed Parsley had run off with a local teen-ager, was the long and short of it. "Have I ever seen this girl?" Alexandra asked.

"Oh certainly," Jane said. "She was always in that gang in front of the Superette after about eight at night, waiting for a drug pusher I suppose. A pale smudgy face wider than it was high, somehow, with dirty flaxen hair just hanging down any old how, and dressed like a little female lumberjack."

"No love beads?"

Jane answered seriously. "Well, no doubt she owned some, to wear when she wanted to go to a debutante party. Can't you picture her? She was one of those picketing the town meeting last March and threw sheep's blood they got at the slaughterhouse all over the war memorial."

"I can't, honey, maybe because I don't want to. These kids in front of the Superette always frighten me, I just hustle out between them without looking to the right or the left."

"You shouldn't be frightened, they're not even seeing you. To them you're just part of the landscape, like a tree."

"Poor Ed. He did look so harassed lately. When I saw him at the concert, he even seemed to want to cling to *me*. I thought that was being disloyal to Sukie, so I shook him off."

"The girl isn't even from Eastwick, she was always hanging around here but she lived up in Coddington Junction, some perfectly awful broken home in a trailer there, living with her common-law stepfather because her mother was always on the road doing something in a carnival, they call it acrobatics."

Jane sounded so prim, you would think she was a virgin spinster if you hadn't seen her functioning with Darryl Van Horne. "Her name is Dawn Polanski," Jane was going on. "I don't know if her parents called her Dawn or she called herself that, people like that do give themselves names now, like Lotus Blossom and Heavenly Avatar or whatever."

Her toughened little hands had been incredibly busy, and when the cold semen had spurted out, it was Jane who had appropriated most of it. Other women's sexual styles are something you are left mostly to guess at and perhaps wisely, for it can be *too* fascinating. Alexandra tried to blink the pictures out of her mind and asked, "But what are they going to *do*?"

"I daresay they have no idea, after they go to some motel and screw till they're sick of it. Really, it *is* pathetic." It was Jane who had stroked her first, not Sukie. Picturing Sukie, the soft white flame her body had been, posing on the slates, opened a little hollow space in Alexandra's abdomen, near her left ovary. Her poor insides: she was sure one day she'd have an operation, and they'd open it all too late, just crawling with black cancer cells. Except they probably weren't black but a brighter red, and shiny, like cauliflower of a bloody sort. "Then I suppose," Jane was saying, "they'll head for some big city and try to join the Movement. I think Ed thinks it's like joining the army: you find a recruitment center and they give you a physical and if you pass they take you in."

"It seems so deluded, doesn't it? He's too old. As long as he stayed around here he seemed rather young and dashing, or at least *int*eresting, and he had his church, it gave him a forum of sorts...."

"He hated being respectable," Jane broke in sharply. "He thought it was a sellout."

"Oh my, what a world," Alexandra sighed, watching a gray squirrel make his stop-and-start wary way across the tumbled stone wall at the edge of her yard. A batch of her bubbies was baking in the ticking kiln in the room off the kitchen; she had tried to make them bigger, but as she did so the crudities of her self-taught technique, her ignorance of anatomy, seemed to matter more. "What about Brenda, how is she taking it?"

"About as you'd expect. Hysterically. She was virtually openly condoning Ed's carrying on on the side but she never thought he'd leave her. It's going to be a problem for the church, too. All she and the kids have is the parsonage and it's not theirs, of course. They'll have to be kicked out eventually." The calm crackle of malice in Jane's voice took Alexandra a bit aback. "She'll have to get a job. She'll find out what it's like, being on your own."

"Maybe we..." *Should befriend her*, was the unfinished thought.

"*Never*," telepathic Jane responded. "She was just too fucking smug, if you ask me, being Mrs. Minister, sitting there like Greer Garson behind the coffee urn, snuggling up to all the old ladies, you should have seen her breeze in and out of that church during our rehearsals. I know," she said, "I shouldn't take such satisfaction in another woman's comeuppance, but I do. You think I'm wrong. You think I'm wicked."

"Oh no," Alexandra said, insincerely. But who is to say what wicked is? Poor Franny Lovecraft could have broken her hip that night and be on a walker till she stepped into her grave. Alexandra had come to the phone holding a wooden stirring spoon and idly, as she waited for Jane to be milked of all her malice, she bent the thing with her mind waves so that its handle curled back like a dog's tail and rested in the carved bowl of the spoon. Then she bade the snakelike circle coil slowly up her arm. The abrasive caress of the wood set her teeth on edge. "And how about Sukie?" Alexandra asked. "Isn't she sort of left too?"

"She's delighted. She encouraged him, she told me, to find what he could with this Dawn creature. I think she'd had her little ride with Ed."

"But does that mean she's going to go after Darryl now?" The spoon had draped itself around her neck and was touching its bowl end to her lips. It tasted of salad oil. She flickered her tongue against its wood and her tongue felt feathery, forked. Coal was nuzzling against her legs, worriedly, smelling magic, which had a tiny burnt odor like a gas jet when first turned on.

"I daresay," Jane was saying, "she has other plans. She's not as attracted to Darryl as you are. Or as I am, for that matter. Sukie likes men to be *down*. Keep your eye on Clyde Gabriel, is my advice."

"Oh that awful wife," Alexandra exclaimed. "She should be put out of her misery." She was scarcely minding what she was saying, for to tease Coal she had put the writhing spoon on the floor and the hair on his withers had bristled; the spoon lifted its head, and Coal's lips tugged up from his teeth, and his eyes kindled to attack.

"Let's do it," Jane Smart briskly replied.

Distracted by this sharp new wickedness in Jane, and a bit frightened by it, Alexandra let the spoon unbend; it dropped its head and clattered flat on the linoleum. "Oh I don't think it's for us to do," she protested, mildly.

"I always did despise him and am not in the least surprised," Felicia Gabriel announced in her flat self-satisfied manner, as if addressing a small crowd of friends who unanimously thought she was wonderful, though in fact she was speaking to her husband, Clyde.

He had been trying to comprehend through his drunken post-supper fog a *Scientific American* article on the newer anomalies of astronomy. She stood with a nagging expectant tension in the doorway of the shelf-lined room he tried to use as a study now that Jenny and Chris were no longer around to pollute it with electronic noises, with Joan Baez and the Beach Boys.

Felicia had never outgrown the presumingness of a pretty and vivacious high-school girl. She and Clyde had gone through the public schools of Warwick together, and what a fetching live-wire she had been, in on every extracurricular activity from student council to girls' volleyball and a straight A average to boot, not to mention being the first female captain ever of the debating team. A thrilling voice that would lift out above all the others in the impossibly high part of "The Star-Spangled Banner": it cut right through him like a knife. She had had dozens of boyfriends; she had been a real catch. He kept reminding himself of this. At night, when she fell asleep beside him with that depressing promptitude of the virtuous and hyperactive, leaving him to wrestle for hours alone with the demons of insomnia an evening's worth of liquor had planted in his system, he would examine her still features by moonlight, and the shadowed fit of her shut lids in their sockets and of her lips buttoned over some unspoken utterance of dream debate would disclose to his inspection an old perfection of nicely whittled bones. Felicia seemed frail when unconscious. He would lie propped up on one elbow and gaze at her, and the form of the peppy teenager he had loved would be restored to him, in her fuzzy pastel sweaters and her long plaid skirts swinging down the halls lined with tall green metal lockers, along with a sensation of being again his gangling "brainy" teenaged self; a giant insubstantial column of lost and wasted time would arise from the bedroom walls so that they seemed to be lying like two crumpled bodies at the base of an airshaft. But now she stood erect before him, unignorable, dressed in the black skirt and white sweater in which she had chaired the evening's meeting of the Wetlands Watchdog Committee, where she had heard the news about Ed Parsley, from Mavis Jessup.

"He was *weak*," she stated, "a weak man somebody had once told he was handsome. He never looked handsome to me, with that pseudo-aristocratic nose and those slidy eyes. He never should have entered the ministry, he had no call, he thought he could charm God just as he charmed the old ladies into overlooking that he was a hollow man. To me—Clyde, *look* at me when I'm talking—he utterly failed to project the qualities of a man of God."

"I'm not sure the Unitarians care that much about God," he mildly answered, still hoping to read. Quasars, pulsars, stars emitting every millisecond jets of more matter than is contained in all the planets: perhaps in such cosmic madness he himself was looking for the old-fashioned heavenly God. Back in those innocent days when he had been "brainy" he had written for special credit in biology a long paper called "The Supposed Conflict Between Science and Religion," concluding that there was none. Though the paper had been given an A+, thirty-five years ago, by pie-faced, effeminate Mr. Thurmann, Clyde saw now that he had lied. The conflict was open and implacable and science was winning.

"Whatever they care about it's more than staying young forever, which is what drove Ed Parsley into the arms of that pathetic little tramp," Felicia announced. "He must have taken a good look one day at that perfectly deplorable Sukie Rougemont you're so fond of and realized that she was over thirty and he better find a younger mistress or he'd be dragged into growing up himself. That saint Brenda Parsley, why she put up with it I have no idea."

"Why? Why not? What options did she have?" Clyde hated to hear her rant yet he could not resist replying now and then.

"Well, she'll kill him. This new one will absolutely kill him. He'll be dead inside of a year in some hovel where she's led him, his arms full of needle marks, and Ed Parsley will get none of my sympathy. I'll spit on his grave. Clyde, you must stop reading that magazine. What did I just say?"

"You'll thspit on his grave."

Semiconsciously he had imitated a slight strangeness in her diction. He looked up in time to see her remove a piece of tinted fuzz from between her lips. She rolled the fuzz into a tight pellet with rapid nervous fingers at her side while she talked on. "Brenda Parsley was telling Marge Perley it might have been that your friend Sukie gave him a push so she could give this Van Horne creature her undivided attention, though from what I hear around town his attention is divided . . . three ways every . . . Thursday night."

The uncharacteristic hesitation in her phrasing led him to look up from the jagged graphs of pulsar flashes; she had removed something else from her mouth and was making another pellet, staring him down as if daring him to notice. When she had been a high-school girl she had had shining round eyes, but now her face, without growing fat, with every year was pressing in upon these lamps of her soul; her eyes had become piggy, with a vengeful piggy glitter.

"Sukie's not a friend," he said mildly, determined not to fight. *Just this once, not a fight*, he Godlessly prayed. "She's an employee. We have no friends."

"You better *tell* her she's an employee because from the way she acts down there she's the veritable queen of the place. Walks up and down Dock Street as if she owns it, swinging her hips and in all that junk jewelry, everybody laughing at her behind her back. Leaving her was the smartest thing Monty ever did, about the *only* smart thing he ever did, I don't know why those women bother to go on living, whores to half the town and not even getting paid. And those poor neglected children of theirs, it's a positive crime."

At a certain point, which she invariably pressed through to reach, he couldn't bear it any more: the mellowing anaesthetic effect of the Scotch was abruptly catalyzed into rage. "And the reason we have no friends," he growled, letting the magazine with its monstrous celestial news drop to the carpet, "is you talk too Goddamn much."

"Whores and neurotics and a disgrace to the community. And *you*, when the *Word* is supposed to give some voice to the community and its legitimate concerns, instead give employment to this, this *person* who can't even write a decent English sentence, and allow her space to drip her ridiculous poison into everybody's ears and let her have that much of a hold over the people of the town, the few good people that are left, frightened as they are into the corners by all this vice and shamelessness everywhere."

"Divorced women have to work," Clyde said, sighing, slowing his breathing, fighting to keep reasonable, though there was no reasoning with Felicia when her indignation started to flow, it was like a chemical, a kind of chemical reaction. Her eyes shrank to diamond points, her face became frozen, paler and paler, and her invisible audience grew larger, so she had to raise her voice. "Married women," he explained to her, "don't have to do anything and can fart around with liberal causes."

She didn't seem to hear him. "That dreadful man,"

she called to the multitudes, "building a tennis court right into the wetlandth, they thay"—she swallowed— "they say he uses the island to smuggle drugs, they row it in in dorieth when the tide ith high—"

This time there was no hiding it; she pulled a small feather, striped blue as from a blue jay, out of her mouth, and quickly made a fist around it at her side.

Clyde stood up, his feelings quite changed. Anger and the sense of entrapment fell from him; her old pet name emerged from his mouth. "Lishy, what on earth...?" He doubted his eyes; saturated with galactic strangeness, they might be playing tricks. He pried open her unresisting fist. A bent wet feather lay upon her palm.

Felicia's tense pallor relaxed into a blush. She was embarrassed. "It's been happening lately," she told him. "I have no idea why. This scummy taste, and then these *things*. Some mornings I feel as if I'm choking, and pieces like straw, dirty straw, come out when I'm brushing my teeth. But I know I've not eaten anything. My breath is terrible. Clyde! I don't know what's *hap*pening to me!"

As this cry escaped her, Felicia's body was given an anxious twist, a look of being about to fly off somewhere, that reminded Clyde of Sukie: both women had fair dry skin and an ectomorphic frame. In high school Felicia had been drenched in freckles and her "pep" had been something like his favorite reporter's nimble, impudent carriage. Yet one woman was heaven and the other hell. He took his wife into his arms. She sobbed. It was true; her breath smelled like the bottom of a chicken coop. "Maybe we should get you to a doctor," he suggested. This flash of husbandly emotion, in which he enfolded her frightened soul in a cape of concern, burned away much of the alcohol clouding his mind.

But after her moment of wifely surrender Felicia stiffened and struggled. "*No.* They'll make out I'm crazy and tell you to put me away. Don't think I don't know your thoughts. You wish I was dead. You bastard, you *do.* You're just like Ed Parsley. You're all bastards. Pitiful, corrupt...all you care about ith awful women...." She writhed out of his arms; in the corner of his eye her hand snatched at her mouth. She tried to hide this hand behind her but, furious above all at the way that truth, for which men die, was mixed in with her frantic irrelevant self-satisfaction, he gripped her wrist and forced her clenched fingers open. Her skin felt cold, clammy. In her unclenched palm lay curled a wet pinfeather, as from a chick, but an Easter chick, for the little soft feather had been dyed lavender.

"He sends me letters," Sukie told Darryl Van Horne, "with no return address, saying he's gone underground. They've let him and Dawn into a group that's learning how to make bombs out of alarm clocks and cordite. The System doesn't stand a chance." She grinned monkeyishly.

"How does that make you feel?" the big man smoothly asked, in a hollow psychiatric voice. They were having lunch at a restaurant in Newport, where no one else from Eastwick was likely to be. Elderly waitresses in starchy brown miniskirts, with taffeta aprons tied behind in big bows evocative of Playboy bunny tails, brought them large menus, printed brown on beige, full of low-cal things on toast. Her weight was not among Sukie's worries: all that nervous energy, it burned everything up.

She squinted into space, trying to be honest, for she sensed that this man offered her a chance to be herself. Nothing would shock or hurt him. "It makes me feel relieved," she said. "That he's off my hands. I mean, what he wanted wasn't something a woman could give him. He wanted power. A woman can give a man power over herself in a way, but she can't put him in the Pentagon. That's what excited Ed about the Movement as he imagined it, that it was going to replace the Pentagon with an army of its own and have the same, you know, kind of thing—uniforms and speeches and board rooms with big maps and all. That really turned me off, when he started raving about that. I like *gentle* men. My father was gentle, a veterinarian in this little town in the Finger Lakes region, and he loved to read. He had all first editions of Thornton Wilder and Carl Van Vechten, with these plastic covers to protect the jackets. Monty used to be pretty gentle too, except when he'd get his shotgun down and go out with the boys and blast all these poor birds and furry things. He'd bring home these rabbits he had blasted up the ass, because of course they were trying to run away. Who wouldn't? But that only happened once a year—around now, as a matter of fact, is what must have made me think of it. That hunting smell is in the air. Small game season." Her smile was marred by the paste of cracker and bean spread that clung in dark spots between her teeth; the waitress had brought this free hors d'oeuvre to the table and Sukie had stuffed her face.

"How about old Clyde Gabriel? He gentle enough for you?" Van Horne lowered his big woolly barrel of a head when he was burrowing into a woman's secret life. His eyes had the hot swarming half-hidden look of children's when they put on Halloween masks.

"He might have been once, but he's pretty far gone. Felicia has done bad things to him. Sometimes at the paper, when some little layout girl just beginning the job has, I don't know, put a favored advertiser in a lower-left corner, he goes, really, wild. The girl has nothing to do but burst into tears. A lot of them have quit."

"But not you."

"He's easy on me for some reason." Sukie lowered her eyes—a lovely sight, with her reddish arched brows and her lids just touched with lavender make up and her sleek shimmering apricot hair demurely backswept and held in place on both sides by barrettes whose copper backs were echoed by a necklace close to her throat of linked copper crescents.

Her eyes lifted and flashed their green. "But then I'm a good reporter. I really am. Those baggy old men in Town Hall who make all the decisions—Herbie Prinz, Ike Arsenault—they really like me, and tell me what's up."

While Sukie consumed the crackers and bean spread, Van Horne puffed on a cigarette, doing it awkwardly, in the Continental manner, the burning tip cupped near the palm. "What's with you and these married types?"

"Well, the advantage of a wife is she saves you from making any decisions. That's what was beginning to frighten me about Brenda Parsley: she really had ceased to be any check on Ed, they were so far gone as a couple. We used to spend whole nights in these awful fleabags together. And it wasn't as if we were making love, after the first half-hour; he was going on about the wickedness of the corporate power structure's sending our boys to Vietnam for the benefit of their stockholders, not that I ever understood how it was benefiting them exactly, or got much impression that Ed really cared about those boys, the actual soldiers were just white and black trash as far as he was concerned...." Her eyes had dropped and lifted again; Van Horne felt a surge of possessive pride in her beauty, her vital spirit. His. His toy. It was lovely how in a pensive pause her upper lip dominated her lower. "Then *I*," she said, "had to get up and go home and make breakfast for the kids, who were terrified because I'd been gone all night, and stagger right off to the paper—*he* could sleep all day. Nobody knows what a minister is supposed to be doing, just give his silly sermon on Sundays, it's really such a ripoff."

"People don't terrifically mind," Darryl said sagely, "being ripped off, is something I've discovered over the years." The waitress with her varicose legs exposed to mid-thigh brought Van Horne skinned shrimp tails on decrusted triangles of bread, and Sukie chicken à la king, cubed white meat and sliced mushrooms oozing in their cream over a scalloped flaky patty shell, and also brought him a Bloody Mary and her a Chablis spritzer paler than lemonade, because Sukie had to go back and write up the latest wrinkle in the Eastwick Highway Department's budget embarrassments as winter with its blizzards drew ever closer. Dock Street had been battered this summer by an unusually heavy influx of tourists and eight-axle trucks, so the slabs of mesh-reinforced concrete over the culverts there by the Superette were disintegrating; you could look right down into the tidal creek through the potholes. "So you think Felicia's an evil woman," Van Horne pursued, apropos of wives.

"I wouldn't say evil, exactly . . . yes I would. She really is. She's like Ed in a way, all causes and no respect for actual people around her. Poor Clyde sinking right in front of her eyes, and she's on the phone with this petition to restore a dress code at the high school. Coat and ties for the boys and nothing but skirts for the girls, no jeans or hotpants. They talk about fascists a lot now but she really is one. She got the news store to put *Playboy* behind the counter and then had a fit because some photography annual had a little tit and pussy in it, the models on some Caribbean beach, you know, with the sun sparkling all over them through a Polaroid filter. She actually wants poor Gus Stevens put in jail for having this magazine on his rack that his suppliers just brought him, they didn't ask. She wants *you* put in jail, for that matter, for unauthorized landfill. She wants everybody put in jail and the person she really *has* put in jail is her own husband."

"Well." Van Horne smiled, his red lips redder from the tomato juice in his Bloody Mary. "And you want to give him a parole."

"It's not just that; I'm at*trac*ted," Sukie confessed, suddenly close to tears, this whole matter of attraction so senseless, and silly. "He's so grateful for just the ... the minimum."

"Coming from you, minimum is pretty max," Van Horne said gallantly. "You're a winner, tiger."

"But I'm not," Sukie protested. "People have these fantasies about redheads, we're supposed to be hot I suppose, like those little cinnamony candy hearts, but really we're just people, and though I bustle around a lot and try, you know, to look smart, at least by Eastwick standards, I don't think of myself as having the *real* whatever it is—power, mystery, womanliness—that Alexandra has, or even Jane in her kind of lumpy way, you know what I mean?" With other men also Sukie had noticed this urge of hers to talk about the two other witches, to seek coziness conversationally in evoking the three of them, this triune body under its cone of power being the closest approach to a mother she had ever had; Sukie's own mother—a busy little birdy woman physically like, come to think of it, Felicia Gabriel, and like her fascinated by doing good—was always out of the house or on the phone to one of her church groups or committees or boards; she was always taking orphans or refugees in, little lost Koreans were the things in those years, and then abandoning them along with Sukie and her brothers in the big brick house with its back yard sloping down to the lake. Other men, Sukie felt, minded when her thoughts and tongue gravitated to the coven and its coziness and mischief, but not Van Horne; it was his meat somehow, he was like a woman in his steady kindness, though of course terribly masculine in form: when he fucked you it hurt.

"They're dogs," he said now, simply. "They don't have your nifty knockers."

"Am I wrong?" she asked, feeling she could say anything to Van Horne, throw any morsel of herself into that dark cauldron of a simmering, smiling man. "With Clyde. I mean, I know all the books say you should *never*, with an employer, you lose your job then afterwards, and Clyde's so desperately unhappy there's something dangerous about it in any case. The whites of his eyeballs are yellow; what's that a sign of?"

"Those whites of his eyeballs were marinating," Van Horne assured her, "when you were still playing with Barbie dolls. You go to it, girl. Easy on the guilt trip. We didn't deal the deck down here, we just play the cards."

Thinking that if they talked about it any more, her affair with Clyde would be as much Darryl's as hers, Sukie steered the conversation away from herself; for the rest of the luncheon Van Horne talked about himself, his hopes of finding a loophole in the second law of thermodynamics. "There *has* to be one," he said, beginning to sweat and wipe his lips in excitement, "and it's the same fucking loophole whereby everything crossed over from nonbeing. It's the singularity at the bottom of the Big Bang. Yeah, and what *about* gravity? These smug scientists everybody thinks are so sacred talk as if we've all understood it ever since Newton rigged those formulas but the fact is it's a *hell*uva mystery; Einstein says it's like a screwy graph paper that's getting bent all the time but, Sukie baby, don't drift off, it's a *force*. It lifts the tides; step out of an airplane it'll suck you right down, and what kind of a force is it that operates across space instantly and has nothing to do with the electromagnetic field?" He was forgetting to eat; flecks of spit were appearing on the lacquered tabletop. "There's a formula out there, there's gotta be, and it's going to be as elegant as good old $E = mc^2$. The sword from the stone, you know what I mean?" His big hands, disturbing like the leaves of those tropical house plants that look plastic though we know they're natural, made a decisive sword-pulling motion. Then, with salt and pepper and a ceramic ashtray bearing a prim pink image of Newport's historical Old Colony House, Van Horne tried to illustrate subatomic particles and his faith that a combination could be found to generate electricity without further energy input. "It's like jujitsu: you toss the guy over your shoulder with more force than he came at you with. Levering. You gotta *swing* those electrons." His repulsive hands showed how. "You think just mechanically or chemically on this, you're licked; the old second law's got you every time. You know what Cooper pairs are? No? You're kidding. You a journalist or not? The news isn't all who's screwing who, you know. They're pairs of loosely bound electrons that make up the heart of superconductors. Know anything about superconductors? No? O.K., their resistance is zero. I don't mean it's very small, I mean it's *zero*. Well, suppose we found some Cooper *trip*lets. You'd have resistance of *less* than zero. There's gotta be an element, like selenium was for the Xerox process. Those assholes up in Rochester didn't have a thing until they hit upon selenium, out of the blue, they just fell into it. Well, once we get our equivalent of selenium, there's no stopping us, Sukie babes. You get down there under the chemical skin, every roof in the world can become a generator with just a coat of paint. This photovoltaic cell they use in the satellites is just a sandwich, really. What you need isn't ham, cheese, and lettuce—translate that silicon, arsenic, and boron—what you need is ham salad, where the macro arrangement isn't an issue. All *I* have to do is figure out the fucking mayonnaise."

Sukie laughed and, still hungry, took a breadstick from a miniature beanpot on the table and unwrapped it and began to nibble. To her it all sounded like fantastical presumption. There were all these men in Rochester and Schenectady, she had grown up with the type, science majors with little straight mouths and receding hairlines and those plastic liners in their shirt pockets in case their pens leaked, working away systematically at these problems, with government funds and nice little wives and children to go home to at night. But then she recognized this thought as sheer prejudice left over from her old life, before sheer womanhood had exploded within her and she realized that the world men had systematically made was all dreary poison, good for nothing really but battlefields and waste sites. Why couldn't a wild man like Darryl blunder into one of the universe's secrets? Think of Thomas Edison, deaf because as a boy he had been lifted into a cart by his ears. Think of that Scotsman, what was his name, watching the steam lift the lid of the kettle and then cooking up railroads. It was on the tip of her tongue to tell Van Horne how for fun she and Jane Smart had been casting spells on Clyde's awful wife; using a Book of Common Prayer Jane had stolen from the Episcopalian church where she sometimes pinch-hit as choir director, they had solemnly baptized a cookie jar Felicia and would toss things into it—feathers, pins, sweepings from Sukie's incredibly ancient little house on Hemlock Lane.

There, not ten hours after her lunch with Darryl Van Horne, she entertained Clyde Gabriel. The children were asleep. Felicia had gone off in a caravan of buses from Boston, Worcester, Hartford, and Providence to protest something in Washington: they were going to chain themselves to pillars in the Capitol and clog everything, human grit in the wheels of government. Clyde could stay the night, if he arose before the first child awoke. He made a touching mock-husband, with his bifocals and flannel pajamas and a little partial denture that he discreetly wrapped in a Kleenex and tucked into a pocket of his suit coat when he thought Sukie wasn't watching.

But she was, for the bathroom door didn't altogether close, due to the old frame of the house settling over the centuries, and she had to sit on the toilet some minutes waiting for the pee to come. Men, they were able to conjure it up immediately, that was one of their powers, that thunderous splashing as they stood lordly above the bowl. Everything about them was more direct, their insides weren't the maze women's were, for the pee to find its way through. Sukie, waiting, peeked out; Clyde, with an elderly tilt to his head and that bump on the back of his skull studious men have, crossed the vertical slit that she could see of her bedroom. From the angle of his arms she saw he was taking a thing out of his mouth. There was a brief pink glint of false gum and then he was slipping his little packet of folded Kleenex into the side pocket of his coat where he would not forget it when he groped out of her room at dawn. Sukie sat with her lovely oval knees together and her breath held: since girlhood she had liked to spy on men, this other race interwoven with hers, so full of bravado and dirty tough talk but such babies really, as they proved whenever you gave them your breasts to suck or opened your crotch for them to go down on, the way they burrowed there and wanted to crawl back in. She liked to sit just as she was only on a chair and spread her legs so her bush felt all big and the curls of it glittery and let them just lap and kiss and eat. Hair pie, a boy she used to know in New York State called it.

The pee at last came. She turned off the bathroom light and went into the bedroom, where the only illumination arose from the street lamp up at the corner of Hemlock Lane and Oak Street. She and Clyde had never spent a night together before, though lately they had taken to driving into the Cove woods at lunchtime (she walking along Dock Street as far as the war monument and he picking her up in his Volvo there); the other day she had grown bored with kissing his sad dry face with its long nostril hairs and tobaccoey breath and, to amuse herself and him, had unzipped his fly and swiftly, sweetly (she herself felt) jerked him off, coolly watching. These comic jets of semen, like the cries of a baby animal in the claws of a hawk. He had been flabbergasted by her witch's trick; when he laughed his lips pulled back strangely, exposing back rows of jagged teeth with pockets of blackened silver. That had been a little frightening, corrosion and pain and time all bared. She felt timid again, stepping unseeing into her own room with this man in it, her eyes not yet adjusted from the bathroom. Where Clyde sat in the corner his pajamas glowed like a fluorescent bulb that has just been switched off. A red cigarette tip glowed near his head. She could see herself, her white flanks and nervous ribbed sides, more clearly than she saw him, for several mirrors—gilt-framed, ancient, inherited from an Ithaca aunt—hung on her walls. These mirrors were mottled with age; the damp plaster walls of old stone houses had eaten the mercury off their backs. Sukie preferred such mirrors to perfect ones; they gave her back her beauty with less cavil. Clyde's voice growled, "Not sure I'm up to this."

"If not you, who?" Sukie asked the shadows.

"Oh, I can think of a number," he said, nevertheless standing and beginning to unbutton his pajama top. The glowing cigarette had been transferred to his mouth and its red tip bounced as he spoke.

Sukie felt a chill. She had expected to be folded instantly into his arms, with long, starved, bad-breath kisses such as they had shared in the car. Her prompt nakedness put her at a disadvantage; she had devalued herself. These frightful fluctuations a woman must endure on the stock exchange of male minds, up and down from minute to minute, as their ids and superegos haggle. She had half a mind to turn and closet herself again in the bright bathroom, and damn him. He had not moved. His dehydrated once-handsome face, taut at the cheekbones, was scrunched wiseguy-style around the cigarette, one eye held shut against the smoke. That was how he would sit editing copy, his soft pencil scurrying and slashing, his jaundiced eyes sheltered under a green eyeshade, his cigarette smoke loosing drifting galactic shapes in the cone of his desk light, his cone of power. Clyde loved to cut, to find an entire superfluous paragraph that could be disposed of without a seam; though lately he had grown tender with her own prose, correcting only the misspellings. "How big a number?" she asked. He thought she was a whore. Felicia must keep telling him that. The chill Sukie had felt: was it the cold of the room, or the thrilling sight of her own white flesh simultaneously haunting the three mirrors?

Clyde killed his cigarette and finished undoing his

pajamas. Now he was naked too. The amount of pallor in the mirrors doubled. His penis was impressive, lank like him, dangling in that helpless heavy-headed way penises have, this most precarious piece of flesh. His skin slithered anxiously against hers as he at last attempted an embrace; he was bony but surprisingly warm.

"Not too big," he answered. "Just enough to make me jealous. God, you're lovely. I could cry."

She led him into bed, trying to suppress any movements that might wake the children. Under the covers his head with its sharp angles and scratchy whiskers rested heavily on her breast; his cheekbone grated on her clavicle. "This shouldn't make you cry," she said soothingly, easing bone off bone. "It's supposed to be a happy thing." As Sukie said this, Alexandra's broad face swam into her mind: broad, a bit sun-browned even in winter from her walks outdoors, the gentle clefts at her chin and the tip of her nose giving her an impassive goddesslike strangeness, the blankness of one who holds to a creed: Alexandra believed that nature, the physical world, was a happy thing. This huddling man, this dogskin of warm bones, did not believe that. The world for him had been rendered tasteless as paper, composed as it was of inconsequent messy events that flickered across his desk on their way to the moldering back files. Everything for him had become secondary and sour. Sukie wondered about her own strength, how long she could hold these grieving, doubting men on her own chest and not be contaminated.

"If I could have you every night, it might be a happy thing," Clyde Gabriel conceded.

"Well, then," Sukie said, in a mother's tone, staring frightened at the ceiling, trying to launch herself into the agreed-upon surrender, that flight into sex her body promised others. This man's body out of its half-century released a complex masculine odor that included the rotted scent of whiskey—a taint she had often noticed, bending over him at the desk as his pencil jabbed at her typewritten copy. It was part of him, something woven in. She stroked the hair on his skull with its long bump of intelligence. His hair was thinning: how fine it was! As if every hair truly had been numbered. His tongue began to flick at her nipple, rosy and erect. She caressed the other, rolling it between thumb and forefinger, to arouse herself. His sadness had been cast into her, and she could not quite shake it. His climax, though he was slow to come in that delicious way of older men, left her own demon unsatisfied. She needed more of him, though now he wanted to sleep. Sukie asked, "Do you feel guilty toward Felicia, being with me this way?" It was an unworthy, flirtatious thing to say, but sometimes after being fucked she felt a desperate sliding, a devaluation too steep.

The room's single window held stony moonlight. Bald November reigned outside. Lawn chairs had been taken in, the lawns were dead and flat as floors, the outdoors was bare as a house after the movers had come. The little pear tree bejewelled with fruit had become a set of sticks. A dead geranium stood in a pot on the window sill. The narrow cupboard beside the cold fireplace held green string. A charm slept beneath the bed. Clyde fetched his answer up from a depth near dreams. "No guilt," he said. "Just rage. That bitch has gabbled and prattled my life away. I'm usually numb. Your being so lovely wakes me up a little, and that's not good. It shows me what I've missed, what that self-righteous boring bitch has made me miss."

"I think," Sukie said, still flirtatious, "I'm supposed to be a little extra, I'm not supposed to make you *an*-

gry." Meaning, too, that she was not the one to take him on and get him out from under, he was too sad and poisoned; though she did feel wifely stirrings, still, viewing such men in their dailiness—that stoop their shoulders have when they got up from a chair, the shamefaced awkward way they step in and out of their trousers, how docilely they scrape their whiskers off their faces every day and go out in the world looking for money.

"It makes me dizzy, what you show me," Clyde said, lightly stroking her firm breasts, her flat long abdomen. "You're like a cliff. I want to jump."

"Please don't jump," Sukie said. She heard a child, her youngest, turning in her bed. The house was so small, they were all in one another's arms at night, through the papered odd-shaped walls.

Clyde fell asleep with his hand on her belly, so she had to lift his heavy arm—the soft rasp of his snoring stopped, then resumed—to slide herself from the sway-backed bed. She tried to pee again and failed, took her nightie and bathrobe from the back of the bathroom door, and checked on the restless child, whose covers had all been kicked in the agitation of some nightmare to the floor. Back in bed Sukie lulled herself by flying in her mind to the old Lenox place— the tennis games they could play all winter now that Darryl extravagantly had installed a great canvas bubble-top held up by warm air, and the drinks Fidel would serve them afterwards with their added color-spots of lime and cherry and mint and pimiento, and the way their eyes and giggles and gossip would interlace like the wet circles their glasses left on the glass table in Darryl's huge room where Pop Art was gathering dust. Here, the women were free, on holiday from the stale-smelling life that snored at their sides. When Sukie slept, she dreamed of yet another woman,

Felicia Gabriel, her tense triangular face, talking, talking, angrier and angrier, her face coming closer, the tip of her tongue the color of a bit of pimiento, wagging in relentless level indignation behind her teeth, now flickering between her teeth, touching Sukie here, there, maybe we shouldn't, but it does feel, who's to say what's natural, whatever exists has to be natural, and nobody's watching anyway, nobody, oh, such a hard rapid little red tip, so considerate really, so good. Sukie briefly awoke to realize that the climax Clyde had failed to give her the apparition of Felicia had sought to. Sukie finished the effort with her own left hand, out of rhythm with Clyde's snores. The tiny staggering shadow of a bat passed in front of the moon and this too Sukie found consoling, the thought of something awake besides her mind, as when a late-night trolley car screeched around a distant unseen corner in the night when she was a girl in New York State, in that little brick city like a fingernail at the end of a long icy lake.

Being in love with Sukie made Clyde drink more; drunk, he could sink more relaxedly into the muck of longing. There was now an animal inside him whose gnawing was companionable, a kind of conversation. That he had once longed for Felicia this way made his situation seem all the more satisfactorily hopeless. It was his misfortune to see through everything. He had not believed in God since he was seven, in patriotism since he was ten, in art since the age of fourteen, when he realized he would never be a Beethoven, a Picasso, or a Shakespeare. His favorite authors were the great seers-through—Nietzsche, Hume, Gibbon, the ruthless jubilant lucid minds. More and more he blacked out somewhere between the third and fourth Scotches, unable to remember next morning what book he had been holding in his lap, what meetings Felicia had returned from, when he had gone to bed, how he had moved through the rooms of the house that felt like a vast and fragile husk now that Jennifer and Christopher were gone. Traffic shuddered on Lodowick Street outside like the senseless pumping of Clyde's heart and blood. In his solitary daze of booze and longing he had pulled down from a high dusty shelf his college Lucretius, scribbled throughout with the interlinear translations of his studious, hopeful college self. *Nil igitur mors est ad nos neque pertinet hilum, quandoquidem natura animi mortalis habetur.* He leafed through the delicate little book, its Oxford-blue spine worn white where his youthful moist hands had held it over and over. He looked in vain for that passage where the swerve of atoms is described, that accidental undetermined swerve whereby matter complicates, and all things are thus, through accumulating collisions, including men in their miraculous freedom, brought into being; for without this swerve all atoms would fall ever downwards through the *inane profundum* like drops of rain.

It had been his habit for years to step out into the relative quiet of the back yard before going up to bed and to gaze for a minute at the implausible spatter of stars; it was a knife edge of possibility, he knew, that allowed these fiery bodies to be in the sky, for had the primeval fireball been a shade more homogeneous no galaxies could have formed and had it been a shade less the galaxies would have billions of years ago consumed themselves in a heterogeneity too rash. He would stand by the corroding portable barbecue grill, never used now that the kids were gone, and remind himself to wheel it into the garage now that winter was in the air, and never manage to do it, night after night, lifting his face thirstily to that enigmatic miracle arching overhead. Light sank into his eyes that had started on its way when cave men prowled the vast world in little bands like ants on a pool table. Cygnus, its unfinished cross, and Andromeda, its flying V with, clinging near the second star, the bit of fuzz that—his neglected telescope had often made clear—is a spiral galaxy beyond the Milky Way. Night after night the heavens were the same; Clyde was like a photographic plate exposed again and again; the stars had bored themselves into him like bullet holes in a tin roof.

Tonight his old college *De Rerum Natura* folded its youthfully annotated pages and slipped between his knees. He was thinking of going out for his ritual stargaze when Felicia barged into his study. Though of course it was not his study but theirs, as every room in the house was theirs, and every flaking clapboard and bit of crumbling insulation on the old single-strand copper wiring was theirs, and the rusting barbecue and above the front doorway the wooden eagle plaque with its red, white, and blue weathered in the rain of atoms to rose, yellow, and black.

Felicia unwound striped wool scarves from around her head and throat and stamped her booted feet in indignation. "There are *such* stupid people running this town; they actually voted to change the name of Landing Square to Kazmierczak Square, in honor of that idiotic boy who went off and got himself killed in Vietnam." She pulled off her boots.

"Well," Clyde said, determined to be tactful. Since Sukie's flesh and fur and musk had flooded those cells of his brain set aside for a mate, Felicia seemed diaphanous, an image of a woman painted on tissue paper that might blow away. "That area hasn't really been a boat landing for eighty years. It got all silted in the blizzard of '88." He was innocently proud to be specific; along with astronomy, Clyde, in the days when his head was clear, used to be interested in terrestrial disasters: Krakatoa blowing its top and shrouding the Earth in dust, the Chinese flood of 1931 that killed nearly four million, the Lisbon earthquake of 1755 that struck when all the faithful were in church.

"But it was so *pleas*ant," Felicia said, giving that irrelevant quick smile which showed she thought her words inarguable, "up there at the end of Dock Street, with the benches for the old people, and that old granite obelisk that didn't look like a war memorial at all."

"It might still be pleasant," he offered, wondering if one more inch of Scotch would mercifully knock him out.

"No it won't," Felicia said definitely. She stripped off her coat. She was wearing a broad copper bracelet that Clyde had never seen before. It reminded him of Sukie, who sometimes left her jewelry on but nothing else and walked in nakedness glinting, in the shadowy rooms where they made love. "Next thing they'll want to be naming Dock Street and then Oak Street and then Eastwick itself after some lower-class dropout who couldn't think of anything better to do than go over there and napalm villages."

"Kazmierczak was a pretty good kid, actually. Remember, a few years back, he was their quarterback, and on the honor roll at the same time? That's why people took it so hard when he got killed last summer."

"Well *I* didn't take it hard," Felicia said, smiling as if her point had been clinched. She came near the fire he had built in the grating, to warm her hands now that her mittens were off. She half-turned her back and fiddled with her mouth, as if disentangling a hair from her lips. Clyde didn't know why this by now familiar gesture angered him, since of all the unattractive traits that had come upon her with age this one affliction could not be construed as her fault. In the morning he would see feathers, straw, pennies still slick with saliva stuck to her pillow and want to shake her awake, his own head thundering. "It's not ath if," she insisted, "he was even born and bred in Eastwick. His family moved here about five years ago, and his father refuthes to get a job, just works on the highway crew long enough to get another six months of unemployment. He was at the meeting tonight, wearing a black tie with egg stains all over it. Poor Mrs. K., she tried to dress up so as not to look like a tart but I'm afraid she failed."

Felicia had a considerable love for the underprivileged in the abstract but when actual cases got close to her she tended to hold her nose. There was a fascinating spin to Felicia and Clyde couldn't always resist giving a poke to keep her going. "I don't think Kazmierczak Square has such a bad ring to it," he said.

Felicia's beady furious eyes flashed. "No you wouldn't. You wouldn't think Shithouse Square had such a bad ring to it either. You don't give a damn about the world we pass on to our children or the wars we inflict on the innocent or whether or not we poison ourselves to death, you're poisoning yourself to death right now tho what do you care, drag the whole globe down with you ith the way you look at it." The diction of her tirade had become thick and she carefully lifted from her tongue a small straight pin and what looked like part of an art-gum eraser.

"Our children," he sneered. "I don't see them around to receive the world in whatever shape we pass it on." He drained the glass of Scotch—a taste of smoke and heather amid the cubes of fluoridated water. Ice rattled against his upper lip; he thought of

Sukie's lips, their cushiony expression of pleasure even when she was trying to be solemn and sad. He made her sad, was one of his sorrows. Her lipstick tasted ever so faintly of cherry and sometimes left a line across her two front teeth. He stood to replenish his glass, and staggered. Bits of Sukie—her plump parallel toes tipped with scarlet, her copper necklace of crescents, the pale orange tufts in her armpits—fluttered about him unsteadily. The bottle lived on a lower shelf, beneath a long uniform set of Balzac like so many miniature brown coffins.

"Yes, that's another thing you can't stand, the way Jenny and Chris have gone off, as if you can keep children home forever, as if the world doesn't have to *change* and *grow*. Wake up, Clyde. You thought life was going to be just like those children's books Mommy and Daddy kept piling on your bed every time you were sick, all those Wee Astronomers and Children's Classics and coloring books with safe little outlines and nice pointy crayons in their snug little boxes, when the fact is it's an *or*ganism, Clyde—the world is an organism, it's vital, it's sensitive, it's moving *on*, Clyde, while you sit over there playing with that silly little paper of yours as if you were still Mommy's pet sick in bed. Your so-called reporter Sukie Rougemont was there tonight at the meeting, her piggy little nose in the air, giving me that I-know-something-you-don't-know-look."

Language, he was thinking, perhaps *is* the curse, that took us out of Eden. And here we are trying to teach it to these poor good-natured chimpanzees and grinning dolphins. The Johnnie Walker bottle chortled obligingly in its tilted throat.

"Don't you think, *ooh*," Felicia was going on, exclaiming as the vortex of fury gripped her, "don't you think I don't know about you and that minx, I can read you like a book and don't you forget it, how you'd like to fuck her if you had the guts but you don't, you don't."

The picture of Sukie as she was, blurred and gentle and with a sort of distended amazement in her expression beneath him, when she was being fucked, came into his mind and the strong honey of it paralyzed his tongue, which had wanted to protest, *But I do.*

"You sit here," Felicia was going on, with a chemical viciousness that had become independent of her body, a possession controlling her mouth, her eyes, "you sit here mooning about Jenny and Chris who've at least had the guts and the sense to kiss this Godforsaken town good-bye forever and try to make careers for themselves where things are *hap*pening, you sit here mooning but you know what they used to say to me about you? You really want to know, Clyde? They would say, 'Hey, Mom, wouldn't it be great if Dad would leave us? But, you know,' they would have to add, 'he just doesn't have the guts.'" Scornfully, as if still in the voice of others: "'He just doesn't—have—the guts.'"

The polish, Clyde thought, the polish of her rhetoric was what made it truly insufferable: the artful pauses and repetitions, the way she had picked up the word "guts" and turned it into a musical theme, the way she was making her orotund points before a huge mental audience rapt to the uttermost tier of the bleachers. A crowd of thumbtacks had come up from her gullet during the climax of her peroration, but not even this had stopped her. Felicia spat them swiftly into her hand and tossed them into the log fire he had built. They faintly sizzled; their colored heads blackened. "No gutth at all," she said, extracting one last tack and flicking it through the gap between the bricks and the fire screen, "but he wants to turn the entire town into a memorial for this horrible war. It must all fit, it must be, what do they call it, a syndrome. A drunken weakling wants the entire world to go down with him. Hitler, that's who you remind me of, Clyde. Another weak man the world didn't stand up to. Well, it's not going to happen this time." Now the imaginary crowd had gotten behind her—troops she was leading. *"We're standing up to evil,"* she called, her eyes focused above and beyond his head.

And she stood with legs braced as if he might try to knock her down. But he had taken a step her way because the fire, under its mouthful of wet tacks, seemed to be dying. He pulled back the screen and gave the spread logs a poke with the brass-handled poker. The logs snuggled closer, with sparks. He was reminded of himself and Sukie: a curious benison attendant upon sex with Sukie was how sleepy her proximity made him; at the slithering touch of her skin a blissful languor would steal upon him, after a life of insomnia. Before and after sex her naked body rode so lightly at his side he seemed to have found his spot in space at last. Just thinking of this peace the red-haired divorcee bestowed drew a merciful blankness across his brain.

Perhaps minutes passed. Felicia was vehemently talking. His children's vigorous contempt for him had become involved with his criminal willingness to sit in a chair while unjust wars, fascist governments, and profit-greedy exploiters ravaged the world. The poker's smooth heft was still in his hand. In its chemical indignation her face had gone white as a skull; her eyes burned like the tiny flames of votive candles deep in the waxy pockets they have hollowed. Her hair seemed to be standing up in a ragged, skimpy halo. Most horribly, things kept coming out of her mouth—parrot feathers, dead wasps, bits of eggshell all mixed in an unstoppable thin gruel she kept wiping from her chin

in a rhythmic gesture like cocking a gun. He saw these
extrusions as a sign; this woman was possessed, she bore
no relation to the woman he in good faith had married.
"Hey come on, Lishy," Clyde begged, "let's cool it. Let's
call it a day." The chemical and mechanical action that
had replaced her soul surged on; in her trance of indignation she had ceased to see and hear. Her voice would
wake the neighbors. Her voice was growing louder, fed
inexhaustibly from within. His drink was in his left
hand; he lifted the poker in his right and slashed it down
across her head, just to interrupt the flow of energy for
a moment, to plug the hole through which too much
was pouring. The bone of her skull gave off a surprising high-pitched noise, as if two blocks of wood had been
playfully knocked together. Her eyeballs rolled upward,
displaying their whites, and her lips parted involuntarily, showing on her tongue an impossibly blue small
feather. He knew he was making a mistake but the
silence felt heaven-sent. His own chemicals took over;
he hit her head with the poker again and again, pursuing it in its slow fall to the floor, until the sound the
blows made was more liquid than that of wood knocking wood. He had plugged this hole in cosmic peace
forever.

An immense sheath of relief slid upward from Clyde
Gabriel, a film slipping from his sweat-coated body
like a polyethylene protecting bag being pulled from
a clean suit. He sipped on the Scotch and avoided
looking at the floor. He thought of the stars outside
and of the impervious pattern they would be making
on this night of his life as on every other in the aeons
since the galaxy condensed. Though he still had a lot
to do, and some of it very difficult, a miraculously
refreshed perspective gave each of his actions a
squared-off clarity, as if indeed he had been returned
to those illustrated children's books Felicia had scorn-

fully conjured up. How curious of her to do so: she had been right, he had loved those days of staying home from school sick. She knew him too well. Marriage is like two people locked up with one lesson to read, over and over, until the words become madness. He thought she whimpered from the floor but decided it was only the fire digesting a tiny vein of sap.

As a conscientious, neatness-loving child Clyde had relished architectural drawings—ones that showed every molding and lintel and ledge and made manifest the triangular diminishments of perspective. With ruler and blue pencil he used to extend the diminishing lines of drawings in magazines and comic books to the vanishing point, even when the point lay well off the page. That such a point existed was a pleasing concept to him, and perhaps his first glimpse into adult fraudulence was the discovery that in many flashy-looking drawings the artists had cheated: there was no exact vanishing point. Now Clyde in person had arrived at this place of final perspective, and everything was ideally lucid and crisp around him. Vast problematical areas—next Wednesday's issue of the *Word*, the arrangement of his next tryst with Sukie, that perpetual struggle of lovers to find privacy and a bed that did not feel tawdry, the recurrent pain of putting back on his underclothes and leaving her, the necessity to consult with Joe Marino about the no-longer-overlookable decrepitude of this house's old furnace and deteriorating pipes and radiators, the not dissimilar condition of his liver and stomach lining, the periodic blood tests and consultations with Doc Pat and all the insincere resolutions his deplorable condition warranted, and now no end of complication with the police and the law courts—were swept away, leaving only the outlines of this room, the lines of its carpentry clean as laser beams.

He tossed down the last of his drink. It scraped his guts. Felicia had been wrong to say he didn't have any. In setting the tumbler on the fireplace mantel he could not avoid the peripheral vision of her stocking feet, fallen awkwardly apart as if in mid-step of an intricate dance. She had in truth been a nimble jitterbugger at Warwick High. That wonderful pumping, wah-wahing big-band sound even little local bands could fabricate in those days. The tip of her girlish tongue would show between her teeth as she set herself to be twirled. He stooped and picked up the Lucretius from the floor and returned it to its place on the shelf. He went down into the cellar to look for a rope. The disgraceful old furnace was chewing its fuel with a strained whine; its brittle rusty carapace leaked so much heat the basement was the coziest part of the house. There was an old laundry room where the previous owners had left an antique Bendix with wringers and an old-fashioned smell of naphtha and even a basket of clothespins on the round tin lid of its tub. The games he used to play with clothespins, crayoning them into little long-legged men wearing round hats somewhat like sailor hats. Clothesline, nobody uses clothesline any more. But here was a coil, neatly looped and tucked behind the old washer in a world of cobwebs. The transparent hand of Providence, Clyde suddenly realized, was guiding him. With his own, opaque hands—veiny, gnarled, an old man's claws, hideous—he gave the rope a sharp yank and inspected six or eight feet of it for frayed spots that might give way. A rusty pair of metal shears lay handy and he cut off the needed length.

As when climbing a mountain, take one step at a time and don't look too far ahead up the path: this resolve carried him smoothly back up the stairs, holding the dusty rope. He turned left into the kitchen and looked up. The ceiling here had been lowered in renovation and presented a flimsy surface of textured cellulose tiles held in a grid of aluminum strapping. The house had nine-foot plaster ceilings in the other downstairs rooms; the ornate chandelier canopies, none of which still held a chandelier, might not take his weight even if he climbed a stepladder and found a protuberance to knot the clothesline around.

He went back into his library to pour one more drink. The fire was burning a bit less merrily and could do with another log; but such an attention lay on that vast sheet of concerns no longer relevant, no longer his. It took some getting used to, how hugely much no longer mattered. He sipped the drink and felt the smoky amber swallow descend toward a digestion that was also off the board, in the dark, not to occur. He thought of the cozy basement and wondered whether, if he promised just to live there in one of the old coal bins and never go outdoors, all might be forgiven and smoothed over. But this cringing thought polluted the purity he had created in his mind minutes ago. Think again.

Perhaps the rope was the problem. He had been a newspaperman for thirty years and knew of the rich variety of methods whereby people take their own lives. Suicide by automobile was actually one of the commonest; automotive suicides were buried every day by satisfied priests and unaffronted loved ones. But the method was uncertain and messily public and at this vanishing point all the aesthetic prejudices Clyde had suppressed in living seemed to be welling up along with images from his childhood. Some people, given the blaze in the fireplace, the awful evidence on the floor, and the thoroughly wooden house, might have made a pyre for themselves. But this would leave Jenny and Chris with no inheritance and Clyde was *not* one of those like Hitler who wanted to take the world with him; Felicia had been crazy in this comparison. Further, how could he trust himself not to save his scorched skin and flee to the lawn? He was no Buddhist monk, trained in discipline of that craven beast the body and able to sit in calm protest until the charred flesh toppled. Gas was held to be painless but then he was no mechanic either, to find the masking tape and string putty to seal off the many windows of the kitchen whose roominess and sunniness had been one of the factors in Felicia's and his decision to buy the house thirteen years ago this December. All of this year's December, it occurred to him with a guilty joy, December with its short dark tinselly days and ghastly herd buying and wooden homage to a dead religion (the dime-store carols, the pathetic crèche at Landing—Kazmierczak—Square, the Christmas tree erected at the other end of Dock Street in that great round marble urn called the Horse Trough), all of December was among the many things now off Clyde's sublimely simplified calendar. Nor would he have to pay next month's oil bill. Or gas bill. But he disdained the awkward wait gas would require, and he did not want his last view of reality to be the inside of a gas oven as he held his head in it on all fours in the servile position of a dog about to be fed. He rejected the messiness with knives and razor blades and bathtubs. Pills were painless and tidy but one of Felicia's causes had been a faddish militance against the pharmaceutical companies and what she said was their attempt to create a stoned America, a nation of drug-dependent zombies. Clyde smiled, the deep crease in his cheek leaping up. Some of what the old girl said had made sense. She hadn't been entirely babble. But he did not think she was right about Jennifer and Chris; he had never expected or desired them to stay home forever, he was offended only by Chris's going into such a flaky profession as the stage and Jenny's moving so far away, to Chicago no less, and letting herself be bombarded by X-rays, her ovaries exposed so she might never bear him any grandchildren. They too were off the map, grandchildren. Having children is something we think we ought to do because our parents did it, but when it is over the children are just other members of the human race, rather disappointingly. Jenny and Chris had been good quiet children and there had been something a bit disappointing in that too; by being good they had been evading Felicia, who when younger and not so plugged into altruism had had a terrible temper (sexual frustration no doubt at the root of it, but how can any husband keep a woman protected and excited at the same time?), and in the process the children had evaded him also. Jenny when about nine used to worry about death and once asked him why he didn't say prayers with her like the other daddies and though he didn't have much of an answer that was the closest together they had ever drawn. He had always been trying to read and her coming to him had been an interruption. With a better pair of parents Jenny could have grown to be a saint, such light pale clear eyes, a face as smooth as a photographed face after the retoucher is done with it. Until he had had a girl baby Clyde had never really seen female genitals, so sweet and puffy like twin little pale buns off a pastry tray.

The town had grown very silent around them, around him: not a car was stirring on Lodowick Street. His stomach hurt. It usually did, this time of night: an incipient ulcer. Doc Pat had told him, If you *must* keep drinking, at least eat. One of the unfortunate side effects of his affair with Sukie was skipping lunch in order to fuck. She sometimes brought a jar of cashews but with his bad teeth he wasn't that fond of nuts any more; the crumbs got under the appliance and cut his gums.

Amazing, women, the way loving never fills them up. If you do a good job they want more the next minute, as bad as getting out a newspaper. Even Felicia, for all she said she hated him. This time of night he would be having one more nip by the dying fire, giving her time to get herself into bed and fall asleep waiting for him. Having talked herself out, she toppled in a minute into the oblivion of the just. He wondered now if she had been hypoglycemic: in the mornings she had been clearheaded and the ghostly audience she gave her speeches to had dispersed. She had never seemed to grasp how much she infuriated him. Some mornings, on a Saturday or Sunday, she would keep her nightie on as provocation, by way of making up. You would think a man and woman living together so many hours of their lives would find a moment to make up in. Missed opportunities. If tonight he had just ridden it out and let her get safely upstairs... But that possibility, too, along with his grandchildren and the healing of his liquor-pitted stomach and his troubles with his little denture, was off the map.

Clyde had the sensation of there being several of him, like ghost images on TV. This time of night he, in a parade of such ghost images, would mount the stairs. The stairs. The limp dry old rope still dangled in his hand. Its cobwebs had come off on his corduroy trousers. Lord give me strength.

The staircase was a rather grand Victorian construction that doubled back after a midway landing with a view of the back yard and its garden, once elaborate but rather let go in recent years. A rope tied to the base of one of the upstairs balusters should provide enough swing room over the stairs below, which could serve as a kind of gallows platform. He carried the rope upstairs to the second-floor landing. He worked rapidly, fearing the alcohol might overtake him with a blackout. A square knot was right over left, then left over right. Or was it? His first attempt produced a granny. It was hard to move his hands through the narrow spaces between the squared baluster bases; his knuckles got skinned. His hands seemed to be a great distance from his eyes, and to have become luminous, as though plunged into an ethereal water. It took prodigies of calculation to figure where the loop in the rope should come (not more than six or eight inches under the narrow facing board with its touchingly fine Victorian molding, or his feet might touch the stairs and that blind animal his body would struggle to keep alive) and how big the loop for his head should be. Too big, he would fall through; too snug, he might merely strangle. The hangman's art: the neck should break, he had read more than once in his life, thanks to a sudden sharp pressure on the cervical vertebrae. Prisoners in jail used their belts with blue-faced results. Chris had been in Boy Scouts but that had been years ago and there had been a scandal with the scoutmaster that had broken up the den. Clyde finally produced a messy kind of compound slip knot and let the noose hang over the side. Viewed from above, by leaning over the banister, the perspective was sickening; the rope lightly swayed and kept swaying, turned into a pendulum by some waft of air that moved uninvited through this drafty house.

Clyde's heart was no longer in it but with the methodical determination that had put ten thousand papers to bed he went into the warm cellar (the old furnace chewing, chewing fuel) and fetched the aluminum stepladder. It felt feather-light; the might of angels was descending upon him. He also carried up some lumber scraps and with these set the ladder on the carpeted stairs so that, one pair of plastic feet resting three risers lower than the other on pieces of wood, the step-less crossbraced rails were vertical and the entire tilted *A*-shape would topple over at a nudge. The last thing he would see, he estimated, would be the front doorway and the leaded fanlight of stained glass, its vaguely sun-riselike symmetrical pattern lit up by the sodium glow of a distant street lamp. By light nearer to hand, scratches on the aluminum seemed traces left by the swerving flight of atoms in a bubble chamber. Every-thing was touched with transparency; the many taper-ing, interlocked lines of the staircase were as the architect had dreamed them; it came to Clyde Gabriel, rapturously, that there was nothing to fear, of course our spirits passed through matter like the sparks of divinity they were, of course there would be an afterlife of infinite opportunities, in which he could patch things up with Felicia, and have Sukie too, not once but an infinity of times, just as Nietzsche had conjectured. A lifelong fog was lifting; it was all as clear as rectified type, the meaning that the stars had been singing out to him, *candida sidera*, tingeing with light his sluggish spirit sunk in its proud muck.

The aluminum ladder shivered slightly, like a highstrung youthful steed, as he trusted his weight to it. One step, two, then the third. The rope nestled dryly around his neck; the ladder trembled as he reached up and behind to slip the knot tighter, snug against what seemed the correct spot. Now the ladder was swinging violently from side to side; the agitated blood of its jockey was flailing it toward the hurdle, where it lifted, as he had foreseen, at the most delicate urging, and fell away. Clyde heard the clatter and thump. What he had not expected was the burning, as though a hot rasp were being pulled up through his esophagus, and the way the angles of wood and carpet and wallpaper whirled, whirled so widely it seemed for a second he had sprouted eyes in the back of his head. Then a redness in his overstuffed skull was followed by blackness, giving way, with the change of a single letter, to blankness.

"Oh baby, how horrible for you," Jane Smart said to Sukie, over the phone.

"Well it's not as if I'd had to see any of it myself. But the guys down at the police station were plenty vivid. Apparently she didn't have any face *left*." Sukie was not crying but her voice had that wrinkled quality of paper that has been damp and though dry will never lie flat again.

"Well she was a *vile* woman," Jane said firmly, comforting, though her head with its eyes and ears was still back in the suite of Bach unaccompanieds—the exhilarating, somehow malevolently onrushing Fourth, in E-flat Major. "So boring, so self-righteous," she hissed. Her eyes rested on the bare floor of her living room, splintered by repeated heedless socketing of her cello's pointed steel foot.

Sukie's voice faded in and out, as though she were letting the telephone drop away from her chin. "I've never known a man," she said, a bit huskily, "gentler than Clyde."

"Men are violent," Jane said, her patience wearing thin. "Even the mildest of them. It's biological. They're full of rage because they're just accessories to reproduction."

"He hated even to correct anybody at work," Sukie went on, as the sublime music—its diabolical rhythms, its wonderfully cruel demands upon her dexterity—slowly faded from Jane's mind, and the sting from the side of her left thumb, where she had been ardently pressing the strings. "Though once in a while he would blow up at some proofreader who had let just *oo*dles of things slip through."

"Well darling, it's obvious. That's why. He was keeping it all inside. When he blew up at Felicia he had thirty years' worth of rage, no wonder he took off her head."

"It's not fair to say he took off her head," Sukie said. "He just kind of—what's that phrase everybody's using these days?—*was*ted it."

"And then wasted himself," prompted Jane, hoping by such efficient summary to hasten this conversation along so she could return to her music; she liked to practice two hours in the mornings, from ten to noon, and then give herself a tidy lunch of cottage cheese or tuna salad spooned into a single large curved lettuce leaf. This afternoon she had set up a matinee with Darryl Van Horne at one-thirty. They would work for an hour on one of the two Brahmses or an amusing little Kodály Darryl had unearthed in a music shop tucked in the basement of a granite building on Weybosset Street just beyond the Arcade, and then have, their custom was, Asti Spumante, or some tequila milk Fidel would do in the blender, and a bath. Jane still ached, at both ends of her perineum, from their last time together. But most of the good things that come to a woman come through pain and she had been flattered that he would want her without an audience, unless you counted Fidel and Rebecca padding in and out with trays and towels; there was something precarious about Darryl's lust that was flattered and soothed by the three of them being there together and that needed the most extravagant encouragements when Jane was with him by herself. She added to Sukie irritably, "That he was clear-minded enough to carry it through is what I find surprising."

Sukie defended Clyde. "Liquor never made him

confused unusually, he really drank as a kind of medicine. I think a lot of his depression must have been metabolic; he once told me his blood pressure was one-ten over seventy, which in a man his age was really wonderful."

Jane snapped, "I'm sure a lot of things about him were wonderful for a man of his age. I certainly preferred him to that deplorable Ed Parsley."

"Oh, Jane, I know you're dying to get me off the phone, but speaking of Ed..."

"Yess?"

"Have you been noticing how close Brenda has grown to the Neffs?"

"I've rather lost track of the Neffs, frankly."

"I know you have, and good for you," Sukie said. "Lexa and I always thought he abused you and you were much too gifted for his little group; it really was just jealousy, his saying your bowing or whatever he said was prissy."

"Thank you, sweet."

"Anyway, the two of them and Brenda are apparently thick as thieves now, they eat out at the Bronze Barrel or that new French place over toward Pettaquamscutt all the time and evidently Ray and Greta have encouraged her to put in for Ed's position at the church and become the new Unitarian minister. Apparently the Lovecrafts are all for it too and Horace you know is on the church board."

"But she's not ordained. Don't you have to be ordained? The Episcopalians where I fill in are very strict about things like that; you can't even join as a member unless a bishop has put his hands somewhere, I think on your head."

"No, but she *is* in the parsonage with those brats of theirs—abso*lu*tely undisciplined, neither Ed or Brenda believed in ever saying No—and making her the new minister might be more graceful than getting her to leave. Maybe there's a course or something you can take by mail."

"But can she preach? You *do* have to preach."

"Oh I don't think that would be any real problem. Brenda has wonderful posture. She was studying to be a modern dancer when she met Ed at an Adlai Stevenson rally; she was in one of the warm-up acts and he was to ask the blessing. He told me about it more than once, I used to wonder if he wasn't still in love with her after all."

"She is a ridiculous vapid woman," Jane said.

"Oh Jane, don't."

"Don't what?"

"Don't sound like that. That's the way we used to talk about Felicia, and look what happened."

Sukie had become very small and curled over at her end of the line, like a lettuce leaf wilting. "Are you blaming *us*?" Jane asked her briskly. "Her sad sot of a husband I would think instead should be blamed."

"On the surface, sure, but we *did* cast that spell, and put those things in the cookie jar when we got tiddly, and things did keep coming out of her mouth, Clyde mentioned it to me so innocently, he tried to get her to go to a doctor but she said medicine ought to be entirely nationalized in this country the way it is in England and Sweden. She hated the drug companies, too."

"She was full of hate, darling. It was the hate coming out of her mouth that did her in, not a few harmless feathers and pins. She had lost touch with her womanhood. She needed pain to remind her she was a woman. She needed to get down on her knees and drink some horrible man's nice cold come. She needed to be beaten, Clyde was right about that, he just went at it too hard."

"Please, Jane. You frighten me when you talk like that, the things you say."

"Why *not* say them? Really, Sukie, you sound infantile." Sukie was a weak sister, Jane thought. They put up with her for the gossip she gathered and that kid-sister shine she used to bring to their Thursdays but she really was just a conceited immature girl, she couldn't please Van Horne the way that Jane did, that burning stretching; even Greta Neff, washed-out old bag as she was with her granny glasses and pathetic pedantic accent, was more of a woman in this sense, a woman who could hold whole kingdoms of night within her, burning. "Words are just words," she added.

"They're not: they make things *hap*pen!" Sukie wailed, her voice shrivelled to a pathetic wheedle. "Now two people are dead and two children are orphans because of us!"

"I don't think you can be an orphan after a certain age," Jane said. "Stop talking nonsense." Her *s*'s hissed like spit on a stove top. "People stew in their own juice."

"If I hadn't slept with Clyde he wouldn't have gone so crazy, I'm sure of it. He loved me so, Jane. He used to just hold my foot in his two hands and kiss between each pair of toes."

"Of course he did. That's the kind of thing men are supposed to do. They're supposed to adore us. They're shits, try to keep that in mind. Men are absolutely shits, but we get them in the end because we can suffer better. A woman can outsuffer a man every time." Jane felt huge in her impatience; the black notes she had swallowed that morning bristled within her, alive. Who would have thought the old Lutheran had so much jism? "There will always be men for you, sweetie," she told Sukie. "Don't bother your head about

Clyde any more. You gave him what he asked for, it's not your fault he couldn't handle it. Listen, truly. I must run." Jane Smart lied, "I have a lesson coming in at eleven."

In fact her lesson was not until four. She would rush back from the old Lenox place aching and steamy-clean and the sight of those grubby little hands on her pure ivory keys mangling some priceless simpli-fied melody of Mozart's or Mendelssohn's would make her want to take the metronome and with its heavy base mash those chubby fingers as if she were grinding beans in a pestle. Since Van Horne had come into her life Jane was more passionate than she had ever been about music, that golden high-arched exit from this pit of pain and ignominy.

"She sounded so harsh and strange," Sukie said to Alexandra over the phone a few days later. "It's as if she thinks she has the inside track with Darryl and is fighting to protect it."

"That's one of his diabolical arts, to give each of us that impression. I'm really quite sure it's me he loves," said Alexandra, laughing with cheerful hopelessness. "He has me doing these bigger pieces of sculpture now, varnished papier-mâché is what this Saint-Phalle woman uses, I don't know how she does it, the glue gets all over your fingers, into your hair, *yukk*. I get one side of a figure looking right and then the other side has no shape at all, just a bunch of loose ends and lumps."

"Yes he was saying to me when I lose my job at the *Word* I should try a novel. I can't imagine sitting down day after day to the same story. And the people's names—people just don't *exist* without their real names."

"Well," Alexandra sighed, "he's challenging us. He's stretching us."

Over the phone she did sound stretched—more diffuse and distant every second, sinking into a translucent quicksand of estrangement. Sukie had come back to her house after the Gabriels' funeral, and no child was home from school yet, yet the little old house was sighing and muttering to itself, full of memories and mice. There were no nuts or munchies in the kitchen and as the next best consolation she had reached for the phone. "I miss our Thursdays," she abruptly confessed, childlike.

"I know, baby, but we have our tennis parties instead. Our baths."

"They frighten me sometimes. They're not as cozy as we used to be by ourselves."

"*Are* you going to lose your job? What's happening with that?"

"Oh I don't know, there are so many rumors. They say the owner rather than find a new editor is going to sell out to a chain of small-town weeklies the gangsters operate out of Providence. Everything is printed in Pawtucket and the only local news is what a correspondent phones in from her home and the rest is statewide feature articles and things they buy from a syndicate and they give them away to everybody like supermarket fliers."

"Nothing is as cozy as it used to be, is it?"

"*No,*" Sukie blurted, but could not quite, like a child, cry.

A pause occurred, where in the old days they could hardly stop talking. Now each woman had her share, her third, of Van Horne to be secretive about, their solitary undiscussed visits to the island which in stark soft gray December had become more beautiful than ever; the ocean's silver-tinged horizon was visible now from those upstairs Arguslike windows behind which Van Horne had his black-walled bedroom, visible through the leafless beeches and oaks and swaying larches surrounding the elephantine canvas bubble that held the tennis court, where the snowy egrets used to nest. "How was the funeral?" Alexandra at last asked.

"Well, you know how they are. Sad and gauche at the same time. They were cremated, and it seemed so strange, burying these little rounded boxes like Styrofoam coolers, only brown, and smaller. Brenda Parsley said the prayer at the undertaker's, because they haven't found a replacement for Ed yet, and the Gabriels weren't anything really, though Felicia was always going on about everybody else's Godlessness. But the daughter wanted I guess some kind of religious touch. Very few people came, actually, considering all the publicity. Mostly *Word* employees putting in an appearance hoping to keep their jobs, and a few people who had been on committees with Felicia, but she had quarrelled you know with almost everybody. The people at Town Hall are delighted to have her off their backs, they all called her a witch."

"Did you speak to Brenda?"

"Just a bit, out at the cemetery. There were so few of us."

"How did she act toward you?"

"Oh, very polished and cool. She owes me one and she knows it. She wore a navy-blue suit with a ruffled silk blouse that did look sort of wonderfully ministerial. And her hair done in a different way, swept back quite severely and without those bangs like the woman in Peter, Paul, and Mary that used to make her look, you know, puppyish. An improvement, really. It was Ed used to make her wear those miniskirts, so he'd feel more like a hippie, which was really rather humiliating, if you have Brenda's piano legs. She spoke quite well, especially at the graveside. This lovely fluting voice floating out over the headstones. She talked about how much into community service both the deceased were and tried to make some connection between their deaths and Vietnam, the moral confusion of our times, I couldn't quite follow it."

"Did you ask her if she hears from Ed?"

"Oh I wouldn't dare. Anyway I doubt it, since *I* never do any more. But she did bring him up. Afterwards, when the men were tugging the plastic grass around, she looked me very levelly in the eye and said his leaving was the best thing ever happened to her."

"Well, what else can she say? What else can any of us say?"

"Lexa sweet, whatever do you mean? You sound as though you're weakening."

"Well, one does get weary. Carrying everything alone. The bed is so cold this time of year."

"You should get an electric blanket."

"I have one. But I don't like the feeling of electricity on top of me. Suppose Felicia's ghost comes in and pours a bucket of cold water all over the bed, I'd be electrocuted."

"Alexandra, don't. Don't scare me by sounding so depressed. We all look to you for whatever it is. Mother-strength."

"Yes, and that's depressing too."

"Don't you believe in any of it any more?"

In freedom, in witchcraft. Their powers, their ecstasy.

"Of course I do, poops. Were the children there? What do they look like?"

"Well," Sukie said, her voice regaining animation, giving the news, "rather remarkable. They both look like Greek statues in a way, very stately and pale and perfect. And they stick together like twins even though the girl is a good bit older. Jennifer, her name is, is in her late twenties and the boy is college-age, though he's not in college; he wants to be something in show business and spends all his time getting rides back and forth between Los Angeles and New York. He was a stagehand at a summer-theatre place in Connecticut and the girl flew in from Chicago where she's taken a leave from her job as an X-ray technician. Marge Perley says they're going to stay here in the house a while to get the estate settled; I was thinking maybe we should do something with them. They seem such babes in the woods, I hate to think of their falling into Brenda's clutches."

"Baby, they've surely heard all about you and Clyde and blame you for everything."

"Really? How could they? I was being nothing but kind."

"You upset his internal balances. His ecology."

Sukie confessed, "I don't like feeling guilty."

"Who does? How do you think I feel, poor dear quite unsuitable Joe keeps offering to leave Gina and that swarm of fat children for me."

"But he never will. He's too Mediterranean. Catholics never get conflicted like us poor lapsed Protestants do."

"Lapsed," Alexandra said. "Is that how you think of yourself? I'm not sure I ever had anything to lapse from."

There entered into Sukie's mind, broadcast from Alexandra's, a picture of a western wooden church with a squat weatherbeaten steeple, high in the mountains and unvisited. "Monty was very religious," Sukie said. "He was always talking about his ancestors." And on the same wavelength the image of Monty's drooping milk-smooth buttocks came to her and she knew at last for certain that he and Alexandra had had an affair. She yawned, and said, "I think I'll go over to Darryl's and unwind. Fidel is developing some wonderful new concoction he calls a Rum Mystique."

"Are you sure it isn't Jane's day?"

"I think she was having her day the day I talked to her. Her talk was really excited."

"It burns."

"Exactly. Oh, Lexa, you really should see Jennifer Gabriel, she's delicious. She makes me look like a tired old hag. This pale round face and these pale blue eyes like Clyde had and a pointy chin like Felicia had and the most delicate little nose, with a fine straight edge like something you would sculpture with a butter knife but slightly dented into her face, like a cat's if you can picture it. And such skin!"

"Delicious," Alexandra echoed, driftingly. Alexandra used to love her, Sukie knew. That first night at Darryl's, dancing to Joplin, they had clung together and wept at the curse of heterosexuality that held them apart as if each were a rose in a plastic tube. Now there was a detachment in Alexandra's voice. Sukie remembered that charm she made, with its magical triple bow, and reminded herself to take it out from under her bed. Spells go bad, lose efficacy, within about a month, if no human blood is involved.

And a few more days later Sukie met the female Gabriel orphan walking without her brother along Dock Street: on that wintry, slightly crooked sidewalk, half the shops shuttered for the winter and the others devoted to scented tinted candles and Austrian-style Christmas ornaments imported from Korea, these two stars shone to each other from afar and tensely let gravitational attraction bring them together, while the windows of the travel agency and the Superette, of the Yapping Fox with its cable-knit sweaters and sensible plaid skirts and of the Hungry Sheep with its slightly slinkier wear, of Perley Realty with its faded snapshots of Cape-and-a-halfs and great dilapidating Victorian gems along Oak Street waiting for an enterprising young couple to take them over and make the third floor into apartments, of the bakery and the barbershop and the Christian Science reading room all stared. The Eastwick branch of the Old Stone Bank had installed against much civic objection a drive-in window, and Sukie and Jennifer had to wait as if on opposite banks of a stream while several cars nosed in and out of the slanted accesses carved into the sidewalk. The downtown was much too cramped and historic, the objectors, led by the late Felicia Gabriel, had pointed out in vain, for such a further complication of traffic.

Sukie at last made it to the younger woman's side, around the giant fins of a crimson Cadillac being guardedly steered by fussy, dim-sighted Horace Lovecraft. Jennifer wore a dirty old buff parka wherein the down had flattened and one of Felicia's scarves, a loose-knit purple one, wrapped several times around her throat and chin. Several inches shorter than Sukie, she seemed an undernurtured waif, her eyes watery and nostrils pink. The thermometer that day stood near zero.

"How's it going?" Sukie asked, with forced cheer.

In size and age this girl was to Sukie as Sukie was to Alexandra; though Jennifer was wary she had to yield to superior powers. "Not so bad," she responded, in a small voice whittled smaller by the cold. She had acquired in Chicago a touch of Midwestern nasality in her pronunciation. She studied Sukie's face and took a little plunge, adding confidingly, "There's so much stuff; Chris and I are overwhelmed. We've both been living like gypsies, and Mommy and Daddy kept *ev*erything—drawings we both did in kindergarten, our grade-school report cards, boxes and boxes of old photographs...."

"It must be sad."

"Well, that, and *frus*trating. They should have made some of these decisions themselves. And you can see how things were let slide these last years; Mrs. Perley said we'd be cheating ourselves if we didn't wait to sell it until after we can get it painted in the spring. It would cost maybe two thousand and add ten to the value of the place."

"Look. You look frozen." Sukie herself was snug and imperial-looking in a long sheepskin coat, and a hat of red fox fur that picked up the copper glint of her own. "Let's go over to Nemo's and I'll buy you a cup of coffee."

"Well..." The girl wavered, looking for a way out, but tempted by the idea of warmth.

Sukie pressed her offensive. "Maybe you hate me, from things you've heard. If so, it might do you good to talk it out."

"Mrs. Rougemont, why would I hate you? It's just Chris is at the garage with the car, the Volvo—even the car they left us was way overdue for its checkup."

"Whatever's wrong with it will take longer to fix than they said," Sukie said authoritatively, "and I'm sure Chris is happy. Men love garages. All that banging. We can sit at a table in the front so you can see him go by if he does. Please. I want to say how sorry I am about your parents. He was a kind boss and I'm in trouble too, now that he's gone."

A badly rusted '59 Chevrolet, its trunk shaped like gull wings, nearly brushed them with its chrome protuberances as it lumbered up over the curb toward the browny-green drive-in window; Sukie touched the girl's arm to safeguard her. Then, not letting go, she urged her across the street to Nemo's. Dock Street had been widened more than once as motor traffic increased in this century; its crooked sidewalks had been pared in places to the width of a single pedestrian and some of the older buildings jutted out at odd angles. Nemo's Diner was a long aluminum box with rounded corners and a broad red stripe along its sides. In midmorning it held only the counter crowd—underemployed or retired men several of whom with casual handlift or nod greeted Sukie, but less gladly, it seemed to her, than before Clyde Gabriel had let horror into the town.

The little tables at the front were empty, and the picture window that overlooked the street here sweated and trickled with condensation. As Jennifer squinted against the light, small creases leaped up at the corners of her ice-pale eyes and Sukie saw that she was not quite so young as she had seemed on the street, swaddled in rags. Her dirty parka, patched with iron-on rectangles of tan vinyl, she laid a bit ceremoniously across the chair beside her, and coiled the long purple skein of scarf upon it. Underneath, she wore a simple gray skirt and white lamb's-wool sweater. She had a tidy plump figure; and there was a roundness to her that seemed too simple—her arms and breasts and cheeks and throat all defined with the same neat circular strokes.

Rebecca, the slatternly Antiguan Fidel was known to keep company with, came with crooked hips and her heavy gray lips twisted wryly shut on all she knew. "Now what you ladies be liking?"

"Two coffees," Sukie asked her, and on impulse also ordered johnnycakes. She had a weakness for them; they were so crumby and buttery and today would warm her insides.

"Why did you say I might hate you?" the other woman asked, with surprising directness, yet in a mild slight voice.

"Because." Sukie decided to get it over with. "I was your father's—whatever. You know. Lover. But not for long, only since summer. I didn't mean to mess anybody up, I just wanted to give him something, and I'm all I have. And he *was* lovable, as you know."

The girl showed no surprise but became more thoughtful, lowering her eyes. "I know he was," she said. "But not much recently, I think. Even when we were little, he seemed distracted and sad. And then smelled funny at night. Once I knocked some big book out of his lap trying to cuddle and he started to spank me and couldn't seem to stop." Her eyes lifted as her mouth shut on further confession; there was a curious vanity, the vanity of the meek, in the way her nicely formed, unpainted lips sealed so neatly one against the other. Her upper lip lifted a bit in faint distaste. "*You* tell me about him. My father."

"What about him?"

"What he was like."

Sukie shrugged. "Tender. Grateful. Shy. He drank too much but when he knew he was going to see me he would try not to, so he wouldn't be—stupid. You know. Sluggish."

"Did he have a lot of girlfriends?"

"Oh no. I don't think so." Sukie was offended. "Just me, was my conceited impression. He loved your mother, you know. At least until she became so— obsessed."

"Obsessed with what?"

"I'm sure you know better than I. With making the world a perfect place."

"That's rather nice, isn't it, that she wanted it to be?"

"I suppose." Sukie had never thought of it as nice, Felicia's public nagging: a spiteful ego trip, rather, with more than an added pinch of hysteria. Sukie did not appreciate being put on the defensive by this bland little ice maiden, who from the sound of her voice might be getting a cold. Sukie volunteered, "You know, if you're single in a town like this you pretty much have to take what you can find."

"No I don't know," said Jennifer, but softly. "But then I guess I don't know much about that sort of thing altogether."

Meaning what? That she was a virgin? It was hard to know if the girl was empty or if her strange stillness manifested an exceptionally complete inner poise. "Tell me about you," Sukie said. "You're going to become a doctor? Clyde was so proud of that."

"Oh, but it's a fraud. I keep running out of money and flunking anatomy. It was the chemistry I liked. The technician job is really as far as I'm ever going to go. I'm stuck."

Sukie told her, "You should meet Darryl Van Horne. He's trying to get us all *un*stuck."

Jennifer unexpectedly smiled, her little flat nose whitening with the tension. Her front teeth were round as a child's. "What a grand name," she said. "It sounds made up. Who is he?"

But she must, Sukie thought, have heard about our sabbats. The girl was difficult to see through; patches of an unnatural innocence, as though she had been skipped by life, blocked telepathy as lead blocks X-rays. "Oh, a sort of eccentric youngish middle-aged man who's bought the old Lenox place. You know, the big brick mansion toward the beach."

"The haunted plantation, we used to call that. I was fifteen when my parents moved here and really never got to know the area terribly well. There's an enormous amount to it, though it looks like nothing on the map."

Insolent tropical Rebecca brought their coffee in Nemo's heavy white mugs, and the golden johnny-cakes; along with the pronounced warm fragrances of these there carried across the glazed table a spicy sour smell that Sukie linked to the waitress herself, her broad pelvis and heavy coffee-colored breasts, as she leaned over to set the mugs and plates in place. "Is there anything wanting now of you ladies' happiness?" the waitress asked, looking down upon them from the great slopes of herself. Her head looked rather small and sinewy—her black hair done in corn rows of tight braids—upon the mass of her flesh.

"Is there any cream, Becca?" Sukie asked.

"I get you de one." Putting down the little aluminum pitcher, she told them, "You can say 'cream' if you likes, milk is what de boss puts in every mornin'."

"Thank you, darling, I *meant* milk." But for a little joke Sukie quickly said to herself the white spell *Sator arepo tenet opera rotas*, and the milk poured thick and yellow, cream. Curdled flecks rotated on the circular surface of her coffee. Johnnycake turned to buttery fragments in her mouth. Indian ghosts of cornmeal slipped through the forest of her tastebuds. She swallowed and said, of Van Horne, "He's nice. You'd like him, once you got over his manner."

"What's wrong with his manner?"

Sukie wiped crumbs from her smiling lips. "He comes on rough, but it's a put-on really. He's really no threat, anybody can manage Darryl. A couple of my girlfriends and I play tennis with him in this fantastic big canvas bubble he's put up. Do you play?"

Jennifer's round shoulders shrugged. "A little. Mostly at summer camp. And a bunch of us used to go use the U. of C. courts occasionally."

"How long are you going to be around, before you go back to Chicago?"

Jennifer was watching the curds swirl in her own coffee. "A while. It may take until summer to sell the house, and Chris has nothing much to do as it turns out and we get along easily; we always have. Maybe I won't go back. As I said, it wasn't working out that great at Michael Reese."

"Were you having man trouble?"

"Oh *no*." Her eyes lifted, displaying below her pale irises arcs of pure youthful white. "Men don't seem all that interested in me."

"But why not? If I may say so, you're lovely."

The girl lowered her eyes. "Isn't this funny milk? So thick and sweet. I wonder if it's gone bad."

"No, I think you'll find it very fresh. You haven't eaten your johnnycake."

"I nibbled at it. I never was that crazy about them, they're just fried dough."

"That's why we Rhode Islanders like them. They come as they are. I'll finish yours if you don't want it."

"I must do something wrong that men sense. I used to talk about it with my friends sometimes. *My* girl-friends."

"A woman needs woman friends," Sukie said complacently.

"I didn't have that many of those either. Chicago is a tough town. These birdlike little ethnic women studying all night and full of all the answers. If you ask them anything personal, though, like what you're doing wrong with these men you have to meet, they clam right up."

"It's hard to be right with men, actually," Sukie told her. "They're very angry with us because we can have babies and they can't. They're terribly jealous, poor dears: Darryl tells us that. I don't really know whether or not to believe him; as I say, a lot of him is pure put-on. At lunch the other day he was trying to describe his theories to me, they all have to do with some chemical whose name begins with 'silly.'"

"Selenium. It's a magical element. It's the secret of those doors in airports that open automatically in front of you. Also it takes the green color out of glass that iron gives it. Selenic acid can dissolve gold."

"Well, my goodness, you do know a thing or two. If you're that into chemistry, maybe you could be Darryl's assistant."

"Chris keeps saying I should just hang out in our house with him a while, at least until we sell it. He's fed up with New York, *it's* too tough. He says the gays control all the fields he's interested in—window dressing, stage design."

"I think you should."

"Should what?"

"Hang around. Eastwick's amusing." Rather impatiently—the morning was wasting—Sukie brushed all the johnnycake crumbs from the front of her sweater. "This is *not* a tough town. This is a *sweet*ie-pie town." She washed down the crumbs in her mouth with a last sip of coffee and stood.

"I feel that," the other woman said, getting the signal and beginning to gather up her scarf, her pathetic patched parka. Dressed and on her feet, Jenny performed a surprising, thrilling mannish action: she took Sukie's hand in a firm grip. "Thank you," she said, "for talking to me. The only other person who has taken any interest in us, except for the lawyers of course, is that nice lady minister, Brenda Parsley."

"She's a minister's wife, not a minister, and I'm not sure she's so nice either."

"Her husband behaved horribly to her, everybody tells me."

"Or she to him."

"I *knew* you'd say something like that," Jennifer said, and smiled, not unpleasantly; but it made Sukie feel naked, she could be seen right through, with no lead vest of innocence to protect her. Her life was lived in full view of the town; even this little stranger knew a thing or two.

Before Jennifer flicked the scarf into place Sukie noticed that around her neck hung a thin gold chain of the type that for some people supports a cross. But at the base of the girl's slender soft white throat hung the Egyptian tau cross, its loop at the top like the head of a tiny man—an ankh, symbol of life and death both, an ancient sign of mysteries come newly into vogue.

Seeing Sukie's eyes linger there, Jennifer looked oppositely at the other's necklace of copper moons and said, "My mother was wearing copper. A broad plain bracelet I'd never seen before. As if—"

"As if what, dear?"

"As if she were trying to ward something off."

"Aren't we all?" said Sukie cheerily. "I'll be in touch about tennis."

The space inside Van Horne's great bubble was acoustically and atmospherically weird: the sounds of shouts and of balls being hit seemed smothered even as they rang out, and a faint prickly sensation of pressure weighed on Sukie's freckled brow and forearms. The amber hair of these forearms stood up as if electrified. Beneath the overarching firmament of dun canvas everything seemed in slightly slow motion; the players moved through an aura of compression, though in fact the limp dome stayed inflated because the air within it, pumped by a tireless fan through a boxy plastic mouth sealed by duct tape low in one corner, was warmer than the winter air outside. Today was the shortest day of the year. An earth hard as iron lay locked beneath a sky whose mottled clouds spit snow like ashes sucked up a chimney and then dispersed with the smoke. Thin powdery lines appeared next to brick edges and exposed tree roots but melted in the wan noon sun; there was no accumulation, though every shop and bank with its seasonal pealing and cotton mimicry was inviting Christmas to be white. Dock Street, as early darkness overtook the muffled shoppers, looked harried, its gala lights a forestallment of sleep, a desperate hollow-eyed attempt to live up to some promise in the bitter black air. Playing tennis in their tights and leg warmers and ski sweaters and double pairs of socks stuffed into their sneakers, the young divorced mothers of Eastwick were taking a holiday from the holiday.

Sukie feared guiltily that she might have spoiled it for the others by bringing Jennifer Gabriel along. Not that Darryl Van Horne had objected to her suggestion over the phone; it was his nature to welcome new recruits and perhaps their little circle of four was becoming narrow for him. Like most men, especially wealthy men, especially wealthy men from New York City, he was easily bored. But Jennifer had taken the liberty of bringing her brother along, and Darryl would surely be appalled by the entry into his home of this boy, who was in the newest fashion of youth inarticulate and sullen, with glazed eyes, a slack fuzzy jaw, and tangled curly hair so dirty as to be scarcely blond. Instead of tennis sneakers he had worn beat-up rubber-cleated running shoes that even in the chill vastness of the bubble gave off a stale foul smell of male sweat. Sukie wondered how pristine Jennifer could stand a housemate so slovenly. Monty for all his faults had been fastidious, always taking showers and rinsing out coffee cups she had abandoned on an end table after a phone conversation. The boy had borrowed a racket and shown no ability to hit the ball over the net, and no embarrassment at his inability, only a sluggish petulance. Ever the courteous host and seeming gentleman, Darryl, though all suited up to play, in an outfit of maroon jogging pants and purple down vest that made him look like a macaw, had suggested that the four females enjoy a set of ladies' doubles while he took Christopher away for a tour of the library, the lab, the little conservatory of poisonous tropical plants. The boy followed with languid ingratitude as Darryl gestured and spouted words; through the walls of the bubble they could hear him exclaiming all the way up the path to the house. Sukie did feel guilty.

She took Jenny as her partner in case the girl proved inept, though in warming up she had shown a firm stroke from both sides; in play she showed herself to be a spunky sound-enough player, though without much range—which may have been partly deference to Sukie's leggy, reaching style. At about the age of eleven, Sukie, learning the game on an old, rhododendron-screened macadam court a friend of her family's had on his lakeside estate, had been complimented by her father for a spectacular, lunging "get"; and ever after she had been a "fetching" style of player, even lagging in one corner and then the other to make her returns seem spectacular. It was the ball right in on her fists Sukie sometimes couldn't handle. She and Jenny quickly went up four games to one on Alexandra and Jane, and then the tricks began. Though the object coming into Sukie's forehand was an optic-yellow Wilson, what she got her racket on—knees bent, head down, power flowing forward and up for a topspin return—was a gob of putty; the weight of it took a chip out of her elbow, it felt like. What dribbled up to the net between Jennifer's feet was inarguably, again, a tennis ball. On the next point the serve came to her backhand and, braced against another lump of putty, she felt something lighter than a sparrow fly from her strings; it disappeared into the shadowy vault of the dome, beyond the ring of clear plastic portholes that admitted light, and fell far out of bounds in the form of an optic-yellow Wilson.

"Play fair, you two fiends," Sukie shouted across the net.

Jane Smart called back flutingly, "Keep your eye on the ball, sugar, and bad things won't happen."

"The hell you say, Jane Pain. I put perfect swings into both those shots." Sukie was angry because it wasn't *fair*, when her partner was an innocent. Jennifer, who had been poised on the half-court line, had seen only the outcome of these shots and turned now to show Sukie a forgiving, encouraging face, heart-shaped and flushed a bright pink. On the next exchange, the girl darted to the net after a weak return from Jane, and Sukie willed Alexandra to freeze; Jenny's sharp volley thudded against the big woman's immobilized flesh. Released from the spell in a twinkling, Alexandra rubbed the stung spot on her thigh.

Reproachfully she told Sukie, "That would have really hurt if I weren't wearing woolies under my tights."

A welt would arise there, though, and Sukie apologetically pleaded, "Come on, let's just play real tennis." But both opponents were sore now. A grinding pain seized Sukie's joints as she stretched to volley an easy shot coming over the center of the net; pulled up short, she helplessly watched the blurred ball bounce on the center stripe. But she heard Jenny's feet drum behind her and saw the ball, miraculously returned, drop between Jane and Alexandra, who had thought they had the point won. This brought the game back to deuce, and Sukie, still staggered by that sudden ache injected into her joints but determined to protect her partner from all this *malefica*, said the blasphemous backwards words *Retson Retap* three times rapidly to herself and created an air pocket, a fault in the crystal of space, above their opponents' forecourt, so that Jane double-faulted twice, the ball diving in mid-trajectory as from a table edge.

That made the game score five to one and brought the serve to Jenny. When she tossed the ball up, it became an egg and spattered all over her upturned face, through the gut strings. Sukie threw down her racket in disgust and it became a snake, that then had nowhere to slither to, the great bubble being sealed all along the edge; frantically the creature, damned at the dawn of creation, whipped its S's and zetas of motion back and forth across the blood-colored AsPhlex that framed the green court, its diagrammed baselines and boundaries. "All right," Sukie announced. "That does it. The game's over." Little Jenny with an inadequate feminine handkerchief was trying to wipe away from around her eyes the webby watery albumen and the yolk with its fleck of blood. The egg had been fertilized. Sukie took the hanky from her and dabbed. "I'm sorry, so sorry," she said. "They just can't stand to lose, they are terrible women."

"At least," Alexandra called across the net apologetically, "it wasn't a *rot*ten egg."

"It's all right," Jennifer said, a little breathless but her voice still level. "I knew you all have these powers. Brenda Parsley told me."

"That idiotic blabbermouth," Jane Smart said. The other two witches had come around the net to help wipe Jennifer's face. "We don't have any powers she doesn't, now that she's been left."

"Is that what does it, being left?" Jenny asked.

"Or doing the leaving," Alexandra said. "The strange thing is it doesn't make any difference. You'd think it would. Anyway, I'm sorry about the egg. But my thigh's going to be black and blue tomorrow because Sukie wouldn't let me move; it wasn't really playing the game."

Sukie said, "It was as much playing the game as what you were doing to me."

"You mis-hit those shots plain and simple," Jane Smart called over; she had gone to the edge of the court to look for something.

"I thought too," said Jennifer softly, courting the others, "your head came up, at least on the backhand."

"You weren't watching."

"I was. And you have a tendency to straighten your knees at impact."

"I *don't*. You're supposed to be my *part*ner. You're supposed to en*cour*age me."

"You were wonderful," the girl said obediently.

Jane returned holding in her cupped palm a little heap of black sand she had scraped up with her fingernails at the side of the court. "Close your eyes," she ordered Jennifer, and threw the sand directly into her face. Magically, the glutinous remains of egg evaporated, leaving, however, the grit, which gave the smooth upturned features a startled barbaric look, as if wearing a speckled mask.

"Maybe it's time for our bath," Alexandra remarked, gazing maternally at Jennifer's gritty face.

Sukie wondered how they could have their usual bath with these strangers among them and blamed herself, for having been too forthcoming in inviting them. It was her mother's fault; back home in New York State there had always been extra people at the dinner table, people in off the street, possible angels in disguise to her mother's way of thinking. Aloud Sukie protested, "But Darryl hasn't played yet! Or Christopher," she added, though the boy had been lackadaisical and arrogantly inept.

"They don't seem to be coming back," Jane Smart observed.

"Well we better go do something or we'll all catch cold," Alexandra said. She had borrowed Jenny's damp handkerchief (monogrammed *J*) and with an intricately folded corner of it was removing, grain by grain, the sand from the girl's docile round face, tilted up toward this attention like a pink flower to the sun.

Sukie felt a pang of jealousy. She swung her arms and said, "Let's go up to the house," though her muscles still had lots of tennis in them. "Unless somebody wants to play singles."

Jane said, "Maybe Darryl."

"Oh he's too marvellous, he'd slaughter me."

"I don't think so," Jenny said softly, having observed their host warm up and as yet unable to see, fully, the wonder of him. "You have much better form. He's quite wild, isn't he?"

Jane Smart said coldly, "Darryl Van Horne is quite the most civilized person I know. And the most tolerant." Irritably she went on, "Lexa dear, do stop fussing with that. It'll all come off in the bath."

"I didn't bring a bathing suit," said Jennifer, her eyes wide and questing from face to face.

"It's quite dark in there, nobody can see anything," Sukie told her. "Or if you'd rather you can go home."

"Oh, no. It's too depressing. I keep imagining Daddy's body hanging in midair and that makes me too scared to go up and start sorting the things in the attic."

And it occurred to Sukie that whereas the three of them all had children they should be tending to, Jennifer and Christopher *were* children, tending to themselves. She suffered a sad vision of Clyde's prick, a father's, which could have been her own father's and in truth *had* seemed a relic of sorts, with a jaundiced tinge on its underside when erect and enormously long gray hairs, like hairs from an old woman's head, snaking down from the testicles. No wonder he had overreacted when she spread her legs. Sukie led the other women out of the tennis bubble, whose oval door unzipped from either side and had to be used quickly, to keep warm air from escaping.

The dying December day nipped at their faces, their sneakered feet. Coal, that loathsome Labrador of Alexandra's, and Darryl's blotchy nervous collie, Needlenose, who had together trapped and torn apart some furry creature in the island's little woods, came and romped around them, their black muzzles bloody. The earth of the once gently bellied lawn leading up to the house had been torn by bulldozers to build the court this fall and the clumps of sod and clay, frozen hard, made a moonscape treacherous to tread. Tears of cold in Sukie's eyes gave her companions a rainbow aura and it hurt her cheeks to talk. On the firmness of the driveway she broke into a sprint; at her back the others followed like a single clumsy beast on the gravel. The great oak door yielded to her push as if sensate, and in the marble-floored foyer, with its hollow elephant's foot, a sulphurous pillow of heat hit her in the face. Fidel was nowhere in sight. Following a mutter of voices, the women found Darryl and Christopher sitting on opposite sides of the round leather-topped table in the library. Old comic books and a tea tray were arranged on the table between them. Above them hung the melancholy stuffed moose and deer heads that had been left by the sporting Lenoxes: mournful glass eyes that did not blink though burdened with dust. "Who won?" Van Horne asked. "The good or the wicked?"

"Which witch is which?" Jane Smart asked, flinging herself down on a crimson beanbag chair under a cliff of bound arcana, pale-spined giant volumes identified in spidery Latin. "The fresh blood won," she said, "as it usually does." Fluffy, malformed Thumbkin had been standing still as a statuette on the hearth tiles, so close to the fire the tips of her whiskers seemed to spark; now with great dignity she stalked over to Jane's ankles and, as if Jane's white athletic socks were scratching posts, sunk the arcs of her claws deeply in, her tail at the same time shivering bolt upright as though she were blissfully urinating. Jane yowled and with the toe of one sneakered foot hoisted the animal high into space. Thumbkin spun like a great snow-flake before noiselessly landing on her double paws over near where the brass-handled poker, tongs, and ash shovel glittered in their stand. The offended cat's eyes blinked and then joined their brass glitter; the vertical pupils narrowed in their yellow irises, con-templating the gathering.

"They began to use dirty tricks," Sukie tattled. "I feel gypped."

"That's how you tell a real woman," joked Darryl Van Horne in his throaty, faraway voice. "She always feels gypped."

"Darryl, don't be dreary and epigrammatical," Alexandra said. "Chris, does that tea taste as good as it looks?"

"'TsO.K.," the boy managed to get out, sneering and not meeting anyone's eye.

Fidel had materialized. His khaki jacket looked more mussed than usual. Had he been with Rebecca in the kitchen?

"*Té para las señoras y la señorita, por favor,*" Darryl

told him. Fidel's English was excellent and increasingly idiomatic, but it was part of their master-servant relationship that they spoke Spanish as long as Van Horne knew the words.

"*Sí, señor.*"

"*Rápidamente,*" Van Horne pronounced.

"*Sí, sí.*" Away he went.

"Oh isn't this cozy!" Jane Smart exclaimed, but in truth something about it dissatisfied Sukie and made her sad: the whole house was like a stage set, stunning from one angle but from others full of gaps and unresolved shabbiness. It was an imitation of a real house somewhere else.

Sukie pouted, "I didn't get the tennis out of my system. Darryl: come down and play singles with me. Just until the light goes. You're all suited up for it and everything."

He said gravely, "What about young Chris here? He hasn't played either."

"He doesn't want to I'm sure," Jennifer interjected in a sisterly voice.

"I stink," the boy agreed. He really was blah, Sukie thought. A girl his age would be so amusing, so alert and socially sensitive, gathering in impressions, turning them into flirtation and sympathy, making the room her web, her nest, her theatre. Sukie felt herself quite frantic, standing and tossing her hair, verging on rudeness and exhibitionism, and she didn't quite know what to blame, except that she was embarrassed at having brought the Gabriels here—never again!—and hadn't had sex with a man since Clyde committed suicide two weeks ago. She had found herself lately at night thinking of Ed, wondering what he was doing off in the underground with that little low-class smudge Dawn Polanski.

Darryl, intuitive and kind for all his coarse manner,

rose in his red jogging pants and put his purple down vest back on, plus a Day-Glo orange hunting cap with a bill and earflaps that he sometimes wore for a joke, and took up his racket, an aluminum Head. "One quick set," he warned, "with a seven-point tie breaker, if it goes to six-six. First ball turns into a toad, you forfeit. Anybody want to come watch?" Nobody did, they were waiting for their *té*. Lonely as a married couple then, the two of them went out into the dimming gray afternoon—the silent woods and bushes lavender and the sky an enamelled green in the east—down to the dome with its graveyard closeness and quiet.

The tennis was grand; not only did Darryl play like a robot, clumsy-looking but infallible, but he drew forth from Sukie amazing shots, impossible gets turned into singing winners, the segmented breadths and widths of the court miniaturized by her unnatural speed and adroitness. The ball hung like a moon as she raced for it; her body became an instrument of thought, present wherever she willed it. She even brought off a few backhand overheads. She felt herself stretch at the top of her serves like a bow releasing an arrow. She was Diana, Isis, Astarte. She was female grace and strength shed, for this silver moment, of its rough garb of servitude. Gloom gathered in the corners of the dun bubble; the portholes of sky hovered overhead like a mammoth crown of aquamarines; her eyes could no longer see the dark opponent scrambling and thumping and heaving on the far side of the net. The ball kept coming back, and with pace, springing up at her face like a predator repeatedly reborn from the painted asphalt. Hit, hit, she kept hitting, and the ball got smaller and smaller—the size of a golf ball, the size of a golden pea, and at last there was no bounce on the inky far side of the net, just a leathery swallowing sound, and the game was over. "That was bliss," Sukie announced, to whoever was there.

Van Horne's voice scraped and rumbled forward, saying, "I was a pal to you, how's about being a pal to me?"

"O.K.," Sukie said. "What do I do?"

"'Kiss my ass," he said huskily. He offered it to her over the net. It was hairy, or downy, depending on how you felt about men. Left, right...

"And in the middle," he demanded.

The smell seemed to be a message he must deliver, a word brought from afar, not entirely unsweet, a whiff of camel essence coming through the flaps of the silken tents of the Dragon Throne's encampment in the Gobi Desert.

"Thanks," Van Horne said, pulling up his pants. In the dark he sounded like a New York taxi driver, raspy. "Seems silly to you, I know, but it gives me a helluva boost."

They walked together up the hill, Sukie's sweat caking on her skin. She wondered how they would manage the hot tub with Jennifer Gabriel there and showing no disposition to leave. Back in the house, the loutish brother was alone in the library, reading a big blue volume that Sukie in a glance over his shoulder saw to be bound comic books. A caped man in a blue hood with pointed ears: Batman. "The complete fucking set," Van Horne boasted. "It cost me a bundle, some of those old ones, going back to the war, that if I'd had the sense to save as a kid I could have made a fortune on. Christ I wasted my childhood waiting for next month's issue. Loved The Joker. Loved The Penguin. Loved the Batmobile in its underground garage. You're both too young to have gotten the bug."

The boy uttered a complete sentence. "They used to be on TV."

"Yeah, but they camped it up. They didn't have to do that. They made it all a joke, that was damn poor taste. The old comic books, there's real evil there. That white face used to haunt my dreams, I'm not kidding. How do you feel about Captain Marvel?" Van Horne pulled from the shelves a volume from another set, bound in red rather than blue, and with a comic fervor boomed, "Sha-ZAM!" To Sukie's surprise he settled himself in a wing chair and began to leaf through, his big face skidding with pleasure.

Sukie followed the faint sound of female voices through the long room of moldering Pop Art, the small room of unpacked boxes, and the double doors leading to the slate-lined bath. The lights in their round ribbed wells had been rheostatted to low. The stereo's red eye was watching over the gentle successions of a Schubert sonata. Three heads of pinned-up hair were disposed upon the surface of steaming water. The voices murmured on, and no head turned to watch Sukie undress. She slid from her many stiff layers of tennis clothes and walked through the humid air naked, sat on the stone edge, and arched her back to give herself to the water, at first too fiery to bear but then not, not. Oh. Slowly she became a new self. Water like sleep sucks our natural heaviness away. Alexandra's and Jane's familiar bodies bobbed about her; their waves and hers merged in one healing agitation. Jennifer Gabriel's round head and round shoulders rested in the center of her vision; the girl's round breasts floated just beneath the surface of the transparent black water and in it her hips and feet were foreshortened like a misbegotten fetus's. "Isn't this lovely?" Sukie asked her.

"It is."

"He has all these controls," Sukie explained.

"Is he going to come in with us?" Jennifer asked, afraid.

"I think not," Jane Smart said, "this time."

"Out of deference to you, dear," Alexandra added.

"I feel so safe. Should I?"

"Why not?" one of the witches asked.

"Feel safe while you can," another advised.

"The lights are like stars, aren't they? Random, I mean."

"Watch this." They all knew the controls now. At the push of a finger the roof rumbled back. The first pale piercings—planets, red giants—showed early evening's mothering turquoise dome to be an illusion, a nothing. There were spheres beyond spheres, each transparent or opaque as the day and year turned.

"My goodness. The outdoors."

"Yess."

"Yet I don't feel cold."

"Heat rises."

"How much money do you think he put into all this?"

"Thousands."

"But why? For what purpose?"

"For us."

"He loves us."

"Only us?"

"We don't really know."

"It's not a useful question."

"Aren't you content?"

"Yes."

"Yess."

"But I'm thinking Chris and I should be getting back. The pets should be fed."

"What pets?"

"Felicia Gabriel used to say we shouldn't waste protein on pets when everybody in Asia was starving."

"I didn't know Clyde and Felicia had pets."

"They didn't. But shortly after we got here somebody put a puppy in the Volvo one night. And a cat came to the door a little later."

"Think of us. We have children."

"Poor neglected little scruffy things," Jane Smart said in a mocking tone that indicated she was imitating another voice, a voice "out there" raised in hostile gossip against them.

"Well I was raised very protectively," Sukie offered, "and it got to be oppressive. Looking back on it I don't think my parents were doing me any favors, they were working out some problems of their own."

"You can't live others' lives for them," said Alexandra driftingly.

"Women must stop serving everybody and then getting even psychologically. That's been our politics up to now."

"Oh. That does feel good," Jenny said.

"It's therapy."

"Close the roof again. I want to feel *cozy*."

"And shut off the fucking Schubert."

"Suppose Darryl comes in."

"With that hideous kid."

"Christopher."

"Let them."

"Mm. You're strong."

"My art, it giffs me muskles efen ünter me fingernails, like."

"Lexa. How much tequila was in your tea?"

"How late does the supermarket toward Old Wick stay open?"

"I have no idea, I absolutely have stopped going

there. If the Superette downtown doesn't have it, we don't eat it."

"But they have hardly any fresh vegetables and no fresh meat."

"Nobody notices. All they want are those frozen dinners so they don't have to come to the table and interrupt TV, and hero sandwiches. The onions they slop in! I think it's what made me stop kissing the brats good night."

"My oldest, it's incredible, nothing but crinkle chips and Pecan Sandies since he was twelve and still he's six foot two, and not a cavity. The dentist says he's never seen such a beautiful mouth."

"It's the fluoride."

"I *like* Schubert. He isn't always *after* you like Beethoven is."

"Or Mahler."

"Oh my God, Mahler."

"He really is monstrously too much."

"My turn."

"*My* turn."

"Ooh, lovely. You've found the spot."

"What does it mean when your neck always hurts, and up near your armpits?"

"That's lymph. Cancer."

"Please, don't even joke."

"Try menopause."

"I wouldn't care about that."

"I look forward to it."

"You do wonder, sometimes, if being fertile isn't overrated."

"You hear terrible things about IUDs now."

"The best subs, funnily enough, are from that supertacky-looking pizza shack at East Beach. But they close October to August. I hear the man and his wife go to Florida and live with the millionaires in Fort Lauderdale, that's how well they do."

"That one-eyed man who cooks in a tie-dyed undershirt?"

"I've never been sure if it's really one eye or is he always winking?"

"It's his wife does the pizzas. I wish I knew how she keeps the crusts from getting soggy."

"I have all this tomato sauce and my children have gone on strike against spaghetti."

"Give it to Joe to take home."

"He takes enough home."

"Well, he leaves you something, too."

"Don't be coarse."

"*What* does he take home?"

"Smells."

"Memories."

"Oh. My goodness."

"Just let yourself float."

"We're all here."

"We're right with you."

"I feel that," Jenny said in a voice even smaller and softer than her usual one.

"How very lovely you are."

"Wouldn't it be funny to be that young again?"

"I can't believe I ever was. It must have been somebody else."

"Close your eyes. One last nasty piece of grit right here in the corner. There."

"Wet hair is really the problem, this time of year."

"The other day my breath froze my scarf right to my face."

"I'm thinking of getting mine layered. They say the new barber on the other side of Landing Square, in that little long building where they used to sharpen saws, does a wonderful job."

"On women?"

"They have to, men have stopped getting them. They've upped the price, though. Seven fifty, that's without any wave or wash or anything."

"The last thing I did for my father was wheel him into the barber for a haircut. He knew it was his last, too. He announced it to everybody, all these men sitting around. 'This is my daughter, who's bringing me in for the last haircut I'll have in my life.'"

"Kazmierczak Square. Have you seen the new sign?"

"Horrible. I can't believe it'll last."

"People forget. The schoolchildren now, World War Two to them is just a myth."

"Don't you wish you still had skin like this? Not a scar, not a mole."

"Actually, there is a little pink thing I noticed the other day, up high. Higher."

"Oh yess. That hurt?"

"No."

"Good."

"Did you ever notice, once you start investigating yourself for lumps like they say you should, they seem to be everywhere? The body is just *ter*ribly complicated."

"Please don't even make me think about it."

"In the new dictionary they got at the paper there are these transparencies bound in with regular pages at the entry 'Man,' only a woman's body is there too. Veins, muscles, bones, each on a sheet of their own, it's incredible. How it all fits."

"I don't think it's really complicated, it's just our thinking about it makes it complicated. Like a lot of things."

"How wonderfully round they are. Perfect semicircles."

"Hemispheres."

"That sounds so political."

"Hemispheres of influence."

"That *is* one of the unjoys. Erogenous-zone sag. I looked at my bottom in the mirror the other day and here were these definite undeniable puckers. Maybe that's why I have a stiff neck."

"Nemo's makes a pretty good sausage sub."

"Too many hot red peppers. Fidel is getting to Rebecca. He's flavoring her."

"What color do you think their babies would be?"

"Beige."

"Mocha."

"Does that feel too intrusive?"

"Not exactly."

"How well she speaks!"

"Oh God: the trouble with being young and beautiful is nobody helps you really appreciate it. When I was twenty-two and at my peak I guess all I did was worry about pleasing my mother-in-law and if I was as good in bed as these whores Monty knew in college."

"It's like being rich. You know you have something and you get uptight about being taken advantage of."

"Darryl doesn't seem to let it worry him."

"How rich *is* he, really?"

"He still hasn't paid Joe's bill, I know."

"That's how the rich are. They hold their money and collect the interest."

"Pay attention, love."

"How can I not?"

"My fingertips are all shrivelled."

"Maybe it's time we see if amphibians can lay their eggs on land."

"Okey-dokey."

"Here we go."

Splashing, they emerged cumbersomely: silver born

in a chemical tumult from lead. They groped for towels.

"Where *is* he?"

"Asleep? I gave him a pretty strenuous game, if I do say so."

"They say, unless you use oil afterwards, water isn't good for your skin past a certain age."

"We have ointments."

"We have buckets of ointments."

"Just stretch out. Are you still relaxed?"

"Oh yes. I really am."

"Here's another, just under your pretty little boob. Like a tiny pink snout." Dark as the room was, it did not seem strange that this could be seen, for the pupils of the four of them had expanded as if to overflow their gray, hazel, brown, and blue irises. One witch pinched Jennifer's false teat and asked, "Feel anything?"

"No."

"Good."

"Feel any shame?" another asked.

"No."

"Good," pronounced the third.

"*Is*n't she good?"

"She is."

"Just think, 'Float.'"

"I feel I'm flying."

"So do we."

"All the time."

"We're right with you."

"It's killing."

"I love being a woman, really," Sukie said.

"You might as well," Jane Smart said dryly.

"I mean, it's not just propaganda," Sukie insisted.

"My baby," Alexandra was saying.

"Oh" escaped Jenny's lips.

"Gently. Gentler."

"This is paradise."

"Well, *I* thought," Jane Smart said over the phone emphatically, as if certain of being contradicted, "she was a bit *too* ingratiating. Too demure and Alice-in-Wonderlandish. I think she's up to something."

"But what would that be? We're all poor as church mice and a town scandal besides." Alexandra's mind was still in her workroom, with the half-fleshed-out armatures of two floating, lightly interlocked women, wondering, as she patted handfuls of paste-impregnated shredded paper here and there, why she couldn't muster the confidence she used to bring to her little clay figurines, her little hefty bubbies meant to rest so securely on end tables and rumpus-room mantels.

"Think of the situation," Jane directed. "Suddenly she's an orphan. Obviously she was making a mess of things out in Chicago. The house is too big to heat and pay taxes on. But she has nowhere else to go."

Lately Jane seemed intent on poisoning every pot. Outside the window, the sparrow-brown twigs of an as yet snowless winter moved in a cold breeze, and the swaying birdfeeder needed refilling. The Spofford children were home for Christmas vacation but had gone ice-skating, giving Alexandra an hour to work in; it shouldn't be wasted. "I thought Jennifer was a nice addition," she said to Jane. "We mustn't get ingrown."

"We mustn't ever leave Eastwick either," Jane surprisingly said. "Isn't it horrible about Ed Parsley?"

"What about him? Has he come back to Brenda?"

"In pieces he'll come back" was the cruel reply. "He and Dawn Polanski blew themselves up in a row house in New Jersey trying to make bombs." Alexandra remembered his ghostly face the night of the concert, her last glimpse of Ed, his aura tinged with sickly green and the tip of his long vain nose seeming to be pulled so that his face was slipping sideways like a rubber mask. She could have said then that he was doomed. Jane's harsh image of coming back in pieces sliced Alexandra, her crooked arm and hand floating away with the telephone and Jane's voice in it, while her eyes and body let the window mullions pass through them like the parallel wires of an egg slicer. "He was identified by the fingerprints of a hand they found in the rubble," Jane was saying. "Just this hand by itself. It was all over television this morning, I'm surprised Sukie hasn't called you."

"Sukie's been a little huffy with me, maybe she felt upstaged by Jennifer the other night. Poor Ed," Alexandra said, feeling herself drift away as in a slow explosion. "She must be devastated."

"Not so it showed when I talked to her a half-hour ago. She sounded mostly worried about how much of a story the new management at the *Word* would want; there's this boy in Clyde's office now younger than we are, he's been sent by the owners, who everybody thinks are front men for the Mafia that hangs out, you know, on Federal Hill. He's just out of Brown and knows nothing about editing."

"Does she blame herself?"

"No, why would she? She never urged Ed to leave Brenda and run off with that ridiculous little slut, she was doing what she could to hold the marriage together. Sukie told me she told him to stick with Brenda and the ministry at least until he had looked into public relations. That's what these ministers and priests who leave the church go into, public relations."

"I don't know, general involvement," Alexandra weakly said. "Did they find Dawn's hands too?"

"I don't know what they found of Dawn's but I

don't see how she could have escaped unless..." *Unless she were a witch* was the unspoken thought.

"Even that wouldn't do much against cordite, or whatever they call it. Darryl would know."

"Darryl thinks I'm ready for some Hindemith."

"Sweetie, that's wonderful. I wish he'd tell me I'm ready to go back to my bubbies. I miss the money, for one thing."

"Alexandra S. Spofford," Jane Smart chastised. "Darryl's trying to do something wonderful for you. Those New York dealers get ten thousand dollars for just a doodle."

"Not my doodles," she said, and hung up depressed. She didn't want to be a mere ingredient in Jane's poison pot, part of the daily local stew, she wanted to look out of her window and see miles and miles of empty golden land, dotted with sage, and the tips of the distant mountains a white as vaporous as that of clouds, only coming to a point.

Sukie must have forgiven Alexandra for being too taken with Jenny, for she called after Ed's memorial service to give an account. Snow had fallen in the meantime: one does forget that annual marvel, the width of it all, the air given presence, the diagonal strokes of the streaming flakes laid across everything like an etcher's hatching, the tilted big beret the bird-bath wears next morning, the deepening in color of the dry brown oak leaves that have hung on and the hemlocks with their drooping deep green boughs and the clear blue of the sky like a bowl that has been decisively emptied, the excitement that vibrates off the walls within the house, the suddenly supercharged life of the wallpaper, the mysteriously urgent intimacy the potted amaryllis on the window enjoys with its pale phallic shadow. "Brenda spoke," Sukie said. "And some sinister fat man from the Revolution, in a beard and ponytail. Said Ed and Dawn were martyrs to pig tyranny, or something. He became quite excited, and there was a gang with him in Castro outfits that I was afraid would start beating us up if anybody muttered or got out of line somehow. But Brenda was quite brave, really. She's gotten rather wonderful."

"She has?" A sheen, was how Alexandra remembered Brenda: a sleekly blond head of hair done up in a tight twist, turning away at the concert party amid the peacock confusion of auras. From other encounters her mind's eye could supply a long, rather chalky face, with complacent lips more brightly painted than one quite expected, with that vehement gloss of a rose about to drop its petals.

"She has her outfit down to a T now—dark suits with padded shoulders, and a silk necktie in front so broad it looks like a napkin she forgot to take out after eating lobster. She spoke for about ten minutes, about what a caring minister Ed had been, *so* interested in Eastwick and its delicate ecology and its conflicted young people and all that, until his conscience— and here, on the word 'conscience,' Brenda got her voice to break, you would have loved it, she dabbed with her hanky at her eyes, just one tear from each eye, ex*actly* enough—until his conscience, she said, demanded he take his energies away from the confines of this town, where they were so much appreciated"—Sukie's powers of mimicry were in full gear now; Alexandra could see her upper lip crinkling and protruding drolly—"and devote them, these wonderful energies, to trying to correct the *dread*ful, my dear, malaise that is poisoning the heartblood of our nation. She said our nation is laboring under a malignant spell and looked me right in the eye."

"What did you do?"

"Smiled. It wasn't *me* who got him down there in New Jersey with the bomb squad, it was Dawn. Very little mention of her, by the way, when the fat man got done. Like none. Apparently they never found any pieces of her, just bits of clothing that could have come out of a closet. She was such a scruffy little thing maybe she sailed out through the roof. The Polanskis or whatever their name is, the stepfather and the mother, showed up, though, dressed like something out of a Thirties movie. I guess they don't get out of their trailer that often. I kept looking at the mother wondering about these acrobatics she does for the circus, I must say she's kept her figure; but her *face*. Frightening. So tough it was growing things all over it like you have on your heel from bad shoes. Nobody knew what to say to them, since the girl was just Ed's floozie and not even officially dead at that. Even Brenda didn't quite know how to handle it at the door, since the family was at the root of her troubles in a way, but I must say, she was magnificent— very courteous and *grande dame*, gave them her sympathy with a glistening eye. Brenda's not our sort, I know, but I really do admire the way she's picked herself up and made something of her situation. Speaking of situations…"

"Yes?" Alexandra asked on cue. The pause had been a probe to see if she was still paying attention. Alexandra had been idly making dots with her fingertips on the fogged patches in the lower panes of her kitchen window—semiconscious conjurings of snow, or Sukie's freckles, or the holes in the telephone mouthpiece, or the paint dabs with which Niki de Saint-Phalle decorated her internationally successful "Nanas." Alexandra was glad Sukie was talking to her again; she sometimes feared that if it were not for Sukie she would lose all contact with the world of daily events and go off sailing into the stratosphere just like little Dawn blown out of that house in New Jersey.

"I've been fired," Sukie said.

"Baby! You haven't! How could they, you're the only undreary thing about that paper now."

"Well, maybe you could say I quit. The boy who's taken Clyde's place, with some Jewish name I can't remember, Bernstein, Birnbaum, I don't even *want* to remember it, cut my obituary of Ed from a column and a half to two little dumb paragraphs; he said they had a space problem this week because another poor local has been killed in Vietnam but I know it's because everybody's told him Ed had been my lover and he's afraid of my going overboard in print and people tittering. A long time ago Ed had given me these poems he wrote in the style of Bob Dylan and I *had* put a couple of them in but wouldn't have complained if they'd come and asked me to cut those; but they even took out how he founded the Fair Housing Group and was in the top third of his class at Harvard Divinity School. I said to the boy, 'You've just come to Eastwick and I don't think you realize what a beloved figure Reverend Parsley was,' and this brat from Brown smiled and said, 'I've heard about his being beloved,' and I said, 'I quit. I work hard on my copy and Mr. Gabriel almost never cut a word.' That made this insufferable child smile all the more and there was nothing to do but walk out. Actually, before I walked out I took the pencil out of his hand and broke it right in front of his eyes."

Alexandra laughed, grateful to have such a spirited friend, a friend in three dimensions unlike those evil clown faces in her bedroom. "Oh Sukie, you honestly did?"

"Yes, and I even said, 'Go break a leg,' and threw the two pieces on his desk. The smug little kike. But now what do I do? All I have is about seven hundred dollars in the bank."

"Maybe Darryl..." Alexandra's thoughts did fly to Darryl Van Horne at all hours: his overeager face with its flecks of spit, and certain dusty corners of his home awaiting a woman's touch, and such moments as the frozen one after he had laughed his harsh brittle bark, when his jaw snapped shut and the world as it were had to come unstuck from a momentary spell. These images did not visit Alexandra's brain by invitation or with a purpose but as one radio station overlaps another as we travel a winding road. Whereas Sukie and Jane seemed to have gathered fresh strength and vehemence from their rites on the island, Alexandra found her independent existence had gone from clay to paper in substance and her sustaining ties with nature had slackened. She had let her roses head into winter unmulched; she had not composted the leaves as in other Novembers; she kept forgetting to fill the birdfeeder and no longer bothered to rap on the window to drive the greedy gray squirrels away. She dragged herself about with a lassitude that even Joe Marino noticed, and that discouraged him. Boredom in a wife is part of the social contract, but boredom in a mistress undermines a man. All Alexandra wanted was to soak her bones in the teak hot tub and lean her head on Van Horne's hairy matted torso while Tiny Tim warbled over the stereo, "Livin' in the sunlight, lovin' in the moonlight, havin' a wonderful time!"

"Darryl has his hands full," Sukie told her. "The town is about to shut off his water for nonpayment of his bill and he's, at my suggestion I guess, hired Jenny Gabriel to be his lab assistant."

"At your suggestion?"

"Well, she *was* this technician out in Chicago, and now here she is pretty much all alone...."

"Sukie, your darling guilt. Aren't you sly?"

"I thought I owed her a *lit*tle something, and she does look awfully cute and serious in this little white coat over there. A bunch of us were over there yesterday."

"There was a party over there yesterday and nobody told me?"

"Not a real party. Nobody got undressed."

She must get hold of herself, Alexandra told herself. She must find a new center to her life.

"It was for less than an hour, baby, honest. It just happened. The man from town water was there too, with a court order or whatever they have to have. Then he couldn't find the turn-off and accepted a drink and we all tried on his hardhat. You know Darryl loves you best."

"He doesn't. I'm not as pretty as you are and I don't do all the things for him that Jane does."

"But you're his body type," Sukie reassured her. "You look good together. Sweetie, I really ought to run. I heard that Perley Realty might take on a new trainee in anticipation of the spring rush."

"You're going to sell real estate?"

"I might have to. I have to do something, I'm spending millions on orthodontia, and I can't imagine why; Monty had beautiful teeth, and mine aren't bad, just that slight overbite."

"But is Marge—what did you say about Brenda?—our sort?"

"If she gives me a job she is."

"I thought Darryl wanted you to write a novel."

"Darryl wants, Darryl wants," Sukie said. "If Darryl'll pay my bills he can have what he wants."

Cracks were appearing, it seemed to Alexandra after Sukie hung up, in what had for a time appeared perfect. She was behind the times, she realized. She wanted

things never to change, or, rather, to repeat always
in the same way, as nature does. The same tangle of
poison ivy and Virginia creeper on the tumbled wall
at the edge of the marsh, the same glinting mineral
mix in the pebbles of the road. How magnificent and
abysmal pebbles are! They lie all around us billions
of years old, not only rounded smooth by centuries
of the sea's tumbling but their very matter churned
and remixed by the rising of mountains and their
chronic eroding, not once but often in the vast receding cone of aeons, snow-capped mountains arisen
where Rhode Island and New Jersey now have their
marshes, while oceans spawned diatoms where now
the Rockies rise, fossils of trilobites embedded in their
cliffs. Museums had dazed Alexandra as a girl with
their mineral exhibits, interlocked crystalline prisms
in colors vulgar save that they came straight from
nature, lepidolite and chrysoberyl and tourmaline with
their regal names, all struck off like giant frozen sparks
in the churning of the earth, the very granite outcrops
around us fluid, the continents bobbing in basalt. At
times she felt dizzy, tied to all this massive incremental
shifting, her consciousness a fleck of mica. The sensation persisted that she was not merely riding the
universe but a partner to it, herself enormous within,
capable of extracting medicine from the seethe of
weeds and projecting rainstorms out of her thought.
She and the seethe were one.

In winter, when the leaves fell, forgotten ponds
moved closer, iced-over and brilliant, through the
woods, and the summer-cloaked lights of the town
loomed neighborly, and placed a whole new population of shadows and luminous rectangles upon the
wallpaper of the rooms her merciless insomnia set her
to wandering through. Her powers afflicted her most
at night. The clown faces created by the overlapping

peonies of her chintz curtains thronged the shadows and chased her from the bedroom. The sound of the children's breathing pumped through the house, as did the groans of the furnace. By moonlight, with a curt confident gesture of plump hands just beginning to show on their backs the mottling of liver spots, she would bid the curly-maple sideboard (which had been Oz's grandmother's) move five inches to the left; or she would direct a lamp with a base like a Chinese vase—its cord waggling and waving behind it in mid-air like the preposterous tail plumage of a lyrebird—to change places with a brass-candlestick lamp on the other side of the living room. One night a dog's barking in the yard of one of the neighbors beyond the line of willows at the edge of her yard irritated her exceptionally; without sufficient reflection she willed it dead. It had been a puppy, unused to being tied, and she thought too late that she might as easily have untied the unseen leash, for witches are above all adepts of the knot, the *aiguillette*, with which they promote enamorments and alliances, barrenness in women or cattle, impotence in men, and discontent within marriages. With knots they torment the innocent and entangle the future. The puppy had been known to her children and next morning the youngest of them, baby Linda, came home in tears. The owners were sufficiently incensed to have the vet perform an autopsy. He found no poison or sign of disease. It was a mystery.

The winter passed. In the darkroom of overnight blizzards, New England picture postcards were developed; the morning's sunshine displayed them in color. The not-quite-straight sidewalks of Dock Street, shovelled in patches, manifested patterns of compressed bootprints, like dirty white cookies with treads. A jag-

ged wilderness of greenish ice cakes swung in and out
with the tides, pressing on the bearded, barnacled
pilings that underlay the Bay Superette. The new
young editor of the *Word*, Toby Bergman, slipped on
a frozen slick outside the barber shop and broke his
leg. Ice backup during the owners' winter vacation on
Sea Island, Georgia, forced gallons of water to seep
by capillary action between the shingles of the Yapping Fox gift shop and to pour down the front inside
wall, ruining a fortune in Raggedy Ann dolls and
découpage by the handicapped.

The town in winter, deprived of tourists, settled
more compactly upon itself, like a log fire burning
late into the evening. A dwindled band of teen-agers
hung out in front of the Superette, waiting for the
psychedelic-painted VW van the drug dealer from
south Providence drove. On the coldest days they stood
inside and, until chased by the choleric manager (a
moonlighting tax accountant who got by on four hours
sleep a night), clustered in the warmth to one side of
the electric eye, beside the Kiwanis gumball machine
and the other that for a nickel released a handful of
stale pistachios in shells dyed a psychedelic pink. Martyrs of a sort they were, these children, along with the
town drunk, in his basketball sneakers and buttonless
overcoat, draining blackberry brandy from a paper
bag as he sat on his bench in Kazmierczak Square,
risking nightly death by exposure; martyrs too of a
sort were the men and women hastening to adulterous
trysts, risking disgrace and divorce for their fix of
motel love—all sacrificing the outer world to the inner,
proclaiming with this priority that everything solid-
seeming and substantial is in fact a dream, of less
account than a merciful rush of feeling.

The crowd inside Nemo's—the cop on duty, the
postman taking a breather, the three or four burly types

collecting unemployment against the spring rebirth of construction and fishing—became as winter wore on so well known to one another and the waitresses that even ritual remarks about the weather and the war dried up, and Rebecca filled their orders without asking, knowing what they wanted. Sukie Rougemont, no longer needing gossip to fuel her column "Eastwick Eyes and Ears" in the *Word*, preferred to take her clients and prospective buyers into the more refined and feminine atmosphere of the Bakery Coffee Nook a few doors away, between the framer's shop run by two fags originally from Stonington and the hardware store run by a seemingly endless family of Armenians; different Armenians, in different sizes but all with intelligent liquid eyes and kinky hair glistening low on their foreheads, waited on you each time. Alma Sifton, the proprietress of the Bakery Coffee Nook, had begun in what had been an old clam shack, with simply a coffee urn and two tables where shoppers who didn't want to run the gauntlet of stares in Nemo's might have a pastry and rest their feet; then more tables were added, and a line of sandwiches, mostly salad spreads (egg, ham, chicken), easily dished up. By her second summer Alma had to build an addition to the Nook twice the size of the original and put in a griddle and microwave oven; the Nemo's kind of greasy spoon was becoming a thing of the past.

Sukie loved her new job: getting into other people's houses, even the attics and cellars and laundry rooms and back halls, was like sleeping with men, a succession of subtly different flavors. No two homes had quite the same style or smell. The energetic bustling in and out of doors and up and down stairs and saying hello and good-bye constantly to people who were themselves on the move, and the gamble of it all appealed to the adventuress in her, and challenged her charm. Her sitting hunched over at a typewriter inhaling other people's cigarette smoke all day had not been healthy. She took a night course in Westerly and passed her exam and got her real-estate license by March.

Jane Smart continued to give lessons and fill in on the organ at South County churches and to practice her cello. There were certain of the Bach unaccompanied suites—the Third, with its lovely bourrée, and the Fourth, with that opening page of octaves and descending thirds which becomes a whirling, inconsolable outcry, and even the almost impossible Sixth, composed for an instrument with five strings—where she felt for measures at a time utterly *with* Bach, his mind exactly coterminous with hers, his vanished passion, lesser even than dust dispersed, stretching her fingers and flooding her cerebral lobes with triumph, his insistent questioning of the harmonics an operation of her own perilous soul. So this was the immortality men had built their pyramids and rendered their blood sacrifices for, this rebirth of a drudging old wife-fucking Lutheran *Kapellmeister* in the nervous system of a late-twentieth-century bachelor girl past her prime. Small comfort it must bring to his bones. But the music did talk, in its syntax of variation and reprise, reprise and variation; the mechanical procedures accumulated to form a spirit, a breath that rippled the rapid mathematics of it all like those footsteps wind makes on still, black water. It was communion. Jane did not see much of the Neffs, now that they were involved in the circle Brenda Parsley had gathered around her, and would have been endlessly solitary but for the crowd at Darryl Van Horne's.

Where once there had been three and then four, now there were six, and sometimes eight, when Fidel and Rebecca were enlisted in the fun—in the game of touch football, for instance, that they played with a beanbag in the echoing length of the big living room,

the giant vinyl hamburger and silkscreened Brillo
boxes and neon rainbow all pushed to one side, jum-
bled beneath the paintings like junk in an attic. A
certain contempt for the physical world, a voracious
appetite for immaterial souls, prevented Van Horne
from being an adequate caretaker of his possessions.
The parqueted floor of the music room, which he had
had sanded and polyurethaned at significant expense,
already held a number of pits gouged by the endpin
of Jane Smart's cello. The stereo equipment in the
hot-tub room had been soaked so often there were
pops and crackles in every record played. Most spectacularly, a puncture had mysteriously deflated the
tennis-court dome one icy night, and the gray canvas
lay sprawled there in the cold and snow like the hide
of a butchered brontosaurus, waiting for spring to
come, since Darryl saw no point in bothering with it
until the court could be used as an outdoor court
again. In the touch-football games, he was always one
of the quarterbacks, his nearsighted bloodshot eyes
rolling as he faded back to pass, the corners of his
mouth flecked with a foam of concentration. He kept
crying out, "The pocket, the pocket!"—begging for
protection, wanting Sukie and Alexandra, say, to block
out Rebecca and Jenny moving in for the tag, while
Fidel circled out for the bomb and Jane Smart cut
back for the escape-hatch buttonhook. The women
laughed and bumbled at the game, unable to take it
seriously. Chris Gabriel languidly went through the
motions, like a disbelieving angel, misplaced in all this
adult foolishness. Yet he usually came along, having
made no friends his own age; the small towns of
America are generally empty of people his age, at
college as they are, or in the armed forces, or beginning their careers amid the temptations and hardships
of a city. Jennifer worked many afternoons with Van

Horne in his lab, measuring out grams and deciliters of colored powders and liquids, deploying large copper sheets coated with this or that doped compound under batteries of overhead sunlamps while tiny wires led to meters monitoring electrical current. One sharp jump of the needle, Alexandra was led to understand, and more than the riches of the Orient would pour in upon Van Horne; in the meantime, there was an acrid and desolate chemical stink dragged up from the dungeons of the universe, and a mess of unscrubbed aluminum sinks and spilled and scattered elements, and plastic siphons clouded and melted as if by sulphurous combustion, and glass beakers and alembics with hardened black sediments crusted to the bottoms and sides. Jenny Gabriel, in a stained white smock and the clunky big sunglasses she and Van Horne wore in the perpetual blue glare, moved through this hopeful chaos with a curious authority, sure-fingered and quietly decisive. Here, as in their orgies, the girl—more than a girl, of course; indeed, only ten years younger than Alexandra—moved uncontaminable and in a sense untouched and yet among them, seeing, submitting, amused, unjudging, as if nothing were quite new to her, though her previous life seemed to have been one of exceptional innocence, the very barbarity of the times serving, in Chicago, to keep her within her citadel. Sukie had told the others how the girl had all but confided, in Nemo's, that she was still a virgin. Yet the girl disclosed her body to them with a certain shameless simplicity during the baths and the dances and submitted to their caresses not insensitively, and not without reciprocating. The touch of her hands, neither brusquely powerful like that of Jane's callused tips nor rapid and insinuating as with Sukie, had a penetration of its own, a gentle lingering as if in farewell, a forgiving slithering inquisitive something, ever less tentative, that pushed through to the bone. Alexandra loved being oiled by Jennifer, oiled while lying stretched on the black cushions or on several thicknesses of towels spread on the slates, the dampness of the bath enfolded and lifted up amid essences of aloe and coconut and almond, of sodium lactate and valerian extract, of aconite and cannabis indica. In the misted mirrors that Van Horne had installed on the outside of the shower doors, folds and waves of flesh glistened, and the younger woman, pale and perfect as a china figurine, could be seen kneeling in those angled deep distances mirrors create. The women developed a game called Serve Me, a sort of charade, though nothing like the charades Van Horne tried to organize in his living room when they were drunk but which collapsed beneath their detonations of mental telepathy and the clumsy fervor of his own mimicry, which disdained word-by-word enactments but sought to concentrate in one ferocious facial expression such full titles as *The History of the Decline and Fall of the Roman Empire* and *The Sorrows of Young Werther* and *The Origin of Species. Serve me*, the thirsty skins and spirits clamored, and patiently Jennifer oiled each witch, easing the transforming oils into the frowning creases, across the spots, around the bulges, rubbing against the grain of time, dropping small birdlike coos of sympathy and extollation.

"You have a lovely neck."

"I've always thought it was too short. Stubby. I've always hated my neck."

"Oh, you shouldn't have. Long necks are grotesque, except on black people."

"Brenda Parsley has an Adam's apple."

"Let's not be unkind. Let's think serene-making thoughts."

"Do me. Do me next, Jenny," Sukie nagged in a piping child's voice; she reverted quite dramatically, and while stoned was not above sucking her thumb.

Alexandra groaned. "What indecent bliss. I feel like a big sow rolling around."

"Thank God you don't smell that way," Jane Smart said. "Or does she, Jenny?"

"She smells very sweet and clean," Jenny primly said. From within that transparent bell of innocence or unknowing her slightly nasal voice came from as if far away, though distinctly; in the mirrors she was, kneeling, the shape and size and luster of one of those hollow porcelain birds, with holes at either end, from which children produce a few whistled notes.

"Jenny, the backs of my thighs," Sukie begged. "Just slowly along the backs, incredibly slowly. And use your fingernails. Don't be afraid of the insides of the thighs. The backs of the knees are wonderful. *Won*derful. Oh my God." Her thumb slid into her mouth.

"We're going to wear Jenny out," Alexandra warned in a considerate, drifting, indifferent voice.

"No, I like it," the girl said. "You're all so appreciative."

"We'll do you," Alexandra promised. "As soon as we get over this drugged feeling."

"I don't really care about being rubbed that much," Jenny confessed. "I'd rather do it than have it done to me, isn't that perverse?"

"It works out very well for us," Jane said, hissing the last word.

"Yes it does," Jenny agreed politely.

Van Horne, out of respect perhaps for the delicate initiate, seldom bathed with them now, or if he did he left the room swiftly, his hairy body wrapped from waist to knees in a towel, to keep Chris entertained with a game of chess or backgammon in the library.

He made himself available afterwards, however, wearing clothes of increasing foppishness—a silk paisley strawberry-colored bathrobe, for instance, with bell-bottom slacks of a fine green vertical stripe protruding below, and a mauve foulard stuffed about his throat—and affecting an ever-more-preening manner of magisterial benevolence, to preside over tea or drinks or a quick supper of Dominican *sancocho* or Cuban *mondongo*, of Mexican *pollo picado con tocino* or Colombian *soufflé de sesos*. Van Horne watched his female guests gobble these spicy delicacies rather ruefully, puffing tinted cigarettes through a curious twisted horn holder he lately brandished; he had himself lost weight and seemed feverish with hopes for his selenium-based solution to the problem of energy. Away from this topic, he often fell apathetically silent, and sometimes left the room abruptly. In retrospect, Alexandra and Sukie and Jane Smart might have concluded that he was bored with them; but they were themselves so far from bored with him that boredom did not enter their imaginations. His vast home, which they had nicknamed Toad Hall, expanded their meagre domiciles; in Van Horne's realm they left their children behind and became children themselves.

Jane came faithfully for her sessions of Hindemith and Brahms and, most recently attempted, Dvořák's swirling, dizzying Concerto for cello in B Minor. Sukie as that winter slowly melted away began to trip back and forth with notes and diagrams for her novel, which she and her mentor believed could be preplanned and engineered, a simple verbal machine for the arousal and then the relief of tension. And Alexandra timidly invited Van Horne to come view the large, weightless, enamelled statues of floating women she had patted together with gluey hands and putty knives and wooden salad spoons. She felt shy, having him to her house, which needed fresh paint in all the downstairs rooms and new linoleum on the kitchen floor; and between her walls he did seem diminished and aged, his jaw blue and the collar of his button-down Oxford frayed, as if shabbiness were infectious. He was wearing that baggy green-and-black tweed jacket with leather elbow-patches in which she had first met him, and he seemed so much an unemployed professor, or one of those sad men who as eternal graduate students haunt every university town, that she wondered how she had ever read into him so much magic and power. But he praised her work: "Baby, I think you've found your *shtik*! That sort of corny carny quality Lindner has, but with you there's not that metallic hardness, more of a Miró feeling, and sexy—sex-*ee*, hoo boy!" With an alarming speed and clumsiness, he loaded three of her papier-mâché figures into the back seat of his Mercedes, where they looked to Alexandra like gaudy little hitchhikers, corky bright limbs tangled and the wires that would suspend them from a ceiling snarled. "I'm driving to New York day after tomorrow more or less, and I'll show these to my guy on Fifty-seventh Street. He'll nibble, I'll bet my bottom buck; you've really caught something in the cultural works now, a sort of end-of-the-party feel. That unreality. Even the clips of the war on TV look unreal, we've all seen too many war movies."

Out in the open air, next to her car, dressed in a sheepskin coat with grimy cuffs and elbows, the matching sheepskin hat too small for his bushy head, he looked to Alexandra beyond capture, a lost cause; but, with an unpredictable lurch, he yielded to the bend of her mind and came back into the house with her and, breathing wheezily, up to her bedroom, to the bed she had lately denied to Joe Marino. Gina was pregnant again and that made it just too heavy. Darryl's potency had something infallible and unfeeling about it, and his cold penis hurt, as if it were covered with tiny little scales; but today, his taking her poor creations so readily with him to sell, and his stitched-together, slightly withered appearance, and the grotesque peaked sheepskin hat on his head, all had melted her heart and turned her vulva super-receptive. She could have mated with an elephant, thinking of becoming the next Niki de Saint-Phalle.

The three women, meeting downtown on Dock Street, checking in with one another by telephone, silently shared the sorority of pain that went with being the dark man's lover. Whether Jenny too carried this pain her aura did not reveal. When discovered by an afternoon visitor in the house, she always was wearing her lab coat and a frontal, formal attitude of efficiency. Van Horne used her, in part, because she was opaque, with her slightly brittle, deferential manner, her trait of letting certain vibrations and insinuations pass right through her, the somehow schematic roundness to her body. Within a group each member falls into a slot of special usefulness, and Jenny's was to be condescended to, to be "brought along," to be treasured as a version of each mature, divorced, disillusioned, empowered woman's younger self, though none had been quite like Jenny, or had lived alone with her younger brother in a house where her parents had met violent deaths. They loved her on their own terms, and, in fairness, she never indicated what terms she would have preferred. The most painful aspect of the afterimage the girl left, at least in Alexandra's mind, was the impression that she had trusted them, had confided herself to them as a woman usually first confides herself to a man, risking destruction in the determination to *know*. She had knelt among them like a docile slave and let her white round body shed the glow of its perfection upon their darkened imperfect forms sprawled wet on black cushions, under a roof that never slid back after, one icebound night, Van Horne had pushed the button and a flash made a glove of blue fire around his hairy hand.

Insofar as they were witches, they were phantoms in the communal mind. One smiled, as a citizen, to greet Sukie's cheerful pert face as it breezed along the crooked sidewalk; one saluted a certain grandeur in Alexandra as in her sandy riding boots and old green brocaded jacket she stood chatting with the proprietress of the Yapping Fox—Mavis Jessup, herself divorced, and hectic in complexion, and her dyed red hair hanging loose in Medusa ringlets. One credited to Jane Smart's angry dark brow, as she slammed herself into her old moss-green Plymouth Valiant, with its worn door latch, a certain distinction, an inner boiling such as had in other cloistral towns produced Emily Dickinson's verses and Emily Brontë's inspired novel. The women returned hellos, paid bills, and in the Armenians' hardware store tried, like everybody else, to describe with finger sketches in the air the peculiar thingamajiggy needed to repair a decaying home, to combat entropy; but we all knew there was something else about them, something as monstrous and obscene as what went on in the bedroom of even the assistant high-school principal and his wife, who both looked so blinky and tame as they sat in the bleachers chaperoning a record hop with its bloodcurdling throbbing.

We all dream, and we all stand aghast at the mouth of the caves of our deaths; and this is our way in. Into the nether world. Before plumbing, in the old outhouses, in winter, the accreted shit of the family would mount up in a spiky frozen stalagmite, and such phenomena help us to believe that there is more to life than the airbrushed ads at the front of magazines, the

Platonic forms of perfume bottles and nylon night-gowns and Rolls-Royce fenders. Perhaps in the passageways of our dreams we meet, more than we know: one white lamplit face astonished by another. Certainly the fact of witchcraft hung in the consciousness of Eastwick; a lump, a cloudy density generated by a thousand translucent overlays, a sort of heavenly body, it was rarely breathed of and, though dreadful, offered the consolation of completeness, of rounding out the picture, like the gas mains underneath Oak Street and the television aerials scraping *Kojak* and Pepsi commercials out of the sky. It had the uncertain outlines of something seen through a shower door and was viscid, slow to evaporate: for years after the events gropingly and even reluctantly related here, the rumor of witchcraft stained this corner of Rhode Island, so that a prickliness of embarrassment and unease entered the atmosphere with the most innocent mention of Eastwick.

iii. Guilt

> Recall the famous witch trials: the most acute and
> humane judges were in no doubt as to the guilt of the
> accused; the "witches" *themselves did not doubt it*—and
> yet there was no guilt.
>
> —*Friedrich Nietzsche, 1887*

"YOU HAVE?" Alexandra asked Sukie, over the phone.
It was April; spring made Alexandra feel dopey and
damp, slow to grasp even the simplest thing through
the omnipresent daze of sap running again, of organic
filaments warming themselves once again to crack the
mineral earth and make it yield yet more life. She had
turned thirty-nine in March and there was a weight
to this too. But Sukie sounded more energetic than
ever, breathless with her triumph. She had sold the
Gabriel place.

"Yes, a lovely serious rather elderly couple called
Hallybread. He teaches physics over at the University
in Kingston and she I think counsels people, at least
she kept asking me what *I* thought, which I guess is
part of the technique they learn. They had a house

236

in Kingston for twenty years but he wants to be nearer the sea now that he's retired and have a sailboat. They don't mind the house's not being painted yet, they'd rather pick the color themselves, and they have grandchildren and step-grandchildren that come and visit so they can use those rather dreary rooms on the third floor where Clyde kept all his old magazines, it's a wonder the weight didn't break the beams."

"What about the emanations, will that bother them?" For some of the other prospects who had looked at the house this winter had read of the murder and suicide and were scared off. People are still superstitious, even with all of modern science.

"Oh yes, they had read about it when it happened. It made a big splash in every paper in the state except the *Word*. They were amazed when somebody, not me, told them this had been the house. Professor Hallybread looked at the staircase and said Clyde must have been a clever man to make the rope just long enough so his feet didn't hit the stairs. I said, Yes, Mr. Gabriel had been very clever, always reading Latin and these abstruse astrological things, and I guess I began to look teary, thinking of Clyde, because Mrs. Hallybread put her arm around me and began to act, you know, like a counsellor. I think it may have helped sell the house actually, it put us on this footing where they could hardly say no."

"What are their names?" Alexandra asked, wondering if the can of clam chowder she was warming on the stove would boil over. Sukie's voice through the telephone wire was seeking painfully to infuse her with vernal vitality. Alexandra tried to respond and take an interest in these people she had never met, but her brain cells were already so littered with people she had met and grown to know and got excited by and even loved and then had forgotten. That cruise

on the *Coronia* to Europe twenty years ago with Oz
had by itself generated enough acquaintances to pop-
ulate a lifetime—their mates at the table with the edge
that came up in rough weather, the people in blankets
beside them on the deck having bouillon at elevenses,
the couples they met in the bar at midnight, the stewards, the captain with his square-cut ginger beard,
everyone so friendly and interesting because they were
young, young; youth is a kind of money, it makes
people fawn. Plus the people she had gone to high
school and Conn. College with. The boys with motorcycles, the pseudo-cowboys. Plus a million faces on
city streets, mustached men carrying umbrellas, cur-
vaceous women pausing to straighten a stocking in
the doorway of a shoe store, cars like cartons of faces
like eggs driving constantly by—all real, all with names,
all with souls they used to say, now compacted in her
mind like dead gray coral.

"Kind of cute names," Sukie was saying. "Arthur
and Rose. I don't know if you'd like them or not, they
seemed practical more than artistic."

One of the reasons for Alexandra's depression was
that Darryl had some weeks ago returned from New
York with the word that the manager of the gallery
on Fifty-seventh Street had thought her sculptures
were too much like those of Niki de Saint-Phalle. Furthermore, two of the three had returned damaged;
Van Horne had taken Chris Gabriel along to help
with the driving (Darryl became hysterical on the Connecticut Turnpike: the trucks tailgating him, hissing
and knocking on all sides of him, these repulsive obese
drivers glaring down at his Mercedes from their high
dirty cabs) and on the way home they had picked up
a hitchhiker in the Bronx, so the pseudo-Nanas riding
in the back were shoved over to make room. When
Alexandra had pointed out to Van Horne the bent

limbs, the creases in the fragile papier-mâché, and the one totally torn-off thumb, his face had gone into its patchy look, his eyes and mouth too disparate to focus, the glassy left eye drifting outward toward his ear and saliva escaping the corners of his lips. "Well Christ," he had said, "the poor kid was standing out there on the Deegan a couple blocks from the worst slum in the fucking country, he coulda got mugged and killed if we hadn't picked him up." He thought like a taxi driver, Alexandra realized. Later he asked her, "Why don'tcha try working in wood at least? You think Michelangelo ever wasted his time with gluey old newspapers?"

"But where will Chris and Jenny go?" she mustered the wit to ask. Also on her mind uncomfortably was Joe Marino, who even while admitting that Gina was in a family way again was increasingly tender and husbandly toward his former mistress, coming by at odd hours and tossing sticks at her windows and talking in all seriousness down in her kitchen (she wouldn't let him into the bedroom any more) about his leaving Gina and their setting themselves up with Alexandra's four children in a house somewhere in the vicinity but out of Eastwick, perhaps in Coddington Junction. He was a shy decent man with no thought of finding another mistress; that would have been disloyal to the team he had assembled. Alexandra kept biting back the truth that she would rather be single than a plumber's wife; it had been bad enough with Oz and his chrome. But just thinking a thought so snobbish and unkind made her feel guilty enough to relent and take Joe upstairs to her bed. She had put on seven pounds during the winter and that little extra layer of fat may have been making it harder for her to have an orgasm; Joe's naked body felt like an incubus and when she opened her eyes it seemed his hat was still on his head, that absurd checked wool hat with the tiny brim and little iridescent brown feather.

Or it may have been that somewhere someone had tied an *aiguillette* attached to Alexandra's sexuality.

"Who knows?" Sukie asked in turn. "I don't think they know. They don't want to go back where they came from, I know that. Jenny is so sure Darryl's close to making a breakthrough in the lab she wants to put all her share of the house money into his project."

This did shock Alexandra, and drew her full attention, either because any talk of money is magical, or because it had not occurred to her that Darryl Van Horne needed money. That *they* all needed money—the child-support checks ever later and later, and dividends down because of the war and the overheated economy, and the parents resisting even a dollar raise in the price of a half-hour's piano lesson by Jane Smart, and Alexandra's new sculptures worth less than the newspapers shredded to make them, and Sukie having to stretch her smile over the weeks between commissions—was assumed, and gave a threadbare gallantry to their little festivities, the extravagance of a fresh bottle of Wild Turkey or a jar of whole cashews or a tin of anchovies. And in these times of national riot, with an entire generation given over to the marketing and consumption of drugs, ever more rarely came the furtive wife knocking on the back door for a gram of dried orchis to stir into an aphrodisiac broth for her flagging husband, or the bird-loving widow wanting henbane with which to poison her neighbor's cat, or the timid teen-ager hoping to deal for an ounce of distilled moonwort or woadwaxen so as to work his will upon a world still huge in possibilities and packed like a honeycomb with untasted treasure. Nightclad and giggling, in the innocent days when they were freshly liberated from the wraps of housewifery, the witches used to sally out beneath the crescent moon to gather such herbs where they nestled at the rare and delicate starlit junction of suitable soil and moisture and shade. The market for all their magic was drying up, so common and multiform had sorcery become; but if they were poor, Van Horne was rich, and his wealth theirs to enjoy for their dark hours of holiday from their shabby sunlit days. That Jenny Gabriel might offer him money of her own, and he accept, was a transaction Alexandra had never envisioned. "Did you talk to *her* about this?"

"I told her I thought it would be crazy. Arthur Hallybread teaches physics and he says there is absolutely no foundation in electromagnetic reality for what Darryl is trying to do."

"Isn't that the sort of thing professors always say, to anybody with an idea?"

"Don't be so defensive, darling. I didn't know you cared."

"I don't care, really," Alexandra said, "what Jenny does with her money. Except she *is* another woman. How did she react when you said this to her?"

"Oh, you know. Her eyes got bigger and stared and her chin turned a little more pointy and it was as if she hadn't heard me. She has this stubborn streak underneath all the docility. She's too good for this world."

"Yes, that is the message she gives off, I suppose," Alexandra said slowly, sorry to feel that they were turning on her, their own fair creature, their *ingénue*.

Jane Smart called a week or so later, furious. "Couldn't you have *guessed*? Alexandra, you *do* seem abstracted these days." Her *s*'s hurt, stinging like match tips. "She's moving in! He's invited her and that foul little brother to move in!"

"Into Toad Hall?"

"Into the old *Len*ox place," Jane said, discarding the pet name they had once given it as if Alexandra were stupidly babbling. "It's what she's been angling for all along, if we'd just opened our foolish eyes. We were so *nice* to that vapid girl, taking her in, doing our thing, though she always *did* hold back as if really she were above it all and time would tell, like some smug little Cinderella squatting in the ashes knowing there was this glass slipper in her future—oh, the *priss*iness of her now is what gets me, swishing about in her cute little white lab coat and getting *paid* for it, when he owes everybody in town and the bank is thinking of foreclosing but it doesn't want to get stuck with the property, the upkeep is a *night*mare. Do you know what a new slate roof for that pile would run to?"

"Baby," Alexandra said, "you sound so financial. Where did you learn all this?"

The fat yellow lilac buds had released their first small bursts of heart-shaped leaves and the arched wands of forsythia, past bloom, had turned chartreuse like miniature willows. The gray squirrels had stopped coming to the feeder, too busy mating to eat, and the grapevines, which look so dead all winter, were beginning to shade the arbor again. Alexandra felt less sodden this week, as spring muddiness dried to green; she had returned to making her little clay bubbies, getting ready for the summer trade, and they were slightly bigger, with subtler anatomies and a deliberately Pop intensity to their coloring: she had learned something over the winter, by her artistic misadventure. So in this mood of rejuvenation she had trouble quickly sharing Jane's outrage; the pain of the Gabriel children's moving into a house that had felt fractionally hers sank in slowly. She had always held to the conceited fantasy that in spite of Sukie's superior beauty and liveliness and Jane's greater intensity and commitment to witchiness, she, Alexandra, was Darryl's favorite—in size and in a certain psychic breadth most nearly his match, and destined, somehow, to *reign* with him. It had been a lazy assumption.

Jane was saying, "Bob Osgood told me." He was the president of the Old Stone Bank downtown: stocky, the same physical type as Raymond Neff, but without a teacher's softness and that perspiring bullying manner teachers get; solid and confident, rather, from association with money Bob Osgood was, and utterly, beautifully bald, with a freshly minted shine to his skull and a skinned pinkness catching at his ears and his eyelids and nostrils, even his tapering quick fingers, as if he had stepped fresh from a steam room.

"You *see* Bob Osgood?"

Jane paused, registering distaste at the direct question as much as uncertainty how to answer. "His daughter Deborah is the last lesson on Tuesdays, and picking her up he's stayed once or twice for a beer. You know what an impossible bore Harriet Osgood is; poor Bob can't get it up to go home to her."

"Get it up" was one of those phrases the young had made current; it sounded a bit false and harsh in Jane's mouth. But then Jane *was* harsh, as people from Massachusetts tend to be. Puritanism had landed smack on that rock and after regaining its strength at the expense of the soft-hearted Indians had thrown its steeples and stone walls all across Connecticut, leaving Rhode Island to the Quakers and Jews and antinomians and women.

"Whatever happened to you and those nice Neffs?" Alexandra asked maliciously.

Harshly Jane laughed, as it were hawked into the mouthpiece of the telephone. "*He* can't get it up at all these days; Greta has reached the point where she tells anybody in town who'll listen, and she practically asked the boy doing checkout at the Superette to come back to the house and fuck her."

The *aiguillette* had been tied; but who had tied it? Witchcraft, once engendered in a community, has a way of running wild, out of control of those who have called it into being, running so freely as to confound victim and victimizer.

"Poor Greta," Alexandra heard herself mumble. Little devils were gnawing at her stomach; she felt uneasy, she wanted to get back to her bubbies and then, once they were snug in the Swedish kiln, to raking the winter-fallen twigs out of her lawn, and attacking the thatch with a pitchfork.

But Jane was on her own attack. "Don't give me that pitying earth-mother crap," she said, shockingly. "What are we going to *do* about Jennifer's moving in?"

"But sweetest, what can we do? Except show how hurt we are and have everybody laughing at us. Don't you think the town won't be amused enough anyway? Joe tells me some of the things people whisper. Gina calls us the *streghe* and is afraid we're going to turn the baby in her tummy into a little pig or a thalidomide case or something."

"Now you're talking," Jane Smart said.

Alexandra read her mind. "Some sort of spell. But what difference would it make? Jenny's there, you say. She has *his* protection."

"Oh it will make a difference believe you me," Jane Smart pronounced in one long shaking utterance of warning like a tremulous phrase drawn from a single swoop of her bow.

"What does Sukie think?"

"Sukie thinks just as I do. That it's an outrage. That

we've been betrayed. We've nursed a viper, my dear, in our bos*ooms*. And I don't mean the vindow viper."

This allusion did make Alexandra nostalgic for the nights, which in truth had become rarer as winter wore on, when they would all listen, nude and soaking and languid with pot and California Chablis, to Tiny Tim's many voices surrounding them in the stereophonic darkness, warbling and booming and massaging their interiors; the stereophonic vibrations brought into relief their hearts and lungs and livers, slippery fatty presences within that purple inner space for which the dim-lit tub room with its asymmetrical cushions was a kind of amplification. "I would think things will go on much as before," she reassured Jane. "He loves *us*, after all. And it's not as if Jenny does half the things we do for him; it was us she liked to cater to. The way that upstairs rambles, it's not as if they'll all be sharing quarters or anything."

"Oh Lexa," Jane sighed, fond in despair. "It's really *you* who're the innocent."

Having hung up, Alexandra found herself less than reassured. The hope that the dark stranger would eventually claim her cowered in its corner of her imagining; could it be that her queenly patience would earn itself no more reward than being used and discarded? The October day when he had driven her up to the front door as to something they mutually possessed, and when she had to wade away through the tide as if the very elements were begging her to stay: could such treasured auguries be empty? How short life is, how quickly its signs exhaust their meaning. She caressed the underside of her left breast and seemed to detect a small lump there. Vexed, frightened, she met the bright beady gaze of a gray squirrel that had stolen into the feeder to rummage amid the sunflower-seed husks. He was a plump little gentle-

man in a gray suit with white shirtfront, come bright-
eyed to dine. The effrontery, the greed. His tiny gray
hands, mindless and dry as bird feet, were arrested
halfway to his chest by sudden awareness of her gaze,
her psyche's impingement; his eyes were set sideways
in the oval skull so as to seem in their convexity opaque
turrets, slanted and gleaming. The spark of life inside
the tiny skull wanted to flee, to twitch away to safety,
but Alexandra's sudden focus froze the spark even
through glass. A dim little spirit, programmed for
feeding and evasion and seasonal copulation, was
meeting a greater. *Morte, morte, morte,* Alexandra said
firmly in her mind, and the squirrel dropped like an
instantly emptied sack. One last spasm of his limbs
flipped a few husks over the edge of the plastic feeder
tray, and the luxuriant frosty plume of a tail flickered
back and forth a few more seconds; then the animal
was still, the dead weight making the feeder with its
conical green plastic roof swing on the wire strung
between two posts of an arbor. The program was can-
celled.

Alexandra felt no remorse; it was a delicious power
she had. But now she would have to put on her Wellingtons and go outside and with her own hand lift
the verminous body by its tail and walk to the edge
of her yard and throw it into the bushes over the stone
wall, where the bog began. There was so much dirt
in life, so many eraser crumbs and stray coffee grounds
and dead wasps trapped inside the storm windows,
that it seemed all of a person's time—all of a woman's
time, at any rate—was spent in reallocation, taking
things from one place to another, dirt being as her
mother had said simply matter in the wrong place.

Comfortingly, that very night, while the children
were lurking around Alexandra demanding, depend-

ing upon their ages, the car, help with their home-
work, or to be put to bed, Van Horne called her, which
was unusual, since his sabbats usually arose as if spon-
taneously, without the deigning of his personal invitation, but through a telepathic, or telephonic, merge
of the desires of his devotees. They would find themselves there without quite knowing how they came to
be there. Their cars—Alexandra's pumpkin-colored
Subaru, Sukie's gray Corvair, Jane's moss-green Valiant—would take them, pulled by a tide of psychic
forces. "Come on over Sunday night," Darryl growled,
in that New York taxi-driver rasp of his. "It's a helluva
depressing day, and I got some stuff I want to try out
on the gang."

"It's not easy," Alexandra said, "to get a sitter on
a Sunday night. They've got to get up for school in
the morning and want to stay home and watch Archie
Bunker." In her unprecedented resistance she heard
resentment, an anger that Jane Smart had planted
but whose growth was being fed now with her own
veins.

"Ah come on. Those kids of yours are ancient, how
come they still need sitters?"

"I can't saddle Marcy with the three younger, they
don't accept her discipline. Also she may want to drive
over to a friend's house and I don't want her not to
be able to; it's not fair to burden a child with your
own responsibilities."

"What gender friend the kid seeing?"

"It's none of your business. A girlfriend, as it happens."

"Christ, don't snap at *me*, it wasn't me conned you
into having those little twerps."

"They're *not* twerps, Darryl. And I do neglect them."

Interestingly, he did not seem to mind being talked
back to, which she had not done before: perhaps it

was the way to his heart. "Who's to say," he responded mildly, "what's neglect? If my mother had neglected me a little more I might be a better all-round guy."

"You're an O.K. guy." It felt forced from her, but she liked it that he had bothered to seek reassurance.

"Thanks a fuck of a lot," he answered with a jolting coarseness. "We'll see you when you get here."

"Don't be huffy."

"Who's huffy? Take it or leave it. Sunday around seven. Dress informal."

She wondered why next Sunday should be depressing to him. She looked at the kitchen calendar. The numerals were interlaced with lilies.

Easter evening turned out to be a warm spring night with a south wind pulling the moon backwards through wild, blanched clouds. The tide had left silver puddles on the causeway. New green marsh grass was starting up in the spaces between the rocks; Alexandra's headlights swung shadows among the boulders and across the tree-intertwined entrance gate. The driveway curved past where the egrets used to nest and now the collapsed tennis-court bubble lay creased and hardened like a lava flow; then her car climbed, circling the mall lined by noseless statues. As the stately silhouette of the house loomed, the grid of its windows all alight, her heart lifted into its holiday flutter; always, coming here, night or day, she expected to meet the momentous someone who was, she realized, herself, herself unadorned and untrammelled, forgiven and nude, erect and perfect in weight and open to any courteous offer: the beautiful stranger, her secret self. Not all the next day's weariness could cure her of the exalted expectation that the Lenox place aroused. Your cares evaporated in the entry hall, where the sulphurous scents greeted you, and an apparent elephant's-foot umbrella stand holding a cluster of old-fashioned knobs and handles on second glance turned out to be a single painted casting, even to the little strap and snap button holding the umbrella furled—one more mocking work of art.

Fidel took her jacket, a man's zippered windbreaker. More and more Alexandra found men's clothes comfortable; first she began to buy their shoes and gloves, then corduroy and chino trousers that weren't so nipped at the waist as women's slacks were, and lately the nice, roomy, efficient jackets men hunt and work in. Why should they have all the comfort while we martyr ourselves with spike heels and all the rest of the slave-fashions sadistic fags wish upon us?

"*Buenas noches, señora,*" Fidel said. "*Es muy agradable tenerla nuevamente en esta casa.*"

"The mister have all sort of gay party planned," Rebecca said behind him. "Oh there big changes afoot."

Jane and Sukie were already in the music room, where some oval-backed chairs with a flaking silvery finish had been set out; Chris Gabriel slouched in a corner near a lamp, reading *Rolling Stone*. The rest of the room was candlelit; candles in all the colors of jellybeans had been found for the cobwebbed sconces along the wall, each draft-tormented little flame doubled by a tin mirror. The aura of the flames was an acrid complementary color: green eating into the orange glow yet constantly repelled, like the viscid contention amid unmixing chemicals. Darryl, wearing a tuxedo of an old-fashioned double-breasted cut, its black dull as soot but for the broad lapels, came up and gave her his cold kiss. Even his spit on her cheek was cold. Jane's aura was slightly muddy with anger and Sukie's rosy and amused, as usual. They had all, in their sweaters and dungarees, evidently underdressed for the occasion.

The tuxedo did give Darryl a less patchy and shambling air than usual. He cleared his froggy throat and announced, "Howzabout a little concert? I've been working up some ideas here and I want to get you girls' feedback. The first number is entitled"—he froze in mid-gesture, his sharp little greenish teeth gleaming, his spectacles for the night so small that the pale-plastic frames seemed to have his eyes trapped—"'The A Nightingale Sang in Berkeley Square Boogie.'"

Masses of notes were struck off as if more than two hands were playing, the left hand setting up a deep cloudy stride rhythm, airy but dark like a thunderhead growing closer above the treetops, and then the right hand picking out, in halting broken phrases so that the tune only gradually emerged, the rainbow of the melody. You could see it, the misty English park, the pearly London sky, the dancing cheek-to-cheek, and at the same time feel the American rumble, the good gritty whorehouse tinkling only this continent could have cooked up, in the tasselled brothels of a southern river town. The melody drew closer to the bass, the bass moved up and swallowed the nightingale, a wonderfully complicated flurry ensued while Van Horne's pasty seamed face dripped sweat onto the keyboard and his grunts of effort smudged the music; Alexandra pictured his hands as white waxy machines, the phalanges and flexor tendons tugging and flattening and directly connected to the rods and felts and strings of the piano, this immense plangent voice one hyperdeveloped fingernail. The themes drew apart, the rainbow reappeared, the thunderhead faded into harmless air, the melody was restated in an odd high minor key reached through an askew series of six descending, fading chords struck across the collapsing syncopation.

Silence, but for the hum of the piano's pounded harp.

"Fantastic," Jane Smart said dryly.

"Really, baby," Sukie urged upon their host, exposed and blinking now that his exertion was over. "I've never heard anything like it."

"I could cry," Alexandra said sincerely, he had stirred such memories within her, and such inklings of her future; music lights up with its pulsing lamp the cave of our being.

Darryl seemed disconcerted by their praise, as if he might be dissolved in it. He shook his shaggy head like a dog drying itself, and then seemed to press his jaw back into place with the same two fingers that wiped the corners of his mouth. "That one mixed pretty well," he admitted. "O.K., let's try this one now. It's called 'The How High the Moon March.'" This mix went less well, though the same wizardry was in operation. A wizardry, Alexandra thought, of theft and transformation, with nothing of guileless creative engendering about it, only a boldness of monstrous combination. The third offering was the Beatles' tender "Yesterday," broken into the stutter-rhythms of a samba; it made them all laugh, which hadn't been the effect of the first and which wasn't perhaps the intention. "So," Van Horne said, rising from the bench. "That's the idea. If I could work up a dozen or so of these a friend of mine in New York says he has an in with a recording executive and maybe we can raise a modicum of moolah to keep this establishment afloat. So what's your input?"

"It may be a bit...special," Sukie offered, her plump upper lip closing upon her lower in a solemn way that looked nevertheless amused.

"What's special?" Van Horne asked, pain showing, his face about to fly apart. "Tiny Tim was special. Liberace was special. Lee Harvey Oswald was special.

To get any attention at all in this day and age you got to be way out."

"This establishment needs moolah?" Jane Smart asked sharply.

"So I'm told, toots."

"Honey, by whom?" Sukie asked.

"Oh," he said, embarrassed, squinting out through the candlelight as if he could see nothing but reflections, "a bunch of people. Banker types. Prospective partners." Abruptly, in tune perhaps with the old tuxedo, he ducked into horror-movie clowning, bobbing in his black outfit as if crippled, his legs hinged the wrong way. "That's enough business," he said. "Let's go into the living room. Let's get *smashed*."

Something was up. Alexandra felt a sliding start within her; an immense slick slope of depression was revealed as if by the sliding upwards of an automatic garage door, the door activated by a kind of electric eye of her own internal sensing and giving on a wide underground ramp whose downward trend there was no reversing, not by pills or sunshine or a good night's sleep. Her life had been built on sand and she knew that everything she saw tonight was going to strike her as sad.

The dusty ugly works of Pop Art in the living room were sad, and the way several fluorescent tubes in the track lighting overhead were out or flickered, buzzing. The great long room needed more people to fill it with the revelry it had been designed for; it seemed to Alexandra suddenly an ill-attended church, like those that Colorado pioneers had built along the mountain roads and where no one came any more, an ebbing more than a renunciation, everybody too busy changing the plugs in their pickup truck or recovering from Saturday night, the parking places outside gone over to grass, the pews with their racks still stocked with hymnals visible inside. "Where's Jenny?" she asked aloud.

"The lady still cleaning up in de labora*tory*," Rebecca said. "She work so hard, I worry sickness take her."

"How's it all going?" Sukie asked Darryl. "When can I paint my roof with kilowatts? People still stop me on the street and ask about that because of the story I wrote on you."

"Yeah," he snarled, ventriloquistically, so the voice emerged from well beside his head, "and those old fogies you sold the Gabriel dump to bad-mouthing the whole idea, I hear. Fuck 'em. They laughed at Leonardo. They laughed at Leibniz. They laughed at the guy who invented the zipper, what the hell was his name? One of invention's unsung greats. Actually, I've been wondering if microörganisms aren't the way to go—use a mechanism that's already set in place and self-replicates. Biogas technology: you know who's way ahead in that department? The Chinese, can you believe it?"

"Couldn't we just use less electricity?" Sukie asked, interviewing out of habit. "And use our bodies more? Nobody needs an electric carving knife."

"You need one if your neighbor has one," Van Horne said. "And then you need another to replace the one you get. And another. And another. Fidel! *Deseo beber!*"

The servant in his khaki pajamas, abjectly shapeless and yet also with a whisper of military menace, brought drinks, and a tray of *huevos picantes* and palm hearts. Without Jenny here, surprisingly, conversation lagged; they had grown used to her, as someone to display themselves to, to amuse and shock and instruct. Her wide-eyed silence was missed. Alexandra, hoping that art, any art, might staunch the internal bleeding of her melancholy, moved among the giant hamburgers and ceramic dartboards as if she had never seen them before; and indeed some of them she hadn't. On a four-foot plinth of plywood painted black, beneath a plastic pastry bell, rested an ironically realistic replica—a three-dimensional Wayne Thiebaud—of a white-frosted wedding cake. Instead of the conventional bride and groom, however, two nude figures stood on the topmost tier, the female pink and blonde and rounded and the black-haired man a darker pink, but for the dead-white centimeter of his semi-erect penis. Alexandra wondered what the material of this fabrication was: the cake lacked the scoring of cast bronze and also the glaze of enamelled ceramic. Acrylicked plaster was her guess. Seeing that no one but Rebecca, passing a tray of tiny crabs stuffed with *xuxu* paste, was observing her, Alexandra lifted the bell and touched the frostinglike rim of the object. A tender dab of it came away on her finger. She put the finger in her mouth. Sugar. It was real frosting, a real cake, and fresh.

Darryl, with wide splaying gestures, was outlining another energy approach to Sukie and Jane. "With geothermal, once you get the shaft dug—and why the hell not? they make tunnels twenty miles long over in the Alps every day of the week—your only problem is keeping the energy from burning up the converter. Metal will melt like lead soldiers on Venus. You know what the answer is? Unbelievably simple. Stone. You got to make all your machinery, all the gearing and turbines, out of stone. They can do it! They can chisel granite now as fine as they can mill steel. They can make springs out of poured cement, would you believe?—particle size is what it all boils down to. Metal has had it, just like flint when the Bronze Age came in."

Another work of art Alexandra hadn't noticed

before was a glossy female nude, a mannequin without
the usual matte skin and the hinged limbs, a Kienholz
in its assaultiveness but smooth and minimally defined
in the manner of Tom Wesselmann, crouching as if
to be fucked from behind, her face blank and bland,
her back flat enough to be a tabletop. The indentation
of her spine was straight as the groove for blood in a
butcher's block. The buttocks suggested two white
motorcycle helmets welded together. The statue stirred
Alexandra with its blasphemous simplification of her
own, female form. She took another margarita from
Fidel's tray, savored the salt (it is a myth and absurd
slander that witches abhor salt; saltpeter and cod liver
oil, both associated with Christian virtue, are what
they cannot abide), and sauntered up to their host. "I
feel sexy and sad," she said. "I want to take my bath
and smoke my joint and get home. I swore to the
babysitter I'd be home by ten-thirty; she was the fifth
girl I tried and I could hear her mother shouting at
her in the background. These parents don't want them
to come near us."

"You're breaking my heart," Van Horne said, looking sweaty and confused after his gaze into the geothermal furnace. "Don't rush things. I don't feel
smashed yet. There's a schedule here. Jenny's about
to come down."

Alexandra saw a new light in Van Horne's glassy
bloodshot eyes; he looked scared. But what could scare
him?

Jenny's tread was silent on the carpeted curved
front staircase; she came into the long room with her
hair pulled back like Eva Perón's and wearing a
powder-blue bathrobe that swept the floor. Above each
of her breasts the robe bore as decoration three
embroidered cuts like large buttonholes, which
reminded Alexandra of military chevrons. Jenny's face,

with its wide round brow and firm triangular chin, was shiny-clean and devoid of make-up; nor did a smile adorn it. "Darryl, don't get drunk," she said. "You make even less sense when you're drunk than when you're sober."

"But he gets in*spi*red," Sukie said with her practiced sauciness, feeling her way with this new woman, in residence and somehow in charge.

Jenny ignored her, looking around, past their heads. "Where's dear Chris?"

From the corner Rebecca said, "Young man in de liberry reading his magazines."

Jenny took two steps forward and said, "Alexandra. Look." She untied her cloth belt and spread the robe's wings wide, revealing her white body with its round-nesses, its rings of baby fat, its cloud of soft hair smaller than a man's hand. She asked Alexandra to look at that translucent wart under her breast. "Do you think it's getting bigger or am I imagining it? And up here," she said, guiding the other woman's fingers into her armpit. "Do you feel a little lump?"

"It's hard to say," Alexandra said, flustered, for such touching occurred in the steamy dark of the tub room but not in the bald fluorescent light here. "We're all so full of little lumps just naturally. I don't feel anything."

"You aren't *con*centrating," Jenny said, and with a gesture that in another context would have seemed loving took Alexandra's wrist in her fingers and led her right hand to the other armpit. "There's sort of the same thing there too. Please, Lexa. Concentrate."

A faint bristle of shaven hair. A silkiness of applied powder. Underneath, lumps, veins, glands, nodules. Nothing in nature is quite homogeneous; the universe was tossed off freehand. "Hurt?" she asked.

"I'm not sure. I feel *some*thing."

"I don't think it's anything," Alexandra pronounced.

"Could it be connected with this somehow?" Jenny lifted her firm conical breast to further expose her transparent wart, a tiny cauliflower or pug face of pink flesh gone awry.

"I don't think so. We all get those."

Suddenly impatient, Jenny closed her bathrobe and pulled the belt tight. She turned to Van Horne. "Have you told them?"

"My dear, my dear," he said, wiping the corners of his smiling mouth with a trembling thumb and finger. "We must make a ceremony of it."

"The fumes today have given me a headache and I think we've all had enough ceremonies. Fidel, just bring me a glass of soda water, *aqua gaseosa, o horchata, por favor. Pronto, gracias.*"

"The wedding cake," exclaimed Alexandra, with an icy thrill of clairvoyance.

"Now you're cooking, little Sandy," Van Horne said. "You've got it. I saw you poke and lick that finger," he teased.

"It wasn't that so much as Jenny's manner. Still, I can't believe it. I know it but I can't believe it."

"You better believe it, ladies. The kid here and I were married as of yesterday afternoon at three-thirty p.m. The craziest little justice of the peace up in Apponaug. He stuttered. I never thought you could have a stutter and still get the license. D-d-d-do you, D-D-D-D-D—"

"Oh Darryl, you didn't!" Sukie cried, her lips pulled so far back in a mirthless grin that the hollows at the top of her upper gums showed.

Jane Smart hissed at Alexandra's side.

"How could you two do that to us?" Sukie asked. The word "us" surprised Alexandra, who felt this announcement as a sudden sore place in her abdomen alone.

"So sneakily," Sukie went on, her cheerful party manner slightly stiff on her face. "We would at least have given her a shower."

"Or some casserole dishes," Alexandra said bravely.

"She did it," Jane was saying seemingly to herself but of course for Alexandra and the others to overhear. "She actually managed to pull it off."

Jenny defended herself; the color in her cheeks was high. "It wasn't so much managing, it just came to seem natural, me here all the time anyway, and naturally..."

"Naturally nature took its nasty natural course," Jane spit out.

"Darryl, what's in it for you?" Sukie asked him, in her frank and manly reporter's voice.

"Oh, you know," he said sheepishly. "The standard stuff. Settle down. Security. Look at her. She's beautiful."

"Bullshit," Jane Smart said slowly, the word simmering.

"With all respect, Darryl, and I *am* fond of our little Jenny," Sukie said, "she *is* a bit of a blah."

"Come on, cut it out, what sort of reception is this?" the big man said helplessly, while his robed bride beside him didn't flinch, taking shelter as she always had behind the brittle shield of innocence, the snobbery of ignorance. It was not that her brain was less efficient than theirs, within its limits it was more so; but it was like the keyboard of an adding machine as opposed to that of typewriters. Van Horne was trying to collect his dignity. "Listen, you bitches," he said. "What's this attitude that I owe you anything? I took you in, I gave you eats and a little relief from your lousy lives—"

"Who made them lousy?" Jane Smart swiftly asked. "Not me. I'm new in town."

Fidel brought in a tray of long-stemmed glasses of champagne. Alexandra took one and tossed its contents at Van Horne's face; the rarefied liquid fell short, wetting only the area of his fly and one pants leg. All she had achieved was to make him seem the victim and not herself. She threw the glass vehemently at the sculpture of intertwined automobile bumpers; here her aim was better, but the glass in mid-flight turned into a barn swallow, and flicked itself away. Thumbkin, who had been licking herself on the satin love seat, worrying with avid tongue the tiny pink gap in her raiment of long white fur, perked up and gave chase; with that comical deadly solemnity of cats, green eyes flattened across the top, she stalked along the back of the curved four-cushion sofa and batted in frustration at the air when she reached the edge. The bird took shelter by perching upon a hanging Styrofoam cloud by Marjorie Strider.

"Hey, this isn't at all the way I pictured it," Van Horne complained.

"How *did* you picture it, Darryl?" Sukie asked.

"As a blast. We thought you'd be pleased as hell. You brought us together. You're like Cupids. You're like the maids of honor."

"I *never* thought they'd be pleased," Jenny corrected. "I just didn't think they'd be quite so ill-mannered."

"Why *would*n't they be pleased?" Van Horne held his rubbery strange hands open in a supplicatory fashion, arguing with Jenny, and they did look the very tableau of a married couple. "We'd be pleased for *them*," he said, "if some schnook came along and took 'em off the market. I mean, what's this jealousy bag, with the whole damn world going up in napalm? How fucking bourgeois can you get?"

Sukie was the first to soften. Perhaps she just wanted to nibble something. "All right," she said. "Let's eat the cake. It better have hash in it."

"The best. Orinoco beige."

Alexandra had to laugh, Darryl was so funny and hopeful and discombobulated. "There is no such thing."

"Sure there is, if you know the right people. Rebecca knows the guys who drive that crazy-painted van down from south Providence. *La crème de la crooks*, honest. You'll fly out of here. Wonder what the tide's doing?"

So he did remember: her braving the ice-cold tide that day, and him standing on the far shore shouting "You *can* fly!"

The cake was set on the tablelike back of the crouching nude. The marzipan figures were removed and broken and passed around for them to eat in a circle. Alexandra got the prick—tribute of a sort. Darryl mumbled "*Hoc est enim corpus meum*" as he did the distribution; over the champagne he intoned, "*Hic est enim calix sanguines mei.*" Across from Alexandra, Jenny's face had turned a radiant pink; she was allowing her joy to show, she was dyed clear through by the blood of triumph. Alexandra's heart went out to her, as if to a younger self. They all fed cake to one another with their fingers; soon its tiered cylinders looked eviscerated by jackals. Then they linked dirty hands and, their backs to the crouching statue, upon whose left buttock Sukie with lipstick and frosting had painted a grinning snaggle-toothed face, they danced in a ring, chanting in the ancient fashion, "*Emen hatan, Emen hetan*" and "*Har, har, diable, diable, saute ici, saute là, joue ici, joue là!*"

Jane, by now the drunkest of them, tried to sing

all the stanzas to that unspeakable Jacobean song of songs, "Tinkletum Tankletum," until laughter and alcohol broke her memory down. Van Horne juggled first three, then four, then five tangerines, his hands a frantic blur. Christopher Gabriel stuck his head out of the library to see what all the hilarity was about. Fidel had been holding back some marinated capybara balls, which now he served forth. The night was becoming a success; but when Sukie proposed that they all go have a bath now, Jenny announced with a certain firmness, "The tub's been drained. It had gotten all scummy, and we're waiting for a man from Narragansett Pool Hygiene to come and give the teak a course of fungicide."

So Alexandra got home earlier than expected and surprised the babysitter intertwined with her boyfriend on the sofa downstairs. She backed out of the room and reëntered ten minutes later and paid the embarrassed sitter. The girl was an Arsenault and lived downtown; her friend would drive her home, she said. Alexandra's next action was to go upstairs and tiptoe into Marcy's room and verify that her daughter, seventeen and a woman's size, was virginally asleep. But for hours into the night the vision of the pallid undersides of the Arsenault girl's thighs clamped around the nameless boy's furry buttocks, his jeans pulled down just enough to give his genitals freedom while she had been stripped of all her clothes, burned in Alexandra's brow like the moon sailing backwards through tattered, troubled clouds.

They met, the three of them, somewhat like old times, in Jane Smart's house, the ranch house in the Cove development that had been such a comedown, really, for Jane after the lovely thirteen-room Victorian, with its servants' passageways and ornamental

ball-and-stick work and Tiffany-glass chandeliers, that
she and Sam in their glory days had owned on Vane
Street, one block back from Oak, away from the water.
Her present house was a split-level ranch standing on
the standard quarter-acre, its shingled parts painted
an acid blue. The previous owner, an underemployed
mechanical engineer who had finally gone to Texas
in pursuit of work, had spent his abundant spare time
"antiquing" the little house, putting up pine cabinets
and false boxed beams, and knotty wainscoting with
induced chisel scars, and even installing light switches
in the form of wooden pump handles and a toilet
bowl sheathed in oaken barrel staves. Some walls were
hung with old carpentry tools, plow planes and frame
saws and drawknives; and a small spinning wheel had
been cunningly incorporated into the banister at the
landing where the split in levels occurred. Jane had
inherited this fussy overlay of Puritania without overt
protest; but her contempt and that of her children
had slowly eroded the precious effect. Whittled light
switches were snapped in rough haste. Once one stave
had been broken by a kick, the whole set of them
collapsed around the toilet bowl. The cute boxy toilet-
paper holder had come apart too. Jane gave her piano
lessons at the far end of the long open living room,
up six steps from the kitchen-dinette-den level, and
the uncarpeted living-room floor showed the ravages
of an apparently malign fury; the pin of her cello had
gouged a hole wherever she had decided to set her
stand and chair. And she had roamed the area fairly
widely, rather than play in one settled place. Nor did
the damage end there; everywhere in the newish little
house, built of green pine and cheap material in a set
pattern like a series of dances enacted by the construction crews, were marks of its fragility, scars in
the paint and holes in the plasterboard and missing

tiles on the kitchen floor. Jane's awful Doberman pinscher, Randolph, had chewed chair rungs and had clawed at doors until troughs were worn in the wood. Jane really did live, Alexandra told herself in extenuation, in some unsolid world part music, part spite.

"So what shall we do about it?" Jane asked now, drinks distributed and the first flurry of gossip dispersed—for there could be only one topic today, Darryl Van Horne's astounding, insulting marriage.

"How smug and 'at home' she was in that big blue bathrobe," Sukie said. "I hate her. To think it was me that brought her to tennis that time. I hate myself." She crammed her mouth with a handful of salted pepita seeds.

"And she was quite competitive, remember?" Alexandra said. "That bruise on my thigh didn't go away for weeks."

"That should have told us something," Sukie said, picking a green husk from her lower lip. "That she wasn't the helpless little doll she appeared. It's just I felt so guilty about Clyde and Felicia."

"Oh *stop* it," Jane insisted. "You *did*n't feel guilty, how *could* you feel guilty? It wasn't your screwing Clyde rotted his brain, it wasn't you who made Felicia such a horror."

"They had a symbiosis," Alexandra said consideringly. "Sukie's being so lovely for Clyde upset it. I have the same problem with Joe except I'm pulling out. Gently. To defuse the situation. People," she mused. "People *are* explosive."

"Don't you just *hate* her?" Sukie asked Alexandra. "I mean, we all understood he was to be yours if he was to be anybody's, among the three of us, once the novelty and everything wore off. Isn't that so, Jane?"

"It is not so" was the definite response. "Darryl and I are both musical. And we're dirty."

"Who says Lexa and I aren't dirty?" Sukie protested.

"You work at it," Jane said. "But you have other tendencies too. You both have goody-goody sides. You haven't committed yourselves the way I have. For me, there is nobody except Darryl."

"I thought you said you were seeing Bob Osgood," Alexandra said.

"I said I was giving his daughter Deborah piano lessons," Jane responded.

Sukie laughed. "You should see how uppity you look, saying that. Like Jenny when she called us all ill-mannered."

"And didn't she boss him around, in her chilly little way," Alexandra said. "I knew they were married just from the way she stepped into the room, making a late entrance. And he was different. Less outrageous, more tentative. It was sad."

"We *are* committed, sweetie," Sukie said to Jane. "But what can we do, except snub them and go back to being our old cozy selves? I think it may be nicer now. I feel closer to the two of you than for months. And all those hot hors d'oeuvres Fidel made us eat were getting to my stomach."

"What can we *do*?" Jane asked rhetorically. Her black hair, brushed from a central part in two severe wings, fell forward, eclipsing her face, and was swiftly brushed back. "It's obvious. We can *hex* her."

The word, like a shooting star suddenly making its scratch on the sky, commanded silence.

"You can hex her yourself if you feel that vehement," Alexandra said. "You don't need us."

"I do. It needs the three of us. This mustn't be a little hex, so she'll just get hives and a headache for a week."

Sukie asked after a pause, "What *will* she get?"

Jane's thin lips clamped shut upon a bad-luck word, the Latin for "crab." "I think it's obvious, from the other night, where her anxieties lie. When a person has a fear like that it takes just the teeniest-weeniest psychokinetic push to make it come true."

"Oh, the poor child," Alexandra involuntarily exclaimed, having the same terror herself.

"Poor child nothing," said Jane. "She is"—and her thin face put on additional hauteur—"Mrs. Darryl Van Horne."

After another pause Sukie asked, "How would the hex work?"

"Perfectly straightforwardly. Alexandra makes a wax figure of her and we stick pins in it under our cone of power."

"Why must *I* make it?" Alexandra asked.

"Simple, my darling. You're the sculptress, we're not. And you're still in touch with the larger forces. My spells lately tend to go off at about a forty-five degree angle. I tried to kill Greta Neff's pet cat about six months ago when I was still seeing Ray, and from what he let drop I gather I killed all the rodents in the house instead. The walls stank for weeks but the cat stayed disgustingly healthy."

Alexandra asked, "Jane, don't you ever get scared?"

"Not since I accepted myself for what I am. A fair cellist, a dreadful mother, and a boring lay."

Both the other women protested this last, gallantly, but Jane was firm: "I give good enough head, but when the man is on top and in me something resentful takes over."

"Just try imagining it's your own hand," Sukie suggested. "That's what I do sometimes."

"Or think of it that *you're* fucking *him*," Alexandra said. "That he's just something you're toying with."

"It's too late for all that. I like what I am by now.

If I were happier I'd be less effective. Here's what I've done for a start. When Darryl was passing the marzipan figures around I bit off the head of the one representing Jenny but didn't swallow it, and spit it out when I could in my handkerchief. Here." She went to her piano bench, lifted the lid, and brought out a crumpled handkerchief; gloatingly she unfolded the handkerchief for their eyes.

The little smooth candy head, further smoothed by those solvent seconds in Jane's mouth, did have a relation to Jenny's round face—the washed-out blue eyes with their steady gaze, the blond hair so fine it lay flat on her head like paint, a certain blankness of expression that had something faintly challenging and defiant and, yes, galling about it.

"That's good," Alexandra said, "but you also need something more intimate. Blood is best. The old recipes used to call for *sang de menstruës*. And hair, of course. Fingernail clippings."

"Belly-button lint," chimed in Sukie, silly on two bourbons.

"Excrement," Alexandra solemnly continued, "though if you're not in Africa or China that's hard to come by."

"Hold on. Don't go away," Jane said, and left the room.

Sukie laughed. "I should write a story for the Providence *Journal-Bulletin*, 'The Flush Toilet and the Demise of Witchcraft.' They said I could submit features as a free-lancer to them if I wanted to get back into writing." She had kicked off her shoes and curled her legs under her as she leaned on one arm of Jane's acid-green sofa. In this era even women well into middle age wore miniskirts, and Sukie's kittenish posture exposed almost all the thigh she had, plus her freckled, gleaming knees, perfect as eggs. She was in a wool pullover dress scarcely longer than a sweater, sharp orange in color; this color made with the sofa's vile green the arresting clash one finds everywhere in Cézanne's landscapes and that would be ugly were it not so oddly, boldly beautiful. Sukie's face wore that tipsy slurred look—eyes too moist and sparkling, lipstick rubbed away but for the rims by too much smiling and chattering—that Alexandra found sexy. She even found sexy Sukie's least successful feature, her short, fat, and rather unchiselled nose. There was no doubt, Alexandra thought to herself dispassionately, that since Van Horne's marriage her heart had slipped its moorings, and that away from the shared unhappiness of these two friends there was little but desolation. She could pay no attention to her children; she could see their mouths move but the sounds that came out were jabber in a foreign language.

"Aren't you still doing real estate?" she asked Sukie.

"Oh I am, honey. But it's *such* thin pickings. There are these hundreds of other divorcees running around in the mud showing houses."

"You made that sale to the Hallybreads."

"I know I did, but that just about brought me even with my debts. Now I'm slipping back into the red again and I'm getting desperate." Sukie smiled broadly, her lips spreading like cushions sat on. She patted the empty place beside her. "Gorgeous, come over and sit by me. I feel I'm shouting. The acoustics in this hideous little house, I don't know how she can stand hearing herself."

Jane had gone up the little half-flight of stairs to where the bedrooms were in this split-level, and now returned with a linen hand towel folded to hold some delicate treasure. Her aura was the incandescent purple of Siberian iris, and pulsed in excitement. "Last night," she said, "I was so upset and angry about all this I couldn't sleep and finally got up and rubbed myself all over with aconite and Noxema hand cream, with just a little bit of that fine gray ash you get after you put the oven on automatic cleaner, and flew to the Lenox place. It was wonderful! The spring peepers are all out, and the higher you get in the air the better you can hear them for some reason. At Darryl's, they were all still downstairs, though it was after midnight. There was this kind of Caribbean music that they make on oil drums pouring full blast out of the stereo, and some cars in the driveway I didn't recognize. I found a bedroom window open a couple of inches and slid it up, ever so carefully—"

"Janie, this is so thrilling!" Sukie cried. "Suppose Needlenose had smelled you! Or Thumbkin!"

For Thumbkin, Van Horne had solemnly assured them, beneath her fluffy shape was the incarnate soul of an eighteenth-century Newport barrister who had embezzled from his firm to feed his opium habit (he had been hooked during spells of the terrible toothaches and abscesses common to all ages before ours) and, to save himself from prison and his family from disgrace, had pledged his spirit after death to the dark powers. The little cat could assume at will the form of a panther, a ferret, or a hippogriff.

"A dab of Ivory detergent in the ointment quite kills the scent, I find," Jane said, displeased by the interruption.

"Go on, go on," Sukie begged. "You opened the window—do you think they sleep in the same bed? How can she stand it? That body so cold and clammy under the fur. He was like opening the door of a refrigerator with something spoiling in it."

"Let Jane tell her story," Alexandra said, a mother to them both. The last time she had attempted flight, her astral body had lifted off and her material body had been left behind in the bed, looking so small and pathetic she had felt a terrible rush of shame in mid-air, and had fled back into her heavy shell.

"I could hear the party downstairs," Jane said. "I think I heard Ray Neff's voice, trying to lead some singing. I found a bathroom, the one that *she* uses."

"How could you be sure?" Sukie asked.

"I know her style by now. Prim on the outside, messy on the inside. Lipsticky Kleenexes everywhere, one of those cardboard circles that hold the Pill so you don't forget the right day lying around all punched out, combs full of long hair. She dyes it, by the way. A whole bottle of pale Clairol right there on the sink. And pancake make-up and blusher, things I'd *die* before ever using. I'm a hag and I know it and a hag is what I want to look like."

"Baby, you're beautiful," Sukie told her. "You have raven hair. And naturally tortoiseshell eyes. And you take a tan. I wish I did. Nobody can take a freckled person quite seriously, for some reason. People think I'm being funny even when I feel lousy."

"What did you bring back in that sweetly folded towel?" Alexandra asked Jane.

"That's *his* towel. I stole it," Jane told them. Yet the delicate script monogram seemed to be a *P* or a *Q*. "Look. I went through the wastebasket under the bathroom sink." Carefully Jane unfolded the rose-colored hand towel upon a spidery jumble of discarded intimate matter: long hairs pulled in billowing snarls from a comb, a Kleenex bearing a tawny stain in its crumpled center, a square of toilet paper holding the vulval image of freshly lipsticked lips being blotted, a tail of cotton from a pill bottle, the scarlet pull thread of a Band-Aid, strands of used dental floss. "Best of all," Jane said, "these little specks—can you see them? Look close. Those were in the bathtub, on the bottom and stuck in the ring—she doesn't even have the decency to wash out a tub when she uses it. I dampened the towel and wiped them up. They're leg hairs. She shaved her legs in the bath."

"Oh that's nice," Sukie said. "You're scary, Jane. You've taught me now to always wash out the tub."

"Do you think this is enough?" Jane asked Alexandra. The eyes that Sukie had called tortoiseshell in truth looked paler, with the unsteady glow of embers.

"Enough for what?" But Alexandra already knew, she had read Jane's mind; knowing chafed that sore place in Alexandra's abdomen, the sore place that had begun the other night, with too much reality to digest.

"Enough to make the charm," Jane answered.

"Why ask me? Make the charm yourself and see how it goes."

"Oh no, dearie. I've already said. We don't have your—how can I put it?—access. To the deep currents. Sukie and I are like pins and needles, we can prick and scratch and that's about it."

Alexandra turned to Sukie. "Where do you stand on this?"

Sukie tried, high on whiskey as she was, to make a thoughtful mouth; her upper lip bunched adorably over her slightly protruding teeth. "Jane and I have talked about it on the phone, a little. We *do* want you to do it with us. We do. It should be unanimous, like a vote. You know, by myself last fall I cast a little spell to bring you and Darryl together, and it worked up to a point. But only up to a point. To be honest, honey, I think my powers are lessening all the time. Everything seems drab. I looked at Darryl the other night and he looked all slapped together somehow—I think he's running scared."

"Then why not let Jenny have him?"

"*No*," Jane interposed. "She mustn't. She stole him.

She made fools of us." Her *s*'s lingered like a smoky odor in the long ugly scarred room. Beyond the little flights of stairs that went down to the kitchen area and up to the bedrooms, a distant, sizzling, murmuring sound signified that Jane's children were engrossed in television. There had been another assassination, somewhere. The President was giving speeches only at military installations. The body count was up but so was enemy infiltration.

Alexandra still turned to Sukie, hoping to be relieved of this looming necessity. "You cast a spell to bring me and Darryl together that day of the high tide? He wasn't attracted to me by himself?"

"Oh I'm sure he was, baby," Sukie said, but shruggingly. "Anyway who can tell? I used that green gardener's twine to tie the two of you together and I checked under the bed the other day and rats or something had nibbled it through, maybe for the salt that rubbed off from my hands."

"That wasn't very nice," Jane told Sukie, "when you knew I wanted him myself."

This was the moment for Sukie to tell Jane that she liked Alexandra better; instead she said, "We *all* wanted him, but I figured you could get what you wanted by yourself. And you did. You were over there all the time, fiddling away, if that's what you want to call it."

Alexandra's vanity had been stung. She said, "Oh hell. Let's do it." It seemed simplest, a way of cleaning up another tiny pocket of the world's endless dirt.

Taking care not to touch any of it with their hands, lest their own essences—the salt and oil from their skins, their multitudinous personal bacteria—become involved, the three of them shook the Kleenexes and the long blond hairs and the red Band-Aid thread and, most important, the fine specks of leg bristle, that jumped in the weave of the towel like live mites, into a ceramic ashtray Jane had stolen from the Bronze Barrel in the days when she would go there after rehearsal with the Neffs. She added the staring sugar head she had saved in her mouth and lit the little pyre with a paper match. The Kleenexes blazed orange, the hairs crackled blue and emitted the stink of singeing, the marzipan reduced itself to a bubbling black curdle. The smoke lifted to the ceiling and hung like a cobweb on the artificial surface, papery plasterboard roughed with a coat of sand-impregnated paint to feign real plaster.

"Now," Alexandra said to Jane Smart. "Do you have an old candle stump? Or some birthday candles in a drawer? The ashes must be crushed and mixed into about a half-cup of melted wax. Use a saucepan and butter it thoroughly first, bottom and sides; if any wax sticks, the spell is flawed."

While Jane carried out this order in the kitchen, Sukie laid a hand on the other woman's forearm. "Sweetie, I know you don't want to do this," she said.

Caressing the delicate tendony offered hand, Alexandra noticed how the freckles, thickly strewn on the back and the first knuckles, thinned toward the fingernails, as if this mixture had been insufficiently stirred. "Oh but I do," she said. "It gives me a lot of pleasure. It's artistry. And I love the way you two believe in me so." And without forethought she leaned and kissed Sukie on the complicated cushions of her lips.

Sukie stared. Her pupils contracted as the shadow of Alexandra's head moved off her green irises. "But you had liked Jenny."

"Only her body. The way I liked my children's bodies. Remember how they smelled as babies?"

"Oh Lexa: do you think any of us will ever have any more babies?"

It was Alexandra's turn to shrug. The question seemed sentimental, unhelpful. She asked Sukie, "You know what witches used to make candles out of? Baby fat!" She stood, not altogether steadily. She had been drinking vodka, which does not stain the breath or transport too many calories but which also does not pass like a stream of neutrinos through the system altogether without effect. "We must go help Jane in the kitchen."

Jane had found an old box of birthday candles at the back of a drawer, pink and blue mixed. Melted together in the buttered saucepan, and the ashes from their tiny pyre stirred in with an egg whisk, the wax came out a pearly, flecked lavender-gray.

"Now what do you have for a mold?" Alexandra asked. They rummaged for cookie cutters, rejected a pâté mold as much too big, considered demitasse cups and liqueur glasses, and settled on the underside of an old-fashioned heavy glass orange-juice squeezer, the kind shaped like a sombrero with a spout on the rim. Alexandra turned it upside down and deftly poured; the hot wax sizzled within the ridged cone but the glass didn't crack. She held the top side under running cold water and tapped on the edge of the sink until the convex cone of wax, still warm, fell into her hand. She gave it a squeeze to make it oblong. The incipient human form gazed up at her from her palm, dented four times by her fingers. "Damn," she said. "We should have saved out a few strands of her hair."

Jane said, "I'll check to see if any is still clinging to the towel."

"And do you have any orangesticks by any chance?" Alexandra asked her. "Or a long nail file. To carve

with. I could even make do with a hairpin." Off Jane
flew. She was used to taking orders—from Bach, from
Popper, from a host of dead men. In her absence
Alexandra explained to Sukie, "The trick is not to
take away more than you must. Every crumb has some
magic in it now."

She selected from the knives hanging on a magnetic
bar a dull paring knife with a wooden handle bleached
and softened by many trips through the dishwasher.
She whittled in to make a neck, a waist. The crumbs
fell on a ScotTowel spread on the Formica countertop.
Balancing the crumbs on the tip of the knife, and with
the other hand holding a lighted match under this
tip, she dripped the wax back onto the emerging figurine to form breasts. The subtler convexities of belly
and thighs Alexandra also built up in this way. The
legs she pared down to tiny feet in her style. The
crumbs left over from this became—heated, dripped,
and smoothed—the buttocks. All the time she held
in her mind the image of the girl, how she had glowed
at their baths. The arms were unimportant and were
sculpted in low relief at the sides. The sex she firmly
indicated with the tip of the knife held inverted and
vertical. Other creases and contours she refined with
the bevelled oval edge of the orangestick Jane had
fetched. Jane had found one more long hair clinging
to the threads of the towel. She held it up to the
window light and, though a single hair scarcely has
color, it appeared neither black nor red in the tint of
its filament, and paler, finer, purer than a strand from
Alexandra's head would have been. "I'm quite certain
it's Jenny's," she said.

"It better be," Alexandra said, her voice grown
husky through concentration upon the figure she was
making. With the edge of the soft fragrant stick that

pushed cuticles she pressed the single hair into the yielding lavender scalp.

"She has a head but no face," Jane complained over her shoulder. Her voice jarred the sacred cone of concentration.

"We provide the face" was Alexandra's whispered answer. "We know who it is and project it."

"It feels like Jenny to me already," said Sukie, who had attended so closely to the manufacture that Alexandra had felt the other woman's breath flitting across her hands.

"Smoother," Alexandra crooned to herself, using the rounded underside of a teaspoon. "Jenny is smooooth."

Jane criticized again: "It won't stand up."

"Her little women never do," Sukie intervened.

"Shhh," Alexandra said, protecting her incantatory tone. "She must take this lying down. That's how we ladies do it. We take our medicine lying down."

With the magic knife, the *Athame*, she incised grooves in imitation of Jenny's prim new Eva Perón hairdo on the little simulacrum's head. Jane's complaint about the face nagged, so with the edge of the orangestick she attempted the curved dents of eye sockets. The effect, of sudden sight out of the gray lump, was alarming. The hollow in Alexandra's abdomen turned leaden. In attempting creation we take on creation's burden of guilt, of murder and irreversibility. With the tine of a fork she pricked a navel into the figure's glossy abdomen: born, not made; tied like all of us to mother Eve. "Enough," Alexandra announced, dropping her tools with a clatter into the sink. "Quickly, while the wax has a little warmth in it still. Sukie. Do you believe this is Jenny?"

"Why...sure, Alexandra, if you say so."

"It's important that *you* believe. Hold her in your hands. Both hands."

She did. Her thin freckled hands were trembling.

"Say to it—don't smile—say to it, 'You are Jenny. You must die.'"

"You are Jenny. You must die."

"You too, Jane. Do it. Say it."

Jane's hands were different from Sukie's, and from each other: the bow hand thick and soft, the fingering hand overdeveloped and with golden glazed calluses on the cruelly used tips.

Jane said the words, but in such a dead determined tone, just reading the notes as it were, that Alexandra warned, "You must believe them. *This is Jenny.*"

It did not surprise Alexandra that for all her spite Jane should be the weak sister when it came to casting the spell; for magic is fueled by love, not hate: hate wields scissors only and is impotent to weave the threads of sympathy whereby the mind and spirit move matter.

Jane repeated the formula, there in this ranch-house kitchen, with its picture window, spattered by hardened bird droppings, giving on a scrappy yard nevertheless graced at this moment of the year with the glory of two dogwoods in bloom. The day's last sunlight gleamed like a background of precious metal worked in fine leaf between the drifting twists of the dark branches and the sprays, at the branches' ends, of four-petalled blossoms. A yellow plastic wading tub, exposed to the weather all winter and forever outgrown by Jane's children, rested at a slight tilt beneath one of the trees, holding a crescent of filthy water that had been ice. The lawn was brown and tummocky yet misted by fresh green. The earth was still alive.

The voices of the other two recalled Alexandra to

herself. "You too, sweetie," Jane told her harshly, handing her bubby back to her. "Say the words."

They were hateful, but on the other hand factual; Alexandra said them with calm conviction and hastily directed the spell to its close. "Pins," she told Jane. "Needles. Even thumbtacks—are there some in your kids' rooms?"

"I hate to go in there, they'll start yammering for dinner."

Alexandra said, "Tell them five more minutes. We must finish up or it could—"

"It could what?" Sukie asked, frightened.

"It could backfire. It may yet. Like Ed's bomb. Those little round-headed map pins would be nice. Even paper clips, if we straighten them. But one good-sized needle is essential." She did not explain, *To pierce the heart.* "Also, Jane. A mirror." For the magic did not occur in the three dimensions of matter but within the image matter generated in a mirror, the astral identity of mere mute things, an existence added on to existence.

"Sam left a shaving mirror I sometimes use to do my eyes."

"Perfect. Hurry. I have to keep my mood or the elementals will dissipate."

Off Jane flew again; Sukie at Alexandra's side tempted her, "How about one more splash? I'm having just one more weak bourbon myself, before I face reality."

"This is reality, I'm sorry to say. A half-splash, honey. A thimble of vodka and fill the rest up with tonic or 7 Up or faucet water or anything. Poor little Jenny." As she carried the wax image up the six battered steps from the kitchen into the living room, imperfections and asymmetries in her work cried out to her—one leg smaller than the other, the anatomy where hips and thighs and abdomen come together not really understood, the wax breasts too heavy. Whoever had made her think she was a sculptress? Darryl: it had been wicked of him.

Jane's hideous Doberman, released by some door she had opened along the upstairs hall, bounded into the living room, the claws of his feet scrabbling on the naked wood. His coat was an oily black, close and rippling and tricked out like some military uniform with orange boots and patches of the same color on his chest and muzzle and, in two round spots, above his eyes. Drooling, he stared up at Alexandra's cupped hands, thinking something to be eaten was held there. Even Randolph's nostrils were watering with appetite, and the folded insides of his aroused erect ears seemed extensions of ravenous intestines. "Not for you," Alexandra told him sternly, and the dog's glassy black eyes looked polished, they were trying so hard to understand.

Sukie followed with the drinks; Jane hurried in with a two-sided shaving mirror on a wire stand, an ashtray full of multicolored tacks, and a pincushion in the form of a little cloth apple. The time was a few minutes to seven; at seven the television programs changed and the children would be demanding to be fed. The three women set the mirror up on Jane's coffee table, an imitation cobbler's bench abandoned by the mechanical engineer as he cleared out for Texas. Within the mirror's silver circle everything was magnified, stretched and out of focus at the edges, vivid and huge at the center. In turn the women held the doll before it, as at the hungry round mouth of another world, and stuck in pins and thumbtacks. "Aurai, Hanlii, Thamcii, Tilinos, Athamas, Zianor, Auonail," Alexandra recited.

"Tzabaoth, Messiach, Emanuel, Elchim, Eibor, Yod, He, Vou, He!" Jane chanted in crisp sacrilege.

"Astachoth, Adonai, Agla, On, El, Tetragrammaton, Shema," Sukie said, "Ariston, Anaphaxeton, and then I forget what's next."

Breasts and head, hips and belly, in the points went. Distant indistinct shots and cries drifted into their ears as the television program's violence climaxed. The simulacrum had taken on a festive encrusted look— the bristle of a campaign map, the fey gaudiness of a Pop Art hand grenade, a voodoo glitter. The shaving mirror swam with reflected color. Jane held up the long needle, of a size to work thick thread through suede. "Who wants to poke this through the heart?"

"You may," Alexandra said, gazing down to place a yellow-headed thumbtack symmetrical with another, as if this art were abstract. Though the neck and cheeks had been pierced, no one had dared thrust a pin into the eyes, which gazed expressionless or full of mournful spirit, depending on how the shadows fell.

"Oh no, you don't shove it off on me," Jane Smart said. "It should be all of us, we should all three put a finger on it."

Left hands intertwining like a nest of snakes, they pushed the needle through. The wax resisted, as if a lump of thicker substance were at its center. "*Die,*" said one red mouth, and another, "*Take that!*" before giggling overtook them. The needle eased through. Alexandra's index finger showed a blue mark about to bleed. "Should have worn a thimble," she said.

"Lexa, now what?" Sukie asked. She was panting, slightly.

A little hiss arose from Jane as she contemplated their strange achievement.

"We must seal the malignancy in," Alexandra said. "Jane, do you have Reynolds Wrap?"

The other two giggled again. They were scared, Alexandra realized. Why? Nature kills constantly, and we call her beautiful. Alexandra felt drugged, immobilized, huge like a queen ant or bee; the things of the world were pouring through her and reemerging tinged with her spirit, her will.

Jane fetched too large a sheet of aluminum foil, torn off raggedly in panic. It crackled and shivered in the speed of her walk. Children's footsteps were pounding down the hall. "Each spit," Alexandra quickly commanded, having bedded Jenny upon the trembling sheet. "Spit so the seed of death will grow," she insisted, and led the way.

Jane spitting was like a cat sneezing; Sukie hawked a bit like a man. Alexandra folded the foil, bright side in, around and around the charm, softly so as not to dislodge the pins or stab herself. The result looked like a potato wrapped to be baked.

Two of Jane's children, an obese boy and a gaunt little girl with a dirty face, crowded around curiously. "What's *that*?" the girl demanded to know. Her nose wrinkled at the smell of evil. Both her upper and lower teeth were trussed in a glittering fretwork of braces. She had been eating something sweet and greenish.

Jane told her, "A project of Mrs. Spofford's that she's been showing us. It's very delicate and I know she doesn't want to undo it again so please don't ask her."

"I'm *starv*ing," the boy said. "And we *don't* want hamburgers from Nemo's again, we want a home-cooked meal like other kids get."

The girl was studying Jane closely. In embryo she had Jane's hatchet profile. "Mother, are you drunk?"

Jane slapped the child with a magical quickness, as if the two of them, mother and daughter, were parts of a single wooden toy that performed this action over and over. Sukie and Alexandra, whose own starved children were howling out there in the dark, took this signal to leave. They paused on the brick walk outside the house, from whose wide lit windows spilled the spiralling tumult of a family quarrel. Alexandra asked Sukie, "Want custody of this?"

The foil-wrapped weight in her hand felt warm.

Sukie's lean lovely nimble hand already rested on the door handle of her Corvair. "I would, sweetie, but I have these rats or mice or whatever they are that nibbled at the other. Don't they adore candle wax?"

Back at her own house, which was more sheltered from the noise of traffic on Orchard Road now that her hedge of lilacs was leafing in, Alexandra put the thing, wanting to forget it, on a high shelf in the kitchen, along with some flawed bubbies she hadn't had the heart to throw away and the sealed jar holding the polychrome dust that had once been dear old well-intentioned Ozzie.

"He goes everywhere with her," Sukie said to Jane over the phone. "The Historical Society, the conservation hearings. They make themselves ridiculous, trying to be so respectable. He's even joined the Unitarian choir."

"Darryl? But he has utterly no voice," Jane said sharply.

"Well, he has a little something, a kind of a baritone. He sounds just like an organ pipe."

"Who told you all this?"

"Rose Hallybread. They've joined at Brenda's too. Darryl apparently had the Hallybreads over to dinner and Arthur wound up telling him he wasn't as crazy as he had first thought. This was around two in the morning, they had all spent hours in the lab, boring

Rose silly. As far as I could understand, Darryl's new idea is to breed a certain kind of microbe in some huge body of water like Great Salt Lake—the saltier the better, evidently—and this little bug just by breeding will turn the entire lake into a huge battery somehow. They'd put a fence around it, of course."

"Of course, my dear. Safety first."

A pause, while Sukie tried to puzzle through if this was meant sarcastically and, if so, why. She was just giving the news. Now that they no longer met at Darryl's they saw each other less frequently. They had not officially abandoned their Thursdays, but in the month since they had put the spell on Jenny one of the three had always had an excuse not to come. "So how *are* you?" Sukie asked.

"Keeping busy," Jane said.

"I keep running into Bob Osgood downtown."

Jane didn't bite. "Actually," she said, "I'm unhappy. I was standing in the back yard and this black wave came over me and I realized it had something to do with summer, everything green and all the flowers breaking out, and it hit me what I hate about summer: the children will be home all day."

"Aren't you wicked?" Sukie asked. "I rather enjoy mine, now that they're old enough to talk adult talk. Watching television all the time they're much better informed on world affairs than I ever was; they want to move to France. They say our name is French and they think France is a civilized country that never fights wars and where nobody kills anybody."

"Tell them about Gilles de Rais," Jane said.

"I never thought of him; I did say, though, that it was the French made the mess in Vietnam in the first place and that we were trying to clean it up. They wouldn't buy that. They said we were trying to create more markets for Coca-Cola."

There was another pause. "Well," Jane said. "Have you seen her?"

"Who?"

"*Her*. Jeanne d'Arc. Madame Curie. How does she look?"

"Jane, you're amazing. How did you know? That I saw her downtown."

"Sweetie, it's obvious from your voice. And why else would you be calling me? How was the little pet?"

"Very pleasant, actually. It was rather embarrassing. She said she and Darryl have been missing us *so* much and wish we'd just drop around some time informally, they don't like to think they have to extend a formal invitation, which they *will* do soon, she promised; it's just they've been terribly busy lately, what with some very hopeful developments in the lab and some legal affairs that keep taking Darryl to New York. Then she went on about how much she loves New York, compared with Chicago, which is windy and tough and where she never felt safe, even right in the hospital. Whereas New York is just a set of cozy little villages, all heaped one on top of the other. Et cetera, et cetera."

"I'll never set foot in that house again," Jane Smart vehemently, needlessly vowed.

"She really did seem unaware," Sukie said, "that we might be offended by her stealing Darryl right out from under our noses that way."

"Once you've established in your own mind that you're innocent," Jane said, "you can get away with anything. How did she look?"

Now the pause was on Sukie's side. In the old days their conversations had bubbled along, their sentences braiding, flowing one on top of the other, each anticipating what the other was going to say and delighting in it nonetheless, as confirmation of a pooled identity.

"Not great," Sukie pronounced at last. "Her skin seemed...transparent, somehow."

"She was always pale," Jane said.

"But this wasn't just pale. Anyway, baby, it's May. Everybody should have a little color by now. We went down to Moonstone last Sunday and just soaked in the dunes. My nose looks like a strawberry; Toby kids me about it."

"Toby?"

"You know, Toby Bergman: he took over at the *Word* after poor Clyde and broke his leg on the ice this winter? His leg is all healed now, though it's smaller than the other. He never does these exercises with a lead shoe you're supposed to do."

"I thought you hated him."

"That was before I got to know him, when I was still all hysterical about Clyde. Toby's a lot of fun, actually. He makes me laugh."

"Isn't he a lot...younger?"

"We talk about that. He'll be two whole years out of Brown this June. He says I'm the youngest person at heart he's ever met, he kids me about how I'm always eating junk food and wanting to do crazy things like stay up all night listening to talk shows. I guess he's very typical of his generation, they don't have all the hangups about age and race and all that that we were brought up on. Believe me, darling, he's a big improvement on Ed and Clyde in a number of ways, including some I won't go into. It's not complicated, we just have fun."

"Super," Jane said in dismissal, dropping the *r*. "Did her...spirit seem the same?"

"She came on a little less shy," Sukie said thoughtfully. "You know, the married woman and all. Pale, like I said, but maybe it was the time of day. We had a cup of coffee in Nemo's, only she had cocoa because she hasn't been sleeping well and is trying to do without caffeine. Rebecca was all over her, insisted we try these blueberry muffins that are part of Nemo's campaign to get some of the nice-people luncheon business back from the Bakery. She hardly gave *me* the time of day. Rebecca. She just took one bite of hers, Jenny this is, and asked if I could finish it for her, she didn't want to hurt Rebecca's feelings. Actually, I was happy to, I've been *rav*enous lately, I can't imagine what it is, I can't be pregnant, can I? These Jews are real potent. She said she didn't know why, but she just hadn't had much of an appetite lately. Jenny. I wondered if she was fishing, to see if I knew why by any chance. She may know in her bones about the... the thing we did, I don't know. I felt sorry for her, the way she seemed so apologetic, about not having an appetite."

"It really is true, isn't it?" Jane observed. "You pay for every sin."

There were so many sins in the world it took Sukie a second to figure out that Jane meant Jenny's sin of marrying Darryl.

Joe had been there that morning and they had had their worst scene yet. Gina was in her fourth month by now and it was starting to show; the whole town could see. And Alexandra's children were about to be let out of school and would make these weekday trysts in her home impossible. Which was a relief to her; it would be a great relief, frankly, for her not to have to listen any more to his irresponsible and really rather presumptuous talk of leaving Gina. She was sick of hearing it, it meant nothing, and she wouldn't want it to mean anything, the whole idea upset and insulted her. He was her lover, wasn't that enough? *Had* been her lover, after today. Things end. Things begin, and things end. All grown-ups know that, why didn't he? Caught as he was so severely, rotated on the point of her tongue as on a spit, Joe became hot, and walloped her shoulder a few times with a fist kept loose enough not to hurt, and ran around the room naked, his body stocky and white and two dark swirls of hair on his back suggesting to her eyes butterfly wings (his spine its body) or a veneer of thin marble slices set so the molten splash of grain within made a symmetrical pattern. There was something delicate and organic about the hair on Joe's body, whereas Darryl's had been a rough mat. Joe wept; he took off his hat to beat his head on a doorframe: it was parody and yet real grief, actual loss. The room, the Williamsburg-green of its old woodwork and the big peonies of its curtains with their concealed clown faces and the cracked ceiling that had mutely and conspiratorially watched over their naked couplings, was part of their grief, for little is more precious in an affair for a man than being welcomed into a house he has done noth-ing to support, or more momentous for the woman than this welcoming, this considered largesse, her house his, his on the strength of his cock alone, his cock and company, the smell and amusement and weight of him—no buying you with mortgage pay-ments, no blackmailing you with shared children, but welcomed simply, into the walls of yourself, an admis-sion dignified by freedom and equality. Joe couldn't stop thinking of teams and marriage; he wanted his own penates to preside. He had demeaned with "good" intentions her gracious gift. In his anguish he sur-prised Alexandra by getting erect again, and since his time was short now, their morning wasted in words, she let him take her his favorite way, from behind, she on her knees. What a force of nature his pounding was! How he convulsed, shooting off! The whole episode left her feeling tumbled and cleansed, like a towel from the dryer needing to be folded and stacked on some airy shelf of her sunny, empty home.

The house, too, seemed happier for his visit, in this interval before the eternity of their parting sank in. The beams and floorboards of this windy, moistening time of the year chatted among themselves, creaking, and a window sash when her back was turned would give a swift rattle like a sudden bird cry.

She lunched on last night's salad, the lettuce limp in its chilled bath of oil. She must lose weight or she couldn't wear a bathing suit all summer. Another failing of Joe's was his forgivingness of her fat—like those primitive men who turn their wives into captives of obesity, mountains of black flesh waiting in their thatched huts. Already Alexandra felt slimmer, lightened of her lover. Her intuition told her the phone would ring. It did. It would be Jane or Sukie, lively with malice. But from the grid pressed against her ear emerged a younger, lighter voice, with a tension of timidity in it, a pocket of fear over which a membrane pulsed as at a frog's throat.

"Alexandra, you're all avoiding me." It was the voice Alexandra least in the world wanted to hear.

"Well, Jenny, we want to give you and Darryl privacy. Also we hear you have other friends."

"Yes, we do, Darryl loves what he calls input. But it's not like ... we were."

"Nothing's ever quite the same," Alexandra told her. "The stream flows; the little bird hatches and breaks the egg. Anyway. You're doing fine."

"But I'm not, Lexa. Something's very wrong."

Her voice in the older woman's mind's eye lifted toward her like a face holding itself up to be scrubbed, a grit of hoarseness upon its cheeks. "What's very wrong?" Her own voice was like a tarpaulin or great dropcloth which in being spread out on the earth catches some air under it and lifts in a bubble, a soft wave of hollowness.

"I'm tired all the time," Jenny said, "and not much appetite. I'm subconsciously so hungry I keep having these dreams of food, but when I sit down to the reality I can't make myself eat. And other things. Pains in the night that come and go. My nose runs all the time. It's embarrassing; Darryl says I snore at night, which I never did before in my whole life. Remember those lumps I tried to show you and you couldn't find?"

"Yes. Vaguely." The sensations of that casual hunt rushed horribly into her fingertips.

"Well, there are more. In the, in the groin, and up under my ears. Isn't that where the lymph nodes are?"

Jenny's ears had never been pierced, and she was always losing little childish clip-on earrings in the tub room, on the black slates, among the cushions. "I really don't know, honey. You should see a doctor if you're worried."

"Oh I did. Doc Pat. He sent me to the Westwick Hospital to have tests."

"And did the tests show anything?"

"They said not really; but then they want me to have more tests. They're all so cagey and grave and talk in this funny voice, as though I'm a naughty child who might pee on their shoes if they don't keep me at a distance. They're scared of me. By being sick at all I'm showing them up somehow. They say things like my white-cell count is 'just a bit out of the high normal range.' They know I worked at a big city hospital and that puts them on the defensive, but I don't know anything about systemic disorders, I saw fractures and gallstones mostly. It would all be silly except at night when I lie down I can *feel* something's not right, something's working at me. They keep asking me if I'd been exposed to much radiation. Well of course I'd worked with it at Michael Reese but they're *so* careful, draping you in lead and putting you in this thick glass booth when you throw the switch, all I could think of was, in my early teens just before we moved to Eastwick and were still in Warwick, I had an awful lot of dental X-rays when they were straightening my teeth; my mouth was a mess as a girl."

"Your teeth look lovely now."

"Thank you. It cost Daddy money he didn't really have, but he was determined to have me beautiful. He *loved* me, Lexa."

"I'm sure he did, darling," Alexandra said, pressing down on her voice; the air caught under the tarpaulin was growing, struggling like a wild animal made of wind.

"He loved me so much," Jenny was blurting. "How could he do that to me, hang himself? How could he leave me and Chris so alone? Even if he were in jail for murder, it would be better than this. They wouldn't have given him too much, the awful way he did it couldn't have been premeditated."

"You have Darryl," Alexandra told her.

"I do and I don't. You know how he is. You know him better than I do; I should have talked to you before I went ahead with it. You might have been better for him, I don't know. He's courteous and attentive and all that but he's not there for me somehow. His mind is always elsewhere, with his projects I guess. Alexandra, *please* let me come and see you. I won't stay long, I really won't. I just need to be... touched," she concluded, her voice retracted, curling under almost sardonically while voicing this last, naked plea.

"My dear, I don't know what you want from me,"

Alexandra lied flatly, needing to flatten all this, to erase the smeared face rising in her mind's eye, rising so close she could see flecks of grit, "but I don't have it to give. Honestly. You made your choice and I wasn't part of it. That's fine. No reason I should have been part of it. But I can't be part of your life now. I just can't. There isn't that much of me."

"Sukie and Jane wouldn't like it, your seeing me," Jenny suggested, to give Alexandra's hard-heartedness a rationale.

"I'm speaking for myself. I don't want to get re-involved with you and Darryl now. I wish you both well but for my sake I don't want to see you. It would just be too painful, frankly. As to this illness, it sounds to me as if you're letting your imagination torment you. At any rate you're in the hands of doctors who can do more for you than I can."

"Oh." The distant voice had shrunk itself to the size of a dot, to something mechanical like a dial tone. "I'm not sure that's true."

When she hung up, Alexandra's hands were trembling. All the familiar angles and furniture of her house looked askew, as if wrenched by the disparity between their moral distance from her—things, immune from sin—and their physical closeness. She went into her workroom and took one of the chairs there, an old arrow-back Windsor whose seat was spattered with paint and dried plaster and paste, and brought it into the kitchen. She set it below the high kitchen shelf and stood on it and reached up to retrieve the foil-wrapped object she had hidden up there on returning from Jane's house this April. The thing startled her by feeling warm to her fingers: warm air collects up near a ceiling, she thought to herself in vague explanation. Hearing her stirring about, Coal padded out from his nap corner, and she had to lock

him in the kitchen behind her, lest he follow her outdoors and think what she was about to do was a game
of toss and fetch.

Passing through her workroom, Alexandra stepped
around an overweening armature of pine two-by-fours
and one-by-twos and twisted coathangers and chicken
wire, for she had taken it into her head to attempt a
giant sculpture, big enough for a public space like
Kazmierczak Square. Past the workroom lay, in the
rambling layout of this house lived in by eight generations of farmers, a dirt-floored transitional area
used formerly as a potting shed and by Alexandra as
a storage place, its walls thick with the handles of
shovels and hoes and rakes, its stepping-space narrowed by tumbled stacks of old clay pots and by opened
bags of peat moss and bone meal, its jerrybuilt shelves
littered with rusted hand trowels and brown bottles
of stale pesticide. She unlatched the crude door—
parallel beaded boards held together by a Z of bracing
lumber—and stepped into hot sunlight; she carried
her little package, glittering and warm, across the lawn.

The frenzy of June growth was upon all the earth:
the lawn needed mowing, the border beds of button
mums needed weeding, the tomato plants and peonies
needed propping. Insects chewed at the silence; sunlight pressed on Alexandra's face and she could feel
the hair of her single thick braid heat up like an electric coil. The bog at the back of her property, beyond
the tumbled fieldstone wall clothed in poison ivy and
Virginia creeper, was in winter a transparent brown
thicket floored, between tummocks of matted grass,
with bubbled bluish ice; in summer it became a solid
tangle of green leaf and black stalk, fern and burdock
and wild raspberry, that the eye could not travel into
for more than a few feet, and where no one would
ever step, the thorns and the dampness underfoot

being too forbidding. As a girl, until that age at about
the sixth grade when boys become self-conscious about
your playing games with them, she had been good at
softball; now she reared back and threw the charm—
mere wax and pins, so light it sailed as if she had flung
a rock on the moon—as deep into this flourishing
opacity as she could. Perhaps it would find a patch of
slimy water and sink. Perhaps red-winged blackbirds
would peck its tinfoil apart to adorn their nests. Alexandra willed it to be gone, swallowed up, dissolved,
forgiven by nature's seethe.

The three at last arranged a Thursday when they
could face one another again, at Sukie's tiny house
on Hemlock Lane. "Isn't this cozy!" Jane Smart cried,
coming in late, wearing almost nothing: plastic sandals
and a gingham mini with the shoulder straps tied at
the back of the neck so as not to mar her tan. She
turned a smooth mocha color, but the aged skin under
her eyes remained crêpey and white and her left leg
showed a livid ripple of varicose vein, a little train of
half-submerged bumps, like those murky photographs with which people try to demonstrate the existence of the Loch Ness monster. Still, Jane was vital,
a thick-skinned sun hag in her element. "God, she
looks terrible!" she crowed, and settled in one of Sukie's
ratty armchairs with a martini. The martini was the
slippery color of mercury and the green olive hung
within it like a red-irised reptile eye.

"Who?" Alexandra asked, knowing full well who.

"The darling Mrs. Van Horne, of course," Jane
answered. "Even in bright sunlight she looks like she's
indoors, right there on Dock Street in the middle of
July. She had the gall to come up to me, though I was
trying to duck discreetly into the Yapping Fox."

"Poor thing," Sukie said, stuffing some salted pecan

halves into her mouth and chewing with a smile. She wore a cooler shade of lipstick in the summer and the bridge of her little amorphous nose bore flakes of an old sunburn.

"Her hair I guess has fallen out with the chemotherapy so she wears a kerchief now," Jane said. "Rather dashing, actually."

"What did she say to you?" Alexandra asked.

"Oh, she was all isn't-this-nice and Darryl-and-I-never-see-you-any-more and do-come-over-we're-swimming-in-the-salt-marsh-these-days. I gave her back as good as I got. Really. What hypocrisy. She hates our guts, she must."

"Did she mention her disease?" Alexandra asked.

"Not a word. All smiles. 'What lovely weather!' 'Have you heard Arthur Hallybread has bought himself a darling little Herreshoff daysailer?' That's how she's decided to play it with us."

Alexandra thought of telling them about Jenny's call a month ago but hesitated to expose Jenny's plea to mockery. But then she thought that her true loyalty was to her sisters, to the coven. "She called me a month ago," she said, "about swollen glands she was imagining everywhere. She wanted to come see me. As if I could heal her."

"How very quaint," Jane said. "What did you tell her?"

"I told her no. I really don't want to see her, it would be too conflicting. What I *did* do, though, I confess, was take the damn charm and chuck it into that messy bog behind my place."

Sukie sat up, nearly nudging the dish of pecans off the arm of her chair but deftly catching it as it slipped. "Why, sugar, what an extraordinary thing to do, after working so hard on the wax and all! You're losing your witchiness!"

"I don't know, am I? Chucking it doesn't seem to have made any difference, not if she's gone on chemotherapy."

"Bob Osgood," Jane said smugly, "is good friends with Doc Pat, and Doc Pat says she's really riddled with it—liver, pancreas, bone marrow, earlobes, you name it. *Entre nous* and all that, Bob said Doc Pat said if she lives two more months it'll be a miracle. She knows it, too. The chemotherapy is just to placate Darryl; he's frantic, evidently."

Now that Jane had taken this bald little banker Bob Osgood as her lover, two vertical dents between her eyebrows had smoothed a little and there was a cheerful surge to her utterances, as though she were bowing them upon her own vibrant vocal cords. Alexandra had never met Jane's Brahmin mother but supposed this was how voices were pushed into the air above the teacups of the Back Bay.

"There are remissions," Alexandra protested, without conviction; strength had flowed out of her and now was diffused into nature and moving on the astral currents beyond this room.

"You great big huggable sweet thing you," Jane Smart said, leaning toward her so the line where the tan on her breasts ended showed within the neck of loose gingham, "whatever has come over our Alexandra? If it weren't for this creature you'd be over there now; *you'd* be the mistress of Toad Hall. He came to Eastwick looking for a wife and it should have been you."

"We *wanted* it to be you," Sukie said.

"Piffle," Alexandra said. "I think either one of you would have grabbed at the chance. Especially you, Jane. You did an awful lot of cocksucking in some noble cause or other."

"Babies, let's not bicker," Sukie pleaded. "Let's have

our cozy time. Speaking of seeing people downtown, you'll never guess who I saw last night hanging around in front of the Superette!"

"Andy Warhol," Alexandra idly guessed.

"Dawn Polanski!"

"Ed's little slut?" Jane asked. "She was blown up by that explosion in New Jersey."

"They never found any parts of her, just some clothes," Sukie reminded the others. "Evidently she had moved out of this pad they all shared in Hoboken to Manhattan, where the real cell was. The revolutionaries never really trusted Ed, he was too old and too square, and that's why they put him on this bomb detail, to test his sincerity."

Jane laughed unkindly, but with that toney vibrato to her cackle now. "The one quality I never doubted in Ed. He was sincerely an ass."

Sukie's upper lip crinkled in unspoken reproval; she went on, "Apparently there was no sincerity problem with Dawn and she was taken right in with the bigwigs, tripping out every night somewhere in the East Village while Ed was blowing himself up in Hoboken. Her guess is, his hands trembled connecting two wires; the diet and funny hours underground had been getting to him. He wasn't so hot in bed either, I guess she realized."

"It dawned on her," Jane said, and improved this to, "Uncame the Dawn."

"Who told you all this?" Alexandra asked Sukie, irritated by Jane's manner. "Did you go up and talk to the girl at the Superette?"

"Oh no, that bunch scares me, they even have some blacks in it now, I don't know where they come from, the south Providence ghetto I guess. I walk on the other side of the street usually. The Hallybreads told me. The girl is back in town and doesn't want to stay with her stepfather in the trailer in Coddington Junction any more, so she's living over the Armenians' store and cleaning houses for cigarette or whatever money, and the Hallybreads use her twice a week. I guess she's made Rose into a mother confessor. Rose has this awful back and can't even pick up a broom without wanting to scream."

"How come," Alexandra asked, "you know so much about the Hallybreads?"

"Oh," said Sukie, gazing upward toward the ceiling, which was tinkling and rumbling with the muffled sounds of television, "I go over there now and then for R and R since Toby and I broke up. The Hallybreads are quite amusing, when she's not in one of her moods."

"What happened between you and Toby?" Jane asked. "You seemed so...satisfied."

"He got fired. This Providence syndicate that owns the *Word* thought the paper wasn't sexy enough under his management. And I must say, he did do a lackadaisical job; these Jewish mothers, they really spoil their boys. I'm thinking of applying for editor. If people like Brenda Parsley can take over these men's jobs I don't see why I can't."

"Your boyfriends," Alexandra observed, "don't have very good luck."

"I wouldn't call Arthur a boyfriend," Sukie said. "To me being with him is just like reading a book, he knows so much."

"I wasn't thinking of Arthur. Is he a boyfriend?"

"Is he having any bad luck?" Jane asked.

Sukie's eyes went round; she had assumed everybody knew. "Oh nothing, just these fibrillations. Doc Pat tells him people can live with them years and years, if they keep the digitalis handy. But he hates the fibrillating; like a bird is caught in his chest, he says."

Both her friends, with their veiled boasting of new lovers, were in Alexandra's eyes pictures of health— sleek and tan, growing strong on Jenny's death, pulling strength from it as from a man's body. Jane svelte and brown in her sandals and mini, and Sukie too wearing that summer glow Eastwick women got: terrycloth shorts that made her bottom look high and puffbally, and a peacocky shimmering dashiki her breasts twitched in a way that indicated no bra. Imagine being Sukie's age, thirty-three, and daring wear no bra! Ever since she was thirteen Alexandra had envied these pert-chested naturally slender girls, blithely eating and eating while her own spirit was saddled with stacks of flesh ready to topple into fat any time she took a second helping. Envious tears rose itching in her sinuses. Why was she mired so in life when a witch should dance, should skim? "We *can't* go on with it," she blurted out through the vodka as it tugged at the odd angles of the spindly little room. "We *must* undo the spell."

"But how, dear?" Jane asked, flicking an ash from a red-filtered cigarette into the paisley-patterned dish from which Sukie had eaten all the pecans and then (Jane) sighing smokily, impatiently, through her nose, as if, having read Alexandra's mind, she had foreseen this tiresome outburst.

"We *can't* just kill her like this," Alexandra went on, rather enjoying now the impression she must be making, of a blubbery troublesome big sister.

"Why not?" Jane dryly asked. "We kill people in our minds all the time. We erase mistakes. We rearrange priorities."

"Maybe it's not our spell at all," Sukie offered. "Maybe we're being conceited. After all, she's in the hands of hospitals and doctors and they have all these instruments and counters and whatnot that don't lie."

"They *do* lie," Alexandra said. "All those scientific things lie. There *must* be a form we can follow to undo it," she pleaded. "If we all three *con*centrated."

"Count me out," Jane said. "Ceremonial magic really bores me, I've decided. It's too much like kindergarten. My whisk is still a mess from all that wax. And my children keep asking me what that thing in tinfoil was; they picked right up on it and I'm afraid are telling their friends. Don't forget, you two, I'm still hoping to get a church of my own, and a lot of gossip does *not* impress the good folk in a position to hire choirmasters."

"How can you be so callous?" Alexandra cried, deliciously feeling her emotions wash up against Sukie's slender antiques—the oval tilt-top table, the rush-seat three-legged Shaker chair—like a tidal wave carrying sticks of debris to the beach. "Don't you see how horrible it is? All she ever did was he asked her and she said yes, what else could she say?"

"I think it's rather amusing," Jane said, shaping her cigarette ash to a sharp point on the paisley saucer's brass edge. "'Jenny died the other day,'" she added, as if quoting.

"Honey," Sukie said to Alexandra, "I'm honestly afraid it's out of our hands."

"'Never was there such a lay,'" Jane was going on.

"You didn't do it, at worst you were the conduit. We all were."

"'Youths and maidens, let us pray,'" quoted Jane, evidently concluding.

"We were just being *used* by the universe."

A certain pride of craft infected Alexandra. "You two couldn't have done it without me; I was *so* energetic, such a good organizer! It felt *won*derful, administering that horrible power!" Now it felt wonderful, her grief battering these walls and faces and things—

the sea chest, the needlepoint stool, the thick lozenge
panes—as if with massive pillows, the clouds of her
agitation and remorse.

"Really, Alexandra," Jane said. "You don't seem
yourself."

"I know I don't. I've felt terrible for days. I don't
know what it is. My left ovary, before every other
period, it really hurts. And at night, the small of my
back, such pain I wake up and have to lie curled on
my side."

"Oh you poor big sad yummy thing," Sukie said,
getting up and taking a step so the tips of her breasts
jiggled the shimmering dashiki. "You need a back
rub."

"Yes I do," Alexandra pouted.

"Come on. Stretch out on the sofa. Jane, move over."

"I'm so scared." Sniffles spiced Alexandra's words,
stinging high in her nostrils. "Why would it be just
the ovary, unless..."

"You need a new lover," Jane told her, dropping
the *r* in her curt fashion. How did she know? Alexandra had told Joe she didn't want to see him any
more but this time he had not called back, and the
days of his silence had become weeks.

"Hitch up your pretty blouse," Sukie said, though
it was not a pretty blouse but one of Oz's old shirts,
with collar points that refused to lie down, because
the plastic stays were lost, and an indelible food stain
near the second button. Sukie bared the bra strap,
the snaps were undone, a pang of expansion flooded
Alexandra's chest cavity. Sukie's narrow fingers began
to work in circles. The rough cushion Alexandra's
nose was against smelled comfortingly of damp dog.
She closed her eyes.

"And maybe a nice thigh rub," Jane's voice declared.
Clinks and a rustle described how she set down her

glass and crushed out her cigarette. "Our lumbar tension builds up at the backs of our thighs and needs to be released." Her fingers with their hardened tips tried to release it, pinching, caressing, trailing the nails back and forth for a *pianissimo* effect.

"Jenny—" Alexandra began, remembering that girl's silky massages.

"We're not hurting Jenny," Sukie crooned.

"DNA is hurting Jenny," Jane said. "D'naughty DNA."

In a few minutes Alexandra had been tranced nearly to sleep. Sukie's awful-looking Weimaraner, Hank, trotted into the room with his lolling lilac-colored tongue and they played this game: Jane set a row of Wheat Thins along the backs of Alexandra's legs and Hank licked them off. Then they placed some on Alexandra's back, where her shirt had been tugged up. His tongue was rough and wet and warm and slightly adhesive, like a huge snail's foot; back and forth it flipflopped on the repeatedly set table of Alexandra's skin. The dog, like his mistress, loved starchy snacks but, surfeited at last, he looked at the women wonderingly and begged them with his eyes—balls of topaz, with a violet cloud at each center—to desist.

Though the other churches in Eastwick suffered a decided falling-off in attendance during the summer rebirth of sun worship, Unitarian services, never crowded, held their own; indeed they were augmented by vacationers from the metropolises, comfortably fixed religious liberals in red slacks and linen jackets, splashy-patterned cotton smocks and beribboned garden hats. These and the regulars—the Neffs, the Richard Smiths, Herbie Prinz, Alma Sifton, Homer and Franny Lovecraft, the young Mrs. Van Horne, and a relative newcomer in town, Rose Hallybread, without her agnostic husband but with her protégée, Dawn Polanski—were surprised, once "Through the Night of Doubt and Sorrow" had been wanly sung (Darryl Van Horne's baritone contributing scratchy harmony in the balcony choir), to hear the word "evil" emerge from Brenda Parsley's mouth. It was not a word often heard in this chaste nave.

Brenda looked splendid in her open black robe and pleated jabot and white silk cravat, her sun-bleached hair pulled tightly back from her high and shining forehead. "There is evil in the world and there is evil in this town," she pronounced ringingly, then dropped her voice to a lower, confiding register that yet carried to every corner of the neoclassic old sanctuary. Pink hollyhocks nodded in the lower panes of the tall clear windows; in the higher panes a cloudless July day called to those penned in the white box pews to get out, out into their boats, onto the beach and the golf courses and tennis courts, to go have a Bloody Mary on someone's new redwood deck with a view of the Bay and Conanicut Island. The Bay would be crackling with sunshine, the island would appear as purely verdant as when the Narragansett Indians lived there. "It is not a word we like to use," Brenda explained, in the diffident tone of a psychiatrist who after years of mute listening has begun to be directive at last. "We prefer to say 'unfortunate' or 'lacking' or 'misguided' or 'disadvantaged.' We prefer to think of evil as the absence of good, a momentary relenting of its sunshine, a shadow, a weakening. For the world *is* good: Emerson and Whitman, Buddha and Jesus have taught us that. Our own dear valiant Anne Hutchinson believed in a covenant of grace, as opposed to a covenant of works, and defied—this mother of fifteen and gentle midwife to sisters uncounted and uncountable—the sexist world-hating clergy of Boston in behalf of her belief, a belief for which she was eventually to die."

For the last time, thought Jenny Van Horne, *the exact blue of such a July day falls into my eyes. My lids lift, my corneas admit the light, my lenses focus it, my retinas and optic nerve report it to the brain. Tomorrow the Earth's poles will tilt a day more toward August and autumn, and a slightly different tincture of light and vapor will be distilled.* All year, without knowing it, she had been saying good-bye to each season, each subseason and turn of weather, each graduated moment of fall's blaze and shedding, of winter's freeze, of daylight gaining on the hardening ice, and of that vernal moment when the snowdrops and croci are warmed into bloom out of matted brown grass in that intimate area on the sunward side of stone walls, as when lovers cup their breath against the beloved's neck; she had been saying good-bye, for the seasons would not wheel around again for her. Days one spends so freely in haste and preoccupation, in adolescent self-concern and in childhood's joyous boredom, *there really is an end to them, a closing of the sky like the shutter of a vast camera.* These thoughts made Jenny giddy where she sat; Greta Neff, sensing her thoughts, reached into her lap and squeezed her hand.

"As we have turned outward to the evil in the world at large," Brenda was splendidly saying, gazing upward toward the back balcony with its disused pipe organ, its tiny choir, "turned our indignation outward toward evil wrought in Southeast Asia by fascist politicians and an oppressive capitalism seeking to secure and enlarge its markets for anti-ecological luxuries, while we have been so turned we have been guilty—yes, guilty, for guilt attaches to omissions as well as *com-missions*—guilty of overlooking evil brewing in these very homes of Eastwick, our tranquil, solid-appearing

homes. Private discontent and personal frustration
have brewed mischief out of superstitions which our
ancestors pronounced heinous and which indeed"—
Brenda's voice dropped beautifully, into a kind of
calm soft surprise, a teacher soothing a pair of parents
without gainsaying a dreadful report card, a female
efficiency-expert apologetically threatening a bluster-
ing executive with dismissal—"*are* heinous."

*Yet behind that shutter must be an eye, the eye of a great
Being,* and in a premonition not unlike her father's
some months before Jenny had come to repose a faith
in that Being's custody of her even while her new
friends, and those humanoid machines at the Westwick Hospital, fought for her life. Having herself
worked in a hospital those years, Jenny knew how
bleakly statistical in the end were the results obtained
by all that so amiably and expensively administered
mercy. What she minded most was the nausea, the
nausea that went with the drugs and now with the
radiation directed into her semiweekly as she lay
strapped and swathed upon that giant turntable of
chrome and cold steel, which lifted her this way and
that until she felt seasick. The clicked-off seconds of
its radioactive humming could not be cleansed from
her ears and persisted even in sleep.

"There is a brand of evil," Brenda was saying, "we
must fight. It must not be tolerated, it must not be
explained, it must not be excused. Sociology, psychology, anthropology: in this one instance all these
creations of the modern mind must be denied their
mitigations."

I will never see icicles dripping from the eaves again,
Jenny thought, *or a sugar maple catching fire. Or that
moment in late winter when the snow is all dirty and eaten
by thaw into rotten, undercut shapes.* These realizations
were like a child's finger rubbing a hole in a befogged

windowpane above a radiator on a bitterly cold day; through the clear spot Jenny looked into a bottomless never.

Brenda, her hair shimmering down to her shoulders—had it been like that at the beginning of the service, or had it come unpinned in her ardor?—was rallying invisible forces. "For these women—and let us not in our love of our sex and pride in our sex deny that they *are* women—have long exerted a malign influence in this community. They have been promiscuous. They have neglected at best and at worst abused their children, nurturing them in blasphemy. With their foul acts and unspeakable charms they have driven some men to deranged acts. They have driven some men—I firmly believe this—have driven some men to their deaths. And now their demon has alighted—now their venom has descended—their wrath hath—" As from the bell of a hollyhock a bumblebee sleepily emerged from between Brenda's plump painted lips and dipped on its questing course over the heads of the congregation.

Jenny tittered, to herself. Greta's hand gave another squeeze. On her far side Ray Neff snorted. Both the Neffs wore glasses: oval steel-rimmed grannies for Greta, squarish rimless on Ray. Each Neff seemed a single big lens, *and I sit between them*, Jenny thought, *like a nose*. An aghast silence focused upon Brenda, erect in her pulpit. Above her head hung not the tarnished brass cross that had been suspended there for years in irrelevant symbolism but a solid new brass circle, symbol of perfect unity and peace. The circle had been Brenda's idea. She took a shallow breath and tried to speak out through the something else gathering in her mouth.

"Their wrath has tainted the very air we breathe," she proclaimed, and a pale blue moth, and then its little tan sister, emerged; the second fell to the lectern, which was miked, with an amplified thud, then found its wings and beat its way toward the sky locked high behind the tall windows.

"Their jealouthy hath poithoned uth all—" Brenda bent her head, and her mouth gave birth to an especially vivid, furry, foul-tasting monarch butterfly, its orange wings rimmed thickly in black, its flickering flight casual and indolent beneath the white-painted rafters.

Jenny felt a tense swelling within her poor wasting body, as if it were a chrysalis.

"Help me," Brenda brokenly uttered down toward the lectern, where the crisp pages of her sermon had been speckled with saliva and insect slime. She seemed to be gagging. Her long platinum-blond hair swung and the brass O shone in the shafts of sunlight. The congregation broke its stunned silence; voices were raised. Franny Lovecraft, in the loud tones of the deaf, suggested that the police be called. Raymond Neff took it upon himself to leap up and shake his fist in the sun-riddled air; his jowls shook. Jenny giggled; the hilarity pressing within her could no longer be stifled. It was, somehow, the animation of it all that was so funny, the irrepressible cartoon cat that rises from being flattened to resume the chase. She burst into laughter—high-voiced, pure, a butterfly of sorts—and yanked her hand from Greta's sympathetic, squeezing grasp. She wondered who was doing it: Sukie, everybody knew, would be in bed with that sly Arthur Hallybread while his wife was at church; sly old elegant Arthur had been fucking his physics students for thirty years in Kingston. Jane Smart had gone all the way up to Warwick to play the Hammond organ for a cell of Moonies starting up in an abandoned Quaker meetinghouse; the ambience (Jane had

told Mavis Jessup, who had told Rose Hallybread, who
had told Jenny) was depressing, all these brainwashed
upper-middle-class kids with Marine haircuts, but the
money was good. Alexandra would be making her
bubbies or weeding her mums. Perhaps none of the
three was willing this, it was something they had loosed
on the air, like those nuclear scientists cooking up the
atomic bomb to beat Hitler and Tojo and now so
remorseful, like Eisenhower refusing to sign the truce
with Ho Chi Minh that would have ended all the trouble, like the late-summer wildflowers, goldenrod and
Queen Anne's lace, now loosed from dormant seeds
upon the shaggy fallow fields where once black slaves
had opened the gates for galloping squires in swal-
lowtail coats and top hats of beaver and felt. At any
rate it was all so *funny*. Herbie Prinz, his jowly greedy
thin-skinned face liverish in agitation, pushed past
Alma Sifton and beat his way down the aisle and nearly
knocked over Mrs. Hallybread, who like the other
women was instinctively covering her mouth as, stiff-
backed, she rose to flee.

"Pray!" Brenda shouted, seeing she had lost control
of the occasion. Something was pouring over her lower
lip, making her chin shine. "Pray!" she shouted in a
hollow man's voice, as if she were a ventriloquist's
dummy.

Jenny, hysterical with laughter, had to be led outside, where the apparition of her staggering between
the bespectacled Neffs nonplussed the God-fearing
burghers washing their automobiles at this hour along
Cocumscussoc Way.

Jane Smart retired when her children did, often
going straight to bed after tucking the two littlest in
and falling asleep while the older ones watched an
illicit half-hour of *Mannix* or some other car-chase

series set in southern California. Around two or two-thirty she would awaken as abruptly as if the telephone had rung once and then fallen silent, or as if an intruder had tested the front door or carefully broken a windowpane and was holding his breath. Jane would listen, then smile in the dark, remembering that this was her hour of rendezvous. Arising in a translucent nylon nightie, she would settle her little quilted satin bed jacket around her shoulders and put milk on the stove to heat for cocoa. Randolph, her avid young Doberman, would come rattling his claws into the kitchen and she would give him a Chew-Z, a rock-hard bone-shaped biscuit to gnaw on; he would take the bribe into his corner and make evil music upon it with his long teeth and serrated purplish lips. The milk would boil, she would take the cocoa up the six steps to the living-room level and release her cello from its case—its red wood lustrous and alive like a superior kind of flesh. "Good baby," Jane might say aloud, since the silence in the flat tracts of the development all around—no traffic, no children crying; Cove Homes rose and retired in virtual synchrony—was so absolute as to be frightening. She would scan her splintered floor for a hole to brace her pin in and, dragging music stand and three-way floorlamp and straightbacked chair into place, would play. Tonight she would tackle the Second of Bach's suites for unaccompanied cello. It was one of her favorites; certainly she preferred it to the rather stolid First and the dreadfully difficult Sixth, black with sixty-fourth notes and impossibly high, written as it had been for an instrument with five strings. But always, in even Bach's most clockworklike ringing of changes, there was something to discover, something to *hear*, a moment when a voice cried out amid the turning of the wheels. Bach had been happy at Köthen, but for his wife

Maria's sudden death and the so *simpatico* and musical Prince Leopold's marriage to his young cousin, Henrietta of Anhalt; Bach called the little bride an "*amusa*," that is, a person opposed to the muses. Henrietta yawned during courtly concerts, and her demands deflected princely attention away from the *Kapellmeister*, a deflection that helped prompt his seeking the cantorship in Leipzig. He took the new post even though the unsympathetic princess herself surprisingly died before Bach had left Köthen. In the Second Suite, there was a theme—a melodic succession of rising thirds and a descent in whole tones—announced in the prelude and then given an affecting twist in the allemande, a momentary reversal (up a third) of the descent; thus a poignance was inserted in the onrolling *(moderato)* melody, which returned and returned, the matter under discussion coming to a head of dissonance in the *forte d♯-a* chord between a trilled *b* natural and a finger-stinging run, *piano*, of thirty-second notes. The matter under discussion, Jane Smart realized as she played on and the untasted cocoa grew a tepid scum, was death—the mourned death of Maria, who had been Bach's cousin, and the longed-for death of Princess Henrietta, which would indeed come. Death was the space these churning, tumbling notes were clearing, a superb polished inner space growing wider and wider. The last bar was marked *poco a poco ritardando* and involved intervals—the biggest a *D-d'*—which sent her fingers sliding with a muffled screech up and down the neck. The allemande ended on that same low tonic, enormously: the note would swallow the world.

Jane cheated; a repeat was called for (she *had* repeated the first half), but now, like a traveller who by the light of a risen moon at last believes that she is headed somewhere, she wanted to hurry on. Her fingers felt inspired. She was leaning out above the music; it was a cauldron bubbling with a meal cooked only for herself; she could make no mistakes. The courante unfolded swiftly, playing itself, twelve sixteenths to the measure, only twice in each section stricken to hesitation by a quarter-note chord, then resuming its tumbling flight, the little theme almost lost now. This theme, Jane felt, was female; but another voice was strengthening within the music, the male voice of death, arguing in slow decided syllables. For all its fluttering the courante slowed to six dotted notes, stressed to accent their descent by thirds, and then a fourth, and then a steep fifth to the same final note, the ineluctable tonic. The sarabande, *largo*, was magnificent, inarguable, its slow skipping marked by many trills, a ghost of that dainty theme reappearing after a huge incomplete dominant ninth had fallen across the music crushingly. Jane bowed it again and again—low $C^\#$-B^b-g—relishing its annihilatory force, admiring how the diminished seventh of its two lower notes sardonically echoed the leap of a diminished seventh ($C^\#$-b^b) in the line above. Moving on after this savoring to the first minuet, Jane most distinctly heard—it was not a question of hearing, she *embodied*—the war between chords and the single line that was always trying to escape them but could not. Her bow was carving out shapes within a substance, within a blankness, within a silence. The outside of things was sunshine and scatter; the inside of everything was death. Maria, the princess, Jenny: a procession. The unseen inside of the cello vibrated, the tip of her bow cut circles and arcs from a wedge of air, sounds fell from her bowing like wood shavings. Jenny tried to escape from the casket Jane was carving; the second minuet moved to the key of D major, and the female caught within the music raced in sliding steps of tied notes but then was returned, *Menuetto I da capo*, and swallowed by its darker colors and the fierce quartet of chords explicitly marked for bowing: *f-a aufstrich, Bᵇ-f-d abstrich, G-g-e aufstrich; A-e-c**. Bow sharply, up, down, up, and then down for the three-beat *coup de grâce*, that fluttering spirit slashed across for good.

Before attempting the gigue, Jane sipped at her cocoa: the cold circle of skin stuck to her slightly hairy upper lip. Randolph, his Chew-Z consumed, had loped in and lain near, on the scarred floor, her tapping bare toes. But he was not asleep: his carnelian eyes stared directly at her in some kind of startlement; a hungry expression slightly rumpled his muzzle and perked up his ears, as pink within as whelk shells. These familiars, Jane thought, they remain dense— chips of brute matter. He knows he is witnessing something momentous but does not know what it is; he is deaf to music and blind to the scrolls and the glidings of the spirit. She picked up her bow. It felt miraculously light, a wand. The gigue was marked *allegro*. It began with some stabbing phrases—dit-*duh* (a-d), dit-*duh* (bᵇ-c*), dit dodododo dit *duh*, dit…On she spun. Usually she had trouble with these gappy sharped and flatted runs but tonight she flew along them, deeper, higher, deeper, *spiccato, legato*. The two voices struck against each other, the last revival of that fluttering, that receding, returning theme, still to be quelled. So this was what men had been murmuring about, monopolizing, all these centuries, death; no wonder they had kept it to themselves, no wonder they had kept it from women, let the women do their nursing and hatching, keeping a bad thing going while they, *they*, men, distributed among themselves the true treasure, onyx and ebony and unalloyed gold, the substance of glory and release. Until now Jenny's death had been simply an erasure in Jane's mind, a nothing;

now it had its tactile structure, a branched and sumptuous complexity, a sensuous downpulling fathoms more flirtatious than that tug upon our ankles the retreating waves on the beach give amid the tumbling pebbles, that wonderful weary weighty sigh the sea gives with each wave. It was as if Jenny's poor poisoned body had become intertwined, vein and vein and sinew and sinew, with Jane's own, like the body of a drowned woman with seaweed, and both were rising, the one eventually to be shed by the other but for now interlaced, one with the other, in those revolving luminescent depths. The gigue bristled and prickled under her fingers; the eighth-note thirds underlying the running sixteenths grew ominous; there was a hopeless churning, a pulling down, a grisly *fortissimo* flurry, and a last run down and then skippingly up the scale to the cry capping the crescendo, the thin curt cry of that terminal *d*.

Jane did both repeats, and scarcely fumbled anything, not even that tricky middle section where one was supposed to bring the quickly shifting dynamics through a thicket of dots and ties; who ever said her *legato* sounded *détaché*?

The Cove development lay outside in the black windows pure as a tract of antarctic ice. Sometimes a neighbor called to complain but tonight even the telephone was betranced. Only Randolph kept an eye open; as his heavy head lay on the floor one opaque eye, flecks of blood floating in its darkness, stared at the meat-colored hollow body between his mistress's legs, his strident rival for her affection. Jane herself was so exalted, so betranced, that she went on to play the first movement of the cello part for the Brahms E Minor, all those romantic languorous half-notes while the imaginary piano pranced away. What a softy

Brahms was, for all his flourishes: a woman with a beard and cigar!

Jane rose from her chair. She had a killing pain between her shoulder blades and her face streamed with tears. It was twenty after four. The first gray stirrings of light were planting haggard shapes on the lawn outside her picture window, beyond the straggly bushes she never trimmed and that spread and mingled like the different tints of lichen on a tombstone, like bacterial growths in a culture dish. The children began to make noise early in the morning, and Bob Osgood, who had promised to try to meet her for "lunch" at a dreadful motel—an arc of plywood cottages set back in the woods—near Old Wick, would call to confirm from the bank; so she could not take the phone off the hook and sleep even if the children were quiet. Jane felt suddenly so exhausted she went to bed without putting her cello back in its case, leaving it leaning against the chair as if she were a symphony performer excused from the stage for intermission.

Alexandra was looking out the kitchen window, wondering how it had become so smeared and splotched with dust—could rain itself be dirty?—and therefore saw Sukie park and come in along the brick walk through the grape arbor, ducking her sleek orange head in avoidance of the empty birdfeeder and the low-hanging vines with their ripening green clusters. It had been a wet August so far and today looked like more rain. The women kissed inside the screen door. "You're *so* nice to come," Alexandra said. "I don't know why it should scare me to look for it alone. In my own bog."

"It *is* scary, sweet," Sukie said. "For it to have been so effective. She's back in the hospital."

"Of course we don't really know that it was it."

"We do, though," Sukie said, not smiling and her lips therefore looking strange, bunchy. "We know. It was it." She seemed subdued, a girl reporter again in her raincoat. She had been rehired at the *Word*. Selling real estate, she had told Alexandra more than once over the telephone, was just too chancy, too ulcer-producing, waiting for things to click, wondering if you might have said something more subliminally persuasive in that crucial moment when the clients first see the house, or when they're standing around in the basement with the husband trying to look sage about the pipes and the wife terrified of rats. And then when a deal does go through the fee usually has to be split three or four ways. It really was giving her ulcers: a little dry pain just under the ribs, higher than you'd imagine, and worst at night.

"Want a drink?"

"Afterwards. It's early. Arthur says I shouldn't drink a drop until my stomach gets back in shape. Have you ever tried Maalox? God, you taste chalk every time you burp. Anyway"—she smiled, a flash of her old self, the fat upper lip stretched so its unpainted inner side showed above her bright, big, outcurved teeth— "I'd feel guilty having a drink without Jane here."

"Poor Jane."

Sukie knew what she meant, though it had happened a week before. That dreadful Doberman pinscher had chewed Jane's cello to pieces one night when she didn't put it back in its case.

"Do they think it's for good this time?" Alexandra asked.

Sukie intuited that Alexandra meant Jenny in the hospital. "Oh, you know how they are, they would never say that. More tests is all they ever say. How're your own complaints?"

"I'm trying to stop complaining. They come and go. Maybe it's premenopausal. Or post-Joe. You know about Joe?—he really *has* given up on me."

Sukie nodded, letting her smile sink down slowly over her teeth. "Jane blames *them*. For all our aches and pains. She even blames them for the cello tragedy. You'd think she could blame herself for that."

At the mention of *them*, Alexandra was momentarily distracted from the sore of guilt she carried sometimes in the left ovary, sometimes in the small of her back, and lately under her armpits, where Jenny had once asked her to investigate. Once it gets to the lymph glands, according to something Alexandra remembered reading or seeing on television, it's too late. "Who of them does she blame specifically?"

"Well for some reason she's fastened on that grubby little Dawn. I don't think myself a kid like that has it in her yet. Greta is pretty potent, and so would Brenda be if she could stop putting on airs. From what Arthur lets slip, for that matter, Rose is no bargain to tangle with: he finds her a very tough cookie, otherwise I guess they'd have been divorced long ago. She doesn't want it."

"I do hope he doesn't go after her with a poker."

"Listen, darling. That was never *my* idea of the way to solve the wife problem. I was once a wife myself, you know."

"Who wasn't? I wasn't thinking of you at all, dear heart, it was the house I'd blame if it happened again. Certain spiritual grooves get worn into a place, don't you believe?"

"I don't know. Mine needs paint."

"So does mine."

"Maybe we should go look for that thing before it rains."

"You *are* nice to help me."

"Well, I feel badly too. In a way. Up to a point. And I spend all my time chasing around in the Corvair on wild-goose chases anyway. It keeps skidding and getting out of control, I wonder if it's the car or me. Ralph Nader hates that model." They passed through the kitchen into Alexandra's workroom. "What on earth is *that*?"

"I wish I knew. It began as an enormous something for a public square, visions of Calder and Moore I suppose. I thought if it came out wonderfully I could get it cast in bronze; after all the papier-mâché I want to do something permanent. And the carpentry and banging around are good for sexual deprivation. But the arms won't stay up. Pieces keep falling off in the night."

"They've hexed it."

"Maybe. I certainly cut myself a lot handling all the wire; don't you just hate the way wire coils and snarls? So I'm trying now to make it more life-size. Don't look so doubtful. It might take off. I'm not totally discouraged."

"How about your little ceramic bathing beauties, the bubbies?"

"I can't do them any more, after that. I get physically nauseated, thinking of her face melting, and the wax, and the tacks."

"You ought to try an ulcer some time. I never knew where the duodenum *was* before."

"Yes, but the bubbies were my bread and butter. I thought some fresh clay might inspire me so I drove over to Coventry last week and this house where I used to buy my lovely kaolin was all in this tacky new aluminum siding. Puke green. The widow who had owned it had died over the winter, of a heart attack hauling wood the woman of the family that has it now said, and her husband doesn't want to be bothered with selling clay; he wants a swimming pool and a patio in the back yard. So that ends that."

"You look great, though. I think you're losing weight."

"Isn't that another of the symptoms?"

They made their way through the old potting shed and stepped into the back yard, which needed a mowing. First the dandelions had been rampant, now the crabgrass. Fungi—blobs of brown loaded by nature with simples and banes and palliatives—had materialized in the low damp spots of this neglected lawn during this moist summer. Even now, the mantle of clouds in the distance had developed those downward tails, travelling wisps, which mean rain is falling somewhere. The wild area beyond the tumbled stone wall was itself a wall of weeds and wild raspberry canes. Alexandra knew about the briars and had put on rugged men's jeans; Sukie however was wearing under her raincoat a russet seersucker skirt and frilly maroon blouse, and on her feet open-toed heels oxblood in color.

"You're too pretty," Alexandra said. "Go back to the potting shed and put on those muddy Wellingtons somewhere around where the pitchfork is. That'll save your shoes and ankles at least. And bring the long-handled clippers, the one with the extra hinge in the jaw. In fact, why don't you just fetch the clippers and stay here in the yard? You've never been that much into nature and your sweet seersucker skirt will get torn."

"No, no," Sukie said loyally. "I'm curious now. It's like an Easter-egg hunt."

When Sukie returned, Alexandra stood on the exact spot of grass, as best she remembered, and demonstrated how she had thrown the evil charm to be rid of it forever. The two friends then waded, clipping and wincing as they went, out into this little wilderness where a hundred species of plants were competing for sunlight and water, carbon dioxide and nitrogen. The area seemed limited and homogeneous—a smear of green—from the vantage of the back yard, but once they were immersed in it it became a variegated jungle, a feverish clash of styles of leaf and stem, an implacable festering of protein chains as nature sought not only to thrust itself outward with root and runner and shoot but to attract insects and birds to its pollen and seeds. Some footsteps sank into mud; others tripped over hummocks that grass had over time built up of its own accumulated roots. Thorns threatened eyes and hands; a thatch of dead leaves and stalks masked the earth. Reaching the area where Alexandra guessed the tinfoil-wrapped poppet had landed, she and Sukie stooped low into a strange vegetable heat. The space low to the ground swarmed with a prickliness, an air of congestion, as twigs and tendrils probed the shadows for crumbs of sun and space.

Sukie cried out with the pleasure of discovery; but what she gouged up from where it had long rested embedded in the earth was an ancient golf ball, stippled in an obsolete checkered pattern. Some chemical it had absorbed had turned the lower half rust color.

"Shit," Sukie said. "I wonder how it ever got out here, we're miles from any golf course." Monty Rougemont, of course, had been a devoted golfer, who had resented the presence of women, with their spontaneous laughter and pastel outfits, on the fairway in front of him or indeed anywhere in his clubby paradise; it was as if in discovering this ball Sukie had come upon a small segment of her former husband, a message from the other world. She slipped the remembrance into a pocket of her rain coat.

"Maybe dropped from an airplane," Alexandra suggested.

Gnats had discovered them, and pattered and nipped at their faces. Sukie flapped a hand back and forth in front of her mouth and protested, "Even if we do find it, baby, what makes you think we can undo anything?"

"There must be a form. I've been doing some reading. You do everything backwards. We'd take the pins out and remelt the wax and turn Jenny back into a candle. We'd try to remember what we said that night and say it backwards."

"All those sacred names, impossible. I can't remember half of what we said."

"At the crucial moment Jane said 'Die' and you said 'Take that' and giggled."

"Did we really? We must have got carried away."

Crouching low, guarding their eyes, they explored the tangle step by step, looking for a glitter of aluminum foil. Sukie was getting her legs scratched above the Wellingtons and her handsome new London Fog was being tugged and its tiny waterproofed threads torn. She said, "I bet it's caught halfway up some one of these fucking damn prickerbushes."

The more querulous Sukie sounded, the more maternal Alexandra became. "It could well be," she said. "It felt eerily light when I threw it. It sailed."

"Why'd you ever chuck it out here anyway? What a hysterical thing to do."

"I told you, I'd just had a phone conversation with Jenny in which she'd asked me to save her. I felt guilty. I was afraid."

"Afraid of what, honey?"

"You know. Death."

"But it isn't *your* death."

"Any death is your death, in a way. These last weeks I've been getting the same symptoms Jenny had."

"You've *al*ways been that way about cancer." In exasperation Sukie flailed with the long-handled clippers at the thorny round-leafed canes importuning her, pulling at her raincoat, raking her wrists. "Fuck. Here's a dead squirrel all shrivelled up. This is a real dump out here. Couldn't you have found the damn thing with second sight? Couldn't you have made it, what's the word, levitate?"

"I tried but couldn't get a signal. Maybe the aluminum foil bottled up the emanations."

"Maybe your powers aren't what they used to be."

"That could be. Several times lately I tried to will some sun, I was feeling like such a maggot with all this dampness; but it rained anyway."

Sukie's thrashing grew more and more irritable. "Jane levitated her whole self."

"That's Jane. She's getting very strong. But you heard her, she doesn't want any part of reversing this spell, she *likes* the way things are going."

"I wonder if you've overestimated how far you can throw. Monty used to complain about golfers looking for their balls, how they'd always walk miles past where it could possibly be."

"To me it feels like we've *under*estimated. As I said, it really flew."

"You work out that way then, and I'll retrace a little. God, these fucking prickers. They're *hate*ful. What *good* are they, anyway?"

"They feed the birds. And rodents and skunks."

"Oh, great."

"Some aren't raspberries, I was noticing, they're wild roses. When we first moved to Eastwick, Ozzie and me, every fall I'd make jelly out of the rose hips."

"You and Oz were just too dear."

"It was pathetic, I was such a housewife. You're a saint," she told Sukie, "to be doing this. I know you're bored. You can quit any time."

"Not such a saint, really. Maybe I'm scared too. Here it is, anyway." She sounded nowhere near as excited as when she had found the golf ball fifteen minutes earlier. Alexandra, scratched and impeded by (her sensation was) some essential and unappeasable rudeness in the universe, pushed her way to where the other woman stood. Sukie had not touched the thing. It lay in a relatively open spot, a brackish patch supporting on its edges some sea milkwort; a few frail white flowers put forth their attractions in the jungle shadows. Stooping to touch the crumpled Reynolds Wrap, not rusted but dulled by its months in the weather, Alexandra noticed the damp dark earth around it crawling with mites of some kind, reddish specks collected like filings around a magnet, scurrying in their tiny world several orders lower, on the terraces of life, than her own. She forced herself to touch the evil charm, this hellishly baked potato. When she picked it up, it weighed nothing, and rattled: the pins inside it. She gently pried open the hollow aluminum foil. The pins inside had rusted. The wax substance of the little imitation of Jenny had quite disappeared.

"Animal fat," Sukie at last said, having waited for Alexandra to speak first. "Some little bunch of jiggers out here thought it was yummy and ate it all up or fed it to their babies. Look: they left the little hairs. Remember those little hairs? You'd think they would have rotted or something. That's why hair clogs up sinks, it's indestructible. Like Clorox bottles. Some day, honey, there will be nothing in the world but hair and Clorox bottles."

Nothing. Jenny's tallow surrogate had become nothing.

Raindrops like pinpricks touched their faces, now that the two women were standing erect amid the brambles. Such dry microscopic first drops foretell a serious rain, a soaker. The sky was solid gray but for a thin bar of blue above the low horizon to the west, so far away it might be altogether out of Rhode Island, this fair sky. "Nature is a hungry old thing," Alexandra said, letting the foil and pins drop back into the weeds.

"And thirsty," Sukie said. "Didn't you promise me a drink?"

Sukie wanted to be consoling and flirtatious, sensing Alexandra's sick terror, and did look rather stunning, with her red hair and monkeyish lips, standing up to her breasts in brambles, in her smart raincoat. But Alexandra had a desolate sensation of distance, as if her dear friend, fetching yet jaded, were another receding image, an advertisement, say, on the rear of a truck pulling rapidly away from a stoplight.

One of Brenda's several innovations was to have members of the church give an occasional sermon; today Darryl Van Horne was preaching. The well-thumbed big book he opened upon the lectern was not the Bible but a red-jacketed *Webster's Collegiate Dictionary*. "Centipede," he read aloud in that strangely resonant, as it were pre-amplified voice of his. "Any of a class (Chilopoda) of long flattened many-segmented predaceous arthropods with each segment bearing one pair of legs of which the foremost pair is modified into poison fangs."

Darryl looked up; he was wearing a pair of half-moon reading glasses and these added to the slippage of his face, its appearance of having been assembled of parts, with the seams not quite smooth. "You didn't know that about the poisonous fangs, did you? You've never had to look a centipede right in the eye, have you? *Have* you, you lucky people!" He was boomingly addressing perhaps a dozen heads, scattered through the pews on this muggy day late in August, the sky in the tall windows the sullen no-color of recycled paper. "Think," Darryl entreated, "think of the evolution of those fangs over the aeons, the infinity— don't you hate that word, 'infinity,' it's like you're supposed to get down on your knees whenever some dumb bastard says it—the infinity—and I guess my saying it makes me one more dumb bastard, but what the hell else can you say?—*think* of all those little wriggling struggles behind the sink and down in the cellar and the jungle that ended in this predaceous arthropod's—isn't that a beautiful phrase?—this predaceous arthropod's mouth, if you want to call it a mouth, it isn't like any of our ruby lips, I tell you, before those two front legs somehow got the idea of being poisonous and the trusty old strings of DNA took up the theme and the centipedes kept humping away making more centipedes and finally they got modified into fangs. *Poi*sonous fangs. Hoo boy." He wiped his lips with forefinger and thumb. "And they call this a Creation, this mess of torture." The sermon title announced in movable white letters on the signboard outside the church was "THIS IS A TERRIBLE CRE-ATION."

The scattered listening heads were silent. Even the woodwork of the old structure failed to creak. Brenda herself sat mute in profile beside the lectern, half hidden by a giant spray of gladioli and ferns in a plaster urn, given in memory this Sunday of a stillborn son Franny Lovecraft had once produced, fifty years ago. Brenda looked pale and listless; she had been indisposed off and on for much of the summer. It had been an unhealthy wet summer in Eastwick.

"You know what they used to do to witches in Germany?" Darryl asked loudly from the pulpit, but as though it had just occurred to him, which probably it had. "They used to sit them on an iron chair and light a fire underneath. They used to tear their flesh with red-hot pincers. Thumbscrews. The rack. The boot. Strappado. You name it, they did it. To simpleminded old ladies, mostly." Franny Lovecraft leaned toward Rose Hallybread and whispered something in a loud but unintelligible rasp. Van Horne sensed the disturbance and in his vulnerable shambling way went defensive. "O.K.," he shouted toward the congregation. "So what? Well, you're going to say, this is human nature. This is human history. What does this have to do with Creation? What's this crazy guy trying to tell me? We could go on and on till nightfall with tortures human beings have used against each other under the sacred flag of one form of faith or another. The Chinese used to tear the skin off a body inch by inch, in the Middle Ages they'd disembowel a guy in front of his own eyes and cut his cock off and stuff it in his mouth for good measure. Sorry to spell it out like that, I get excited. The point is, all this stacked end to end multiplied by a zillion doesn't amount to a hill of beans compared with the cruelty natural organic friendly Creation has inflicted on its creatures since the first poor befuddled set of amino acids struggled up out of the galvanized slime. Women never accused of being witches, pretty little blonde dollies who never laid an evil eye on even a centipede, die every day in pain probably just as bad as and certainly more prolonged than any inflicted by the good old *Hexestuhl*. It had big blunt studs all over it, I don't know what the thermodynamic principle was. I don't want to think about it any more and I bet you don't either. You get the idea. It was terrible, terrible; Jesus it was terrible." His glasses fell forward on his nose and in readjusting them he seemed to press his whole face back together. His cheeks looked wet to some in the congregation.

Jenny was not here; she was back in the hospital, with uncontrollable internal bleeding. This was the sermon's undercurrent. Ray Neff was not here today either—he had accepted an invitation from Professor Hallybread to go sailing in Arthur's newly bought gaff-rigged Herreshoff 12½' across to Melville. Greta was here, though, sitting alone. It was hard to know about Greta—what she thought, what she wanted. Her being German, though her accent was never as bad as the people poking fun of it would have had you believe, put a kind of grid across her soul when you tried to look inside. Straight straw-dull hair, cut short, and amazing eyes the blue of dirty dishwater behind her granny glasses. She never missed a Sunday, but it may have been simply the unreflective thoroughness of her race, the German race, that admirable machine always waiting for a romantic demon to seize the levers.

Van Horne had been silent a while, pawing through the dictionary clumsily, as if his hands were gloves. Old Mrs. Lovecraft could now be heard as she leaned over to Mrs. Hallybread and distinctly asked, "Why is he using those filthy words?" Rose Hallybread looked exceedingly amused; she was a tall woman with a tiny head set in a nest of wiry gray and black hair frizzed way out. Her very small face was the color of a walnut, creased and recreased by decades of sun worship; what she whispered back was inaudible. On her other side sat Dawn Polanski; the girl had fascinating wide Mongolian cheekbones and smudged-looking skin and that impervious deadpan calm of the lawless. Between them she and Rose did pack a lot of psychic power.

Van Horne dimly heard the commotion and looked

up, blinked, pushed his glasses higher on his nose, and apologetically pronounced, "I know this is taking plenty long enough but here, right on one page, I've just come across 'tapeworm' and 'tarantula.' 'Tarantula: any of various large hairy spiders that are typically rather sluggish and though capable of biting sharply are not significantly poisonous to man.' Thanks a lot. And his limp little buddy up here: 'Any of numerous cestode worms (as of the genus *Taenia*) parasitic when adult in the intestine of man or other vertebrates.' Numerous, mind you, not just one or two oddballs tucked back in some corner of Creation, anybody can make a mistake, but a lot of them, a lot of *kinds*, a terrific idea, Somebody must have thought. I don't know about the rest of you gathered here, wishing I'd pipe down and sit down probably, but I've always been fascinated by parasites. I mean fascinated in a negative way. They come in so many sizes, for one thing, from viruses and bacteria like your friendly syphilis spirochete to tapeworms thirty feet long and roundworms so big and fat they block up your big intestine. Intestines are where they're happiest, by and large. To sit around in the slushy muck inside somebody else's guts—that's their catbird seat. You doing all the digesting for 'em, they don't even need stomachs, just mouths and assholes, pardon my French. But boy, the ingenuity that old Great Designer spent with His lavish hand on these humble little devils. Here, I scribbled down some notes, out of the *En-cy-clo-pedia*, as Jiminy Cricket used to say, if I can read 'em in this lousy light up here; Brenda, I don't see how you do it; week after week. If I were you I'd go on strike. O.K. Enough horsing around.

"Your average intestinal roundworm, about the size of a lead pencil, lays its eggs in the feces of the host; that's simple enough. Then, don't ask me how—there's a lot of unsanitary conditions in the world, once you get out of Eastwick—these eggs get up into your mouth and you swallow 'em, like it or not. They hatch in your duodenum, the little larvae worm through the gut wall, get into a blood vessel, and migrate to your lungs. But you don't think that's where they're gonna retire and live off their pension, do you? No sir, my dear friends, this little mother of a roundworm, he chews his way out of his cozy capillary there in the lungs and gets into an air sac and climbs what they call the respiratory tree to the epiglottis, where you go and swallow him again!—can you believe you'd be so stupid? Once he's had the second ride down he *does* settle in and becomes your average mature wage-earning roundworm.

"Or take—hold it, my notes are scrambled—take an appealing little number called the lung fluke. Its eggs get out in the world when people cough up sputum." Van Horne hawked by way of illustration. "When they hatch in fresh water that's lying around in these crummy, sort of Third-World places, they move into certain snails they fancy, in the form now of larvae, these lung flukes, follow me? When they've had enough of living in snails they swim out and bore into the soft tissues of crayfish and crabs. And when the Japanese or whoever eat the crayfish or crabs raw or undercooked the way they like it, in they go, these pesky flukes, and chew out through the intestines and diaphragm to get into good old lung and begin this sputum routine all over again. Another of these watery little jobbies, *Diphyllobothrium latum* if I can read it right, the little swimming embryos are eaten first by water fleas, and then fish eat the water fleas, and bigger fish eat *those* fish, and finally man bites the bullet, and all the while these itty-bitty monsters instead of being digested have been chewing their way out through the various stomach linings and are *thriv*ing. Hoo boy. There're a ton of these stories, but I don't want to bore anybody or, you know, overmake my point here. Wait, though. You got to hear this. I'm quoting. '*Echinococcus granulosus* is one of the few tapeworms parasitizing man in which the adult worm inhabits the intestine of the dog, while man is one of the several hosts for the larval stage. Moreover, the adult worm is minute, measuring only three to six millimeters. In contrast, the larva, known as a hydatid cyst, may be large as a football. Man acquires infection'—get this—'from contact with the feces of infected dogs.'

"So here you have, aside from a lot of feces and sputum, Man, allegedly made in the image of God, as far as little *Echinococcus* is concerned just a way station on the way to the intestines of a dog. Now you mustn't think parasites don't dig each other; they do. Here's a cutie pie called *Trichosomoides crassicauda*, of whom we read, quote, 'The female of this species lives as a parasite in the bladder of the rat, and the degenerate male lives inside the uterus of the female.' So degenerate, even the Encyclopedia thinks it's degenerate. And, hey, how about this?—'What might be termed sexual phoresis is seen in the blood fluke *Schistosoma haematobium*, in which the smaller female is carried in a ventral body-wall groove, the gynecephoric canal, of the male.' They had a drawing in the book I wish I could share with you good people, the mouth up at the tip of something like a finger and this big ventral sucker and the whole thing looking like a banana with its zipper coming undone. Trust me: it is *nasty*."

And to those who were sitting restless now (for the sky in the top panes of the windows was brightening as if a flashlight were shining behind the paper, and the hollyhock tops nodded and shuffled in a clearing breeze, a breeze that nearly capsized Arthur and Ray out in the East Passage, near Dyer Island: Arthur was unaccustomed to handling the lively little daysailer; his heart began to fibrillate; a bird beat its wings in his chest and his brain chanted rapidly, *Not yet, Lord, not yet*) it appeared that Van Horne's face, as it bobbed back and forth between his scrambled notes and a somehow blinded outward gaze toward the congregation, was dissolving, was thawing into nothingness. He tried to gather his thoughts toward the painful effort of conclusion. His voice sounded forced up from far underground.

"So to wind this thing up it's not just, you know, the nice clean pounce of a tiger or a friendly shaggy lion. That's what they sell us with all those stuffed toys. Put a kid to bed with a stuffed liver fluke or a hairy tarantula would be more like it. You all eat. The way you feel toward sunset of a beautiful summer day, the first g-and-t or rum-and-Coke or Bloody Mary beginning to do its work mellowing those synapses, and some nice mild cheese and crackers all laid out like a poker hand on the plate on the glass table out there on the sundeck or beside the pool, honest to God, good people, that's the way the roundworm feels when a big gobbety mess of half-digested steak or moo goo gai pan comes sloshing down to him. He's as real a creature as you and me. He's as noble a creature, designwise—really *lov*ingly designed. You got to picture that Big Visage leaning down and smiling through Its beard while those fabulous Fingers with Their angelic manicure fiddled with the last fine-tuning of old *Schistosoma*'s ventral sucker: that's Creation. Now I ask you, isn't that pretty terrible? Couldn't you have done better, given the resources? I sure as hell could have. So vote for me next time, O.K.? Amen."

In every congregation there has to be a stranger. The solitary uninvited today was Sukie Rougemont, sitting in the back wearing a wide-rimmed straw hat to hide her beautiful pale orange hair, and great round spectacles, so she could see to read the hymnal and to take notes on the margin of her mimeographed program. Her scurrilous column "Eastwick Eyes and Ears" had been reinstated, to make the *Word* more "sexy." She had gotten wind of Darryl's secular sermon and come to cover it. Brenda and Darryl, from their position on the altar dais, must have seen her slip in during the first hymn, but not Greta nor Dawn nor Rose Hallybread had been aware of her presence, and since she slipped out in the first stanza of "Father, Who on Man Doth Shower," no confrontation between the factions of witches occurred. Greta had begun to yawn unstoppably, and Dawn's lusterless eyes furiously to itch, and the buckles of Franny Lovecraft's shoes had come undone; but all of these developments might be laid to natural causes, as might Sukie's discovering, the next time she looked in the mirror, eight or ten more gray hairs.

"Well, she died," Sukie told Alexandra over the phone. "At about four this morning. Only Chris was with her, and he had dozed off. It was the night nurse coming in realized she had no pulse."

"Where was Darryl?"

"He'd gone home for some sleep. Poor guy, he really had tried to be a dutiful husband, night after night. It had been coming for weeks, and the doctors were surprised she had hung on so long. She was tougher than anybody thought."

"She was," Alexandra said, in simple salute. Her own heart with its burden of guilt had moved on, into an autumn mood, a calm of abdication. It was past Labor Day, and all along the edges of her yard spindly wild asters competed with goldenrod and the dark-leaved, burr-heavy thistles. The purple grapes in her arbor had ripened and what the grackles didn't get fell to form a pulp on the bricks; they were really too sour to eat, and this year Alexandra didn't feel up to making jelly: the steam, the straining, the little jars too hot to touch. As she groped for the next thing to say to Sukie, Alexandra was visited by a sensation more and more common to her: she felt outside her body, seeing it from not far away, in its pathetic specificity, its mortal length and breadth. Another March, and she would be forty. Her mysterious aches and itches continued in the night, though Doc Paterson had found nothing to diagnose. He was a plump bald man with hands that seemed inflated, they were so broad and soft, so pink and clean. "I feel rotten," she announced.

"Oh don't bother," Sukie sighed, herself sounding tired. "People die all the time."

"I just want to be held," Alexandra surprisingly said.

"Honey, who doesn't?"

"That's all she wanted too."

"And that's what she got."

"You mean by Darryl."

"Yes. The worst thing is—"

"There's worse?"

"I really shouldn't be telling even you, I got it from Jane in absolute secrecy; you know she's been seeing Bob Osgood, who got it from Doc Pat—"

"She was pregnant," Alexandra told her.

"How did you know?"

"What else could the worst thing be? So sad," she said.

"Oh I don't know. I'd hate to have been that kid. I don't see Darryl as cut out for fatherhood somehow."

"What's he going to do?" The fetus hung disgustingly in Alexandra's mind's eye—a blunt-headed fish, curled over like an ornamental door knocker.

"Oh, I guess go on much as before. He has his new crowd now. I told you about church."

"I read your squib in 'Eyes and Ears.' You made it sound like a biology lecture."

"It was. It was a wonderful spoof. The kind of thing he loves to do. Remember 'The A Nightingale Sang in Berkeley Square Boogie'? I couldn't put anything in about Rose and Dawn and Greta, but honestly, when they put their heads together the cone of power that goes up is absolutely *elec*tric, it's like the aurora borealis."

"I wonder what they look like skyclad," Alexandra said. When she had this immediate detached vision of her own body it was always clothed, though not always clothed in what she was wearing at the time.

"Awful," Sukie supplied. "Greta like one of those lumpy rumpled engravings by the German, you know the one—"

"Dürer."

"Right. And Rose skinny as a broom, and Dawn just a little smoochy waif with a big smooth baby tummy sticking out and no breasts. Brenda—Brenda I could go for," Sukie confessed. "I wonder now if Ed was just my way of communicating with Brenda."

"I went back to the spot," Alexandra confessed in turn, "and picked up all the rusty pins, and stuck them in myself at various points. It still didn't do any good. Doc Pat says he can't find even a benign tumor."

"Oh sweetie *pie*," Sukie exclaimed, and Alexandra realized she had frightened her, the other woman wanted to hang up. "You're really getting weird, aren't you?"

Some days later Jane Smart said over the phone, her voice piercing with its indignation, "You *can't* mean you haven't already heard!"

More and more, Alexandra had the sensation that Jane and Sukie talked and then one or the other of them called her out of duty, the next day or later. Maybe they flipped a coin over who got the chore.

"Not even from Joe Marino?" Jane was going on. "He's one of the principal creditors."

"Joe and I don't see each other any more. Really."

"What a shame," Jane said. "He was so dear. If you like Italian pixies."

"He loved me," Alexandra said, helplessly, knowing how stupid the other woman felt her to be. "But I couldn't let him leave Gina for me."

"Well," Jane said, "that's a rather face-saving way of putting it."

"Maybe so, Jane Pain. Anyway. Tell me your news."

"Not just *my* news, the whole *town's* news. He's left. He's skipped, sugar pie. *Il est disparu.*" Her *s*'s hurt, but they seemed to be stinging that other body, which Alexandra could get back into only when she slept.

From the wrathfully personal way Jane was taking it Alexandra could only think, "Bob Osgood?"

"*Dar*ryl, darling. Please, wake up. Our dear Darryl. Our leader. Our redeemer from Eastwick *ennui*. And he's taken Chris Gabriel with him."

"Chris?"

"You were right in the first place. He was one of those."

"But he—"

"Some of them can. But it isn't real to them. They don't bring to it the illusions that normal men do."

Har, har, diable, diable, saute ici, saute là. There she had been, Alexandra remembered, a year ago, mooning over that mansion from a distance, then worrying about her thighs looking too fat and white when she had to wade. "Well," she said now. "Weren't we silly?"

"'Naïve' is the way I'd rather put it. How could we *not* be, living in a ridiculous backwater like this? Why are we here, did you ever ask yourself that? Because our husbands planted us here, and we like dumb daisies just *stay.*"

"So you think it was little Chris—"

"All along. Obviously. He married Jenny just to cinch his hold. I could kill them both, frankly."

"Oh Jane, don't even say it."

"And her money, of course. He needed that pathetic little money she got from the house to keep his creditors at bay. And now there's all the hospital bills. Bob says it's a terrible mess, the bank is hearing from everybody because they're stuck with the mortgage on the Lenox place. He did admit there may be just enough equity if they can find the right developers; the place would be ideal for condominiums, if they can get it by the Planning Board. Bob thinks Herbie Prinz might be persuadable; he takes these expensive winter vacations."

"But did he leave all his laboratory behind? The paint that would make solar energy—"

"Lexa, don't you understand? There was never anything there. We *imagined* him."

"But the pianos. And the art."

"We have no idea how much of that was paid for. Obviously there are *some* assets. But a lot of that art surely has depreciated dreadfully; I mean, really, stuffed penguins spattered with car paint—"

"He loved it," Alexandra said, still loyal. "He didn't fake that, I'm sure. He was an artist, and he wanted to give us all an artistic experience. And he did. Look at your music, all that Brahms you used to play with him until your awful Doberman ate your cello and you began to talk just like some unctuous *bank*er."

"You're being very stupid," Jane said sharply, and hung up. It was just as well, for words had begun to stick in Alexandra's throat, the croakiness of tears aching to flow.

Sukie called within the hour, the last gasp of their old solidarity. But all she could seem to say was "Oh my God. That little wimp Chris. I never heard him put two words together."

"I think he *wanted* to love us," Alexandra said, able to speak only of Darryl Van Horne, "but he just didn't have it in him."

"Do you think he wanted to love Jenny?"

"It could be, because she looked so much like Chris."

"He was a model husband."

"That could have been irony of a sort."

"I've been wondering, Lexa, he must have known what we were doing to Jenny, is it possible—"

"Go on. Say it."

"We were doing his *will* by, you know—"

"Killing her," Alexandra supplied.

"Yes," said Sukie. "Because he wanted her out of the way once he had her legally and everything was different."

Alexandra tried to think; it had been ages since she had felt her mind stretch itself, a luxurious feeling, almost muscular, probing those impalpable tunnels of the possible and the probable. "I really doubt," she decided, "that Darryl was ever organized in that way. He had to improvise on situations others created, and couldn't look very far ahead." As Alexandra talked, she saw him clearer and clearer—felt him from the inside, his caverns and seams and empty places. She had projected her spirit into a place of echoing desolation. "He couldn't create, he had no powers of his own that way, all he could do was release what was already there in others. Even us: we had the coven before he came to town, and our powers such as they are. I think," she told Sukie, "he wanted to be a woman, like he said, but he wasn't even that."

"Even," Sukie echoed, critically.

"Well it *is* miserable a lot of time. It honestly is." Again, those sticks in the throat, the gateway of tears. But this sensation, like that resistant one of trying to think again, was somehow hopeful, a stiff beginning. She was ceasing to drift.

"This might make you feel a little better," Sukie told her. "There's a good chance Jenny wasn't so sorry to die. Rebecca has been doing a lot of talking down at Nemo's, now that Fidel has run off with the other two, and she says some of the goings-on over there after we left would really curl your hair. Apparently it was no secret from Jenny what Chris and Darryl were up to, at least once she was safely married."

"Poor little soul," Alexandra said. "I guess she was one of those perfectly lovely people the world for some reason never finds any use for." Nature in her wisdom puts them to sleep.

"Even Fidel was offended, Rebecca says," Sukie was saying, "but when she begged him to stay and live with her he told her he didn't want to be a lobsterman or a floor boy over at Dataprobe, and there was nothing else the people around here would let a spic like him do. Rebecca's heartbroken."

"Men," Alexandra eloquently said.

"Aren't they, though?"

"How have people like the Hallybreads taken all this?"

"Badly. Rose is nearly hysterical that Arthur is going to be involved financially in the terrible mess. Apparently he got rather interested in Darryl's selenium theories and even signed some sort of agreement making him a partner in exchange for his expertise; that was one of Darryl's things, getting people to sign pacts. Her back evidently is so bad now she sleeps on a mat on the floor and makes Arthur read aloud to her all day, these trashy historical novels. He can never get away any more."

"Really, what a boring terrible woman," Alexandra said.

"Vile," Sukie agreed. "Jane says her head looks like a dried apple packed in steel wool."

"How *is* Jane? Really. I fear she got rather impatient with me this morning."

"Well, she says Bob Osgood knows of a wonderful man in Providence, on Hope Street I think she said, who can replace the whole front plate of her Ceruti without changing the timbre, he's one of those sort of hippie Ph.D.'s who've gone to work in the crafts to spite their father or protest the System or something. But she's patched it with masking tape and plays it chewed and says she likes it, it sounds more human. I think she's in terrible shape. *Very* neurotic and paranoid. I asked her to meet me downtown and have a sandwich at the Bakery or even Nemo's now that Rebecca doesn't blame us for everything any more, but she said no, she was afraid of being seen by those *others*. Brenda and Dawn and Greta, I suppose. I see them all the time along Dock Street. I smile, they smile. There's nothing left to fight about. Her color"— back to Jane—"is frightening. White as a clenched fist, and it's not even October."

"Almost," Alexandra said. "The robins are gone, and you can hear the geese at night. I'm letting my tomatoes rot on the vine this year; every time I go into the cellar these jars and jars of last year's sauce reproach me. My awful children have absolutely rebelled against spaghetti, and, I must say, it does pack on the calories, which is scarcely what I need."

"Don't be silly. You *have* lost weight. I saw you coming out of the Superette the other day—I was stuck in the *Word*, interviewing this incredibly immature and pompous new harbormaster, he's just a kid with hair down to his shoulders, younger than Toby even, and just happened to look out the window— and thought to myself, 'Doesn't Lexa look *fab*ulous.' Your hair was up in that big pigtail and you had on that brocaded Iranian—"

"Algerian."

"—Algerian jacket you wear in the fall, and had

Coal on a leash, a long rope."

"I had been at the beach," Alexandra volunteered. "It was lovely. Not a breath of wind." Though they talked on some minutes more, trying to rekindle the old coziness, that collusion which related to the yield-ingness and vulnerability of their bodies, Alexandra and—her intuition suddenly, unmistakably told her—Sukie as well deadeningly felt that it had all been said before.

There comes a blessed moment in the year when we know we are mowing the lawn for the last time. Alexandra's elder son, Ben, was supposed to earn his allowance with yard work, but now he was back in high school and trying to be a fledgling Lance Alworth at football practice afterwards—sprinting, weaving, leaping to feel that sweet hit of leather on outstretched fingertips ten feet off the ground. Marcy had a part-time job waitressing at the Bakery Coffee Nook, which was serving evening meals now, and regrettably she had become involved with one of those shaggy sinister boys who hung out in front of the Superette. The two younger children, Linda and Eric, had entered the fifth and seventh grades respectively, and Alexandra had found cigarette butts in a paper cup of water beneath Eric's bed. Now she pushed her snarling, smoking Toro, which hadn't had its oil changed since the days of Oz's home maintenance, once more back and forth across her unkempt lawn, littered with long yellow featherlike willow leaves and all bumpy as the moles were digging in for the winter. She let the Toro run until it had burned up all its gas, so none would clog the carburetor next spring. She thought of drain-ing the sludgy ancient oil but that seemed *too* good and workmanlike of her. On her way back to the kitchen from the gardening-tool shed she passed through her workroom and saw her stalled armature at last for what it was: a husband. The clumsily nailed and wired-together one-by-twos and two-by-fours had that lankiness she admired and that Ozzie had displayed before being a husband had worn his corners down. She remembered how his knees and elbows had jabbed her in bed those early years when nightmares twitched him; she had rather loved him for those nightmares, confessions as they were of his terror as life in all its length and responsibility loomed to his young manhood. Toward the end of their marriage he slept like a thing motionless and sunk, sweating and exuding oblivious little snuffles. She took his multicolored dust down from the shelf and sprinkled a little on the knotty piece of pine two-by-four that did for the armature's shoulders. She worried less about the head and face than the feet; it was the extremities, she realized, that mattered most to her about a man. Whatever went on in the middle, she had to have in her ideal man a gauntness and delicacy in the feet—Christ's feet as they looked overlapped and pegged on crucifixes, tendony and long-toed and limp as if in flight—and something hardened and work-broadened about the hands; Darryl's rubbery-looking hands had been his most repulsive feature. She worked her ideas up sketchily in clay, in the last of the pure white kaolin taken from the widow's back yard in Coventry. One foot and one hand were enough, and sketchiness didn't matter; what was important was not her finished product but the message etched on the air and sent to those powers that could form hands and fingers to the smallest phalange and fascia, those powers that spilled the marvels of all anatomies forth from Creation's berserk precise cornucopia. For the head she settled on a modest-sized pumpkin she bought at that roadside stand on Route 4, which for ten months of the year looks hopelessly dilapidated and abandoned but comes to life at harvest time. She hollowed

out the pumpkin and put in some of Ozzie's dust, but
not too much, for she wanted him duplicated only in
his essential husbandliness. One crucial ingredient was
almost impossible to find in Rhode Island: western
soil, a handful of dry sandy sage-supporting earth.
Moist eastern loam would not do. One day she happened to spot parked on Oak Street a pickup truck
with Colorado plates, those white numbers on a green
silhouette of mountains. She reached inside the back
fender and scraped some tawny dried mud down into
her palm and took it home and put it in with Ozzie's
dust. Also she needed a cowboy hat for the pumpkin,
and had to go all the way to Providence in her Subaru
to search for a costume store that would cater to Brown
students with their theatricals and carnivals and protest demonstrations. While there, she thought to en-
roll herself as a part-time student in the Rhode Island
School of Design; she had gone as far as she could as
a sculptress with being merely primitive. The other
students were scarcely older than her children, but
one of the instructors, a ceramist from Taos, a leathery limping man well into his forties and weathered
by the baths and blasts of life, took her eye, and she
his, in her sturdy voluptuousness a little like that of
cattle (which Joe Marino had hit upon in calling her,
while rutting, his *vacca*). After several terms and
turnings-away they did marry and Jim took her and
his stepchildren back west, where the air was ecstat-
ically thin and all the witchcraft belonged to the Hopi
and Navajo shamans.

"My God," Sukie said to her over the phone before
she left. "What was your secret?"

"It's not for print," Alexandra told her sternly. Sukie
had risen to be editor of the *Word*, and in keeping
with the shamelessly personal tone of the emerging
postwar era had to run scandal or confession every
week, squibs of trivial daily rumor that Clyde Gabriel

would have fastidiously killed.

"You must imagine your life," Alexandra confided to the younger woman. "And then it happens."

Sukie relayed this piece of magic to Jane, and dear angry Jane, who was in danger of being an embittered and crabbed old maid, so that her piano students associated the black and white of the keys with bones and the darkness of the pit, with everything dead and strict and menacing, hissed her disbelief; she had long since disowned Alexandra as a trustworthy sister.

But in secrecy even from Sukie she had taken splinters of the cello-front replaced by the dedicated hippie restorer on Hope Street and wrapped them in her dead father's old soot-colored tuxedo and stuffed into one pocket of the jacket some crumbs of the dried herb Sam Smart had become, hanging in her ranch-house basement, and into the other pocket put the confetti of a torn-up twenty-dollar bill—for she was tired, boringly tired, of being poor—and sprinkled the still-shiny wide lapels of the tuxedo with her perfume and her urine and her menstrual blood and enclosed the whole odd-smelling charm in a plastic cleaner's bag and laid it between her mattress and her springs. Upon its subtle smothered hump she slept each night. One horrendously cold weekend in January, she was visiting her mother in the Back Bay, and a perfectly suitable little man in a tuxedo and patent-leather pumps as shiny as boiling tar dropped in for tea; he lived with his parents in Chestnut Hill and was on his way to a gala at the Tavern Club. He had heavy-lidded protruding eyes the pale questioning blue of a Siamese cat's; he did not drop by so briefly as to fail to notice—he who had never married and who had been written off by those he might have courted as hopelessly prissy, too sexless even to be called gay—something dark and sharp and dirty in Jane that might stir the long-dormant amorous part of his being. We wake at different times, and the gallantest flowers are those that bloom in the cold. His glance also detected in Jane a brisk and formidable potential administrator of the Chippendale and Duncan Phyfe antiques, the towering cabinets of Chinese lacquerwork, the deep-stored cases of vintage wine, the securities and silver he would one day inherit from his parents, though both were still alive, as were indeed two of his grandparents—ancient erect women changeless as crystal in their corners of Milton and Salem. This height of family, and the claims of the brokerage clients whose money he diffidently tended, and the requirements of his delicate allergic nature (milk, sugar, alcohol, and sodium were among the substances he must avoid) all suggested a manageress; he called Jane next morning before she had time to fly away in her battered Valiant and invited her for drinks that evening at the Copley bar. She refused; and then a picture-book blizzard collapsed on the brick precincts and held her fast. His call that evening proposed lunch upstairs at the snowbound Ritz. Jane resisted him all the way, scratching and singeing with her murderous tongue; but her accent spoke to him, and he made her finally his prisoner in a turreted ironstone fantasy in Brookline designed by a disciple of H. H. Richardson.

Sukie sprinkled powdered nutmeg on the circular glass of her hand mirror until there was nothing left of the image but the gold-freckled green eyes or, when she slightly moved her head, her monkeyish and over-lipsticked lips. With these lips she recited in a solemn whisper seven times the obscene and sacred prayer to Cernunnos. Then she took the tired old plaid plastic place mats off the kitchen table and put them into the trash for Tuesday's collection. The very next day a jaunty sandy-haired man from Connecticut showed up at the *Word* office, to place an ad: he was looking for a pedigreed Weimaraner to mate with his bitch. He was renting a cottage in Southwick with his small children (he was recently divorced; he had helped his wife go belatedly to law school and her first action had been to file for mental cruelty) and the poor creature had decided to come into heat; the bitch was in torment. This man had a long off-center nose, like Ed Parsley; an aura of regretful intelligence, like Clyde Gabriel; and something of Arthur Hallybread's professional starchiness. In his checked suit he looked excessively alert, like a gimcrack salesman from upstate New York or a song-and-dance man about to move sideways across a stage, strumming a banjo. Like Sukie, he wanted to be amusing. He was really from Stamford, where he worked in an infant industry, selling and servicing glamorized computers called word processors. On hers she now rapidly writes paperback romances, with a few taps of her fingertips transposing paragraphs, renaming characters, and glossarizing for re-use standard passions and crises.

Sukie was the last to leave Eastwick; the afterimage of her in her nappy suede skirt and orange hair, swinging her long legs and arms past the glinting shopfronts, lingered on Dock Street like the cool-colored ghost the eye retains after staring at something bright. This was years ago. The young harbormaster with whom she had her last affair has a paunch now, and three children; but he still remembers how she used to bite his shoulder and say she loved to taste the salt of the sea-mist condensed on his skin. Dock Street has been repaved and widened to accept more traffic, and from the old horse trough to Landing Square, as it tends to be called, all the slight zigzags in the line of the curb have been straightened. New people move to town; some of them live in the old Lenox mansion, which has indeed been turned into condominiums. The tennis court has been kept up, though the perilous experiment with the air-supported canvas canopy has not been repeated. An area has been dredged and a dock and small marina built, as tenant inducement. The egrets nest elsewhere. The causeway has been elevated, with culverts every fifty yards, so it never floods—or has only once so far, in the great February blizzard of '78. The weather seems generally tamer in these times; there are rarely any thunderstorms.

Jenny Gabriel lies with her parents under polished granite flush with the clipped grass in the new section of Cocumscussoc Cemetery. Chris, her brother and their son, has been, with his angelic visage and love of comic books, swallowed by the Sodom of New York. Lawyers now think that Darryl Van Horne was an assumed name. Yet several patents under that name do exist. Residents at the condo have reported mysterious crackling noises from some of the painted window sills, and wasps dead of shock. The facts of the financial imbroglio lie buried in vaults and drawers of old paperwork, silted over in even this short a span of time and of no great interest. What is of interest is what our minds retain, what our lives have given to the air. The witches are gone, vanished; we were just an interval in their lives, and they in ours. But as Sukie's blue-green ghost continues to haunt the sun-struck pavement, and Jane's black shape to flit past the moon, so the rumors of the days when they were solid among us, gorgeous and doing evil, have flavored the name of the town in the mouths of others, and for those of us who live here have left something oblong and invisible and exciting we do not understand. We meet it turning the corner where Hemlock meets Oak; it is there when we walk the beach in off-season and the Atlantic in its blackness mirrors the dense packed gray of the clouds: a scandal, life like smoke rising twisted into legend.

About the Author

John Updike was born in 1932, in Shillington, Pennsylvania. He graduated from Harvard College in 1954, and spent a year as a Knox Fellow at the Ruskin School of Drawing and Fine Art in Oxford, England. From 1955 to 1957 he was a staff member of *The New Yorker*, to which he has contributed short stories, poems, and book reviews. Since 1957 he has lived in Massachusetts.